Douglas Reeman

THE DEEP
SILENCE

RENDEZVOUS -
SOUTH ATLANTIC

ARROW

This edition published by Arrow in 2004
an imprint of The Random Group,
20 Vauxhall Bridge Road, London SW1V 2SA

Papers used by Random House UK Ltd are natural
recyclable products made from wood grown in
sustainable forests. The manufacturing processes
conform to the environmental regulations of the
country of origin.

A catalogue record for this book is available from the
British Library

Printed and bound in Great Britain by
Bookmarque Ltd, Croydon, Surrey

ISBN 0 09 190135 9

THE DEEP SILENCE

Contents

1

The Black Pig

The bleak waters of the Gareloch were speckled with countless tiny whitecaps as the stiff south-westerly wind bore up from the Firth of Clyde and flattened the gorse of the distant hills like wet fur. Firmly anchored at her usual moorings, the submarine depot ship caught the dancing reflections in her tall sides, which shone with spray and the drizzle which had been falling steadily since first light.

Yet, in spite of the wind and the damp air, it was warm, even humid, for early March, and the wide stateroom of the captain commanding the submarine squadron seemed still and lifeless, and the windows which overlooked the broad expanse of open water were misty with condensation.

The captain, a compact little man with sparse greying hair, sat watchfully behind his littered desk and studied his unexpected visitor with unrelaxed caution. Senior officers were not unusual aboard the depot ship, and with the growing importance of the submarine arm of the Navy they were almost a weekly disturbance to the intricate and dedicated routine. But Vice-Admiral Ronald Vane was not just another visitor on some fact-finding tour or other. As the prime organiser and guardian of the new nuclear arm to the submarine fleet he represented something special, whose word was worth full attention.

He was known to be an unpredictable man, and his sudden arrival from London by helicopter that morning, unheralded and without the normal ceremonial, had been a bad beginning to the day.

Even allowing for the eccentricities which were to be

expected from any admiral, Vane was an unusual man. He was small and thin, and dressed in a grey pin-striped suit, the wide lapels and baggy trousers of which would not have been out of place in the twenties. It was still creased from the cramped flight in the helicopter, and the captain wondered what made a man of such power and importance dress in a manner which would be shunned by his own steward.

The admiral turned suddenly, his eyes bright in his pale, lined face. 'When did the *Temeraire* come alongside?'

The captain sighed and relaxed slightly. Perhaps it was a courtesy visit after all. It seemed as if every possible person had come to see the latest addition to the new nuclear force, from technical experts to hopeful newspaper correspondents. The *Temeraire* was, after all, something very special. One of the latest hunter-killer submarines, fully equipped with a fantastic range of homing torpedoes and ultra-sensitive sonar detection gear, she was fully powered with a nuclear reactor which was at the head of its field.

'She came in at dawn, sir.' The captain pushed a thick folder across his desk. 'She's completed a full three months' trials and working up, and I'm sending her on to Rosyth for a final check-up for defects.'

The admiral ignored the folder. 'I'm afraid that's no longer possible. In my briefcase I have a new set of orders for the captain. He will be required to sail tomorrow at dawn.' His tone was flat and uncompromising. 'I suppose you can see to all his requirements?'

The captain stared at him with amazement. 'But it needs another month at least, sir! There are always teething troubles at this stage. We've ironed out a lot of them, of course, but the *Temeraire*'s brand new, and we can't afford to take chances!'

The admiral eyed him coldly. 'Fortunately, the choice is not yours, Captain.' He turned his back and wiped the haze from the window with his sleeve. He was looking straight down on to the vessel in question, and he found himself wondering what gave her the strange air of menace. Her rounded black hull was devoid of all the usual clutter of conventional submarines, and, apart from the tall, wafer-thin tower, there was nothing to break her smooth outline but for the hydroplanes which were folded on either side of her bows like two sharp ears.

8

There was silence in the cabin, and then the captain said, 'Where will she be sailing, if I may ask?'

The admiral stared fixedly at the black shape below him for several more seconds. In the far distance the tannoy squeaked and a metallic voice intoned, 'Up spirits! Up spirits!'

Then he said with sudden impatience, 'I'd like to go aboard at once. It will save time and repetitions.'

The captain controlled his irritation and picked up his cap. 'If you'll come with me, sir.'

The admiral followed the other officer out into the noise and bustle of the upper deck where oilskinned sailors moved busily beneath the swaying derricks as fresh stores were swung out to the waiting submarines. There was the sickly smell of rum in the air, and as the admiral passed the main galley he saw the cooks putting the finishing touches to the midday meal.

Then down a steep gangway and along a well-worn catwalk where a saluting sentry led the way across to the *Temeraire*. She began to look her size, the admiral thought. Her four and a half thousand tons made her almost four times as big as her conventionally powered contemporaries, but like an iceberg most of her bulk was concealed beneath the waters of the Gareloch.

He could see the scrapes and slime on her fat hull, the scratches on the black paint below the tower, or *fin* as it was now called, and it was hard to imagine her as being so completely new and untried.

A young, harassed lieutenant was supervising the loading of a large packing case, and he looked up startled as the captain snapped, 'I'm going below. I take it your C.O. is still aboard?'

The officer nodded, his eyes wandering to the admiral with the uncertainty of a man who has been told only part of the truth. 'Yes, sir.'

The admiral climbed through the screen door of the fin and peered down the oval hatch at his feet. He was a sceptical man, but even so was instantly impressed. The average submarine was constructed something like an underground train with one central passageway running from stem to stern. From his position above the hatch the admiral could see down and down as the ladders pointed the way through three decks and into another world. He followed his guide below and across the

9

gleaming control room. Even without the watchkeepers at their stations it was somehow alert and exciting. Rows of shining dials and repeaters, the sheathed periscopes and radar scanners, all gave the impression of immense power and strength. He wondered what else apart from size made the *Temeraire* so different from the other boats which still made up the bulk of the fleet. He decided it must be the smell.

Normally a submarine was pervaded by the unchanging odour of diesel oil and machinery. Here there was nothing of the kind. It was more of a sweetly antiseptic smell, mixed with that of sweat and cooking, a strange, unreal essence like the steel shell which contained it.

A petty officer handed the admiral a small film badge without a word and another to the captain. The latter pinned his to his jacket and said without humour, 'The usual precaution, sir. Just to make sure you don't become radio-active without anybody noticing!'

They passed down a narrow, brightly lit passageway, the sides of which were covered by pastel-coloured plastic, and which again gave the air of unreality. Outside a door labelled *Captain* the admiral said flatly, 'David Jermain, isn't it?'

The other man nodded. 'He's had command right from the time the keel was laid, sir.' He tapped on the door. 'This'll be a shock for him. The whole crew is about worn-out by the trials. They should have been going on leave from Rosyth.'

The admiral merely blinked. 'The world is unfortunately full of surprises. Not all of them pleasant!'

*   *   *

Commander David Jermain waited until the admiral had seated himself in the small cabin and watched his hands busy with the lock of his briefcase. Once he glanced across the little admiral's head to catch the captain's eye, but the latter merely shrugged, as if the visit was a complete mystery to him also.

The admiral drew out a narrow folder and cleared his throat. Then surprisingly he glanced around the cabin and said crisply, 'You seem very comfortable here?'

Jermain smiled gently. 'I've not had a great time to get used to it yet, sir.'

The admiral studied him thoughtfully. Jermain was an impressive figure, a man who somehow suited the boat. He was over six feet in height, with a slight stoop to his broad shoulders, the mark of many months in submarines. The admiral knew that over half of Jermain's thirty-six years had been given to the Navy, and of that more than ten years had been in submarines. In spite of his high technical ability, which the admiral knew from his records, Jermain had a strange old-world appearance which made him instantly arresting. He had a thoughtful, grave face with deep lines on either side of his mouth. But his brown eyes were faintly humorous, and when he had smiled his whole countenance had become almost youthful. His dark hair was rather too long for the admiral's taste, but it seemed to suit him nevertheless. He recalled that Jermain was a Cornishman. That probably explained it, he decided. The bleak coasts of Cornwall had produced so many sailors, navymen and pirates alike that it was easy to visualise some of Jermain's heritage.

He realised that the others were watching him and he said rather sharply, 'I am afraid that I have new orders for you, Jermain.' He dropped the folder on the small desk. 'You must complete storing and take on a fresh outfit of torpedoes and proceed to sea tomorrow at dawn.'

Jermain's eyebrows lifted slightly. 'Destination, sir?' He was still on his feet, his tall frame loose and relaxed, yet giving the impression of vigilance, like a cat.

The admiral coughed. 'Singapore. The situation in the Far East has been deteriorating lately, as you are no doubt aware. The Americans, quite rightly, expect us to do our fair share in reinforcing the nuclear screen in the area, so for that reason I cannot afford to give you any more time to complete your final trials. *Temeraire* can get a fair amount of help from the Singapore base in the way of small repairs and so forth, does that suit you?'

Jermain stared at the folio. 'I don't have much choice, do I, sir?'

'No, you do not.' The admiral glanced at his watch. 'You'll be under the local control of Vice-Admiral Sir John Colquhoun when you get there. He is having a difficult time of his own without your adding to it!' He gave a brief smile. 'Our government is bent on cutting down the naval and military strength in the area, and I am afraid that Sir John's own command is an obvious choice for the axe! However, that does not concern you. The Chinese Communist government is making fresh infiltrations and troubles which we think may endanger the peace of the Far East as a whole. The Americans are keen to contain this threat, but to do so they must have our backing. Anyway, it's all in your orders.'

'My number one has left the boat, sir.' Jermain tried to read beyond the admiral's calm eyes. 'He has been appointed to take command of the *Phoenix*, this boat's sister ship.'

The admiral replied coolly, 'I know. I ordered it myself. I'm sending you Lieutenant-Commander Ian Wolfe as your new number one.' He paused. 'Your brother-in-law, I believe?'

Jermain dropped his eyes. 'He was, sir. Married my sister about three years ago. They're divorced now.' He continued quickly, 'I thought he was in line for a command of his own, too?'

The admiral looked down at his feet. 'A further cruise as your, er, understudy might well be to his advantage, Jermain.' He stood up. 'Anyway, I want this boat ready on time. Forget the little nagging problems and concentrate on getting her shaken down into a fully operational boat! If World War Three broke out this afternoon I suspect that you would be the first to badger me to be allowed to get into action! Well, this is an emergency. We don't want another Malaysia or another Viet Nam in the Far East, and if a show of real force in the right place and at the right time can prevent it, then I think your, er, temporary inconvenience will be well worth while!'

Jermain said, 'It is asking a lot of a brand-new boat, sir.'

'I believe in asking a lot, Jermain. It's the only way I get results!' He grinned unfeelingly. 'Send me a signal when you sail. I must get back to the Admiralty, or the Ministry of Defence as our political guardians now choose to call it.' He chuckled. 'Although what we are supposed to be defending is sometimes a complete puzzle to me!'

Jermain groped for his cap. 'I'll see you over the side, sir.'

'Please, no.' The admiral tucked his briefcase under his arm. 'I don't want any ceremony. There are too many starving

12

defence correspondents slopping gin in the depot ship's ward-room by now. One sight of me and the whole thing will be out on their front pages!' He paused momentarily by the door, his eyes searching. 'When you get to Singapore you'll be working with the Americans, something which is nothing new for you with the Holy Loch just over the hill. But Singapore itself is undergoing a reappraisal by our government, and the sub-marine section in the Far East will become less dependent on any base there.'

Jermain frowned. 'Vice-Admiral Colquhoun has always been fully responsible for our operations out there, sir.'

The admiral shrugged. 'Things change. God knows, I've seen enough during *my* service!'

He stepped over the coaming. 'I'll go now. There's a lot to do.'

Jermain listened to their footsteps fading along the passage-way and then sat down to read the folio. After a while he picked up a telephone and said, 'This is the captain. I want all officers in the wardroom in fifteen minutes.'

*   *   *

The *Temeraire*'s wardroom ran almost the full width of the hull and was free of all the usual clutter to be found in the old-type submarines. The overhead pipes, the mass of complex wiring, in fact all but fittings essential for the comfort of the occupants, were discreetly covered by pleasantly coloured panels of bright plastic, and even the steel cupboards and bulk-head furniture were disguised in imitation graining to give the impression of well-polished woodwork. The lighting was con-cealed and carefully angled so that the whole wardroom was evenly lit, as if from an open sky. Only the gentle whirr of fans and the faint quiver of the toughened hull against its fenders reminded the silent officers of their other world.

Jermain dropped into a chair at the head of the table and laid the folio in front of him. He glanced around at the eight expec-tant faces. Apart from the missing second-in-command, there was still one absent. He cleared his throat. 'I see that the sub is adrift. But I shall have to carry on without our junior officer.'

There were a few laughs, and then Lieutenant Drew, the

anti-submarine officer, said gruffly, 'I sent him ashore for some spares, sir.'

Jermain nodded. It wás strange how he never got used to Drew's harsh Australian accent. He was a tough, restless man who seemed unable to relax at any time.

He continued, 'Any plans which you may have had must go by the board.' He saw Kitson, the electrical officer, glance quickly at his golf clubs propped in one corner. 'We have fresh sailing orders, and it will be up to each one of us to get the crew cracking in time.'

Jermain had their full attention now. When he had first entered the wardroom he had immediately noticed the air of relaxed ease, almost of gaiety after the three months of strain and hard work. In addition to the rigorous trials there had been the irritations of having a mass of passengers. Technicians and surveyors from the dockyard, experts from the base, and engine specialists from Rolls-Royce. Every inch of space had seemed to be full of men with notebooks and slide-rules, so that tempers had become frayed and even small problems had provoked open clashes.

Like his officers, Jermain had imagined that apart from putting right a few minor defects all these irritations had gone for good. The admiral had made it all sound so smooth, so easy. It was as if the *Temeraire* was a mere counter on a map, instead of being the most sophisticated and complicated weapons system ever to put to sea.

He said, 'We are going to Singapore, and we sail at first light tomorrow.' He looked at Lieutenant Mayo, the heavily bearded navigating officer. 'As soon as you've had lunch get straight over to the depot ship and collect everything you want.'

Mayo was as dark and brooding as his deep voice, but like the rest of the *Temeraire*'s team was hand-picked for his job. He grimaced and plucked at his beard. 'Singapore is it? God, that's a bit hard!'

Jermain looked next at Griffin, the doctor. 'Is everyone fit, Doc?'

Griffin was all arms and legs, so that he appeared to have difficulty in folding himself into his chair. He had round, liquid eyes, and seemed quite unmoved by the submarine's sudden orders. He smiled vaguely. 'I've not done a thing since

I came aboard, sir. Apart from handing out a few pieces of Elastoplast and a couple of crates of contraceptives that is!'

Mayo scowled. 'The Black Pig is the best contraceptive ever invented! Christ, you never get ashore long enough to do any damage!'

Jermain smiled inwardly. When he had first conned the *Temeraire* into the Gareloch from the builders' yard a dockyard manager had said with awe, 'God, look at this black pig!' So the name had stuck.

It was indeed fortunate that the doctor had no outstanding cases. A relief crew was at Rosyth awaiting the submarine's arrival and would no doubt be on leave up to the exact time of takeover. The admiral's orders made it clear that no delays would be tolerated. They sailed on time, no matter what.

Lieutenant-Commander Ross, the engineer, rolled an empty glass in his strong hands and studied Jermain's features for several seconds. The oldest officer aboard, he looked even older than his forty-four years. His craggy face was lined and grey from his trade, and he spoke with a sharp staccato tone used to carrying above even the most violent piece of machinery. Not that he had to worry about noise in the *Temeraire*. On her trials she had exceeded all expectations, and when running deep had eluded two stalking frigates overhead, in spite of the fact that both commanders had been given the submarine's exact course and depth.

Ross said sharply, 'Bloody typical! Twenty million pounds of equipment and they want to throw it about like so much scrap!'

Jermain shrugged. 'I'd possibly agree with you, Chief, if I thought it would solve anything.'

Ross added stubbornly, 'I can just see it. We'll get to Singapore and the base will have damn all! Just a few spares off the steam submarines from the First World War!'

Jermain sighed and flicked over the pages of the folio. Ross was a good engineer. The best he had met. But he liked to have the last word.

Sub-Lieutenant Luard, the supply officer, leaned back and closed his eyes as if to get a better understanding of what the orders would mean to him. Normally he was a cheerful, buoyant member of the wardroom, and was quite oblivious of the

15

crew's friendly contempt. They had nicknamed him 'The Ace' because of his dashing, neatly cropped beard and his habit of wearing an obsolete submariner's sweater on every possible occasion. He was said to look more like the old wartime submarine commanders than those gentlemen in question.

He said wearily, 'Thank God I've nearly finished stocking up!' Luard was only recently risen from the lower deck, and in moments of stress displayed a distinct Cockney accent. At other times he managed to keep it well under control. In his mind's eye he could see every item of food required to sustain eleven officers and seventy-nine ratings across thousands of miles of unseen ocean. Only that forenoon he had checked in some five and a half tons of fresh meat, six hundred dozen eggs and, most important, one hundred gallons of good navy rum. A nuclear boat was always supposed to be ready for a long cruise at any time, but nobody ever took it seriously. Until now. . . .

Jermain said, 'There'll be a new number one coming aboard shortly. Some of you may know Ian Wolfe. He's a first-class officer, and well able to take over at short notice.' He listened to his own voice, and wondered.

He had not seen Wolfe for over a year, and then only a brief moment. What was the real reason for his command being delayed? They had been friends for many years. At Fort Blockhouse, in the Mediterranean, wherever the Navy spread its influence, they were always bumping into each other.

Then Wolfe had married Sarah, his sister, and the knots had strengthened even more. Until they had started working on the nuclear boats with the Americans at the Holy Loch.

Looking back, it was hard to gauge the exact moment when things had started to go wrong. Jermain had returned from a long training cruise to find Wolfe beside himself with anxiety and despair. It had all seemed so confused and pointless. Sarah had left him, and it appeared that things had been bad for some time. When it became obvious that she had left him for another man, an American officer from the Holy Loch, Wolfe's bitterness had changed to an all-consuming anger. He had shut himself off from Jermain's friendship, and when the opportunity had arisen he had left for another course at the opposite end of the country. After that they had drifted apart. Sarah

16

wrote an occasional brief letter, and when the divorce came and went without fuss or publicity, the letters became even less frequent. Jermain was still baffled. He and his sister had always been so close. When their father had died just after the war, their mother had married again, and somehow along the way the threads of family had been broken for good. Jermain's home was in Polruan, overlooking the old town of Fowey and the gentle, unchanging estuary. But now there was no home, and no link with the old life. Just the *Temeraire*. The Black Pig.

He looked slowly around the table. 'It seems likely that more pressure will be brought on the government to restrict the use of Singapore as a base in its fullest sense. Boats like ours which can go for a year without refuelling if so required are quite obviously the answer. The Americans have been working towards this ideal for some time.' He broke off and stared at Lieutenant Oxley, the sonar officer.

Oxley was a debonair, outwardly casual man who made everything he did appear easy. It was an act, but as he avoided making mistakes it was a harmless enough affectation. He would certainly be earmarked for command, if he stayed out of trouble. He asked in his quiet drawl, 'But I still don't see the jolly old point of our dashing off to Singapore right now, sir. I mean, what about our people's leave and so forth? The lads aren't going to like it at all!'

Jermain showed his teeth. 'An understatement. However, it will be up to each of you to explain it to your own men. This is a picked crew. If you like, the cream of the Navy. They're not children who have to be pampered with promises! I will address the men later, but I shall want you to tell them the bones of this change right away. There'll be letters to write and various other arrangements they'll want to make before we sail.'

Ross said dourly, 'Bloody poor show! They never have any respect for how the lads feel!'

Jermain stood and picked up the folio. 'There'll be another briefing during the dog watches.'

Mayo, the navigating officer, plucked his beard and said dreamily, 'Sixteen thousand miles. I take it we'll be going round the Cape?'

Jermain nodded, satisfied that his bombshell had at last been

17

accepted as unavoidable. 'That's so, Pilot. Should take about five weeks.'

The petty officer steward poked his head around the curtained doorway. 'Are we ready for lunch now, gentlemen?'

Ross snorted. 'I just lost *my* appetite!'

Luard looked up from his notebook and scowled. 'That's typical! Rack your bloody brains to arrange a suitable and nutritious menu and *you* lose your bloody appetite!'

Jermain walked back to his cabin, their laughter hanging in the air behind him. It all seemed smooth enough. Perhaps the admiral was right about the way to handle matters after all.

He looked round the deserted control room and tried to think clearly about the days which lay ahead. He had told the others that the crew were the pick of the Navy. So they were. But they were also human, and like the boat had been under constant strain.

He bit his lip and walked back to his cabin. There was so much to plan and arrange. There would be time for suppositions later.

*   *   *

By early evening the drizzle had ceased and the wind had all but blown itself out. In the grey light the Gareloch shone dully like old pewter, its surface broken here and there by querulous little clusters of gulls which rode up and down on the gentle swell in search of scraps from the anchored ships.

Lieutenant-Commander Ian Wolfe paid off the taxi and stood for several minutes looking along the nearest wooden pier. But for a dockyard policeman near the barbed-wire gate at the far end the place seemed deserted, and beyond the gates and the low sheds of the wharves Wolfe could see the tall, stately hull of the depot ship, her ensign making a rare patch of colour at her stern.

He sighed and picked up his suitcases. His trim, athletic build made him appear taller than he was, and at first glance his open face and even, impassive features did little to mark him apart from any other naval officer of his age and rank. But closer inspection laid bare the unnatural tenseness in the set of his jaw, a certain controlled hardness in his grey eyes which might strike a stranger as being more unexpected than a physical deformity.

Wolfe felt tired and strained, and stared towards the distant town of Faslane with something like distaste. The long journey from the south of England had left him empty and irritable, and he had to quell the urge to speak his resentments aloud.

He strode towards the pier, his steps ringing hollowly on the wet timbers, his eyes fixed on the distant flag. He had been in Chatham when he had received his fresh orders for the *Temeraire*. He wondered why the change of events had not affected him more. Collins, the officer who had been given command of *Phoenix*, the new nuclear boat building at Barrow, had taken what should have been his. Not that there was any point in laying the blame at his doorstep. Their Lordships were quite oblivious to personal hopes and thwarted ambitions. Officers came and went, slotted and docketed like so many items of equipment.

It would be strange to serve with David Jermain again. He quickened his pace in time with his thoughts, his brain already exploring a new threat, a fresh change of fears. For months Wolfe had totally immersed himself in the study of his trade. He had ploughed fixedly through transistor theory, digital computing, Boolean logic and electronic circuitry, and the hundred and one other brain-wrenching problems he was required to master for his final command. And every hour of the day and night he was haunted by her face, the girl he had loved and lost to the American. Sarah, the strange, restless girl whose gipsy-style beauty had made him a slave at first sight when he had shared a leave with Jermain in the Cornish cottage.

He had imagined that a total involvement with his work would ease, if not actually banish, the misery from his mind. He never found theory easy to absorb, and he was more at home on an open bridge than in a classroom. He had been shocked to find that the reverse had happened.

The early warnings had shown themselves in lack of sleep. Then he had made stupid mistakes and omissions in his work, and twice he had lost his temper with the hard-pressed instructors.

But when he had found himself drinking just that bit more

heavily each night in his quarters he had seen the warnings for himself. Almost guiltily he had contacted a private psychologist in London, and while his classmates enjoyed their brief weekends with their families or friends, Wolfe made his secret visits to the quiet consulting room in London.

The thought of being discharged from the Navy had forced him to take this final step. He knew well enough that his career was the only thing holding him together.

Now he was joining Jermain as second-in-command. For a 'refresher' prior to actual command, as the admiral had so dryly indicated. Or was it merely to satisfy the Staff that he was only fit for second fiddle? Or nothing at all!

He stopped dead, the sweat like ice beneath his cap. He forced his nerves to return to normal with something like physical effort. It would be good to see David again, but for the nagging fear of his reminding him of Sarah.

Wolfe often wondered what Jermain really thought about him and his sister. Jermain had never married, had seemed strangely content with the almost monastic existence of a naval officer. Yet Wolfe knew that it was largely because of Sarah that Jermain had missed several promising chances. He had seemed determined that she would never be alone, and had sent for her to live near whatever base his ship was using. Wolfe guessed that because of this close tie Jermain would be feeling a sense of loss in his own way.

He noticed suddenly that there was a small group of figures huddled behind a hut at the side of the pier entrance. They were young teenagers in crumpled windcheaters and jeans, their bodies jammed together for warmth and comfort. Wolfe saw that two of them carried a rain-faded C.N.D. banner, and some of the others were listening to a raucous transistor radio.

He realised it was Sunday tomorrow. The usual invitation to ban-the-bomb enthusiasts to congregate around the Holy Loch or the Gareloch and chant their slogans to all and sundry.

Temeraire was probably the only British nuclear boat alongside at the moment, so this little gathering was no doubt for her benefit, he thought.

He felt the old anger moving again. Any little thing seemed to set it going. These long-haired teenagers, for instance. They would chant and protest like sheep until the *Temeraire* sailed.

Then it would be quite all right apparently for the other conventional submarines to stay in the Gareloch unmolested! As if being blasted to bloody fragments wasn't bad enough!

He swung round with a start as a young sub-lieutenant stepped from the group and saluted. He was a pale, almost delicate-looking youth, with the wide apprehensive eyes of a startled fawn. He said, 'Can I give you a hand with the bags, sir? I expect you'll be going aboard *Temeraire*?'

They fell in step as the policeman opened the gates and glanced at their passes. Wolfe had thought he would resent an early intrusion to his brooding, but the boy's casual acceptance seemed somehow soothing.

His name was apparently Max Colquhoun, the *Temeraire*'s most junior officer. He had been despatched ashore for some spares and was now returning to the ship.

Wolfe asked, 'Have you been aboard long?'

Colquhoun shrugged. 'Since she commissioned. My first real appointment actually.'

Wolfe smiled in spite of his tension. How the submarine service was changing, and changing fast. Gone were the days of oily hands, dirty sweaters and weeks-old beards. It was a clean, businesslike trade where young officers went in at the bottom and studied more like apprentices than junior watch-keepers of the old days. He asked, 'You knew I was coming then?'

Colquhoun sounded vaguely defensive. 'The gatekeeper just told me.'

'And those layabouts you were talking to. What the hell did you find to speak about?'

'Nothing really.' Colquhoun quickened his pace as a seaman ran down the brow from the depot ship to collect the bags.

His voice sounded sharper, Wolfe thought, like a little boy caught out. He sighed inwardly. What the hell! The sub-lieutenant could chat to Jesus Christ for all he cared!

On the other side of the big ship's main deck Wolfe stood looking down at the dull-painted submarine. Inside that fat hull was escape. A complete isolation which was more definite than distance or time. This was all he required. The London psychologist could go to hell from now on.

He clambered across the catwalk and returned the trot

sentry's salute. A small group of men were mustered by the *Temeraire*'s ensign staff, and an officer watched the depot ship's yard, waiting for the official Sunset to be sounded and the flag lowered.

Wolfe swung round and found his hand gripped firmly by another.

Jermain said quietly, 'Good to have you aboard, Ian. The Pig will go like blazes now!'

Overhead from the depot ship's rail a bugle blared the Alert. But Wolfe did not hear it, nor did he trust himself to speak. He looked at Jermain's grave face and knew that he too was glad to be here. Not only that, he *needed* to be here.

*   *   *

Jermain paused in the forward torpedo space and watched as Wolfe ran his hand over one of the polished breeches. He had taken Wolfe on a quick conducted tour of the boat, down through the three decks, the crew spaces and storerooms, the galley and the control room. Approximately in the centre of the submarine was a massive bulkhead which separated the living and storage quarters from the vessel's driving power and the secret reactor room. The watertight door in the bulkhead was known jokingly as Checkpoint Charlie, and no unauthorised persons were ever allowed access to the engineer's private world beyond.

Now, in the very stem of the hull, behind the six torpedo tubes, he awaited Wolfe's first reactions.

Wolfe said suddenly, 'There's still a lot to get used to.'

Jermain studied him thoughtfully. His friend was changed even more than he had expected. It was nothing you could lay a name to. He seemed as alert as ever, and his keen interest was obvious. But there was something lacking. He seemed without his old dry humour, as if it had been forcibly removed.

He said, 'You'll soon catch on. It'll be a good chance to put your hard work into practice.'

They climbed up past the sick bay, where an attendant was polishing glass beakers, and back up another ladder towards the wardroom. Jermain glanced into each compartment as he passed and tried to gauge the reactions of his men to the sailing orders. It was always difficult to tell with men like these. An individual who was nursing some grievance or fear might be slow to display it before the rest.

The coxswain, a thickset giant of a man, padded from the chief petty officers' mess and called, 'All the men are off shore now, sir. Except for the postman, an' he's just taken the mail to the dock office.' He stared at Wolfe with a pair of bright, clear eyes. 'I hope you'll be happy aboard, sir.'

Jermain grinned. 'No doubt you'll look after him!'

The coxswain rocked back on his heels. 'That's right, sir. Twine's the name. Any time you want anything done aboard, just drop me the wink!'

They passed on, leaving the massive C.P.O. standing by his mess.

Wolfe remarked, 'They seem a happy lot.'

'They'll need to be, Ian. Cooped up aboard on trials is bad enough, but a further long cruise without even surfacing will test their will to survive!'

They entered the wardroom, where Baldwin, the petty officer steward, was busy refilling glasses for the assembled officers.

Jermain said quietly, 'If you want to drink, Ian, now's the time.' He did not see the quick hardness appear in the other's eyes. 'The ratings are all right for their rum when we're at sea, but for us it's almost a teetotal cruise. We're kept on the hop too much for a bout of mess life!'

Wolfe relaxed slightly and forced his mouth to smile as he was introduced to the other officers. They appeared to be a good bunch, he thought. The engineer officer looked a bit of a binder, and the navigating officer, Mayo, might well prove an irritating companion with his gloomy face and deep, husky voice.

Jermain took a glass and raised it to the light. 'A toast, gentlemen. To Singapore, and whatever lies beyond!'

They drank in silence, and then Colquhoun's voice broke into the pause, as if he was unable to control it. 'Sir, I understand we're sailing tomorrow morning?'

Lieutenant Oxley, the sonar officer, grinned. 'God, has the penny dropped?'

Colquhoun ignored him and kept his eyes fixed on the captain. His face was quite white, and Jermain could see the muscles twitching at the corners of his mouth. 'Could I ask for a transfer, sir?'

Jermain lifted his hand as several of the others started to speak. 'What's the matter, Sub? I'd have thought you'd have liked the idea, your father being the vice-admiral there?'

Colquhoun dropped his eyes and seemed to go limp. 'I— I'm sorry, sir. I just thought . . .'

Mayo banged down his glass. 'God Almighty! You should be proud of the chance to sail on this trip, Sub! I don't know what's got into you!'

Jermain stared at the sub-lieutenant. 'I'm afraid it's too late for second thoughts now, Sub. The mail is posted, the shore telephone disconnected.' He glanced at the bulkhead clock. 'And in four hours the Chief here will be pulling the first control rods in the reactor to start it "cooking". And then at 0600 we slip and proceed as ordered.' He picked up his cap. 'Now, if you'll excuse me I'm going to the depot ship to pay my respects to Captain S/M.'

Colquhoun looked at Jermain's broad shoulders, then with the others still staring at him gave a short gulp and ran from the wardroom.

Lieutenant-Commander Ross peered at his glass. 'I have a feeling that this trip'll separate the men from the boys,' he said dreamily.

2

An Ugly Word

Jermain stepped into the control room and glanced briefly at the clock. Ten minutes to go.

The brightly lit compartment seemed full of intent figures, each man busy with his own private checks and double checks as orders were passed back and forth through the boat's maze of telephones and radio handsets.

Jermain acknowledged the formal greetings and walked through into the chart-room where Mayo was stooping over the glass-topped table, a pair of dividers in his thick hand. He looked up and said, 'Wind's freshened during the night, Captain. Gone round to the south too.'

Jermain nodded and flicked over the pages of the log. He could feel the tension rising within him like a flood, his heart pounding in time to the relayed orders and muffled clatter of machinery. He never got used to it. Never felt quite sure that all would go exactly as the last time.

It was not just holding command, with all that it could mean to a man's nerves, it went far deeper. The power and meaning of the *Temeraire*, her stupendous cost and value, her very presence was always hanging over him like some untamed beast. Jermain often had the nagging feeling that if he once relaxed or turned his back, like the over-confident lion tamer in the cage, he would never get a second chance.

He looked at Mayo's bearded face and wondered if he ever had the same qualms.

A messenger peered in at them. 'Five minutes, sir!'

Jermain had already been right round the boat. There was nothing more he could do. Lieutenant-Commander Ross had reported that the sealed reactor had gone 'critical' and there was power to respond to all orders. On the deck above, Lieutenant Drew was supervising the wires which still held the boat to her parent ship, and was no doubt cursing the rain and cold in his rich Queensland vocabulary.

Jermain buttoned his oilskin around his throat and checked his glasses before slinging them on his chest. Through the door he could see the coxswain sitting by his wheel beside the planesman, the pair of them looking more like pilot and co-pilot of some weird aircraft than seamen.

Behind them, his face masklike in the overhead lights, Wolfe stood with his arms folded, his eyes fixed on some point above the helmsman's head. At his elbow, a messenger waited for any sudden change of orders or swift emergency.

Jermain took a last look round. Nothing had been overlooked, as far as he could tell. They were all trained men. They must be treated as such.

He walked to the foot of the long, shining ladder and began to climb. In passing he tried to catch Wolfe's eye, but the man seemed absorbed in his duties and did not turn his head.

Up and up. Through the surface navigation bridge, where a messenger and a communications rating stood shivering below the open hatch and the angry-looking sky above.

Jermain stepped from the ladder and into the tiny cockpit at the tip of the fin, the highest point in the boat. He waited a few seconds for his eyes to get accustomed to the gloom, and then he peered over the screen towards the forecasing where seamen moved restlessly around the wires, their caps making bright splashes of white against their shining oilskins and the black hull below them.

It was a bad morning, he thought. The low scudding clouds and steady drizzle seemed to try to prevent the daylight from reaching the water, and only across the distant, craggy hills could he see any sort of detail.

The fin swayed lazily in the swell, and the starboard side squeaked against the depot ship's fenders. Jermain could see the usual cluster of figures atop the big ship's rail, including the white cap and gold leaf of Captain S/M, who was no doubt watching everything like an anxious mother.

Lieutenant Victor, the assistant torpedo anti-submarine

26

officer, stood at his side, shifting from one foot to the other. Unlike any of the others, Victor found his rank and appointment hard to carry. He had come up the hard way from the lower deck only three years earlier, and at thirty-two was already deeply lined, and his hair was thin and greying. He had been happy as a rating, and had accepted each small promotion with satisfaction, if not actual surprise. Then with the growing technical requirements of the Service he had been recommended for a commission. At first he had been flattered, and his wife had been quick to urge him onwards, to take the one irrevocable step.

Gone was the coarse but good-humoured life of the petty officers' mess, the 'middle of the road' which had always seemed so clear and safe. The wardroom cult was harder to understand, the social divisions more difficult to overcome.

Victor was a good technical man, but his lack of imagination was a tremendous handicap for his new role. As a rating he had always understood that once a man was an officer he was in a world apart, a world so tight and unified that it faced outwards with calm dignity and constant self-control. Yet, in spite of similar uniforms and ranks, the officers were as unlike each other as chalk and cheese. At the top of the tree were the professional, Dartmouth-trained executive types, men like Jermain and Wolfe, and Oxley, the sonar expert. Then there were the indestructible and essential branch officers, engineers like Ross, and Griffin, the doctor. At the bottom of the ladder were the others. Victor knew he had over-simplified it all, but he could find no other explanation. Why else was it, for instance, that even now he was inwardly sweating as he stared at the captain's shoulders? As if expecting a reprimand, or some patronising comment. He knew he was being unfair to Jermain, but at the same time he did not want another letdown.

Once, when he had been first commissioned, Victor had been serving in a small patrol submarine at Gosport. He had just begun to feel at home, settled at last in his new uniform. The boat's captain had been a young lieutenant, a casual, self-assured officer who had apparently done all he could to make Victor welcome. Then one night there had been a wardroom party ashore and Victor had got very drunk. Happily he had stood on a table singing one old song after another while the other officers and their wives had watched him spellbound.

They had applauded him, and clapped his shoulder. For Victor the sun was truly at its zenith. When he had sailed on trials the following morning he had heard the captain speaking to the first lieutenant about the incident.

The latter had remarked casually, 'Our new Fourth Hand seems to have a fund of songs, sir.'

The captain's reply had been icy and irritable. 'All the same, these bloody rankers! Give 'em an inch and they soon revert to type!'

Victor awoke from his brooding thoughts with a jerk as Jermain said, 'Let go springs!'

The wires grated across the steel hull, and from aft Petty Officer Jeffers, the second coxswain, yelled, 'Grab 'old of that wire, Archer! Stone me! You're like a bleedin' tart in a trance this mornin'!'

Jermain smiled briefly. 'Stand by!'

He lifted his glasses and swung them over the anchorage. Two dark frigates, still undisturbed at their moorings, and a small coastal minesweeper waiting to guide them down the channel.

There was a momentary break in the clouds, and a shaft of silver light played across the choppy water and lit up the *Temeraire*'s white number, S-191, on the side of her fin.

A few gulls circled overhead, and Jermain saw a scruffy drifter pushing down-channel towards Helensburgh.

He cupped his hands. 'Slack off the headrope!'

He saw Drew goading his small party in the bows, and watched as the dripping wire went slack and allowed the bows to swing slowly with the wind away from the depot ship's side.

Unlike older submarines, *Temeraire* had only one screw. It made her control and speed more silent at depth, but handling her on the surface was another matter.

The Captain S/M's voice floated from above. 'Good luck, David! Have one for me when you touch land again!'

Jermain lifted his hand but did not take his eyes from the widening gap of sloshing water. 'Slow ahead! Let go aft!'

The plating beneath his boots trembled only slightly, and he found that he was holding his breath. 'Port ten!'

With a gentle slop of spray around her bows the submarine

28

began to circle away from the protection of the depot ship's side. Once clear, the wind and rain splattered into the small cockpit and rattled against the glass screen.

Jermain squinted at the gyro repeater, watching the minesweeper turn obediently as if on a string. 'Midships. Steer one five zero.' He half listened to his orders being repeated into the handset and wondered how Wolfe was coping below. He seemed collected enough. This trip, unwanted or not, might be the making of him.

The mooring wires had been lashed and stowed, and Drew clattered up the ladder and said breathlessly, 'All secure for sea, Skipper!' He peered across at his assistant. 'Christ, Jeff, you look like death this fine mornin'!' He grinned at Jermain. 'Still, he's not a bad bloke!'

Victor's thin mouth twisted into a smile. He wanted to reply with some cutting remark, something to whittle Drew down to size. Victor hated his brash familiarity before the captain, his earthy behaviour with the men.

Jermain said calmly, 'Take over the con. I'm going to the control room.'

Drew rubbed his gloved hands. 'Aye, aye, Skipper. One five zero an' follow me leader!' He waited until Jermain had lowered himself through the hatch and then yelled down to Petty Officer Jeffers, 'Get those men fell in for leavin' harbour! This'll be the last fresh air they get for a bit!' To Victor he added, 'This is more like it, eh?'

The other man ducked as a curtain of spray lifted over the fin and soaked his face. 'If you say so.'

Drew winked at the signalman who swayed nearby with a small hand-lamp. 'That's what I like to hear, man! A real spirit of adventure! No wonder we've lost the bloody empire!'

Without either pipes or bugles to pay her respect the Temeraire passed quietly down-channel, a black silhouette like some child's drawing, her wash hardly disturbing the moored yachts and still-sleeping warships.

*　　*　　*

Four hours had passed since the Temeraire had slipped her moorings, and with a stiffening wind pushing to meet her she thrust her rounded snout into each successive roller with something like anger.

Thirty feet above the deck in the open cockpit Jermain felt the spray and rain stinging his cheeks like wet sand, and he sensed the old exultation slowly replacing the strain, as alcohol will unwind a man's taut nerves.

Wedged by his side Wolfe stared into the weather and wiped the lenses of his glasses before training them across the screen. As the submarine pushed steadily down the Firth of Clyde he could see the unbroken line of the coast some four miles to port, whilst looming out of the spray like a grey smudge on the opposite beam he could just make out the lonely rock cluster of Ailsa Craig. A mile ahead of the yawing submarine the little minesweeper still manfully led the way, her frail wooden hull shining like glass as she rolled from one sickening arc to another.

Jermain shouted, 'When we dive it'll be as peaceful as a vault! You can pour a cup of coffee and hardly see a ripple!'

Wolfe nodded and swallowed a momentary pang of nausea. Too long in a classroom, he thought bitterly. Too long with memories and tortured hopes for company.

Jermain glanced sideways at his friend. 'How does it feel to be back?'

Wolfe considered the question. After the first tensions of getting under way, the unfamiliar feel of the control room, and the strange, alien faces of the men around him, he had slowly managed to find himself once more.

Once clear of the loch and butting into the open water he had handed over to the O.O.W. and joined the rest of the officers at a hasty breakfast. Hasty because the *Temeraire* was heading to sea, and there would be enough time later for looking inwards. Now the officers and men not required for immediate duty squeezed into the small surface navigation bridge below the cockpit, taking that last look at the land. By the ladder, smoking and hardly speaking, the next batch of men would wait their turn.

Wolfe replied, 'Good. It feels good.'

Jermain squinted over the bows, watching the dark-sided waves with their angry, curling crests. Submerged it would be peaceful, and there would be time to start work again. In her natural element the submarine looked clean and different, her

30

rounded hull gleaming like the skin of a whale, with the surging water creaming back and over her sloping foredeck in an inverted horseshoe of frothing foam and spray.

He said, 'Increase revs for fifteen knots. Inform the escort, Bunts.'

The rating with the signal lamp nodded and cradled it in the crook of his arm. As the lamp clicked busily Jermain saw an answering stab of light from the minesweeper's swaying bridge. He said, 'I think if I had to go back to general service I'd spew my guts out!'

The rating intoned, 'Signal from escort, sir. "What is your diving position and time?"'

Jermain glanced at his watch and replied, 'We will be abeam of Portpatrick at 1230. Ten miles offshore we'll make the first test dive.' He added, 'Check with Lieutenant Mayo. With this damned wind in our teeth I may have to crack on speed a bit to make the correct area on time.'

Wolfe eyed him evenly. 'You always were a perfectionist. No wonder they gave you command!'

Jermain smiled quietly. 'I have my moments.'

After a few moments the light passed his signal to the escort. Then he added, 'Once in Singapore, I shouldn't wonder if they fly you home for your own boat, Ian. You deserve it.'

'Maybe.' Wolfe watched a determined-looking gull circling above the corkscrewing periscopes. 'It's this trip or bust for me. I'll never take a shore job.' He forced a smile, but there were lines of strain around his eyes. 'Can you see me in gaiters and sword at Whale Island? Or lecturing to a lot of bloody recruits?'

One of the two bridge lookouts said sharply, 'There's a sail fine on the port bow, sir!'

A sail? Jermain swung his glasses. 'Out in this weather?'

The brown hills and a solitary church steeple swam momentarily across the lenses, and then as the waves leapt into frightening size under the powerful glasses he saw the brief flash of dark red and a small flapping triangle of sail. It rose and dipped in the deep swell, but it was moving, and moving fast.

Jermain said, 'Damned fools! They'll have one hell of a time trying to beat back!'

31

A messenger at the intercom said, 'Turning on to new course, sir. Two one zero. Increasing revolutions for sixteen knots.'

'Very good.' Jermain seized the screen as a big wave broke across the bow and thundered against the foot of the fin. It was like a solid object, and he heard some of the men below laughing at each other's reactions.

Wolfe asked suddenly, 'Do you think there's more to our voyage than we've been told?' He shrugged. 'Or shouldn't I ask at this point?'

Jermain lifted his glasses again. The sail was fairly flying over the yellow-fanged waves. Like the fin of some giant shark. He felt vaguely uneasy, yet could not explain it.

He said slowly, 'As my Number One you have every right to know. But it's all pretty vague. Apart from a few routine details I've told you all I know. But the Chinese are getting restless. The Americans seem to think they'll try another push further north.'

Wolfe groaned. 'Not Formosa, surely?'

Jermain shook his head. 'Not this time. Something real is my guess. The games are over. The Chinese are getting tired of the cold war. They want to draw their little empire together with a piece of force.'

Wolfe frowned. Jermain's obvious interest made him realise just how out of touch he had become. 'You mean Korea again?'

Jermain did not answer. He said sharply, 'That damned fool! He'll be across our bows in a moment!'

Wolfe followed his gaze. The dinghy was moving closer each minute, so that he could actually see the small varnished hull plunging like a polished walnut beneath the bright sail. He could see three, maybe four, figures aboard, their backs arched across the weather side to hold the boat on its careering course.

'He might pass ahead.' Wolfe looked at Jermain's face. It was then that he realised something of the strain and responsibility which lurked behind those calm features.

Wolfe asked quickly, 'Shall I signal the escort to head the boat off?'

'No chance now. It'd take some time to turn round in this. The poor bastard is rolling his guts out as it is!' He glared at the dripping compass repeater. 'Alter course two points to starboard. Maybe the fool hasn't seen us yet.' His eye fell on the

32

signalman. 'Well, don't stand there gaping, man! Flash up the escort and tell them our new course!'

Jermain felt the tension growing around him. Below through the hatch he could hear the men whispering quietly. The captain was jumpy. The old man was losing the touch! He forced himself to grin. 'Not that I should care, I suppose. The old Black Pig would push that dinghy over like a matchbox!' The men laughed, but every eye rested on the red sail.

'Dinghy's going about, sir!' The lookout caught his breath. 'No it isn't, sir! The madman's coming straight for us!'

Wolfe watched spellbound. Through his glasses he could see the tense but determined faces below the sail, the way one of them was pointing at the submarine. It reminded him of an old painting of a whaleboat plunging on its quarry.

'Slow ahead!' Jermain ground his teeth as the eager wind pushed the sea heavily over the bows and swung the fin through one more sickening angle. He felt helpless, unable to control the four and a half thousand tons of steel below his skidding boots as it pushed on to some invisible meeting point on the sea ahead.

Wolfe said, 'Will you heave to, sir?'

Jermain shook his head. 'With this wind and sea running we'd slew right round.' He waved his arm through the rain. 'We'd be run aground in fifteen minutes hereabouts! It's shoal water out there!'

The bosun's mate asked, 'What orders, sir? Control room is asking for instructions.'

Overhead, the slim attack periscope squeaked slightly in its mounting, and Jermain guessed that the O.O.W. or Mayo was already watching the start of the inevitable.

Jermain said coldly, 'Close up the emergency deck party. And signal the escort to stand by to pick up survivors.'

Wolfe watched Jermain's impassive face and felt strangely moved. What a rotten beginning, he thought. What a bloody senseless waste.

*   *   *

In the control room Lieutenant Oxley, the O.O.W., stooped down to peer through the partly raised periscope, his sleek head

33

shining in the bright lights. He pursed his lips and murmured, 'Talk about David and Goliath!' He straightened up and glanced quickly at the gyro repeater. 'A collision course if I ever saw one!'

Max Colquhoun looked pale and tired as he watched Oxley's face beside the grease-smeared periscope. Apart from his general duties about the boat he was also assistant to Oxley in dealing with the complex sonar system which singled out *Temeraire* and her rare class. *Temeraire*'s function was to hunt and kill other submarines. To do this she had to be swift and silent, so silent that she remained undetected by her prey as well as by any possible hunter on the surface. Able to operate in great depths far below the isothermal barrier, she was virtually beyond the reach of any conventional sonar, yet could find and kill her enemies with calculated ease.

Oxley said, 'Come and take a look, Max.'

Colquhoun took the training handles of the periscope and peered through the spray-dappled lens. He saw the dinghy instantly, and felt his stomach contract as if from a blow.

The intercom barked, 'Emergency deck party close up at the double!'

Oxley grinned. 'That's you, Max! Watch you don't get your feet wet!'

Jeffers, the second coxswain, a squat, blue-jowled petty officer, was already climbing the ladder, his body deformed by his orange lifejacket, his cap tugged down over his eyes. He looked at Colquhoun and said, 'I'll lead the way, sir. It may be a bit dicky up top!'

The little party assembled in the lower part of the fin, four seamen and the petty officer, all jammed together and staring at each other like strangers.

Jeffers shrugged and knocked off the clips of the screen door. The wind was like ice after the swaying warmth of the control room, and Colquhoun stared out at the curved deck with something like shock. Below decks the submarine seemed vast and remote. Standing in the narrow doorway it was like standing on a partly submerged rock. He watched the hissing rollers breaking across the wet steel and the hostile sea beyond.

'Right then!' Jeffers stepped over the coaming and grasped

34

the handrail which encircled the fin. 'Let's go and take a look at the silly bastards!'

The dinghy was less than fifty feet from the port bow, and appeared to be higher than the submarine's deck. As Colquhoun and his men appeared around the fin the boat's occupants gave a small cheer, their voices whipped across the water like the cries of sea birds.

Colquhoun could see the escort vessel plunging back along her course, her stern rising clear of the wavetops, while from her bridge came the metallic garble of a loud-hailer.

The dinghy's sail changed shape, and two of the occupants hoisted up a crude banner which whipped out stiffly like a sheet of metal in the wind.

Jeffers groaned and dashed the spray from his face. 'Bugger me! They're ban-the-bomb merchants!'

Rider, one of the seamen, yelled, 'Some of 'em have been hanging about the base for ages!'

Jeffers snapped, 'I don't give a pig's arse *who* they are! They're done for if they touch the Black Pig!'

The waving dinghy sailors froze as if they too had suddenly realised the depth and size of the great monster which pushed towards them. Arms waved, and there was some attempt to retrim the sail. But it was too late. Like a leaf in a millrace the little boat began to tilt.

Jeffers snatched the grapnel and line from Rider. ''Ere! Let me 'ave a go!'

There was a sodden thump as the boat's drop-keel struck the curved bow, then it seemed to rush along the submarine's deck like a thing gone mad. The grapnel fastened into the gunwale and the seamen took the strain.

Colquhoun had a vague picture of staring faces and wet, shining oilskins as his little group struggled to pull the four figures clear of the stranded boat. From above he could hear the captain's voice, sharp yet controlled, as he swung the hull slightly off course to ease the strain of the wind and jubilant spray.

The four dinghy sailors stood dazedly against the fin, held in position by two of the seamen. Jeffers and the others man-handled the dinghy around the sheltered side of the swaying tower, the waves reaching at their skidding feet as they cursed

35

and panted with their captive. More men appeared from the open door, and knives flashed in the dull light as they cut away the sail and rigging. Now that the immediate danger was over the seamen were even joking with each other and throwing pointed insults at the unexpected visitors.

Jermain swung down the bridge ladder and steadied himself against the safety rail. It had been a near thing. His relief was giving way to a cold and unreasonable anger, and he snapped, 'Signal the escort to come up astern! We can put these four aboard their dinghy and drop them back by line.'

Jeffers rubbed his hands. 'They're lucky to be alive, sir.'

Jermain ignored him and pulled himself around the fin to confront the dripping and exhausted figures who were still pinioned against the streaming steel. He stared at their faces. All young. All frightened but defiant. He started. One of them was a girl, her forehead bleeding from her hasty rescue.

Jermain shouted above the wind, 'I hope you're satisfied? You damn nearly got killed!'

One of the youths said, 'It was worth it.' He grinned in spite of his discomfort. 'Thanks for being so decent about it.'

Jermain pointed towards the madly swinging escort. 'Save your excuses for him!' He turned his back and climbed up the ladder to rejoin Wolfe behind the screen.

Wolfe scowled. 'Little fools! I hope the authorities clap 'em in jail for a bit!'

Jermain fretted with impatience as the dinghy bobbed astern on a grass line towards the waiting escort. The little mine-sweeper had a scrambling net down. There would be another rough handling for the four youngsters before they were through. The dinghy would be a write-off. It was to be hoped that the brief demonstration would compensate the owner.

He replied slowly, 'Unlikely. It would be bound to get into the Press. I imagine that the admiral is unwilling for any extra publicity about our movements!'

He broke off as he saw the girl in the tossing dinghy turn to blow him an impudent kiss. In spite of his anxiety Jermain grinned. 'Well, they've got guts, whatever their motives!'

Wolfe turned away, masking his anger. He was worried, too. He had been leaning over the screen as Jermain had gone down to the deck after the rescue. Even with the wind whining over the bridge he had heard one of the young men from the dinghy say to his friends, 'Poor old Max! I thought he was going to have a fit when he saw us!'

Max. Max Colquhoun. Wolfe recalled with sudden clarity the young officer waiting by the pier in deep conversation with the small group of would-be demonstrators. The connection was obvious.

He wondered if he should mention it to Jermain. If an officer was stupid enough to blab about *Temeraire*'s movements he was a menace to everyone aboard. He thought of Jermain's other problems and decided against it. He watched Colquhoun pass below with the relieved deck party and nodded to himself.

I'll be watching you, my lad. Just one false move. Just one....

*   *   *

Lieutenant-Commander Colin Ross sauntered across the control room and paused outside the chart-room door. He was carrying a pair of disposable bootees which were worn by all persons required to pass through Checkpoint Charlie as a protection against possible contamination. He waited until Jermain looked up from the chart table and then gestured towards the bulkhead clock.

'Are we in position?'

Jermain smiled. In spite of the engineer's abrupt manner of speaking, he knew that Ross was a reserved, even shy, man. He was showing all the usual signs to be expected before the first dive.

'Coming up, Chief.' He tapped the chart. 'Portpatrick is ten miles abeam. Is your department ready?'

Ross sniffed. 'All checked and compensated. I'll be damn glad to get down. This motion is playing hell with my digestion!'

'Very well. Sound off diving stations.' Jermain picked up his glasses and walked briskly through the control room towards the ladder. The tannoy grated, 'Diving stations! Diving stations!' There was the usual flurry of padding feet, the click of equipment, and then the orderly shut down of all but essential traffic. Throughout the hull the various heads of departments reported their men closed up and standing by.

37

Wolfe was standing straddle-legged in the centre of the space, the trim book in his hands. 'Turn out the fore-planes!'

Jermain asked, 'All set, Number One?'

Wolfe licked his lips. 'I've just made another check, Captain. I've allowed for all extra stores and spares, as well as all other big items.'

'Good. It'll be different from the last time now that we've got rid of all the passengers.'

Wolfe allowed his brow to relax slightly. 'Ninety men aboard. That's ninety multiplied by about one hundred and fifty pounds.' He closed the book. 'That should do it.'

Jermain began to climb. 'Very well. Rig for diving.' He reached the surface navigating bridge and stared through the salt-smeared glass. The upper cockpit was empty, and here only the lookouts and the signalmen still waited until the last moment.

The shoreline was almost hidden in a fresh rain squall, and Jermain wondered briefly if the dinghy sailors were being well looked after in the distant minesweeper.

Below he heard the snap of metal as the watertight doors were moved and tested. If anything went wrong in the dive they would be slammed shut in an instant, sealing the compartments into separate zones of safety, or individual tombs.

The intercom announced, 'Hydroplanes tested and correct!'

'Very good.' A pause. A quick look round with the glasses. A brief picture of a jumbled town, far away, like an aerial map. A few gulls, a streamer of smoke from the escort's short funnel.

'Signal escort, Bunts. Am commencing first dive. Depth sixty feet.'

The light clattered, then there was an answering flash across the tumbling water. Jermain wondered if anyone in the distant town would see the light and spare them a thought. He found that his throat was dry. He glanced sideways at the signalman, a competent, trusting face. No sign of doubt or uncertainty.

He snapped, 'Slow ahead. Open main vents. Take her down to sixty feet!'

He listened to his orders being repeated.

'Clear the bridge!' He stabbed the red button and heard the banshee klaxon echoing through his command. The lookouts vanished, and he pressed it a second time.

Jermain felt the deck tremble very slightly and begin to tilt. He followed the others and slammed the hatch with the locking wheel. Down to the foot of the fin and another hatch to be sealed.

In the control room all was quiet but for the gentle whirr of fans and the occasional creak of metal. It was hard to realise that the boat was diving but for the slight angle and the telltale needles on the gauges.

Side by side the helmsman and planesman sat at their controls, their bodies hunched as if they were actually riding the Black Pig.

Down, down. Thirty feet. Forty-five. Fifty.

The planesman swung his controls and sighed, the sound very loud.

The orders were passed, voices hushed as if in church.

'Flood auxiliary tanks.'

'Engine room reports that shaft seals are one hundred per cent, sir.'

Jermain wiped his face with his hands. 'Very good.'

Although the hull was massively constructed to withstand the *pull* of eighty thousand pounds to the square inch, it had its weak points. The seals around the single shaft, for instance. But so far everything was fine.

'Steady at sixty feet, Captain.'

'Very well. Raise the radar mast and check on escort. Then make her a signal of our depth and speed.'

The dials flickered, the lights on the panels winked and obeyed each set move.

Jermain looked at his watch. 'Pressure in the boat.'

There was a mere hiss as air pressure was raised and measured.

The tannoy said, 'All compartments check!'

Wolfe listened to the rapid replies. 'No leaks, pressure constant, sir. All stations have checked.'

Jermain nodded and felt a nerve jumping at the corner of his eye. He looked across at Mayo's bearded face. 'Ready, Pilot?'

Mayo stretched and watched the helmsman. 'Yes, sir. Course one seven five. Revs for twenty-five knots.'

Oxley wrote rapidly in the log. It was somehow final.

Jermain waited a moment longer. Gone was the wind and choppy sea. Here all was calm and ordered. He felt a sensation of inner pride in this machinery-crammed world.

He said, 'Make a signal to escort. Will proceed as scheduled. Thank you and goodbye.' He watched the signalman writing busily. 'No, scrub out that "goodbye". Better make it "until next time".'

The deck trembled suddenly as the power began to increase. The build-up of speed would carry them clear of the busy traffic lanes, down to the open sea of the Atlantic and still further south.

'Up periscope.' He leaned his forehead against the rubber pad and peered through the powerful lenses. He saw the little escort turning stoically through a black-sided roller. Her shape blurred even as he watched. By nightfall she would be tied up at her berth, her crew scattered through the bars and cinemas.

'Signal from escort, sir. "*Bon voyage* and keep clear of dinghies!"'

Jermain smiled wearily. 'Down periscope. Secure radar.' He looked across at Wolfe. 'Take her down to eighty feet and fall out diving stations. Commence passage routine.'

Fiske, the petty officer cook, raised his head through the hatch and blinked at the activity. In a stage whisper he asked, 'Is it all right to get the lamb chops goin'?'

Oxley stared at him and said, 'Plenty of gravy, Chef.'

The cook vanished. For him the business of diving was just a plain inconvenience.

*   *   *

Jermain finished writing his personal diary as Ross leaned inwards through the cabin door and said, 'Running like a dream. I just wondered if you were going to perform the usual rite?'

Jermain smiled and gestured to the cupboard. 'Help yourself, Chief. That was a pretty good dive.'

Ross poured two horses' necks and stood them on the deck. He pointed at them and exclaimed, 'Look at that! Not a quiver!'

'Cheers!' Jermain tilted the glass. Probably the last one

before Singapore. 'We'd better go to lunch, Chief. There are a few points I want to discuss with you this afternoon about store space.' He looked up as Lieutenant Kitson, the electrical officer, hovered awkwardly in the entrance.

Kitson was a thickset, sad-looking man who appeared too clumsy for the task of controlling every electrical device and supervising many hundreds of miles of wiring which fed the boat like arteries. Yet he was as alert as he was busy, and even found the time to act as the *Temeraire*'s entertainments and sports officer. The latter duty was almost as demanding as the first. To keep the men fit and free from boredom the boat was equipped with films and taped music, as well as keep-fit devices and a whole cabinet of correspondence courses which covered just about everything from gardening to public speaking.

Jermain grinned. 'Not now. If one of your lads has broken the rowing machine it'll just have to wait till one of the artificers can fix it!'

Kitson did not smile. 'I'm sorry, sir. I *must* speak to you.'

Ross stood up and drained his glass. 'I'll be off.'

'No, Chief. This may concern you too.' Kitson shifted uncomfortably.

Jermain eyed him steadily. 'Well, what is it?'

'I've just finished my rounds, sir.' He held out his gloved hand across which there was a smear of fresh paint. 'I found this on the steering circuit, just forrard of the reactor control compartment.'

Ross scowled. 'So what? Christ, with all the dockyard mateys we've had aboard, I'm surprised there's any paint at all!'

Kitson swallowed hard. 'The paint was over the circuit wiring, sir.'

Jermain leaned forward. 'Just what are you telling me?'

'The paint was put there deliberately, sir.' He looked as if he was going to be sick. 'Underneath it the wires were half sawn through!'

Ross trembled. 'Do you know what you're saying, man?'

Kitson faced him stubbornly. 'The paint was still wet. There have been no strangers aboard for twenty-four hours.'

Jermain stared past him, his eyes empty of expression. 'Thank you. Carry on to your lunch now, will you? I don't have to tell you to keep quiet about this.'

When Kitson had gone Ross exploded, 'God Almighty, he's saying it's one of the crew! That would be sabotage!'

Jermain pushed away the half-empty glass. 'An ugly word, Chief. I'll have to think about it.'

3

Taking the Strain

Lieutenant-Commander Ian Wolfe walked wearily into the deserted wardroom and stared for several seconds at the table. He had just completed the 1800 to 2000 watch in the control room, yet somehow the thought of food and rest seemed to jar on his nerves. The long table was laid for two only. For himself and his watchkeeping companion, Sub-Lieutenant Colquhoun. Every officer did two hours on watch and six off, working in pairs. Apart from the doctor, and Luard, the supply officer, no one was exempt, and even Ross and Kitson, the electrical officer, stood their watches in addition to their other duties. The latter seemed to enjoy the change, and kept their watches alive with questions and playful mistakes as they grappled with the mysteries of navigation and seamanship.

Wolfe slumped in a chair and heard Baldwin, the senior steward, stirring into action behind his pantry hatch. It was hard to get used to the wardroom's sudden emptiness after the close-knit world of conventional submarines. Here there were double cabins for the officers, places where they could hide their faces from their companions and find moments of peace.

Colquhoun entered the wardroom and sat at the other side of the table, an old magazine already open at his side. Wolfe watched him thoughtfully and pondered back over the last seven days. Seven days since leaving the Gareloch, many hours of silent running south and further south, while the daily routine went on, and the captain put the boat through one exercise and drill after another.

When Wolfe had handed over the watch to Lieutenant Oxley the *Temeraire*'s position had been off the West African coast, two hundred miles from Senegal, while to the east lay the Cape Verde Islands. Nearly three and a half thousand miles since they had last seen the Scottish hills, yet with little or nothing to show any change.

Every day of the voyage Jermain would bring the boat up to periscope depth, and only the brief glimpse through the powerful lenses would show any sort of difference. Gone were the short, steep waves of the Irish Sea, the great, sullen rollers of the Atlantic. Now the sea was bright blue and unbroken, with a sky which was so clear it seemed to mock at their stealthy passage.

At first there had always been a queue of seamen to peer through the periscopes on such occasions, but now there were hardly any who seemed interested. This was their world, and they were looking inwards, at each other, at themselves. Even now, in the lower crew space, there was a cinema show taking place, which accounted for the air of desertion. Jules Verne would never have visualised such an improbability, Wolfe thought. The big, whale-shaped submarine gliding through the dark water at some twenty knots while her crew whistled and jeered at the exploits of an escapist film show.

Baldwin pattered into the wardroom and placed some soup on the table. Wolfe sipped slowly and watched his silent companion. Nerves were getting tense already, and there had been several small outbreaks of temper. The captain never let up on the drills, and Wolfe guessed that it was partly to keep the men from getting bored, as well as his own way of carrying on with tests and trials left over from the curtailed working-up exercises.

Wolfe's thoughts kept returning to the unknown saboteur. The idea of such a man sharing his every hour aboard grated on his mind like a saw. And the more he thought about it, the more he found himself watching Colquhoun.

Ever since the young officer's first outburst when Jermain had confirmed the sailing orders Wolfe had watched him and worried. He had pondered on Colquhoun's friendship with the C.N.D. demonstrators, and added to it his belief that Colquhoun was in real fear of going to Singapore, where his father was a very senior officer.

Colquhoun looked tired and pale, and his eyes were only

moving slowly across the open magazine, as if he was incapable of making the effort to read.

Jermain had approached the problem very carefully. He had spoken to each officer, and to all the senior ratings. It was to be kept quiet, a close watch was to be maintained and, above all, everything was to carry on as normal. It was unlikely that the culprit would strike again yet. His own life would be in danger, too. But once in Singapore anything might happen.

In spite of every precaution, however, Wolfe had sensed a difference in the boat. In the Navy the lower-deck telegraph was usually very active. Here, confined within the Black Pig's fat hull, the rumours moved quietly and uneasily, like an unseen gas.

Cruising on the surface it might have been different, Wolfe decided. A touch of spray, the sight of another ship, no matter how distant, would take the edge off the tension. But the *Temeraire* was not just a submersible boat, she was a submarine. She was built to stay under water, and her speed and manoeuvrability depended on it.

He looked up at the brightly coloured reproduction of Turner's *Fighting Temeraire* which hung facing him on the opposite bulkhead. It depicted the old ship of the line being towed up the Thames to the breaker's yard in 1838. She was being towed by a steam tug, and Wolfe wondered if people shook their heads then over the change from sail to coal, as they did over nuclear power. It again reminded him of Colquhoun's quiet evasiveness that night on the pier, and he heard himself say sharply, 'I suppose you'll see your father when we reach Singapore?'

Colquhoun did not look up. 'I expect so, Number One.'

He could feel Wolfe watching him like a cat, and he had to force himself to stare blindly at the open pages. Each swing of the *Temeraire*'s big screw was carrying him closer and closer. He had not seen his father for nearly a year, and even although he knew the separation could not last for ever, he had enjoyed every minute of it.

Colquhoun was the vice-admiral's only son. Like all his remembered ancestors it was expected that he too would enter the Navy as the only career. Colquhoun had fought his father right up to the last. He had never wanted to follow in his footsteps, and the conflict of wills leading up to his own final capitulation had broadened his resentment into hatred.

His father had been a submarine ace in the Second World War, yet it was hard to think of him as ever being young like Oxley, or Drew. It was equally difficult to compare him with Jermain's calm composure, or any of the other commanding officers he had met.

He glanced quickly across at Wolfe. He could well imagine his father being something like *him*, he thought bitterly.

Wolfe seemed to be two persons. Watchful and competent one minute, then giving way to short bursts of violent sarcasm, just like his father.

He thought about the dinghy escapade and the girl, Julie, who had nearly lost her life in the mad seconds before she was hauled aboard. He would just have to forget her now. Before, with the submarine going from the Gareloch or from Rosyth it had been easy to see her, to make the most of her exciting company. But she moved with a group, and Colquhoun tortured himself a little longer as he thought of her at this moment. Probably laughing and dancing with one of the others, while he might already be a faded memory.

They had met at the little club in Rosyth, a place frequented by students and others like Colquhoun who sought after their true identities. He had known it was wrong to tell them about the *Temeraire*'s sailing time, but how was he to know that her destination was Singapore and not Rosyth as originally planned?

He felt the cold resentment and hostility welling up as he saw Wolfe studying him with those grey, empty eyes. Perhaps he imagined that *he* had committed the sabotage! Colquhoun felt like laughing. It was probably a poor sailor who did not want to leave his wife, or some fool working off an old, vague grievance. It never failed to annoy him. The way that some people reacted to these small acts of wilful damage. It never seemed to occur to anyone that these clean and tidy ratings who said 'Aye, aye, sir' and saluted you at the right moments, who were competent and skilled at their jobs, had any problems of their own. Only occasionally, when a man came to his particular officer and asked his advice about mortgages, an unfaithful wife, about promotion prospects or changing his religion did the hidden part of the iceberg show itself.

Colquhoun pushed the picture of the unknown culprit from his thoughts and considered how he would react when he again met his father.

Vice-Admiral Sir John Colquhoun, a compact, steely-eyed man who seemed so like the many framed paintings of past Colquhouns in the old Hampshire home which had been in the family for generations. Before Nelson had joined the Navy, before the Dutch had sailed insolently up the Thames, there had been a Colquhoun in the Service. Now, in his fifties, the admiral seemed as far off and unreal as one of those paintings.

Colquhoun could remember his father's rage when he had found him at home during his very first leave from Dartmouth. He had been reading a book about ballet, but if he had been studying a work of absolute filth and depravity his father could not have appeared more furious.

'My God! What sort of a son have I produced? You're too spineless for a son of mine!' And so on and so forth.

Colquhoun usually gave in, if only for his mother's sake. She was quiet and frail, unable any longer to withstand the admiral's sudden changes of temperament.

He did not really know why he had entered the submarine service. Whether it was because or in spite of his father's past record was a point he could not decide. His mother had said, 'Your father will be proud of you, Max.' But the admiral had been strangely silent on the matter. Did he perhaps see his son's progress as some sort of challenge? It was indeed odd to realise that only within the same service had Colquhoun been able to show any sort of independence from his father.

He could well imagine what he would have thought of Julie. Like all his other girl friends, Colquhoun thought bitterly. The admiral used such words as *decadent* and *gutless,* and a *disgrace to their country*! He seemed to expect the whole country to be permanently under arms.

Colquhoun realised that Wolfe was saying, 'I thought your sonar department was a bit sloppy this morning, Sub. If we're called on to go into some sort of action you'll not get any second chances!'

Colquhoun kept his face non-committal. There had been another drill involving both the sonar and T.A.S. departments, and one of his men, a young seaman named Lightfoot, had made a complete hash of his settings. The result had been swift and disturbing. All the little pent-up tensions had flared and died like star shells, with voice-pipes and intercom snapping and barking complaints and reprimands until the error was sorted out and rectified.

He replied carefully, 'Lieutenant Oxley was in charge. He didn't seem too worried.'

'Covering up for you, I shouldn't wonder!' Wolfe seemed to control himself with an effort. 'Just keep an eye on your men in future. They don't respect softness.'

The first lieutenant stood up suddenly and walked from the wardroom.

Alone at the table Colquhoun stayed staring after him. When he gets a command of his own, that's one submarine I'll *not* join, he thought grimly.

*　　　*　　　*

Two decks below Colquhoun's lonely table the second crew space was equally quiet, and for a normally crowded compartment almost deserted.

It was crossed and lined by tiers of neat bunks and brightly enamelled lockers, and piped music insinuated itself from the tannoy loudspeakers at either end. Several seamen were sitting in their underwear around one of the tables intent on the serious game of uckers, and another solitary sailor was carving a model ship from a piece of wood.

Ordinary Seaman John Lightfoot lay in his bunk, his hands behind his head, and tried to make himself fall asleep. Through an open hatch in the deckhead he could hear the crack of gunfire and the muffled thunder of horses as the main body of the crew settled down to enjoy the Western in the main crew space.

Lightfoot was twenty years old, with wide eyes and a troubled mouth which added to his appearance of nervous expectancy. He tried to turn his mind away from his nagging, insistent apprehension, and he was almost inclined to leave the bunk and join the others at the table.

It was seven days since he had tried to cut through the wiring. Seven wretched and fearful days of waiting to be discovered

48

and unmasked in front of the others. But although rumour passed upon rumour, nothing had happened. Sometimes he imagined that people were watching him, speaking about him behind his back and waiting for him to slip up. Innocent remarks became barbed and full of meaning. Casual comment could become immediately suspect. Nervously, like a badly injured man feeling the extent of his wounds, Lightfoot explored the terrible events which had driven him to an act of sabotage.

From the film show above he imagined he could hear a familiar laugh, and he felt the tears of anger and shame pricking his eyes like needles. Able Seaman Bruce, the tough, devil-may-care Scouse from the dock area of Liverpool who had started him on this nightmare train of events.

Unlike Bruce and the majority of the crew Lightfoot was a 'pressed' man. He had been happy in general service, but like many others of the sonar branch had been forced into the submarine fleet without consultation. The submarine service was growing too rapidly to depend on volunteers, and Lightfoot had found himself installed in the unnatural surroundings of submarine life for a period of five years.

His early misgivings had given way to awe and pride, and within a few weeks he had settled down completely. A Londoner, Lightfoot had rarely made the long journey south from the Gareloch when his brief leaves became due. He had been content to wander around the strange Scottish countryside, which in itself was as different to him as the submarine herself.

His home was in Battersea, that soot-encrusted area of decaying buildings which sprawled between the great railway yards of Clapham Junction and the Thames. The place was slow to change even in the face of the advancing blocks of soulless council flats, and the Lightfoot family had survived want and unemployment, wars and personal unrest in the same street for four generations. In his mind's eye he could see his mother, old before her time, in the peeling kitchen of the little terraced house. It was sandwiched between one of the many railway arches and a soap factory, and when the fast trains went through the junction every piece of furniture would rattle and a fine film of dust would defy even his mother's busy efforts.

49

He did not know to this day if his family were glad he had joined the Navy. They could do with the extra space he had left behind, but in some strange way seemed to resent his efforts to break away from the dreary surroundings which were their lot. When he had gone home with the new gold-wire tally on his cap, *H.M. Submarines*, for all to see, his mother had said flatly, 'Well, I suppose you know what you're doing.' His father, on strike from the bus depot, had remarked, 'Dead cushy from what it was in *my* day!'

Lightfoot had not understood this hostility. He wanted them to be pleased. To wish him luck. It was strange how the ties of family seemed to hold him still, in spite of the distance.

Bruce, or Porky as he was called because of his capacity to hold his beer, had come into his life during one of those rare fits of depression which occurred each time he saw the men reading their letters from home. There was never a letter from Battersea. Just a card at Christmas and one for his birthday. Yet Lightfoot dutifully posted a regular allowance to his mother and waited for recognition. Bruce had said on that first afternoon, 'Wot's eatin' you then?' He was hard-faced, with the belligerent look of a fighter. His Liverpool accent was as sharp as his eye, but he seemed genuinely interested in Lightfoot's problems.

Then he had said, 'Forget it, kid! I told my folks to get stuffed when I was thirteen!' He had shown his strong, uneven teeth. 'Jesus, the old man nearly threw a fit!' He had squatted on the bunk, his eyes dreamy. 'This regiment's a pushover if you keep out of trouble aboard ship. Then, once ashore, you do what the bloody hell you like! You come on a run ashore with me, kid. I'll show you!'

And he had, too. Lightfoot had got drunk for the first time, but true to his word, Porky Bruce had shepherded him back to the *Temeraire* and safely past the cold eye of the duty petty officer. He had undressed him and cleaned the vomit from his shoes with the calm indifference of an old campaigner.

They made a strange pair. Lightfoot, wide-eyed and desperately keen to prove himself; Bruce, brash and casual, with the hard-won knowledge of the lower deck to carry him through. Bruce seemed to have two faces. He worked on the sonar with Lightfoot and was extremely competent. Yet he made his skill appear like insolence, his brisk familiarity with his instruments seemed as if he was cocking a snook at his immediate superiors.

He had educated Lightfoot in his trade, and in the same manner had looked after him ashore. He had even laid low a marine outside a pub just to show his youthful companion how easy it was.

Only once on board the *Temeraire* had he shown the latent force to his mess mates. A seaman had jokingly remarked about Lightfoot's constant shoregoing habits with his unlikely friend. Bruce had seized the man and had shaken him gently like a rat, his face only inches away. 'Me an' the kid is oppos, see?' Shake. Shake. 'When I want your friggin' advice I'll ask for it, see?' Another shake. 'Any more squit from you an' I'll mark you for life!'

And that was that.

Then had come the night when things had changed. They had been together in a small pub outside Faslane. A dull place, full of sailors who were drinking because there seemed nothing else to do. Somehow or other they had got into conversation with a middle-aged civilian who told them he was a salesman. He had offered to drive them to his hotel where he had some bottles of better stuff than they were getting in the pub.

Several drinks later they had gone out to the man's car, and with a roar of noise had started down the open road away from the town. After a while Bruce had said thickly, 'Must get out. I'm burstin'!'

Lightfoot could remember every moment which followed. The car's sudden acceleration, a momentary glimpse of Bruce's startled face in the swinging headlights as he stood swaying at the side of the road.

Lightfoot had not grown up in the slums without learning that such men existed. In fact, when he was only ten his best friend had been picked up by some man and taken behind the hoardings off the Falcon Road.

Lightfoot remembered the man's hot, frantic hand, the noise of the engine and the weird moonscape within the powerful headlights. He had wriggled on the swaying seat, struggling first with anger then with fear as the car drove faster and faster in time with the man's voice.

It had only taken a few seconds, yet it had lasted a lifetime.

51

When Bruce had come panting along the road he had found the car against a tree and Lightfoot standing motionless beside it.

The man lay a few feet away, his skull crushed against a piece of stone. In the headlights' reflected glare they could see the blood shining on the grass, the pebble-like stare in the man's dead eyes.

'I killed him!' Lightfoot had listened to his own voice like a stranger. 'He tried to . . .' He had staggered vomiting against the car. 'I pushed him hard and his door opened.'

The headlights had died at that instant and he remembered Bruce saying harshly, 'Serve the bastard right!' The next piece of the pattern was harder to remember.

Bruce stumbling in the darkness, making sure that they had left nothing in the car. Then the pair of them running like hunted animals beside the road, and ducking as an occasional car drove past. As they had reached the outskirts of the town a police car and ambulance had swept down the same road, sirens wailing and lights flashing.

They had returned to the submarine and climbed into their bunks. Bruce had merely paused to say in a fierce whisper, 'Take my word on it! The scuffers will never connect us with it!' That was all he seemed to care about it.

Looking back it was hard to understand what he had really hoped to gain by the sabotage. When the *Temeraire* had returned from her last batch of trials Lightfoot had waited for the police to board the boat and take him away. Nothing had happened at all. Everything seemed to be dwarfed by the news that the boat was sailing immediately for the Far East.

Lightfoot knew he would be unable to stand the waiting any longer. He had to delay the departure so that he could make his way to London and explain to his family before they heard the story from someone else.

Again he felt the tears welling up behind his eyes. He had even made a mess of that. He had dodged the trot sentry and found his way aft unseen. He had been at work with a hacksaw when Bruce had appeared at his side.

' 'Ere! Cut that out, you young twit!' He had spoken in a grating whisper. 'I saw you was missin' an' I guessed what you might try!' He had seized his wrist in a vice-like grip. '*I'm* in this too, remember! I told you before, the scuffers'll never latch on to us. An' anyway that bloody queer deserved what he got!' Briskly he had smeared paint across the half-cut wires. 'Now git forrard an' for Chrissake take a grip on yourself!'

The worst of it was, Bruce really did not care about it. He was up there in the film show hooting his head off as if he hadn't a care in the world.

Every time there was a pipe over the intercom or a petty officer called his name Lightfoot nearly fainted. He felt trapped and alone, with no one who could help but Bruce.

The leading hand of the mess, a tall Devonian named Haley, sauntered past the bunk. 'You okay, youngster?' He peered in at him. 'You look two-blocks to me!'

Lightfoot bit his lip. 'I'm all right, Hookey. Something I ate, I expect.'

Haley nodded sagely. 'That bloody Porky been feedin' you some of his rum again?' He grinned and walked over to join the others.

Lightfoot remained staring at the bunk above. He had to get a grip on himself. Had to.

The intercom broke into the music. 'D'you hear there! Ordinary Seaman Lightfoot muster outside the wardroom!'

Lightfoot shut his eyes and felt the nausea closing over him.

*   *   *

Colquhoun looked up from his thoughts as he heard the quiet knock on the wardroom door. 'Come in.'

Lightfoot paused uncertainly in the entrance, his cap held awkwardly in his hands, his eyes flickering around the deserted wardroom like, Colquhoun thought, a trapped animal.

'You sent for me, sir?' Lightfoot's voice was husky.

Colquhoun stared at him. Usually he saw the young seaman as a hunched figure over the sonar controls or another familiar face moving through the boat on some mission or other. Tonight he looked strange and quite different. His hair was dishevelled, as if he had just got out of bed, and there were dark shadows under his eyes.

'Just wanted a quiet word, Lightfoot.'

The young seaman waited, the well-lit wardroom spinning around him like some maddened whirlpool. Only the seated officer remained unmoving and still, like an inquisitor.

'I was a bit worried about the drill this morning.'

Lightfoot waited for Colquhoun to continue. Any second now. The accusation, the beginning of the end.

Colquhoun stood up. 'Are you feeling all right?' He saw the boy swallow hard. 'You look like death.'

'I'm fine, sir.' Lightfoot tried to bring the moisture back to his dry lips. 'Just a bit tired.'

'I'm sorry I dragged you up here then. It was just to say that we're having another drill tomorrow, and I thought it best to go over what went wrong this morning.'

'Is that all, sir?' Lightfoot stared at him as if mesmerised.

Colquhoun gave a small smile. He could remember the angry confusion and then Wolfe's 'They don't respect softness!' 'Some people take the view that it's quite important. I just wanted to make sure that nothing goes wrong in *our* section again.' He brushed his fair hair from his eyes. 'It makes for a quieter life that way!'

Lightfoot held himself upright with physical effort. He was safe for a while longer. In fact, the young sub-lieutenant was trying to be friendly. It did not seem possible. He managed to reply, 'It was my fault, sir. I slipped up. The valve casing was loose and the vibration was getting on my nerves.' He faltered, looking for the right words. 'I'm sorry if I fouled up the exercise.'

He looked so miserable that Colquhoun felt vaguely sorry for him. As soon as he had ordered a messenger to pipe for Lightfoot he had relented. He was not even sure of the real reason. He saw the boy's eyes wandering about him as if marking the differences between his own way of life and those of Colquhoun.

'Have you settled down all right?'

Lightfoot nodded. 'I like it very much, sir. It's a bit different from what I'm used to.'

Colquhoun knew something of his background and said, 'Well, I expect even Battersea will seem good enough when you get back from this cruise!'

Lightfoot's chin lifted slightly. 'I didn't mean my home, sir. I was talking about leaving general service and coming to submarines!'

God, you bloody fool! Colquhoun felt a flush rising to his cheeks. He wanted so much to feel at home with these men, to understand them. If he had to be in the Navy he did not want to be just another officer, like so many he had met.

He said hurriedly, 'You must think I'm an idiot! I didn't mean to sound like that.'

Lightfoot studied him gravely. 'You don't have to worry, sir. I'm used to it.' He shrugged. 'Anyway, you're an officer.'

Colquhoun laughed in spite of his embarrassment. 'Well, I suppose that means something!'

There was an awkward silence. Then Colquhoun said, 'When we get to Singapore I expect there'll be a good deal of sport going on.' He made up his mind. 'Do you like sailing?'

It was Lightfoot's turn to smile. 'Never had much chance, sir. The Thames is pretty crowded off Nine Elms!'

'I asked for that.' Colquhoun tried to picture the seaman in the dismal surroundings which still seemed to haunt him. 'I'd be glad to have you in my dinghy crew if you like. Are you interested?'

Lightfoot thought briefly of Bruce and what he would say. Bloody officers! They're all bastards! Then he said quickly, 'Thanks. I'd like to have a go very much, sir!'

He looked closely at Colquhoun's pale face. It was difficult to spot where the difference lay. Perhaps in his easy, assured manner as much as in his accent. He thought that Colquhoun was not terribly good at his job, but then junior officers never seemed to be, anywhere. But he was different from the others. Not so sharp, not so quick with a reprimand when one was required and earned. He had heard Bruce say of him, ' 'E's as soft as 'addock-water! 'E wouldn't be where 'e was if 'is old man wasn't a bleedin' admiral!'

Lightfoot felt a nerve jump in his cheek as Colquhoun said casually, 'Let's hope we don't have any more wilful damage at Singapore. That might put the lid on everything!'

He shifted uneasily. 'This chap, sir. I—I mean, this one who did the damage.' He forced himself to meet Colquhoun's gaze. 'Do you reckon they'll find him?'

Colquhoun heard a buzz of noise through the door. The film must be ending. He glanced at his watch. 'Probably. We'll just have to keep our eyes open, won't we?'

55

'What would make a man do it, sir? Maybe he had a reason.'

Colquhoun watched him evenly. 'But no valid excuse, I expect.'

Lightfoot stepped back as Lieutenant Drew sauntered through the door and then said, 'Well, I'll check the gear tomorrow morning, sir. Before the drills start.'

Drew raised an eyebrow as the young seaman hurried away. 'One of your friends, Sub?' He grinned. 'Or are you just instilling a bit of discipline?'

Colquhoun did not reply. He was still staring at the open door, the picture of Lightfoot's face etched in his mind like a photograph. My God, he thought suddenly. It was Lightfoot! His guilt had been as naked on his face as if he had openly admitted to the sabotage attempt.

Colquhoun sat quite still, dazed with the shock of his unexpected knowledge.

*　　　*　　　*

The following morning, as soon as breakfast had been completed and the boat cleaned for another day, the drills started all over again.

Precisely at 0930 Jermain entered the control room and consulted the log. Then to Mayo, the O.O.W., he said, 'Bring her up to periscope depth, Pilot. It's time to take a look around.'

Jermain half-listened to the brisk pattern of commands behind him. Everything seemed to be running smoothly this time, he thought. And the sonar department had reported another ship some five miles away on the port bow. She would make a good mock target for the torpedo crew, something stronger than a figment of the imagination.

'Sixty feet, sir!'

'Very good. Up periscope.' He crouched down, his eye screwed against the slim monocular attack periscope. He blinked as a shaft of blinding sunlight lanced through the lens and then swung the handles towards the reported bearing.

There she was. A low-lying freighter with a long trail of greasy smoke hanging in her wake like a banner. She looked at peace with the world, no doubt making for Sierra Leone, he decided.

He turned the periscope through a full circle. The sea was flat and empty, a moving pattern of blue silk, glittering in a thousand hues in the reflected sunlight. He settled again on the lonely merchantman.

'Down periscope. Exercise Action Stations!' The alarm shrilled momentarily in the boat's still air, and he watched the clock as men hurried quietly to their positions.

'Steer one four zero. Reduce speed to twelve knots!'

Wolfe picked up his notebook and stood by his side, his eyes expressionless as he watched the coxswain easing the wheel over.

Jermain said, 'We'll attack with two tubes, and then run deep as if she had a destroyer escort, Number One.' He broke off as the reports began to come in.

'Target is bearing Red four five. Range ten thousand yards. Approximate course and speed zero five zero, six knots.'

Wolfe said sharply, 'I'd like to have a word with you after the drill, sir.'

Jermain broke into his train of thoughts and stared at him. 'Something wrong?'

'Young Colquhoun, sir. I think he's slack. I'll have to bear down on him for a while!'

Jermain felt a twinge of irritation but replied evenly, 'Has he done something stupid?'

Wolfe frowned. 'It's his whole attitude. Last night I saw him chatting to one of the men in the wardroom. I think he did it to spite *me*. I'd already told him not to try and curry favour with the men under him. But he's too damn clever for his own good!'

The petty officer at the plot said, 'Target holding course and speed, sir.'

Jermain snapped, 'Start the attack!' Then quietly to Wolfe, 'For God's sake, Ian, you can cope with that surely?'

'Well, I'm new aboard here. I thought it might come better from you!'

Mayo called, 'Ready, sir!' He was watching Wolfe's face with considerable interest.

'Up periscope!' Jermain tried to shut out Wolfe's set features and forget the ominous tension in his voice. He had sounded as if the matter was really important, not merely an

57

everyday problem. Perhaps he was not yet ready for sea service again? Maybe the admiral had been trying to tell him just that when he had changed the orders.

The old freighter swam across the cross-wires and settled as if caught in a mesh.

'Stand by One and Two tubes!' He glanced quickly at a messenger. 'Check with the T.A.S. officer and tell him I want a complete timing of the attack. Down periscope!'

He expected to see that Wolfe had returned to his duties, but instead he stood facing him as stubbornly as before.

Jermain said evenly, 'Look, why not forget about it for a day or two? We've another three weeks yet before Singapore. You don't want to be too hard on a man, or an officer, until you've had time to test his metal!'

'If you think so, sir.' Wolfe sounded unconvinced. 'But if I was his commanding officer . . .'

The strain and responsibility of the past two weeks tore at Jermain's reserve like a steel barb. He stepped closer to the other man, his voice lowered to a whisper. 'Until that time, Number One, I suggest you try to keep a sense of proportion!'

He swung round as the messenger said breathlessly, 'Lieutenant Drew reports that the drill took fifteen seconds, sir!'

Jermain found that his hands were shaking from the sudden burst of anger, but he managed to control his reply. 'Good. Now we'll carry out the second part of the exercise.'

He strode to the intercom. 'Shut off for depth-charging! We will now carry out an emergency dive!' He heard the click of controls and the gentle hiss of compressed air, then he said, 'Right. Take her down to six hundred feet!'

Mayo said, 'Six hundred feet, sir! That's equal to our record dive on trials!'

The deck tilted very slightly, and with all the watertight doors and hatches slammed and clipped shut the air seemed suddenly flat and lifeless.

Jermain counted the seconds, his eyes fixed on the big depth gauges above the helmsman's head. Perhaps this extreme dive would help to drive out some of the stupid and petty irritations, he thought. Wolfe's sudden and unexpected outburst had been as unnerving as a mechanical failure, even more so because there was nothing in his face to show the reason for it. He

58

seemed to have momentarily forgotten Colquhoun, he thought. Anyway, he was watching the diving operations and showed no sign of either anger or resentment. He had changed. *How* he had changed!

'Two hundred feet, sir!' The planesman's voice sounded taut.

Down, down, deeper into a sea which must have already lost sight of the sun and the calm sky above.

'Three hundred feet, sir!'

Jermain glanced at the clock. 'Increase to fifteen knots.'

In his mind's eye he could picture the *Temeraire*'s great bulk gliding down like a graceful whale, a shadow growing in the darkness. Gone would be her fat, even humorous surface outline. Down here she was in her true element. A hunter. A killer.

'Four hundred feet, sir!'

It was incredible to realise that only twenty years earlier, when men like Colquhoun's father had stalked enemy shipping, the diving depth had rarely gone beyond two hundred feet, and usually it had been half that amount. At this great depth their hulls would have been crushed, then burst apart by the mounting pressure. And the Black Pig could do better. Much better.

'Five hundred feet, sir!'

'Very good. Increase to twenty knots.' The greater thrust from the big screw would give the planesman an easier task as he guided the massive hull downwards.

Mayo coughed. 'It's a weird feeling! Apart from the dials we might be at periscope depth!'

The deck gave a slight quiver, and from beyond the chart-room came a dull, drawn-out groan of metal under pressure.

'Six hundred feet, sir!'

'Good.' Jermain could feel his shirt clinging to his back. 'Check all compartments!'

He looked across at Wolfe's stiff shoulders. 'After this we'll return to cruising depth and give the men a break.'

The messenger said, 'Chief Engineer on this telephone, sir.'

Jermain took it quickly. 'Well, what is it? And why don't you use the intercom and save time?'

Ross sounded far away. 'You'll not be wanting a full broadcast, sir. I've just finished my check down aft, sir. I'm not happy.'

Jermain felt the eyes of the others on his face, reading his lips like blind men.

Ross continued, 'Below the generator room there's a definite seepage. My lads are checking again now, but I'm pretty sure.'

Jermain stared at the handset. 'Do you mean a fracture in the hull itself, Chief?' He heard Mayo gasp and saw one of the seamen put his hand to his mouth.

Ross sounded firm. 'I can find no other reason, sir.'

Jermain bit his lip and tried to form a mental picture of the small, box-like compartment just aft of the reactor room. A small leak was to be expected at this stage and under these conditions. But a flaw in the hull! He felt his mouth go dry.

Even with every possible care such things could happen. Other nuclear boats like the *Dreadnought* and the *Resolution* had been docked with hairline cracks in their hull structures. But they had been in good hands, and their faults had been contained, if not completely cured, in dockyards equipped to deal in such matters. But out here, thousands of miles from any proper aid and attention, *Temeraire* had no such advantage.

Ross said suddenly, 'I suggest you reduce speed to twelve knots, to cut vibration, but keep at this depth for another twenty minutes or so. Then I'll come and tell you what I think.' A small pause. 'But if you want my advice you'll go up top and make a signal that you're returning to base!'

Jermain put down the handset and walked to the centre of the control room. He felt the content of Ross's report like a pain, as if the *Temeraire*'s very arteries had been injured and the extent of her damage was finding its way to him.

He looked at Wolfe. 'Open up the boat, Number One. I'm afraid those watertight doors will not keep this rumour under control!'

4

Sword and Medals

Vice-Admiral Sir John Colquhoun, Flag Officer Commanding the Far East Inshore Squadron, marched into the cool interior of his wide reception room and stood for a few moments to regain his breath. Normally he would have felt the old exhilaration of Sunday morning with the firm traditions of parades and divisions, but on this particular day he seemed unable to control his irritation and sense of annoyance.

Forrest, his elegant but harassed flag lieutenant, followed him into the room and made a quick gesture to a waiting steward who was hovering near the window which ran the full side of the far wall. The steward skilfully rolled up the blinds so that the glittering expanse of Singapore anchorage was displayed like a framed panorama, the moored warships and shimmering white buildings beyond pinned down by the sun's persistent glare, and made unreal by its intensity.

The admiral sighed and plucked quickly at his crisp white uniform. Beneath it his body felt dry and prickly from standing too long in the sun while the marine band went through its repertoire and the long ranks of sailors waited for inspection and the final ordeal at the mercy of the base chaplain. But Sunday was Sunday, and neither weather nor any of his other problems were allowed to alter the admiral's set routine.

He unbuckled his sword and threw it on to a chair. The steward was already pouring gin into an iced glass, and the flag lieutenant was shifting from one foot to the other as he waited for his master's next possible demand.

Sir John Colquhoun was a compact, impressive figure in his well-cut uniform, and the pale, steady eyes which gazed out over the harbour gave little indication of his uncertainty and anger. He stared steadily at the empty buoys directly opposite his new headquarters and thought back over the past months, so that without difficulty he could picture the old but impressive bulk of his flagship, the aircraft carrier which had sailed so recently on her last voyage to the breaker's yard.

Far away in London, a stroke of a pen, a unanimous decision at government level had changed life for him, and indeed for many others. The empty buoys seemed to symbolise his sense of isolation and loss as much as the sterile building over which his flag now flew. The thought of being tied to a desk, with all the clutter of charts and meaningless wall graphs, made him feel his age and awoke the old bitterness like some nagging illness.

He snapped, 'Is the *Temeraire* alongside?'

The flag lieutenant read the signs and said carefully, 'She passed Beaulieu Point just before this morning's parade, sir. She picked up her moorings an hour ago.'

The admiral crossed to the open window and swung the giant telescope on its tripod until it settled on the squat, grey outline of the submarine depot ship. There was a sense of anti-climax in what he saw. The nuclear submarine was just another black shape. In the old but powerful lens he could see the slime on her hull, the signs of endurance of nearly five weeks underwater. All the same, it was an impressive achievement, he thought. The speed of her voyage from Scotland would have been thought impossible to a point of fantasy in the submarines of his day.

He said slowly, 'Did you tell the depot ship that I want the *Temeraire*'s captain over here?'

'Yes, sir. He has to pay his respects to Captain S/M and the Admiral Superintendent and so forth, but he should be here in a few minutes.'

'Good. We'll see if our important visitor is impressed!'

The flag lieutenant sighed and held the iced glass limply in his hand. He could not start his first drink of the day before the admiral, and the sight of the ice cubes already melting in the humid air filled him with gloom. The important visitor to whom the admiral referred with such open scorn was not the *Temeraire*'s captain, but the man who had been given the full honours only two hours previously.

James Conway, known in the popular Press as 'Big Jim', had been in Singapore for over a week. As a Member of Parliament and the government's trusted representative of the new Defence Commission, he seemed to symbolise, in the admiral's eyes at least, all the stupidity and irrational behaviour of a government solely interested in destroying its own power overseas for all time. The flag lieutenant had had to bear the weight of his superior's displeasure and was beginning to wonder if it would ever end.

The admiral closed the telescope and ran his fingers over the worn engraving on its mounting. 'Presented to Lieutenant Michael Colquhoun, 1898'. He wondered briefly what his father would have thought about the new Navy. He glared at the flat, burnished water and tried to picture it as it had once been. Battleships and cruisers, trots of rakish destroyers and all the countless attendant craft.

Now, apart from two destroyers, the depot ship and her small brood of submarines, the anchorage seemed almost deserted. The main bulk of the Far East Fleet was made up in small patrol ships, minesweepers and the like. All excellent ships for hunting pirates and checking the flow of refugees and smugglers throughout the vast areas of the China Seas, but hardly suitable for showing the flag.

When his carrier had been at her moorings there had at least been something visible. A hint of what could be expected if one or more of the uneasy hotchpotch of small nations which lived off the admiral's command stepped out of line.

He touched his glass with his tongue. 'Where is our Defence expert at this moment?'

The young officer glanced at his watch. 'With the C.-in-C., sir. But he'll be joining you for lunch in an hour.'

The admiral groaned. 'I suppose he's bringing his bloody wife with him?'

The flag lieutenant hid a smile. 'I expect so, sir.'

'I don't know which of 'em is worse! Her with her good works, and her "My Jim works so hard, you know!", or that bloody husband of hers.' He glared at his glass. 'What *was* he in the last war?'

'I understand that he was a sergeant in the infantry, sir.'

'God Almighty! And to think that a man like that can come out here and tell us what to do!' He waved his hand vaguely across the window and the giant wall chart with its flags and coloured counters. 'To listen to him you'd think that our main work was to keep the local Chinese in employment in the ruddy dockyard, rather than patrol and protect one of the most difficult and dangerous sea areas in the world!'

The flag lieutenant said, 'I believe he won the Military Medal, sir.'

'So did thousands of others, Forrest! I hope you're not suggesting that makes all of *them* fit for running the Royal Navy!'

He warmed to his theme. 'Have you seen the way he panders to the locals? With his attendant photographers and whatnot. He deliberately takes off his jacket just to be seen talking in his braces to a lot of bloody dockyard workers! I think I'll have a stroke if he stays here much longer!'

An impeccable marine orderly stepped through the door. 'Beggin' yer pardon, sir. Commander Jermain is waitin' to pay 'is respects.'

The admiral's eyes glinted. 'Show him in!' He grinned at his flag lieutenant. 'We'll show these ruddy humbugs, eh?'

He wiped the smile from his face and stood quite still beneath one of the overhead fans as Jermain walked slowly into the room. In a quick appraisal the admiral noted the signs of strain and tiredness on his face, the white uniform which still showed traces of being too long in a metal case.

The admiral realised just as quickly that some of his own tension had been caused by this anticipated meeting. He felt something like relief and said, 'Good to have you here, Jermain!' He held out his hand. 'Now while we've having a drink I'll try and put you in the picture before my other guest arrives.'

The steward moved busily with the glasses, and the admiral continued evenly, 'As you know, Jermain, your arrival is quite an event. But it means more than you can possibly imagine.' He studied the other man's grave features, noticing the lines of tension around his eyes. He hurried on, 'I came out here to organise and control the Inshore Squadron.' He pointed at the chart. 'That covers about everything really. I've had patrol

64

boats winkling out terrorists and gunrunners around Malaysia, and up north there are frigates and destroyers on the Japan run. There have been a few submarines, of course, but the Americans do most of the heavy work. They are, of course, better placed for the longer patrols.' His voice hardened. 'However, your *Temeraire* puts a different complexion on things. Even though you may work with the U.S. Fleet, you'll be under my control. It's absolutely essential that we can hold our end up, show the world that we are still capable out here!'

Jermain felt the tiredness pricking the back of his eyes and allowed the gin to move across his dry throat. The long cruise was over. The bright sunlight and heady salt air had made him feel drunk, like a man who has been too long away from natural living. From the very instant that the *Temeraire* had pushed her way into the anchorage, past the saluting warships, acknowledging the twittering pipes and lordly bugles, it seemed as if he had not found a second to stop and collect his thoughts.

Almost dazedly he had stepped ashore, the unfamiliar sword dangling at his side, to pay his respects to Singapore's chain of command. The Admiral Superintendent, the captain of the Submarine squadron, the captain of the base itself. The Commander-in-Chief had sent a brief but courteous welcome by messenger. He was known to be an understanding and competent admiral who no doubt was well aware that Jermain would be tired enough without adding to his ordeal by a long audience at this stage.

Jermain half listened to what the vice-admiral was saying. None of it counted, he thought bitterly. The sooner he put a stop to it the better it would be.

He said, 'I had hoped that the Captain S/M would have contacted you, sir.' He saw a glint of annoyance in the admiral's pale eyes. 'This has been a difficult trip, and, in my opinion, far too soon, before the *Temeraire* was ready for it.'

Sir John Colquhoun eyed him coldly. 'What do you mean?'

Jermain tried again. 'During a deep dive in the South Atlantic we found what may prove to be hull damage, sir. At six hundred feet there was a definite seepage.' He felt the ache of despair closing in on him. 'It's all in my report. I was under radio silence, otherwise I would have requested permission to return to the U.K.'

65

The admiral stared at him. 'Surely there must be some mistake?'

Jermain shrugged. 'We cannot be sure without proper docking facilities, sir. It would mean a complete infra-red analysis of the hull and dockyard services for this type of boat.'

The admiral rubbed his chin, his eyes unwinking and bright. 'But you only *think* it's a fracture, Captain?'

Jermain replied quietly, 'My engine-room staff have carried out a full check as far as they are able, sir. There is a seepage at extreme depths. Of course, it *could* be a faulty welding which may be concealed behind one of the frames. But it's far too risky to take chances.'

'Six hundred feet, you say?' The admiral walked to the chart. 'But on the trials there was no trouble, I take it?'

'Nothing you would not expect, sir.' Jermain tried to imagine how the admiral's mind was working. What did it matter about depth or what anyone else had seen? This was now, and vital.

'Well, that's a relief, Captain. You had me a bit worried there!' The admiral laughed shortly, but his eyes were cold. 'Six hundred feet in a brand-new boat must be expected to cause some teething troubles, after all! My God, when I commanded a little S-boat in the last war I sank over forty thousand tons of enemy shipping without ever diving below *one* hundred feet!'

Jermain said sharply, 'This is different, sir. My command is too new for chances. I would suggest that I am ordered home immediately.'

The admiral's smile faded. 'If I choose to do so, you will be the first to know, I can assure you!' He calmed himself with an effort. 'Some of you young officers forget the meaning of your training. The *Temeraire* is not just a plum command, it's a responsibility, a means to an end!' He pointed at the chart 'For months now the Chinese have been moving men and ships up to the north. To the Yellow Sea and beyond. Intelligence reports suggest more trouble in Korea, but whatever it is, we must keep every ship at first-degree readiness! My God, boy, a nuclear ship like yours is absolutely invaluable at the moment!'

The flag lieutenant said quietly, 'There have been Chinese submarines in the area too, Captain. We must be able to detect and track them, before they start to interfere with our own traffic.'

The admiral snapped, 'When I want your information service I'll ask for it, Forrest!' He turned to Jermain. 'These youngsters don't understand the submariner's mind, do they?'

Jermain swayed. All the weeks of worry and preparations, the strain of testing and gauging every small piece of equipment, had been bad enough. Then with the unexpected orders, the problems of welding a tired and resentful crew into a ready-made combat team, the burden had grown almost too heavy. He said stubbornly, 'It's not a question of over-caution on my part, sir.'

He did not get any further.

'I'm sure you're saying what you think is best, Captain. However, you must allow me to be the judge of that!' The admiral touched the array of medals on his tunic. 'We have to make a show of force in this area. The Chinese *and* the Americans understand that sort of thing! They have a saying out here, "An empty hand is never licked", well, I can assure you it's never been more true!'

Jermain took another drink from the flag lieutenant and saw the brief look of sympathy in the man's eyes. He heard the admiral say, 'After all, Jermain, it may only be a matter of a few weeks. It'll be a good training for your men. I'd have thought you'd have welcomed it?'

He made it sound so reasonable that Jermain found himself checking back along his thoughts, as he had been doing since that last dive. He could still hear the urgency in Ross's tone and feel the sick disappointment in his own heart.

As the admiral talked so it became more obvious what was making him so definite and insistent, Jermain decided. He was one of those admirals, thankfully rare, who could only measure strength and power by visible evidence. Big ships, massive formations. It was rumoured that the admiral had all but lost his appointment under the government's sweeping changes, the pruning of each and every branch of the Services. More and more responsibility for Far Eastern strategy was being left to the American Seventh Fleet, and Jermain could well imagine what *Temeraire*'s timely arrival could mean.

67

'I shall, of course, obey your instructions, sir.' Jermain saw a flicker of hostility in the admiral's eyes, but he continued doggedly, 'But my men are tired, and quite unprepared for this change of events. A lot of the crew are married. They'll be wondering about their families, getting them out here, and so forth.'

The admiral snorted. 'A lot of old women! This whole command is bogged down with bloody wives and children as it is! Heavens, Jermain, for every active officer or man there are about one hundred hangers-on! It's worse than a damned holiday camp!' He stared hard at the bright water beyond the building. 'The trouble is they're too soft today! Must have their wives and television sets just outside the dockyard gates! In my day we were grateful just to stay alive!'

Jermain said, 'But during the war . . .'

The admiral's face hardened. 'There's a war on *now*, damn it! Every hour of the day we're being hampered by terrorists, and our ships are stalked by Red warships! I would have imagined that the Americans' experience in Viet Nam was warning enough of what can happen!'

The flag lieutenant said hurriedly, 'The staff car has just arrived, sir.'

The admiral swallowed hard. 'That'll be our gallant Member of Parliament!' He fixed Jermain with a steady stare. 'Nothing you have said or heard must leak out, especially in front of *him*!'

Jermain replied stiffly, 'I am under your orders, sir.'

'Good. I was beginning to wonder!' The admiral added as an afterthought, 'I shan't ask you to do anything foolhardy, Captain. It is what you represent that counts!'

The flag lieutenant announced, 'Mr. James Conway, sir!'

The admiral switched on his smile. 'Delighted to have you here! I want you to meet the captain of the *Temeraire*!'

*   *   *

Ordinary Seaman John Lightfoot levelled his camera and squinted at the group of Chinese children who made up the sole audience of a giant Sikh street salesman. The man was holding several bottles of what appeared to be colourless medicine and his voice was as serious and confidential as if he had been addressing a crowd of hundreds.

Lightfoot sighed and rewound the camera before moving on with the slow, aimless throng in which he was carried like a leaf on a stream. He had been ashore for about an hour, but already his mind was pleasantly confused by the strange sounds and dialects, the bright colours and jumbled excitement of the stalls and open-fronted shops. It seemed as if all the world had gathered in this place. Above the narrow street he could see the bright blue sky, from which the afternoon sun blazed down on the drifting dust and defied the efforts of the small sea breeze to break through its power.

And everywhere there were British servicemen. Soldiers and airmen, and, of course, a generous sprinkling of white-clad sailors. It was strange to see British women in such quantities, Lightfoot thought. Against the background of oriental sounds it was odd to hear Yorkshire or Scottish dialects, and not a few from his own town.

Military and naval patrols stood quietly at street corners, swinging their sticks or fingering their pistols as they casually surveyed the passing crowds, and Lightfoot was reminded of the coxswain's short speech before the *Temeraire*'s libertymen had been allowed ashore.

The big chief petty officer had rocked back on his heels as he had run a critical eye over the assembled sailors. Apart from a few technical ratings and the duty officer, every man jack was being let ashore on this first day in Singapore.

Twine, the coxswain, had said, 'Now just remember, lads, this ain't Guzz or Pompey. This is Singapore, the main British base in these parts, and a place crawlin' with every kind of trouble an' temptation!' He had paused to allow the titters to die away. 'In addition it's full of pongos an' a whole heap of so-called sailors who ain't been to sea since they joined. These barrack-stanchions will more'n likely try to start a fight. If they do, it'll be up to you to sort it all out neat an' proper. Either move off at the sight of trouble or *win*! I don't want to see a lot of you skates bein' dragged aboard by the shore patrol an' bringin' disrespect on the Black Pig, got it?' His eyes had moved slowly along the ranks. 'The captain 'as made sure of full liberty. It's up to you to watch yourselves!'

69

Lieutenant Oxley, the duty officer, had added, 'Be on the watch for anyone trying to get information about you and the *Temeraire*. This may look like home, but it's terrorist country, and don't you forget it!'

Then the chattering, cheerful throng of men had surged ashore to the waiting trucks which would carry them the thirteen miles into town. Away from the work and strain, out of the steel shell which had become their world.

Lightfoot was surprised to find that he had at last started to relax. Shortly after the submarine had picked up her moorings alongside the depot ship he had nearly fainted with horror. Within minutes of the last line going over the side he had seen two grave-faced men in civilian clothes come down the brow with the Captain S/M. Then he had heard a petty officer say grimly, ''Ere they come. The bloody security boys!'

The men in question had gone to the wardroom, but after enduring an agony of suspense Lightfoot had heard nothing more. He had mentioned their arrival to Bruce who had made investigations of his own. Later Bruce had said calmly, 'Just routine. They're here to make sure you don't cut any more wires!' He had still been laughing when they had found their way ashore together.

But within fifteen minutes of de-bussing in the town Bruce had got involved with a dark-eyed Malay girl who had beckoned invitingly from a window above the street. Bruce had said huskily, 'Just the job! I bin waitin' weeks for this!'

He had told Lightfoot to follow his example, but when he had stammered out excuses the big seaman had just grunted, 'Suit yourself! But even if you catch a dose off one of 'em it only means a couple of needles in yer arse!' He had gone off chuckling with plans for a rendezvous later in the day.

Lightfoot wished he had had the nerve to follow his friend. If only to see what it was like. He grinned at the thought and realised it was the first time anything had made him smile since before the night of the car smash and the man lying dead beside the road.

Anyway, it was good to be alone for a bit. At first the sun and strange air had made him feel sick, but now as he sauntered along the street with his camera at the ready he felt a real sense of peace.

He thought momentarily of Colquhoun and wondered why he had shown such an interest in him. Admittedly he had not mentioned the dinghy-sailing again, but then he was no doubt too busy. Especially as his old man was a vice-admiral right here in Singapore.

He heard someone call his name, and a seaman called Archer panted up beside him. 'Here! Hold on, mate!' He fell in step with him. 'I missed you when you got off the bus. I've been trying like hell to catch you up.'

Lightfoot watched him cautiously. There was no need for such a display of friendship, he thought. Archer, known as Gipsy because of his swarthy skin and slicked-back hair, had never bothered to speak to him before, even when cooped up in the boat for five weeks underwater! He said, 'I'm going to meet Porky Bruce.' It sounded defensive and he blushed angrily.

Archer eyed him lazily. 'It was you I wanted.'

They had reached a narrow sidestreet and without warning Archer piloted him down it, brushing aside a whining carpet salesman as if he had been a piece of cardboard.

Archer seemed strangely excited. 'Look, I won't beat about the bush, mate.' He gestured crudely. 'I got a nice bit of crumpet stowed away, just whimpering for it!' He grinned. 'But I'm a bit short of the ready, see?'

Lightfoot stared at him. Archer was a senior seaman with far more pay than he ever earned. 'I can let you have a bit . . .'

Archer cut him short. 'I want the lot, mate.' He eyed him with mock surprise. 'You don't get it, do you?' He leaned forward. 'I was there, mate. Don't you understand, I was *there*!'

Lightfoot shook his head, but his madly pumping heart made him sway on his feet. 'I don't know what you're talking about!' But his voice was broken and defeated.

Archer's eyes were unwinking and completely devoid of pity. 'I was in the pub when you went off with that bloody queer. I suppose you robbed the bastard before you done him in?' He lifted his hand. 'Don't bother to explain, mate! Just so long as you understand how we stand!' He winked. 'With them two security blokes aboard it would be too damn easy to drop a hint in the right place, an' we don't want *that*, do we?'

The grinning seaman seemed to be standing behind a mist,

71

and Lightfoot blindly pulled out his frayed wallet, his ears still ringing with Archer's casual threat. 'This is all I've got.' He watched wretchedly as the man pulled the notes out. 'I was going to buy a present for my mother.'

It sounded so strange in the face of what had happened that Archer said, 'In that case, have ten bob on me, mate!'

Leaving Lightfoot staring at the empty wallet, Archer strolled back towards the sunshine. He paused and called, 'Don't lose that nice camera! I might take a fancy to it later on!'

So there was no escape after all. If he had gone straight to the authorities at the time things might have been different. After all, it *was* an accident! He remembered the man's clawing fingers and felt the helpless anger rising to mock him once more.

If it hadn't been for Bruce he would have turned himself in.

Lightfoot walked blindly through the crowd, but this time there was no pleasure in his heart.

*   *   *

The reception for the *Temeraire*'s officers was held that same evening at Vice-Admiral Colquhoun's headquarters. The guests filled the big reception room and flowed out over the wide terrace beyond. In the evening's purple light the water below the balustrade looked cool and inviting, and the brightly lit warships across the anchorage shimmered above their own reflections.

In a slightly self-conscious group the submarine's officers in their white uniforms stood out against the women's coloured dresses and the gently perspiring marine orchestra.

Jermain felt as if his smile was welded to his mouth as the flag lieutenant made one introduction after another. Even the friendly reception and the soothing effect of cool champagne did little to ease the nagging concern for his command.

He glanced at his officers. They at least seemed to be enjoying themselves, he thought. Even Wolfe appeared relaxed and calm, and was in deep conversation with the Member of Parliament he had met earlier. The latter was a heavily built man with a shining red face and a laugh which came regularly and without effort, as if it was switched on for the occasion.

Sir John Colquhoun, resplendent in full mess dress and a chest of miniature decorations, beamed across at him and said, 'A good turn out, eh, Jermain?'

He nodded. 'Yes, sir.' He thought of Lieutenant Victor, the duty officer, imprisoned in the cool safety of the *Temeraire*'s wardroom. Whereas the others pitied him his lonely vigil, Jermain would willingly have traded duties with him.

Conway, the M.P., was saying loudly, 'I'll be having a look at your ship as soon as I can squeeze it in.'

Wolfe replied, 'There's quite a bit to see.'

Conway shook his head and sighed. 'I'm afraid I don't get much time for luxuries, old chap.'

An anxious little woman in an expensive scarlet dress said quickly, 'Jim's so busy these days, you know! The P.M. is always giving him such hard jobs!'

Jermain smiled in spite of his tense nerves. That must be Mrs. Conway. He saw the vice-admiral's eyes harden and heard him say, 'We're not exactly relaxing here ourselves!'

Conway wagged a finger. 'Now then, Sir John! We've been over all that! There have to be cuts in our expenses, and let's face it, the Navy has never been one for economising!'

Sir John Colquhoun was about to make a sharp retort when his eye fell on his son, who until this moment had been hidden by the others. 'Well, hello, Max.' He held out his hand. 'How are you shaping up?'

Jermain only half caught the young officer's mumbled reply. He studied them thoughtfully. The slim uncertainty of the sub-lieutenant against his father's bluff, almost belligerent, confidence. Yet there was some small likeness, Jermain decided. The same pale eyes, the same tilt of the head.

The admiral looked across at him and said offhandedly, 'I hope you can make a man of him, Jermain! Although I expect it'll be an uphill task!'

Jermain said calmly, 'I have no complaints, sir. We're all learning aboard the *Temeraire*!'

For one brief instant Jermain saw the doubt in the admiral's eyes, then he said, 'We shall see.'

Jermain realised that the M.P. was speaking to him.

'I'm very interested in your ship, Captain. I like to keep in

73

touch. Mind you, I'm still to be convinced of the worth of such a vessel!'

Wolfe interrupted sharply, 'I suppose that if war broke out tomorrow the government would expect a graph made of tonnage sunk against man-hours and rum consumed!'

Conway grinned. 'You should be in Parliament!'

Oxley plucked at his tunic and drawled, 'Well, I didn't get into my ice-cream suit just to listen to my betters arguing.' He looked at the admiral. 'With your permission, sir, I'd like to go and try my prowess on the dance floor?'

Conway's grin broadened. 'Another one ripe for politics, eh?'

Oxley eyed him coolly. 'Actually, I hope to follow my father into the House of Lords!'

Jermain caught Wolfe's eye and said quickly, 'I think we had all better circulate, Number One. Before any eggs get broken!'

But the admiral said testily, 'You stay and talk, Jermain. Time enough for that sort of thing later!'

Conway became serious. 'Are you satisfied with the *Temeraire*?'

Jermain saw the admiral stiffen. He replied, 'She's a magnificent submarine. Still ripe from trials, of course, but a major step forward in every way.' From the corner of his eye he saw the admiral relax slightly.

What the hell did words matter anyway? The admiral was doing what he thought was best for public relations, and so presumably was the M.P.

Conway took another glass of champagne. 'You hear all this talk of safety and radiation leakage, it's all a bit confusing for the layman.'

'There's no danger on that score.' Jermain watched Lieutenant Drew guiding a laughing girl around the floor. Against his white tunic her tanned skin looked like silk.

He said absently, 'The nuclear submarine used to be a freak. Now it's a fact of life. We have to live with it.'

Conway frowned. 'And what will you be doing here?'

Jermain waited for the admiral to say something, but he appeared to be in deep conversation with Conway's wife. He said at length, 'Certain exercises with the Americans. I've not had my final instructions yet.'

74

The big man nodded. 'Good. We must show the Americans we can be relied on, militarily speaking!'

A colonel of marines with an upturned, ginger moustache paused to say a word with the admiral, and Jermain saw Conway stiffen as if in defence. For a moment Jermain saw through the big man's guard and felt strangely affected. Conway was not finding his work as easy as the admiral thought. At heart he might still be a sergeant, and his apparent ease with men like Sir John Colquhoun and the unknown colonel was a hard-won battle.

Conway saw Jermain's quiet scrutiny and laughed shortly. 'That young officer of yours. Is his father really a lord?'

Jermain smiled. 'I believe so. I'd never really thought about it.'

'I agree with the admiral about one thing, Captain. You are an unusual man.' Conway laughed again to hide his sudden embarrassment. 'I think the *Temeraire* is in very safe hands!'

Just as quickly the guard dropped back into place. 'Well, I must be off. I've a lot to do before tomorrow!'

The admiral looked round. 'Thank goodness *he's* gone!' Then he turned as his flag lieutenant appeared at his elbow. 'Well?'

'The signal, sir.' The flag lieutenant held out a pad and glanced meaningly at Jermain.

Jermain watched the admiral scanning the signal pad and wondered. The lieutenant had said *the* signal. It was too pat, too coincidental with the M.P.'s exit.

The admiral cleared his throat. 'It's from London, Jermain. Your orders are to sail tomorrow for an exercise with the Americans.' He skimmed quickly over the preliminaries. '*Temeraire* will proceed to U.S. Fleet area Romeo Tango Five for Exercise Flashpoint.' He gave a small smile. 'I hope you put on a good show!'

Jermain took the single copy of the signal and read it slowly. 'Did you confirm this with London, sir? Are they aware of my report?'

The admiral snapped, 'Of course I did. You are supposed to be fully operational for this sort of thing. Anyway, it's confirmed under my responsibility!'

'I see.' Jermain felt the anger boiling inside him like fire.

The words, the careful deceit, made him reckless. 'My own responsibility is to my command, sir. There may be flaws in the hull, as I know you are aware.'

'I am more interested in possible flaws in the crew, Jermain. In any case you'll be better off at sea. The Singapore government is worried about your being here in the harbour. Rumours about contamination and all that rot. That fool Conway wouldn't like any trouble with the local government at this stage of his work. He said as much earlier.'

'Very well, sir. But my decision must be upheld should I have to break off the exercise.'

'I don't think that will be necessary, Jermain.' The admiral's tone was final. 'The sooner you get this job done, the quicker I can arrange your passage home.'

Jermain walked through the laughing guests and leaned against the cool balustrade. The anchorage was quite dark now, but against the floodlit hull of the depot ship he could clearly see the *Temeraire*'s black whaleback and the number on her fin.

Only aboard her did he feel in control of things. Here nothing was certain, and little seemed to go below face value.

But the orders were definite enough. The area referred to was three days' sailing to the north east off Hainan Island and close to the coast of North Viet Nam. The Americans were used to this sort of exercise, and as the admiral had remarked, the sooner it was completed, the earlier they could leave.

But Jermain knew from past experience that nothing was ever that simple.

5

Romeo Tango Five

Jermain rolled over in his bunk and groped wearily for the telephone. He had been in a deep sleep so that he was not even sure if the insistent buzz had been part of some disordered dream. 'Captain speaking.' He peered at the luminous face of his watch and tried again to clear his brain.

From the control room he heard Oxley's calm voice. 'Five-thirty, sir. We'll be coming up to the rendezvous in fifteen minutes.'

Jermain switched on the bunkside light and stared emptily at his small cabin. The charts and open logbooks were still as he had left them only four hours earlier. One hundred and fifty feet above his bunk the early sun would be feeling its way across the water. There might still be the vicious little squall which had blown up when they had left Singapore nearly three days ago, and which had greeted the probing periscope each time they had planed upwards to take a look at the outside world.

He realised that Oxley was still waiting at the other end of the line. 'Very good. Were the hands called early?'

'Yes, sir.' Oxley sounded a bit peeved. 'Shall I have some breakfast sent along to you, too?'

'No.' Jermain dropped the handset and swung his long legs over the side of the bunk. The canned air of his cabin felt cold to his skin, and he shivered slightly as he pulled on his shirt. He had been sweating in his exhausted sleep, and as he groped for the rest of his clothing his mind reluctantly returned to the nagging problems which waited for every awakening like playful tormentors.

77

To go to sea immediately after the enforced voyage from Scotland had been bad enough. There were faults to rectify, spare fittings to be installed, and the thousand and one other items which always dogged the captain of a new vessel.

But Vice-Admiral Colquhoun's bombshell had been almost too much to bear. Fleet manœuvres were a nightmare at the best of times, with every senior officer breathing down the neck of his next subordinate. For the admiral to throw the *Temeraire* into some pressurised Anglo-American exercise with neither preparation nor discussion was asking for trouble of the worst kind.

The admiral had saved his worst act until the very moment of departure. As the submarine had tugged at her moorings and men had scampered along the casing in readiness for letting go, he had presented himself at the brow with the calm statement that he intended to accompany *Temeraire* to the exercise area.

Jermain took two of the little tablets which Griffin had given him to help him keep going. He washed them down with a glass of water and grimaced at himself in the bulkhead mirror.

Sir John Colquhoun had been like a child with a new toy. As the boat had moved free from her moorings and the tense business of conning the great black hull safely through the harbour traffic had begun, he had wandered happily through the boat, stopping every so often to peer into a compartment at a startled rating or to watch an officer at his controls, usually with a 'Don't mind me, boy! Just act as if I wasn't here!' As if the sight of a flag officer wasn't bad enough, he had changed into a roll-necked sweater, commenting, 'Can't get used to all this clinical stuff! When I was in submarines we had to *dress* the part!'

He seemed to be enjoying himself well enough, Jermain thought. He had refused to accept or even share one of the cabins, but insisted on using one of the wardroom spare bunks which were kept for excess passengers of more lowly state.

Consequently, it was impossible to enter the wardroom, even during the night watches, without Sir John's face popping out from between the bunk curtains with some comment or jocular criticism.

78

It was getting on everyone's nerves. Jermain knew that the admiral's son hardly ever entered the wardroom and had been seen snatching a quick meal during his watch. Ross too avoided the admiral, but for different reasons. Whenever the admiral was able to corner the chief engineer he would ask some question about the complex machinery or some detail concerning the reactor, and after the chief's lengthy explanations Sir John would wave his hand and say cheerfully, 'I'm afraid it's all new to me! Completely new!'

Jermain had even heard Lieutenant Drew taking advantage of the admiral's impossible questions. The T.A.S. officer had answered two questions in Jermain's presence with such sincerity and eloquence that the admiral had been deeply impressed. Only Jermain knew that the Australian's answers had been so much gibberish. After the last occasion he had reprimanded Drew, and the latter had said gloomily, 'It's just that he gets on my wick, sir!'

And then of course there were the two security officers. Usually seated in the ship's office or at the wardroom table, they never seemed to separate. They had checked the men's service records and questioned the heads of departments. They had even insisted that Lieutenant Kitson should show them the actual place where the wiring had been tampered with. Naturally they had not found the culprit. Like the admiral, they had only succeeded in getting on everybody's nerves.

The previous afternoon Jermain had approached the admiral about the matter. The latter had been standing in the small chart-room making his own calculations of the course and speed.

After a while he had said playfully, 'I'm just a passenger, Jermain. You mustn't ask me things like that!'

Jermain had replied coldly, 'The security officers are aboard at your insistence, sir. I only wanted them to make a check when we entered Singapore.'

The admiral had stared at him for several seconds. 'They know their job, Jermain. While this boat is under my control I want it free of trouble, see?' There the matter had ended.

Jermain picked up his cap and walked through the passageway to the control room. It would soon be time to go to periscope depth and the control-room lighting was dimmed to a

79

warm orange glow to ease the strain on the eyes of the watch-keeping officers.

Oxley said formally, 'Course zero one zero, sir. Speed twenty knots.'

Jermain nodded and walked slowly through the control room. The men looked clean and fresh-faced, but their expressions were tense and strained, and he knew that they were all thinking about the exercise and about showing their paces in front of the Americans.

In the chart-room he found Wolfe and Mayo leaning over the table. He felt them watching him as he checked the course and the *Temeraire*'s position, as he had done every day since her keel had first felt salt water.

It was still hard to realise that the world outside the hull had changed yet again. He stared at the pencilled lines, the neat crosses which marked each interval of their most recent journey. Out of Singapore, and in silence across the South China Sea. Northward up the coast of unhappy Viet Nam, and then east-wards towards the mass of the Chinese mainland, where Hainan Island hung like an ulcer from the parent body.

On the exercise chart this area was marked as Romeo Tango Five. In such areas the Americans searched and probed continu-ously, like wrestlers circling for openings in their opponents' guard. Along three thousand miles of little-known coastline their nuclear submarines patrolled and watched, tested their weapons and waited for that one dreaded day when their terrible power would be flung against China and any other potential enemy.

Temeraire's part in Exercise Flashpoint was small but vital. She had been ordered to shadow one such Polaris submarine to a proposed firing position one hundred miles south of Hainan Island. While the bigger and more cumbersome American sub-marine manœuvred into her pinpointed firing zone, *Temeraire* would cover her with a protective sonar screen so that she could do her deadly work undisturbed.

A day after leaving Singapore Jermain had made his first rendezvous with a small task force of the U.S. Seventh Fleet. At the prescribed time he had surfaced between two parallel lines of sleek warships while helicopters hovered like giant locusts overhead and on the deck of a nearby cruiser a naval band played 'Rule Britannia'. It was a bizarre and slightly un-nerving experience.

The admiral in charge of the force had been dropped neatly on the swaying fin from one of the helicopters, and after a brief but searching inspection had given Jermain his instructions. He had been more than surprised to meet Sir John Colquhoun. To Jermain he had said quietly, 'Don't they trust you alone, Captain?' Then with a grin he had added, 'I'll be happy to take him off your hands if he's willing to leave!'

But Sir John had not been willing. He had queried several points in the American plan, not least the selection of the exercise area.

The American admiral had studied him gravely. 'It's like this, Sir John. By 1970 there will be one hundred and seventy-two nuclear submarines in the world. In thirty years maybe double that figure. And now, this very day, the Red Chinese are the fourth largest submarine power! We have to be ready for anything. We have to learn to use what we have at our disposal right now!' He had let his eyes move across the chart as if to see more clearly the sleeping mass of China. 'You never know what the Reds'll try next. But the only thing they respect is power, and plenty of it! So just to keep 'em in line we must lean on them once in a while!'

After he had been hoisted back to his helicopter Jermain had thought about his last words. But Sir John had said stiffly, 'Bloody Americans! You'd think they owned the world!'

Jermain sighed and picked up the intercom handset. 'This is the captain speaking.' He heard his voice echoing through the compartments of the hull and could imagine his men watching and listening. 'In a few moments we will make contact with the American Polaris boat which some of you saw two days ago.'

The big, rocket-firing submarine had been at the rear of the fast-moving formation, and repeatedly Jermain had found his eyes drawn to her with cold fascination. Larger than the *Temeraire* she showed little outward sign of her devastating power. Jermain knew from past experience that beneath her rounded hull were two erect lines of Polaris missiles. Sixteen rockets, each with a range of over two and a half thousand miles. Such a craft could reach inland and destroy anything and everything. Yet in the harsh sunlight she looked dangerously normal, with her high-mounted planes shining on either side of her fin like two scythes.

He continued, 'We will patrol an area to the north of her and south of Hainan Island. A conventional submarine will carry out an attack through our screen. It will be up to us to find and destroy the attacker before it makes a successful contact with the Polaris boat.' He glanced at his watch. 'You will now go to action stations. I will keep you informed at each stage of the operation.' He wanted to wish them luck, to tell them he was relying on them. But they were all experts at their own jobs. It would seem superfluous, even apprehensive of trouble.

He nodded towards Wolfe, who pressed the emergency buzzer.

Chief Petty Officer Harris, the radio supervisor, stood up from his control panel and wiped his hands on his thighs. 'All checked, sir.' He stared suspiciously at a small loudspeaker at his side, the ear of the acoustic radio through which they could talk with or listen to the other submerged boat.

'Boat at action stations, sir.'

'Very good.' Jermain glanced at Wolfe. 'It's a damned eerie feeling, isn't it? Two great submarines making a rendezvous in the middle of nowhere!'

The acoustic radio crackled and Jermain stared at it as the voice said slowly, 'NEMESIS calling BLUEBOY. Do you read me? Over.'

Harris cleared his throat. 'BLUEBOY to NEMESIS. Read you loud and clear. Over.'

Mayo called from the chart-room, 'Right on course, sir!'

From the sonar compartment Oxley's voice came calmly through the intercom. 'We have the Polaris boat, sir. Range ten thousand yards. Course zero nine zero. Speed twenty plus.'

Harris repeated the information and Jermain heard the American say, 'Right on the button! Nice to have you around, pal!'

Then a new voice, clipped and precise. Even the weird distortion caused by five miles of water could not hide the tension in his speech. 'Hallo, BLUEBOY. This is the captain. We will carry out phase one at two zero zero feet. Over and out.'

82

Jermain stood beside the sheathed periscopes, his eyes watchful. 'Take her down, Number One. Two hundred feet. Steer zero four five and reduce to twelve knots.' The dials flickered and the deck tilted very slightly.

The admiral's voice broke into his thoughts. 'What's happening, Jermain?'

'We're cutting across the American's stern. Then I will turn on a parallel course between him and the mainland.'

The admiral sounded excited. 'How close inshore will you go?'

Jermain had to force his mind away from the tactical problems to concentrate on the admiral's question. 'Seventy-five miles at the nearest, sir. We're right over the start of the Continental Shelf hereabouts.' He gestured towards the depth recorder. 'We've got a thousand fathoms under the keel. Just five miles further inshore and the shelf rises to less than fifty fathoms.' He watched the admiral's pale eyes, but in his thoughts he could see the great undersea cliff rising in a green wall, against which a submarine would be like so much tin.

Oxley's voice again. 'Starting the sweep, sir. No contact.'

The admiral remarked, 'Bloody tame after all this waiting! When you think back to the war, Jermain, what a difference! The stalking and listening. The days of misery while the depth-charges rattled the teeth in your head!' He rubbed his hands. 'But at the end of it all, the ship in your cross-wires! That was the moment.'

Mayo called, 'Altering course, sir. Zero nine zero.'

Twine at his wheel intoned, 'Course zero nine zero, sir.'

Jermain peered at his watch. 'Any contact yet?' He bit his lip. The admiral's constant muttering was getting him rattled. Oxley would rightly resent any unnecessary questioning. He snapped, 'Belay that!'

The intercom came to life. 'Nemesis has changed course for second run, sir.' Oxley sounded tired. 'Bearing two two five, twelve thousand yards.'

Jermain glanced at the petty officer by the plot. 'Got that?'

'Yes, sir.' He ran his rule carefully across the glass-topped table. 'She'll be exercising her missile crews now, sir.'

Jermain tried not to look at the clock. Minutes dragged past

83

and still nothing happened. Six miles away the Polaris submarine was going about her business, her crew of over a hundred men no doubt absorbed in the intricate drill of preparing the missiles for a mock launching. But where was the attacker?

He checked the chart and tried to think it out step by step. The *enemy* was a conventionally-powered killer submarine with a maximum speed of perhaps eighteen knots. Her skipper would be well aware of the practice area and could guess to within a few miles their approximate position. Whereas his position was a complete mystery. He had a dozen choices, and he only needed one break in the screen to make a quick attack.

Jermain bit his lip. Where would *I* go?

He made a decision. 'Take her up to one hundred feet, Number One.' He heard the slight hiss of pressurised air and saw the slender needles begin to swing back.

The admiral said, 'Aren't we expected to stay at two hundred feet?'

'This is supposed to be the real thing, sir. The enemy won't stick to the rules.'

Jermain forgot the admiral as Wolfe reported, 'One hundred feet, sir!'

Jermain crossed to his side and said quietly, 'The crafty bastard will probably keep close to the surface as he makes his run in.'

Wolfe nodded. 'More than likely. He'll take his time so that his screws and motors make as little sound as possible.'

'Suppose he closes from Hainan Island?' Jermain was thinking aloud. 'He would stand a much better chance. He'll know that we're unlikely to cross the Continental Shelf into shallow water. But *he* could do it very easily.'

Wolfe's eyes glowed. 'It's a thought. Sonar echoes would be distorted anyway by the shelving bottom. He'd be up to us with his own detection gear and we'd be on equal footing!'

Jermain smiled. 'I agree. That's what I would do.' He peered down at the chart. 'Alter course to zero one zero. We'll close in a bit.'

The sounding recorder began to swing as if caught by a magnet.

Mayo said doubtfully, 'Fifty fathoms, sir.'

Jermain picked up the engine-room handset. 'Is everything all right, Chief?'

Ross answered immediately, as if he had been sitting with the phone in his hand. 'Running like a clock, sir.'

'We're turning towards the land and into shallow water, Chief. If we draw blank or the sonar gets a strong echo in the original area I'll turn back and go to maximum speed. So be prepared!'

He heard Ross chuckle and felt slightly relieved. Ross said, 'Like looking for a nigger in a coal-hole, sir!'

Oxley's voice caught his attention. 'Getting distorted echoes, sir. Could be a throwback. But definitely not another vessel.'

'Keep searching. I shall make another sweep to the westward in ten minutes.'

The admiral had sat on a stool as if the suspense was getting him down. He remarked, 'The Americans will have something to crow about if they break through your screen, Jermain.'

So it's *my* screen now, is it? Jermain said aloud, 'I don't suppose the *target* will be too pleased, sir!'

The admiral ignored him. 'I can just hear that idiot Conway if the *Temeraire* makes a hash of this! He'll probably withdraw every blasted British warship from the Far East!' He glared at the round-eyed control-room messenger, the only man present who was not employed and therefore listening. 'What do these mildew-minded little shop stewards know about this sort of thing, eh?'

With her searching sonar swinging around her like an invisible shield the submarine prowled nearer and nearer to the shoreline. No one spoke any more, and men became conscious of the silence, of heart-beats, and the endless, dragging minutes.

*   *   *

Right forward, in the *Temeraire*'s underbelly, Max Colquhoun sat stiffly in his steel chair, his eyes moving restlessly across the shoulders of the sonar operator. By his side Oxley lounged with his chin on his chest, his fingers drumming a little tattoo on his microphone. On the tall panels the lights flickered and the operators' headsets squeaked and muttered with all the noises from the sea around them. It was a strange world,

85

Colquhoun thought. As if the whole crushing force of the sea was filled with unknown chattering creatures.

Petty Officer Irons, the senior sonar rating, readjusted his dials and said briefly, 'There it goes again, sir.' The microphone at his elbow relayed the strange bleeping sound which had earlier aroused Oxley's attention.

It reminded Colquhoun of a disturbed bird in a hedgerow. Chirping irritably before dropping once more into a doze.

Oxley said, 'I still can't make it out.' He glanced at the sounding gauge. 'God, we're in forty fathoms now!' He yawned and stretched his legs. 'Why didn't I stay in *ordinary* boats? What could be better than a rainy day in Gosport, sipping beer in the old Anglesey?'

Irons said sharply, 'There it goes again, sir.' He paused and then added, 'I think it came from a slightly different bearing.' His fingers readjusted the red dial. 'Three five five degrees or thereabouts.' He twisted round to look at Oxley's frowning face. 'I'm sorry, sir, but it only makes a sound for a few seconds!'

Colquhoun said, 'Well, there's nothing on the surface. We'd have heard it long ago.'

Oxley stared at him. 'Sub, you can be very helpful at times.' He ignored Colquhoun's expression of surprise and switched on his intercom. 'Captain, sir? I think I've found out what the strange echoes are.' He winked at Colquhoun. 'I think there are fishing boats overhead. Maybe several over a wide area. Small boats without their engines running would be almost impossible to detect at this stage.'

Jermain's tone was patient. 'So what did you hear?'

'I read some months ago that the Russians have been using some sort of underwater fishing gear. It makes a *fish sound* and helps to attract any nearby shoals to the area.' He scowled at Irons, who was openly grinning at him. 'Well, that's what I read sir.'

Jermain did not laugh. 'You could be right. I should have thought of that. There are no Russian trawlers in this area, but no doubt the Chinese have this gadget, too.'

Another pattern of bleeps rattled in the microphones, and Irons rubbed his ears angrily. 'Hell, that was close!' He glared at the panel. 'I hope the bastards catch a bloody whale!'

Without warning the gauge on the centre of the panel gave a sharp jerk and then settled firmly at an angle. Irons crouched low and began to move his dials with set concentration. Through his teeth he said, 'Strong echo, sir! Bearing Green one zero zero! Extreme range but *definite*!'

Oxley came to life. 'Continue tracking!' In the intercom he said sharply, 'Definite contact, sir! Extreme range, bearing Green one zero zero!'

As if in reply the intercom crackled, 'Start the attack!'

Oxley grinned. 'Soon be over now!'

*　　　*　　　*

Jermain listened to the brisk passing of orders as the helm went over and like a circling aircraft the *Temeraire* swam round in a tight turn on to the new bearing. Half aloud he said, 'Just as I thought. The enemy must have known about the fishing boats and has been sculling about behind them all day. Just waiting his chance!'

'Course one one zero, sir.'

'Very good. Increase to twenty knots!' He looked at Wolfe. 'As soon as we cross into deep water I'll dive to three hundred feet!'

Wolfe nodded and tapped the planesman's shoulder.

The admiral was on his feet. 'Can you head him off?'

'Should be easy, sir. He's taken too long to make his attack. Nemesis will be making her next turn in five minutes, so he'll have to crack on speed. I shall close the range as for two homing torpedoes and then loose a grenade.' He smiled in spite of his earlier uncertainty. 'All parties will hear the grenade and know that the hunter has been hunted!'

He watched the gyro repeater as the admiral said, 'That'll make 'em sit up! You see now why I wanted your boat on this exercise? To me it's more than a show of force, Jermain, it's the only way to prove our worth out here!' He rubbed his hands. 'I might get a couple more nuclear boats under my command in the near future. That'll stop any possible chance of our authority being undermined!'

Mayo called, 'Crossing the Shelf now, sir! Eight hundred fathoms in five minutes!'

87

Jermain heard Drew's harsh voice on the intercom as he goaded his torpedo party into the final part of the attack drill. He did not really care what the admiral saw in the exercise. The important thing was that the crew had behaved extremely well, and at no time had a single defect been reported. Now perhaps they could get on with the business of training undisturbed.

The sounding recorder began to swing slowly and then more steeply as the sea bed fell away. Maybe at their present depth of one hundred feet they would make a slight shadow across the treacherous cliff edge as they swam into safer waters.

Without warning there was an insane screech of metal, like a bandsaw across solid steel, and as the deck gave a warning tilt to port the nerve-searing sound was followed by a violent, shuddering lurch which threw some of the men from their feet.

Jermain reeled against the periscopes, his ribs aching from a blow against the greased metal, his mind momentarily stunned as the hull received a full jolt as if from a solid object. For an instant he imagined that they had collided with another submarine. Already the depth gauge was rotating wildly, and he heard Wolfe yelling hoarsely at the coxswain.

Jermain forced his mind to hold steady. 'Slow ahead! Watch your gauges!'

Jeffers, the second coxswain, sounded breathless. 'Can't hold her, sir! The planes is jammed!'

'Diving, sir!' Wolfe was gripping the planesman's seat, his eyes glued to the dials.

Jermain felt the deck corkscrewing beneath him and heard Wolfe say tightly, 'One hundred and fifty feet, sir! One hundred and seventy-five feet!'

As if to emphasise the danger, the hull shuddered again and more violently. It was like hearing an oil drum being beaten with a giant hammer. And in between each boom there was the screech of metal, grating at the hull like steel tentacles.

'Emergency surfacing drill, Number One!' Jermain listened to his own voice and found time to wonder. It sounded calm and unemotional, yet he could feel his nerves screaming in time to the *Temeraire*'s struggles with the thing which was trying to destroy her. 'Close all watertight doors!' The control room seemed to become smaller as the oval doors were clipped shut.

Wolfe added, 'Still diving, sir. Two hundred and seventy-five feet!'

Jeffers gasped as his control wheel slackened for a few seconds and then locked again. Every eye was fixed on the dials, and each ear was numbed by the regular booming impacts against the tough steel.

Jermain said, 'Must be one of those fish-buoys! We've got it wrapped round the fin and the after hydroplane!'

He could feel the sweat pouring between his shoulders like ice water, could sense the horror around him which already fringed on the edge of panic. The young messenger was gripping a petty officer's sleeve, his eyes filling his face like mirrors of terror, and in the chart-room entrance Mayo stood with his arms wide against the tilting hull as if he had been crucified.

Ross's voice came on the intercom. 'I'm blowing everything, sir! Can you try and free the aft-planes?'

Jermain said, 'Try opposite helm, Coxswain! See if you can shake it off!'

Twine swung the wheel, his eyes steady as he watched the gyro repeater. Twisting and turning like a snared fish the submarine thrashed wildly from one side to the other.

Only the admiral appeared unmoved, Jermain noticed. He stood against the plot table, his pale eyes empty of expression, like a man already dead.

'Four hundred feet, sir!' The man's voice sounded fractured.

Jermain dashed the sweat from his eyes and listened to the banshee screech against the hull. Down and down. Nearly five thousand feet to the bottom. No one had ever lived from a last dive. Friends of those lost in early disasters spoke glibly of a 'quick death', but who could tell? Jermain saw a seaman staring at the curved side as if expecting to see it cave in at any second.

'Four hundred and fifty feet, sir!'

There was a long-drawn-out rattle and then a violent jerk which nearly threw Jermain to the deck.

Jeffers yelled, 'It's free, sir! She's answerin'!'

The sounds were changing again. Now it seemed as if a giant piece of metal was being bounced along the casing, its trailing cable rattling jubilantly behind it.

Jermain said flatly, 'Hold her, Number One. I don't want to pop up like a cork!' He saw the needle begin to turn in

89

their favour, and heard a seaman sobbing quietly behind him. He added, 'Keep her at periscope depth.' Over his shoulder he snapped, 'All sections report damage and injuries!'

Voices crackled and hummed through the intercom system, voices unrecognisable in strain and relief.

'Open up the boat. Stand by emergency deck party!'

Jeffers did not turn. 'Shall I be relieved, sir?'

Jermain shook his head. 'No, I want you there at the planes. We're not out of the wood yet!'

Wolfe said, 'No apparent damage, sir. Two torpedomen slightly injured in the fore-ends.'

'Very well. Pass the word for the doctor.'

Oxley's voice sounded loud over the speaker. 'Lost contact, sir. The submarine must have turned away.'

Twine said between his teeth, 'Not bleedin' well surprised, with all this row goin' on!'

Jermain met Wolfe's eye and wondered if he too had been struck by Oxley's behaviour. With the boat diving headlong for the bottom Oxley could still retain an interest in his hard-won target.

The deck party were already mustering below the bridge ladder, their expressions mixed between shock and surprise at being alive.

Sub-Lieutenant Colquhoun slung his leg over the coaming of the control-room door, his fingers fumbling with his life-jacket. He did not seem to see either Jermain or his father, but stared blindly at his waiting men.

The admiral broke his silence and said tightly, 'Well, Jermain, I hope you're satisfied!'

Jermain tore his eyes from the depth gauge. 'About what, sir?' He saw the anger flickering in the admiral's eyes, like reflections in the side of an ice floe.

'By your pig-headed stupidity you've not only lost the submarine contact, you also damn nearly sunk this boat!' He waved his hands around him. 'You should have stuck to the instructions!'

'We would have made no contact, sir.' Jermain eyed him angrily. 'At least, it would have been too late to intercept.'

Sir John Colquhoun turned away. 'We don't know for sure that Oxley did make a true contact. It might be just one more piece of damned incompetence!' He seemed to be talking to himself now. 'The humiliation! Your excuses'll cut no ice with me, I can assure you!'

'Sixty feet, sir!' Wolfe was watching the admiral, his features grim.

'Up periscope.' Jermain staggered, and for a moment he thought the steering had jammed. But as the periscope hissed from its well he saw that the weather had worsened, and in spite of the watery sunlight the lenses seemed to be shrouded in heavy mist. But it was rain, steady, torrential rain, which was beating the sea's surface into froth and fine spray.

He straightened his shoulders. 'Can't see a thing. Surface!'

He brushed past the admiral and stopped beside the deck party. 'You will have to get out on the hull. It'll not be easy, and speed will be essential.' He looked at Colquhoun's pale face. 'But no risks, understand?' He saw him nod, but there was little understanding in his eyes.

Mayo yelled, 'I'm sending up an additional rating to replace Jeffers, sir!'

The hull staggered, and Jermain swarmed up the ladder, knocking off the first set of clips and opening the hatch in automatic movements. Up the ladder with the deck party panting at his feet and then through the second hatch and on to the surface navigation bridge. The water was still draining away, and the fin's fibreglass covering was thick with crusted salt and trailers of weed.

With the rain beating savagely at his head and shoulders Jermain pulled himself the last few feet into the open cockpit at the top of the fin. The rain was as deafening as it was heavy, and the masked sunlight shimmered around the wallowing hull and made the sea seem like steam. As if the sea was angry to lose its victim and its rage had been transformed into heat.

Jermain clambered over the edge of the screen, his eyes straining astern. He saw the raw welts on the black whaleback where the trapped cable had scored through the paintwork to the metal itself. And then bobbing astern like a sea-anchor he saw the dull-coloured buoy and the last coil of wire which appeared to be holding it to the boat's vertical rudder.

He shouted above the hissing rain, 'Pass the word to the control room! We must retain this speed the whole time. If we stop the buoy may sink and wrap itself around the screw, then we are done for! Not that the Communists would mind towing us into port!' The joke had no effect, and he heard his instructions being relayed tonelessly through the intercom.

Lieutenant Victor squeezed into the cockpit. 'Number One sent me up to lend a hand, sir.' He blinked at the sea and added, 'God, what a mess!'

Jermain turned to Colquhoun. 'Are you ready?'

Colquhoun nodded dumbly.

'Right then. Take your men down to the rear of the fin, just like you did when the dinghy came aboard. I suggest you rig a tackle to the handrail and pay out two men towards the vertical rudder. Once there they should be able to hack that wire free without too much difficulty.' He gripped the boy's arm. 'I'll trim the boat as high as I can, but the men who do the job will be swimming for part of the time, so hold on to their lifelines like hell!'

'Yes, sir. I'll go myself.'

Jermain watched the little group climb down to the partly submerged deck and waited as they rigged the lifeline and huddled together for a last conference.

During all the confusion no one had reported hearing the end of the exercise, which was hardly surprising. The attacking submarine was to detonate two grenades to signify a successful strike, and no doubt at this very moment her captain was congratulating himself at this unexpected result.

Jermain gritted his teeth and plucked his sodden shirt away from his chest. All it needed now was for the unseen fishing boats to arrive and demand damages!

6

Human Error

Max Colquhoun shouted above the noise of the dinning rain, 'Right then! Pay out the lifelines and make sure there's no slack!' He looked directly at the seaman who was to accompany him along the wave-washed deck. 'We'll take one hacksaw each and work in relays!'

The man, Gipsy Archer, bared his teeth and wiped the water from his black hair. 'Should get a tot of neaters for this, sir!'

Colquhoun tore off his streaming clothes and stood swaying on the steel casing. Under his bare feet it felt like ice. Then he tightened his underpants around his waist and tied one of the lifelines hard against his hips. He had to work fast, and not give himself time to waver in front of the watching men.

At first he had thought his legs would not even carry him down to this treacherous place, and his offer to do the job himself had seemed all the more a cruel mockery. He missed the tough competence of Petty Officer Jeffers, whose seamanship appeared to come as much from instinct as from any set drill.

He blinked the spray from his eyes and handed Archer the end of a loose rope bridle. Like lumberjacks on a giant log they would walk down the sides of the hull, held apart by the bridle and steadied by the slender lifelines.

He tried to grin. 'Right, Gipsy! Let's see how good a seaman you are!'

Archer shrugged and moved the hacksaw on to one hip. Against his tanned and tattooed body Colquhoun seemed frail and delicate. He had volunteered to accompany the officer not out of loyalty but for the sheer guts of the thing. He was proud of his strength, and was always ready to match it against the other seamen.

Slipping and sliding they moved away from the swaying fin, each step taking them nearer the deeply shelving whaleback towards the stern where the angry water boiled across the steel like a mill-race.

Colquhoun winced as the backwash surged around his legs. It was very cold in comparison to the rain, and he could feel his breath wheezing in his lungs with each precarious movement. Once when he looked back he saw Able Seaman Rider taking charge of the line party and, above him, silhouetted against the sheeting rain and washed-out sky, the watchful figure of the captain.

Just this once they were depending on him, he thought desperately. Perhaps it was that thought alone which was making him keep going. Yet his father had not said a word, not even wished him luck. The memory of the admiral's angry face in the control room made him suddenly bitter. But why should it matter? He had known their meeting would be just as it was.

A wave curled lazily over the hull and pushed him kicking against the *Temeraire*'s rough flank. For an instant he saw the sea right below him and felt his shins grate cruelly on the metal.

Archer pulled on the bridle and yelled, 'You takin' a dip then?' He was actually grinning.

With sudden determination Colquhoun fought his way along the casing, ignoring the cuts and bruises on his hands and feet and concentrating on the tall rudder blade which seemed to cruise quite independently from the rest of the boat. He was quite frozen now, yet his senses seemed sharper instead of dulled by his constant pounding. He could see the score marks left by the snared cable and even small patterns of rust around the horizontal rudder.

He paused, sobbing for breath. Without looking at his companion he gasped, 'We'll jump together! For God's sake don't slip or we'll miss the rudder and fall into the screw!'

Archer scowled, 'I ain't stupid, *sir*!'

Momentarily blinded by the criss-cross of surging water Colquhoun leapt towards the upright sheet of steel with its

94

mocking halter of wire cable. For a brief instant he thought he had missed his direction and fell kicking into the maelstrom, his mouth filling with salt as he screamed meaningless words and curses into the sea itself. The bridle pulled him against the rudder fin with a savage jerk, and he saw his own blood running freely into the creamy froth around the bar-taut line. But they had made it.

Working at top speed they freed themselves from the bridle and clung on either side of the rudder, blind to everything but the cable and the job in hand.

Colquhoun sawed at the wire for a full minute and then croaked, 'You take over!' As Archer carried on with the muscle-wrenching work Colquhoun found his eyes drawn down and behind his perch to where the distorted sunlight cast an occasional glow on the great whirling propeller blades. One slip . . . He shuddered.

Back below the fin, Rider tested the lifelines and shouted, 'Play 'em like fish, lads! Don't jerk 'em off!' He looked round startled as two more figures emerged from the screen door.

Lightfoot and Bruce stood staring at the drama, and then the latter growled, 'We come up to lend a hand!'

Rider nodded, his panting making him bend over. 'Good! It's about time you bloody sonar people did somethin'!'

Bruce spat on his hands and seized one of the lines. To Light-foot he said, 'Looks like they're nearly through.'

Lightfoot took his place behind him and braced his legs against the hull's uneasy roll. He was almost blinded by the rain, and he stumbled awkwardly as the churned waves swept up and over the casing, trying to push the men from their hold.

He had almost lost his head when the *Temeraire* had tilted crazily towards the bottom. The men in the sonar compartment had stared at each other without recognition, their faces like masks of terror, too shocked to comprehend what was really happening.

There was always the risk, of course. It was mentioned in the training depots in a matter-of-fact, clinical fashion, as if it only happened on very rare occasions, and then only to others.

All Lightfoot's past anguish, his terror of the seaman, Archer, had vanished as the boat had plummeted down. His world had been confined to the small steel room with its glittering, mocking equipment and the men who sat like caged wax-works.

Over the intercom, from another part of the sealed hull, he had heard sharp, brittle orders being passed and snatches of meaningless conversation. Then every so often the captain's voice would penetrate his whirling mind, so that he waited for it, like the word of God.

When eventually the wire cable had slipped free from its first hold and the deck had swung slowly upwards he had felt a hand on his shoulder and heard Colquhoun say, 'It'll be all right now. You see!'

Perhaps he did not know what he was saying, and maybe he was not even aware he had spoken. But the quiet encouragement in his tone had made all the difference to Lightfoot.

The events were like dream sequences. Short, vivid pictures. Fierce, inexplicable sounds. And now they were out in the air, being lashed from all sides by rain and blown spray.

He wondered vaguely what Bruce was thinking as he cradled the line in his big hands. Had he been shocked out of what had gone before?

When Lightfoot had told him about Archer's threats Bruce had been unusually quiet and calm. They had spoken in whispers as the submerged submarine had sped northwards from Singapore and the men around them slept in their bunks. Lightfoot had tried to explain his own feelings and what he ought to have done.

Bruce had said sharply, 'Makes no difference now, wack. What's done is done.' Then with a flare of his old belligerence he had added, 'Leave him to me!'

But again, nothing had happened. If anything, Bruce had appeared to make a point of avoiding Gipsy Archer. Perhaps Bruce never intended to say anything, Lightfoot thought bitterly. After all, Archer had said nothing about him at all. So if he did not know Bruce was connected with the accident and the man's death, why should Bruce take any action at all?

A freak gust of wind cleared the rain and spray from the rudder, and Lightfoot felt a cold hand tightening around his heart. Gipsy Archer was the man on the rudder beside Colquhoun. Even through the downpour there was no mistaking his dark features and the arrogant tilt of his head. And he was tied to the line which Bruce held with such earnest concentration.

He opened his mouth to attract Bruce's attention, but at that moment he felt the line go slack as Bruce pulled violently, the full power of his shoulders against it.

Archer was just about to slide down the rudder blade as his last thrust with the hacksaw severed the wire. There was a loud twang and the bobbing fish-buoy curtsied free and sank in the submarine's wake. But Archer seemed to lose his hold, and as the rest watched with fascinated horror he slithered down the blade, his legs and arms kicking madly, his skin bleeding from a dozen places as he fought to save himself.

Bruce muttered hoarsely, 'The wire must have cut him down!' But when he glanced round Lightfoot saw that his eyes were cold and indifferent.

Another series of shouts made him turn again, and Rider yelled, 'Gipsy's caught hold of the sub!'

Archer made one final effort. Reaching up he seized Colquhoun's ankle and with all his strength pulled himself clear of the water.

Colquhoun was already weakened by the effort of holding on, and this last strain was more than enough. Lightfoot saw him struggle to reach down as if to assist the big seaman, but Archer pushed his hand aside, and using the officer like a ladder he dragged himself to safety.

Whether the strain on the lifeline was too much, or whether it had got frayed by the friction with the rudder, no one could be sure. Just before another fierce squall swept the watching men Lightfoot saw Colquhoun's hand begin to slip, and watched sickened as his legs disappeared into the creaming water below him.

He heard Jermain shout, 'Stop engine! Stand by with heaving lines!'

But even Lightfoot knew that would not be enough. In this weather, and allowing for the way already on the submarine, it would be some time before the captain could go about and find a single, drowning man.

Looking neither right nor left, Lightfoot ran back along the casing, and when his legs could no longer cope with the sluicing water he took a deep breath and dived clear of the hull.

Colquhoun was held afloat by his lifejacket, but limp and

only half conscious he allowed his head to loll as the water washed over him. He opened his eyes and stared at Lightfoot, and tried to speak as the boy turned him on his back and trod water.

The latter said hoarsely, 'S'all right, sir! I'm a good swimmer!'

Colquhoun retched. 'You might have been killed!' Then as the memory crowded his mind, 'Is Archer safe?'

Lightfoot paddled round to peer at the submarine's misty shape as it moved slowly out of the squall. 'He's okay.' So he should be too, he thought with sudden fury. He had knocked Colquhoun off the rudder in his efforts to save himself.

A yellow liferaft splashed alongside and bobbed obediently on its line. Hands were reaching down, and familiar faces moved vaguely around the two sodden figures as they were hauled up on to the casing.

Bruce hissed at him, 'You young *fool*!' but Lightfoot could not look at him. It needed time and it needed thinking about. But whichever way you looked at it, Bruce had tried to murder Archer.

Colquhoun found himself wrapped in a blanket and sitting in the wardroom while Griffin, the doctor, poured something fiery between his lips. He became aware that he was surrounded by a quiet watching group of figures. Baldwin, the steward, grinning all over his freckled face. Lieutenant Drew giving him an admiring smile, and Griffin watching like a hen with a day-old chick.

Drew said, 'You did a good job, Max! I thought that god-damn wire was with us for ever!'

Griffin frowned severely. 'You'll have to rest Too much excitement in one day for anyone!'

Then Colquhoun saw his father. The admiral was standing in the wardroom entrance, his hand gripping the curtain as if for support. He looked suddenly old, Colquhoun thought.

The admiral said, 'I'm glad you're all right, my boy.'

Colquhoun tried to define his feelings but could sense nothing. He replied, 'It was damn cold, sir.'

The admiral saw the others watching him and seemed to pull himself together. 'You should never have gone. The men could have managed it on their own!'

Colquhoun lay back and closed his eyes. That was more like it, he thought. Even now his father appeared unable to find a single word of warmth or pleasure.

The sudden realisation that it no longer seemed to matter filled Colquhoun with astonishment. It was as if his ordeal had been a test, a last chance to prove his individuality. The ideas became vague and distorted, and he heard the doctor say, 'I'll take him to the sick bay. I think he's had enough!'

But Colquhoun's eyes were shut, so he did not realise that the last remark was directed at his father.

*   *   *

Jermain wedged himself in the corner of the cockpit and tried to peer through the hissing curtain of rain. Through the hatch at his feet he could hear the clatter of orders, the questions and answers being passed back and forth over the intercom, but his mind still rebelled against the necessary routine and he was unable to free himself from a feeling of uncertainty.

A messenger called above the downpour, 'Steering and hydroplane tested and answering correctly, sir!'

'Very good!' Jermain stared at the rain and marvelled at the way it seemed to enclose the slow-moving hull like a steel fence. It should have been a bright clear morning, yet from his perch at the tip of the swaying fin it might have been any time, on any sea.

He snapped, 'Tell the first lieutenant to speed up the checks. I want a quick report from all sections on damage.'

The man ducked out of sight and Jermain returned to his thoughts. It was like some inner sense of danger. Something uncertain yet real.

He could feel Lieutenant Victor shifting his feet behind him and wondered what he was thinking about the *Temeraire*'s failure during their first real exercise.

He sighed and rested his arms on the wet steel and stared directly ahead. It was like being aloft on a small, isolated light-house or on some forgotten rock, he thought. There was no sense of belonging to the hull which was all but hidden by the seething water.

Victor whispered loudly, 'The admiral's coming up, sir!'

Jermain tightened his jaw and waited in silence as Sir John Colquhoun hoisted himself through the hatch to stand beside him. The admiral looked angry. As if he was only controlling himself with real effort.

Jermain said, 'I understand your son is all right, sir.'

'So it would appear.' The admiral glared at the strange mirage of rain and spray without any sort of recognition in his pale eyes. 'What the hell are you waiting about for?'

'I'm checking for damage, sir. In addition, I'd like to get a look at those fishing boats.'

The admiral did not seem to hear. 'What a bloody mess!'

'I thought our people behaved very well, sir. And your son made a fine display of courage.' Jermain's face was impassive.

'He was lucky!' The admiral ignored the hardness which had crept into Jermain's eyes. 'Right now I'm more worried about this exercise! All I've got to offer the Americans is your brief sonar report. At best it will prove that we could have destroyed the attacker but for this unfortunate bit of mishandling.'

The messenger reported, 'No damage, sir!'

The admiral snorted. 'I hate to think what would happen on active service!'

The radio supervisor scrambled through the hatch and stood stiffly in the rain in the crowded cockpit. He seemed afraid of touching the admiral with his own body, Jermain thought.

Jermain asked flatly, 'Well, Harris, what is it?'

The chief petty officer tried to shield his signal pad from the rain. 'Signal from Nemesis, sir. Exercise cancelled.'

Jermain frowned. Cancelled? Surely it should have been *completed?*

The radio supervisor glanced quickly at the admiral's face. 'The attacking submarine was diverted back to base with engine trouble, sir.' Harris gulped. 'All units to clear exercise area.'

The admiral snatched the pad and read through it searchingly. He exploded, 'This is the last straw, Jermain! First you disobey instructions only to get tangled in a lot of wire which a first-year subbie could have avoided!' He waved the pad.

Now *this*! And to think I might have believed your findings! Damn it, man, there was no submarine at all!'

Jermain said, 'My sonar department is very efficient, sir. Every officer and rating is hand-picked.'

'I don't care if they are all university graduates!' The admiral seemed unaware of the silent men around him. 'I was prepared to overlook your efforts with an inexperienced crew and a new boat, even to the point of making some suitable signal to the Americans in the way of an apology!' He glared at Jermain's grave features. 'And what a bloody fool I would have looked, eh? Telling 'em about your wonderful sonar report when there *was* no submarine!'

The messenger's voice was hushed. 'Control room request instructions, sir.'

The admiral took a grip of himself. 'I suggest you submerge and return to base post-haste, Jermain! At least nobody outside the Service will know of your escapade!'

Jermain looked across his shoulder and said calmly, 'Retain course and speed. We will remain at Action Stations.' He returned the admiral's look of open amazement. 'I am not satisfied, sir. If Lieutenant Oxley obtained a contact, then there must be an explanation.' His mouth tightened. 'As you reminded me earlier when I asked for your assistance, sir, you are a passenger in this boat. I take full responsibility.'

The admiral could only stare at him for several seconds. Then he said, 'You'll be sorry for this, Jermain. You will pay an expensive price for your show of independence!'

Jermain allowed his stomach muscles to relax slightly as the admiral ducked through the hatch. For a full minute he allowed the rain to wash over his face and chest, like an athlete after some test of endurance. Then he said, 'I think the squall is moving over. Be ready to dive.' He heard Victor mumble an assent and half smiled to himself. It was as if Victor was afraid to speak too openly with him now, in case some of the shame rubbed off on him, too.

Maybe it had been a bit of useless defiance. The admiral was right about one thing at least. The Navy would have no time at all for a captain who had blotted his copybook so openly!

He watched the rain moving diagonally away from the hull.

The fin and the small length of exposed casing began to steam immediately as the sun felt its way through the spray and wind-blown salt, and Jermain noticed for the first time that he had been standing in the downpour in his shirt and shorts. He felt the warmth soaking his body, and with it came another pang of uneasiness. There was something wrong with the pattern in his mind, yet he still could not explain it.

Perhaps if he had tried to describe his feelings to the admiral an open clash might have been avoided. But he recalled the man's stony expression when his son had led his small party to cut free the treacherous wire, and knew it was pointless to continue that line of thought.

Sir John Colquhoun had been prepared to be his friend on his own set conditions. The *Temeraire* was not important as a weapon, nor even part of a new strategy. To the admiral it had represented only the chance of holding on to an obsolete com-mand and the opportunity of displaying its potential in the face of the Americans, who challenged his control in the area. Not even the near death of his only son had been able to move him from the apparent realisation that his position and authority might be damaged rather than heightened by this most unfor-tunate of circumstances.

He saw the rain moving slowly away, and as if at a signal the wind too began to diminish. The sea's surface smoothed itself under the gathering sunlight, so that it glimmered like milk beneath a low but impenetrable haze.

The radar would have saved any further search, but to use it would certainly be asking for real trouble. Radar transmis-sions could be detected immediately, and any unfriendly war-ship in the vicinity would be quick to take an interest.

Jermain tugged his cap over his eyes. There I go again. Was it caution or imagination?

Victor spoke quickly, 'There's one of them, sir! Fine on the port bow!'

Jermain rested his elbows on the screen and levelled his glasses. At first he thought it was a slow-moving aircraft. But as the haze twisted and danced across the lenses he saw that he was looking at the mast and upper yard of a small ship. Far beyond it was a second one, cut off and lost like part of a mirage.

Jermain glanced briefly at the gyro repeater. 'Steer one one zero.' He stared hard at the floating masthead. Probably one of the trawlers. Yet it was apparently stationary and quite unmoved by the loss of a buoy and a few hundred feet of wire cable. Aloud he said, 'I'd have thought there'd be a bit of excitement! After all, the Black Pig is no lightweight. It must have given them a bit of a jolt, too!'

Victor said uneasily, 'We're getting a bit close, sir.'

Poor bastard thinks I'm round the bend. Jermain turned and smiled. 'Not quite what I expected. I must admit!'

At that moment the haze seemed to fall apart like a transparent curtain and there, rocking gently above its own reflection, was the other ship.

At first Jermain imagined that it was some sort of modern trawler. But even as he moved his glasses along her high, raked stem and over the compact bridge he saw the sudden flurry of foam beneath her stern and the telltale surge of power from the hidden screws.

Abaft her squat funnel was a long, white-painted deckhouse, and as the ship gathered way Jermain saw the sides of the structure fall away to reveal the gun mounting which even now was swinging towards him.

He shouted, 'Diving alarm! Clear the bridge!' He heard the lookouts stumbling down the ladder and Victor's heavy breathing as he groped for the button.

'AOOGAH! AOOGAH!' The klaxon screamed its warning just as the sea lit up with a bright orange flash. The shell passed directly above the fin with the sound of tearing silk, and Jermain felt the shock-wave slashing at his shoulders as he tried to keep his glasses trained on the other ship.

He yelled, 'Hard a-starboard! Full ahead!'

As Victor repeated his orders Jermain turned to watch the slender waterspout as it fell slowly on to the calm sea across the other beam. A few feet lower and the shell would have cut through the fin like a knife through butter.

The water around the hull was already boiling in torment as the tanks were flooded, and the hydroplanes took control and thrust the submarine's bows down.

Another bright flash, and the whole hull shook like a mad thing as the shell exploded within twenty feet of the side.

All at once the air was full of screaming splinters and the stench of salt and cordite. Water seemed to be falling everywhere, and Jermain almost fell as the deck tilted forward and down.

He took a last quick look at the other vessel. She was moving fast and was barely a quarter of a mile away now. Just one hit was all she needed. Just one!

Jermain jumped for the hatch and then stopped in his tracks his eyes fixed on Victor's upturned face and the long pattern of blood which poured from beneath his spread-eagled body. Victor was staring at him, his eyes filled with shocked horror and disbelief. He was opening and shutting his mouth, but no words came, and when he tried to move his legs towards the hatch the stream of blood became a torrent. It was then that he began to scream.

Jermain forced his mind under control and with steady, deliberate movements lifted the other man's legs over the coaming, shutting his ears to the terrible screams which went on and on and which seemed to exclude every other sound. And all the time Victor's unblinking eyes were fixed on him, hating, pleading and despairing with each passing second.

Hands reached up through the hatch, and with one final scream Victor was dragged down the tilting ladder. Jermain jumped after him, his shocked eyes only half taking in the water as it cascaded over the lip of the cockpit to shred away the bright scarlet stain from the steel plates.

Behind him the two hatches slammed shut, muffled and final as the boat continued in her steep dive.

In the control room the men at the controls worked their wheels and instruments as if detached entirely from the huddled group around the foot of the bridge ladder. Two seamen trying to hold Victor's thrashing body, Griffin, tense and controlled as he searched for the wounds, and the men who had carried the officer down the ladder, their clothes streaked with blood, their faces shocked and drained of colour.

Jermain said tightly, 'Three hundred feet, Number One. Alter course to one seven zero. Maximum revolutions!'

He saw Wolfe studying his face and heard the confident clicks from the diving panel. He forced himself to watch the gauges, to listen to the efforts of his command to obey him.

Like a far-off diesel train he heard the ship's thrashing screws as she passed somewhere overhead. For an instant he felt something like madness sweeping through his mind, the urge to hit back, and kill and keep on killing until the sea was empty.

'Three hundred feet, sir.' He caught Wolfe's eye and added flatly, 'Tell the sonar to track the other ship. He might try and detect our position.'

He saw Griffin stand up from the silent men by the ladder and knew that Victor was dead.

The doctor said slowly, 'Three splinters in his back, sir.' He stared down at the dead man. 'I don't know how he survived as long as he did.'

Jermain looked at Victor's face. It was like a stranger's. Not like a human being at all. Just an effigy. A thing.

He replied, 'Take him to the sick bay, Doc. I'll be along later.'

What was there to say? Jermain stared at the waiting men. They seemed shocked, dulled by the savage turn of events.

Wolfe said quietly, 'That was close, sir.'

Jermain eyed him emptily. 'They were waiting for us.' He looked across towards the wardroom entrance where he could see the admiral silhouetted against the light. 'It was no imagination. Neither was that submarine.'

'Would you like me to take over?' Wolfe sounded strained. 'Poor old Victor.'

Jermain felt the anger returning like a flood. 'Just carry on with your watch, Number One.' He did not recognise the harshness in his voice. 'And get that blood mopped up. There'll be time enough for grief and recriminations later on!'

He forced himself to walk unhurriedly to the chart-room. Once there he leaned on the table and stared fixedly at the chart. He tried to focus his eyes, to visualise how and why such a trap had been sprung. Only *Temeraire*'s unexpected arrival and her tangling in the fish-buoy had averted what might have been much worse. Where better to destroy a loaded Polaris submarine than in the middle of a set exercise?

Jermain found neither consolation nor pride in what had happened. His training, even his old instinct, did not allow for Victor's sudden death.

In his mind he could still picture those wide, desperate eyes, and in the silence of the chart-room he imagined he could hear the echoes of far-off screams.

*　　　*　　　*

Lieutenant Commander Ian Wolfe walked slowly into the wardroom and then paused uncertainly. The admiral was seated at the head of the empty table, a small book open in front of him. It was just after one o'clock in the morning, and the boat seemed silent and subdued as it cruised steadily towards Singapore. Wolfe was to take over his watch at two o'clock, yet for some reason felt unable to sleep. Ever since the previous morning when he had parcelled up Victor's few belongings he had been feeling restless and vaguely apprehensive. He was not sure he knew the full reasons for this, but he was unwilling to take the risk of facing his innermost thoughts in the small world of his cabin.

The admiral looked up and nodded towards a chair. 'Take a seat, Number One.' His eyes looked bright in the single reading light beside the table. 'It seems too quiet to sleep.'

Wolfe slumped in a chair and took a cigarette from a tin on the table. The last thing he wanted was to speak with the admiral, to take sides, to offer any sort of opinion on what had happened.

Perhaps it was his lack of feeling over Victor's death which troubled him most, he thought moodily. Over the whole boat there was an air of dejection rather than sadness. The swift horror of Victor's fate hung over officers and men alike, yet there appeared to be more than sorrow. It was like watching guilty men, Wolfe decided.

Victor had not been very popular in the wardroom. He had been withdrawn and defensive, and quick to show resentment if even a casual comment was challenged. Wolfe knew that some of the officers were now very conscious of his isolation amongst them, and were troubled because of it.

Wolfe, on the other hand, had made little effort to increase his own personal contact with any of them. It was enough to perform his duty, to use the passing time to prepare himself for the real challenge which still eluded him. A command of his own. There was no room for stupid and empty arguments, no point in allowing himself to become involved.

The admiral was watching him. 'I suppose you're wondering what will happen when we reach base?' He raised one eyebrow and smiled. 'I don't think you have anything to reproach yourself for. You handled the diving of the boat very well indeed. I shall certainly mention the fact at the enquiry.'

Wolfe pricked up his ears. So there was to be an enquiry now? He kept his voice non-committal. 'I believe the captain has made a full report, sir. I can't think of anything to add.'

The admiral smiled. 'Now then, Number One! You don't have to prove your loyalty to me, you know! I admire you for it, but we must face the facts.'

Wolfe stared at him. 'Victor was killed by some sort of Chinese patrol boat, sir. It might just as easily have killed the captain, too.'

'Quite so.' The smile was clamped on the admiral's face. 'But I was referring to the whole affair.' He waved his hands. 'In my position you get to see the whole picture of operations like a panorama!'

Wolfe tried to relax his stiff muscles. His headache had returned and he wanted to massage his forehead, but the other man's unwinking gaze made him resist it.

He said slowly, 'I understand the Chinese were on some sort of operational patrol. When we surfaced and moved amongst them they opened fire. It's not the first time there's been such a clash, sir. The Americans are always running foul of these bloody scavengers!'

'Maybe. But only the captain and poor Victor know for sure what really happened. And Victor is dead.'

Wolfe stirred uneasily. You bastard. You dirty-minded little bastard! He tried to see beyond the admiral's cold eyes, to be one jump ahead.

The admiral said calmly, 'I shall, of course, put in a good word for Jermain. There is no point in being vindictive. No point at all. But *Temeraire* is far too valuable to be used like a battering ram, don't you agree?'

The question came out with a snap and Wolfe felt pinned down by the admiral's relentless stare. 'But the other submarine, sir? The one Oxley detected.' Wolfe tried to avoid the point-blank question. It was an open challenge, to test which way his loyalty would go. He thought quickly of Jermain's impassive face after Victor had died, of the sharpness in his tone. Perhaps he was rattled, even unprepared for his massive weight of responsibility. He tried to halt his line of reasoning, to blot out the picture of Jermain's masklike features. He had been like a stranger, a man apart.

The headache was getting worse, throbbing at his skull like insistent hammers.

'The submarine?' The admiral shrugged. 'Underwater echoes are unreliable at the best of times, Number One. I can remember when I took my little S-boat off the Dogger Bank after a Jerry destroyer. I thought I was being tagged by an enemy submarine but at the same time I used my head and acted with the right spirit!' His face was flushed. 'Got him with a full salvo! A copybook attack!' He became serious again. 'I admire any man who tries to uphold the honour of the Service in front of a foreign power. But any man who *invents* a situation to cover his own mistakes is far more likely to bring discredit rather than praise!'

Wolfe cleared his throat. 'Do you mean the captain, sir?' He regretted the question immediately. He saw the shutters drop behind the admiral's eyes and cursed himself for his stupidity. He could not afford to take sides. There was neither time nor valid reason for it. Jermain had been a friend, a *real* friend. But that was long ago, when the Navy and all that went with it had been another, more enjoyable way of life.

The picture grew in his racing thoughts like a spectre. After all, what had Jermain *really* done when Sarah had left him? Maybe he was bound to take his sister's side. He could even be corresponding with her, sharing her other life just as he had once done. Did anyone know anyone any more? Jermain was a stranger like the others, a man out for himself.

Wolfe felt the sweat gathering on his brow and said harshly, 'I am not really in a position to say anything, sir!'

The admiral gave a thin smile. 'Of course not. You have your own future to contemplate. That is enough for any aspiring officer, eh?'

Wolfe nodded, feeling sick. 'I suppose so.'

Sir John Colquhoun eyed him thoughtfully. 'Have you seen much action, Number One?'

'The usual, sir.' The headache tightened its grip. 'I took part in the Suez campaign, and I was in Malaysia for a while.' He shrugged heavily. 'Yet one is never really expecting trouble until it happens.'

'Perhaps.' The admiral closed his book with a snap. 'But when these incidents occur, even in the Cold War, we must be ready. Instantly prepared for the unexpected! The country is too soft, too indifferent to care about what we are doing. It is a lonely, uphill struggle.' He gave an elaborate sigh. 'But we must accept our responsibilities and face them!'

Wolfe tightened his hands into fists under the table. If he told the admiral about his son's mixing with the C.N.D., *that* might wipe some of the smugness from his words! But he knew he was only deluding himself. Men like the admiral left no room for manœuvre.

He glanced at his watch. 'I think I'll get ready to take over my duty, sir.' He noticed with surprise that the admiral's book was a cheap thriller from the *Temeraire*'s library. He added hastily, 'I'll look in the sick bay and see that your son is all right.'

The admiral opened his book. 'Very well if you think it necessary.'

Wolfe stared at the admiral's lowered head and marvelled. He was even jealous of Jermain because of his own son, he thought. Suddenly Wolfe felt disgust for himself and the way he had failed to stand up to the admiral's thinly veiled attack on Jermain.

He walked quickly into the passageway and half paused beside the captain's door. There was still a light in the cabin, and he could picture Jermain sitting at his little desk, his calm face intent on the never-ending stream of affairs which awaited his attention.

Command of the *Temeraire* had been a culmination of hard work and dedicated concentration on Jermain's part. Now, in the twinkling of an eye, everything had changed. A clash with the admiral, wilful damage and an officer killed. The list seemed endless, yet it was, Wolfe knew, only a beginning.

He wondered if he would have behaved as Jermain had done

under the same circumstances. It would be easy to save face, to admit a sonar fault and promise better for the future. Curiously enough, Victor's death was the least important of the problems. The authorities would say it was unfortunate but unavoidable. A sad loss incurred in the path of duty.

Wolfe remembered the empty cabin with its frayed bathrobe behind the door. The small bundle of personal effects which represented a man's hopes and fears. A few well-thumbed photographs of a wife and children. All wrapped and sealed along with an official letter of grief.

Wolfe rested his head on the cool metal and breathed out hard. It was stupid to think of it. It was nothing to do with him. He still allowed his mind to torture him a little longer. The animal-like screams ringing around the tower, the blood-splattered seamen on the ladder.

He had thought it was Jermain who had been hit. But even now he was afraid to face what his reeling mind knew to be a fact. In some inexplicable way he had been sorry when he had seen that it was Victor and not Jermain who lay twisting on the deckplates.

With a sob he hurried into his cabin and threw himself full length across his bunk.

7

Welcome Back

Jermain returned the salutes of the marine policemen and walked briskly through the wide gates. Beyond the neat barriers of anti-terrorist sandbags he could see the tall white buildings and the painted sign, 'Commander-in-Chief, Far East'. An admiral's flag hung limp in the harsh sunlight above a circle of dried grass, and sailors walked to and fro with messages and folios on errands of varying importance.

Jermain glanced at his watch and grimaced. He was five minutes late already, although he had left the *Temeraire* at her moorings with plenty of time in hand. He had not been to Singapore for several years, and he was stunned by the density of traffic in the jammed streets and the mad abandon of drivers and pedestrians alike. He had sat sweating in his taxi while an accident between another car and a rusty trishaw had been sorted out by an impassive policeman and the two gesticulating culprits. Above him, the hands of the Memorial Hall clock had moved slowly towards eleven o'clock, the time set for the preliminary enquiry at naval headquarters.

Temeraire had docked in the early dawn, this time with neither fuss nor ceremony, and Jermain had been thrown into a full measure of work until the very last moment. Nobody aboard even pretended any more that the submarine would be returning home in the foreseeable future. The ratings received the waiting wads of home mail and retired to their messes in silence, aware perhaps for the first time that there was little hope of a quick reunion with that other, domestic, life.

Jermain saw Lieutenant Oxley and his senior sonar rating, Petty Officer Irons, walking towards him, the latter carrying the leather case of the exercise reports. Oxley was wearing sunglasses but his down-turned mouth showed his irritation and resentment only too clearly.

He saluted in his usual casual manner. 'They've finished with me, sir.' He gestured towards the main building. 'I've been in Sleepy Hollow for two hours with the brains of the operations staff, and now I feel as dim as they are!' He forced a grin. 'I still don't know if they accept my report.'

Irons said respectfully, 'They ran the rule over me an' all, sir.'

Jermain felt the pent-up strain changing to bitter indignation as he listened. It was like being at school again. Like a mischievous, over-imaginative child.

He said, 'I'm going in myself now.'

Oxley shrugged. 'Good luck, sir. I'll be at the Tang-Lin Club for a bit if you'd like to meet me later on? Perhaps I could help to smooth away the wrinkles of pique?'

Jermain smiled tightly. 'I'll see. And thanks.' He walked on, and when he turned the corner he saw they were still staring after him.

What did Oxley really think? he wondered. Did he blame him for this damned enquiry? It might prove to be a slur on him as much as himself.

He slammed angrily through a swing door and into the glacier chill of the air-conditioning before an orderly could open it for him. More stairs, following the neat signs and attentive orderlies. Everyone seemed to be watching him, yet avoiding his eye, and the realisation only added to his mounting anger.

A cool Wren officer stood up from her desk and meaningly glanced at her watch. 'This way, sir.' She smoothed down her jacket. 'The admiral is waiting for you.'

Jermain stared at her slim shoulders. Go on, you bitch! Just tell me I'm late! But she opened the double doors and said evenly, 'Commander Jermain, sir.'

The room was very wide and very quiet. Even the overhead fans seemed muted, and the distant sound of traffic was a discreet murmur.

Sir John Colquhoun was perched on the corner of one of the big map tables, and a stout captain whom Jermain recognised as the C.-in-C.'s Chief of Staff sat behind a littered desk. The Captain S/M was also there and gave Jermain a quick smile of encouragement.

The admiral looked more relaxed and much calmer than he had appeared aboard the submarine. His white uniform was perfect and his face shone as if from a cold shower. He nodded briskly. 'As you can see, Jermain, the C.-in-C.'s not aboard. He's up country on tour as it happens, but I think I can deal with this unfortunate affair.'

Jermain relaxed slightly. So this was how it was to be.

He said formally, 'I apologise for being late, sir. I was delayed by . . .'

Sir John shook his head. 'Late? I hadn't noticed. Ah well, I suppose it takes time to get used to a place.'

The Chief of Staff sighed. 'I've been over your report, Jermain. Very interesting indeed.' He tapped the open folio. 'I am with it until the moment of surfacing, and then I think we're all in the dark. But of course it's not new for a warship of any kind to be fired on. The Chinese like playing at pirates!' He frowned. 'However, I am a bit worried about the sonar contact. I understand that your sonar department is a bit green and could quite likely have got ruffled.' He glanced briefly at the admiral. 'I know myself what it's like in a new boat, and with half the Americans watching for a cock-up!'

The admiral snapped, 'Yes, I think we can discount the contact entirely.'

Jermain swayed back slightly on his heels. 'I disagree, sir. The contact was positive. It *was* a submarine.'

The captain looked down at his desk. 'I see.'

Jermain hurried on. 'Which means in my view one of two things. Either the Chinese were on an exercise and using the Polaris boat as a target, or,' he looked directly at the admiral, 'they were in deadly earnest!'

The admiral began to swing one leg quickly across the other. 'Are you trying to suggest that the Red Chinese would *attack* a Polaris boat, Jermain?'

The Captain S/M shook his head very imperceptibly but Jermain ignored him. It was too late now. It was all or nothing.

'That's about the strength of it, sir.'

The Chief of Staff spread his hands and said, 'But don't you think the Americans were aware of all these risks when they selected this area for an exercise?' He looked up, scowling. 'They're not fools, you know!'

'I know, sir.' Jermain saw the disbelief in the man's eyes and added stubbornly, 'In my opinion the Americans were only on an exercise up to a point. I think that the Polaris submarine was on her normal combat station and that we were the ones *on exercise*!'

The Chief of Staff stood up and began to pace in front of the wall maps. 'So it all hinges on your contact. Out of that assumption you make this statement that the Reds were likely to have a crack at a Polaris boat, and in addition the Americans are deliberately keeping *us* in the dark, right?'

'That's about it, sir.' Jermain felt the anger giving way to despair. They did not want to believe him, and on the face of it he could hardly blame them.

The Captain S/M said quietly, 'Boats from my squadron have sometimes been in that area. I must admit that this idea of yours is new to me.' He looked unhappy and added, 'After all, Jermain, your boat is equipped with the best sonar in the world, and the attacking submarine you say you detected was an ordinary conventional boat. Now how could such a boat hope to get near a nuclear one without being discovered long before she got in range? Even supposing the *Temeraire* had not been there at all, the American boat would surely have pipped her and made off at full speed?' He forced a smile. 'I know I'm old-fashioned, Jermain, but just give me one good explanation.'

Jermain felt tired. 'I can't, sir. I can only give you the facts as I have been taught to translate them.'

The admiral closed his eyes and rocked gently on the table. 'I don't like to say this, Jermain, but it has to be said. There is a great difference between the tactics table and real life. Only experience and time can give you the definite *eye* for the chance, the possibility. Until that time you must rely only on your present reserve of ability and training.'

The Chief of Staff glanced at his clock. 'This is what I propose to do. The *Temeraire* will re-provision and make good any damage and defects during the next few days. Lieutenant Victor's remains can be flown back to U.K. on the next available plane, as we don't want a lot of unnecessary publicity out here.' He knitted his brow in concentration. 'Mr. Conway and his party are still on the base, and this sort of thing won't help him to placate the Singapore government when he's trying to put his case. As you know, Jermain, Conway intends to pare down this command both from the point of view of forces as well as commitments. The Malaysian set-up has changed fast, and although they want our protection they won't want us to provoke their neighbours, the Red Chinese.' He closed the folio with a snap. 'I must say, I agree with them.'

Jermain heard himself ask, 'And what about the emergency? I was sent here because of it.'

The admiral yawned. 'Well, of course that is another matter. The Chinese are moving ships and men into North Korea, or at least the Americans seem to think so. That's really their problem at the moment.' He waved a hand across the charts. 'We have to show our strength in a different way. We must indicate that we are with the Americans, but not *of* them. Our image must be stability.' He smiled. 'I *like* that.' He repeated it half to himself and then added sharply, 'So that covers it, I think. *Temeraire* will await fresh orders. In the meantime I will draft my own report for the pundits of Whitehall, and one for the U.S. Navy. I shall state firmly that your boat did all that was expected, but that whilst surfacing to clear away a fouled fishing cable you were fired on by some unknown vessel and incurred the death of an officer. They are the facts. There is nothing else to add.' He paused and frowned meaningly. 'At *this* stage!'

They were all watching him. Jermain kept his face calm in spite of his inner feelings. 'Is that all, sir?'

'For the present.' The Chief of Staff ruffled his papers. 'In the meantime you will pay special attention to internal security and make sure your men behave themselves ashore. Singapore is crawling with spies and informers as well as ordinary trouble-makers. As soon as you are ready for sea again I will draft some new orders. You will no doubt be going north to work with the Americans for a bit. But all that is confidential.'

The Captain S/M added swiftly, 'My men will do all they can to help, Jermain.'

Jermain thought of his silent crew and the hasty leave-taking from Scotland. And all for this! To be used as a status symbol. He recalled too with sudden clarity the senior American officer under whom he had studied when he had first started his training for nuclear submarines.

The officer had rasped 'You'll be awed and goddamned afraid when you start. Then one day you'll command a boat of your own. When that happens you might think you've made it, that you're one of God's disciples!' He had leaned on his desk and glared at the class. 'The nuclear submarine is a weapon, not a possession or a mark of your own damn prowess! Learn to use it as a weapon! Ride it, and take charge of it! By the time you take control you should be ready to throw it about like a goddamn rifle!'

He answered flatly, 'And my own report, sir. What will happen to that?'

The admiral stood up, his face expressionless. 'I cannot say how it will be received. No doubt Their Lordships will treat the matter with fairness in view of your record and your, er, comparative inexperience in these waters.'

It was over. Jermain turned on his heel and walked back through the doors.

The Wren officer said, 'There's a message for you, Commander. Mr. Conway would like to see you at his house this evening.' She held out a scrap of paper. 'It's all on there.'

Jermain stared unseeingly at the neat writing. Now Conway would want to stick his oar in. Well, if he asks me what I think, I shall tell him!

The Wren said, 'Was it rough, Commander?'

Jermain turned angrily and then checked himself. The Wren was quite pretty, and she sounded as if she cared. He replied, 'I was impressed.'

She smiled and turned away as the telephone began to ring. Over her shoulder she remarked quietly, 'But not, I suspect, *convinced*!'

*   *   *

Jermain signed the last of the official letters and leaned back in his chair. At the other side of the small cabin Wolfe sat in silence, his eyes moving restlessly across the pile of signals on the desk.

The *Temeraire* felt deserted and dead, and only the purring fans gave any hint of activity outside the cabin. The libertymen were ashore along with most of the officers, and with the reactor cool and run down only the minimum of machinery was kept running.

Jermain said wearily, 'That's the lot for the moment. I've made a signal to Flag Officer Submarines requesting a replacement for Victor, though God knows when he'll arrive, or where we'll be when he does!' He waited for some sort of response but Wolfe remained silent and watchful. He seemed too relaxed, too controlled, Jermain thought. It was as if he had lost or deliberately erased all his old personality and only his outward appearance remained the same. He added, 'You feeling all right, Number One?'

Wolfe stirred himself. 'Good enough.'

'I'm sorry I can't take you with me on this visit to Conway's place. I could do with a friendly face.' He straightened his fresh drill uniform and dragged his eyes from the neat bunk. He would far rather spend a few hours on his back, he thought.

Wolfe said flatly, 'I may take a run ashore later, when it's cooler.' He sounded indifferent. 'I don't suppose I'll get much further than the Officers' Club.'

Jermain toyed with his pen. 'I haven't mentioned it before, Ian, but are you still brooding about Sarah?' He saw the caution creep into Wolfe's eyes. 'You should try and make a new start. I think I would.'

'Would you?' Wolfe eyed him emptily. 'It's all right for you. You've never married. It's different when you know what there is to lose.'

Baldwin, the steward, peered through the door, 'Captain, sir? There's a car alongside the depot ship for you.'

Jermain stood up and reached for his cap. He continued slowly, 'I've thought about you and Sarah a lot. Much more than I thought I would. There must have been something to break you up. You were so right for each other, I thought.' He smiled gently. 'Maybe you should have waited a bit instead of rushing madly for a divorce. I mean, it may not have been as black as you imagined?'

Wolfe lurched to his feet. 'Imagined? Coming from you that's pretty damn good!'

Jermain said, 'Hold on, Ian! I only meant . . .'

'I don't care what you meant! I'm sick to bloody death of being lectured! I know what happened. She got tired of waiting about for me, and like all bloody women she thought she'd go and enjoy herself with the first pretty Yank who whistled to her!'

'I think that's ridiculous!' Jermain studied Wolfe with concern. 'She was never like that.'

Wolfe swallowed hard. 'Well, it's my affair. I'd be glad if you'd keep out of it in future!'

Jermain shrugged. 'Suit yourself. But I hate to see you tearing yourself apart over what's over and done with.'

'It'll never be over for me.' Wolfe was staring past him. 'Never in a thousand bloody years!'

By the time Jermain had climbed to the upper deck to where Kitson, the O.O.D., and the trot sentry were waiting to see him over the side, Wolfe seemed to have returned to normal.

Jermain turned by the gangway. 'All the same, Ian, I don't want you to get the idea you're on your own. It's unhealthy, and in our present circumstances potentially dangerous.'

Wolfe lifted his hand in salute and said quietly, 'I think I can hold down my job, sir!'

Jermain felt the sun playing across his neck and with it the old nagging feeling of irritation. It had been a mistake to have Wolfe aboard. He would have been better off in a boat full of strangers, where he could feel his own way in his own time. He hurried across the depot ship's wide deck and down the brow towards the jetty.

The sun was already low in the sky, but a total absence of wind did little to clear away the humidity of the day. Flags hung limp on their masts, and two large junks hovered motionless on the still water of the harbour like timeless reminders of the East and all its problems.

There was an open sports car standing beside a tall gantry and a small group of white-clad sailors were hanging around it as if in hopes of getting a lift into town. The group seemed to melt into the dusty jetty itself as Jermain approached the car, the oak leaves on his cap apparently being enough to dispel any such beliefs.

Jermain pulled up with a start. The driver of the car was a girl, who was leaning against the passenger seat and watching him from behind a pair of dark glasses. She was wearing a plain, sleeveless dress and her skin was evenly tanned and looked very smooth.

She said, 'I've come to collect you.' She pushed open the door and revved the engine noisily. 'I thought you'd prefer this to an official car.'

He slid in beside her and pulled his cap tighter on his head as she rammed the car into gear and drove bumpily across the jetty railway tracks. As she drove through the maze of sheds and parked cranes Jermain watched her from the corner of his eye. It seemed an age since he had been with a girl of any sort, let alone as attractive as this one. In her middle twenties, he thought. Probably one of the girls from the Defence Commission. The short brown hair which framed her face was bleached by the sun and her bare legs were strong and well formed.

She drove past the security guards with a casual wave and gathered speed across the causeway. She said suddenly, 'Are you looking forward to this evening?'

'I'm prepared for it, if that's the same thing.' Jermain tensed in his seat as the car sped past a ramshackle taxi with inches to spare.

She laughed. 'You're not a bit what I expected!'

Jermain frowned. 'How do you mean?'

'I was just talking with some of your men back there. They're as scared as hell of you!'

'Rubbish!' Jermain felt vaguely pleased. 'They've no cause to be!'

The girl turned to look at him, her eyes hidden by the glasses. Her mouth was turned down in a mock grimace. 'They like you. That's the main thing. Pretty rare out here.'

'And how long have you been here?' Jermain was getting out of his depth.

'Oh, about six months. I've been helping to pave the way for the Commission and all that.' She laughed at some inner joke. 'It's a bit of a hoot really!'

I can imagine, Jermain thought. She would have the pick of every eligible officer on the base.

She said after a few moments, 'I understand you've already met everyone who matters here?'

'If you are referring to your boss, Mr. Conway, well yes, I have.'

She looked sideways at him. 'What's the matter, Commander? Don't you like him?' She grinned. 'He's waiting for you right now. He'll have his "Man of the People" suit on, I expect, all creased in the right places!'

Jermain said dryly, 'You don't sound very loyal.'

'Oh, he's sweet really! You should get on well together.'

She jammed down the clutch and changed gear, her skirt riding carelessly around her thighs. Jermain noticed that her skin was the same even tan all over, and he had a tantalising picture of her stretched out on some beach, the clean limbs naked to the sun.

He said quickly, 'Do you like your job, whatever it is?'

'At times.' She touched her lower lip with one finger. 'It's all very secret, of course. Even the tape-recorders have to be blindfolded!'

Jermain realised with a jerk that the car had covered several miles without his noticing the distance. Houses and open shops flashed past, and the car's low bonnet seemed to cleave its way through a mad maelstrom of scurrying Chinese, loaded handcarts and the white and khaki of off-duty servicemen.

He said, 'Will you be there this evening?'

'For a bit. But I have a date tonight.' She glanced at him. 'But don't worry, you'll get a car to take you back to the base.'

Jermain lapsed into silence. She reminded him of the girl in the dinghy which had crashed into the *Temeraire*'s bows. There was something so fresh and natural about her, and he felt strangely unnerved. It was, of course, ridiculous even to think along these lines. He had been too long under strain, too long at sea. That was all there was to it.

She said, 'I was sorry to hear about the officer who was killed.'

Jermain stiffened. 'There's not much security around here!'

'I thought I might go and see his widow when I get back tc

U.K., to see if there's anything I can do to help.'

She sounded so completely genuine in her concern that Jermain felt confused. 'I'm sorry.' He turned to stare at her. 'I didn't mean to yell at you.'

Her lips parted across her even teeth. 'Like your men said. You really are a *pig* when you want to be!' But she was smiling.

Jermain grinned in spite of his embarrassment. 'I must say, I'd rather have you as a companion than some idiotic Member of Parliament!'

The car screeched sideways between two open gates where a dozing native constable leaned against a tree, and ground to a violent halt outside a square, shuttered house. She said, 'We've arrived, Commander!'

Jermain stood beside the car as she climbed from the driving seat and pushed the hair from her forehead. She was taller than he had imagined, and beneath the crumpled dress he could see the smooth lines of her body, the firmness of her breasts.

She stood looking at him. 'Now tell me, Commander, do you really *like* what you see?'

He coughed. 'Was I staring?'

She nodded gravely. 'A trifle.' She turned as Conway appeared at the top of the entrance stairway. 'Well, I must be off. Need a shower.' She gave Jermain a mock salute. 'May see you later, then?'

Jermain stared at Conway. He was indeed wearing a creased suit and his tie was hanging loosely around his shoulders.

Conway held out his hand. 'Come into the house, Commander.' He guided Jermain into the cool passageway. 'I see you got the car all right.'

Jermain asked carefully, 'Who was that girl?'

Conway grimaced. 'That was Jill. My daughter!'

*   *   *

Max Colquhoun wandered thoughtfully through the deserted control room and shone his torch across the gleaming panels. It was unnaturally peaceful in the boat and he found himself wondering why he had offered to relieve Kitson as officer-of-the-day. The latter had hurried ashore immediately, loaded down with golf clubs and a tennis racquet. It was too late in the evening to play anything, Colquhoun thought, but no doubt Kitson was eager to arrange a full programme of games while the submarine was in port.

The ensign had been lowered, and he felt that he might easily be the only soul aboard. From the direction of the chief and petty officers' mess he caught the distant strain of dance music and then he heard a man whistling in time with the radio. He felt vaguely comforted and paused to massage his back. He could feel the angry bruises and the dressing which Griffin had pasted across the cuts he had sustained on the rudder. It was odd how the others looked on him as some sort of hero. He had not even been able to save Archer when the lifeline had parted. He conjured up a stark picture of the water rising to meet him and the suffocating crush of salt in his lungs. It had been a near thing all right. Maybe that was why he did not want to join the others ashore. He needed to reassemble himself. To sort out his confused thoughts.

He climbed down a ladder and stood for a few moments looking along the full length of the upper crew space. The lines of empty bunks seemed to be waiting expectantly for their drunken owners when the libertymen came off shore. Perhaps they would feel the benefit of a good 'booze-up'. Some of the gloom and apprehension left by Victor's death and the boat's near disaster might be lost in a bout of drunkenness and all that went with it. Then only the married men would still be affected, Colquhoun thought. They always seemed to be more worried with mortgages and children's schooling than anything that occurred within the Service.

He was about to carry on with his rounds when he saw a solitary figure squatting beside one of the mess tables. It was Lightfoot. He was leaning on his elbows, his eyes unseeing as he stared down at a crumpled sheet of notepaper. Beside it, neatly arranged like part of a pattern, was an equally grubby envelope.

Colquhoun felt a sudden pang of guilt. Apart from the usual tongue-tied words he had hardly found a suitable opportunity to thank the boy for saving his life. That was one of the troubles with the Navy. Outstanding acts of kindness or bravery were hardly mentioned. It was simply not done. Small gripes and irritations, on the other hand, found plenty of outlets in ward-room and lower deck alike.

He tucked his cap under his arm and coughed quietly. 'Hello, Lightfoot. I'd have thought you'd be ashore with your mates?' He smiled. 'You're not duty, are you?'

Lightfoot looked up startled and half rose to his feet.

Colquhoun slung one leg over a bench seat and tossed his cap on the table. 'Don't get up for me. This is *your* home!'

Lightfoot sat down with a jerk, like a puppet, the strings of which have been severed. He said, 'I didn't hear you, sir.'

He stuffed the letter inside his shirt. 'I stood in for another bloke. I didn't feel like a run ashore.'

Colquhoun nodded. 'Like me.' He had another disconnected picture of his father sitting in state in his spacious headquarters. Maybe that was why he had taken Kitson's duty. To avoid meeting his father. Not that he need have bothered, he thought bitterly. The admiral had sent neither invitation nor greeting since he had left the boat.

Lightfoot said suddenly, 'Are you feeling all right now, sir?'

'Not too. bad, thanks.' Colquhoun saw with a start that the young seaman's eyes were red-rimmed. As if tears were not far away. He added quietly, 'Nothing wrong, is there?'

'It's me mum, sir.' Lightfoot tapped his pocket. 'She's dead.' He stared wretchedly at the table. 'The first letter I've ever had from me father and it's to tell me that she's dead!' He sounded stunned.

Colquhoun leaned forward. 'I'm terribly sorry.' He saw the boy's eyes studying him emptily. 'Really. I mean it.'

Lightfoot said, 'She worked her guts out for us. For *him* in particular.' He closed his eyes and two bright tears showed on his lashes. 'The lousy, stinking bastard!'

'I don't quite understand? Do you mean your father?'

'That's who I mean all right!' Lightfoot brushed his eyes with the back of his hand. 'Never given her nothing! Just moan, moan, moan! Pub every night, even when we were kids. Even when he was on strike or laid off he always had his fags and beer. Never mind about Mum!' He shook with an inner con-vulsion. 'Now *this*! On top of everything else!'

Colquhoun swallowed. 'I was going to write to her, too.' It had been a lie but he found that he meant it. 'To tell her what you did.'

'D'you mean it, sir?' The washed-out eyes were staring at him.

'You saved my life, and don't forget it.' He forced a smile. 'I know *I* won't.' He became serious. 'I'll tell you what I'll do. I'll get the captain to make a signal and have you flown home. He's bound to release you.'

Lightfoot's head dropped. 'You don't understand, sir. This letter is asking for more money. Mum's been buried already!' He stared hard at the table. 'Dead and buried, and I never knew!'

Colquhoun did not know what to say to him. The boy's father could have contacted the authorities. A signal would have been flashed to *Temeraire*. Perhaps too late for him to be flown back in time for the funeral. But it would have been a worthwhile try.

'He says he can't afford all the expenses for the burial, sir.' He gritted his teeth. 'The bastard! I'll bet he was at the Falcon for his pint just as usual!'

There was a thump overhead and the sound of a door slamming. The first of the returning libertymen no doubt, Colquhoun thought. The duty P.O. could deal with them on his own. In fact, he was better suited for the job. A quick thump on the chin would not be taken amiss from a petty officer by an unruly sailor on the rampage. But Lightfoot was in no state to be here when his messmates returned. Understanding or not, their fogged questions and commiserations would turn into a nightmare.

He said quickly, 'I suggest you come with me. You can sit in my cabin for a bit until things quieten down.' He picked up his cap. 'Sub-Lieutenant Luard won't be aboard for hours yet. He's dated a little nurse from the hospital.' He remark seemed to fall flat, but Lightfoot was already on his feet, his face suddenly defenceless.

'Thank you, sir. I'd like that.'

Colquhoun led the way past the empty galley with its gleaming stove and regimented pots. 'It's time we had a yarn about that dinghy sailing, too,' he said easily. 'You need time to think. To get your system clear.'

He switched on his cabin light and gestured towards a chair. 'Help yourself.' Another switch connected the cabin with the boat's piped music. 'As you can see, your officers are not as tidy as you chaps!'

Lightfoot perched on the edge of his chair, his eyes wandering around the chaos of discarded uniforms, magazines and the usual junior officer's clutter.

Colquhoun pulled open a drawer. 'This is strictly against regulations, but I think you can do with a drink.' He poured two measures of gin. 'It's on its own, I'm afraid, but Mr. Luard has scoffed all the tonic!'

Lightfoot took the glass and turned it in his hands as if it was some delicate crucible.

Colquhoun said, 'Well, here's to us. Thanks to you, I'm able to say this. And I'll not forget what you did for me!'

He felt himself knocked sideways as the door burst open behind him. The pain was all the more intense because the door's edge had struck his bruised back, and with a gasp he found himself on top of Lightfoot, his hands and face soaked with gin.

He staggered to his feet and turned round. 'What the hell d'you think you're doing?' He paused as he saw that it was the first lieutenant's square shoulders which were framed in the rectangle of light from the passageway. Behind him, his face bobbing anxiously from one side to the other, was Mason, the duty petty officer.

Wolfe was wearing a lightweight shoregoing suit and seemed to be breathing very heavily. For several seconds he stood in the doorway, his hands on his hips, his hair falling across his forehead

He said at length, 'So this is where you are!' He put his head on one side but the passage light threw a shadow across his face. 'I might have bloody well guessed it!'

Colquhoun felt the blood rising to his face. 'Now just a minute, Number One!'

Wolfe threw back his head and roared, 'Say *sir* when you address me, *Mister* Colquhoun!' He walked stiffly into the cabin, his eyes moving round the place like a dog searching for clues. 'I have just come aboard in time it seems!' He peered down at Lightfoot who was standing stockstill as if mesmerised. 'Who are you staring at?'

'I was just discussing a personal matter with . . .'

'Keep *silence*!' Wolfe stood inches away from Colquhoun, his chest heaving with anger. 'I came aboard to find the trot sentry swilling tea in the radio room and the duty P.O. sculling about the crew space like a first-year recruit!' His voice dropped so that he sounded almost reasonable. 'And where was the duty officer?' He took a half-pace forward and Colquhoun could feel the man's fury, could almost taste the drink in his throat. Wolfe yelled, '*Where was he?*' He did not wait for an answer. 'He was in his bloody cabin with his young friend!' He glared round at the wretched Mason.

The petty officer said thickly, 'But, sir, I was just explainin'.'

Wolfe thundered, 'Save it, Mason!' He swung round. 'And as for you, Sub-Lieutenant Colquhoun, I can only say it is *exactly* what I expected! Not content with balling up your duties and sheltering behind your father's rank, you apparently think you can get away with this sort of thing!'

Colquhoun tried to control the tremor in his voice. 'Are you implying that we, that I . . .'

Wolfe prodded him in the chest. 'Yes, you bloody little ponce, that's exactly what I *am* suggesting!'

Colquhoun thought of his father's cold eyes, of Lightfoot's pathetic gratitude, of all the other tormenting acts and incidents which had dogged him for so long. His first fear was slowly giving way to anger. Not a reasonable reaction to Wolfe's insinuations, but something worse, like madness.

In a surprisingly clear voice he said, 'As officer-of-the-day, I am placing you under arrest, sir! In my opinion you are under the influence of drink and therefore in an unfit state to perform your duties.'

Mason stared at Lightfoot and muttered, 'My Gawd!'

Wolfe swayed against the bunk. 'You're doing *what*?'

Colquhoun felt the strength leaving his legs but continued quickly, 'I would advise you to go to your quarters and await the commanding officer's return.'

Wolfe looked as if he was going to hit him. Then, to Colquhoun's shocked surprise, he said quite calmly, 'Suit yourself.

It'll all be the same in a hundred years!'

He left the cabin, and Petty Officer Mason said shakily, 'I 'ave a feelin' that this is goin' to be one of them nights, sir!'

8

And Goodbye

The Malay houseboy cleared away the plates and then placed a larger silver coffee-pot on the table.

Conway, whose wife had quietly left the room a few moments earlier, loosened his tie which he had previously knotted for her benefit, and grinned across at Jermain. 'That feels better! I like to unwind when I'm out of the public eye!'

Jermain allowed his body to relax slightly. It had been a simple but excellent meal and not a bit as he had imagined it would be.

When he had first arrived at the house he had expected Conway to brush aside the preliminaries with his usual outspoken forcefulness and then continue along much the same lines as the admiral. But it was not to be. Both Conway and his rather frail wife had been more than pleasant. The big M.P. had questioned him about the *Temeraire* and her crew, and his wife had rambled vaguely through her memories of Cornwall when she heard that it was Jermain's home.

It seemed that Mrs. Conway was not very strong and Singapore's harsh climate, coupled with her husband's whirl of activities, left her little in reserve. She apparently retired to bed early, no doubt to wonder at Big Jim's widening horizons.

Conway pushed a cigar-box along the dark table-top. 'Try one of these if you like. I'm not a cigar man myself.' He pulled an old pipe from his breast pocket. 'I make the most of this at these moments. If I smoke it in public my lass says it's just to impress the voters!' He grinned to himself. 'She's a cheeky one!'

Jermain dropped his eyes. Jill Conway had joined them for pre-dinner drinks and then after a brief explanation to her father had driven back into town. To her date. She had been wearing a short dress of black silk, against which her tanned skin and supple arms had shown to perfection. Without the sunglasses her eyes were large and candid, and Jermain had observed that they were a strange grey-green, like light shining through clear water.

He realised that he too had pulled out his own pipe and he smiled awkwardly. 'Me too. I enjoy my old pipe.'

The coffee and brandy warmed Jermain's stomach like soothing fire. He said, 'I'm very glad I came. The first time I've relaxed for some time.'

Conway swilled the brandy around his glass and frowned. 'I asked you here because I was impressed when we last met.' He looked directly across the table. 'I'm not being pompous. It's a fact. You and I have a lot in common, you know. We're both doing something we like, but neither of us has all that much co-operation, right?'

Jermain eyed him steadily. 'I'm not sure I follow you.'

'That's all right. I'm not trying to trap you. You're too smart for that.' He leaned on one elbow and watched the smoke drifting from his pipe and vanishing into the fans. 'It's very hard to make some of the old stagers out here understand what the government is trying to do. Any sort of change is suspect. Any kind of reorganisation is shunned. You can't reason with men like them. Sir John Colquhoun, f'rinstance. Thinks he's only second to God. And that's just due to seniority!' He grinned openly. 'Don't worry! I'm not asking you to take sides. You've had enough of that since you came out here!' He became serious. 'I read your report. A lot of it was complete mumbo-jumbo to me, but I have my own experts to worry over that!'

Jermain sat very still. Conway was not so empty as he had first appeared. As he had *made* himself appear.

As if reading his mind Conway continued, 'I came up the hard way, Jermain. Hard and rough. Before the war I was a truck driver up in Manchester. I got a reputation for looking after the lads when there was a strike in the offing or when the bosses got a bit mean. It just seemed to happen to me. Then there was the war.' His eyes were glazed as he stared into the

129

smoke. 'Dunkirk taught me a lot of things. That was where I learned to love the Navy, when there was only the bloody sea at my back! It also taught me a lot more. About government stupidity, and the crass negligence which had got us all in that unholy mess!'

He paused to pour some more brandy. 'There was a young subaltern in charge of my lot. No more than a kid. Rather like your young Colquhoun, in point of fact. I was just a lance-corporal at the time. Green as grass, and sick of the whole business. We had one empty Bren and half a dozen rifles between the lot of us. And coming smack down the road was a great Jerry tank! I nearly wet my pants, I can tell you! We'd been fighting and running for six days, and I was all in. We still had half a mile go to to the sea where the Navy was waiting to lift us off. Half a bloody mile, and this tank squatting there like a great iron toad. I knew we'd never make it. We'd be like the others. Just dusty corpses on that ruddy road!' He drank fiercely. 'I looked at this kid, this poor, terrified subaltern who'd hardly got his boots dirty since leaving Sandhurst, and I asked him what we should do. He just looked at me. I can see him now. Just looked at me as if I should have known what to do.'

Jermain waited. 'What happened?'

Conway shrugged. 'He ran up the road and threw himself across the tracks of the tank. He was carrying our last grenades. Just before they blew the tracks off the tank he was smashed to pulp. Ground down like a beetle!' He shook his head. 'I'll never forget him. Never.'

'He must have been a brave fellow.' Jermain was reluctant to speak. To break the spell.

Conway snorted. 'Maybe. But it was a damn stupid waste! When the war was over I was full up to here! I wanted to try and put things right. To make sure it couldn't happen again! I pushed my way into politics. You have to push in our party Of course, my old mates despised me for it. Thought I was "ratting" on them. But I pressed on. And I made it.' He peered at Jermain's grave features. 'The country can't afford hundreds of useless bases just for the personal importance of a few brass-hats! So what we have must be good. It must be better than anyone else's!' He smiled awkwardly. 'Like your submarine.

It's probably worth more than all the other ships in the Far East Fleet at this moment!'

He continued in his thick voice, 'But we must not think of the Far East merely in terms of power and conflict. That's where *we* come in, we're not too involved as yet. The Americans and the Chinese *are* involved, and both are resigned to confrontation at the best, and at worst,' he shrugged, 'World War Three, is my guess.'

Jermain said slowly, 'And you read my report?'

'I did. It worried me. It still does.' He leaned back in his chair and plucked his shirt away from his ribs. 'I get all my reports direct from Whitehall. I like it that way. I don't have to crawl to Sir John for scraps of information which will probably be useless anyway! I like to cut through the red tape.' He winked. 'Or is it *blue* tape in the Navy?'

Jermain smiled. 'I know what you mean.'

Conway wagged his pipe. ' 'Course, they're not all like that. A contact of mine, a Vice-Admiral Vane, he's a sharp one if you like!'

Jermain pictured the little admiral standing in his cabin aboard *Temeraire* with the Gareloch swilling against the moored hull. It seemed so long ago. So remote.

'Vane has seen your report. He thinks as I do. That the Chinese are up to something.' He laughed shortly. 'If your guess is wrong, then we're none the worse off, as I see it.'

'And if I'm right?' Jermain found he was leaning forward.

'One of my jobs out here is to put out feelers. Not a direct peace offensive, but a kind of neutralising probe, as the newspapers would say.'

Jermain could feel the excitement rising within him. 'Let me guess. You're talking about Korea?'

'Right first time. If we could find some way to bring the North and South together after all this time it would be a major step towards peace out here. It would be like uniting Berlin, or clearing up the mess in Viet Nam.' His eyes gleamed. 'That's why our Defence Commission has to show first that we are willing to pare down military strength to basic requirements.' He grinned widely. 'This is all top secret, of course!'

Jermain returned his smile. 'So is the *Temeraire*!'

'Just so. That was why I wanted to see you. You'll be getting fresh orders soon, as you know. You'll be going up north for a bit to work with the Americans again.'

'You know more than I do.' Jermain stared at him.

'Have to, in my job. I can tell you too that I'll be up there myself. I'll be contacting a few people from the other side. All very cloak-and-dagger!'

'A bit risky, isn't it?'

'I don't think so. I'd not be taking my daughter otherwise, would I?'

Jermain persisted, 'You think that the Chinese would try something to break up any sort of interchange?'

'Wouldn't you, for God's sake? They're bound to suspect our motives. But we'll take it step at a time. Nice an' easy!'

'Where do I come in?' Jermain watched the other man's mind at work behind his dreamy eyes.

'Maybe nowhere. But you might be our only real link. You'll get more orders and counter-orders I expect. The Americans will be told about your sonar contact. They might take it as a hint to clear their Polaris submarines out of any area where they might be detected. If the Chinese could provoke an incident on Korea's doorstep during our peace feelers, it would be a disaster.' He tapped out his pipe. 'They've been moving troops into North Korea for weeks. It's not just for the hell of it!'

A car screeched to a halt outside the house and Conway grinned. 'Jill's back. The date can't have been up to much!' He eyed Jermain thoughtfully. 'Not much like her dad, is she? I've done my best for her, but she's earned all that she's got.' He cocked his head on one side. 'When I was driving a truck I never thought my kid would go to university and get an honours degree and all the rest of it. It was just a pipe dream then.'

'Does she help you a good deal?' Jermain heard a telephone ringing and the girl's voice answering it.

Conway frowned. 'She does a hell of a lot. She tackles the welfare side of the job. You know, all the clutter about rehousing and re-employing local families who lose their jobs when we close down a base here and there.'

The door opened and the girl stood framed in the entrance. She spoke to her father, but her eyes were on Jermain. 'That was the *Temeraire* on the phone. They want Commander Jermain back aboard right away.' Jermain was halfway to his

132

feet as she continued, 'Something about an argument.' She raised her eyebrows. 'Is that serious?'

Conway led the way to the door. 'Depends who is doing the arguing, my girl!'

He turned to Jermain. 'Sorry about this. I was enjoying our talk. I'll send for the car.'

The girl was already down the steps. 'I'll drive him, Dad. It'll be quicker.' She looked at Jermain. 'The fresh air will help to clear your mind for the fray!'

*   *   *

Jermain sat with his fingers interlaced on his desk blotter and stared steadily at Wolfe. The first lieutenant was standing directly in front of him, his cap under his arm, his eyes fixed on some point above Jermain's right shoulder.

It was morning and beyond the closed door Jermain could hear the muffled sounds of normality and purpose. The squeak of a hoist, the casual mutter of conversation from the men at work. Up on deck, their bodies bared to the early sunshine, more men would be busy with paint-brushes restoring the fat hull to its old dull lustre and removing the telltale scars of shell splinters. But down in the cabin it was still and quiet, with only the fans and their own breathing to break the spell.

Jermain said evenly, 'I've just seen young Colquhoun and heard all that he had to say. Now what is your story?'

'I'm not a bit surprised at his attitude.' Wolfe seemed very calm. 'I've been riding him pretty hard since I joined the boat because of his general slackness. As you know, he thinks the Navy owes him a living!'

'I'm afraid I don't know.' Jermain felt tired. He had driven back from Conway's house in almost complete silence. Wrapped in his own thoughts, yet all the time conscious of the girl beside him. Only when the car had jolted to a halt on the jetty had she interrupted his ruminations.

'You know, Commander, you really care about your men, don't you?'

Jermain had dragged his eyes from the depot ship's pale side where the quartermaster watched them in silence. 'Does that surprise you?'

She smiled. 'With most of the men I've met, it's just show. Only for the record!'

He had seen her eyes shining in the reflected headlamps, had wanted to stay and be alone with her. He had replied slowly, 'I'm sorry to drag you out here like this. I had hoped we might talk some more.' He had felt foolish under the calm scrutiny. 'But then I expect you're pretty hard to pin down?'

She had switched on the engine, her face in deep thought, as if weighing his words. 'Perhaps I'll see you around, Commander. It's a small town, for all its noise!'

Jermain had watched her drive back towards the gates and had climbed up the steep brow to the depot ship.

An apprehensive group had been waiting for him in the *Temeraire*'s wardroom. Colquhoun, flushed but defiant. Griffin, the doctor, still dressed in mess kit and smelling of someone's perfume, and Oxley, who seemed to have taken charge of the situation.

Jermain had listened to each and all of them, his first fears giving way to disappointment and then anger. He had made no judgement at that moment. Tempers were too frayed, opinions too vague for real assessment. But alone for a moment with Griffin he had asked sharply, 'Well, was he drunk?'

Surgeon Lieutenant Toby Griffin often appeared offhand and easy-going, but when it came to his own trade he was very exact. 'I examined Number One as soon as I came aboard, sir. In my opinion he had not had very much to drink.'

Jermain's mind had moved quickly to the next point. 'So all this about the O.O.D. putting him under arrest might have been to cover up something else?' It was an unfair question, but to avoid this matter getting beyond the *Temeraire*'s hull speed and clarity were essential.

Griffin had repeated, 'He was not, in my opinion, too drunk to know what he was doing. But I do think he was suffering a form of intoxication.' He had hurried on as Jermain's face had become grimmer. 'Maybe he had been taking drugs, for a headache perhaps? Anything like that added to a few normal drinks could produce the same result. I know for a fact he had eaten nothing all day. He seemed to be worried about something'

Now, in the calm of the morning it was hard to imagine anything abnormal had ever occurred. If anything, Wolfe seemed more amused than angry.

Jermain started again. 'Tell me in your own words what happened.'

Wolfe shrugged. 'I went ashore. When I returned aboard the boat was a shambles. No trot sentry, and the duty petty officer out of the rig-of-the-day lounging about the mess decks. Then I found Colquhoun in his cabin.' He breathed out hard. 'Drinking, if you please, with a junior rating!' He shifted his glance momentarily to Jermain's face. 'Now, if that's normal, just say so!'

Jermain said, 'Colquhoun states that you were insulting and made certain allegations. In other words, you were drunk.'

Wolfe sighed. 'He must be off his head. I was angry right enough, and with good reason He just lost his head, that's all.'

'I see.' He tapped his desk. 'Well, I've told Colquhoun what *I* think about it.' Jermain watched for some sign of uncertainty, but Wolfe's gaze was steady. 'He was upset, over-anxious, and in his position it seemed quite reasonable. The rating, Lightfoot, had had some bad news from home. Colquhoun thought he was doing the right thing.'

Wolfe said stiffly, 'So you're taking his side?' He shrugged. 'I spoke my mind to him, and he took the easy way out, or so he thought.'

Jermain eyed him coldly. 'Don't be such a bloody fool! You know it's not as simple as that. I know he acted hastily, but he hasn't your experience. This is a new crew, untried, and unsettled by all trouble we've been having. I expect you to set them an example and not add to their problems!'

Wolfe nodded. 'I know it's hard for you. I'm sorry. It can't be easy to have to back an incompetent officer just because his father is your admiral.' He sounded quite reasonable.

Jermain stood up, his eyes blazing. 'You know damn well there's nothing like that about it!'

'I'm sorry, sir. I must have misunderstood.' Wolfe studied him flatly.

'If this thing goes any further it might mean a court martial. I intend to see that it does not!' Jermain made himself sit down again. 'For one thing, I have already spoken sharply to Colquhoun and explained in no uncertain terms that there are required ways of behaving. That it is not his lot to entertain ratings in his cabin, no matter how deserving it might appear to be.' He added harshly, 'And I am not convinced that your attitude was blameless either!'

Wolfe drew himself up very stiffly. 'Then there is to be an enquiry, sir?'

'No.' Jermain got a brief picture of Colquhoun's pale face, his mouth set in a stubborn line as he had listened to his words that morning. He continued, 'To behave as you did in front of two ratings is far more damaging. And at this stage of events I would have expected you to act differently.'

'So I suppose it's all over the boat now.' Wolfe gave a small sigh. 'Well, I suppose I might have guessed that would happen. I underestimated Colquhoun, it seems.'

Jermain ignored him. 'Mason, the duty P.O., is slow, but one hundred per cent reliable. It won't go beyond him. As for Lightfoot. We shall just have to hope that he has too much on his mind to complicate matters.'

'And you're doing this for me? Because of our friendship?'

Jermain leaned back in his chair. 'Partly, perhaps. I want you to get over your old troubles, and I need you to help me run this boat. In the next few weeks, maybe even days, we shall be required to act as a combat-ready submarine, and all that it entails. If I lost interest it would mean a court martial, and that would do more than damage reputations, it would injure the efficiency of the *Temeraire*.' His tone hardened. 'And that I will not tolerate, do you understand?'

'Perfectly, sir.'

'In any case, if there was an enquiry outside this boat it might wreck your chances of a command at any time.'

'You are implying that they might doubt my sanity, sir?' Wolfe's eyes were very bright. 'I consider that I acted as any responsible officer would under the same circumstances. I may have made a joke to Colquhoun, but if he implied that I said more, then I shall deny it.'

'Colquhoun has merely stated that he thought you were too drunk to know what you were doing. We've all been under strain, so let's leave it at that!' Jermain dropped his voice. 'But I will not destroy everything we've worked for just because of a few petty jealousies and hatreds! I have lost an officer killed.

I am not losing more officers in a legal tangle to suit you, Colquhoun or anybody else, is that understood?'

Wolfe nodded. 'Yes, sir.'

'Very well.' Jermain softened his voice slightly, hating the barrier between them. 'And try not to let your domestic affairs interfere with your life now.'

He stared hard at Wolfe's impassive face and wondered. He wanted to ask him about the pills Griffin had said he was taking. To break through and find the man he had known so well in the past. But he could not bring himself to do it. Not here and now. Wolfe had enough on his mind for a bit.

Colquhoun had acted hastily and without thought. In submarines discipline was often at variance with the rest of the Service, but, nevertheless, he obviously felt he had no alternative. If they could get to sea again things might be different.

Of one thing he was certain. If Wolfe left the *Temeraire* under a cloud he was finished. Finally and for good. The Navy looked after its own in so many ways but was equally ruthless with those who betrayed its code and ritualistic management.

Jermain was equally certain that if Wolfe let his emotions betray himself in the open once more, it would be the *Temeraire*'s captain whose sword would lie on the court-martial table. The same rules covered all men.

He added, 'I saw Conway last night. I gather we might be used in something big pretty soon. When it comes we must be ready.'

Wolfe replied calmly, 'Yes, sir. I heard that you had come back with his daughter.' There was no emotion in his voice yet Jermain felt a sting in his brief comment.

He said wearily, 'Very well, Number One. You can return to your duties. I hope this incident will be forgotten, and quickly!'

Wolfe paused with his hand on the door handle. 'About my wife, sir. Your sister, that is.' He watched Jermain dispassionately. 'I realise you think she was a blameless angel. Even taking into consideration that she nearly left me on two previous occasions and that she eventually went off with her Yank, I still believe she was talked into it. But I was left out of the matter. Shut off like a damned schoolboy!' He continued in the same flat voice, 'So you see, I've had a lot to consider.'

'I know. And I'm sorry.'

Wolfe opened the door, then said dryly, 'Good. That makes me feel a lot better.'

When the door had closed Jermain dropped his head on to his hands. It was no good. Wolfe was sick with bitterness and self-pity. He might even be a danger to others if pressed too much.

He found his eyes drawn towards his personal signal pad, but instantly dismissed the sudden impulse. He remembered Wolfe's face as he had stepped aboard in Scotland. The look of need and reprieve.

Like the *Temeraire* herself, he had to be given his chance.

*   *   *

The battered sports car wound its way through the press of traffic and somehow managed to filter into a narrow side street. Jermain sat fascinated as a yelling trishaw driver appeared beside his door, and wondered what would happen if the car actually came to a halt. He imagined that the surging mass of people and vehicles would pile up and up into an immovable tangle until the street was filled.

His mind was still confused with the speed of events which had taken him from the busy activity of the *Temeraire*'s clinical atmosphere to this open car and the girl who sat seemingly relaxed behind the wheel.

He had received a brief telephone call whilst working through a mass of reports at his desk. She had sounded casual, and her invitation to 'take a look round' had been matter of fact, as if she did not really care one way or the other.

Jermain had paid a hasty visit to a Chinese tailor and was already beginning to regret his choice in clothing. The light-weight suit was pretty good for length, but across the shoulders it left nothing to spare, and once when he had leaned forward to fill his pipe he had felt an ominous split beneath his arm. But he was happy in spite of his uncertainty. Pleased that she had remembered him at all.

She said suddenly, 'There's a place down here where we can eat. Nothing fancy. But it's fairly quiet.' She did not wait for a reply but swung the wheel towards an even narrower street where the overhanging houses made as if to touch each other.

Above the shaded walls the evening sky was still bright and clear, like a strip of blue silk, and the narrowness of the street seemed to hold all the smells and sounds of the East, to tempt them from every direction at once.

Jermain stood beside the car and stared at the low-windowed foodstalls and the small shops which crouched in total darkness away from the harsh light of the main road. There was a strong scent of fish and spices, and the fragrant odours of cooking meat and charcoal burners. It was all just about as far as you could get from the ordered life of the submarine, Jermain thought.

A grey-bearded Chinese in a white smock bowed politely as the girl led the way into one of the small restaurants. It consisted of half a dozen booths, all but one of which were empty.

Jill Conway sat opposite him, her eyes grave as she watched his face. 'Will this suit you, Commander?'

'The name is David.' He smiled awkwardly. 'The other is a bit formal!'

She nodded. 'David. It suits you.' She looked up at the old proprietor. 'The usual, please.' She added for Jermain's benefit, 'It saves time this way. You can ponder over a Chinese menu for years and you nearly always end up with the same.'

Unaccountably, Jermain felt a pang of jealousy. She was known here. Her casual confidence made him picture her with someone else, sitting just as he was. He said, 'This is fine. I was going to take you to the club. All the trimmings, but this is much better.'

She smiled. 'I guessed that. I also guessed that you would hate going to the club as much as I would!' She seemed to notice his suit for the first time. 'Out of uniform it would be hard to guess what you do for a living.' She placed her head on one side. 'But there's definitely something about the sea in you.' Her mouth quivered in a grin. 'A sort of homespun charm!'

The meal when it came was good and served with all the usual ceremony. It was *satay*, the neatly skewered meat all the more succulent when dipped in the hot peanut sauce. Jermain found that he was very hungry, and once when he met the girl's eyes he saw that she was watching him with open amusement.

She said, 'You look as if you've not eaten for days!'

He dabbed his mouth carefully. 'Like everything else aboard ship, eating becomes routine.' He added slowly, 'Besides which, the company is not so attractive.'

'Thank you.' She toyed with her plate. 'I've enjoyed being with you. But then I knew I would. I always know.'

Once more the pang. Jermain kept his voice non-committal. 'I imagine you get a lot of entertaining?'

'What a delightful way of putting it! Actually it's pretty much of a bore. All talk. Not much else.'

The little Chinese had placed a pot of tea on the table yet Jermain had hardly noticed. He was suddenly aware of the darkening shadows outside the window. Of the relentless passing of time.

She said, 'I guess I'll have to be getting back soon.'

Jermain controlled his disappointment. 'Well, thanks for everything. I must have bored you sick with all my talk about the *Temeraire*.' He forced a grin. 'It was good of you to listen!'

She shook her head. 'I'd have told you if I was bored. I was surprised that I was so interested.' Impulsively she laid her hand on his. 'But I'm leaving with my father tomorrow morning. I have to make a few calls.'

Jermain stared at her hand. 'I know. I'm only sorry we didn't have more time.'

'I know. I am too. You meet someone. For some reason you seem to click.' She shrugged. 'Then you move on.' Her eyes moved over his face. 'I'm not just saying this. I mean it.'

'I knew you would be leaving soon. I just hoped . . .'

She smiled gently. 'What did you hope?'

Jermain dropped his eyes. What was the point of going on? She belonged to another world. Another kind of generation. He answered, 'It was nothing. I was just being stupid!'

She pulled her hand away and began to rummage through her handbag. Without looking up she said quietly, 'What would you think of a girl who was conceited enough to expect a man to wait for her after she'd been out enjoying herself late at night?'

Jermain felt a surge of excitement, but replied carefully, 'It all depends. If she was important to the man I think he'd be only too happy.'

She looked up quickly, her face serious. 'I don't want it to end like this. Not just here and now.'

He smiled. 'Just give me the address. I'll wait for you if it takes until dawn!'

Her guard was down and she seemed confused but strangely pleased. 'I have to go to the United Nations place outside the town.' She looked uncertain. 'It's a long way, David.'

'I'll find it.' They were both staring at each other as if surprised at their own voices. 'Don't you worry about me.'

She swallowed hard. 'Well, that's settled then. But I won't blame you if you change your mind. I've got a damned cheek really!'

Jermain stood up and paid the watching proprietor. 'What time shall I come?'

'I'll make some excuse and leave the party about ten. You can wait in the old car if you like.' She touched his arm impulsively. 'It's crazy, isn't it?'

'Not to me.' He guided her to the car. 'You go and get to your party, Jill. I'll take a taxi back to the boat. I'll pass the time with a bit of work!'

She studied him seriously. 'It must be the heat, but I wish I was coming with you!'

Jermain watched her drive back into the traffic, her hair rippling against her face, then after a moment he walked in the opposite direction.

*   *   *

The taxi sped along the tree-lined road, its headlights reflecting on the overhanging branches and the tangle of thick brush which seemed to be only temporarily held at bay by the strip of tarmac. The turbaned Sikh behind the wheel drove extremely fast, his massive head bowed slightly towards a small radio which swung from the driving mirror, his shoulders twitching in time to the discordant music.

In the back seat Jermain clung to a side strap and tried to think clearly about the immediate future. When he had returned to the *Temeraire* he had found the new orders waiting for him as if to curb his small moment of freedom and pleasure.

The *Temeraire* was to proceed to sea the following day. The destination was Taiwan, where she would join up with units of the American Seventh Fleet.

He had called his senior officers together and told them the news. Wolfe had accepted it with something like relief, Jermain thought. No questions or regrets. Just a few bald comments of duty and nothing more.

Ross, the engineer officer, on the other hand, had been openly pessimistic. 'It's not that I wish to criticise the motives behind these orders, sir.' He had stared woodenly at Jermain. 'It's just that I'm not happy about the condition of the hull. We've had no real check-up since that leak. On real sea duty anything might come to light!'

Jermain had known it was an unspoken criticism of himself. Only he as captain could have stood out for the submarine's immediate return home for docking and inspection. But on the face of it there was neither opportunity nor real evidence. It might well be as the admiral had said. Just a fluke. A settling down of a new boat. Either way, there was no time left for manoeuvre. The Americans expected British co-operation. Any sign of prevarication would certainly be taken as unwillingness to help in the delicate situation which threatened the peace and security of the Far East.

Bleakly Jermain had stated what he expected of each and every man aboard. He had made each point clearly so that there should be no argument later as to where the blame would lie. He knew that he had driven a wedge between himself and the others, but there was no other way. Weakness led to slackness, which in turn could destroy all of them.

It seemed a far cry from the excitement and adulation of the early days in *Temeraire*, he thought grimly. Then just to be aboard the new boat had been enough. The actual purpose of her role had seemed too remote to contemplate.

The taxi squealed up a steep drive towards a brightly lit house. There appeared to be a light in every window and the wide forecourt was crammed with cars. Jermain paid off the driver and walked slowly towards the familiar silhouette of the old sports car. Already he was feeling foolish and began to wish he had not let the taxi leave without him.

He ran his hand over the car seat. Tomorrow it would belong to someone else. And, like himself, would be forgotten. He eased himself behind the wheel and stared towards the stars.

It had been easy to forget his real responsibilities. But there was no escape from any one of them.

He tried to think about Taiwan and the voyage which lay ahead. It would be strange to work with the Americans again. To be committed to a course of action instead of merely contemplating a vague possibility.

He heard the muffled beat of dance music and imagined Jill Conway in someone's arms. It would be better to leave now, he decided. There was no point in hoping for the impossible. Just his being here could only cause her embarrassment and humiliation.

'So you came, David!' Her voice came out of the darkness and jolted him from his brooding thoughts.

She was wearing a long dress of some dark colour so that her face and arms seemed to shine in the dim light. Jermain could smell her perfume, the same that she had worn that afternoon.

He started to climb from the car but she said quickly, 'You drive. For some unaccountable reason I think I may have had a bit too much to drink!'

Jermain started the engine and drove carefully through the gates. Beside him the girl lay back in her seat, her face upturned towards the night sky. He said, 'You should wear a coat. It's cool now.'

She laughed. 'I don't care about anything. You came. You said you would come and you did!' She swayed against him as the car took the first curve, and Jermain felt her head rest momentarily on his shoulder. She added, 'I thought that party would never end!'

When they reached the outskirts of the town she sat upright and peered through the screen. 'Take the next road on the right.' She sounded tense. 'Just along here.'

Jermain followed the line of buildings and said, 'This isn't the way to your house.'

'I know. Before my father came out here I shared a flat with two other girls. I told you.'

Jermain felt her staring at him. 'Yes, you did.'

'Well, that's where we're going.' She lapsed into silence.

They passed a parked police Land Rover with its occupants smoking quietly beside the road and then swung into a small

143

cluster of low buildings. It was very quiet. As if there was nobody else alive.

Without speaking Jermain followed the girl up some stone steps and then waited as she switched on a light and flooded the small apartment with personality.

She waved vaguely 'They're away. Now we can find a bit of peace.'

Jermain stood uncertainly in the centre of the room and watched her as she moved round him. He saw that the dress was deep blue and that she looked both beautiful and unreachable.

She stopped in front of him and then gave him a push. 'For God's sake sit down!'

Jermain fell on to a sofa and felt his jacket give in to the unexpected treatment. He peeled it off and held it up. 'I had a feeling it was a bad bargain!'

She did not reply. She was still standing in the middle of the room, her arms hanging quite limp at her sides.

Jermain stood up and walked towards her. Her eyes were fixed on his face, her expression a mixture of concern and excitement. She did not move or resist as he cupped his hands around her bare shoulders and pulled her to him.

Then, suddenly, she pressed her face against his chest, her voice muffled and unsteady. 'It has to be now, David. There might never be another time!'

He could feel her shaking, just as he could sense his own longing. It was like pain. Like finality.

'Are you sure?' He no longer recognised his voice and the words seemed drowned by his heart-beats.

She pushed herself away but would not look at him. She nodded violently. 'Now. It must be!'

Then she walked quickly from the room, so that for a brief instant Jermain thought he had imagined it all. The seconds dragged into minutes, then something made him follow her, as if at some kind of signal.

The blue dress lay discarded on the floor, her shoes where she had kicked them in one corner of the room.

Her eyes were wide and unblinking as she studied his face. She said, 'Don't say anything, David. Just come to me!'

He crossed to the bed and ran his hand gently across her

144

throat and breasts. He felt her shudder, felt his own longing roaring in his brain like unquenchable fire. Then his ready-made suit lay beside her dress and his body against hers.

As if from a long way off he heard her say, 'Hold me!' Her arms were about his neck, pulling him down, and she quivered as if from pain as he found her mouth and felt her tongue against his own.

Long after the first desperate passion had passed they lay quite still, their bodies together, their limbs entwined like part of the whole.

Jermain touched her spine and she moved her face against his shoulder. He knew that she was asleep but for a long time he held her against him, watching her, feeling the warmth and perfection of her body.

He knew that this could never be the end of it. Not now. Not ever.

9

'If You Can't Take a Joke . . .'

The tannoy speaker on the control-room bulkhead hummed into life. 'During the dog watches there will be a talk on astronomy given by Lieutenant Mayo. The film show tonight will be a Western, called *Waggons West*.'

The men on watch glanced at each other and grinned. It was back to normal. The private, regulated life of a small town.

Max Colquhoun shifted his weight to the other foot and peered at the clock. Another hour of the watch still to run. Through the open hatch at the end of the control room came the heady aroma of rum as Sub-Lieutenant Luard supervised the forenoon issue, and above the faint hum of machinery Colquhoun could hear the distant clatter of dishes from the galley. He looked down at the chart. Two days out from Singapore, with the submarine's silent power pushing them swiftly north-eastwards across the vast open waters of the South China Sea. Some two hundred miles away on the port beam was Hainan Island, which before had been just a name on a map. Now Colquhoun could never think of it without remembering Victor's sudden death and the nightmare struggle with the wire on the rudder. Yet he was able to think of it more objectively, even calmly. He felt stronger within himself, and perhaps for the first time sensed a feeling of belonging to the *Temeraire* as a vital member of her community.

Right now he was in sole command of the control room. The boat was running smoothly at a depth of one hundred and fifty feet, and the men at the controls were relaxed and easy with the now familiar instruments around them.

Colquhoun still shared his watch with the first lieutenant,

but Wolfe had made a curt excuse and had gone to the sick bay to see Griffin.

That was another strange thing, Colquhoun thought. He had expected the captain to keep them apart, to avoid another clash like the night Wolfe had come aboard in such a dangerous mood. But it seemed that Jermain intended to ignore the affair. To kill it and keep it in its right perspective. The more Colquhoun thought about it, the more he felt doubts about his own behaviour. He had heard that Wolfe was going through some personal misery which had been at the root of his sudden rage. Colquhoun still did not know how else he could have coped with the situation, but he knew deep down that it was not yet over completely.

He had tried to make contact with Wolfe. To clear the air once and for all. The day the submarine had sailed from Singapore he had found the first lieutenant alone in the chart-room. He had said quickly, 'I'm sorry about the row, sir. I expect you think I acted stupidly. Looking back, I guess we both got a bit worked up!'

Wolfe had glanced from the chart, his brows wrinkled slightly as if to grasp what he was talking about. Then he had given a mere shrug. 'Oh that. Well, we live and learn, I suppose.' He had tapped the chart. 'It'll be strange to work with the Americans again.' His face had hardened. 'Like old times for me.'

And that was all. No recriminations. No further comment. But on the other hand he had stayed aloof and detached during all watches, and in the wardroom. Colquhoun had observed that he rarely seemed to speak to anyone, but went about his work with the quiet concentration of a man completely absorbed in his own personal sphere.

Then there was Lightfoot. It was odd the way he kept crowding into Colquhoun's thoughts. On the last day in Singapore Colquhoun had kept his word and taken the boy sailing in a borrowed dinghy. The latter had said nothing at all about Wolfe's insinuations, but if anything it seemed to have drawn them closer together. In his cabin later Luard had said awkwardly, 'I saw you out with that chap Lightfoot, Max. Taking a bit of a chance, aren't you?'

Colquhoun had stared at him with surprise. It was rarely

147

that Luard ever spoke of anything in such a serious tone. 'What of it?'

Luard had tried to pass it off. 'You know how it is. People talk. You should know. It *happens*!'

Colquhoun walked thoughtfully across the deck and peered over the helmsman's shoulder. It happens. What did it mean?

He tried to analyse his own feelings and motives towards Lightfoot. It seemed ridiculous that he should feel so close to him, to someone so removed from his own way of life. Yet it was true. In the dinghy Lightfoot had patiently followed his instructions, yet once he had grasped the problems of sailing the boat he acted more as an equal than a subordinate being offered a favour. He had a quick, alien wit and a surprising interest in all that went on around him, and was quite unlike any other rating Colquhoun had met.

They had grounded the boat on a sandbar and lounged in their swimming trunks, basking in the hot sun. Often Colquhoun found himself wondering about the clumsy attempt to sabotage the submarine's steering and tried to imagine Lightfoot as the culprit. It surprised him to find that it no longer seemed to matter. The boy had had some desperate reason, probably connected with his family. Right or wrong in his line of reasoning, Colquhoun knew that he would keep it to himself. Lightfoot had saved his life. And in some inexplicable way he seemed to need Colquhoun's friendship, just as he knew his own feelings were reaching out in the same direction. It made him feel guilty and yet elated. It was like some inner challenge which set him apart from the others.

The planesman whispered between his teeth, 'Captain's comin' up, sir!'

Colquhoun pulled himself from his rambling thoughts and glanced quickly towards the watertight door.

Jermain ducked his head down as he stepped through the oval frame and seemed quietly surprised as Colquhoun reported, 'Course zero four zero, sir. One hundred and fifty feet at twenty-five knots.'

'Where's Number One?'

Colquhoun said, 'Sick bay, sir. Just slipped away for a minute or two.'

Jermain smiled. 'Can you manage her on your own, Sub?'

'Just about.' Colquhoun relaxed slightly. There was something very reassuring about Jermain. He was never sarcastic or overbearing. In fact, he did not seem to fit any mould at all. Even his interview after the clash with Wolfe had been patient and devoid of threats. Rather like a schoolmaster with a promising but tactless pupil, Colquhoun decided.

Jermain walked through to the chart-room and checked the log. 'We'll go to periscope depth in half an hour, Sub. We'll raise the radio mast and get ready to receive our first American signals.' He seemed more preoccupied than usual, as if his mind was only half on his duties.

Colquhoun watched his face with close interest. It was like being allowed to share something private. Jermain rarely showed anything but complete dedication to his daily routine, and this trace of uncertainty seemed to add to rather than detract from his stature.

Jermain ran his finger down the neat line of pencilled figures and calculations left by the navigating officer and tried to relate them to what might lie ahead. In a day and a half they should reach the American operational base at Taiwan, and from there almost anything might come their way. He made an effort to build some enthusiasm out of the new destination as he had always been able to do in the past. It ought to be a great experience to use his new submarine alongside a fully trained and operational force. It should be a challenge, a rightful culmination to the months of training. Even Taiwan itself would be entirely new for all of them. The island which guarded the Formosa Strait and the main approaches to Communist China. Its ancient and feared General Chiang Kai-shek, whose gaunt shadow seemed to hang over the scene like some grotesque cardboard cut-out, supported by American money and materials of war, was a predominant factor in the undeclared battle between East and West. Yet as Jermain stared at the chart and the calculations. he could feel neither excitement nor pride.

He had slept badly, tossing and turning in his bunk, and jerking awake at the most normal shipboard sounds. Time and time again he had pictured the girl in his mind, had almost sensed her touch and the warm softness of her body.

An hour before the *Temeraire* had sailed Jermain had gone

aboard the depot ship for his final briefing, but after leaving the operations-room he had come face to face with Conway. The meeting had been so unexpected that Jermain had been conscious of a sudden feeling of guilt. It was entirely new to him, and for a few moments he had been almost unnerved.

Conway had been carrying his briefcase and was dressed for his flight to the north. He had said, 'I had to come and see you before I pushed off, Commander. There was a lot I wanted to say to you, but it seems we're bound for separate points of the compass.' He had given his lopsided grin. 'Very nautical, eh?'

Together they had leaned on the rail and stared down at the black submarine. A blue haze had hung around the diesel generator outlet, and men had been moving purposefully about the upper deck loosening the mooring wires and stowing away the final stores for the journey.

Conway had said suddenly, 'I hear you had a good time with Jill. She hasn't said much, but I think she was sorry she couldn't spend more time with you.'

Jermain had tensed at the mention of her name. It was obvious that Conway knew nothing of his daughter's later meeting with him. Of the fact that they had slept together.

Conway had hurried on, 'Yes, I wish you could have seen a bit more of her. She needs someone a bit mature. Someone who's just not another young hanger-on.' He had glanced sideways at Jermain. 'I'm not suggesting that you're an old man, it's just that she's had a bad time in the past. Her mother and I have had a few worried moments, I can tell you.'

'In what way?' Jermain could not meet the other man's gaze. He had wanted to change the subject or to end the conversation altogether.

'When she was at university she met this man. He was much older than she was, and, worse still, he was married. He was a tutor of some sort, but I didn't hear about it until the whole thing blew up. Well, of course it had to end, but I don't think she ever really got over it. She went completely off the rails for months. Drank too much, mixed with all the wrong people, you know the sort of thing.' He had seemed unable to stop talking, and Jermain had guessed Conway had bottled it all up within himself for a long time.

'Somehow I managed to get her fixed up with my department. It's got a pretty wide range of work, and above all it keeps her busy and occupied most of the time. But every so often I see the signs, and I get worried as hell all over again She's all I've got. I just want her settled.'

At that moment Oxley had called up from the casing, 'Fifteen minutes to go, sir!'

Conway had added, 'I hope I've not embarrassed you, Commander? I thought you might understand.'

'I think I do.' Jermain had tried not to think of the girl's body naked on the bed like a pale crucifix. He had known he was doing wrong, and Conway's confidence had added to his sense of guilt.

Perhaps she had been using him as another 'experience', and he had remembered with sudden clarity that once during the night she had clung to his shoulder and called 'John'. At the time he had put it down to the excitement, the all-devouring elation which had left them weak and at peace together. But Conway's words had changed all that. She must have been thinking back to that other man, to those precious days which Jermain could never share. A passing substitute, the momentary recapture of a dream. He had felt sick.

Conway had held out his hand. 'Good luck, Commander. I hope we meet again with more time to spare.' By the time Jermain had climbed down to the submarine's casing Conway had vanished.

Jermain had tried more than ever to push himself harder into his work, but even that evaded him. The boat was running like silk, there seemed little to do but think and brood over what had happened.

If only he could have seen her just once more. In the dawn light he had dressed quickly beside the bed while the girl watched him through half-closed eyes. They hardly spoke, but once when he stooped over her she gripped his hand so fiercely that her nails broke the skin.

She had shown no regrets. Neither did she seem to care what he might have thought of her willingness to sleep with him.

Each was wrapped in his and her private thoughts, and when the actual moment of departure came there was no longer any time for words.

She had held his hand under her breast and watched the emotions crossing his face. 'I won't get up till you've gone.' Her voice had been low and husky. 'There's no point in adding to the pain.'

'I have to see you again.' His voice had sounded as hopeless as he had felt. The waiting submarine, the remorseless passing of time, added to his feeling of inevitability and loss. 'I have to!'

She had kissed him quickly and hard, and then pulled the sheet up to her chin so that in the half-light she looked defence-less, like a child. 'You might forget me by tomorrow.' She had shivered beneath the sheet. 'It might all be different then.'

'What about you, Jill? How will you feel?'

Her words still stayed with him, awake or in his restless sleep. 'At this very moment I cannot bear the thought of your leaving this room. I cannot pretend to know how I will feel tomorrow.' She had turned her face on to the pillow so that her hair had hidden her eyes. 'Now go quickly, David. I'm not strong enough for farewells!'

Jermain realised that Colquhoun was speaking again.

'I saw the two security men go ashore, sir. Does that mean they're satisfied with everything?' Colquhoun was watching him closely.

Jermain shrugged. 'Maybe. Anyway, I'm glad to be shot of them. To get the boat welded into some sort of order again.'

Colquhoun gave a quick grin. 'No admiral either, sir!'

Some of the tension drained out of Jermain's face and he smiled. 'Did you see your father before we sailed?'

'I saw the *admiral*, sir.' Colquhoun looked away. 'I took a present up to the house to be posted back to my mother. My father was having a conference but condescended to come out for a few minutes.' His voice became bitter. 'He said I was wasting my time in submarines and that I should go back to general service.'

Jermain said gently, 'He means well, I expect. He probably expects big things from you.'

Colquhoun sighed. 'I find his reasoning beyond me.'

Jermain turned away. Don't look to me for guidance, he thought. I imagined that I knew myself. Now I am not sure of anything!

*   *   *

Wolfe returned to the control room and glanced quickly at the clock. A few minutes to go and then the boat would be gliding upwards to listen to the far-off world of command and naval strategy. He felt depressed and uneasy, and his conversation with Griffin, the doctor, had gone entirely the wrong way.

He had found Griffin seated at a table in the sick bay, apparently absorbed in studying a small carved figurine. He had said cheerfully, 'Picked it up in the market in Singapore, Number One. Only cost a few bob. Marvellous piece of work.'

Wolfe had said, 'Probably made in Birmingham! They're all bloody sham!'

Griffin had sighed and placed the figurine carefully in a drawer. 'It's like that, is it?' He had studied Wolfe carefully. 'What can I do for you?'

'I have a headache. I want a few tablets for it.' Wolfe had felt angry beneath Griffin's cool scrutiny. 'For God's sake, it's only a headache!'

'Did I suggest otherwise?' Griffin had pulled out his keys. 'I'll fix you up certainly. But have you had any sort of treatment recently? Are you sure it's nothing worse?'

'Look, if you don't want to give me a simple remedy then say so! I can manage without a lecture!'

Griffin did not seem to hear him. 'Serving in submarines affects different people different ways. It can produce the same effect as, say, alcohol. A man can show his real character, just as he will do under the influence of drink or drugs. What he can cover up under normal conditions can overpower his usual control and become all-important and outsize, so that he can think of little else.'

Wolfe remembered his angry sarcasm. 'And how long have *you* been in submarines, Doctor?'

'Two years, on and off.' Griffin had eyed him calmly. 'But you don't have to be able to dig holes in the ground to learn about architecture!' He had given him the tablets. 'These should do the trick, but if they don't I'll give you a going over.'

Wolfe had snapped, 'Should I rely on your judgement?'

'It seems that I must rely on *you*, Number One, so why not?'

The petty officer of the watch said, 'Time, sir!'

Wolfe started. 'Very well. Take her up to periscope depth.' He felt easier in his mind when something was happening. He watched the gauges and listened to the gentle hiss of pressurised air.

'Sixty feet, sir.'

Wolfe grunted. 'Up periscope!' For several seconds he swung the big periscope in a slow circle, his eyes squinting against the glare. The sea was flat and glittering with a million bright mirrors. Like the pale sky it was empty. Not a gull or even a piece of flotsam marred the probing lenses.

He said, 'Raise the radio mast and inform the W/T room.'

He heard Jermain's voice at his side. 'All quiet, Number One?'

'Yes, sir. It's a pity we can't raise the radar mast, too. It would save all this scratching around for information.'

'I agree.' Jermain seemed distant. 'But our orders do not change on that point. Any radar transmissions could easily be detected.' He added suddenly, 'I hear you were in the sick bay?'

Wolfe caught sight of Colquhoun across the captain's shoulder. 'Just for a moment. Did he say I have been adrift for the whole watch?' Even as he said it, Wolfe cursed himself. There I go again. What the hell is the matter with me? A matter-of-fact question becomes a major issue. Perhaps Griffin is right after all.

Jermain replied calmly, 'He made his report, nothing more.'

Wolfe said, 'Just a headache. What with one thing and another ...'

The radio supervisor interrupted by poking his head through the radio-room hatch. 'Signal coming in now, Captain! From American Group Ten.'

Jermain pursed his lips. 'It feels strange.'

'I'll bet the Yanks have been waiting for this.' Wolfe scowled as he listened to the muted stammer of Morse. 'They'll just love to throw *us* around!'

Jermain said, 'I'd have thought they'd be more occupied in other directions.' He broke off as the radio supervisor called, 'We'll have it all in another minute, sir.'

Jermain said, 'Right. Let's have the code book and all the combat material in the chart-room. I have a feeling this is more than a social call!'

*   *   *

Able Seaman Bruce spooned down the last of his tinned pineapple and wiped his thick fingers on the front of his shirt. He looked around the mess table and continued with the story. 'Yeh, as I was sayin'. I gets this tart back to her place and we starts bargainin' for a fair price. Now, I bin out East afore, an' I know the form . . .'

Haley, the leading hand of the mess, reached for his pipe and said dryly, 'I can imagine!'

Bruce scowled. 'These Chinese toms who hang about the dockyard don't bargain unless it's for a purpose.' He winked across at Lightfoot. 'When they've got a fair idea of the wad you're carryin' they gives a signal, an' out comes a hairy great wog from behind the bleedin' bed! Afore you can say "kiss my arse" he's clobbered you, an' when you awakes in the arms of a shore patrol you got no money, and no enjoyment!'

Dale, another seaman, asked wearily, 'So what happened *this* time?'

Bruce smiled knowingly. 'I dived for the back of the bed, and sure enough there's this tart's bloke hidin' behind the screen. I kicks him once, and hard, then jumps on top of this bird.' He threw back his head and roared. 'I guess if I'd been a bleedin' marine I'd 'ave done the bloke as well!'

Lightfoot eyed him distantly. He had heard much the same story before. The place varied, but the situation was always the same. He stiffened as he heard Archer's familiar voice behind him.

'Anyone got a fag to keep me goin' till the canteen opens?'

Someone threw a tin across the table but Archer seemed reluctant to return to his own mess. He said, 'I heard a buzz that we're staying with the Yanks for six months.'

Dale choked on his cigarette. 'Jesus! I was due for leave. It's not damn well fair!'

Bruce eyed him scornfully. 'Pipe down, *Mrs*. Dale! You shouldn't have joined if you can't take a joke!' He turned his gaze back to Archer, who was now standing directly behind Lightfoot. 'So what else did you hear?'

'That Jimmy the One caught some officer in his bunk with one of the lads.' He laughed harshly. 'I'll bet it's true an' all.'

Lightfoot tensed. He could almost feel the man's breath across his neck. He kept his eyes fixed on Bruce's face and wondered how he could appear so casual. There was absolutely no sign of tension or caution. No sign that he was chatting with a man he had tried to kill.

Bruce continued, 'That's a load of squit! Do you think they could keep it quiet?'

Archer sounded angry. ' 'Course they could! Bloody officers stick together like dung on a blanket! I'll find out who it was before long, you see!'

Lightfoot stared down at his plate. Once again things seemed to be moving too fast for him to regain control. After the incident in Colquhoun's cabin his inner sense had told him to stay away from the officer, to withdraw completely into himself. It had always been his method of keeping straight in the past. But Colquhoun's kindness over his mother's death, his genuine willingness to help, had been difficult obstacles to overcome. Furthermore, he had wanted to accept Colquhoun's invitation to go sailing. He had really wanted to go. It had been a kind of challenge, like when he was a kid, answering a dare to run across the railway track only seconds before a passing train.

At first he had imagined that he was using this unexpected relationship with the young officer as a possible shield against Archer, but deep down he knew it was not so. After all, if anything else went wrong it was obvious that Colquhoun had much more to lose.

The realisation made him feel uneasy and sick. It was as if Archer's crude rumour had been a picture of truth. Suppose

Colquhoun felt that way about him? He screwed up his mind with unusual concentration. It was unnerving even to think of it. And he knew that it was not because Colquhoun would appear like the groping man in the car. He realised, even before he had time to think further about it, that he would have made no protest.

Vaguely he heard Archer say, 'The security blokes 'ave gone. That's somethin'!'

Leading Seaman Haley looked up and smiled. 'I suppose they were on the game, too, eh?'

Archer slammed back, 'You mark my words, this is going to be a rough commission. What with the old man bustin' a gut to show how marvellous the Black Pig is, an' half the crew goin' round the bend, I'm glad I'm a bloody A.B.'

Haley said coldly, 'Bloody marvellous. Like the time you fell off the rudder! A real nice piece of seamanship that was!'

Archer was about to make a retort when the tannoy speaker came alive overhead.

'Stand by for an announcement.'

Archer said excitedly, 'See? What did I tell you?'

Haley growled, 'Stow it!'

Jermain's voice came over the speaker, bringing silence to the crowded mess tables. 'This is the Captain speaking. I have to tell you that I have just received a signal from the American Task Force to which we are now attached.' He paused, and those nearest the speaker could hear the faint rustle of paper. 'We are to proceed at maximum speed to a rendezvous point one hundred miles off the west coast of Korea in the Yellow Sea.' His voice became less formal. 'For the benefit of those who have not been reading the daily reports on the notice boards, it means we have to steam another two thousand miles to the north, without breaking the journey at Taiwan as expected.'

A chorus of groans came from the listening seamen. Bruce muttered, 'Strike me blind! It's gettin' like a flamin' round-the-world cruise!'

Jermain continued, 'The object of this assignment is to patrol and, if necessary, intercept shipping which is reported as being used to ferry guerrillas and political agitators from the Chinese mainland to South Korea.' He cleared his throat. 'It

157

means, of course, that the *Temeraire* will be on a full and active duty, with a possibility of action. This is a picked crew, and I expect nothing but the best from all of you. This is not the sort of work we had been expecting, but as you saw very clearly on our last patrol, when Lieutenant Victor lost his life, it is as real and deadly as any publicised emergency.'

Another voice came on the speaker, and Lightfoot was again reminded of that night in Colquhoun's cabin.

Wolfe sounded unruffled and confident. 'With regard to the captain's announcement. General drill will commence at 1400, and all sections will test and exercise equipment. Damage control and fire-fighting parties will muster in the main crewspace at 1415.' Some of the old sharpness returned to his tone. 'Any defects in either equipment *or* personnel will be promptly dealt with. That is all!'

Bruce said, 'I should think it's a bleedin-nough! Roll on my bloody twelve!'

Lightfoot stayed silent. It was going on and on, with one crisis blending into another. It was like the 'Flying Dutchman' he had been forced to read at school. Only worse.

Archer turned to go but added casually, 'Well, mates, this will give us all a real good chance to get to know each other!' As he passed he brushed against Lightfoot's arm. The latter knew it was no accident, just as he knew that his own danger was still with him.

*   *   *

Jermain rolled up his chart and looked around the wardroom table at his silent officers. 'Well, I think we've gone over all the known possibilities, gentlemen. Any questions?'

Ross shook his head. 'I still think this is more than ridiculous!' He was speaking directly to Jermain, excluding the others. 'If we had gone to Taiwan direct as originally planned we could maybe have used some of the American infra-red gear to check over the hull. I would have felt much happier.'

Jermain nodded. 'Our last patrol seemed to rule out any real danger of hull flaws, Chief. We threw the boat around a good deal. If anything was about to come adrift it would surely have happened then?' He saw his words were having no effect. And why should they? He alone was taking the full weight of responsibility. Was it pride in the boat or personal conceit? He dragged his mind back to the lengthy coded signal. One part of it seemed to overshadow all the rest. But again, was it his own strain, his imagination which was giving it too much emphasis?

Inserted in the patrol orders had been the phrase, 'In response to the request of your Flag Officer Inshore Squadron you will proceed, etc., etc.' It might merely have been a typical piece of American courtesy to a lonely unit of another navy. Or it might have been their way of pointing out that Sir John Colquhoun had insisted on this early venture into well-tried and dangerous territory.

He tried to put himself in Sir John's state of mind. The admiral knew of Conway's secret mission to meet envoys from North Korea at a time when East/West relations were strained to breaking point. He knew too that any success on Conway's part would be a sign for further cuts in the Royal Navy's strength and importance in this and adjacent areas. His own command would be reduced to almost nothing. Yet it seemed impossible that the admiral could use his authority to put the *Temeraire* in a position where she would be implicated in any sort of open clash. A man of his experience and undoubted skill must surely take the long view, with the country's security as his first concern.

He said slowly, 'We will go to patrol routine and bring the men up to a first degree of readiness. I don't imagine the Americans will give us much to do at first, but out here we must be prepared for anything.'

Oxley drawled, 'It seems that their main reason for wanting us is to use a protective screen of long-range sonar. We pick up the ships, and they move in surface craft to investigate and board if necessary, right?'

Jermain smiled. 'That just about sums it up.' It was easy to picture Oxley in later life as an admiral. In spite of his apparent casual attitude to Service life he had a mind which he used to grasp at and use the bare essentials. The rest he discarded as no part of an officer's requirements.

That is how *I* should act and think, Jermain decided. I above all, with this valuable ship and trained complement should be

159

able to ignore vague possibilities and personal standards. It is no part of my work. I am merely a part of a whole. A section of an over-all plan.

Wolfe said suddenly, 'Do you really believe the American Intelligence reports, sir? They see a Communist plot in everything!'

'They've had a lot to put up with, Number One.' Jermain found time to marvel at the way Wolfe appeared to have dismissed completely the near disaster over Colquhoun. He seemed almost at ease, and while Jermain had been running through the orders he had been writing busily in his notebook. There was no sign of uncertainty or of his earlier strain. That at least was a good omen, he thought.

Wolfe said flatly, 'I'll bet the top brass back in Whitehall are congratulating themselves over us. I can just see all the little flags being stuck in maps and memos being passed from desk to desk!' He gave a tight smile. 'When the Navy has been cut down to the *Victory* in Portsmouth Dockyard, Whitehall will still have its full quota of admirals and civil servants!'

Lieutenant Kitson glanced uncomfortably at Ross and then blurted out, 'Of course, if there is some sort of flaw in the hull it would be serious for the electrical department, sir.'

Jermain guessed that Kitson and Ross had been having a private conference of their own. 'I am aware of that. We'll cross our bridges when we come to them.' His tone was final. 'Now, I shall lay off the new course and then inform the engine room of the calculated speed. My immediate guess is around thirty knots.'

Jermain sighed. They were all writing in their notebooks again, the grim possibilities and doubts momentarily held at bay.

Sub-Lieutenant Luard remarked vaguely, 'I suppose I'll have to check through all the menus again. If it's not one thing it's another.'

The others stared at him, and then Lieutenant Drew said dryly, 'Fair makes you sweat, doesn't it? Here we are about to embark on a great campaign, and all you can think about is how many tinned sausages you've got to last the voyage!'

They laughed, and Jermain decided it was time to end the

conference If Drew, whose assistant had been killed, could still make jokes, things could not be too bleak.

*   *   *

For another two days the *Temeraire* thrust further northwards. Like a black shadow, her smooth whaleshape hastening through the depths at a speed which would leave most of her surface contemporaries astern, she moved through the Formosa Strait and up into the East China Sea. Only once a day did she swim upwards to periscope depth, when after a quick look round through her powerful eye the radio mast was raised and for brief moments she was once more in contact with the outside world. But again she was only listening. Like her nuclear power, her voice was silent.

The privileged few who saw the periscope's view of the outer world looked around with mixed feelings. Envy and suspicion, fear and excitement. As the submarine moved further north and away from the remaining shipping lanes each sighting report became a small event. The occasional patrolling frigate or destroyer, the dilapidated freighter and the ghostly silhouettes of junks, each became a need, a certain reminder that there was another life beyond the confines of the *Temeraire*'s hull.

The submarine seemed to have become smaller, and the past air of casual acceptance had given way to a watchful tension. Men rarely bothered to discuss the possibility of returning home in some near future, and the general atmosphere had become brittle, even apprehensive.

Jermain watched the change moving through his command and tried to block each problem before it got out of hand. Arguments flared over small things, and discipline tightened accordingly.

Above all, waiting was the worst part. It gave men too long to wonder and distrust, it helped to break down the established pattern of routine.

It was with something like relief that Jermain received the awaited signal even as he took one of his rare looks through the raised periscope. It was brief. The clipped brevity from that unseen chain of command seemed to add to the impression of tension and urgency.

161

Temeraire would take up a patrol area between the jutting peninsula of Shantung Province in Red China and the twisting coastline of Korea. Less than two hundred miles separated the two countries at this point, so that the *Temeraire*'s patrol line would correspond almost exactly with the thirty-eighth parallel which cut Korea in half, and which had decided that men on one side of it would fear and hate their countrymen on the other.

Eight hours after receiving the signal Jermain conned the submarine on to the first leg of the patrol, and like the remainder of his men, settled down to wait.

10

Decision

Jermain leaned against the chart table and stared through the open door into the control room. From the back of his neck to the soles of his feet he felt as if every muscle was aching in unison, yet he knew that if he returned to his cabin sleep would still elude him.

For five endless days the *Temeraire* had carried out her slow search of the patrol area. Back and forth. Up and down. If the sea remained empty, the radio frequency did not. Each time the submarine raised her radio mast the signals came thick and fast. It was as if the whole Yellow Sea was packed with invisible ships and impatient commanders. Unfamiliar routines and complicated code names became almost commonplace, and even the American voices on the acoustic radio had welded themselves into the daily pattern.

As the coded signals poured in Jermain and his officers plodded through the intelligence reports and conflicting information without rest. Only the submarine herself stayed immune, and her smooth-running complacency helped to add to the frustration and strain of her crew.

The *Temeraire* remained at periscope depth for most of the time now. There was not much point in exercising diving anyway. The Yellow Sea was mostly shallow, and even now there were less than twenty fathoms beneath the ballast keel.

The narrowest point between the Korean coast and the Chinese mainland had been selected as the most likely area for infiltration. It would be quick and hard to detect. Along the Korean shoreline Jermain knew there was a waiting company of American warships, added to which there was a sprinkling of South Korean vessels. Then southwards there was a well-stretched chain of patrol ships, including several American submarines. But the plum piece of the line was the *Temeraire*'s. Alone at the northern end, she swept back and forth in complete silence, her long-range sonar probing and listening, while her periscope kept a regular watch for less formidable vessels.

The next immediate link with the rest of the task force was a South Korean frigate. They had seen her only twice since the beginning of the patrol, and then only as a shadow or a smudge of smoke. She carried an American naval officer for liaison duties, and when the two craft were within range of the acoustic radio it was his voice which entered the submarine's hull, like that of an old friend.

As soon as Jermain contacted any suspicious vessel, all he had to do was whistle up the frigate and allow her to board and search it. It sounded simple.

Only the previous day when they made a brief contact the American officer had said, 'For God's sake sight something soon, so that we can get the hell out of here! If I eat much more rice aboard this bucket I'll be getting slant eyes!' It was not exactly a correct form of signalling, but it showed the listening submariners that they were not the only ones dying of boredom.

Oxley was the officer-of-the-watch and stood in the centre of the control room, his hands deep in his pockets. His eyes looked dark with strain, and Jermain wondered if he was beginning to doubt the efficiency of his sonar devices.

Jermain heard a petty officer report, 'Coming up to twenty-one thirty, sir.' The end of another sweep. Time to make a turn on to a new course. The submarine was now at her nearest point to the Chinese mainland. The first time it had happened there had been an edge of excitement in the boat. Now there was nothing. It was just a fact and little more.

Oxley grunted, 'Very well.' He glanced at the captain.

Jermain walked stiffly into the control room, the sudden movement making his legs throb with pain. 'Up periscope.' He waited as the greased tube slid from its well and then pressed his forehead against the pad. The sea looked like deep purple satin, above which the sky seemed pale by comparison. He switched the periscope to full power and swung it gently in a slow arc. The darker line below the sky was not the horizon. It was the land. Nothing solid or distinct, but just a hint of the vast, endless country beyond. He murmured, 'Carry on.'

Oxley said wearily, 'Starboard fifteen. Steer two two five.'

Jermain moved the periscope in rhythm with the boat's gentle turn and wondered how long this uneasy peace would last. His hand slipped on the handle as the intercom suddenly barked, 'Surface contact, sir! Bearing green one one five! Range twenty thousand yards!'

Jermain swung round and met Oxley's astonished stare. 'Down periscope!' Jermain had to lick his lips to clear their sudden dryness. 'Close up action stations!'

He stood for a few more seconds, his ears deaf to the yammer of alarm bells as he forced his mind to work like a slide-rule. Around and below him doors slammed shut and the narrow passageways were alive with running figures. The telephones and voice pipes crackled to life, and as Oxley vanished towards the sonar compartment Wolfe appeared in the control room, his face crumpled from sleep but his eyes alert and calm.

Jermain said, 'Contact the frigate at once. It may be another scare, Number One. But I have a feeling about this one.'

Oxley's voice came over the intercom. 'Captain, sir. It's a firm contact. Distorted but regular. Maybe three or four small vessels. Moving fast but parallel with us.'

Jermain frowned. Moving fast. That would explain the sudden flurry of echoes hitherto undetected. Probably fast patrol boats. Just the craft for a swift crossing to the other side. And what better time to choose? With darkness closing down and the sea like a millpond.

A messenger opened the radio-room door and scurried away with a signal pad. Before the door closed again Jermain heard the distorted garble from the acoustic radio. The American sounded as if he was speaking through a heavy rainstorm.

'Hello BLUEBOY, this is VIGILANT. Your message received and understood. Suggest you close contact and shadow. Listening out.'

Jermain walked slowly to the chart table. The frigate would be turning away now to contact and alert the rest of the waiting force.

He watched Mayo's hands moving across the chart like busy crabs. 'Alter course, Pilot. We'll move to the west to intercept.'

Mayo did not even look up. After a few more minutes he scribbled on his pad and called, 'Steer two seven zero.'

Jermain found that he could not stay still, and it took real effort to make his movements slow and controlled. 'Increase to twenty-five knots. And tell the chief to be ready for maximum revolutions!' He could imagine Ross sitting in his gleaming domain of steel and brass and wondered if he would appreciate what was happening. At least he would not have to worry about a deep dive. In these waters it was an impossibility.

Oxley again. 'Contact appears to be retaining same course and speed. Bearing now green nine zero.'

Mayo said, 'Contact's moving ahead, sir.'

Jermain nodded. 'Increase to thirty knots.' He felt the smallest tremble run through the deck plates and then nothing. The boat was responding like a thoroughbred.

This brief excitement might make all the difference, he thought. A success, no matter how small, would bind the crew together and make all the other irritations fade away for good.

'Range now fifteen thousand yards.'

Jermain thrust his hands into his pockets and balled his fingers into tight fists. He watched the attack team bending over the plot table as the ranges and bearings poured through the headphones and intercom. The ultimate would be to close and challenge the other ships and, if necessary, to attack. But that was impossible, and the *Temeraire*'s men would have to be content to know that the rest of the plan had worked successfully on their work. Even now the far-off American ships would be wheeling into position to spring their trap. Jermain found himself wondering what Conway would think when he was given definite proof that the Chinese were far from eager to accept a peaceful solution to an undeclared war which they believed they were winning.

He made up his mind. 'Slow ahead. Stand by to raise the search periscope.' He waited as the hull shuddered slightly and the racing screw slowed its pace. He looked at the flickering lights above the plot table and tried to imagine how the other ships would appear in the powerful lenses. Just over seven miles. But with the light fading it might be very difficult.

'Up periscope.' He ducked down and came up with the periscope lenses already to his eyes. He found himself holding his breath, his forehead moist against the pad.

The sea was much darker now. Almost black, its surface heaving like polished ebony. There were a few pale stars in the sky, and around the raised periscope Jermain could see the green glow of dancing phosphorescence. It would have to be a quick look.

He caught his lower lip in his teeth and blinked to clear the film from his eyes. There they were. He counted the bright triangular bow waves which stood out against the darkening sea like tiny breakers. There were eight at least. Very small and extremely fast.

He snapped, 'Down periscope.' Then to Wolfe, 'PT boats, I would guess. An arrowhead formation and well grouped.'

Wolfe shrugged. 'Could be a sort of exercise.' Some of his earlier intolerance crept into his tone. 'The Americans aren't the only navy in these waters!'

Oxley's voice said, 'Contact altering course, sir. Swinging round to the south and still turning!'

Jermain nodded. 'Very well. Increase to twenty-five knots again.' He stared hard at the chart. 'It's my guess the PT boats are going to make a complete turn and head out away from the mainland.' He waited a few more seconds. 'Ask sonar what the hell is going on?'

Oxley sounded unruffled. 'Contact still turning, sir. Present course estimated at one one zero degrees.'

Jermain smiled. 'Reduce speed to fifteen knots. They'll pass clear astern of us now.'

Mayo leaned his elbows on the chart and grimaced. 'And that's all there is to it. The little Chinks will steam happily into an ambush and get a dose of gunfire. Then there'll be a few diplomatic notes exchanged and it'll be all quiet until they think of another way of getting their agents and equipment across!'

Jermain eyed him with amusement. 'You're a cynic, Pilot!'

Wolfe said, 'What now, sir?'

'As Pilot has just remarked, we just applaud from the sidelines. As soon as the PT boats are well away we'll flash a further sighting report and resume patrol. I don't imagine we'll be there much longer.'

The intercom interrupted their speculations. 'Another contact, sir. Faint propeller noises and a good deal of throwback

167

from the shallows, but definite enough.' Oxley sounded entirely absorbed. 'I would think that there is another ship or ships keeping along the coast, close inshore.'

Jermain felt vaguely uneasy as the bearings and tracking information began to form a picture on the plot table. The Chinese coastline at this point was desolate and little used. For five days they had sighted nothing, and the nearest port of any consequence was a hundred and fifty miles to the south west.

He said sharply, 'Take the con, Number One. I'm going forrard to talk with Oxley.' Without waiting for a reply he ducked his head through the door and hurried along the passageway. He caught vague glimpses of his men sitting or standing quietly at their stations, their eyes expectant as he passed. He found Oxley and his operators hunched over their equipment, their faces flickering in the lights thrown back from the dials and gauges.

Even Oxley showed some surprise at Jermain's entrance. He pushed the headset from his ears and said, 'There's no change, sir.'

Jermain glanced round the crowded compartment, the dark figures suddenly taking on personality and meaning. There was Colquhoun, and in front of him, in the operator's seat, young Lightfoot. There was Petty Officer Irons, and another operator, their eyes unblinking as they watched and listened.

Oxley added, 'We'd have to get much closer inshore, sir. The echoes are very distorted at this range. Now, if we were tracking another submarine it'd be different!'

Jermain studied the gauges. The *Temeraire* was cruising in barely ten fathoms of water. And in any case, what explanation could he give for his actions?

He asked, 'Can you make any sort of guess about these ships?'

Oxley shrugged. 'I would say two ships. Both twin screw and doing about fifteen knots. From the rhythm and power I would definitely say that they are warships.' He shook his head. 'No doubt about that, in my view.'

Irons looked over his shoulder and squinted at the captain. 'That's right, sir. Too powerful for coasters or the clapped-out freighters the Chinks use hereabouts!'

Jermain rubbed his chin. It felt rough under his palm but he did not notice it. He said, 'Keep tracking. I'll move in a bit closer, but you'll have to keep contact as best you can.'

Oxley asked, 'What do you have in mind, sir?'

Jermain studied him calmly. 'I wish I knew. But there's far too much activity for mere coincidence. We'll run down the coast, but keep about ten miles offshore. If we stay on roughly a parallel course you should be able to detect any sort of sudden manœuvre on their part.'

He returned to the control room and waited impatiently until Mayo had transformed his ideas into a working plan.

The helmsman listened to the new orders and leaned forward over the wheel. 'Course two four zero, sir.'

Thinking aloud Jermain said, 'We can't raise the fleet without giving our own position away. In this shallow water it's too risky. The Chinese would feel more than justified in lobbing a few depth-charges down on us, on their own back door so to speak!'

Somebody laughed but Wolfe said doggedly, 'Why not let the Yanks handle it from their end?'

'Our last instructions were to track shipping, Number One. So let's do that, shall we?' He smiled at Wolfe's pensive expression. 'It'll do no harm.'

Wolfe said, 'You're really saying that the PT boats were a decoy. That the Yanks will be so busy chasing after them they'll not expect the Reds to try a crossing further south over the wider distance?' He eyed Jermain fixedly. 'Is that it?'

Jermain nodded. 'I could be wrong.'

Surprisingly Wolfe replied, 'I agree with your idea. That's exactly what they would do.' He paused. 'What *I* would do.'

Jermain watched him thoughtfully. Now that he had stopped thinking about himself Wolfe was dropping into his proper role. The realisation made him feel strangely satisfied.

'We'll just have to wait and see,' Jermain replied.

He turned abruptly as the radio supervisor entered the control room. 'What is it, Harris?'

'Just received the fleet broadcast, sir. Usual shipping movements for the most part.'

Jermain looked at the clock. 'God, is it that late already?' It seemed incredible that the normal signals traffic could still be flooding the networks in spite of their own personal tensions.

Harris added doubtfully, 'There's just one thing, sir. The

American Intelligence report that a single ship will be passing through the southern grid between midnight and 0200. The S.S. *Malange*, outward bound from Taiwan to Inch'on in South Korea.'

Wolfe said irritably, 'Well, what of it?'

Harris kept his eyes on the captain. 'There's a Top Secret signal about her, sir. She's carrying a V.I.P., Conway.'

Jermain felt a slight chill in his spine. It would be just like Conway to make his way to South Korea in some unconventional freighter. He had obviously flown north from Singapore and picked up the ship in Taiwan only days ago.

He peered down at the chart and snapped, 'Check these figures, Pilot, and plot the *Malange*'s approximate course, using the American grid reference. You'll have to start with her intended midnight position and work backwards.' To Wolfe he added, 'Finish checking those signals. I want a complete build-up of ship movements in this area.'

Wolfe opened his mouth and then changed his mind and went to the radio room with Harris.

Oxley again. 'Contact still retaining course and speed, sir.'

The petty officer at the plot reported, 'We're getting a good picture, sir.' He peered at his vibrating table. 'The two ships seem to be keeping about three miles offshore. Our range is fourteen thousand yards.'

'Very well.' Jermain watched Mayo's face as he stepped out of the chart-room. 'Well?'

Mayo regarded him calmly. 'The *Malange* will have crossed latitude thirty-five about one hundred and thirty miles west of the Korean coast at midnight, sir. So assuming she's doing between ten and fifteen knots, and not many of her type of scow do much more . . .'

Jermain snapped, 'Cut out the dialogue, Pilot. Just give me the facts!'

Mayo plucked his beard and said coldly, 'So right now she should be about one hundred and seventy miles south east of us.' He coughed noisily and then added, 'Of course, it's all largely guesswork, but give or take twenty miles it's fair enough.'

Jermain brushed past him and walked to the chart table. For a long moment he stood staring down at the pencilled lines, and

170

in his mind's eye he seemed to see the isolated freighter plodding unconcernedly across an empty sea.

But just suppose he had been right about the two mysterious ships which even now were cruising just a few miles abeam? If they turned as suddenly as the others and made a dash into open water they would almost certainly make contact with the *Malange*.

He kept thinking about Conway's quiet optimism, of his hope for some sort of peaceful solution to the East/West conflict. When Jermain had voiced his fears Conway had said, 'I'd not be taking my daughter otherwise. . . .' He had been so sure of his safety and of the value of his mission.

The realisation of his own helplessness made Jermain suddenly angry. If he used his radio he would foul up the whole planned operation, with nothing to offer in return but his own imagination. If he stayed silent and remained on station he would be equally guilty if the Chinese decided to break out from another point.

Mayo had moved to the entrance, his shadow across the chart like a cloud. 'We're in Chinese territorial waters now, sir. In fifteen minutes we shall have to alter course to the seaward.' He studied Jermain's grim features. 'It's already shoaling, and the maximum depth will be less than seven fathoms.'

Jermain was aware of the silence inside the boat. It seemed to be pressing on his eardrums, as if he was submerged in water. It was one problem after another, like a series of maniacal tests.

He replied, 'Very well. But we must try to retain contact with these ships. In open water the detection devices would be doubly effective, but inshore we could be fobbed off by false echoes.'

Mayo sounded cautious. 'The ships may be heading south to Tsingtao, sir.'

Jermain stared at him. 'They've chosen an odd time for it.' He called through the door, 'Try and get the frigate on the acoustic radio. We might still be able to raise her.'

Harris bit his lip. 'Unlikely, sir. The change of water temperature and density inshore won't help, and the distance alone will kill any clear transmission.'

Jermain said sharply, 'Just do as I say.'

Harris glanced at the plot petty officer and gave a brief shrug before returning to the radio room. Through the open door came the usual stammer of Morse and the gentle purr of power from the sets, and Jermain heard Harris speaking quietly to one of the operators. They think I'm going round the bend, he thought bitterly. He watched the clock, mentally counting each dragging second.

Mayo walked to the control room and gave his instructions for alteration. 'Port fifteen. Steady. Steer two one zero.'

Harris reported carefully, 'No response from VIGILANT, sir. Just static.' He waited and then added, 'We could make a quick signal on W/T. It might pass undetected.' He did not sound too hopeful.

Jermain shook his head. 'We'll keep shadowing.'

Wolfe walked across to him. 'The Yanks must have made contact with the PT boats by now. I shouldn't wonder if we get a recall at any moment.'

Jermain nodded. 'Do you think I'm making a mountain out of this?'

Wolfe glanced around the control room before answering. '*Temeraire*'s not really suitable for this sort of caper, sir. It's either the whole works or nothing for us. We've no deck gun like the conventional subs, so we either use the torpedoes or keep clear and listen.' He smiled dryly. 'The top brass hardly had this kind of operation in mind for us!'

The minutes dragged past so that Jermain had the wild impression that every man aboard was waiting for his conviction to crack, for the boat to go about and return to the original patrol area.

Harris reappeared. 'We're getting a lot of garbled signals, sir. The Americans have made some sort of contact to the north. It sounds as if they're having a running skirmish along the coast.'

Jermain walked to the chart. The American patrols were at least doing something. Whatever the outcome of the small clash, it was unlikely that it would make the world headlines. It was amazing how this form of brinkmanship had become personal and accepted by individual commanders instead of being the tool of major statesmen.

In the days of the British Raj the Army had used much

the same system on India's north-west frontier for training infantrymen in the real arts of war. The live bullets from lurking Afghan tribesmen had put many a sweating soldier in his grave with never a mention in the British Press. Today the world powers played the same game, but with more far reaching weapons. One stupid miscalculation might plunge both sides into war, yet the game went on. Viet Nam, Malaysia, and now back to Korea; the deadly moves went on. Test and thrust. Kill and run away. With neither side making either complaint or asking for quarter.

As Wolfe had remarked, *Temeraire* was unsuitable for this work. She was designed for killing submarines and not for local skirmishes. She either used the big stick, or stayed as helpless as a toothless shark.

Oxley's voice came over the intercom. 'Ships seem to be turning, sir. Heading out to sea.'

Jermain banged his hands together. It seemed he had been right.

Oxley added, 'Range closing to about twelve thousand yards, sir.'

'Right, Pilot. Alter course to intercept again. We will keep to the south of these ships and close the range to three miles.' Jermain saw Wolfe's face watching him over Mayo's shoulder. 'It looks as if they're making a dash for it.'

Wolfe waited until Mayo had gone to his chart and then said flatly, 'Will you follow them all the way across, sir?'

'I think not, Number One. Once they're a hundred miles out we can make a W/T sighting report. The Americans have a carrier to the south. Her planes can track the ships and home any surface craft right on to the escape line.' He sighed. 'Then it's up to them what they do.'

The submarine turned in a wide arc and nosed closer to the two fast-moving ships. As each man strained his ears and tried to still the noise of his own heart the distant thrashing of powerful propellers became more apparent.

Mayo stood with his head cocked and muttered, 'Reminds me of the last time, sir. Poor old Victor.'

Jermain did not answer. It was true. The same sound. The steady beat, beat, beat. In his mind he could picture Victor's bloody limbs, the helpless desperation as he had screamed on

173

the ladder. He clenched his fists and forced himself to think.

An hour dragged by, and then another. The cook and his assistants moved quietly through the boat with tea and thick sandwiches which the waiting men took and consumed without pausing in their listening.

Three miles on the *Temeraire*'s port bow the invisible ships retained a steady twenty knots, the sound waves from their screws sweeping over the submarine's hull like hail on a metal roof.

Twice Jermain raised the slender attack periscope, his eye straining to pierce the darkness. If there had been even a hint of a moon he might have seen them, but only the spray from the periscope broke the impenetrable blackness.

Mayo lounged by the chart table, his jaws champing on a sandwich. Between bites he remarked, 'They are staying on our course, sir. They'll pass well to the north of the *Malange*.'

Wolfe said harshly, 'Bloody merchant ships should be forbidden to use these waters! Some of the bastards will trade with anyone. They carried guns to the Indonesians when we were fighting them. They'll hump ammunition and stores for the Reds if the price is right!' He glared at the gyro compass. 'If Conway wants to show how brave he is, and how immune his pink politics will keep him, he wants to go on like he is now!'

Jermain turned away. It was difficult to know if Wolfe's comment was directed at him or just hitting out at large.

Oxley's voice once more. 'Slight alteration, sir. Closing the range.' He cleared his throat. 'Nearest ship closing to five thousand yards.' Another long pause, then, 'Steady on new course, sir.'

Mayo scribbled busily on his pad and passed his findings to Wolfe. 'Bring her round to one one zero, Number One. We'll be on a parallel course again.' He watched his words affecting Jermain's expression. 'They're turning to the south, sir. It's no accident. They both wheeled like bloody soldiers!'

Jermain stared at the plot table. 'Calculate the *Malange*'s present position, Pilot.' He found that his mouth was quite dry, as if he already knew the answer.

Mayo's fingers worked busily, his beard only inches above the chart. He said, 'We're on a converging course, unless

Malange's altered hers.' Mayo brushed a crumb from his lips. 'We'll be within twenty miles of her in two and a half hours.'

Wolfe said, 'She may have turned inshore, sir. Just to be on the safe side.'

Jermain shook his head. 'If her captain has heard of this skirmish he's bound to think he's safe. The PT boats will be two or three hundred miles from his passage route by now. Anyway, he's probably used to it. The Reds don't interfere with local shipping much. It's too useful to them, as you remarked.'

Wolfe grimaced. 'Except that this one has a V.I.P. aboard.'

Jermain eyed him searchingly. Behind Wolfe's controlled features there was something more. Almost as if he was enjoying the situation.

There were no further alterations of course, and apart from a sudden increase of speed, which *Temeraire* matched without effort, the other vessels seemed settled on their objective.

Jermain listened to the quiet reports and watched their combined progress translated into pencilled lines across the chart. Suppose Wolfe's casual remark was right? Would the Chinese really risk an open battle to search out and destroy the *Malange*? Or was their operation merely planned as a complementary one to the PT boats in the north?

If they attacked the freighter it might take all of an hour for help to arrive. An hour in pitch darkness was a lifetime. And if *Temeraire* flashed a radio signal too soon everything would be lost. The two darkened ships might even turn on the submarine with depth-charges. In these shallow waters there was not much Jermain could do then. Except turn tail and run.

He stared hard at the silent figures around him, and knew what he must do.

'We may have to surface later on, Number One.' He was speaking fast, as if he were afraid he might change his mind. 'I shall require a full boarding party to be ready for a sudden emergency. None of the usual gear will be necessary. I want each man armed with a Stirling, and each man to be a volunteer.' He saw the incredulity brighten and then fade in Wolfe's eyes.

Wolfe said, 'Can I say something, sir?'

For an instant Jermain could imagine Wolfe just as he

175

remembered him so long ago. There was concern in his voice. 'Go ahead.'

Wolfe looked away. 'This boat is all that you hoped for. What I hoped for, too. Do you realise what might happen if you are openly challenged by these bastards?' He did not pause. 'You can't fight them with Stirlings. You can't even ask your men to die for nothing! If it comes to an open confrontation what have you left?'

Jermain tightened his jaw. 'I cannot stand by and allow a British merchant ship to be challenged and interfered with, no matter *who* is on board. If these ships attack the *Temeraire* I shall hit back and hard.' His eyes flashed dangerously. 'The tubes are loaded, and I have no doubt that Lieutenant Drew is only too willing to use them after what happened to Victor!'

Wolfe studied him as if for the first time. At length he said softly, 'If you make a mess of this you'll never clear your yard-arm! The brass will crucify you!'

Jermain tried to smile. 'That'll be the least of my worries, Number One!'

He stared at the clock. 'We should make contact with the *Malange* at four o'clock. I shall then make a signal and report what we are doing. After that we're on our own for a while.'

He walked away, and Mayo said quietly to Wolfe, 'Does he mean it?'

Wolfe nodded slowly. 'It's become something personal for him.'

He ignored the mystified expression on Mayo's face and walked slowly towards the diving panel. He had seen the momentary flash of anxiety in Jermain's eyes when Harris had reported Conway's presence aboard the *Malange*. Conway *and* his daughter, no doubt.

Wolfe looked sideways at Jermain's shoulders stooped across the chart table and felt the old wildness returning to his mind. Now *you* know what it feels like!

With a start he realised he was grinning and that a rating was watching him with fixed fascination. Angrily he barked, 'Tell Lieutenant Drew to report to the control room at once!'

He ran his hand across his face and felt the sweat on his fingers like warm blood.

11

Rank and File

'Down periscope!' Jermain wiped the palms of his hands on his thighs and peered quickly at the control-room clock. The time was twenty minutes to four. He walked the three steps to the plot table and stood frowning for a few seconds. Around him in the weird orange glow of the action lights the men on watch looked unreal and ghost like.

'The *Malange* is early.' He spoke what was uppermost in his mind. Minutes earlier Oxley's delicate listening devices had reported the heavy, thrashing beat of a single screw almost dead ahead of the submerged submarine. Moving slowly from right to left. It could be no other ship, but even allowing for miscalculation on Mayo's part she seemed well ahead of time.

Wolfe said, 'I make her present course three two zero, sir.'

Jermain tried not to listen to the other ship's muffled beat. 'That would account for her crossing our course at this point.' He stared at Wolfe's shadowed features. 'But it would mean that she's hopelessly off her proper route!'

Mayo said, 'She is, sir. According to my reckoning she's steering almost north west.' He did not sound as if he believed himself. 'It's ridiculous, sir! She's heading *away* from Korea!'

Jermain swallowed hard. 'Keep checking, Pilot. And let me have any information you can about the other ships.'

Oxley called over the intercom, 'Both other vessels have turned away to the north, sir. Range about six thousand yards.'

Jermain stared hard at the plot table. Like counters on a staff officer's map the ships were moving inexorably in a strange and meaningless formation. He said, 'Alter course, Pilot. We'll close the *Malange* from astern but keep on her starboard quarter.'

He walked to the periscope. 'I want to get a better look at her.'

The boat began to swing on her new track as the periscope broke the surface. Jermain screwed his eye tight against the pad and stared for several seconds at the hard black shape of the other ship. He could see the high white froth at her stern and the paler rectangle of her upperworks framed against the sky. The stars were still there, but even now the sky seemed to be brightening.

'Course two two zero, sir.' Twine sounded tense.

Through the hatch at the end of the control room came the faint click of equipment and the subdued mutter of voices as the boarding party assembled. Volunteers had been taken from each part of the boat and included stokers and signalmen as well as a small handful of seamen.

Jermain snapped, 'Keep those men quiet, Number One! There'll be time for letting off steam later on!' He saw a momentary flash of surprise on Wolfe's face and cursed himself inwardly.

He was getting rattled, and worse, he was showing it to the others. In a steadier tone he added, 'We will raise the periscope every thirty seconds, Number One. In the meantime you can tell the boarding party to finish checking their gear and muster up here below the fin.'

Wolfe replied flatly, 'Do you think you should be sending Colquhoun, sir?'

'Who else is there?' Jermain tore his mind from the nagging problem of the *Malange*'s alteration of course. 'With ten ratings and a good petty officer he should be all right.' He added coldly, 'I can only send those who can be spared.'

Mayo, who had been looking through the periscope, called, 'I think we're running towards a fishing fleet again, sir.'

Jermain took his place and peered at the tiny pinpricks of light which reflected across the lens like fireflies. It was another part of the same nightmare, he thought. All it needed now was for Oxley to pick up those nerve-racking sounds from the fish-buoys.

He stepped clear as the periscope hissed down. 'It will make our approach better this time. The *Malange*'s screw is making enough racket as it is, but the additional craft will help, too.'

He forced a smile. 'Maybe the other ships were put off by the freighter's appearance.'

Oxley called, 'The freighter is fine on the port bow now, sir. Range down to one thousand yards.'

Jermain brushed the hair from his forehead. Nothing was making sense. The *Malange* must have slowed down to cut the range in such a short time.

He saw Colquhoun standing with his men by the bulkhead door and noted the tight set of his mouth. He was carrying a Stirling with both hands, as if his life depended on it.

Jermain called, 'Just take it easy, Sub. When it gets a bit lighter up top I may want you to go across to the *Malange* to bolster morale. You could stop anyone from boarding her with your party, and I will deal with the other opposition until help arrives.'

He saw Jeffers, the second coxswain, tighten his webbing belt and grin broadly. 'Like old times, sir! I ain't shot anyone since I was in Borneo!'

Some of the men tittered and Jermain was thankful. 'Well, I hope that won't be necessary this time.'

Mayo sounded excited. 'Sir! I saw a flash on board the freighter!' He was clinging to the periscope, his beard smeared with grease.

Jermain asked sharply, 'Some sort of signal?'

Mayo swallowed. 'It looked like a shot to me, sir!'

Jermain pushed him aside, his body already stooped over the lens. There was the freighter again. He blinked the sweat from his eye. She looked huge in the crosswires and distorted above her encircling wake of churned spray. He stiffened. There was no mistaking the sudden ripple of orange flashes from her maindeck. They lit up the tall, spindly funnel and the black, eyeless windows of the bridge beyond.

'Down periscope!' He swung round, his mind suddenly ice cool. Either there was already a boarding party aboard the *Malange*, or some sort of mutiny had broken out. Most solitary merchant ships went with fear and caution of pirates and terrorists alike. Their bridges were usually protected with barbed wire and steel gates, behind which their officers were expected to hold out until help was available. But the freighter's absence of distress signals showed that this was no clumsy attack This was well organised and well planned.

He barked, 'Stand by to surface, Number One. I will want the boarders up on the casing abaft the fin as we go alongside. There won't be much time, so two ladders and grapnels will have to suffice.' He stared at Colquhoun's glistening face. 'You take one ladder and Petty Officer Jeffers the second one, right?' He saw Colquhoun nod dazedly. 'My guess is that the sight of the Black Pig right alongside will do the trick.' He wished he felt as calm as he sounded. 'Keep listening to the other two ships and watch the nearest fishing boats. I don't want to foul any nets if I can help it!'

Mayo jumped to obey him and he saw the lights flicking obediently above the diving panel.

'Take the con, Number One. As soon as we surface I shall go to the upper bridge and supervise the boarding from there.'

He climbed up the ladder and knocked off the clips of the lower hatch. Behind him the boarding party milled around uncertainly, fingering their weapons and staring around the control room as if appreciating what awaited them above.

Jermain peered at his watch. 'Surface!' He was already at the upper hatch as the deck tilted sharply, and with a thunder of cascading water the submarine heaved herself bodily through a maelstrom of surging water and bursting air bubbles and broke surface.

Everything was running with water and ice-cold to the touch, but gasping and stumbling the men moved like automatons as they opened the fin door and staggered into the night's clammy embrace.

Even as he reached the open cockpit above the fin, Jermain's ear became attuned to the outside world. The sigh of spray, the rumble of water alongside the submarine's shining flank, and then, sharply insistent, the brittle clatter of small-arms fire.

He wiped his sleeve across the gyro repeater and shouted, 'Port ten! Steer three one five!' The old freighter seemed to hang over him like a cliff and for a heart-stopping moment he imagined that he had misjudged the distance. The lifeboats in their davits, the single line of scuttles, even the sagging guard-rail were visible in the stabbing light and the faint brightening from the sky.

He ground his jaws together with concentration. If the freighter had been a larger ship he would never have managed it. But she was barely ten feet higher than the *Temeraire*'s casing. Even so, the boarders would have to watch out. One false step and a man could fall and be ground between the two hulls.

A lookout at his side nudged him excitedly and levelled a Stirling over the screen. Jermain gauged the final distance and marvelled that no one had noticed the submarine's approach.

'Starboard ten! Stop engine!' He felt the deck quiver and watched narrowly as the black bows began to swing slightly to cut across the freighter's sluggish backwash. The momentum carried the *Temeraire* up and past the high poop, and from the casing he heard Jeffers yell, 'Stand by with them lines!'

Jermain saw the trapped spray leaping like a pack of phantoms right alongside as the two hulls idled together. It was now or never. . . . He shouted, 'Boarders away!' From the corner of his eye he saw the gleaming hooks soaring over the rusting rail, heard the clatter and scrape of weapons as his men waited and then leapt for the twin ladders The deck quivered again, and with a dull boom the rounded hull grated against the freighter's plates.

Jermain realised that he was shaking, and he had to grip the screen with both hands to control it. It seemed crazy and impossible to realise that this was happening. That only feet away were men dedicated to open murder, to whose mercy he had just sent a mere handful of his crew. And Jill, too. He tore his mind away.

'Midships! Slow astern!' The boat began to slide free, her fin almost brushing the overhanging lifeboats.

A messenger at the intercom yelled, 'The two ships is turnin', sir! Swingin' around the fishin' fleet!' He made an effort to control the break in his voice. 'Bearin' red four five! Range six thousand!'

Jermain watched the *Malange*'s wallowing shape swinging across the bows and nodded. 'We will remain surfaced. Tell the first lieutenant to prepare tubes One and Two for firing!'

He had a brief, impossible picture of Sir John Colquhoun's watchful expression when they had taken part in that last exercise. Jermain felt the anger washing away his pent-up anxiety like a cold shower. Perhaps now he would be satisfied, he thought savagely.

He had wanted the *Temeraire* to be baptised, and it looked as if his wish was about to be granted.

The intercom muttered, 'Tubes One and Two ready!'

*　　*　　*

Colquhoun's limbs felt like lead as he pulled himself the last few feet up and over the freighter's bulwark. Below him the taut ladder quivered and then swung heavily against the ship's side as the last of his five men kicked himself clear of the *Temeraire*'s hull and allowed the struggling cluster of dangling figures to pound painfully on the pitted plates.

Colquhoun stumbled down on to the unfamiliar deck and was instantly aware of the sudden and eerie silence. There was a brief, subdued swish of water behind him as the submarine idled astern, and then as the men on the other ladder pounded over the rail he was also conscious of a terrible feeling of loneliness. After nearly a week sealed within the tight world of the submarine the sudden rush of events left him panic-stricken and naked.

Petty Officer Jeffers pushed him unceremoniously to the deck and dropped on his knees beside him. He was already cocking his gun and peering forward towards the bridge. Between sharp breaths he gasped, 'What now, sir? Shall we split up?'

'I—I suppose so!' Colquhoun tried to project his tumbling thoughts beyond the small dark patch of deck below the tall derricks, but he could find nothing but a void of uncertainty and fear.

Jeffers snapped, 'Right! Rider, you take the port side with Stone and Lancing. Cover the bridge and shoot if anything moves this way.'

Colquhoun managed to say, 'But what about the officers up there?'

Jeffers snorted. 'Too late to worry about them, sir. Anyway, I reckon the other bastards are in charge up there. Otherwise the ship'd be on course!'

They both ducked as a sudden burst of automatic fire swept down from a small catwalk abaft the bridge, the flying bullets striking sparks from the hold coamings.

Jeffers yelled, 'See what I mean?' Then to the crouching seamen, 'For Chrissakes open fire! This is no frigging garden party!'

The Stirlings opened up nervously and then joined as one in a dancing pattern of fire across and around the shadowed bridge structure.

Colquhoun rested his head against the cool steel of a hold coaming and tried to control his fierce breathing. It was a nightmare. It could not be happening. He saw the savage fusilade finding and holding the rear of the bridge and heard the clatter of glass as the fast-firing Stirlings swept away the windows. His lungs seemed full of cordite fumes and he had to hold himself physically from hiding his head below the protective steel.

Jeffers roared, 'Move up, lads! We'll cover you from this side!' In a savage whisper he added, 'Come on, sir! Get a grip of yerself!' He shook Colquhoun's arm. 'The lads will be lookin' to you!' Then he rose to his feet, the Stirling jumping in his hands as he poured a blind volley across the exposed deck. 'Take that, you bastards! His voice was wild and unreal. Like a madman's, Colquhoun thought. Then he found that he too was on his feet, running with the others, his voice mocking him in its own insane excitement.

They reached the final hold between themselves and the bridge ladders. Jeffers looked up and jammed another magazine into his smoking gun. He said in an almost matter-of-fact tone, 'We've got 'em foxed for a bit, sir. They can't fire down on us without showin' their 'eads against the white paint up there. Right now we've got to decide what to do next.' He stared sideways at Colquhoun.

The latter looked momentarily over his shoulder as if he still expected to see the *Temeraire*'s fin looming alongside.

Jeffers said calmly, 'It's no use, sir. The skipper'll be too busy to care about us.'

Colquhoun made another effort. In a strangled voice he said, 'I'm sorry. I won't let you down.'

' 'Course you won't.' Jeffers was grinning. 'Just keep with me. I've killed more of these bastards than you've 'ad 'ot dinners, sir!'

Colquhoun shook his head dazedly. These bastards? They

did not know who they were fighting yet. But Jeffers' tough confidence was acting like raw alcohol.

He said quickly, 'They must all be up there. There's been no firing from anywhere else.'

Jeffers gripped his wrist like a steel claw and swung his Stirling across the coaming. '*Still!* not a bloody word, sir!'

The men around them froze and waited, each man fingering his gun and trying to pierce the darkness with his eyes.

Colquhoun heard the slow, scraping movement on the other side of the deck below the bulwark, but as Able Seaman Rider jumped forward with his Stirling raised, Jeffers snarled, 'Get back, you twit! It's one of our lot!'

They pulled the crawling man to safety and turned him over on his back. He was a sturdy, square-faced man in officer's uniform, his head swathed in a rough bandage, the front of which was soaked in blood. In the strange light from the sky overhead the blood glinted on the bandage like black paint.

The man stared up at them, his eyes wide and unblinking. For a second Colquhoun's reeling mind imagined that he was already dead, then he muttered, 'The Navy! For Sweet Jesus' sake, the *Navy!*' He sounded as if he doubted his own reason.

Jeffers shook him gently. 'Take it easy. Just tell us what 'appened!'

The man winced as a shot whined down from the bridge and ricocheted out over the sea. It was met by a savage volley from the watching sailors.

He said slowly, 'I'm Duncan, first mate. We were jumped a day ago just after we had made our signal to the port of destination.' Even dazed and in pain he seemed unable to free his mind from normal, routine phrases. 'There are about twenty of them. Most of 'em were included in the crew.' He grimaced. 'One of the bastards was the steward. He was the only one allowed on the bridge at sea, and he lobbed a grenade right amongst the watch! Killed the old man and most of the others, too!'

Jeffers asked, 'Are you the only one left?'

The mate shook his head. 'The bosun is just below the bridge back there, and I've got seven more lads up forrard behind the winch.' He pulled a big, obsolete Webley from his belt. 'Like me they're down to their last few rounds!' He tried to grin. 'But I've fixed 'em!'

Colquhoun stared over the man's body and tried to see some small movement on the bridge. He heard the mate continue with sudden venom. 'This is a coal-fired ship, y'know. I just happened to be down aft when they rushed the bridge, so I was able to organise a few of the crew myself. Not that they're much use. The usual sweepings. Chinks mostly.' He shuddered. 'I heard them pull the second mate from his bunk. He was screaming like a pig. It sounded as if they were hacking him to death with an axe!'

Jeffers persisted. 'You said you'd fixed them?'

The mate relaxed slightly. 'I closed all the engine-room vents. The bastards will suffocate or blow the bloody boilers now! Either way they can't keep up steam!'

Jeffers nodded. 'So that's it. That explains the loss of speed.'

'What of the passengers? Conway?' Colquhoun felt sick.

The mate shrugged. 'They are in no-man's-land. Their cabins are up there below the radio room. So long as you can keep the bridge isolated they're reasonably safe.' He added grimly, 'Unless they're already butchered!'

A huge Malay in a torn singlet and shorts wriggled around a ventilator and rolled his eyes in the gloom like two marbles. 'Lawd be praised!' He peered at the armed sailors. 'My prayers is answered!'

The mate grinned ruefully. 'This is my bosun.'

Jeffers said urgently, 'The sky's gettin' bright, sir. It'll be dawn shortly. They'll pin us down in the daylight and knock us off like bleedin' flies!' He peered at Colquhoun warily. 'What about it, sir? Shall we make heroes of ourselves?'

Colquhoun fought for time. For just a few seconds to clear his brain and make the nightmare recognisable. 'Who are these people? *What* are they?'

The mate shrugged. 'God knows. Pirates maybe. But they're well organised.'

The bosun nodded. 'We killed a few of 'em, sir. Just a few.' He groped behind him and pulled a sacklike object around the coaming. In the dim light Colquhoun could see the thing's teeth bared in a savage grin, could smell the sweet stench of death. He retched.

Jeffers pushed the corpse away with his foot. 'Well, this one's got a few friends waitin' out there.' He gestured towards the

185

hidden sea. 'So we ain't got much time.'

Colquhoun said in a small voice, 'What do you think is best, Jeffers?'

The petty officer smiled in the gloom. 'Like I said, sir. It's not easy.' He peered up at the dark bridge windows and was immediately met by two swift shots. He ducked and cursed as the bullets screamed past his head and slammed into the deck. 'Nasty,' he said.

Rider wriggled across on his stomach, his Stirling like a toy in his big hands. 'They don't have any more grenades, else we'd have got 'em by now!'

Jeffers' voice was biting. 'That's a bloody big help!'

The seaman laughed quietly. 'No good sittin' like a blue-arsed fly, P.O. We gotta do somethin'!' They both looked at Colquhoun.

The wounded mate said, 'On the starboard side there's a ladder. I had it lashed up the side of the bridge two days ago ready for a bit of red-leading.' He sounded doubtful. 'If you could get a man up there ...'

Jeffers rubbed his chin. 'Just the job, mate. We'll 'ave a go!'

Colquhoun said desperately, 'I'll go.'

Jeffers eyed him quietly. 'Beggin' yer pardon, sir, but I think not.' He chuckled. 'Well, let's face it, sir, officers is officers. They gives orders, they don't go dashing about like bloody marines!' Without waiting for a reply he added in a sharper tone, 'I'll be goin' for the ladder, got it? Rider and 'is mob will rush the port side as soon as I open fire. Porky Bruce can cover me and bring up in the rear.'

Bruce bared his teeth. 'Mind I don't blow your manhood off with me gun, P.O.!'

Colquhoun wiped his face and shuddered. They were joking. Actually joking about almost certain death. He felt Jeffers touch his arm.

'You keep with Bill Rider, sir. 'E's only an A.B., but 'e's more used to this sort of thing. Out in Alex I saw 'im clobber three coppers with a bottle an' go on to smash up a Wog cafe single 'anded!' He grinned. ' 'E's a good bloke in a rough 'ouse!' Then he was gone, and Rider yelled, 'Open fire, you canteen sailors!'

The Stirlings started their maniac chatter once more and the bullets ripped and whined across the bridge like hornets, bringing down shattered woodwork and broken glass like rain on their heads.

Rider gasped, 'Don't forget, sir! This is for real! Don't stop to argue with 'em! Kick their bleedin' faces in!'

Colquhoun nodded numbly. He could picture the little petty officer climbing over the rail and up the flimsy paint ladder beside the bridge. If he was wounded, or even slipped, he would fall straight down into the sea below.

I should have been there! I should be showing these men what to do!

It was not like that other time with the trapped wire on the rudder. Then he had been more afraid of showing fear than of fear itself. This horror was altogether different.

There was a burst of automatic fire from a high angle and Rider yelled, 'The Casing King has made it! Come on, lads! Up them bleedin' stairs!' Then they were all running and screaming like maniacs, their guns firing with neither aim nor care as they tore up the ladder and plunged across the wing of the bridge.

Colquhoun was knocked sideways as his whooping men poured into the crowded wheelhouse. In the growing light he saw several crouching figures outlined against the shattered windows and more sprawled across the littered deck. The air was filled with banging guns and the gasping cries of terror and fury as the two sides came to grips. Here a knife flashed home, cutting short an animal scream of agony. In another corner Colquhoun saw a tall seaman kicking a cowering man in the chest before pouring a full volley into his writhing body. There was blood everywhere, like some ghastly mural, and Colquhoun almost fell as he skidded on a mutilated corpse wearing a captain's uniform.

Through the other side of the bridge Jeffers peered across his smoking Stirling. 'Anyone hurt?'

Rider turned over a body with his foot. 'Nah. Just O'Toole. 'Is guts is playin' up by the smell of it!'

The sailors laughed wildly. As if they were drunk. As if it was all one huge joke.

Jeffers nodded and swung himself through the gap. 'Right

then. Mop up the other ones aft. They'll be poppin' out of the engine room soon, I should think!'

Duncan, the mate, stood silently surveying the carnage. 'Thanks, lads.' He did not seem able to speak.

Jeffers said easily, 'Hold on, chum. We'll get yer ship back for you!'

Colquhoun swallowed the bile in his throat and pushed his way through the wheelhouse door. Outside the air felt cool and damp, and he was startled to see how light it had become in those short, terrifying minutes. Already the sea had lost its deep shadows and the gentle, undulating surface had changed to a pale milky green with a clinging haze hanging lazily above it. In his shocked eyes it seemed too remote, too beautiful and settled for reality. It was like some Japanese water-colour, and even the vague shapes of the motionless fishing boats hung in the distant haze with no more substance than the artist's casual brush strokes.

Jeffers said, 'The mate's put his bosun on the wheel, sir, but there's hardly any steerage way on the ship now. The engine-room mob will be up directly to get a breath of air.' He checked his magazine. 'They'll come shooting!'

Colquhoun took a deep breath. 'Put some men to cover the hatches.' He stared round the deserted decks. 'But we must find Conway and the others!'

Jeffers barked off a string of orders which to Colquhoun's ears sounded like so much gibberish. But the men seemed to come out of their state of crazed elation and pattered away in twos and threes on both sides of the *Malange*'s deck. The petty officer added, 'You check the cabins, sir. I've given you two good lads to help you.' He strode away, his cap tilted over his eyes like a visor.

Able Seaman Bruce watched Colquhoun's strained face and then said, 'The cabins are in one block, as I see it. There's one of our blokes on the far side by the lifeboats.' He gestured with his Stirling. 'You an' me could go right through the central passageway and flush any stragglers out at the other end.' He squinted at the sea. 'How does that suit?'

Colquhoun took a grip on himself. 'Good idea, Bruce.'

Bruce showed his teeth. 'I'll just nip round and warn the other chap.'

He shuffled away, and once more Colquhoun was aware of the terrible silence. There was no sign of the submarine. The ship was alone but for the fishing boats. The latter too could have been deserted and forgotten by their lack of movement.

Bruce came back, breathing hard. 'Okay, sir.'

Colquhoun entered the open door and walked slowly between the cabins which flanked the passageway. There was a deserted pantry, the dishes smashed and scattered on the deck. There was a smear of blood on the handrail, and some empty cartridge cases. Silent witnesses of the horror which had swept through the ship.

Bruce spoke between his teeth. 'Call out, sir! It can't do no 'arm!'

Colquhoun's voice echoed around the passage and seemed to mock back at him. He imagined that each cabin contained either a corpse or a waiting terrorist, that every second invited a new disaster.

Then from the far end of the passage he heard Conway's voice. 'Who is that? Speak up or I'll shoot!'

Colquhoun opened his mouth to call, but as he passed another cabin his eye fell on the mutilated body of the second mate. It was hard to imagine that it had once been human. With a sob he fell against the door, retching uncontrollably.

Bruce yelled, 'It's the Navy! Hold your fire!' Ignoring Colquhoun, he ran forward as the door was pulled open, his small eyes darting from side to side and his gun at the ready.

Colquhoun staggered after him and then halted, staring in the cabin entrance. The wooden panels on the far side were riddled with bullet holes and gun smoke hung trapped in the stale and unmoving air. Conway half lay against the lower bunk, a pistol cradled on his knee. A crumpled form in torn dungarees was lying under the table in a pool of drying blood, an axe still gripped in one clawlike hand.

Colquhoun realised that Conway was wounded, but as he moved forward the big man gasped, 'Help my wife, for God's sake! I can last out!'

The girl, who until now had been standing with her back to a splintered scuttle, stooped down beside her father. She was wearing a short nightdress which had been all but ripped from her body. Across one shoulder Colquhoun saw three deep scratches, like the imprint of an animal's claws. She looked up at him, her eyes shocked but determined.

'No! Leave her alone! She's safe in the next cabin!' But behind her father's back she shook her head sharply, her eyes clouding with tears.

Colquhoun said, 'Let me have a look at you, sir. I think your wife is better left alone for a while.' He tried to lift Conway's hands from his lap, but felt the man shudder as a stream of bright blood spilled through his shirt and cascaded on to the deck.

His mind tried to keep all the other horror at bay as he concentrated on what he had to do. Conway was badly wounded. Possibly in the lower stomach. His wife was obviously dead in the other cabin, and the girl must be near hysteria. He must get a signal to the *Temeraire*. Griffin would know what to do. If there was still any time left for Conway.

Conway looked ashen. 'Burst into the cabins during the night. Lucky I had a gun. God, I thought we were done for ...' He moaned. 'Shooting all night long! Twice they tried to break in here. Lucky I woke up in time!' He stared fixedly at Colquhoun. 'My God! You're one of David Jermain's officers! I remember you!' He broke into a fit of coughing and then muttered, 'I'm so damned hot, boy!' But his hands were like ice.

The girl said, 'The *Temeraire*? Is it really?' The effect of her father's words seemed to have shocked her more than her experience. 'Tell me!'

Colquhoun nodded. 'Yes. The skipper sent me across to help.'

Conway sighed. 'I said to David when I saw him. You are like that young subaltern at Dunkirk.' He leaned his head against his daughter's breast and closed his eyes, all his reserves of strength used up. 'A good boy. But not to be wasted.'

Bruce leaned forward and dug his fingers into Colquhoun's shoulder. 'Sir! The door 'andle! It *moved*!'

They all stared at the small door which apparently connected the cabin with the bathroom. The handle was of bright brass, and as Colquhoun concentrated his stare it seemed to swell and glisten like the sun itself.

Then Bruce said thickly, 'My Gawd! My magazine's

empty!' He gestured wildly. 'Shoot! *Shoot,* sir! Before the bastard does for us!'

The tension and terror broke in Colquhoun's mind like a fractured dam. He felt the gun jumping in his hands, saw the girl holding her fingers over her ears as the staccato rattle filled the cabin with noise and smoke. The unaimed volley cut away the wooden door like paper and burst the lock and handle into flying splinters.

Then the gun fell silent and, mesmerised, Colquhoun watched the shattered door as it opened slowly towards him.

There was distant shouting and the sound of feet on the ladder, then Jeffers panted through the other door, his Stirling across his chest. 'Heard the shootin'! Have you got one of the . . .' His voice trailed away as the door swung inwards with a final jerk and the riddled corpse pitched forward at his feet.

The bullets had torn across the chest and stomach like hideous stitching, almost cutting the man in half. The face was unmarked, and seemed almost peaceful compared with the horror below it.

Jeffers wiped his face with the back of his hand and said harshly, 'I think you'd better let me take the gun, Mr. Colquhoun.' He tucked the Stirling under his arm, his face expressionless as another seaman called:

'I can see the *Temeraire,* P.O.!'

Jeffers said, 'That was the only time you fired, sir.'

Colquhoun did not answer. He was still staring with shocked disbelief at the man on the floor. Able Seaman Archer.

* * *

Jermain ducked his head beneath the glass screen and wiped the lenses of his glasses as a tall curtain of spray lifted lazily from the bows and spattered across the front of the fin. The *Temeraire* was trimmed high in the water, and each thrust from the powerful screw pushed the stem harder into the calm sea and patterned the hull and fin with glistening diamonds of blown salt.

As each dragging minute stripped away the darkness Jermain was conscious of the submarine's vulnerability. On the pale green water, her whale shape outlined in bursting spray, she seemed huge and defenceless. Nevertheless, he allowed his mind to accept that his crude bluff had worked. The two warships which they had dogged all the way from the Chinese coast had swung away to the north, beyond the vague shapes of the fishing boats, as if startled by the unexpected arrival of the giant undersea craft.

A lookout reported, 'Freighter, sir. Bearing green four five!'

He levelled his glasses again. There she was. The old *Malange,* apparently drifting, with hardly a ripple beneath her high bows.

'Starboard ten. Steer zero nine zero.' He shifted the glasses along the freighter's length, noting with cold relief the occasional figure of one of his boarding party and that of a uniformed officer on the bridge. But had he been completely in time?

The radio mast squeaked in its mounting above his head and he imagined Harris and his staff waiting to send off his first signal. He snapped, 'Flash a signal to *Malange,* Bunts. Ask her what is happening.' He saw the hand lamp begin to stammer his message across the narrowing strip of water, and he took time to reassemble his thoughts. Everything had happened so quickly. It was still hard to imagine that it was not just another drill or exercise. He drummed his fingers on the screen. If only both sides would make peace or declare war openly. Then they would know where they stood.

The bridge messenger said, 'Fishing boats have started their engines, sir. Lieutenant Oxley reports continuous and confused propeller noises.'

Jermain nodded. The fishermen would no doubt be unwilling to be involved in anything which might jeopardise their future freedom. Life was difficult enough for them. Preyed upon by the Chinese and Allies alike, they still managed to drag a meagre harvest from the sea to keep themselves and their village intact in a world gone mad. It would pay them to see nothing.

The freighter was much nearer now. Less than half a mile away. Already her gaunt upperworks were haloed in weak sunlight, her upper yards shining like ungainly crucifixes.

He watched the slow stabbing light from her bridge and wondered how Colquhoun was making out.

'Slow ahead. Close up deck party.'

The signalman said, 'All resistance has been overcome. Request medical assistance immediately.' He paused. 'One seaman dead.'

Jermain drew a deep breath. 'Tell the doctor to report to the bridge.'

Below on the submarine's casing he could hear the clatter of feet and the subdued mutter of orders as the two vessels drew close together.

The signalman continued, 'The passenger, Conway, is badly wounded. Can doctor be sent across?' The man watched Jermain's face curiously.

Jermain kept his voice calm. 'Tell them we will . . .' He broke off as the light began to flicker like a mad thing.

With disbelief the signalman shouted, 'They are reporting a submarine, sir! Bearing zero four five!'

Every pair of glasses was blocked by the freighter's motionless bulk, and Jermain felt the sudden threat of that brief signal like the stab of a knife.

The bridge messenger called, 'Sonar reports contact at red four five, sir! Range six thousand yards!'

Almost before the words had dropped from the man's lips the intercom barked, 'Torpedo running on same bearing, sir!'

Jermain pushed past the startled lookouts. 'Signal the *Malange* to abandon ship!' He punched the signalman's arm. 'Immediate!'

But even as the light began to stammer the *Malange* seemed to lift painfully as if on a steep roller. The roar of the exploding torpedo rolled across the water like the clang of a giant anvil, and as Jermain watched he saw the telltale column of spray and brown smoke rising from the far side of the ship even as the shockwave fanned his face with its hot breath.

The intercom was chattering without a break. 'Submarine is still surfaced, sir. Has altered course away. Now steering three four zero!'

All at once Wolfe was in the cockpit at his side, his eyes fixed on the listing ship. 'We could get that sub, sir. With a homing torpedo we could still catch the bastard!'

Jermain dragged his eyes from the freighter and the rising death cloud of smoke. 'The submarine is making for the fishing fleet, Number One. We can't afford the risk of hitting one of those boats. Stand by with a contact torpedo.'

Wolfe stared at him. 'For God's sake, you're not going to let him get away? We could dive now and outdistance him within half an hour!'

Jermain's voice was cold. 'We shall stand by the *Malange* to pick up survivors. Now get below and stand by to fire!'

He could picture the scene below as his orders were relayed to Drew in the torpedo compartment. One torpedo to explode on contact. It was an unlikely chance.

A lookout said thickly, 'She's beginnin' to roll over, sir!'

The freighter was sagging badly, her bows already rising slowly as if in protest. She had bared her bilge keel, and Jermain could see the running figures along the upper deck and the spurting syphons of escaping steam. In a few minutes the sea would reach her boilers. He pounded the screen with his fist as two liferafts splashed over the ship's side, followed by a small handful of leaping figures.

It took physical effort to drag his mind clear of the pitiful scene as the freighter began to capsize. 'Port fifteen. Steer zero one zero.' He crouched over the gyro repeater. 'Report when ready!'

The messenger said, 'Three tube ready, sir!' Another pause. 'Echoes distorted by fishing fleet, sir, but submarine still surfaced and increasing speed. Bearing now green two zero. Range six thousand five hundred.'

Jermain levelled his glasses and stared helplessly at the drifting haze. He could imagine the fishing boats scattering before the escaping submarine, just as he could picture the *Temeraire*'s complex firing controls plotting and estimating the range and bearings. 'Fire when ready, Number One.'

Still the seconds dragged past. Then through the bridge microphone he heard Wolfe's voice, angry and terse. 'Fire Three!'

The hull gave a slight jerk as the single torpedo left the tube. Nothing more. Not a hint of the murderous charge or the small powerful screws behind it.

'Starboard ten. Steer one one zero. Stand by to pick up survivors!'

The minutes passed and eventually the messenger reported,

'No contact, sir.' The torpedo had missed. A homing torpedo would have found and destroyed the other boat whatever her manœuvre, and Jermain was still not sure of his real reason for not firing one.

Almost gently the big submarine nosed its way between the pieces of nodding flotsam and the widening patch of oil and coal dust. The *Malange* had vanished as if it had never been, and the bobbing heads in the water seemed painfully few. Heaving lines were already being thrown, and some of the sailors were lowering themselves into the sea to help the weak and the injured aboard.

Wolfe appeared again on the bridge. He did not look at Jermain but watched intently as the girl was hauled half naked from one of the liferafts.

His voice shook with anger as he said, 'I hope she was worth coming back for! You've thrown everything else away!'

12

Play it Cool

Jermain climbed briskly up the varnished accommodation ladder which hung down the side of the American submarine depot ship. Beneath the soles of his shoes he could feel the rubber treads of the ladder soft and clinging in the blazing afternoon sun, but he made himself run up the last few steps, knowing that otherwise the weariness in his legs would drag him to a halt.

He reached the top and paused on the polished grating, his hand to his cap as the formal salute was given by the waiting side-party of white uniformed seamen and stiff-backed marines. A large, corpulent captain in neatly starched khakis stepped forward and thrust out his hand.

'Welcome to Taiwan, Commander.' He studied Jermain's tired face. 'Sorry we couldn't let you have time to get settled, but the boss wants to see you.'

Jermain looked back over the rail towards the sheltered anchorage where the pale grey warships sweltered in neat ranks beneath their awnings and limp flags. The Nanlien Inlet, on the north-east coast of Taiwan, but to his tired eyes it could almost be Cornwall. On either side of the inlet the lush green trees swept right down to the water, leaving neither beach nor reef to identify it with the Far East. Take away the warships, and ignore the pointed roof-tops of a distant town which showed briefly between the banks of trees, and he might have been back in his childhood.

Jermain said, 'Thank you for your help, sir.' It sounded inadequate.

The *Temeraire* had come alongside the depot ship that forenoon after speeding for two days from that place where the *Malange* had been sent to the bottom with neither warning nor reason. Two days of strain and tension, as each man within the hull waited and wondered what the next landfall would bring.

By some sort of miracle Conway was still alive. During the voyage he had lain in a drugged coma, watched over continuously by Griffin and Jill Conway. To Jermain it seemed incredible that he had carried the girl with him in the same submarine which now lay resting below the depot ship's shadow. Incredible, for he had seen her for barely minutes, and spoken even less.

Once he had torn himself from the inrush of signals and fresh instructions and the urgent business of preparing his reports and had visited the silent group in the sick bay. Conway had looked smaller and older inside the cot and had stared at Jermain's features without recognition.

The girl had said quietly, 'He keeps saying they must have misunderstood him. It's uppermost in his mind.' She had been wearing a sailor's shirt and trousers, her hair still dishevelled with salt water.

Griffin had told him later that he had deliberately kept Conway under strong drugs. The shock of learning of his wife's death would destroy any remaining chance of survival.

Jermain had spoken directly to the girl across the cot. 'I tried, Jill. I tried to get to the ship in time.' How stupid the words had sounded. Like an excuse. Like an epitaph.

She had stared at him gravely. 'I don't want to talk about it, David. Not now. Not here.' She had looked around the sick bay like a trapped and helpless animal. 'If I start to think about what happened I shall break! And he needs me. I *know* he needs me!' She had turned away, her eyes clouding.

Griffin had given a brief shake of the head. 'Later, sir. Maybe later.'

But that time had not come. All too soon they had come into the orbit of the American command and another opportunity had not arrived.

Within minutes the submarine had been swamped by Americans. The *Malange*'s few survivors had been ushered away with swift but gentle efficiency Jermain had been faced by two American liaison officers, one of whom carried the usual bag of waiting information and instructions. When he had finally torn himself away the girl had gone. One of the Americans had patted his arm. 'It'll be okay, Commander. Every goddamn thing will be taken care of!'

After all, what else had he expected? Even his own men seemed to be avoiding his eye. As if they anticipated his fate and wanted no share of his failure.

The captain said abruptly, 'I guess we'd better go right on up.' He led the way past the saluting sailors and through a wide screen door. There was a smell of fresh polish. An air of practised efficiency which Jermain had noticed as he had conned his boat alongside. To the Americans this was no manoeuvre, no show-the-flag mission. This was as near to real war as made no difference.

The captain said over his shoulder, 'Don't pay too much heed to the admiral. He's a great guy in his way, but he likes to act a little!' He chuckled. 'Don't underestimate him either!'

A marine clicked his heels together outside a door with four stars above it. The captain became more formal and said, 'I'll go on in.' He smiled. 'Take it easy, Commander, you're an ally, not a prisoner of war!'

Jermain tried to relax. The captain's words had hit home. He felt alien and unsure of himself. The American flags, the strange accents, even the ship seemed to have a different feel to it. It was stranger still to realise that it was only two months ago he had left that other depot ship in the bleak Gareloch. Two months, and thousands of miles. High hopes and sudden death. The hopeless love of a girl, already lost in a memory.

Beneath the visor of his cap the marine stared at him unwinkingly. Jermain looked down at his own creased white uniform which he had dragged hastily from his metal trunk. Hardly a fitting representative of the Royal Navy, the commander of the *Temeraire*.

The captain walked from the door. 'Okay. You can go in.' He strolled away whistling to himself, and Jermain found himself in the big cabin alone with the American admiral.

Admiral Arnold J. McKelway was a very small man. He was dressed in neat khakis and was chewing thoughtfully on a fat cigar. But his face commanded instant attention. It was tanned and wrinkled like tooled leather, and the eyes which watched

Jermain's approach across the claret-coloured carpet were like bright pieces of washed glass.

McKelway said brusquely, 'Welcome to my command, Jermain. Take a seat before the sweat cuts you down to my size!' He flicked open his shirt across a scrawny chest and directed a portable electric fan across it.

He continued in the same irritable tone, 'I've read your report, Jermain. Quite a potful! The cigar rolled to the opposite side of his mouth. 'Pity about the M.P. But I guess if you feel strongly enough about an ideal you can expect to risk your life once in a while.' He turned over some papers on a table. 'Our boys knocked off a couple of those PT boats you were shadowing. But nothing much else happened. There'll be other times though.'

Jermain clutched the arms of his chair and wondered if he was dreaming. No mention of the way he had left the patrol line. Hardly a regret about the torpedoing of an unarmed freighter.

He said, 'I don't quite understand, sir. Did you read my report about the submarine?'

McKelway's eyebrows lifted slightly. 'Ah yes. The submarine. I read about it.' He shrugged. 'It's a pity you couldn't have got a tinfish into him.'

Jermain rose to his feet. 'Look, sir. I want to make myself clear. The submarine attacked without provocation. But I had to attend to the survivors.'

'So you say, Commander.' McKelway's face was masklike. 'You did what you thought right, so what?' The cigar bobbed up and down in time to his words.

'Well, isn't something going to be done about it?' Jermain's despair was putting an edge in his voice.

'As I see it, Jermain, you were the only one who could have *done* anything, as you put it.' He shrugged. 'But you put your clean, humanitarian principles first.'

'Conway was on an important mission . . .'

McKelway laughed quietly. 'You British kill me, Jermain! You really do! You talk as if we were at peace, or something. Don't you ever read the papers? Hell, where is all that Churchillian stuff about blood and fire?'

Jermain said hotly, 'I am under your orders, sir. But I don't have to accept that kind of reasoning!'

McKelway's face hardened. 'You are under my control only in part, Commander. If you were one of my boys I'd have kicked your ass for you!' He threw the cigar into a wastebasket. 'I have never heard such sanctimonious crap in all my life! Just try to see further than your goddamn British pride, will you?' He stood up and walked to his wall map. 'You say there's no war on? Since the Second World War the United States has lost nearly a quarter of a million boys killed and maimed to defend freedom.' He glared. 'To defend America *and* Britain!' He waved a small hand. 'Hell, I know your country has its own problems, too, but I don't hear your government standing for any outside criticism either!'

Jermain sat down. 'What will happen now?'

'Now?' He rubbed his thigh. 'There will be the usual communiqué.' He tapped a signal pad. 'It's right here.' He skimmed briefly through the typed sentences. 'The S.S. *Malange* was seized by unknown terrorists and was intercepted by Her Majesty's Submarine *Temeraire*. The ship sank after an internal explosion and the survivors were landed at a Taiwan port.' He stared at Jermain's frowning face. 'That about winds it up.'

Jermain felt the walls closing in on him. It was mad. Unreal. No mention of the two shadowing warships. Not a word about the torpedo attack.

He heard himself say flatly, 'I understood you to say that we are fighting a war, sir. This communiqué hardly bears that out!'

The admiral ignored the sarcasm. 'You say this submarine fired a torpedo, Commander?' He spread his hands. 'Well, so did you. But whereas you got no hit, the other skipper managed to sink the freighter.' His face became intent. 'I am trying to get you to see it through the Reds' eyes! If I release this story to the world press, you'll be crucified! The Reds will deny they had a submarine in the area. They'll say that they *wanted* to meet Conway. That their ships were going to welcome the *Malange*, or some such crap.' He stared hard at Jermain. 'And they'll say that *you* torpedoed the *Malange*!'

Jermain's face felt tight with anger. 'But that's ridiculous!'

'Is it?' McKelway sighed. 'You returned with one fish fired.

There's no evidence but your word that a Red submarine ever existed.' He waved down Jermain's angry retort. '*I* believe you. But that doesn't count for much outside the fleet. Who gave the sighting report, anyway?'

'My boarding officer. Colquhoun.' He had a brief picture of Colquhoun's anguished face as he had been pulled from the water. But for Oxley's report he might have disbelieved Colquhoun himself. The young officer seemed completely crushed and broken by Archer's death. He could have been mistaken. No one else in the boarding party seemed sure of anything.

McKelway grunted. 'You also reported a submarine when you were on the exercise with my task force.' He drummed his fingers. 'It's all very strange. And very dangerous.' He seemed to be thinking aloud. 'Your boat is fully equipped with the best detection gear in the world. The Commies have nothing like it; *yet*. But they still got near enough to hit and run. Very strange!'

'Are you saying that I'm mistaken, sir?'

McKelway gave a cold grin. 'I make you mad, Jermain. It's a habit of mine. I can't stand yes-men, and you certainly don't come in that category.' He frowned. 'If there is a submarine on the loose, I *want* it. Otherwise,' he shrugged, 'They'll get cocky and go after big game. A carrier maybe.'

'Or a Polaris submarine!' Jermain felt the sweat running over his chest. The admiral's unruffled manner defeated his own anger.

'Could be.' McKelway glanced at his watch. 'So you see, it's better to play it cool. No need to tell the Reds what we think we know. Let 'em make one more move, and then we'll be ready!'

McKelway walked to a scuttle. 'We're learning, Jermain. But it takes time. We've got to make ourselves fight with *their* weapons.' He looked at the waiting communiqué. 'You failed to fire a homing torpedo because you were afraid of killing a few fishermen. Yet the Reds fired a torpedo smack into the *Malange,* knowing it would kill a lot of their *own* men aboard!' He grinned. 'They weren't to know you were there. A Limey sub right on the doorstep. By putting it in the communiqué it will kill their little plan stone dead. I'll bet they intended to kill Conway if they couldn't take him alive ànd blame it on the Americans, and so drive another wedge between us!' He stared fixedly at Jermain's eyes. 'There's no rift between *us,* is there, Commander?'

Jermain smiled wearily. 'When you put it like that, sir . . .'

'I do put it like that. We can't afford personal misunderstandings any more.' He waved towards the map. 'There's one hell of a lot of people depending on us now.'

McKelway held out his hand. 'Believe me, Jermain, it's best this way. An acceptable solution.'

*   *   *

Everything about the American shore base gave the impression of temporary occupation. Buildings and store sheds were either prefabricated or merely wooden sections bolted to metal frameworks, as if the whole base could be packed up overnight and set down elsewhere at an hour's notice.

A large portion of the *Temeraire*'s crew soon found itself comfortably ensconced in a vast, air-conditioned shack, more like an aircraft hangar than a canteen, and had split into noisy groups amongst their American opposite numbers.

Lightfoot sat quietly sipping a can of ice-cold beer, his eyes moving restlessly around the packed tables with their unfamiliar occupants. A giant jukebox blared jazz continuously so that everyone seemed to be shouting above the din, their faces sweating in spite of the refrigerated air. Chinese girls in PX uniforms ladled out beer and soft drinks, hamburgers and ice cream with stoical calm, apparently immune to the barrage of orders and demands from the waiting men.

A gangling American gunner's mate sat at Lightfoot's table, his jaw working busily on a wad of gum as he acted the part of host and general guide. On his shirt his name-tag read Smirner, but to all and sundry within earshot he was known as Jake.

He said, 'Yeah, we got a good deal here. It's more of a rest camp between trips than a proper base. The ole depot ship deals with the repairs and so forth.' He pushed another can across to Bruce whose face had changed to a mottled scarlet. 'Get it down you, pal. There's plenty more where that came from!'

Leading Seaman Haley tamped down his pipe and sighed

deeply. 'You're off the Polaris boats then?'

Jake grinned. 'Thank Gawd! Each boat's got two crews. As she puts into the inlet one crew comes ashore for a coupl'a months and the relief boys take her out for the next patrol. Real sweet.'

Bruce belched. 'Trust the Yanks! We've been swanning about the bleedin' 'oggin for ages without *any* bloody relief!'

Jake stared. 'What sort of goddamned accent is that, man?'

Haley grinned. 'Liverpool. Where the Beatles come from!'

The American shook his head. 'What d'you know!'

The tannoy doused the jukebox with a metallic roar. 'Now hear this! All enlisted men of the Blue Watch will muster at 1830! Local liberty will cease at 1800.'

The music came back with a triumphant bellow of noise. Jake shrugged. 'That's how it goes! That's our crew. We go aboard this evening an' take over.'

Lightfoot felt the beer rasping in his empty stomach. It had taken less than he had imagined to affect him, but instead of numbing his troubled mind it seemed to bring each item alive with stark and outsize clarity. Through the haze of tobacco smoke Bruce's face hung like a red balloon, his eyes and mouth, even the individual hairs which poked from beneath his tilted cap standing out from the crowded figures around him as if superimposed.

Lightfoot remembered suddenly the nerve-wrenching explosion as the unseen torpedo had struck the freighter. The shock-wave had shaken the hull from stem to stern, like a madman tugging at a well-tuned instrument. He had tried to piece together what had occurred by listening to the staccato comments through the intercom, and gauge the danger from the tight faces around him.

The boarding party had been hauled dripping and coughing down the control-room ladder along with a few Chinese seamen and a man so badly wounded that he looked already dead. There had been a girl, too, and one of the watching men had said, 'Christ! This is more like it! The comforts of home!' But no one had laughed.

Then he had seen Colquhoun, white-faced and shaking as if from cold, his uniform torn and bloodstained, his eyes staring around the boat as if he had never seen it before.

Later the boat had dived and increased speed away from the scene, and Lightfoot had found Bruce sitting wrapped in a grubby towel in the crew space, a cigarette in the centre of his mouth.

Lightfoot had asked, 'What happened to Archer?'

He could still see Bruce as he had been then, less than half an hour after jumping from the capsizing freighter. Bruce had drawn deeply on the cigarette as if considering the matter.

' 'E's kaput! Dead as a bleedin' sardine!' It seemed to amuse him. 'So you see, wack, there's no need to worry any more. We're in the clear for once!'

'How did it happen?' His voice had been unsteady. Looking back, he knew it was because of the uncontrollable relief Bruce's words had brought him. It made him feel unclean and guilty at the same time.

Then Bruce had said coolly, 'Your pal, Mister bloody Colquhoun, done for him!' He had chuckled. 'Cut 'im fair in 'alf with a full magazine!'

Lightfoot had left the crew space, and Bruce had returned calmly to the business of completing his toilet. He had met Petty Officer Jeffers outside the galley, a mug of tea in his hands. But when he had tried to question him Jeffers had answered sharply, 'It's not for me to say, lad. Archer's dead. That's the one thing I do know!' He had wiped his oil-smeared hands on his shirt. 'Now leave me be. I've had a bellyful of questions for one day!'

Rumours sped around the boat like fanned flames, each more positive than the one before. Colquhoun had lost his head and shot Archer by accident. He would be court-martialled. He had reported sighting a submarine on the surface, but Bruce had said it was unlikely, as *he* was with Colquhoun at the time, and the officer was too scared to see anything clearly!

Even the captain did not escape. He had failed to save the freighter. He would be relieved of his command and so forth. . . .

Jake stood up and stared through the smoke. 'Right, you blue-blooded Limeys! Let's see how you make out at bowling. It'll do me good to beat the hell out of you before I sail!' The group broke up noisily and moved towards the end of the canteen.

Bruce tried to follow but collapsed in his chair. His early humour rapidly giving way in a haze of beer.

Lightfoot stood uncertainly beside the table. 'Aren't you going, too?'

Bruce stared up at him morosely. 'Nah. I'll have a few more cans an' then get my head down.' He gave a lopsided grin. 'You still mopin' about Gipsy Archer?' His eyes were red-rimmed and he seemed unable to focus them properly.

Lightfoot watched him cautiously. Bruce was hiding something. His very manner showed that he was bursting apart with some new secret. He sat down and deliberately opened a fresh can and pushed it across.

Bruce lifted it to his lips and allowed the beer to run down his thick chest. Then he started to laugh. There was no sound, but his whole body shook as if he was having some sort of fit.

Between shakes he gasped, 'Your face! Oh, my lovely Jesus, your *face*!' Tears ran down his cheeks and mingled with the beer. 'I wish you could'a been there! Poor old Gipsy. 'E never knew it was comin'!'

Lightfoot opened another can without taking his eyes from the other man. 'What happened?'

''Appened? You may well ask, my old son!' He was half sliding from his chair now. 'I clobbered 'im with the butt of my Stirling and then *leaned* 'im against that bleedin' door! Then all I 'ad to do was tell Colquhoun that there was a bogeyman behind the door an' that my own gun was empty!' He rocked from side to side. ''E was so bloody scared by that time, 'e'd 'ave believed me if I said the 'Oly Ghost was there!' He crossed himself and chuckled again. ''E let rip and blasted Gipsy to bits! Gawd, I nearly peed meself laughin' when I saw Colquhoun's mush after 'e'd done! I don't know 'ow I kept a straight face, I really don't!'

Lightfoot staggered away from the table, his face ashen. 'You're lying! You're just saying that to ...'

Bruce stared at him glassily. 'Like bloody 'ell I am!'

Lightfoot knew that Bruce was in deadly earnest. Any sort of cunning or restraint had gone with the empty beer cans which filled the table. His mind was a complete maelstrom of confusion and horror. He could remember Colquhoun's stricken face, the way the other men had watched him in silence. They were

205

destroying him because of what Bruce had done. What they had both done. He tried to speak but nothing came.

Bruce propped himself on one elbow and muttered, 'Don't you worry about *Mister* Colquhoun, mate. 'E can go to 'ell f'all I care.' Some of his old manner returned momentarily. ' 'Course, if someone told 'im what really 'appened, it wouldn't do no good. It would only drop *you* in the cart. Anyway, I should 'ave to deny it.' He tried to wink. 'We wouldn't want that now, would we?'

Lightfoot walked blindly away from the table and blundered out into the waiting sunlight. Two American shore-patrolmen watched him pass, lazily swinging their sticks and chewing their gum, but he did not even see them.

He walked fast but without direction, his breath gasping in his lungs as the furnace heat pressed down on his head and shoulders. He had to find a way to explain to Colquhoun. There had to be a way.

Back in the canteen, Bruce slept amidst the chaos of beer cans, his head pillowed on his arm. His face was relaxed and smiling, as if he had not a care in the world.

*　　　*　　　*

The car jerked to a halt and the sailor behind the wheel turned in his seat to stare at Jermain through his dark glasses. 'Here it is, Commander. Bungalow Number Thirty. There don't seem to be much sign of life.'

Jermain climbed out of the car and felt the late afternoon sun on his neck. 'Thank you for the ride,' he said.

The American grinned. 'A real pleasure.' The car rolled away in a double-banked cloud of yellow dust, and Jermain was left alone on the road.

The road was very new and as straight as a ruler, with neither tree nor any difference in construction in the neat bungalows to break the harsh, unfinished monotony. But here, during their rest spells ashore, the American officers lived their strange lives in something which seemed a pseudo representation of a piece of America.

Jermain sighed and walked up the path towards the front of the wide bungalow. He pushed through a hanging screen which protected the deep veranda from the dust and flies and found himself in a spacious hallway beyond. Every door was open, and he could feel a stream of fanned air cooling the sweat on his face and hands.

He moved uncertainly into a large living room which looked over the rear of the building and the green hills beyond. Peeping over a line of trees was the newly constructed wall of a canning factory with a brightly painted sign which read: 'Presented by the people of Michigan, U.S.A., as a mark of friendship.' Jermain turned away and found himself staring down at a canopied cot in which a small, round-faced baby was fast asleep. In spite of the surroundings everything was very normal, and very quiet.

Somewhere on the other side of the building a door slammed and he heard a man's voice speaking in a slow, unhurried drawl. 'Now quit fussing, honey. I've packed everything I need for the trip. I'm not leaving you for good, you know!'

A shadow fell across the doorway and Jermain said awkwardly, 'The door was open. I just came in.'

The American was about the same age as himself, and the collar pins in his neat khaki uniform showed him to be the same rank. Oddly enough, his hair was completely grey but cut very short, so that if anything it added to his general appearance of youthful vigour.

'I was kinda expecting you.' He seemed vaguely uncomfortable. 'You must be David Jermain.' His handclasp was firm. 'Jill Conway is in our spare room.' He walked to a table and touched a line of bottles. 'She's asleep right now. The doc gave her a couple of pills.'

Jermain asked, 'Is she all right?'

The American shot him a quick glance. 'It's hard to say. I guess you'd know better than I would.' He poured two large whiskies. 'She came back from the airstrip about an hour ago after seeing her father flown out.'

Jermain dropped his eyes. He still could not understand what had made the girl stay behind in Taiwan when her father was being flown back to England for further treatment. Nothing seemed to make sense any more. Even his journey up here had been in vain. And now this American was acting so strangely. He was obviously a very competent and self-assured officer, yet

Jermain's inner senses told him that he was unsure of himself, even rattled. Could it be because Jill had confided in him? Had told him that she did not in fact wish to see Jermain again?

The American thrust a glass into his hand and said abruptly, 'Look, I don't have much time. I'm skipper of the *Pyramus*, and we're due to sail in an hour.'

Jermain watched him closely. 'A Polaris boat. The one by the depot ship?'

The man nodded. 'That's the one.' He gulped down the drink in one swallow and refilled his glass. 'I guess I owe you an apology, Commander. I wangled it so that Jill Conway could be sent here. I thought she would be company for my wife while I'm away.' He bit his lip. 'Also, I guessed you would come sooner or later.'

Jermain sipped his drink and waited.

The American banged down his glass. 'Hell! I'm one of the guys who is supposed to be capable of handling the most deadly weapon ever invented and I can't even speak my piece.' He called out, 'Come in, darling, I can't cope with this situation!'

The door opened again and he added, 'Meet the wife, Commander.'

Jermain stared, the American and the rest of the room fading into shadows around him. He said quietly, 'Sarah! For God's sake, it's really you?'

Then she was in his arms, her face pressed to his shoulder, the same dark hair hanging rebelliously across her neck.

She stood back and studied him, her face torn between laughing and crying. 'Oh, David! I hated to do this to you! But when I heard your boat had docked here I had to get you to come.' She caught her husband's hand and pulled him towards her. 'This is John.' She looked from one to the other. 'I was so afraid you wouldn't come if you had time to think about it. I did so want everything to be right again.'

Jermain sat down heavily and then looked towards the cot.

His sister nodded. 'Yes, he belongs to us. He's three months old.'

Her husband said, 'His name's David, too.' He grinned with sudden relief. 'For obvious reasons, as I can now appreciate!'

Jermain said dazedly, 'I can't get over it. And yet I knew we would meet again somewhere.' He shook his head. 'I wouldn't have missed this for anything.'

Her husband looked at his watch. 'Well, this is it. I have to go now.'

Jermain saw the quick glance of private anguish pass between them.

She replied steadily, 'I know, John. Are you *sure* you've got everything?'

He winked at Jermain and patted his pockets. 'I guess so.' He picked up his cap, and as if at a prearranged signal a car squealed to a halt outside the house. He said, 'I'll be back in about ten weeks, honey. Just routine stuff.' He walked to the cot and touched his son. 'Take care of your Mom while I'm away.'

Then he kissed her, quickly and without emotion, much like an ordinary man on his way to the office or factory bench.

Jermain guessed that it was part of a careful routine which they had built up to protect themselves from constant heartbreak.

'Well, that's it. I am now Commander John Hurtzig, United States Navy, again.' He grinned and gripped Jermain's hand. 'Next time it'll be longer, I hope. It's good to have you here, and I mean that.'

Then he was gone, and for several seconds they listened to the car's engine speeding down that straight road towards the base.

She poured another drink and said quickly, 'Tell me everything, David. Did you get my letters?' Her voice was husky, and Jermain knew she was still thinking of her husband.

He smiled, 'They haven't caught up with me yet. I am waiting for fresh orders. I don't really know what is going to happen.'

She sat down beside him, her dark eyes pensive. 'I was so worried about you. About what you might think. I knew how you felt about Ian marrying me, and what his friendship meant to you.' She shrugged. 'It's hard to explain. It all seems so long ago.'

He said gently, 'You did what you wanted to do. After all, it was your life.'

She smiled sadly. 'Yes, it was. Now, what about this girl, Jill?' She smiled in spite of her inner anxiety. 'She really is quite a girl. Not a bit what I might have expected for a stick-in-the-mud like you!'

He bit his lip. 'It's nothing like that, Sarah. We met in Singapore. Her father was wounded when the *Malange* was sunk.' The casual words brought it all back like an old pain, and for several seconds he could only stare at the floor like a man coming out of some sick dream.

She said, 'Her mother was killed, too. Mercifully, she died while she was still asleep.' She smiled at Jermain's startled expression. 'Oh yes, she told me all about it.'

'Does she know about you? About your being my sister?'

She nodded. 'The lot. We girls had our heads together for quite a spell. I sat with her until the pills put her to sleep.' She glanced at her watch. 'You can take a peep at her later, if you like.'

Jermain said, 'I shall have to get back to the *Temeraire*. But I can come back if there's nothing fresh to attend to.'

He walked back through the hallway, his arm around her shoulders. At the door she asked suddenly, 'Did you see much of Ian in England? Do you know how he's getting on?'

Jermain swung round to face her, the realisation crowding in on him like a douche of cold water. 'My God, Sarah, I should have told you! He's *here*, as my number one!'

She looked away for a few moments, and when she faced him again her face was calm but resolved. 'Come back soon, David.' She studied his features sadly. 'But keep him away from me.'

He faltered by the door. 'But what happened, Sarah?'

She shook her head. 'Just keep him away.'

13

It Had to Happen One Day

A full week passed and still the *Temeraire* lay at her mooring alongside the U.S. depot ship. The first curiosity aroused by her arrival gave way to casual acceptance as the Americans became once more totally involved in their own affairs. Surface ships and submarines came and went with busy and unexplained purpose, and as the days dragged past the *Temeraire*'s crew became more and more aware of their own futility. When not employed on duties aboard the men found their way inland, each trip ashore adding to the problems of discipline and purpose. Even stable and reliable members of the crew became involved in fights and drunken brawls, either with the Americans or amongst themselves, and the trickle of mail from home only added to the general air of bitterness and discontent.

Then, on the seventh day, the weather broke to add its own weight to the *Temeraire*'s misery. The sky, which had up to now been clear and transparent, was hidden in low cloud, and as the humidity mounted like the interior of a steam bath the rain thundered down as if propelled from a dam. It drove the loungers from the depot ship's maindeck and turned the hills and roadways into rivers of yellow mud. Even inside the submarine's hull there seemed no escape, and the steady deluge battered on the toughened steel, making prisoners of the waiting men.

In his small cabin Jermain sat by the desk, an unlit pipe clamped between his teeth. Although he was dressed only in a pair of slacks his whole body felt stifled and damp with perspiration, and his mind seemed to take an age to deal with even the most routine problem.

Not that there was much to do any more. Several men had been brought before him as defaulters. A Lieutenant Trott had arrived as a hasty replacement for Victor. But otherwise he seemed bound to sit and watch his command falling apart before his eyes, like the hillsides washing away in the rain.

Time and time again he thought of Jill Conway. Nearly every day he had made his way to the bungalow to see her, only to come away feeling empty and discouraged. She seemed like a stranger. Like part of another life. Yet in some strange way he felt she was glad of his visits, if only to keep her own loneliness at bay. There was little news of her father, just the occasional communiqué to say he was 'as comfortable as could be expected'.

He stared round the cabin remembering the excitement when the *Temeraire* had first gone into commission. The speeches, the high hopes. Like the persistent rain they drummed at his mind like taunts.

Beyond the door the intercom intoned. 'Hands to tea. Duty part of the watch muster in the control room.'

The duty watch would probably be the only men aboard, he thought. It was as if they felt some sort of shame for the *Temeraire* and could no longer bear to be aboard for longer than necessary.

Propelled by some inner sense or urgency, Jermain stood up and began to throw on his clothes. He walked through the wardroom where Trott, the new officer, was sitting alone before a cup of tea, and on into the control room. Oxley was mustering the duty hands, a clipboard of papers under his arm.

Jermain said, 'I'll be ashore if I'm wanted. You have the phone number.'

Oxley nodded. 'Aye, aye, sir. No news about our going home, I suppose?'

Jermain caught sight of the assembled men watching him, their faces like strangers, and a flood of resentment made him suddenly angry. 'What's the matter? Isn't there enough work to do here?' He regretted his outburst immediately, but something made him turn on his heel leaving Oxley looking surprised and hurt.

The rain met him with savage glee, and within seconds it had soaked through his coat and made his shoes feel like paper.

With luck there was a solitary car on the jetty and the driver headed away from the sodden base without a word. Jermain sat slumped in the rear seat, his eyes staring over the driver's shoulder at the streaming road.

What the hell was going to happen? If only there was a signal. Send the boat back to England; relieve him of command. *Anything* was better than this waiting!

The car squelched to a halt and the driver pushed open the door.

Jermain tugged his cap over his eyes and hurried the last few steps to the door. It opened before he could touch it and he saw Sarah framed in the yellow lamplight beyond. She closed the door behind him and waited until he had peeled off his dripping coat.

'Thank God you've come, David. Jill just got a message from the base.' She watched him steadily. 'Her father died this morning in hospital.'

'Is she all right?' Jermain felt suddenly calm. Perhaps this was what he had been expecting. Dreading.

'I'm not sure. I was going to telephone the *Temeraire* and send for you. I think she wants to see you.' She moved towards a door. 'I think it's better if you go in alone.' She shivered as the rain slashed at the shutters. 'I'll be with David if you need me.'

Jermain opened the door and stepped quietly inside. With all the shutters closed against the storm the room was deep in shadow. A single lamp burned beside the bed, and the girl was sitting on the window seat, her legs drawn up to her chin. She was wearing the slacks and shirt she had been given aboard the submarine, and she was very still.

Jermain said, 'I just heard. I don't have to tell you how sorry I am.' His voice seemed too loud in spite of the rain.

'I know.' Her eyes shone momentarily in the lamplight. 'But I think we expected it to happen.' Her shoulders moved slightly in what might have been either a shrug or a shudder. 'When I saw him on to the plane he was different. Changed. He didn't want to go on.'

Jermain moved closer. 'He was a good man.'

'I've been trying to prepare myself for this.' Her voice seemed to be coming from a long way off. 'But it's not possible,

213

is it? One minute there's the family. You never think about it really. It's just there.' She moved one hand to her face. 'Then there's nothing. Nothing left.'

'What will you do, Jill? What do you *want* to do?' He felt the urge to hold her, the need to shut out the agony which was tearing her apart.

She did not seem to hear him. 'Do you remember Singapore? That night, that one night we had together?' she stood up and walked away from him. 'I wanted to tell you then, but I couldn't be sure. I thought I was lying to myself, as I lied to you.'

Jermain took a step towards her but she cried, 'No, David! Let me finish in my own way!' They both stood quite still, their shadows touching below the lamp.

Then she continued, 'I was afraid to let myself believe that it could happen so easily. I didn't even wait to find out what *you* thought.' She tried to laugh. 'But I watched you sail that morning and tried to let it die inside me. Then on that ship when your men came aboard. And one of them said, "We're from the *Temeraire*", I knew I couldn't go on without you.' Her voice shook. 'I wanted to tell you all this, here in this house. But I couldn't find the words. Not until now. And now maybe it's too late!' She faced him slowly, her body suddenly erect. 'I told my father about us, about everything.' Her head dropped. 'It seemed to please him.'

She did not resist as he pulled her gently against his body, nor did she look up as he said, 'I told you it couldn't end, Jill. I told you.' Her face felt hot and she was shaking. 'Everything will be all right, you see.' He held her tightly as she began to sob uncontrollably. 'After this things will be different. For both of us.'

The door opened quietly and Sarah said, 'I've got some brandy.' She studied them gravely. 'I'm glad you came, David.'

The girl released herself from his arms and brushed her hand across her face. 'Can you stay, David?'

Jermain looked at his sister. She said, 'I think it would be better. The base can call you if you're needed. I don't like being without a man either when the rain comes.'

They were both looking at him, and Jermain was conscious

of the steady downpour across the metal roof. He thought of the submarine and of his earlier depression, but they no longer seemed important.

'I'd like to very much.'

The girl said quickly, 'I think I'll have a shower. It might make me feel better.'

Jermain followed his sister into the living room and waited as she poured him some brandy. Then she said, 'She wants to cry so let her do it in private. It will do her good. She's been going through hell.'

Jermain stared at the closed door. 'I liked her father. But I'm glad she stayed here instead of flying out with him. There was nothing she could do anyway.'

His sister smiled gently. 'You really are out of touch, David. She stayed to be near *you*. Now that her parents are dead you are all she has to hold on to.' She studied him evenly. 'How do you feel about that?'

Jermain downed the brandy. 'I think you know.'

'Well, that's settled then.' She sighed and looked at the clock. 'I'm going to bed. It's been a long day.' She touched his arm. Don't waste a minute of it, David. I nearly did once. You mustn't make the same mistake.' She brightened. 'Which reminds me, I must go and see if the offspring is asleep through all this!'

She led him to another room. 'Take this one. I don't like to use it while John's away.' She ran her eye around the familiar furniture. 'There's a shower through there.' She kissed him lightly. 'It'll all look better in the morning.'

Jermain stripped off his clothes and stood beneath the cold shower, his mind still dazed by the swift turn of events. She needed him. She had stayed to be near him. There was no mention of love, but it was enough. More than enough.

As he switched off the shower he realised with a start that the rain had stopped also. In the strange room the silence seemed suddenly deafening. Through the shutters he could see the pale bars of moonlight and the stark silhouette of dripping trees behind the house. Everything was motionless, like a dream sequence.

He towelled himself roughly and then threw himself on the bed. She would have to fly back to England. No doubt the flight was already being arranged. He found he could think about it without apprehension. As if he already felt part of her life. He switched off the light and smiled inwardly. Sarah had understood. The sister he had tried to protect and support had made him feel like some immature schoolboy.

He raised himself on his elbows as the door opened and closed in one swift movement. Without speaking the girl crossed the room, her bare feet making no sound. She was wearing what appeared to be a man's bathrobe and her hair was tied back with a piece of ribbon, as if she had just stepped from the shower.

She sat on the edge of the bed and laid her hand on his chest. 'I had to come. You were too near.'

She sat motionless as he untied the bathrobe and let it fall to the floor. In the bright moonlight her naked body gleamed like silver.

He pulled her down beside him and kissed her throat and the shoulder where he had seen the scars. Her hair was damp and her skin felt cool beneath his touch.

Then she threw out her arms, her fingers gripping the sheets as he ran his hand gently over her breasts and down across her stomach. 'Make it last, David! Hurt me if you like, but make it last!'

His shadow blotted out the moonlight, and he felt her body rising to meet and enfold him with an urgency which made him respond with a fierceness he had never known.

Only when he was spent and they lay entwined together, each unwilling to release the other, did she speak again.

'I love you, David. Nothing else matters now.'

He propped himself up and stared down at her. It was complete. He could face everything and anything now.

Her hands moved up behind his neck, and he could feel her breath warm against his chest as she pulled him towards her.

Outside the moon continued to shine on the trees, and beyond the dip in the hills it glittered briefly across the night sea.

The sea was quiet, and holding its secrets for the dawn.

*   *   *

Wolfe awoke with a violent start as his cabin was flooded

with light. 'What the bloody hell!' His mouth felt raw from the gin he had consumed a few hours earlier and inside his head the hammers were busy with their relentless tattoo. He glared at his watch and then at Oxley who stood inside the doorway a jacket over his pyjamas. He added with a gasp of disbelief, 'Hell, it's only four o'clock!'

Oxley glanced quickly at the empty bottle on the deck and the pile of half-smoked cigarettes. He said, 'It's an emergency, Number One. The captain's wanted aboard the depot ship in the operations room.' He added, 'I'm still O.O.D., so I thought you'd better be told at once.'

Wolfe rubbed his eyes to clear away the mist. 'Well, where is the C.O.?'

'Ashore. I have the phone number, but it may take half an hour to get him back here.'

Wolfe rolled off his bunk, his mind working reluctantly. 'I'll bet he's with that bloody girl!' He stumbled to one side as he struggled into his trousers. 'The bitch!'

Oxley was watching him coldly. 'Did you say something?'

Wolfe glared at him. 'Who wants to see the captain anyway? Christ, it's one hell of an hour to call a conference!'

Oxley shrugged. 'It doesn't say on the flimsy, Number One. But there have been lights flashing all over the depot ship. Something big must be happening.'

Wolfe paused. 'What about our own W/T? Have we no signals coming in?'

'No. So it must be something to do with the Americans.'

Wolfe grinned. 'It would be. They get in a bloody flap at the drop of a hat! I expect their ice-cream supply has been buggered up by the Communists!'

Oxley sighed. He had had enough of Wolfe the previous evening. Sitting at dinner he had been speaking with Trott, the new assistant T.A.S. officer. Trott appeared to be an eager and willing addition, but he was undoubtedly very dull. He spoke nostalgically about spring in England. About the cricket score, and every other thing which, unbeknown to himself, was calculated to rub raw the brooding sores of the other officers.

Wolfe had shouted, 'Well, this isn't bloody Lord's, so for God's sake shut it! I wanted a replacement, not a flaming travel courier!'

Trott had retired red-faced and fuming from the table, and the mess had lapsed once more into its new state of gloom and inner deliberation.

Oxley said, 'Shall I call that number?'

Wolfe weighed the words in his mind. He had a clear picture of the girl sitting in the wardroom, her half-naked body smeared with oil and salt, her eyes wide from shock.

He replied coldly, 'No, I'll do it. You acknowledge the message and tell 'em the captain is on his way.' He waited until Oxley had gone and then made himself complete his dressing before he left the cabin.

He reached the radio room where the phone had been connected to the depot ship's switchboard, and after consulting the dutybook he began to dial the number.

In spite of his uncontrollable amusement at the idea of disturbing Jermain, Wolfe's mind kept returning to the other good piece of news he had received two days earlier. The signal had stated clearly that upon return to the United Kingdom Lieutenant-Commander Ian Wolfe would be relieved of his appointment and present himself forthwith for the final Commanding Officers Course. He had been thinking about it when that idiot Trott had started up about England again. What the hell did all that tripe count for? He was going back to work. Real work, with a boat like the *Temeraire* at the end of it. A command of his own.

All the agitation and uncertainty was nearly behind him now. The cruel self-discipline he had exerted upon himself was over. But when he had shared his news with Jermain the latter had seemed caught off guard, even unhappy about it.

Looking back, Wolfe thought he knew why. Jermain stood a good chance of being beached after his affair with the *Malange.* If he left the *Temeraire*, Their Lordships would be hunting for a new, well-tried commanding-officer. Wolfe's heart had given a jump at the sudden realisation that *he* might well be taking Jermain's command, and that Jermain had seen the writing on the wall in the signal's unemotional wording.

The telephone clicked and a voice said, 'Jermain speaking.'

Wolfe said, 'Recall, sir. You're wanted aboard the depot ship immediately.' He grinned at his reflection in the polished panel.

The girl was probably stretched out beside him. Her father dead, yet she couldn't stay away.

Jermain replied, 'I'll come at once. Send a car for me, please.'

Wolfe heard the sound of a door creaking and a woman's voice in the background. His grin widened.

Jermain was covering the mouthpiece with his hand, but nevertheless Wolfe heard him say, 'It's all right, Sarah. It's only the base. You go back to bed.'

Wolfe felt pressure like a steel band tightening round his skull. He could not speak or think clearly. It was as if he had received some sort of seizure. Dimly he heard Jermain say, 'Give me fifteen minutes.' Then the phone went dead.

Oxley appeared by the door. He watched Wolfe curiously and then said, 'I've sent a car.' He frowned. 'Is everything all right, Number One?'

The phone dropped and swung at the end of its flex as Wolfe turned and pushed past the other man. Oxley replaced the instrument and pursed his lips. Another crisis was in the air. It was better than nothing, he decided.

*　　　*　　　*

The operations room was like a great steel cavern which ran the full width of the depot ship's hull. It was crammed with charts and plot tables, with complicated graphs and a barrage of telephones. But the perspex monitoring screens were unlit and unmanned, and all but one of the chart tables covered until the new day.

The air was stale with yesterday's tobacco smoke and the damp odour of condensation and sweat.

Admiral McKelway leaned on his hands across the one lighted table, his face made older by the grey stubble which showed so clearly in the glare. Several staff officers in various stages of undress were grouped around him, and in a far corner a yeoman was busy preparing coffee.

Jermain walked up to the table and waited in silence. He was immediately aware of the tension. As if it was pinned inside the steel room as part of the motionless figures around the table.

McKelway lifted his head and looked at Jermain. 'Sit down,

Commander. Have some coffee.' His head moved sideways like a gun dog's as the teleprinter began its insane clatter behind him. An officer ripped away the message and handed it across to his chief.

Jermain saw the officer glance at the depot ship's captain and give a quick shake of the head.

McKelway's cold eyes flicked away from the paper and back to the chart. In a flat, unemotional tone he said, 'At 0100 this morning an American nuclear submarine failed to make her obligatory signal. I therefore have to assume that she is either in difficulties,' he paused and his eyes fastened on Jermain's face, 'or she has been destroyed!'

Every man in the room but Jermain was already aware of this information, yet the shock of the admiral's words seemed no less than if they were being uttered for the first time.

McKelway continued, 'The U.S.S. *Pyramus* should have discharged her radio-buoy at 0100 in this position.' His wizened finger moved along the chart. 'I know it's early to jump to conclusions, but we cannot afford to take one single chance.'

Jermain stared at the chart, only half his mind following McKelway's dry voice. The *Pyramus* was overdue on station. Somehow Jermain had known which submarine it would be as soon as McKelway had started to speak.

He thought of Sarah's anxious face in the doorway and his own casual words. 'It's only the base. You go back to bed.'

McKelway continued, 'I have the lines open with Washington. I have already been in contact with London.' They were all looking at Jermain. 'What I have to tell you, Jermain, is something which might surprise you, it may even sicken you.' He took a cigar out of his pocket and rolled it absently in his fingers. 'I want you to find that submarine, and I want it found quickly!'

The yeoman said quietly, 'Coffee, gentlemen?'

McKelway lowered himself into a steel chair. 'Might as well. There's a lot of work to be done.' He stared at Jermain. 'I will give you every piece of information I have available, Commander. I'll move heaven and earth to help you in any way I can.' He slammed his fist on the table. 'The *Pyramus* is carrying eighteen Polaris missiles! She has to be located!'

Jermain took a cup and drained the scalding coffee without

even tasting it. He peered down at the coloured chart and said, 'This is the east coast of Korea, sir. What was a Polaris boat sent there for?'

He waited for the lash of McKelway's tongue, but instead the admiral replied evenly, 'That's right. Ask away.' He levered himself forward in his chair. It's been a regular patrol for two years.' The finger moved slowly up the Korean coastline. 'Now look at this. The sea is so deep in some parts it falls away to eighteen hundred fathoms. Ideal country for a deep-running nuclear boat.' The finger moved up and up the coast. 'If you look closely, Jermain, you'll see this valley. It's marked on the chart as the Wantsai Valley, and it runs south east away from the northern end of the Korean mainland. It really is a valley. Some of the surveys have been hazy, but it's a great natural crevasse in the sea bed, some three hundred miles long and never less than thirty miles wide.' He sounded tired. 'It was a natural right from the start. A Polaris submarine was given the Valley as a regular patrol area. Once a Red Alert was given the submarine patrolling the sector could reach her firing position within hours.' He swept his palm upwards across the land mass. 'There are three countries within a hundred miles of the firing point! It's unique. We have North Korea, Russia and China, all comfortably within a small arc of missile range!'

Jermain controlled his breathing with an effort. The admiral's words seemed vast in scale, like the scope of the operations he controlled. He stared at the chart and at the admiral's 'unique' situation. How unlike the other coast of Korea, he thought, where Conway's hopes had died with his wife in the *Malange*. This other coastline was certainly a temptation for any submarine strategist.

The operations officer said suddenly, 'The *Pyramus* may be damaged in some way.' He sounded doubtful. 'In which case there is a certain routine she will have followed. But if she has lost control, then she will have gone straight to the bottom of the Valley. Like the *Thresher,* she'll be scattered in minute fragments, beyond reach, beyond hope.'

McKelway tugged at his collar. 'Christ, it's hot in here!' He looked across at Jermain. 'If you accept this assignment, Commander, you'll be on your own the moment you get under way. Secrecy is our only hope.'

Jermain frowned. 'Do I have any choice, sir?'

'Your people in London have left the choice to you, Jermain. It will be your final responsibility.' He leaned back and watched him calmly.

Jermain said, 'My choice? Must I decide whether one hundred men are to be left trapped or not?' He nodded vehemently. 'Of course I'll go!'

McKelway held up his hand. 'Take it easy, son. There's more to come, a whole lot more!'

A phone buzzed and an officer said, 'Reconnaissance reports a zero, Admiral!'

McKelway did not even blink. 'If the Reds get one peep of what we're doing they'll be in there pitching, Jermain. The *Pyramus* is right on their front doorstep, miles beyond any aid which we can give her. If they guessed the *Pyramus* was crippled and within salvage possibilities they'd go into top gear! Can you imagine what it would mean to the Reds to capture a Polaris boat intact?' He slammed his palms together. 'They would have every goddamn secret in the book. Every detail of our target ability and all the computerised data that goes with it. There would be nothing, but *nothing*, to stop them overtaking our lead in Polaris and nuclear warfare!'

Jermain ran his fingers through his hair. 'When would you want me to sail, sir?'

McKelway glanced at his staff. 'I shall get the final go ahead from Washington in a few hours. You get your boat ready to leave within ten hours, okay?' He added slowly, 'There will be written orders for you by then. Everything legal and tied up!'

Jermain felt a sudden warmth for the small admiral with the weight of command on his slight shoulders.

'Just one more question, sir?' Jermain saw the flash of caution in McKelway's wintry eyes. 'Why me?'

McKelway stood up and took his arm. Together they walked out of the operations room and stood on the damp maindeck below the gaunt derricks.

Then the admiral said quietly, 'I was saving this for later, Jermain.' He leaned on the rail and watched an aproned cook walking towards the galley rubbing the sleep from his eyes. 'I *could* tell you it's because your boat is the latest and best in nuclear submarines. Well, maybe it is at that, but I've got a dozen boats with captains who know that area a whole lot better than *you* do. I could also say it's because I was impressed by your unorthodox style, by the fact that you work things out for yourself as you feel your way. That's unusual nowadays.' He grinned in the grey dawn light 'Seriously, I read your last report and I was impressed. You are a good man for this job. I sincerely believe that.' His tone hardened. 'But my main reason is this. If the *Pyramus* is still intact, but cannot be helped or prevented from falling into enemy hands,' he swung round to face Jermain, 'she must be destroyed.' He gripped Jermain's arms in a tight pincer-hold. 'I am afraid you will have to destroy her, Commander! I cannot and will not ask my own men to destroy their buddies in cold blood!'

Jermain felt the sweat running down his face in spite of the chill air. 'And you think I can, sir?'

McKelway rested his body on the rail and said bitterly, 'You don't know these boys. To you it will be a job. Just a job.' He looked sideways at Jermain's set face. 'It has to be this way, boy. We must always be ready with a final solution.'

Jermain straightened his back. 'I shall return to the *Temeraire*, sir. There's a lot to do.' His voice sounded hollow.

McKelway said quietly, 'This is one hell of an assignment, Commander. Both our governments are prepared to accept this final solution, but in the end it comes down to you and me.' He held out his hand. 'Then it comes down to you alone.' He added, 'I know the *Pyramus*'s skipper well. He's a good boy.'

Jermain had a sudden glimpse of John Hurtzig bending over his son's cot and Sarah's anxious face watching him.

He replied, 'I'll do my best, sir.'

McKelway watched him go, his face lined and sad. 'I never doubted it, boy,' he said quietly. 'Never for a minute!'

*   *   *

Jermain pulled the clean shirt over his head and ran a comb carelessly through his hair. In his cabin mirror he could see Wolfe and Ross watching his every movement, their expressions masking their reactions to his words.

He swung round. 'You will both understand, of course, that

this is all Top Secret. We may still hear that the submarine has been located and all is well. But the Americans are working on the opposite assumption, and so must we.'

Ross folded his notebook and thrust it into his white overalls. 'Well, the reactor is running smoothly, sir. I put my staff to work as soon as I got the word.' He shrugged. 'I would have argued with you over this, in view of the other troubles we've had with the boat, but what can I say now?' He met Jermain's eyes steadily. 'It might be us one day. I'd not like to think that we lack guts when it comes to helping another boat.'

Wolfe said, 'The boat is on stand-by, sir. Two men are stil adrift, but I know where they are. The shore patrol is holdin them for starting a brawl last night.'

Jermain pulled on his jacket and patted his pockets. He had to make sure that everything he needed was on his person. He might be confined to the clothes he stood up in for a very long time. 'Get them back aboard at once, Number One. I want a full complement.'

He was surprised that both Wolfe and Ross had taken his news so calmly and without argument. He wondered what their reactions might be when he told them of the admiral's 'final solution'. He forced the sickening possibility to the back of his mind. He had to find the *Pyramus* first.

A messenger tapped at the door. 'Pardon, Captain. But there's a Commander Martingale to see you.'

A thickset American officer was ushered into the cabin and Jermain said to his own officers, 'This is the other commanding officer of the *Pyramus*. He brought her in from the last patrol.'

The American shook hands, his face grave and lined with worry. He placed a thick folder on Jermain's desk and stared at it. 'This is all the intelligence stuff I've got, Commander. Aerial photographs from our high-fly reconnaissance boys, recognition and rendezvous procedure and so forth. You'll be sailing on the same route as we normally take.' He bit his lip. 'As Hurtzig took.'

He added impetuously, 'I asked the admiral if I could come with you. I'd feel better to know what's happening.' He looked away. 'The old man refused. I guess he has no option.'

A sharp tremor ran through the deck and Ross said, 'Testing main propulsion. I'd better get aft and keep an eye on things.'

Jermain said slowly, 'Remember, this is secret until we sail. I'll tell the men myself. But until then it's a routine patrol.'

Martingale said, 'I hear you stayed with Hurtzig's wife? I had no idea she was your sister.'

He spoke quietly, but Jermain darted a quick glance at Wolfe's face as the man's unexpected words broke the silence like a bomb exploding. He was surprised at the calmness of his own reply. 'I'll take you on deck, Commander. There are a few points I'd like to discuss.'

Wolfe looked at him, his eyes completely steady and composed. 'I'll go round the boat and then check with the shore patrol, sir.'

Jermain nodded and walked through to the passageway. There was not a sign that Wolfe had heard the American's casual reference to Sarah. Not a blink of an eye.

They reached the upper deck and stood in the shadow of the depot ship's side to watch a frigate slipping seawards. Everything was businesslike but unruffled. No inkling of the feverish activity going on in the admiral's operations room or the flood of signals which might mean life or death to Hurtzig and his men.

Martingale said flatly, 'It's beyond me. The *Pyramus* is as safe as a house. I can't think what could have gone wrong.' He clasped Jermain's hand. 'I'll leave you in peace. But I'll be thinking of you.'

Jermain forced a smile. How would Martingale feel if he knew of his orders and the extent they might be carried out? He replied, 'It's nice to be of some use again.'

The American paused on the accommodation ladder and stared down at him. 'I think I know why McKelway wouldn't let me go with you. I guess that's why I wanted to meet you personally.' He looked along the *Temeraire*'s black hull towards the rounded bows and the hidden torpedo tubes. 'It had to happen one day. But that doesn't make it one bit easier for you.' He hurried up the ladder as if he no longer trusted himself to speak.

Oxley walked briskly along the casing and saluted. He was properly dressed and freshly shaved, a different man from the one who had greeted Jermain in the dawn light.

He said, 'Signal, sir. Proceed to sea at 1500 in accordance

225

with operational despatch.' He watched Jermain's face and added, 'Anything to add, sir?'

Jermain looked at his watch. Three hours. Perhaps the Americans were still hoping. He cursed himself for putting the empty faith in his mind.

'The first lieutenant will brief all officers. But once clear of the harbour limits I shall want the boat's number painted out.' They both stared up at the big S.191 on the side of the fin. There would be nothing to betray the *Temeraire*'s identity. She would be like a nameless pirate. An assassin. 'See to it, will you?'

Oxley watched Jermain walk towards the fin and waited as Mayo joined him on the casing. Mayo said, 'What do you make of it, Philip?'

Oxley shook his head. 'It's no bloody half-cock affair this time, Pilot. Did you see the captain's face?' He looked towards the lush hillsides. 'As our allies would say, "this is for real".'

Fifteen minutes after receiving the signal Jermain was summoned again to the depot ship where Admiral McKelway was waiting for him. There was little sign of the strain and anxiety he must be feeling and he was dressed in a fresh set of laundered khakis.

He snapped, 'I have a car waiting, Jermain. I thought you might like to say your farewells to Hurtzig's wife?' He studied him gravely. 'I've already been to see her. I think she deserves that at least.' He led the way to his big staff car and added, 'She'll be going through hell, but she's a navy wife now, and the wife of a commanding officer. If the worst happens it will fall to her to visit the other families.' He rapped on the driver's seat and finished, 'But I don't have to spell it out for you, do I?'

They drove in silence, the trees and white buildings flashing past without meaning. The road was rutted but as bone dry as if there had been no rain at all.

As they stopped outside the bungalow McKelway said briefly, 'Ten minutes, Commander. I have radio contact with the base. I'll yell if I hear anything.'

Jermain stepped into the shaded living room, his body taut and heavy. The two women were standing together by the window watching his face. Sarah said, 'The admiral came here, David. He told me about John.'

Jermain replied, 'I'm sailing almost at once. I just wanted to see you first.' He could not find the words. 'You know I'm going to look for the *Pyramus*?'

She nodded. 'I'm glad it's you, David.' She walked to the door. 'I'll leave you two alone.' She was trying to smile. 'Just bring him back to me, David. To us!' Then she was gone, and the silence moved a step nearer.

When the staff car sounded its horn Jermain left the house like a man in a daze. Later his mind might be able to sort out the swift minutes, recall each precious word.

The girl had said, 'I'll take care of her, David.' Then she had looked up into his face, her eyes steady. 'But come back safely yourself. I need you, too.'

McKelway grunted, 'Let's get moving.' He sounded angry. 'There's been another development, Jermain. I just got it on the radio telephone.' He glared at the driver's back. 'Your top brass are sending a senior officer with you to take overall charge of the operations. I'm sorry, Jermain, I remember what it's like to have a goddamn admiral breathing down my neck!'

Jermain asked flatly, 'Sir John Colquhoun?'

'Exactly. But you don't seem surprised?' McKelway leaned back and lighted a cigar. 'Can you manage him okay?'

Jermain stared at his own reflection in the dusty window. They were all depending on him. Sarah, Jill and the *Pyramus*'s crew. Now Sir John Colquhoun was returning to the *Temeraire*, no doubt at his own insistence. Perhaps it was fitting, Jermain thought bitterly. In a way he was responsible for everything that had happened.

In a hard voice he replied, '*I* command the *Temeraire*, sir.'

The admiral blew out a thin stream of smoke and smiled grimly. 'I guess that answers a whole heap of questions!'

Two hours later McKelway stood alone on the depot ship's bridge and watched the British submarine slip her moorings. Without fuss or undue haste the black whale-shaped hull moved clear and glided towards the wider reaches of the inlet.

A line of blue-shirted seamen stood swaying on her casing, and as she passed the American flagship McKelway heard the shrill twitter of pipes as a last respect was paid.

The officers' white caps looked like small flowers at the tip of the *Temeraire*'s fin, and McKelway guessed that one of them was Jermain.

Across the anchorage a tug hooted. It was a mournful sound, and McKelway suddenly felt helpless and old as he watched the submarine turn slightly and head towards the lazy rollers of the waiting sea. He lowered his glasses and walked back to the operations room. There was nothing he could do now, but wait.

14

Into the Valley

Baldwin, the senior wardroom steward, whipped the breakfast tablecloth over his arm and took a quick glance around the assembled officers before vanishing into his pantry.

Without speaking, Jermain unrolled his chart and spread it on the empty table. He was conscious of the silent, watching officers and of Vice-Admiral Colquhoun who sat at the head of the table, his fingers interlaced across his stomach. For a moment longer he stood looking down at the chart as he assembled his words and listened to the muffled movements from the control room and the subdued murmur of fans.

The deck was quite motionless beneath his feet. There was nothing to betray the fact that the *Temeraire* was cruising at a depth of four hundred feet, her noiseless power thrusting her at a slow but steady ten knots. It would have been better if there was some sort of sensation, he thought vaguely. It had been four days since they had left the Nanlien Inlet, and for the last thirty-six hours they had been creeping slowly north west, listening and probing along the *Pyramus*'s ordered course, not knowing what to expect. Not even knowing if there was anything to find.

Sir John Colquhoun had seemed remarkably relaxed and affable when he had come aboard within minutes of sailing. Again he had insisted on taking a spare berth in the wardroom, and when not asleep could usually be found, as now, like a bemedalled buddha at the table.

When the *Temeraire* had dived for the first time and the complicated checks had been completed, he had joined Jermain in his cabin. He had come straight to the point. 'I've been attending a top-level SEATO conference, Jermain. Otherwise I would have flown down earlier. Much earlier.' He had tapped his fingertips together as he had watched Jermain from beneath lowered brows. 'When I heard about the *Malange* incident I was shocked, naturally. Not so much about Conway, although his death has obviously been a great loss.' His tone had hardened slightly. 'I think your own behaviour and general handling of the situation was lacking in many aspects. I'll go further, it was nothing short of madness.'

Jermain had not replied. But the effort of holding his words had cost him a good deal.

'You've a lot to learn. Such action would not have been tolerated in my time in submarines.' He had sighed. 'However, that part is now over. I can only thank God that we now have this opportunity to prove the *Temeraire*'s worth to the doubters and the critics!' He had added, as if to dismiss the matter, 'There are *some* senior officers who would have had you flown home immediately. It had even crossed my mind to do so. As you know, Jermain, the Board has selected Wolfe for command status. He would be quite capable of taking the boat back to the U.K. without you.'

There had fortunately been an interruption by way of Lieutenant Drew reporting that all tubes had been reloaded with homing torpedoes as instructed. The admiral had been content to keep his distance since that meeting. But his presence was constant, like a threat.

Jermain cleared his throat. 'Well, gentlemen, this is the picture. We will carry on along the Wantsai Valley, making a complete copy of the *Pyramus*'s usual procedure. As you can see from the chart, the Valley ends at a point some forty miles south of Linden Point, or Kokko Kutchi as it's shown here.'

They all craned forward to look at the coast's ragged outline which sprawled diagonally across the chart. All except the admiral, who continued to stare into space, as if his mind was on a higher plane.

'We are now passing through the area where the *Pyramus* should have made her safety signal.' He looked up as Kitson stirred uneasily. 'Do you want to say something?'

Kitson said awkwardly, 'I understood that no nuclear boats ever sent radio signals at sea, sir.'

'This is an exception. Due to the nature of the area and the complex grid layout of the patrol lines, the Polaris boats send up a radio-buoy at *this* point.' He rapped the chart with his pipe stem. 'It is timed to send a short, ten-second signal. After that it floods and sinks. The American's have a series of high-flying reconnaissance aircraft which cover the whole area. They fly from Japan and to within sight of the North Korean coast before they turn and fly back. The schedules are timed so that these buoy signals can be recorded and reported immediately.' He pressed back the chart's folding edges.

Between his hands the Sea of Japan looked empty and impersonal. But in his mind's eye Jermain could picture it as a great submarine mountain range, with the Wantsai Valley running north west through the main part of it. Giant, unknown ridges and deep, plunging crevasses which hid their secrets in perpetual darkness. Maybe there was marine life which men's minds could never understand or discover. He pictured the submarine's slow-moving bulk gliding between the towering sides of the Valley, safely guided by her sensitive navigational systems. Below her keel the bottom dropped away for another ten thousand feet. It did not seem possible.

He continued, 'No such buoy was released or recorded, so we have to assume that the *Pyramus* was damaged in some way. She could have lost control, or the diving planes might have jammed. As you know, at these extreme depths, and at the boat's slow patrol speed, any such trouble might be too swift to rectify.' He looked around their faces. 'However, I am more inclined to believe otherwise. I know that this particular submarine was a well-tried boat. She was recently overhauled, and her crew are extremely competent.' He saw the admiral's eyes swing round and settle on him. 'My guess is that she made some sort of contact, either accidental or planned, with another vessel.'

The admiral wagged his finger and smiled. 'I'm not interrupting, but I should explain to your officers that this *is* only a guess.'

Jermain checked the anger which hovered at the back of his mind. 'Do you wish to add something, sir?'

'Just this. The *Pyramus* is probably sunk. She quite likely made a sudden and unavoidable dive straight to the bottom.'

He spread his hands. 'If so, she's scattered for half a mile like so much scrap!' He looked at the shocked expression on Luard's face. 'If so, we can only locate her whereabouts and return to base. There's nothing anyone can do about it.' He looked at the chart. 'As for the theory that the *Pyramus* was intercepted in some way, well, of course, we must all be prepared for any eventualities. For that reason I suggested that the tubes were loaded with homing torpedoes.' He smiled innocently. 'We don't want any more *enemy* submarines to escape, do we?'

Jermain watched him, his mind suddenly calm. The admiral was actually enjoying it all. But at least he had shown his hand. He said abruptly, 'We shall continue the search until we find her. The American intelligence log suggests one further possibility.' He pointed at the end of the deep soundings on the chart. 'Just here, at the end of the area normally used by the *Pyramus,* the sea bottom is quite flat. From the coast itself the bottom deepens in steps, so that soundings change suddenly and at regular intervals.' He looked hard at each officer in turn as he spoke. 'Just try to picture it. It's like a small plateau, at the end of which the bottom drops away with a jump, down to eight thousand feet. The plateau is at a depth of only two hundred feet, and it was selected as a possible setting-down spot for any submarine in temporary trouble.'

His glance moved across Wolfe's face, but the first lieutenant immediately dropped his eyes to the chart, but not before Jermain had seen the bright intentness in them. 'So if the *Pyramus* has survived a disaster, she might well make for this place. Her captain could put her down on the bottom in comparative safety to effect minor repairs within the hull!' Again the inner pictures of his mind swept up to mock him like a clouded nightmare. Lying for ever, a rusting tomb for her crew, the *Pyramus* would be better to plunge over the edge into the Wantsai Valley. At least the end would be quick.

Drew said slowly, 'Suppose we locate her and we can't do anything to help her, sir?'

Jermain had been expecting it, yet it was still a shock. 'We have to find her first.'

Drew looked doubtful. 'Nasty. Wouldn't care to be in their shoes!'

Jermain felt, drawn and tired. He had hardly found a moment to relax since leaving harbour. Yet he wanted to share his secret with these men. Or was it only to involve them and spread his own sense of shame at what he might have to do?

Oxley, sleek and alert. It would be his sonar which would find the missing *Pyramus*. The invisible waves which reached out from his sensitive devices would search her out, and decide her fate.

Drew, with his rugged Australian face deep in thought. His torpedoes would be the ones. His would be the final voice to urge them on their assassin's journey.

And Wolfe. What went on behind his strange, empty eyes? Was he still brooding over Sarah? Or worse still, was he deluding himself with the promise of his own command?

Jermain remembered his face when he had mentioned the signal from England. A boat of his own at last. And Sir John Colquhoun had mentioned it too, with something like pleasure. The cruel pleasure of a cat with a bird. The admiral at least must know the reality, Jermain thought savagely. That Wolfe could receive that final recommendation only from himself, his commanding officer. And that he could not do.

It was more than a cold-blooded report, and greater than any passing personal assessment.

Jermain had welcomed Wolfe's coming to the boat from the bottom of his heart. It had been like a link with that old past. Someone to share the words of friends and rise above the rigid codes of duty and routine.

But this Wolfe was a stranger. He seemed hard, yet brittle. And his attention to detail bordered on the small-minded rather than the trained and cheerful officer he had once been.

He looked again at the admiral, but he seemed intent on the chart. If it came to an open clash within the boat it would not be difficult for the admiral to drive a wedge between himself and Wolfe. Between captain and crew. He felt a chill on his spine as he recalled McKelway's words. 'You'll be on your own.' Now he knew that he had meant more than just the submarine's solitary search. The *Temeraire*'s captain would be quite alone. Whatever Sir John Colquhoun prescribed or suggested, whatever Wolfe and the others might think, *his* was the final decision.

Abruptly he folded the chart and said, 'That's all, gentlemen. I would like every officer to read and examine the American intelligence reports as soon as possible. I want each one of you to get a clear understanding of what we are doing, and of what we can expect.'

He walked out of the wardroom, and one by one the other officers returned to their duties.

Only Wolfe stayed in his chair, his eyes on the door.

The admiral stood up and stretched comfortably, 'Well, Number One, I don't suppose you've got any illusions about this job, eh?'

Wolfe stared fixedly at the door. 'Two birds with one stone.' Then he seemed to pull himself together, as if he had imagined he was talking to himself. He smiled and said, 'None at all, sir.' He walked from the wardroom, the smile still frozen on his face like a mask.

* * *

Lieutenant Oxley ducked his head through the watertight door and peered quickly around the sonar compartment. The operators looked welded to their seats, their heads hunched over the instrument controls as they had been since the weary search had begun. They worked round the clock, two hours on, four off, with hardly a break to ease the strain of watching and listening.

Colquhoun was sitting in his chair behind the operators, his eyes staring into space. He looked like death, Oxley thought. 'All right, Sub. You can lay aft for a bit.' Oxley saw the younger man stir stiffly in his seat.

Colquhoun said between his teeth. 'It's not time yet. There's another half hour still to run.' He turned his head, and Oxley was shocked to see the redness of his eyes, the deep lines around his mouth.

Oxley snapped, 'Take over the watch, Petty Officer.' Then to Colquhoun he added quietly, 'Come outside.'

Colquhoun followed him obediently, his movements stiff and mechanical.

Oxley lit a cigarette and watched him thoughtfully. 'I've just been to the conference, Sub. The captain appears to think the American boat was interfered with by some sort of enemy action.'

Colquhoun said flatly, 'Is that so?'

Oxley tightened his lips. He might just as well have remarked on the Test-match score, or the state of his bank balance. He glanced quickly around to make sure they were undisturbed. Above his head through an oval hatch he could see the sick-bay entrance where Victor had died. Where Conway had laid in a deep coma awaiting his own fate. The white curtains shimmered in the fanned air and there was a gentle strain of dance music from Griffin's tape-recorder. It was hard to build up a sense of crisis. Harder still to believe that the submarine was in any sort of danger.

He said, 'Now look here, Max. I know you're still brooding about that seaman's death. Maybe you could have avoided it, and maybe you couldn't. It's not for me to say. But right now you've got a job to do. There's no room for self-pity or recriminations now!'

Colquhoun answered quietly, 'I'm surprised you allow me to take charge down here.' His tone was edged with bitterness.

Oxley said calmly, 'I don't have much option, do I?' He laid a hand on his arm and added wearily, 'Look, Max, we're all getting clapped out, but it can't be helped. Just try to think of all of *us*, trapped and waiting for outside help.' He gestured to the curved hull. 'Try and imagine it like that. It's easier to keep control that way.'

Colquhoun shrugged. 'I suppose so.'

'And another thing, Max.' Oxley's voice was cautious. 'Don't try and avoid your father all the time. When you're not actually on duty you scuttle off to your cabin like a hunted dog. You can't run away for ever.'

Colquhoun seemed to jerk himself out of his thoughts. 'Just stay out of my affairs, will you? How the hell can you know what it's been like for me? Do you know what he said to me when he came aboard?' He was starting to shout. 'Well, *do* you?'

Oxley eyed him coolly. 'Tell me, if it makes you feel better!'

'He said that he was surprised I had lasted so long without killing someone! He told me that he had let his judgement as a father overrule his duty for once and that he had managed to hush up any official enquiry!' He stared at Oxley's serious features. 'Can you imagine that? You'd think I killed Archer to spite him!' His eyes suddenly flooded with tears. 'My God, he wants to get his ounce of suffering out of me!'

Oxley looked away, unaccountably embarrassed. 'Pull yourself together! If it's any consolation, I don't hold much brief for the admiral either.' He shrugged. 'But, like God, he's always with us nowadays.' He became suddenly serious. 'And try to think of the men under you, Max. They're not bloody puppets. They're human beings! Right now most of them don't know if they're on their arse or their elbow. It only needs the officers to start bickering and the whole outfit will come apart at the seams.'

Colquhoun wiped his face with his sleeve. 'Well, that doesn't apply to me, thank God. Hardly anyone ever speaks to me now, let alone listens to what I have to say!'

Oxley said sharply, 'Well, go and have a lie down. I'm taking over the watch, so do as I say!'

He slammed through the door, and Colquhoun leaned back against the cool bulkhead, his eyes tightly closed. Why couldn't he be like Oxley? Never ruffled, always self-assured. He had tried so hard to be different from his father's mould, to believe that his own outlook could be transferred into a life he had been too timid to reject. Now, before his eyes, his whole personality seemed to be disintegrating into shame and failure.

By failing to conform to the old and tried codes of wardroom life he had built up a barrier between himself and his contemporaries which he seemed helpless to dislodge. Even Luard who shared his cabin had changed towards him. Whenever they were in the cabin together Luard was either asleep or quick to find an excuse for leaving.

He had tried to use understanding and friendship in his handling of the men, and that too had turned sour. It was as if they mistook friendship for weakness and incompetence.

It was strange that the one person he could talk to was now avoiding him, too. Lightfoot, the boy from the Battersea slums, must be too proud to be soiled by any sort of relationship with him!

Overhead the tannoy squawked. 'Senior hands of messes muster for rum. Damage-control parties will exercise at 1430.'

Colquhoun pounded his fist against the steel door. That's right, he groaned. Carry on as if nothing had ever happened. Routine and drill. Calm, stupid normality, no matter what disaster is waiting for us!

There was a step on the ladder and Lightfoot stood beside him, an enamel jug of tea in his hands. He stared fixedly at Colquhoun's face and then laid the jug carefully on the deck.

'Are you feeling all right, sir?'

Colquhoun could not speak, any more than he could control the stinging tears in his eyes which made Lightfoot swim like a mirage.

The boy fumbled in his pocket and brought out a watch. It was a large, old-fashioned one with a thick chain. He was speaking quickly and urgently, as if he could not control the flow of words. 'I forgot to give you this, sir.' He held it out. 'The mate of the *Malange* give it to me when we fished him out of the water. It belonged to the ship's captain.' He clicked open the back of the watch and added breathlessly, 'It's got the ship's name and the date it was launched engraved on it!' He pushed it into Colquhoun's limp hands. 'The mate wanted you to have it, sir. He said you tried to save his ship. Tried to help.' He dropped his eyes and ended, 'So you did, too!'

Colquhoun stared blindly at the watch. When he spoke his voice was unsteady, like a stranger's. 'You're lying, Lightfoot.' He saw the boy looking at the watch, his eyes wretched. 'He gave it to you for looking after him when he was brought aboard. The doctor told me about it.' His arm moved again to wipe his face. 'Here, take it.'

Lightfoot stared at him with sudden defiance. 'Well, I want you to have it!' He looked around him with something like hatred. 'Christ, you deserve something after what you've been through!' He snatched up the jug and reached for the door. 'I *want* you to have it, see?'

Colquhoun walked slowly away, the watch grasped in his hand like a talisman.

Behind him in the open doorway, Lightfoot watched him go, his lip trembling with anger and emotion. You poor bastard. It's not your fault. It's mine. You tried to help me, and I'm letting you suffer like this!

237

The petty officer called, 'Come on, lad. Chop, chop! Let's have the bloody tea then!'

From his seat at the rear of the compartment Oxley watched the boy's face, and wondered.

* * *

'I believe you wanted to see me, sir?' Jermain closed the wardroom door behind him and watched the admiral warily. Sir John Colquhoun was seated at the table, his jacket unbuttoned, as he pored over a collection of charts and written reports. He was wearing glasses, which gave him a deceptively human appearance.

'Ah yes, Jermain. Come and sit down.'

Jermain eased himself into a chair, the sudden immobility reminding him of his tiredness, of his complete disappointment. Another full day had dragged past since he had addressed his officers in this wardroom, a day of sudden hope and equally sudden despair. The sonar crew had obtained a solid contact during the night, and all the strain and concentration of the slow search had given way to something like excitement. But the contact had proved to be false. An old forgotten wreck, unmarked on the chart, probably a victim of the Second World War.

So the search had continued as before. A crawling examination of the Wantsai Valley, back and forth, with the mean course taking them slowly towards the end of the deep water. Towards the coast.

Sir John removed his glasses and pinched the bridge of his nose. 'It seems to me that our search will be in vain. Sooner or later we will have to turn and retrace our way back to base.' He sighed deeply. 'But I suppose that a negative search is just as final as reporting a few scraps of wreckage. In the end it might be better for all concerned.'

He leafed through a pile of aerial photographs. 'Now these were taken by the American reconnaissance at regular intervals after the *Pyramus* was reported out of contact.' He grimaced. 'Of course they're not much use, the planes fly umpteen miles up to avoid interference. But they do show that the whole area was free of shipping. Apart from fishing boats and so forth.' He eyed Jermain with a slight smile. 'I suppose you still think that the fishing boats had something to do with all this?'

Jermain replied, 'I think it's very possible, sir. There's too much coincidence for comfort. When we were on the exercise off Hainan Island there were fishing boats present. Again when the *Malange* was sunk.' His jaw tightened defiantly. 'It's all we have to go on anyway.'

The admiral leaned back and regarded him calmly. 'I know how you feel, Jermain. You want to prove the boat, to make a place for her in the present situation.' He tapped the table. 'Well, so do I. I've been working for nothing else, in spite of government interference and the American efforts to squeeze us out of the Far East. But the facts of this missing submarine are more obvious. It seems hardly likely that a Polaris boat would be in danger from a lot of Chinese fishermen!'

'We still have to find the *Pyramus*, sir.' It was a stupid comment, but Jermain felt he had to say something if only to check himself. The admiral was goading him. Enjoying every aspect of this hopeless search.

Jermain wanted to ask him openly whether he had done anything to prevent Conway from sailing into an area which he must have known to be potentially dangerous, or if he ever thought beyond the bounds of his own personal advancement.

The admiral wagged one finger. 'It's been over five days now. Even if the *Pyramus* survived one disaster, it is unlikely that the crew is in any shape to save itself.' He shook his head sadly. 'I know how you feel about it, Jermain. Just as we all feel.'

Jermain stood up, sick of the admiral's smooth words and thinly veiled hypocrisy. 'I must get back to the chart-room, sir.'

'Just one more thing, Jermain. It's not really my direct concern, of course, but I think your officers are beginning to doubt the necessity of all this care. You've done your best, *and* we've shown the Americans what the best can be.'

Jermain stared at him with sudden pity. That's all you care, he thought. Impress the Americans, and prove to the world that everything is as it was, and will always remain so.

Sir John continued, 'Now take Conway, for instance. He was not only mistaken about the Far East situation, he was entirely *wrong*. But then you and I know that you can't make

239

national leaders overnight, any more than you can expect a lower-deck rating to transform himself into a good officer.'

Jermain looked away. Don't answer him. Don't allow yourself to be drawn by his remarks.

He answered coldly, 'That is rather a generalisation, surely?' He cursed himself as the admiral gave a small smile.

'I think not. And if you had remembered this small fact I feel that things might have been different for you and the *Temeraire*.' He shrugged as if it was unimportant now. 'This commission has certainly done little for my son, or the two members of your crew who have died.'

Jermain felt the colour stinging his cheeks, but as he opened his mouth to reply the telephone buzzed at his side.

'Captain speaking!' His voice was unnecessarily sharp, and he heard Mayo say cautiously, 'Sonar have just reported some faint H.E. on green four five, sir. Sounds like several small fishing boats.'

Jermain felt suddenly calm. 'Why fishing boats?'

Mayo sounded vague. 'They heard that bleeping sound again, sir. You remember the fish-buoys off Hainan Island?'

Jermain dropped the handset. 'I must go to the control room, sir.'

The admiral stared at his impassive face. 'Well? What is it now?'

'The fish-buoys again, sir. I'm going up to periscope depth.'

The admiral looked uneasy. 'Aren't you taking a bit of a risk?'

'But you said you thought the fishing boats had nothing to do with all this, sir.' Jermain kept his features expressionless. 'I'll take full responsibility.'

The admiral watched him go. Aloud he said to the empty wardroom, 'You certainly will, Jermain. That I promise you!'

*　　*　　*

The atmosphere in the control room was tense. Only the men at the controls seemed normal and absorbed in their duties. The others stood in silence watching Jermain beside the periscope.

Mayo said quietly, 'The nearest vessels are about seven miles away, sir. Of course there may be some others just drifting without engines.'

A petty officer reported, 'No more fish-buoy transmissions, sir.'

They think I'm mad, Jermain thought. He could see several off-duty officers standing beyond the bulkhead door and the sick-berth attendant in his white smock like a watchful ghost.

'Sixty feet, sir.'

Jermain glanced at the clock. Both hands were overlapping and he screwed up his eyes to withstand the glare of the midday sun. 'Up periscope.' He gestured as the air hissed sharply. 'Slowly! Raise it *slowly*!'

He saw the lenses shimmering in distorted green light, and then with a quiet flurry the periscope broke surface. The water was like glass, flat and oily. The sun was hidden by haze-like clouds, so that the sea and sky were bright, yet without colour.

He swung the handles very slowly, his eyes becoming accustomed to the glare even as the first of the distant boats swam across the lenses. For a moment he felt another pang of disappointment. It was just a ragged fishing fleet. Like a thousand others which moved like hungry vagrants in search of food and life.

Jermain said, 'Seem to be about fifty or more. Moving slowly to the north.' He watched some black smoke billow down from one of the boats and hang above the sea like a stain.

He moved the handles to full power and swung the periscope a few more degrees. The boats were well scattered, like flotsam on the flat water. They were moving so slowly that only the occasional splash of foam beneath a stern gave any hint of motion.

Mayo asked, 'Shall I lay off an alteration of course to avoid them, sir?'

Jermain did not answer. The billowing black smoke had moved away slightly, caught in a hot down draught of air. He blinked his eyes rapidly and stared again. He made himself stay quite still, holding his breath, hardly daring to speak as one of the distant boats altered course and moved across his sights. Even at this range there was no mistaking that business-like hull and the high-raked stem.

He slammed back the handles. 'Down periscope. Take her

down to two hundred feet.' He walked quickly to the chart-room. 'Bring me the intelligence pack again!' Mayo followed him, mystified, but Jermain concentrated on his racing thoughts.

It had been right there all the time. He had guessed the most unlikely part, but the obvious facts had been staring him in the face.

He snatched the thick folio from the messenger and pulled the aerial photographs on to the table. 'Give me a pin!'

Nobody moved. They were all staring at him.

With a grunt Jermain snatched the brass dividers and bent over the blurred photographs. As his eyes moved carefully across the scattered shapes he said, 'Now, in nearly all these photographs we can see a collection of fishing boats, right?'

Mayo said, 'Is it the same lot, sir?'

'I think so.' He closed his eyes and tried to picture the scene as he had just seen it through the periscope. 'Roughly the same number anyway.' He pushed the sharp point of the dividers into one of the tiny shapes on the first photograph. 'It was here all the time.' He made another small hole in a second shape, and then a third.

Then he held up the photograph against the chart light, so that the small lamp cast a glow through his three minute holes. It was a perfect triangle.

Mayo said awkwardly, 'I still don't see . . .'

'Neither did I, Pilot!' He took another photograph. 'Look at this one. The same three boats, larger than all the other ones, and in the same position as before.' He squinted at the numbers across the margin. 'Yet this one was taken *one hour* after the first!' He stared round, aware for the first time that the place had filled with watching figures. He said, 'Check each picture, and I think you will find that in every one there appears to be a distinct pattern. Three larger boats of the type I have just seen through the periscope. Of the type which went out to meet the *Malange*.' He saw Wolfe standing silently in the doorway. 'Of the type which fired on us and killed Lieutenant Victor!'

Drew stood beside the chart, an electric razor still grasped in one hand. 'You think there's a connection, sir?'

Jermain watched Mayo's fingers prodding the dividers into

another photograph. 'I've never been more sure. The fishing-buoys, everything, it all fits.'

Mayo straightened his back and nodded. 'The pattern is in all of them, sir. The same three boats are steering in a fixed triangle, and as far as I can make out they're about eight miles apart.'

Jermain said, 'The fish-buoys were a blind. It's my guess they are really some sort of variable depth sonar of an advanced type. By lowering them down through the isothermal barrier they are far more effective than any sort of detection device carried by surface craft. In a place like the Wantsai Valley they are doubly efficient. By relaying cross-bearings to one another, these ships could find and hold even a deep-running submarine.' He looked at Mayo. 'And in the confines of the Valley a damaged submarine would be incapable of avoiding them!'

'So we weren't so stupid after all, sir. The bastards must have been having a dummy-run off Hainan?'

'Something like that.' Jermain felt the excitement stirring his insides. 'The idea is not new, as you know. But out here, in these confined waters, it could be more than effective. It could be fatal!'

He glanced at his watch. 'But whatever they did to the *Pyramus*, they were only half successful. I think they are doing exactly what we are trying to do.' He looked around their faces. 'So it's up to us to find her before they do!'

Wolfe spoke for the first time. 'So what do you intend to do?'

'Take a chance, Number One. We have no other choice.' He leaned over the chart. 'We'll dive to maximum depth and then increase speed to by-pass this search party. Then we'll head direct to the plateau mentioned in the American folio. If the *Pyramus* is anywhere, she *has* to be there.'

Mayo was scribbling rapidly in his logbook. 'What depth, sir?'

Jermain looked directly at Wolfe's set face. 'Nine hundred feet, Pilot.' He continued looking at Wolfe. 'Inform the admiral, Number One. He will want to know what is happening.'

Mayo snapped his book shut. 'That's the deepest yet, sir.' He sounded calm enough, but his eyes were fixed to the chart. He added, 'At the school they said that at this sort of depth it was the same as having a fully loaded car on every square inch of the hull!'

Drew said dryly, 'Shouldn't think there are many cars down there, Pilot!'

Jermain glanced at the curving side to the chart-room and tried to imagine the black water beyond. Then he said sharply, 'Send the hands to action stations.'

As the alarm shattered the boat's silence Jermain walked slowly into the control room. On the strength of his own driving belief, and three pin holes in a blurred photograph, he was committing the *Temeraire* and ninety lives.

Throughout the hull these same men were running quietly to their stations, only half aware of what was happening.

Jermain thought suddenly of the only possible alternative, and dismissed the danger from his mind.

15

A Matter of Trust

Wolfe sat bolt upright in his steel chair behind the helmsman, his eyes unwinking as he watched the depth gauges. How slowly they seemed to creep round, he thought. Down, down. Yet the slender needles appeared to have no connection with reality or the enfolding world outside the hull.

'Six hundred feet, sir.' The rating's voice was hushed, like a visitor in a church, but Wolfe hardly noticed him. His mind and brain were completely controlled and devoid of doubt or uncertainty. Everything around him was clear and crisp, like familiar objects on a bright winter's morning, and his whole body seemed to tingle with excitement.

He checked the slow smile as it spread across his face, and peered intently at the gyro repeater. The tranquilisers were having their effect. He felt like a different person. He thought momentarily of Griffin's earlier unwillingness to supply his needs, and the ease and simplicity with which he had obtained a large packet of pills from the American depot ship just prior to sailing. Like everything else about the Americans, he thought. Slapdash and careless. A bored pharmacist's mate had merely glanced at his uniform and muttered, 'Sign here,' and that was that.

'Seven hundred feet, sir.'

Wolfe took a glance around the control room. The cut-out figures of the men on watch, each wrapped in his own thoughts. The admiral's stocky shape beside the door, his pale eyes swivelling between Jermain and the gauges.

Wolfe allowed his gaze to rest on Jermain's tall figure. He was standing in the centre of the control room, his legs slightly apart, his shoulders hunched as if to test the weight of his command. His face was calm but watchful, and Wolfe could see a nerve jumping very slightly at the corner of his mouth. He's worried, he thought. Like all the rest of them.

'Eight hundred feet, sir.'

Twine, the coxswain, mouthed a silent curse as the metal frames above the control panel groaned as if from pain. Every foot of water added to the pressure, each agonising minute brought some new strain to the hull and men alike.

The intercom said briefly, 'No further contact with surface craft, sir.'

Jermain said quietly, 'Increase to fifteen knots. Steer three zero zero.'

Twine moved the horseshoe-shaped wheel very slightly in his hands, and at his side the planesman took a moment to dash the sweat from his eyes.

The air was damp and clammy, so that the atmosphere felt dank, like a tomb. Every unnecessary fan had been switched off to make the boat as silent as possible, yet Wolfe was unmoved and inwardly scornful of the shining faces around him.

There was a sharp crack, followed by a long-drawn-out humming which echoed along the hull structure like a tin roof shaking in a high wind. Over the open intercom Wolfe heard a man cry out, and behind him the young signalman whispered, 'Jesus Christ!'

'Nine hundred feet, sir.' The rating sounded dazed.

There was another long quiver, and a few flakes of paint floated down from the curved deckhead.

Jermain said, 'Check all compartments.'

The men at the voice-pipes and telephones stirred themselves unwillingly, as if afraid that their ears might miss something.

Mayo called, 'Next alteration, sir. Steer three one zero.'

Wolfe sat back in his chair and watched the controls. Not long now. In his brain he could hear the dull thuds as the torpedoes left the tubes. The distant searing explosions as they found the crippled submarine. He looked quickly at Jermain. He could hardly wait to see his face when the inevitable happened. The good, patient friend, David Jermain, who all this time, over the months of agony and suspense, had aided Sarah in her plans, had secretly sided with her and her bloody American!

He had almost given himself away when the officer from the *Pyramus* had let the cat out of the bag. Somehow he had managed to keep his face calm, perhaps because he already knew half of Jermain's secret.

Now it was almost a pleasure just to sit and watch each moment as it arrived. Two birds with one stone, and what could be more just, or more final? Sarah's lover destroyed by the man in whom she had confided against *him*.

He watched Jermain answering one of the telephones. All his cunning could not help him now. Sucking up to Conway and seducing his daughter had come to no purpose. In addition he had made a bad enemy of the admiral by sticking up for his useless son. The thought of Colquhoun brought back the memory of that night in his cabin with such suddenness that he felt a quiver of blind rage run through him. The bloody insolence of it! And the incredible insult which followed when Jermain refused to take his part against that stupid, gutless little queer!

Jermain said to the admiral, 'The chief has reported some seepage aft, sir. But we're three hundred feet deeper than the last time. I think it'll be all right after all.'

The admiral grunted, 'It's a good time to remember it!'

Wolfe frowned. He remembered the admiral sitting at the table when he had gone to tell him of Jermain's intentions. The admiral had said, 'Well, if he's right about these ships it looks like putting a seal on the *Pyramus*'s fate.'

Then Wolfe had asked, 'My next appointment, sir.' He had tried to sound matter-of-fact. 'When will it be confirmed, do you think?'

The admiral had been evasive. 'It's not for me to say, Number One. Your commanding officer's personal report will carry a good deal of weight. If it's unfavourable,' he had fixed Wolfe with a flat stare, 'then of course that might well be the end of the matter for you. Of course, it can go either way. If a commanding officer is discredited in any manner,' he had shrugged, 'your case might be considered in a different light.'

Wolfe balled his hands into tight fists. The admiral had been passing him a warning. It was obvious. Jermain had not been content to deceive him and drive a wedge between himself and Sarah. No, he had to ruin his career, too! He gritted his teeth until his jaw ached. Well, nothing could help Jermain's plans any more. In a short while he would be discredited by his own eagerness.

Whatever the official report might say, Jermain would be remembered as the man who destroyed an American submarine. That, plus Conway's death and his conflict with the admiral, would finish the destruction.

He glared sideways at Mayo. You'll change your tune, too! He tried to picture the faces of the officers when they all knew what Jermain was going to do.

The navigating officer said, 'We shall be up to the plateau in seventy-five minutes, sir. If you raise her to one hundred feet we can commence the search immediately.' He looked worn out from his continued calculations.

The admiral muttered, 'I hope you're right about all this, Jermain. With those A/S ships coming up astern, I want to find the *Pyramus* quickly and get it over with.' He dropped his voice still further. 'Do you wish me to tell the ship's company what we have to do?'

Jermain gave a small smile. 'I think not, sir. After all, we don't yet know, do we?'

Wolfe moved restlessly in his seat. Go on, my friend. Try and wriggle off this one. There's no one to blame, and nobody to help you now. You are completely alone!

*   *   *

Jermain peered down across Mayo's shoulder at the crisscrossing pencilled lines on the chart. It was nearly two hours since the deep dive to avoid the bogus fishing boats, yet the searching sonar had recorded nothing. With the sureness of a whale the *Temeraire* had planed up from the incredible pressure of the deep valley, her hull seeming to quiver with relief as she crossed the steep-sided cliffs on to the plateau.

Suppose the *Pyramus* had limped further north, seeking escape in the futility of the shallow coastal waters? It was too late to try another area. The bleeping buoys would be swaying through the dark water, like the sticks of blind men in an enclosed room.

Mayo said gruffly, 'There's still a chance, sir.' His pencil made another small cross. 'But this is about our limit. We're within twenty miles of the coast right now.'

Jermain nodded. 'I know. Thank God it's pretty desolate hereabouts. Just a small town over there. All the same, I'll bet they've alerted all the local patrols.'

Mayo yawned. 'It's amazing to think we're here like this. With some useless strip of coast and a whole pile of people intent on killing us if we even show our little fingers above the surface. Why the hell don't we just declare war and be done with it?'

Griffin was standing just inside the door, his face deep in thought. He said, 'That's the stuff, Pilot. Us against the rest. The Good Guys against the Bad Ones!'

The admiral brushed past him, his features lined with irritation. 'Anything new, Jermain?'

'Not yet, sir.'

'For God's sake, there's not much time.' The admiral glared at the chart. 'We'll just have to clear the area if we can't make contact in the next hour.'

Mayo said, 'The A/S boats are coming straight up the Wantsai Valley, sir. Strung out like they are, they can flush out any submarine in their path, or so they seem to hope. The *Pyramus* could either try to avoid the sweep and risk running foul of the steep sides of the Valley. Or she could go ahead of them and get driven into shallow water. Either way, if she's damaged, her chances are pretty small.'

The admiral swung round. 'I'm quite aware of that, Mr. Mayo! Although why you or anyone else should imagine the *Pyramus* is still afloat is quite beyond me!' He looked at Jermain coldly. '*One* hour, Jermain.'

The intercom crackled, 'Contact, sir! Bearing green two zero, range four thousand yards!' A pause, and then Oxley added firmly, 'It's stationary, sir. Definitely the *Pyramus*!'

The admiral said, 'How can he be so damn sure?'

But Jermain was already in the control room, his voice crisp and urgent. 'Start plotting. Alter course and follow sonar. Slow ahead!'

He felt flushed, but his forehead when he wiped it was damp and cold. It must be the *Pyramus*. It had to be.

Mayo reported, 'Course three three zero, sir.' He glanced at the gauges. 'Depth now one hundred and fifty feet.'

'Keep her at that. I want to get as close as I can.' To the radio supervisor he said, 'Start calling her up on the acoustic radio. Keep calling her codename until I tell you otherwise.'

Harris's voice sounded heavy. 'Hello SUNRAY. Hello SUN-RAY. This is BLUEBOY. Are you receiving me? Over!'

The minutes dragged by as the *Temeraire* moved slowly along the bearing.

Harris readjusted his headphones. 'No reply, sir.'

Jermain snapped, 'Keep trying! Just keep calling her!'

'Range now two thousand yards, sir.' Oxley cleared his throat, the sound rasping round the control room like a thunderclap.

Sir John Colquhoun played with the peak of his cap. 'Tell Oxley to keep a constant watch for the ships too, Jermain. They may have increased speed. I don't want to be caught napping!'

Jermain ignored him. The dim hope he had been feeling was slowly giving way to sick apprehension. Try as he might he could not blot out the mental picture of the American submarine with its crew members lying or lolling at their controls, dead even as they waited for help which could never come.

'Range one thousand yards, sir.'

Haris looked round, his face taut and pale. 'Maybe their set is smashed, sir?'

Wolfe eased himself in his chair. 'It's no use. They're finished!'

Jermain glanced at him. 'We'll do another circuit, Number One.'

Wolfe shrugged and said calmly, 'Give me a course, Pilot.'

'Hello SUNRAY, do you read me? This is BLUEBOY.' Harris's voice was getting hoarse, and his constant repetition sounded like an epitaph.

The admiral said sharply, 'It's hopeless, Jermain.' He appeared to have difficulty in keeping his voice down. 'You're just putting off the inevitable. You must realise that.' He glanced at the clock. 'You must haul off and put some distance between us and the *Pyramus*. Even allowing for the missiles being set at safe, there will be one hell of an explosion.'

Jermain felt trapped. Around him he could see the waiting men watching him. Perhaps they guessed what was going to happen. He replied, 'Just a bit longer, sir. We must make sure!'

The admiral regarded him curiously. 'I believe that the skipper is your brother-in-law, Jermain? I know it's not easy for you.' He looked across at Wolfe. 'If you like, I could give the responsibility to the first lieutenant?'

Jermain turned away, sickened. 'Stand by to alter course to zero four five.' He forced himself to add, 'Tell Lieutenant Drew to prepare tubes One and Two for firing.'

Wolfe said quietly, 'I'll tell the hands to stand by for your announcement, sir. You'll want to tell them now, I expect?' His eyes shone like bright stones. 'It'll be something they'll remember!'

Oxley reported, 'We are now passing the *Pyramus*, sir. Abeam to port, one thousand yards. She's about eighty feet below our level of approach.'

Jermain felt the blood pumping through his veins, fogging his mind and vision, blotting out all else but the picture of the *Temeraire*'s smooth shape passing the other submarine. Her slow backwash would reach out and caress the other hull, like a final salute.

The admiral said, 'Carry on, Jermain. You can pull away and fire when you're ready. We can't wait any longer. These are British sailors. I'll not have them involved in more than this specific duty!'

Drew's voice said, 'Bow doors open, sir. One and Two ready!'

Jermain made himself walk to the chart-room where Wolfe had laid the public address handset on the table. He stared down blindly at the chart with its hopeful calculations and wasted efforts. But instead he saw Sarah's face and heard her last words, 'Bring him back to me, David!' And Jill, relaxed in sleep as he had leaned across her body to answer that telephone.

He picked up the handset. 'This is the captain speaking.' He saw the admiral's shoulders relax slightly and watched his quick interchange of glances with Wolfe.

'Hold it, sir!' Harris swung in his chair. 'For God's sake!' He turned his tuning dial, all else forgotten but the sudden wave of static on his speaker.

The voice seemed to come from a long way off. Very small and tired. 'This is SUNRAY. I am receiving you BLUEBOY.' There was a break and the voice continued, 'My God, I must be dreaming!'

Jermain said, 'Close the range, Pilot! Bring her round two points to port!' He strode to Harris's side. 'Here, give me the handset, Chief!'

He spoke very slowly. 'This is BLUEBOY. There is not much time. Just give me your exact position.'

This time it was a different voice, familiar in spite of the static. Jermain could picture him beside the cot looking down at the child, and wondered what sort of hell he had been suffering for these long, waiting days.

'We dived deep to avoid a fishing fleet. There was an explosion, maybe from a single depth-charge. Damage was sustained in the engine room when a salt-water inlet pipe was partially fractured.' He was speaking in sharp, staccato sentences. 'There was also some damage to the sail and the diving planes. Speed was reduced and we could not run deep to avoid further contact with the enemy.' He laughed bitterly. 'Whoever that was!'

Jermain said, 'Can you move?'

'We have been carrying out repairs lying here on the bottom. We had to shut down the reactor to repair the cooling system and the fractured inlet pipe. We will have to use our batteries to restart the reactor, and as you know we can't use our diesel generator submerged. It will take every drop of juice in every reserve battery to get it going. I've tried to cut down everything to save power. There's no ventilation, and every other bit of machinery is off, too. The engine-room crew have been working without a break. Before the reactor cooled they were in a temperature of over one hundred and forty degrees.' He added harshly, 'Six of them are dead.'

Jermain's mind was working like a precision drill. 'How long before you can start up?' He made his voice calmer. 'There is a strong force of anti-submarine craft sweeping up the Valley right now.'

'Christ! I'd have run slap into them!' He paused. 'Give me eight hours. I can probably get "airborne" by then. My speed will still be down to less than ten knots because of the outside damage. But when you've been fighting to stay alive, that seems a helluva lot!'

Jermain saw the admiral's quick shake of the head. He knew what he⁻was thinking. Eight hours. Even half that time would have been too long. The sonar buoys would sniff the *Pyramus* out long before that.

Jermain said quickly, 'Harris, connect this microphone to the public address system. I want the whole crew to hear it!' He turned back to the microphone. 'You will have to blow right up to the surface, right?'

'That's it. I'll run up the snort and start my generators. That will see us back to base okay.' His voice became suddenly tired. 'Who are we kidding? The Reds'll be here before I can get away. You can't fight them all on your own. It was just a last crazy hope, but by God I won't let the bastards take us or our ship!'

His words came back from the *Temeraire*'s hull like an echo. In the torpedo space where the men waited beside the spare torpedoes, in the silent radio room, and amongst the gleaming machinery of the engine room, the men sat or stood listening to the American captain's voice.

Jermain made up his mind. 'I think I can give you those eight hours, John. Nobody knows about us yet. It's just you they're after.' He deliberately turned his back on the admiral's grim features. 'For the next eight hours I will become you. The bait. When I've led the search away from the area you must pull out all the stops and get the hell out of here. By the time they realise what's happened you should be clear enough from the patrol area to whistle up air cover. Now, have you got that?'

He waited, his heart pounding against his ribs.

Hurtzig's voice was muffled. 'Received it loud and clear. I wish you could see my boys, David. I wish I knew how to speak for all of us.'

Jermain said quickly, 'Later will do. Just you get cracking at your end and don't pay any attention to us. It'll be getting dark up top soon, so you should be able to finish your battery charging in safety once the sea's clear.'

The static was beginning to fade out the other man's voice. 'Until the next time, David. Maybe I'll have the right words by then. Over and out.'

The admiral seized his arm and whispered fiercely, 'What the devil do you think you're doing? Do you know what you're saying, man?'

Jermain handed the microphone to Harris and then paused as a ragged burst of cheering echoed over the intercom. He met the admiral's angry stare. 'As you remarked earlier, sir. These are British sailors. I didn't think they'd want to run away and leave men to die.' His tone hardened. 'Any more than they would want to kill them themselves!'

Sir John stared from his face to the microphone. 'So that's why you let the men listen! You deliberately invoked their sympathy!'

Jermain said evenly, 'If you will excuse me, sir.'

The intercom crackled to life. 'Faint hydrophone effect, bearing green one one zero, sir!'

The admiral's face went pale. 'You see! They're here already, you fool!'

Oxley continued, 'Single screw, sir. Maybe small diesel craft.'

Jermain nodded. 'We must take a look. Periscope depth, Number One. Starboard fifteen. Steer three zero zero.' He made himself take time to look at the admiral again. 'Look, sir, if I've done wrong I'll be ready to face the consequences. But my orders,' he paused, '*our* orders were to find and render assistance to the *Pyramus*. We've done the first bit. Now we can carry out the rest. Neither my orders nor the traditions of the Service allow for either cowardice or brutality, sir!'

The admiral followed him into the chart-room. 'How dare you speak to me like that!'

Jermain pulled out a fresh chart. 'Since we are alone, sir, I will just say this. I believe quite sincerely that you intended to destroy the *Pyramus* with or without waiting for her crew to make some effort to escape. She was too deep for her men to get to the surface, and in any case we might not have found them with a tide running. There was in your mind only the one alternative.' He stared hard at the admiral's stricken face. 'Well, I can't see it that way, sir. And if I'm required to answer

254

to a court martial, I will be prepared to state these views.'

A voice called, 'Sixty feet, sir!'

Jermain continued relentlessly, 'No notice was taken of my earlier reports. They were shelved, in case we were "laughed at" by the Americans. No effort was made to understand the requirements and possible uses of my command in these waters, with the result we were operating in shallow water when the *Malange* was sunk.' His voice became scathing. 'My God, a frigate would have been better employed!' He strode away, suddenly aware what the strain and anxiety had cost him.

When he stooped beside the periscope he saw that the admiral was still standing beside the chart, like a man in a state of shock.

'Up periscope.' He swung it on to the bearing and waited for the lens to clear. The cloud was thicker and lower, and already the sea was patchy with dark shadows.

Oxley's voice called, 'The ship has stopped her engine, sir!'

Jermain stared at the small fishing boat which hovered in his cross-wires like a trapped insect. Even as Oxley finished speaking he saw the splash of white at her blunt bow as she dropped anchor and then swung easily on the calm water. Someone was hoisting a riding light, its brightness telling Jermain how quickly the night was closing in.

'Down periscope.' He rubbed his chin. 'It's a small motor fishing boat. No more than fifty feet. Just dropped anchor about half a mile away.'

Mayo said, 'Well, she's not much danger.' He looked darkly at the admiral's motionless shape. 'Not the bloody Red Fleet after all!'

Jermain shook his head. 'I got a good look at her. She's anchored for the night, in my opinion, and she has a radio mast!' He looked at Wolfe's slumped shoulders. 'If *Pyramus* surfaces nearby, even for a second, that fisherman will scream it to the world!'

Mayo asked, 'What will we do, sir? Time's running out fast!'

Jermain smiled grimly. 'I'm aware of that, Pilot!' He stared at the sheathed periscopes. 'It will be dark within half an hour. Dark enough anyway.'

Mayo looked mystified. 'For what, sir?'

'We'll surface and board that fishing boat. We can launch the Gemini dinghy and have some men aboard before they've got their boiled fish on the plates!' He walked across to the plot table, speaking his thoughts aloud. 'She might come in handy. The boarding party can stay behind and make sure the *Pyramus* surfaces all right. If anything fouls up they can pick up survivors. And *we* can be getting on with our part of the operation!' The lines seemed to fade from his face and he appeared almost boyish. 'What do you think of that?'

Mayo's teeth shone through his black beard. 'I'll go across, sir. I'll make a good pirate.'

'Not on, Pilot. You're too valuable here.' He touched his arm. 'But thanks for the show of faith. It may come in handy at my court martial!'

Mayo frowned. 'With all respect, sir, that's a load of crap! If we pull this off, the admiral will be in there reaping the credit.' He shrugged. 'And if we don't, we'll be otherwise engaged and past caring!'

Jermain became serious again. 'Number One, I shall want the dinghy prepared for launching. Fall out the torpedo party and use them. I shall need two officers and four ratings. That should be enough. There won't be more than half a dozen fishermen aboard that tub.'

Wolfe turned and stared at him stonily. He seemed suddenly spent and exhausted, as if the fire was drained out of him. '*Two* officers?'

Jermain snapped, 'Up periscope.' As he took another quick look at the anchored boat he added, 'Yes, Number One. Just in case of accidents, I want someone in charge.'

There was a clatter from forward as the dinghy was man-handled below the main hatch.

He signalled for the periscope to be lowered and continued slowly, 'Colquhoun can take the boarders, but I want *you* in charge. If anything goes wrong when *Pyramus* bounces up it will need someone with real experience to make decisions on the spot.' He eyed him calmly. 'All right?'

Wolfe faced him without a flicker of emotion. 'Is that an order?'

'It's the obvious solution, Number One. When I have headed off the submarine chasers I'll come back for you. If anything goes wrong you can find your own way south east and make contact with friendly forces. Everybody will be too busy looking for us to bother with just one more fishing boat.'

Wolfe glanced casually around the boat. 'And I'm to take Colquhoun. That makes it just about perfect!' He added, 'You're certainly quick to get rid of the bad apples!'

Lieutenant Drew clattered through the open hatch. 'Torpedo party fallen out, sir. Tubes secure.' He glanced quickly between them and added guardedly, 'What now?'

Wolfe picked up his cap. 'I'm leaving.'

He walked calmly away towards the petty officer who had been mustering the small boarding party.

Jermain said heavily, 'Take over from the first lieutenant in the control room. We will continue to circle the fisherman until it gets dark.'

The Australian lifted one eyebrow. 'Number One seems a bit odd?'

'He's tired, that's all.' Jermain stared at Wolfe's shadow beyond the door. If only there was some way of regaining contact with him. Perhaps later there might be time.

Something Sarah had told him when he had tried to question her came into his mind. She had said, 'He seemed to change overnight. He never trusted me, and when I tried to share his problems he just shut himself off. Sometimes he frightened me, David.'

It was odd when you thought about it. Each submarine officer was trained and vetted from every possible angle. At each step in his career he was inspected and reported upon, checked for suitability until his seniority and usefulness put him beyond the reach of the training staff and the would-be medical experts.

Wolfe had been an excellent officer, and as far as his duty was concerned he still was. Yet his very soul was being gnawed away from within. One day it would destroy his outer shell, and when that happened he might well become unsafe, a real danger to those who depended on his judgement.

A perfectly normal officer had been known to crack under the demanding strain of submarine life, when nothing untoward might ever have occurred if he had stayed in conventional craft.

Drew was saying, 'My new cobber, Lieutenant Trott, can take over the tubes then.' He chuckled. 'He's eager enough anyway!'

They both turned as Colquhoun climbed over the coaming, a Stirling dangling from one hand. He said urgently, 'Can I see you, sir?'

Jermain guided him into the chart-room. 'What is it?'

Mayo dropped his parallel rulers and left the compartment without a word. Then Colquhoun burst out, 'I can't do it, sir! Not again!'

Jermain waited, conscious of the ticking clock and the gentle tremble in the deck plates. 'Go on, Max. I'm still listening.'

Colquhoun swayed and then stammered, 'They don't trust me any more, sir. After what happened before. Archer's death. I'm finished, I don't even trust myself now!' He stared wretchedly at Jermain's grave face.

'*I* trust you, Max.' Jermain pointed at the chart. 'I wouldn't send you otherwise.' He remembered Wolfe's bitter 'quick to get rid of the bad apples!' He said, 'What happened to you might have happened to any of us. This new job will certainly help you later if there is any enquiry when we get home.'

Colquhoun sighed. 'I don't want to be helped. If I'm no good, I'd rather not risk any more lives!'

Jermain replied calmly, 'Everything is a risk. Right now, for instance. If I make some sort of error it will cost the lives of every man aboard, and the country will lose a twenty-million-pound boat.' He smiled quietly. 'Whereas you will be spared to tell the whole graphic account for the annals of naval history.'

Colquhoun's jaw dropped. 'But it's different for you, sir.' He struggled to find the words. 'You're the Captain. You know what to do!'

'Do I? What experience do you imagine I've had for this sort of thing, Max? The attack-table at the school, full of little models? Or exercising with a lot of friendly ships and men I've known for most of my life? No, there's no precedent for this. I am trained to use my judgement. The problems I have to face are of other men's making.' He gestured towards the deckhead. 'Like now, for instance. This submarine and the *Pyramus* are tied down by a helpless unarmed fishing boat. We can neither move nor escape without neutralising her first! Ironic, isn't it?'

Colquhoun asked quietly, 'Why are you telling me this, sir?'

'Because I want you to make an effort. Because I rely on you and every other man aboard. I'm like a fighter pilot, Max. I have to do the job I've been selected for. I must never have to ask myself about the parts of the aircraft, the accuracy of the controls. I have to rely on what I have!'

A messenger looked in. 'Mr. Drew says it's dark enough now, Captain!'

'Very good.' Jermain looked at Colquhoun's pale face. 'Forget all the old troubles for the moment. And back up the first lieutenant. He's experienced at this sort of thing, but he can't do it all alone.'

Colquhoun turned on his heel and walked back through the control room. He was only half aware of the watching eyes, the quick pat of encouragement from Drew, and Mayo's, 'You lucky bastard, Max! Yachting while we're playing tag with a lot of gooks!'

Beneath the forward hatch a group of men were checking over the bulbous inflatable dinghy with its paddles and neat outboard motor. Jeffers, the second coxswain, blocked his path, his face creased into a grin. 'I'm not coming this time, sir. Can't be spared.' He pointed at the tall leading seaman with a Stirling under his arm. 'Ted Haley will be with you though, 'e's a good 'and.' He glanced at the other three ratings with a practised eye. 'Cowley's the signalman, and Stoker Mechanic Nettle will be able to cope with the fishing boat's engine.' He darted him a quick glance. 'The other seaman is Lightfoot, sir. 'E volunteered.'

The intercom intoned. 'Stand by to surface! Bridge party close up!'

Colquhoun looked away. 'I don't want him, Jeffers! Get someone else!'

Jeffers shrugged. 'Too late now, sir. Anyway, 'e insisted like. 'E swapped over with another bloke for it!'

Colquhoun turned and made himself meet Lightfoot's gaze. The boy looked weighed down with cross-belt and ammunition, but he was smiling. He said emptily, 'Very well.' He

259

added, 'And thanks, Jeffers, for all you've done for me. For all you've tried to do.'

Jeffers shifted uncomfortably. 'You'll be okay, sir. You see! Anyway, you was right to take this job. You're always better after the second go!'

He stepped back as Wolfe pushed amongst the group, his eyes searching over the dinghy.

He snapped, 'All ready? Grenades and Stirlings?' He tightened his belt. 'Right then. No mistakes, just do as I tell you.' He let his gaze drop on Colquhoun and he added quietly, 'And no shooting. This has to be quiet, see?' Then he smiled. 'You can't live for ever, you know!'

A bell clanged, and Jermain peered through the open door. He was wearing an oilskin and his glasses were slung round his neck.

'I'm going to move in a bit so that you can paddle over. It'll be about five minutes.' He looked at Wolfe searchingly. 'Good luck, Number One.'

Wolfe yawned. 'Thanks.' As Jermain moved back towards the ladder he called gently, 'Give my love to Sarah, will you?'

Jermain stared at him and then climbed slowly up the ladder.

The waiting men stiffened as the admiral's stocky figure filled the doorway. Without pausing he said, 'Can I speak to you a minute?'

Colquhoun looked at Wolfe. The latter said, 'Two minutes. No more!'

The admiral was waiting beyond the heavy steel door, his face in shadows.

Colquhoun asked flatly, 'Well, what is it?' His father did not reply and he added bitterly, 'I suppose you asked that I should be sent on this boarding party? Kill or cure, is that it?'

The admiral said quietly, 'I didn't know about it, Max. I really didn't.' He seemed at a loss for words. 'I just wanted to wish you luck.'

Colquhoun took a grip on himself. 'You what? Are you serious? After all the things you've said about me!' He laughed shortly. 'I'd have thought you'd have been more afraid of my tarnishing the family's name!'

The intercom droned, 'Surfacing!' And the deck gave a sudden lurch.

The admiral stepped forward and gripped his hands. The words were tumbling out of his mouth as if he could no longer control them. 'I've been wrong, Max! I'm out of touch, I can see that now. I wanted it my way, but it was all for you, you must believe that!'

Colquhoun stared at him. His father seemed to be ageing before his eyes.

Wolfe called harshly, 'Come on, Sub! Jump about!'

He replied heavily, 'It's a bit late now.' Then he released his hands from his father's grip and stepped back to the hatch.

16

The Bait

Colquhoun gripped the sides of the dinghy and stared fixedly at the distant riding light. In spite of the steady thrust of paddles and the heavy breathing of the four ratings behind him, the dinghy's progress seemed maddeningly slow.

It had been merely minutes since the *Temeraire* had eased herself carefully to the surface and the main hatch had been flung open. Before the spray had finished cascading on their heads the handling party had heaved the small boat up and over the side of the hull, and urgent hands had pushed Colquhoun and the others after it.

Somehow they had paddled clear, and as they steadied on a course towards the anchored fishing boat the *Temeraire's* black shape had sidled beneath the water in a frothing welter of white spray.

Alone on the surface they had all felt suddenly unprotected and lost. It had been too quick, too violent for consideration. One minute they had been hemmed in by familiar faces, and the next instant the submarine had vanished, as if it had never been.

Wolfe wiped the spray from his face. 'Must be bloody deaf aboard that boat!'

Colquhoun did not reply. The splash and slice of each paddle sounded deafening. The slap of water against the rounded hull even louder. But aboard the fishing boat there was little sign of life, but for the swaying lantern and a thin column of smoke from her galley funnel which rose vertically across the darkening sky, like a stain on an old and faded painting.

Wolfe said, 'Right then. You know what to do. No shooting unless you have to.' His eyes gleamed in the darkness. 'Use your knives, anything, but make it quick!'

Colquhoun swallowed hard and tried to hold back the nausea. When he looked up the fishing boat was almost above him. It was no longer just a threat. It was real.

Leading Seaman Haley hurled his grapnel across the gunwale and pulled the line tight. Then with a few muffled gasps they were all up and on the deserted deck, their weapons ready and cocked.

Wolfe snapped, 'Nettle, take the wheelhouse and guard the radio. Cowley, guard the engine hatch aft!' He gestured at the others. 'Follow me!'

There was a curved hatchway just forward of the tiny wheelhouse, and as their feet thudded across the deck it was flung open and a shaft of lamplight glittered on the levelled weapons.

Wolfe barked, 'Stand still! We will shoot if we have to!' To Colquhoun he added sharply, 'Down you go with Haley. We'll cover you from here!'

Dumbly Colquhoun lowered himself down the steep ladder, his stomach retching uncontrollably. It was a small, box-like cabin, lined with crude bunks, and unbearably hot from a tall charcoal stove which glowed like a furnace. Four roughly dressed men stood in attitudes of fear and shock, and by the stove, a black pot poised in mid-air, was a plump, round-faced woman.

Colquhoun said, 'Does anyone speak English?'

Nobody answered, but as Colquhoun stared at their watching faces he was almost unnerved by a high-pitched wail from one of the bunks.

Haley said gruffly, 'Hell, it's a baby, sir. They look a pretty harmless bunch to me.'

Wolfe called down, 'Nobody's asking you! Just search them for weapons and make sure there's no other exit to this bloody pigsty!'

Haley slung his Stirling and said softly, '*I'll* do it, sir. You just keep a weather eye open.'

Colquhoun watched as the big seaman moved slowly and purposefully around the mesmerised fishermen. All the time he kept talking, empty, casual sentences, like a man with a fret-

263

ful horse. Not one of the men flinched or objected as Haley ran his hands over their rough smocks and quilted jackets, and even the baby fell silent as he lifted each piece of bedding and peered underneath.

'Pongs a bit,' he remarked. 'Still, I don't suppose they notice it.' He looked at the woman. 'I think you're all right, my love.' He grinned encouragingly. 'You just get on with the cooking and forget about us!'

There was a sudden stamp of feet as Wolfe threw himself down the ladder. He pushed Haley roughly aside and barked, 'What the hell is the matter with you?' He glared accusingly at Colquhoun. 'Can't you do *anything*?'

Haley said, 'They're only ordinary fishermen, sir.'

Wolfe eyed him bleakly. 'Did you never hear about the *ordinary* peasants in Viet Nam, Haley? Or in Malaysia, and all the other tin-pot places where they can manœuvre the sympathies of soft-hearted fools like you!' He pushed the woman away from the stove and jerked open her coat. 'She might have a bloody arsenal here for all you care!'

The tallest of the fishermen, obviously the skipper of the boat, began to speak excitedly in a high-pitched twittering tone. He pulled at Wolfe's arm and tried to haul him away from the woman.

Colquhoun's eye was not quick enough to see the blow. In a split second Wolfe had drawn the pistol from his belt and brought the barrel hard across the fisherman's temple. He fell without a further sound, his blood making red diamonds on the deck planking.

Wolfe holstered his gun and snapped, 'They're clean. We'll get back on deck and secure the hatch over this little lot.' He glanced casually at the unconscious fisherman and the woman who was trying to staunch the blood with her apron. 'Next time we'll have a little respect around here!'

Colquhoun reached the gunwale and leaned his hands on the worn woodwork. For several seconds he drew in deep breaths and allowed his taut body to relax. It was even worse than the last time. He could not forget the look on the woman's face, the dark hurt in her eyes as she had stared up at Wolfe. Why did he behave like that? What the hell was the point?

Wolfe's voice seemed to be right in his ear. 'Wake up, Sub,

there's still a lot to do before the Yank tries to surface.' His breathing sounded unsteady. 'We'll form into two watches. I'll take Nettle and Lightfoot. We'll keep anchored until daylight and then move off as arranged. We don't want to excite attention. We'll probably be in sight of land if it's a clear day tomorrow.'

'What about the rendezvous?' Colquhoun could feel the other man watching him. 'Will the captain be able to find us again?'

Wolfe replied coolly, 'You really are a windy character, Sub! Tell me, seriously, what does it feel like to be afraid? I can see from here what it *looks* like!'

Haley coughed discreetly. 'I've put Nettle as lookout, sir. And I've had the dinghy hoisted inboard.'

Wolfe grunted. 'Good. Now check the weapons and grenades. Then we'll open the rations and have a bite to eat.' He added to Colquhoun, 'Should be quite pleasant really. She's a seaworthy little craft!' Then he walked aft towards the wheelhouse.

Haley said quietly, 'All right, sir? Not too rough on you, was he?'

Colquhoun sighed. 'I just don't understand him. He changes like the weather.'

Haley frowned. 'No call for poking that bloke with his pistol. I think the woman was his wife. I'd act the same way if some bloody matelot dropped out of the sky and started pawing her about!'

Wolfe's voice echoed along the deck, 'Come on then! Stop chattering like a pack of old crows and search this boat. Any weapons can be dumped overboard.' He adjusted his belt. 'I'll be in the wheelhouse if you need me, Sub.'

They heard the wheelhouse door slam shut, and then Haley said, 'I'm a bit worried, sir. Suppose the *Temeraire* doesn't come back for us?' He added quickly, 'But what am I spouting about? The admiral will have something to say about that, eh? He'll not want his own son left to find his way home in *this* scow!'

Colquhoun turned his face away. 'That's a great comfort, Haley.'

The tall leading seaman tapped his pipe in his palm and

265

chuckled. 'Well, I'd better arrange the watches, sir. Must have things done navy-style!'

Cowley, a big, square-jawed stoker, came up rubbing his hands. 'She's got an old diesel engine, sir.' He stared dourly at the black water. 'Vintage nineteen 'undred, I should think. Still, it seems to go fair enough.'

Having searched the boat and found nothing more warlike than a rusty shotgun, the *Temeraire*'s boarding party settled down for the night. After a hasty sandwich and a cup of lukewarm tea from a leaking Thermos, Colquhoun made himself comfortable inside the submarine's dinghy abaft the wheelhouse. For a long while he lay staring at the unmoving clouds and listening to each strange and unexplained sound. He heard Nettle, the signalman, whistling softly, and from below decks the sound of a woman's voice. She was either crooning a strange song or sobbing. Colquhoun could not be sure. He kept seeing her face in his thoughts, and the look of fury on Wolfe's features as he had stormed below to search her.

He fell asleep, his head lolling in time to the boat's gentle roll.

Then he felt a hand shaking his arm and he sat bolt upright, his eyes trying to pierce the darkness. Lightfoot was bending over him. 'Time to get up, sir.' The boy sounded nervous. 'The first lieutenant's been yelling for you.'

Colquhoun threw his legs on to the deck and winced. 'For God's sake, what time is it?'

'Nearly one o'clock, sir.' He gestured towards the sea. 'Number One says it's time for the American to come up.'

Together they walked towards the bows. The others were already there, staring at the unbroken water, each apparently wrapped in thought.

Wolfe was hatless and leaning against the stumpy foremast. 'Ah, Sub! Slept well, I hope? Sorry I couldn't arrange tea and toast!' He laughed loudly. 'Well, it won't be long now!'

Haley asked cautiously, 'Do you reckon they'll make it, sir?'

'Not very likely.' Wolfe grinned in the darkness. 'You know what the Yanks are like! It's funny when you think of it. Us stuck up here, and the *Pyramus* somewhere down there. While our own boat is God knows where, getting the hell out of it!'

Colquhoun sensed the apprehension as it transmitted itself

266

amongst the other men, and said quietly, 'They'll be back for us, Number One.'

Wolfe sighed. 'Oh well, if you want to believe in fairy tales!'

There was a sullen rumble deep down in the water and a dull, metallic clatter. It was a feeling more than a sound, and the fishing boat seemed to quiver as if caught in a whirlpool.

Someone shouted, 'There she is! She's blowing to the top now!'

They all stood transfixed as the dark water changed into a beaten maelstrom of seething foam and bursting air bubbles. Then with a mighty roar the streaming bulk of the submarine lifted itself into view. This was no gentle or stealthy surfacing, this was a final desperate lunge to life and freedom. Even in the poor light they could see the jagged outline of the fin with its great gaping holes and shattered plates. Part of the casing was twisted like soft lead, and one of the diving planes looked as if it had been gnawed by some giant shark.

They heard the clang of hatches, and imagined the sick and gasping crew sucking in the air and listening to the sea's noises like men back from the grave. A generator kicked over, and the sour smell of diesel floated between the two craft.

Colquhoun took a deep breath and felt strangely moved. Then he asked, 'Shall we signal them, Number One?'

Wolfe had been staring at the submarine's dark outline as if he was too shocked to move. Colquhoun's question seemed to break the trance, and he answered thickly, 'Do what the hell you like!' Then he marched back towards the wheelhouse.

Haley looked after him and then muttered, 'We could go back home in the *Pyramus*, sir. It might be easier.'

Colquhoun shook his head. 'Our orders are to stay here until we're picked up. If some warships turn up here after all, we might still be able to call up help on the boat's radio.'

Cowley said, 'She's goin' ahead, sir! Look, she's under way again!'

Very slowly, like a wounded whale, the *Pyramus* nudged her bows into the lapping water, and as they strained their eyes to watch, her outline became more indistinct and merged with the night sky.

Haley insisted, 'I'm not questioning the orders, sir.' He seemed to make a decision. 'But I didn't join the Service just to die out here, in a place nobody's ever heard of!'

Colquhoun felt very tired. 'You must make your complaints to the first lieutenant. You should know that, Haley!'

'That's just it, sir.' Haley sounded desperate. 'With all due respect, I think the first lieutenant's past caring.'

'What the hell do you mean, Haley?'

The man stared down at the deck. 'When I went to get him from the wheelhouse just now he was halfway down a bottle of hooch, sir. In my opinion he's hitting it pretty hard!'

Colquhoun felt the fear moving through him like a cold wind. He stared quickly over the bulwark, but the damaged submarine had already vanished. It should have been a moment of triumph for all of them. They had found *Pyramus,* and with any luck, and *Temeraire* acting as bait, she should limp back to base and safety.

But all Colquhoun could feel was despair and the unfairness which had left him once more with impossible decisions to face. He thought of Haley's words and what they must have cost this disciplined seaman's pride to make. 'I didn't join the Service just to die out here!'

Just thinking about the words made him sick with apprehension. In daylight they would see the hostile coastline and the completeness of their own isolation.

He stammered some vague reply and walked quickly to the opposite side of the deck.

Cowley spat over the side. ' 'E'll be a lot of 'elp, I *must* say!'

'That's enough of that!' Haley's voice was sharp, if only to try and restore his own confidence. 'When the time comes he'll do well enough!'

The stoker laughed bitterly. 'Like 'e did for Archer? *That* I can live without, mate!'

Neither of them saw Lightfoot move away to stand silently beside Colquhoun. Not even Colquhoun noticed him or saw the misery on his face, as like the others he stared at the empty sea.

* * *

'Down periscope! Dive to two hundred feet!'

Jermain stepped back, rubbing his eyes as the men around

him relaxed and waited for fresh orders.

Drew's face split into a broad grin. 'I take it that our side has successfully captured the fishing boat?'

'Yes.' Jermain moved his shoulders to ease away the stiffness. 'It's up to us now.'

He stared thoughtfully at the chart and said, 'Alter course to one three zero. That should bring us into contact with the enemy so that we can draw them away from the *Pyramus*.'

'You still believe that she'll make it to the surface, sir?' Mayo looked up from his calculations.

'I'm sure of it.' Jermain was still thinking about the probing search party with which he intended to make contact. He had openly referred to them as the *enemy*. So, in spite of everything, he was already dropping into the part he had been trained for. He added quickly, 'When you've got as far as Commander Hurtzig and his crew towards the edge of the grave, you don't allow a few more risks to get in your way.'

Twine called, 'Steady on one three zero, Captain. Depth two hundred feet.'

'Very good. You can fall out from action stations. Get the men fed as soon as possible. Whatever they have to face now will be better if they've a full belly per man!' Jermain saw some of the men grinning. Just simple, meaningless words, yet they hung to them like liferafts.

A few minutes later Lieutenant Oxley emerged from his cramped compartment stretching and yawning hugely.

Jermain said, 'Although you should be taking over from Number One, I want you to continue with the sonar. Right now you're just about the most vital member of the crew.'

Oxley spread his hands. 'I never doubted it, sir.'

'Your conceit does you credit!' Jermain felt better in spite of his nagging worries. Oxley's casual acceptance of everything was like a tonic.

'I hope Number One is managing all right, sir.' Oxley looked dubious. 'Not a very comfortable job for anyone.'

'I know.' Jermain turned it over again in his mind. He kept thinking of Sarah's words, of his own attitude towards Wolfe. Maybe he had allowed himself to become biased after all. It should be enough to take a man at face value without becoming personally involved.

He said abruptly, 'I'm going to see the admiral. I suggest you have a quick meal.'

Oxley looked at Mayo. 'Shall we dine, Pilot? Nothing like a few overripe kippers to strengthen the soul!'

Mayo groaned. 'Not Spithead Pheasants again surely. Does Luard get everything out of tins for God's sake?'

Jermain found the admiral standing alone in the wardroom staring at the picture of the *Fighting Temeraire*. He said slowly, 'We've altered course, sir. All being well we can draw the A/S boats off without too much danger.'

When Sir John Colquhoun turned Jermain was shocked to see the change which had come over him. He looked shrunken, a mere caricature of the brisk, confident man who had stepped aboard.

The admiral nodded. 'I see. Well, I suppose we can only wait now.'

Jermain waited for the outburst, or some fresh criticism. When nothing happened he added, 'The first lieutenant will be able to keep an eye on the *Pyramus* when she surfaces, sir. Then if other hostile craft show up in spite of our own efforts he can flash a signal for air cover. It might be of little use, but it is a last resort.'

'You've known Wolfe a long time.' The admiral seemed unsure, and it showed in the restlessness of his pale eyes. 'I— I hope he keeps his head.'

'He's been in a lot of domestic trouble, sir. But then you know all about that. But when the chips are down he has always been a very level-headed officer.'

'Yes. I see.' The admiral toyed with the buttons of his jacket. 'I hope he's not worried about this promotion business.'

Jermain shook his head. 'We must just think of this one job now, sir.' He stopped as the chill of realisation crept over him. 'You didn't say anything to him about it, did you, sir?'

The admiral looked away and made a quick, angry gesture with his hand. 'Not exactly! Naturally when he asked me point-blank I had to say something.' He met Jermain's steady eyes with a flash of his old vigour. 'Yes, I *may* have mentioned something of the sort!'

Jermain eyed him coldly. 'Look, sir, I must know. There are men aboard that fishing boat who are relying on his judgement. It may even go further than that.'

'Do you think I don't know that, Jermain?' His face was lined with anxiety. 'My son is back there too, remember that! And you sent him, Jermain! *You* sent him!'

A steward entered the wardroom, faltered at the sound of the raised voices and hurriedly withdrew.

'Yes, I did, sir. Because he is a good officer in many ways. But he has to regain his confidence.' His tone hardened. 'You were his age when you first went into submarines. You must have known this could happen.'

'It was different then.' The admiral moved round the wardroom, his steps slow and unsteady. 'There was a war on. They were a different sort of men then.'

Jermain pushed the pity to the back of his mind. 'I expect your senior officers said that about you, sir. But men don't change. Only the situations and the methods become more complex!'

He wanted to get away, to find the privacy of his cabin for just a few moments. He had to think, to drag upon his inner resources to combat this new danger. But was he really worried about what Wolfe might do? Or was he just concerned because the admiral had revealed what he should have told Wolfe himself?

He said flatly, 'We shall just have to hope for the best, sir.' He made to leave the wardroom but the admiral blocked his path.

'I spoke to my son. He treated me like a stranger!' There was stark misery in his eyes.

'Perhaps he had his own reasons.' Jermain checked the condemnation which nearly slipped from his mouth.

The admiral stared at him wildly and then shouted, 'What the *hell* do you know about it? You don't understand a thing about tradition and continuity! You're like all the rest of the new breed of naval officer! It's just a job to you!'

Jermain replied quietly, 'That's not true. I happen to believe that we can no longer abide by the old standards. It's not only a question of nationality and insular pride. Surely these last few weeks would convince anyone of that fact?' He added calmly, 'I know that I do not have your experience, but it doesn't alter my sense of duty, sir.'

The admiral did not seem to have heard him. He muttered vaguely, 'It was all different before. Then there was a code, even an understanding between enemies. You fought by the rules. It all had some *meaning*!'

Jermain turned to leave. 'It still has meaning, sir. But it isn't just a game. There's too much at stake to lose this fight.'

He walked quickly to his cabin and sat down heavily on the bunk. For several minutes he stared emptily at the opposite bulkhead, his mind awhirl with words and meaningless thoughts.

He tried to picture Wolfe aboard the captured boat, and wondered if his sense of purpose and possible danger had changed him towards young Colquhoun. He remembered too the expression on Wolfe's face as the submarine had made ready to surface. 'Give my love to Sarah.' It had been like a taunt. Like an insult.

Jermain found himself on his feet, his fists clenched at his sides. What was the point of worrying about it now? He could no longer afford the luxury of doubt. He had made the decisions. It was up to him how he played the next move.

The intercom barked, 'Captain in the control room!'

He snatched his unlit pipe from the desk and ran swiftly along the passageway. As he approached the oval door he slowed his pace, and by the time he reached the familiar compartment his face was again calm, his voice steady and even, as he forced himself back into his set role.

Drew said, 'Faint H.E. on green three zero, sir. Fourteen thousand yards. Confused but regular. Must be the fishing fleet.' He sounded breathless, as if he had been running.

Jermain looked at the plot and said quietly, 'Action stations. Bring her up to sixty feet and reduce speed to ten knots.'

Drew swallowed hard. 'That's a bit slow for manœuvring, sir.'

Jermain made his voice patient. 'We have to act out the whole part. They must think that we are crippled, otherwise they'll soon guess there's another submarine in their pond!'

The alarm screamed through the hull, and Drew dragged his eyes from the scampering seamen. 'Fourteen thousand yards. That's one hell of a range, sir. Maybe their sonar won't reach us yet!'

Mayo called, 'Boat at Action Stations, sir!'

He looked jumpy and Jermain said quickly, 'How were the kippers, Pilot? Up to your expectations?'

Mayo looked blank and then grinned. 'Not like Mother used to give me!'

Jermain relaxed slightly. This was the time. The waiting game. If there was open battle, or even a known danger, he could rely on all of them. But right now each man was as brittle as glass.

'Sixty feet, sir.'

He waited until the periscope had hissed from its well and then peered quickly through the lens. Just a few stars between the low clouds. It was very still, and strangely menacing.

'Down periscope.' He walked back to the plot table where a petty officer was staring fixedly at the winking lights. An empty cup stood on the table, and a small dog manufactured from pipe cleaners. Normal, familiar objects left by the watch-keepers.

He glanced across at Drew. It was strange not to see Wolfe's erect figure behind the helmsman. But then nothing was the same any more.

'H.E. closing, sir. Range twelve thousand yards.' Oxley's voice sounded tense.

The admiral entered the control room but seemed unable to find anywhere to stand. Jermain watched him with sudden compassion. He must feel like a piece of extra cargo, he thought briefly. He had allowed his guard to drop in front of Jermain, and was no doubt still brooding about it.

A messenger dropped a torch on the deck plates and Jeffers snarled, 'For Chrissake watch what yer doin', you useless bastard!'

'Range eleven thousand yards, sir.'

Twine stared at the ticking gyro and moved his wheel very slightly. Through his teeth he muttered, 'Can't hear anything yet!'

Jeffers replied with a tight grin, 'You wait, Swain. It'll be like Piccadilly in the rush hour in a minute or two!'

Mayo whispered, 'Maybe they've called it off, sir?'

Oxley's voice came once more. 'Faint sonar transmissions on

same bearing, sir!' A pause. 'Range ten thousand yards. Bearing moving to green three five.'

Mayo opened his mouth to speak but stopped with his jaw hanging down as the sound suddenly penetrated the stillness.

It was very faint, but regular, a stealthy, gentle tapping along the hull.

Jermain made himself stare down at the plot table, but his ears strained towards the threatening sound. He was reminded of his childhood and reading *Treasure Island* for the first time. Of old Blind Pew's stick tapping up the dark street towards the inn and the frightened boy inside.

The petty officer adjusted his headphones and shifted in his seat. 'Bloody hell!'

Jermain glanced at him. 'Worried, P.O.?'

The man grimaced. 'Just the thought of all them torpedoes up in the bow, sir. We could blow this lot of rubbish to kingdom come and hardly notice the difference!'

Jermain smiled. 'I know how you feel. But we have to let them think they're the hunters. Otherwise we'll bring the whole fleet down on our ears!'

The petty officer grinned ruefully. 'Next time I go to the dogs back home I'll be rooting for the poor bloody hare, sir!'

'Nine thousand yards, sir.' Oxley seemed entirely absorbed. 'Mixed transmissions from green two five to green six zero.'

The plot table began to vibrate as the information was fed into it. Mayo said, 'It's a pattern, sir. It looks like the same little group as before.'

The tapping along the hull was louder now, and without a break. It preyed on the eardrums and seemed to blot out everything else. Yet still the unseen hunters retained their course and speed, as if the *Temeraire* was merely part of the imagination.

Drew looked over his shoulder anxiously. 'They're going to pass us, sir. Maybe they're not fooled after all!'

Jermain did not answer him. He was waiting for the next move.

It was almost a relief when Oxley called, 'Ships have altered course, sir! Bearings coming in now!'

The lights on the plot winked malevolently as the approaching ships swung lightly towards the *Temeraire*'s line of approach. They were still in perfect formation, the three lead-ing vessels about six miles apart.

Mayo breathed, 'Come into my parlour . . .'

'H.E. is speeding up, sir! Range closing! All vessels have increased revolutions!'

Jermain wiped his forehead. The game had started. 'Alter course. Steer one zero zero.'

Mayo cocked his head. 'I can hear 'em now!'

Heads tilted. Eyes stared at the curved steel overhead. '*Schoo . . . schoo . . . schoo . . .*' Like the beat of powerful loco-motives. It mingled with the tapping, driving down into the hull, remorseless and without pity for the listening men.

A signalman clasped his hands across his ears, his mouth quivering with fear. The messenger who had earlier incurred Jeffers' anger began to polish the torch on his trousers as if it was the most important thing in the whole world.

'Increase to fifteen knots. Alter course to zero nine zero.' Jermain watched the gyro and then snapped, 'What is the esti-mated range of the nearest ship?'

Mayo said, 'Six thousand yards, sir. That's the centre ship at bearing green nine zero.'

'Well, keep me informed. I'm not a mind reader!' Jermain peered at the table. The three ships had retained their pattern, but were swinging outwards from the central craft like the arms of a trap. *Temeraire's* sudden alteration of course had brought their well-rehearsed drill into full swing, like troops on a parade ground.

'Estimated speed is twenty knots, sir. Still closing.'

Jermain bit his lower lip. 'Increase to eighteen knots. Alter course to zero eight zero!'

Oxley reported, 'All ships are reducing speed, sir!'

Jermain gestured towards the plot. 'Keep checking. I think they're settling down to follow us in comfort.'

Mayo said, 'They'll wait for us to turn south away from the side of the deep channel, sir. Or they can just let us run into the shallows.'

'Faint H.E. bearing red one one zero, sir. Range twelve thousand yards!'

Jermain rubbed his chin. 'That follows. They must have had another single patrol to the north. Just in case.' He listened to

275

the steady flow of bearings and watched the pattern closing in around him, three ships blocking the southern escape route, and a fourth content to tag along on a parallel course to north-west.

Drew scratched his hair noisily. 'All roads lead to Rome! God, I'm as dry as a boot!'

Jermain stared at the clock. The *Pyramus* must be under way by now. Every minute was vital for her safety. 'Right, we'll dive to two hundred feet. That'll give them something to think about. They'll have to use their sonar buoys again, so their speed will be reduced for a while.'

The needles crept round obediently, and Oxley called, 'Still in contact, sir. Slight reduction of revolutions!'

Then Oxley said, 'Ship at red one one zero has increased speed, sir! Range now nine thousand yards!'

Jermain nodded. 'This is it. He's going to make a run over us if he can while the others keep us plotted.'

Mayo sounded hoarse. 'Can't we run deep, sir?'

He shook his head. 'It's too early, Pilot. They'd guess immediately that we are only shamming.'

They all fell silent as the fourth ship's propellers cut through the other sounds. '*Schoo . . . schoo . . . schoo . . .*' Louder and nearer with each steady beat.

'Range now seven thousand yards, sir!'

Jermain did not reply. From the corner of his eye he saw the admiral running a finger around his collar and staring at the deckhead. Of all the people aboard he knows what to expect, Jermain thought coldly. He must be living again all the horrors, all the nerve-stretching agonies of that other war. But this time he was older, and was powerless to retaliate.

'Watch the range, Pilot.' He saw Mayo's eyes gleam in the reflected lights. 'Let this one close to four thousand yards and then increase speed to give us a slight lead on her. We must hang it out as long as possible.'

Mayo grimaced. 'We've only got another three-quarters of an hour, sir. Then we'll have to lift over the edge of the Valley.' He paused. 'Or turn and face this little lot.'

Jermain made himself walk the full length of the control room and back to ease the tension in his limbs. It was like some terrible dream. The powerful little ships above, goading and

276

herding the submarine across the channel like dogs and a wounded bear. Except that *Temeraire* was the wrong target for their efforts. He could well imagine what would have happened once these same craft had found the *Pyramus*. She would have been hunted and finally bracketed by depth-charges. Her captain would have had the choice of being pounded to fragments or surfacing to face surrender and worse. Jermain had little doubt which decision Hurtzig would have taken.

The admiral joined him beside the plot table, his face white in the lamplight. Jermain asked, 'Are you feeling all right, sir?'

'I was just thinking back. All this seems like yesterday, Jermain.' He waved a limp hand. 'Except that we used to have little more than our wits to combat the enemy!' He shuddered slightly. 'I used to hate the depth-charging. We all did. My little S-boat used to operate off the Danish coast and through into the Baltic. Shallow water, and not too much of that either. I had a good first hand at the time. Young chap like Oxley, a real tower of strength. I remember when we were being hunted for a full day after tin-fishing a freighter off Flensburg, he said that it was like being chased by a blind maniac in a pitch-dark room. You never knew what or where he was going to strike next.' He stared at the impassive dials. 'Even now it seems much the same. All this complex gear, and it still comes down to the man in command. Matching his brains against those of the fellow above.'

Jermain frowned. The admiral seemed incapable of remaining silent. He appeared unwilling to face the endless waiting alone.

Jermain said gently, 'I shall be looking to you later on, sir. My experience has all been learned in the training grounds. I'm not much of a judge when it comes down to the time to duck and run.'

The admiral shook his head. 'Not me, Jermain. I feel as old as the sea. It's a new feeling for me.' He looked round startled as Mayo said, 'Range coming down to four thousand, sir.'

Then Jermain ordered, 'Increase to twenty knots.'

Drew swayed about in his seat like an organist as he adjusted his controls and checked the gauges. Then he remarked harshly, 'Much more of this caper and the bastard'll be able to drop rocks on us!'

Jermain walked into the chart-room and picked up the tannoy handset. 'This is the captain speaking. So far we've made a very good job of drawing the hunt away from the *Pyramus*. In a short while now we shall make a sharp turn and head back to the centre of the channel.' He tried not to think of the last time he had used this method of address. Of his men listening to the trapped and desperate Americans. And of the admiral's cold eagerness to fire the torpedoes. He continued quietly, 'There will almost certainly be some sort of depth-charging, but the Black Pig is built for this kind of game, and I have no doubt that she is as eager as we are to get back home, to England.'

He replaced the handset and stood listening to the silence. No cheers, not even a too-bright comment to break the tension.

Mayo said, 'They're closing in for the kill, sir. They've probably signalled for reinforcements to cover the shallows towards the coast by now.'

Jermain nodded. 'Most likely. The more the merrier. It will leave *Pyramus* a nice clear run.'

Mayo pulled at his beard. 'Suppose the American was too far gone to surface, sir? All this danger will be for nothing!' He looked around the compartment. 'It could mean two boats sunk instead of just one!'

Jermain retained a smile on his lips for the benefit of the men watching his face, but his reply was like ice. 'I don't expect to hear that sort of thing from you, Pilot. Just keep those thoughts to yourself.'

He stared hard at the clock and then at the plot table, and the small, glittering lights which represented the eager hunters above. He could wait no longer. The *Temeraire* had been built to withstand a great deal of punishment, but his men were untried. The human mind could take just so much.

He thrust one hand into his pocket and gripped the familiar shape of his pipe. 'Very well, Pilot. Stand by to go about.' He nodded to a watching petty officer who barked into the intercom, 'Shut off for depth-charging! Damage-control parties stand by!'

One last look round. There was no further chance. It had to be right.

Then he said, 'Hard a-starboard! Steer one seven zero!'

The deck tilted steeply as the hull swam round obediently like a whale.

'Take her down to three hundred feet!' Throughout the hull he could feel the thud of watertight doors, the metallic click of hatches. This was the worst part. When men were shut off from their companions and friends. When the world was confined to the walls of a steel cell and the remorseless tap of the enemy's transmissions.

'Ship closing to starboard, sir! Green four five!' The propellers thrashed nearer and nearer, drowning every other sound with their awful symphony.

Jermain looked at the deckhead. 'Hard a-port! Steer one one zero!'

He tried to picture the depth-charges. Three hundred feet at fifty feet a second.

The waiting was over. The time was now.

17

'I Am Not God!'

The two depth-charges, fired from deck mortars, exploded beneath and well ahead of the submerged *Temeraire*. Their twin detonations came as one loud crack which lifted the submarine's bows like a tidal wave and smashed against the toughened steel with a nerve-shattering roar.

Lieutenant Oxley clung to the arms of his seat and held his breath as the sonar compartment tilted sideways and seemed to fall away beneath him. Signal pads and loose fittings slithered from shelves and tables, and from the deckhead the paint chippings floated down like confetti on to the heads of the crouching men around him. He felt the seat pressing into his buttocks as the boat heaved upwards against the enormous pressure of water, and then as his mind grappled to retain control of his shocked senses it slipped away again in a further sickening sweep.

He vaguely remembered the harsh warning across the intercom and his own quick order to his companions. 'Open your mouths wide!' It was said to help withstand these underwater shocks, yet even at the realisation of what was about to happen he found himself considering the futility of his words.

Petty Officer Irons pulled himself upright in his seat and groped for his controls. Aloud he muttered, 'Jesus, I *felt* that!'

Oxley stared down at the bright droplets of blood on his lap and realised with sudden anger that his nose was bleeding. As he felt for his handkerchief he heard the captain's voice over the intercom. 'Starboard fifteen. Steer one nine zero.' Then in the same calm tone, 'Not too close that time.'

There was a sudden jangle of chains from above and Jermain

added sharply, 'Keep silent in the torpedo space! They can hear that row up top!'

Oxley let his eyes move to the deck above. The whole forward space over the sonar compartment was given to the two torpedo sections. Right in the bows, behind the six torpedo tubes, was the loading bay and tube space. Astern of that, long and barren like a garage, was the stowage compartment where racks of spare torpedoes lined the sides of the hull in shining readiness. Now, as the submarine manœuvred hastily to avoid a further attack, the two sections were separated by a closed bulkhead door, connected only by phone and the chattering intercom.

Irons glanced at Oxley. 'I'll bet P.O. Mason is havin' a time up there, sir!'

Oxley twisted his mouth in a smile as he watched the flickering dials on the control panel. Mason was the petty officer in charge of torpedoes. It was a complicated task at the best of times. Now, under sudden attack, and with Lieutenant Trott as his immediate superior instead of the unflappable Drew, he must be suffering, Oxley thought.

One of the operators called, 'H.E. closing from red nine zero, sir!' He craned his head forward intently. 'Bearing steady!'

Oxley watched the information being fed back to the plot in the control room and found time to marvel at the speed with which the attacking ship had gone about. Like a maddened dog after a rabbit, he thought angrily.

He jerked himself out of his brooding thoughts and looked quickly around his men. Their faces were moist with sweat, their movements jerky and only half under control. He barked, 'Stand by for the next attack, lads! Just stay in your positions, no matter what happens! I want to know exactly what everyone is doing!'

Again without warning the depth-charges exploded on either side of the hull. This time the sound was even louder, and the men gasped with pain or rolled drunkenly in their seats. The lights flickered and died, but as the gasps changed to cries of fear they came on again, their bulbs dulled by the splintered paintwork and the humid breaths in the sealed compartment.

The hoisting chains clanged once more through the deck

plating and Oxley heard the quick stampede of feet as the torpedomen ran to quell the noise.

Oxley placed his hands palms downwards on his knees and stared at them with fixed attention. He felt strained and physically sick, and he knew he had to draw on resources as yet unknown to control the shaking in his limbs. His own men were near breaking point. He knew each one of them well enough to realise what this strain was doing to them.

Another pair of explosions rocked the hull sideways and threw two of the men into a yelling heap against the unyielding steel. Oxley could feel the boat sliding away in a downward sweep, and as his eyes sought the depth gauge he saw that the submarine had already dived to four hundred feet. He stared at the needle, mesmerised. In his reeling thoughts he could picture the hull spiralling through the dark water like a falling leaf, out of control, already lost.

Jermain's voice penetrated his shocked mind, as if from another world. 'Hold her at four hundred. Steer one seven zero!' Then, 'Report damage!'

Through the intercom Oxley could hear the squeak of telephones and the murmured replies from the control room. Jermain said, 'Not bad at all, Pilot. Just a few more minutes and we'll be through the worst.'

Then a strange voice came across the intercom, and Oxley had to force his mind to clear completely before he realised that it was Lieutenant Trott, the new officer.

'Captain, sir? If possible I would like permission to open up the rear door to the stowage space.' He sounded nervous but tightly determined. Oxley could hear the petty officer's gruff voice muttering in the background but could not make out what he was saying.

Jermain's voice was sharp. 'You know the orders, Trott. We are still under attack, you know!'

Trott tried again. 'Number Three tube has sprung a leak in the bow door, sir. It must have been after the last attack. There is a definite seepage.'

Jermain's voice was calmer, as if he was using his last reserve of patience to still Trott's worries. 'Just keep the breech closed. We can write off Number Three until we get back to base!'

Oxley gritted his teeth. Jermain must be run off his feet without Trott bleating his stupid head off!

Trott said weakly, 'The breech is open, sir. I discovered the seepage when I was checking for damage. I ordered the men to withdraw the torpedo ready for unloading, but I must have the rear door opened!'

He sounded almost frantic, and for the first time Oxley realised the seriousness of his broken words. Each torpedo was too long to be unloaded without first opening up the two complete sections. Trott had half withdrawn this one, but the bulkhead door prevented its moving any further.

Jermain said, 'Repeat, please! Did you say you've withdrawn the torpedo?'

Trott replied, 'Yes, sir. And it's jammed! I can't get it back.'

Petty Officer Mason's voice took over the intercom. 'It's me, sir, the T.I.' He sounded anxious. 'It's jammed like he says. The tube seepage is exerting some pressure in the bow. The pumps are coping with it for now, but we have to get the breech shut somehow!'

Trott yelled, 'Get away from there, Mason! It's my decision! You stay out of it!'

Irons looked at Oxley and grimaced. 'Christ! He's getting in a panic!'

'Keep trying to replace that torpedo, Trott.' Jermain sounded too calm, Oxley thought. 'There is another ship closing from starboard. You must get that tube sealed! I can't afford to open the whole space. If it flooded the boat would dive for good!' His voice hardened. 'Now take it one step at a time!'

A sonar operator snapped, 'Ship closing fast from green one one zero! Bearing steady!'

Oxley breathed out slowly. 'God, we're right amongst them!'

Vaguely he heard Jermain order another increase of speed. The *Temeraire* was now logging about twenty-five knots! That would give the bastards up there something to ponder over! Just a while longer and the deception could be finished. *Temeraire* would dive deep, and the attackers could think what they liked. They could either carry on with a fruitless search, or claim the boat sunk with all hands! He found that he was smiling openly, like an idiot.

Irons stared up at him. 'Sir, I've just realised something. We can't dive deep! Not with that tube unsealed!'

Even as their eyes met, the thrashing screws of the attacking ship sluiced over the deckhead. It was more muffled by the distance, but none the less deadly.

The charges exploded together near the port beam, so that Oxley felt the pain in his lungs as if he had received the blow himself. The lights faded away, and the men cried out in terror as lamps and gauges shattered overhead and showered them with fragments of glass.

Obediently the emergency lighting came into force, and Oxley stared aghast at the littered compartment, the shocked and bleeding men around him. He gazed blankly at the buckled depth gauge and realised that the boat was porpoising towards the surface. He could feel himself falling backwards in his seat, could sense the sudden change of pressure on his breathing.

Irons croaked, 'Two ships closing fast, sir! Bearing red four five!'

Oxley closed his eyes for a few seconds to search for his inner control. A double attack, with the submarine already shooting towards the surface. It was nearly over. They were finished.

Then he heard Jermain again, level and precise above the roar of the approaching ships. 'Emergency dive! Take her down to eight hundred feet! Steer one six zero!'

The depth gauge quivered uncertainly and then began to move slowly forwards. Oxley stared at the needle, willing it to move faster. Praying that Jermain would be in time.

The roar of depth-charges rolled around the hull and shook the compartment with murderous contempt. More lights shattered, and in the semi-darkness the men clung to any fixed object to stop themselves from being hurled against the treacherous steel.

From far away someone reported, 'Diving correctly, sir! Seven hundred feet!'

Oxley swung round and stared at the intercom speaker as Trott's voice cut through the other sounds and reached out to every quarter of the hull.

'Sir! I can't close the tube! The water's pouring in! *For God's sake, stop the dive!*'

From the control room Jermain sounded empty of emotion. 'How bad is it?'

'It—it's pouring in!' Trott was gabbling, the words mixed up and confused in sudden terror. In the background Oxley could hear the mounting hiss of pressurised water as it ripped past the torpedo and scythed into the small space beyond. He pressed his hand to his forehead and brushed the clammy sweat from his eyes. Once past this depth the water would force into the circular space at the rate of one hundred thousand pounds per minute!

As if in a dream he heard Jermain say, 'Watch the trim!' Just three words, but Oxley knew he was telling the men at the diving controls to make allowance for the tube space filling with water. It was a matter of slide-rule precision. Cold and without feeling. Trott and his six men were already written off, like so much extra ballast in the bows!

Oxley made himself look at the depth gauge. Already the planesman was levelling out towards eight hundred feet. He felt suddenly and uncontrollably sick.

A young sonarman stared at a voice-pipe and croaked, 'Sir! He's calling you!'

Even from his seat behind the panel Oxley could hear Trott sobbing and pleading through the emergency voice-pipe which connected him with the sonar compartment.

Then over the intercom he heard Mason's voice again. Devoid of emotion, it sounded calm and quite controlled. 'Now then, lads! Stand fast! You know we can't get the door open!'

Oxley looked away. Dear God! He could picture Mason with his back to the oval door which led aft, away from the spurting water. Mason, the ordinary, run-of-the-mill petty officer who was now calming his handful of men to stand still and wait for death without panic.

Oxley remembered with sudden clarity that Mason had been the witness to the argument between Colquhoun and the first lieutenant. He recalled too how embarrassed he had been when his small son had been christened in the depot ship's bell back in the Gareloch. He had made an awkward, clumsy speech, after which he had been happy to sink back into the obscurity of his companions.

The sonarman beside the pipe clasped his hands together and said, 'My Christ! *Look!*'

Oxley stared at the water which already seeped through the open voice-pipe, gathering force and power with each dragging second.

In a harsh, strangled tone which he did not recognise he said, 'Close the vent! Shut it, man!'

Irons pushed the man aside and clamped the tube with one savage movement.

For a long moment they all stared at the voice-pipe and listened to a strange hollow clanging overhead. With no hands to still them, the hoisting chains swung gratingly against the projecting torpedo, the sound carrying through the trapped water like the tolling of a funeral bell.

Far away, booming and dull like distant thunder, the baffled depth-charges kept up their steady accompaniment. But throughout the *Temeraire* there was complete silence, but for the steady clanging condemnation from the torpedo space.

*   *   *

'Eight hundred feet, sir.' Petty Officer Jeffers managed to keep his voice calm, but his eyes stayed fixed on the hydroplane telltales, and the knuckles of his hands shone white above his brass wheel.

Jermain took a pace away from the plot table and then stared down at his feet. His shoes crunched on a thick layer of broken glass and metallic dust, and he realised dully that he had hardly moved throughout the whole nerve-racking attack.

Drew cleared his throat and reported, 'I've compensated for the extra weight forrard, sir.' He faltered then continued, 'I think we should retain these revolutions for the moment to give better control.'

Then he turned his head, and Jermain saw the naked misery in his eyes.

'It was my fault, sir!' He could not hold it back any longer. 'I should have told Trott what to expect!'

'You can't allow for everything.' Jermain felt empty and drained. 'He should have known.'

A telephone buzzed and Mayo stood with the handset cradled against his jacket. 'It's the chief, sir.' He watched Jermain's face with a mixture of anxiety and pity. 'He wants a word with you.'

Jermain took the receiver and tried not to listen to the hollow echo from the chains. 'Yes, Chief?'

'That last pattern, sir.' Ross was crisp and normal. 'I think it must have damaged the screw. Nothing vital, but when I went aft I did notice a new sound.' He seemed to be considering the matter. 'It's either a chip out of one of the blades, or maybe one of them is buckled. It will add quite considerably to the noise factor. If you intend to maintain speed I would suggest you run deeper for a while. That is, until the chase is well clear.'

Jermain found that he was weighing each word, dragging every syllable across his aching mind for painful examination. It was difficult to think any more.

He answered slowly, 'Any more trouble with that seepage, Chief?'

Ross said reluctantly, 'No, sir. Nothing to write home about now.'

Jermain bit his lip and stared fixedly at Drew's bent shoulders. How typical, he thought. The one thing which had nagged him since coming out here, yet it had been the unforeseen which had struck without warning. Maybe the bow door on the torpedo tube had been faulty all the time, an overlooked detail from the hasty trials. Now they might never know.

Ross continued quietly, 'I'm sorry about Trott and the others. No one should have to make the decision you did.'

'Keep checking on the screw, Chief.' Jermain dropped the handset and stared emptily at the depth gauges.

The *Temeraire* had pulled it off. By now the American boat would be well clear of the Valley and on her way to safety. He tried to hold on to that fact and ease the pain of the cost to the back of his mind.

The *Temeraire* had suffered with her crew, but her faults could be rectified.

Mayo said, 'Shall we run deep, sir?'

Jermain turned on him. 'Yes, we'll dive to nine hundred feet until we're clear of the area. Then we'll go up to periscope depth and start the high-power pumps in the tube space. We have a damaged screw, and the sound will attract attention unless we are very careful.'

Mayo continued, 'At periscope depth we'll be more vulnerable, sir.'

'God, I know that, Pilot!' His voice seemed to affect Mayo like a blow. 'But I want the tube space pumped dry and inspected for damage, do you understand? If we are challenged again I intend to have something with which to hit back!'

He swung on his heel and looked at the admiral. 'With your permission, sir, I would like to discuss the next phase of this operation.'

The admiral followed him into the chart-room without a word. Once inside Jermain slid the door into place and then said, 'I have carried out the text of my orders, sir. But the damaged screw makes any sort of silent approach extremely difficult.' He made himself speak in a clipped, almost matter-of-fact tone, and he saw the look of stunned disbelief in the admiral's pale eyes.

The latter said thickly, 'What do you want me to say, Jermain? You've had it your way, and it can be said that the whole operation was a success.' He looked away. 'Your decision to dive the boat was the right one. If you had been in the tube space at the time you would have expected nothing different!'

Jermain clenched his fists. Don't say any more, for God's sake! One more piece of consolation, one further word of alleged understanding and *I will break*!

Coldly he answered, 'You are in charge of the operation, sir. You must decide if you think the *Temeraire* should make straight back to base.'

The admiral gasped. 'But the fishing boat, Jermain! My son and the others are still back there!'

Jermain's voice was relentless. 'The decision is the same as mine, sir. Are you prepared to risk the safety of this boat for the sake of a few more men? If it was not your son back there, would you still want to risk disaster?'

'That is unfair!' The admiral began to pace back and forth,

288

his arms swinging in time with his words. 'What are you asking me to do?'

'I am in command of the *Temeraire*, sir. I am not God! The area will be alive with ships by now, and the noise of the damaged screw might well attract attention. I can't even fight back until I've pumped out the tube space.' He leaned against the chart table and felt the weariness spreading through him like a drug.

The admiral replied quietly, 'You once implied that I was old fashioned in my thinking, Jermain. Perhaps you were right.' He looked up, his eyes suddenly bright. 'You stuck out to save the *Pyramus* because they were depending on you. On your faith in your men and in your own judgement. I can see now that their faith was well-founded!'

Jermain dropped his eyes. 'You are telling me to go back, is that it?'

'No, I am not, Jermain. I am telling you that this is still a decision which only you can make. *Must* make!' He shook his head sadly. 'Don't worry, I will promise you my support either way. This time there will be no recriminations from me!'

'Thank you, sir.' Jermain saw the admiral's hands trembling. 'In that case I would like to return for the others immediately.'

The admiral thrust his hands beneath his jacket and nodded firmly. 'I pray that it is what I would have done in your position.' He sat down heavily on the chart locker and stared fixedly at the deck. Then with something of his former strength he barked, 'Now just leave me alone for a few moments, will you!'

Jermain glanced at the chart and then opened the door. In a firm voice he said, 'Bring her round to two eight zero. Fall out Action Stations!'

Behind him he heard the admiral whisper, 'Thank God! *Thank God!*'

Griffin appeared in the control room as the men on watch were relieved. He looked around at the litter of shattered gauges and splintered paint, and then said evenly, 'I'll be standing by when you need me, sir.' He gestured forward. 'We'll take the bodies below once we've got them out.'

Jermain faced him savagely, his nerves screaming. What the

hell did Griffin think they were? So much dead meat to be hidden away for later disposal?

Then he saw the deep concern on the young doctor's face, and all he could bring himself to say was, 'Take care of them, will you?'

Without another word he walked quickly to his cabin and shut the door behind him.

*   *   *

'Time to get up, sir. The sky's getting brighter already.' Leading Seaman Haley placed a metal mug on the deck and rubbed his hands noisily. 'I got the woman to heat some tea for us.'

Colquhoun threw his legs over the edge of the dinghy and staggered to his feet. His body felt bitterly cold, and he realised that his clothing was wet through to his skin.

He took the mug and cradled it gratefully in his hands. 'God, it's cold, Haley! I never thought it would be like this!'

The seaman grimaced. 'If this is the Sea of Japan, you can keep it!'

Colquhoun took a few steps to the low bulwark and stared around him. He could already see the boat taking definite shape and outline, as well as the flat, lapping water around it. The sky was much clearer, and there was a hint of the brightness to come along the vague horizon line.

'Are the fishermen all right?' The memories of the previous night came crowding back, and he added, 'How is the injured one?'

Haley shrugged. 'Seems okay, sir. Probably got a head like a cannon ball.' He peered at the uneasy water. 'We'll be getting the hook up shortly, I suppose. Then we can get under way and meet the old Black Pig. I'll never complain about anything after this!'

Colquhoun tried to stop his teeth from chattering. 'Yes, I'll go and find the first lieutenant.'

Wolfe was sitting in one corner of the minute wheelhouse, his feet propped up on the wheel. He was red-eyed and unshaven, and hardly looked up at Colquhoun's entrance.

'It's getting light, Number One.' Colquhoun noticed that

there was a half-filled tumbler of pale spirit at Wolfe's elbow, and his heavy automatic pistol lay cocked beside it.

Wolfe glanced at him indifferently. 'So I've noticed.' His eye fastened on the metal mug. 'I see you've been crawling to those bloody gooks again!'

'I thought we could do with something hot. I told Haley to fix it.' Colquhoun did not know why he bothered to lie. Nothing he said seemed to make any difference to Wolfe's animosity. 'Shall I get Nettle to start the engine?'

'When I say so.' Wolfe reached beneath his seat and produced a full bottle. He slopped some of the bitter-smelling drink into his glass and held it up to the grey light. 'Rice wine. Not too bad, provided you don't inhale!' He chuckled and took a deep swallow. 'Better than your bloody tea, I can tell you!'

Colquhoun said wearily, 'When are we supposed to rendez-vous?'

'All in good time.' Wolfe's eyes flashed with sudden irrita-tion. Then he added, 'You worry too much, did you know that?' He wagged his glass towards him and some of the drink spilled over his chest. 'What you need is a good woman!' He grinned broadly. 'That's *exactly* what you want.'

'Look, Number One, if you don't want to tell me . . .'

Wolfe leaned forward and studied him intently. 'Now, did I say something to offend you, Sub? I certainly wouldn't want that. You might feel bound to put me under arrest, eh?' He leaned back again and laughed loudly. 'Yes, I think you should find yourself a nice, ambitious woman and settle down! Like me!'

Colquhoun turned to go, but Wolfe shouted, 'You dismiss when I tell you, got it?' Then he became calmer. 'Did you know I was married once, Sub?'

Colquhoun leaned against the stained window and shook his head. 'No.' In spite of Wolfe's even tone he was obviously drunk. Colquhoun was surprised to find that it hardly seemed to matter any more. It was just one more impossible obstacle.

'Oh yes. I never wanted a girl so much in my whole life. I'd have done anything for her. Anything at all.' His head lolled, but he pulled himself together with a jerk. 'Just because I made certain rules, certain definite standards, she started playing around!' He glared at Colquhoun, searching his face. 'The little bitch! She thought I didn't know! But I used to keep a check on her, watched her every move! Of course, I never actually caught her at it, but that was because of her brother, you see.'

Colquhoun tried to follow Wolfe's line of reasoning. 'Whose brother?'

Wolfe heaved himself to his feet, sending the pistol spinning to the deck. 'Don't you get cheeky with me, *Mister* Colquhoun! Just you pay attention!' He was breathing heavily. '*Her* brother, the high and mighty Commander Jermain!'

Colquhoun stared at him. 'I—I didn't know . . .'

'Oh, you didn't know, eh?' Wolfe slumped back on the seat. 'I find that hard to believe.' He took another long swallow and coughed uncontrollably. 'Oh yes, they had it all set up between them. He was jealous of me. Always was, in fact. They thought I'd fight to keep the marriage going by contesting a divorce, knowing that it would ruin me in the Service.' He was quite calm again. 'So I played it by ear. I let them put their story of mental cruelty and all that rubbish across without a murmur!' He smiled at some inner thought. 'I've waited all this time. All this bloody time!'

'Did the captain actually say all this?' Colquhoun tried to gauge Wolfe's reaction to each word. 'I mean, what did he have to gain?'

'I told you! Are you *deaf*?' Wolfe stood up and pressed his hands on the wheel. 'He was jealous! Even after smashing my marriage he was not satisfied. Do you know he actually tried to ruin my chances of getting a command?' He stared at Colquhoun's shocked face and added grimly, 'You may well look surprised, my lad! But after this little lot is over I think we shall see a change for the better!'

'I still don't see what you mean. What made you think the captain could act like that?'

Wolfe seized him by the front of his jacket. 'Who the hell cares what you see? And what the devil do you mean by asking all these questions?' He shook him slowly in time with his words. 'Just you keep a civil tongue in your head in future!' He released his grip and added vaguely, 'Call the hands and prepare to get under way!'

Colquhoun staggered back against the door. 'The rendez-vous, Number One! Have you worked it out yet?'

Surprisingly, Wolfe remained unprovoked by his question. 'Oh, *that*, well, as a matter of fact, I've made other arrangements.' He picked up his pistol and clicked the safety catch back and forth in deep concentration. 'Jermain has no intention of coming back for us. No intention at all. He thinks he can sneak back to base and get all the glory. Oh yes, I've got his measure all right!'

Colquhoun felt the wheelhouse spinning round, and said desperately, 'He will come back! You're wrong!'

'Wrong, am I?' Wolfe watched him pityingly. 'I've been thinking about it all night. He wants to get rid of me, you see.' He grinned widely. 'Don't look so shocked, Sub. He wants to do the same for you, too! He knows the admiral is against him, so this is one clear way to get even with him, too!' He frowned. 'But we're wasting time. We must get under way immediately. I have no intention of letting that bastard get away with it!' He bent down, and Colquhoun heard the clink of glass. Over his shoulder he said sharply, 'Now attend to your duties. I've had just about a bellyful of you!'

Colquhoun climbed blindly down to the deck, his mind awhirl. Wolfe's outburst was all the more terrible because he had tried to make it sound so reasonable. But drunk or mad, it made little difference to the immediate outcome. It was plain that he had no intention of making any rendezvous, just as it was equally obvious that Jermain would not leave them to fend for themselves.

Once during the night he had heard the distant rumble of explosions rolling across the calm water like thunder, and he guessed it was the *Temeraire* under attack as she led the enemy away from the channel. But soon the searching ships would be reinforced, and every extra hour in these waters would bring new danger to the submarine. Jermain would return, but the fishing boat would have gone. He might go on searching until it was too late, and be caught in the shallows like the *Pyramus* had so nearly been.

Haley greeted him eagerly. 'We going now, sir? Are we off to meet the Pig?'

Colquhoun screwed up his mind in an effort to think clearly. 'Soon, Haley. Right now you'd better tell Nettle to start the engine. I'll go forrard and help winch up the anchor.' He was

293

only putting it off. Shelving what had to be done.

A shaft of watery sunlight reflected against the wheelhouse windows, and even as he looked round Colquhoun realised that the little ship had regained her personality and seemed suddenly vulnerable.

The engine coughed twice and then grumbled into life. Fumes lifted above the stern and the deck began to vibrate impatiently.

Cowley, the signalman, spat on his hands and leaned on the winch handle. 'Right! 'Ere we go then!'

Lightfoot watched Colquhoun's worried face and asked quietly, 'Anything wrong, sir?'

Colquhoun looked away. 'Of course not! What the hell should be wrong?' He knew then that he had decided to do nothing. He was already a failure, there was no point in adding to it. If he clashed again with Wolfe everyone would say it was for personal reasons. Because of what had happened before, because of Lightfoot, because of . . . He gritted his teeth and threw his own weight on the winch.

Anyway, he told himself desperately, he was only guessing. Maybe Wolfe was right about the submarine not returning. He was the senior officer, it was his responsibility.

But when he looked quickly at Lightfoot and saw the hurt in his eyes, he felt nothing but shame.

There was a flurry of foam beneath the boat's counter, and as the anchor broke surface Colquhoun saw the water parting across the blunt bows as the small vessel gathered way. Immediately, there was a protesting chorus of shouts and wails from the sealed cabin, which brought an instant response from the wheelhouse.

Wolfe yelled hoarsely, 'Keep those bastards quiet, Sub! One more peep out of them and I'll lob a grenade amongst 'em!'

The wheelhouse window slammed shut, and Haley said, 'That's laying it on a bit thick, isn't it?'

Cowley grinned. 'Serve 'em right!' He glanced nervously over the bow. 'They'll have somethin' to cag about after this!'

The boat settled down to a steady speed, and as the sun lifted above the sharp horizon line the dampened decks gave off a curtain of steam as a warning of the heat to come.

Haley was the first to notice that something was wrong. He

touched Colquhoun's arm and beckoned him away from the others.

'Look, sir, I'm not one to question my officers, but I'm not blind!' In the growing light his face looked crumpled and tired. 'I've been watching the shadows along the deck.' He dropped his voice to a whisper. 'The sun's over the port quarter.' He watched Colquhoun's expression anxiously and then added urgently, 'Well, is it or not, sir?'

'What if it is?' Colquhoun could not meet his stare.

'Hell, sir, that means we're running level with the coast, to the south west!' He glanced nervously at the other men. 'That's away from the channel!'

Colquhoun stared across the bulwark. Just faintly, like a darker patch of low cloud, he could see the line of the coast. Wolfe was keeping his word. Quickly he looked up at the wheelhouse and saw Wolfe's head and shoulders framed in the centre of the window behind the spokes.

Cowley interrupted his thoughts with a wild shout. 'Look, sir! I can see some boats on the starboard bow!'

Colquhoun replied flatly, 'There's a small inlet over there. It'll be the usual coastal traffic!'

Haley stared at him with sudden anger. 'Don't you see what's happening, sir? We're going in the wrong bloody direction! The skipper'll never find us if we stay on this course!'

His words carried to the others, and Nettle, the stoker, who had just emerged from the engine hatch, muttered, 'What's it all mean, Ted?' He tried to laugh. ' 'As Number One got himself lost?'

'Listen to me, lads!' Haley's voice shook with emotion. 'I think we're going the wrong way!' He pointed accusingly at Colquhoun. 'If you don't believe it, ask *him*!'

Colquhoun saw their faces changing to tight hostility. 'What's the good of acting like this?' He looked around him helplessly. 'I'm not in charge! There's nothing I can do!'

Haley exploded, 'For God's sake, sir! Are you going to let this happen? We'll be captured or killed if we keep like this!'

The window above their heads jerked back, and Wolfe snapped, 'I heard that, Leading Hand! I shan't forget this insubordination!' He glared at Colquhoun. 'So you're still trying to make trouble, are you?' He spun the wheel angrily. 'Well, just you listen to me! This boat does what *I* want it to!'

Haley fell back a pace, his eyes shocked. 'My God, he's off his head!'

Wolfe continued calmly, 'Just for the record, I have all your weapons up here, so don't try to do anything foolish!' He closed the window and resumed his study of the horizon.

Haley removed his cap and wiped his forehead. 'For God's sake, what'll we do?' He stared at the others.

Cowley said quietly, ' 'E's an officer. What *can* we do?' He looked accusingly at Colquhoun. 'It's not just us, is it, sir? The lads aboard the *Temeraire*'ll catch it too if they 'ang around lookin' for us.' He tore his eyes away. 'You do what you like. I'm goin' to force me way into the wheelhouse!'

Lightfoot put up his hand. 'Don't do that, Bert! We'll think of something.' He looked imploringly at Colquhoun. 'You'll get us out of it, won't you, sir?'

Haley snarled, '*Him?* He couldn't knock the skin off a rice pudding!' Then he stared wretchedly over the bows towards the distant, slow-moving shapes of two junks. 'It can't happen! Not out here like this!'

Cowley said, 'What about you, Stokes? Could you bust up the engine or somethin'?'

Nettle shook his head. 'No. 'E told me to put the thing full ahead and then clear out.'

Wolfe suddenly yelled, 'Get down behind the bulwark! We'll be passing near these junks soon, and I don't want your stupid faces all over the place!' He brandished his pistol. 'And stay up forrard where I can see you!'

Haley slumped down beside the worn woodwork. 'Jesus! He's grinning! He's actually enjoying himself!'

Lightfoot sat on the deck with his knees drawn up to his chin. He was staring very hard at the wheelhouse, his brow creased in a frown.

'You'll have to help us, sir.' His voice was pitched so low that Colquhoun could hardly hear it. 'Maybe if you speak to the first lieutenant?'

'It's no use!' Colquhoun stared fixedly at a slow moving shadow as it glided across the wheelhouse. The junk's tall sail must be less than twenty yards clear. He added, 'He's mad. He'll do anything now!'

Cowley muttered, 'If the Reds catch us, you know what they'll do to us?' He shuddered. 'I 'ope they kill the officers first, so I can bloody cheer!'

Colquhoun looked round startled as Haley rasped, 'Get down, you young fool!' Then he saw Lightfoot walking very slowly aft towards the wheelhouse, his hands in his pockets, his head sunk forward as if in deep thought.

Wolfe opened the window and called, 'Get back! Keep under cover, you idiot!' When the boy continued to advance he lifted his pistol above the sill. 'Go back, or I'll shoot!'

Lightfoot halted and stared up at Wolfe's livid face. The others, crouching like statues in the bows, heard his voice, clear and steady. 'We want to go back, sir! It's only fair you should think about the rest of us!'

He put his hands behind his back and twined his fingers into a tight knot. Colquhoun could see his wrists shaking with suppressed fear, but somehow he was keeping his voice under control.

Wolfe snarled, 'How dare you speak to me like that? I'm telling you just once more. *Get back!*'

Lightfoot shrugged and then began to advance.

The noise of the shot was like a thunderclap, and for one split second no one really understood what had happened.

Lightfoot seemed to swing round in his stride, as if he had at last decided to obey Wolfe's order. Then, very slowly, he buckled on to his knees, his fingers interlaced across his stomach. Without a sound he pitched forward on to his face and lay quite still.

Colquhoun staggered to his feet, his mind collapsing with shock and sudden madness. Before he realised what he was doing he found himself at the wheelhouse door, tugging at the handle and screaming like a maniac.

He tore it open, his body braced for the bullet's impact, his mind blank to everything but the sight of Lightfoot's form on the sunlit deck.

Wolfe still stood behind the wheel, the gun grasped in one hand. He turned and stared at Colquhoun, his eyes entirely devoid of recognition or knowledge. He said vaguely, 'I didn't want to shoot him. I had to make him understand!'

Blindly Colquhoun wrenched the pistol from his grip, feeling the metal warm against his fingers. He stepped back and raised the gun level with Wolfe's face.

'You bastard! You rotten, lousy bastard!' He was sobbing with each word, so that Wolfe's face was misty above the shaking foresight.

Wolfe opened his eyes very wide. 'My God, Sub, I can't think what's got into you these days!' Then he giggled, a long-drawn, inhuman sound. 'Still, if you must carry on like this, I suppose we'll just have to tolerate it, eh?'

Cowley pushed into the small space and snatched up a Stirling from the deck.

Colquhoun lowered the pistol and stared at it with sick horror. 'I nearly killed him!' He saw Cowley watching him like an unwinking bird. 'Another second and I would have blown his head off!'

Nettle was waiting below the ladder, and Colquhoun said thickly, 'Tie the first lieutenant's hands, Nettle. Then help Cowley to bring the helm round to the south-east.' He did not wait for a reply, but hurried across the deck and dropped to his knees beside Lightfoot's body.

Haley had opened the boy's shirt and was trying to control the stream of blood which seemed to be pouring continuously across the deck planks in a living flood.

Colquhoun lifted Lightfoot's head on to his knees and said, 'Why did you do it, John? For God's sake, why? It was my job. I should have been the one!'

Lightfoot opened his eyes and stared straight up at the empty sky. His face was deathly pale, and there were bright flecks of blood on his lips. He said, 'I had to. *Had* to!' His breathing was very slow. 'You were good to me. You understood me I couldn't let you go on thinking you was no use.'

Haley said tightly, 'Hold on, lad! Just lie quiet!'

But Lightfoot lifted himself on his elbows, his voice desperate. 'You never killed Archer, sir! He was already dead when he was put behind the door! It was nothing to do with you!'

Haley gasped and looked across at Colquhoun. 'So that was how it happened!'

Colquhoun whispered, 'Never mind that! It doesn't matter any more!'

Lightfoot's head fell back on his lap. 'No, it don't matter any more.' He was smiling, but his eyes did not seem to focus properly. 'You'll be all right now, sir! You see!'

He coughed, and this time the blood did not stop.

Colquhoun wiped the boy's face with his handkerchief and leaned forward to keep the sun from his eyes.

Haley said gently, 'It's no use, sir. He's gone.' Then he stood up and walked slowly to the bulwark.

Colquhoun stayed where he was, quite motionless. Only his shadow moved, as the boat turned and swung on to her new course.

18

Someone Should Talk About It!

'Down periscope! Dive to two hundred feet!' Jermain stepped back and said sharply, 'There is a seaplane of some sort bearing green one three five.'

He waited until the deck steadied at the new depth and added, 'the sea's empty. Like a sheet of bloody glass!'

Mayo watched him worriedly. 'What do you think, sir?'

'We'll try another sweep, Pilot. Bring her round two points to port, and tell Oxley to keep a sharp watch. The fishing boat is very small. She might even have some sort of engine trouble.'

He swung on his heel and strode to the chart-room. It gave him the delusion of privacy. A place where he could be alone with his thoughts.

But how much longer could he go on searching? There was no sign of the fishing boat, and every passing minute added to the submarine's own danger. At each furtive search through the periscope there had been some new hint or sign that more ships were coming into the area. Twice he had seen smoke on the burnished horizon. Low, fast-moving smoke, like that of warships. Now there was an aircraft. The enemy had been fooled by the deception, but was still taking no chances.

He swung round as a foot grated on the deck. 'What do you want?' Then he saw that it was the imperturbable Baldwin with a fresh mug of black coffee. 'Thank you. I'm sorry if I sounded rough!'

Baldwin put the mug carefully on the chart table and wiped his hands across his white jacket. ''S'all right, sir. Reckon you've quite a bit on yer mind just now!'

Jermain watched him leave with something like affection. Baldwin, whose duties were so unwarlike, yet were essential to all of them. His world was confined to wardroom cutlery, the proper routine of meals and the collection of mess bills. In all his service he had learned little of the ships which carried him from one end of the world to the other. He had to rely on trust.

The coffee was hot and bitter. Jermain leaned his arms on the table and stared moodily at the straggling outline of the Korean coast.

It was all unreal and fantastic. They had been attacked and had suffered sudden death, yet to the outside world the crisis hardly existed. He thought back to the day they had left the Gareloch, and knew he had felt the same way. The Korean War had ended nearly twenty years ago. Surely nothing more could happen there?

In the control room he heard two ratings removing the last of the broken glass, the sound scraping at his ears like a drill on the nerve of a bad tooth.

From the moment the *Temeraire* had made her stealthy escape from the searching ships overhead the work of putting right the damage had continued without a pause. The men seemed almost glad to do it, if only to keep their minds occupied and away from the unknown dangers.

They had planed up to periscope depth, and Jermain had taken his first look around. After the threatening darkness the blinding daylight came with the shock of an iced shower. The sun so bright that the sea's burnished glare was almost unbearable, and he imagined he could feel its heat through the periscope. And as he stared and searched the empty horizons he was at the same time conscious of the noises inside the hull. The staccato beat of the power pumps, the clatter of feet on the deck below as hatches were thrown open and men waited for the worst job of all.

It should all have been over and finished with. They should have been running deep with the damaged screw whining at full pitch to carry them all to safety. Instead they were still searching, still tied to this damned and mocking Wantsai Valley with all its horrors and nightmare memories.

Jermain had crossed the control room to speak with Mayo

who was standing above the open hatch at the far end. He had been staring down the shining ladder, his face set like a mask. Jermain had been about to speak, but had suddenly looked down to follow his glance.

At the foot of the ladder Griffin's first-aid party were just passing aft with a stretcher. Jermain knew that their sodden, lolling burden had once been Lieutenant Trott. He knew this fact from the uniform. Otherwise there had been no sort of resemblance. No sense of belonging, no part of something once familiar. Just a thing. A staring, open-mouthed remnant.

Now the last of the corpses had been removed from the pumped-out tube space, and there was a smell of disinfectant on the damp air.

Drew had gone forward with Lieutenant Kitson to check the damage to the delicate firing mechanisms and to repair any faults in the circuits. He could hear their tools and hammers rattling through the hull at top speed. At least it was an improvement on the clanging chains, although even now he seemed to hear them, mocking him . . . rebuking him. . . .

He realised that his head had fallen almost on to the chart, and he stood up angrily, shaking himself awake like a dog.

If he gave up the search for Wolfe and the others now he knew he could never forgive himself. The cost was already too high. He had to hold on a little longer.

Even if he was praised for getting the *Pyramus* clear, he would not be able to accept the satisfaction for himself. Sarah's happiness, even the longed for unity with Jill, would be clouded by his own knowledge that he had left his own men to die without reason.

Drew appeared in the doorway. 'Kitson is still working on the circuits, sir. The inrush of water must have cut through some of them like a saw!' He shook his head heavily. 'I'll never forget it!'

Jermain walked past him. It was as if he could no longer stand personal contact. Not yet. Not until the search was over.

'Periscope depth again!' His voice was hard. 'Anything from sonar?'

Mayo shook his head. 'Do you think the seaplane will still be there?'

'How the hell do I know?' Jermain ignored the look on Mayo's face.

'Up periscope!' He leaned on the handles and squinted as his eyes received the full glare of the waiting sun.

The sea was once more clear. Only a few gulls swooped angrily above the periscope, outraged by its intrusion. Jermain watched their grimacing protests as he swung the handles to full power. Tonight these gulls will sleep safely in their nests and crannies ashore. Where will he be? He ground his teeth together with sudden despair. What had happened to the fishing boat? Sunk or captured? Or had Wolfe decided to act independently after all?

He snapped, 'Raise the radio mast! See if you can hear anything.' He thought of the boat's powerful radar, unused and impotent. With that he might find the small boat within minutes. It was tempting, but he knew it was an empty thought. Any such transmission might be instantly detected, then any chance of saving Wolfe and his companions, if there still was one, would be lost for good.

Mayo reported, 'Nothing on sonar, sir.'

'Well, *keep trying*!' He kept his eyes to the periscope and did not see Mayo's face as he looked at Drew. The latter shook his head very slightly. But the gesture seemed to sum up his understanding and his pity for what Jermain was trying to do.

The big lenses moved slowly around the glittering seascape as Jermain searched horizon and sky alike. If an aircraft dived suddenly from the sun there might be precious little time to act. With the sea so clear and calm the *Temeraire*'s bulk would stand out as sharply as if they had been basking on the surface.

Harris burst from the radio room, his lined face alight with excitement. 'Captain, sir! Signal from Flag!' His voice was shattering in the stillness. '*Pyramus* has made her contact! She's out of danger!' He held out the signal pad as if he had to remind himself it was not a dream. 'Flag must have been calling us regularly, sir. This is our recall!'

'Down periscope! Two hundred feet!' Jermain looked coldly at Harris and then moved to the chart table. 'Thank you. You may lower the mast now.'

Harris looked lost. 'I'm sorry, sir, I just thought . . .' His voice trailed away as Mayo shot him a warning frown and, still mystified, he returned to the radio room.

Jermain said, 'Alter course, Pilot. Bring her round to three three zero. Reduce speed to ten knots.' His tone was clipped and final. 'Periscope depth again in fifteen minutes.'

He walked slowly back to the chart-room. The sudden signal had only added to his sense of urgency and despair. Now the whole boat would know that officially the mission was over. The only thing which kept the crew and the *Temeraire* in pressing danger was his own personal stubbornness. Or was it only pride?

The intercom broke into his thoughts. 'Very faint hydrophone effect bearing red four five. Range twenty thousand yards.' Oxley added after a few seconds, 'Could be a small diesel engine, sir!'

Jermain took one quick glance at the chart. It was well away from the area selected for rendezvous but it could be the fishing boat. He felt suddenly sick from the controlled tension. It *had* to be!

'Course to intercept, Pilot!' He pushed past Mayo and snatched up the engine-room handset.

'Captain here! How is the propeller noise, Chief?'

'About the same, sir. But at this speed it's not too bad. More like a whistling than anything.'

He heard Mayo murmur, 'Port twenty. Steady. Steer two eight five!'

Ross added doubtfully, 'If you have to clap on power you'll need to run deep again, sir. The noise would certainly be detectable at present depths.'

'Yes, thank you.' Jermain replaced the handset. So, if this was a false contact he might have to break off the search. Even the admiral, who remained sitting in the deserted wardroom like an old man, would never allow him to risk the boat further.

Mayo said, 'On new course, sir.'

'Very good.' Jermain turned his back on the looming possibility of failure. 'Find out if Kitson has completed his work and then clear for action. There is nothing wrong with the boat's hearing.' He looked around their grim faces. 'I want her teeth ready, too!'

*   *   *

Leading Seaman Haley climbed up the short ladder and eased his body into the wheelhouse. In spite of the fact that every window was fully lowered it was quite airless and as hot as an oven. Colquhoun was standing at the wheel, his slim body stripped to the waist, his skin gleaming with sweat.

Haley said, 'There's some more smoke on the port beam, sir.'

Colquhoun replied, 'Take the wheel.' He picked up the long, battered telescope which he had found in a locker and rested it on the sill of a window. After a few moments he said, 'It's one of those ships.'

Haley knew what he meant well enough, but took the telescope as Colquhoun thrust it into his hands. The dark smudge on the horizon sprung alive in the big glass, and he saw the raked bow slicing through the calm water, the low plume of smoke from her funnel. Like a fast trawler. Like the ones which had hounded the *Temeraire* and had been responsible for Lieutenant Victor's death.

He said slowly, 'The hunt's still going on then. Let's hope she doesn't come over to take a look at *us*.'

Colquhoun answered briefly, 'They'll have us spotted on the radar. They're obviously not bothered.'

Haley moved his legs uneasily. 'Not *yet*!'

Colquhoun ignored him. It was strange how calm he felt. Empty, and completely composed. Like another person.

He said sharply, 'Have you let the fishermen out of their cabin?'

Haley nodded. 'Yes, sir.' The released Koreans were directly below the front of the wheelhouse, watched over by Cowley with his Stirling. Yet Colquhoun had apparently not even seen them. His eyes stayed either on the ancient compass or the harsh light of the horizon. He added cautiously, 'The sun's getting damned high, sir. Do you think we've missed the rendezvous?'

Colquhoun shrugged. 'The compass is well adrift, and the only chart available looks home made. It's got a few crayoned

305

areas for fishing, and not much else. But allowing for the alteration of course and the drift, we're just about on the right track.'

Haley persisted, 'We could be miles off course, as I see it. Even if the skipper does come back for us he'll not find it easy to spot us.' He watched the fast-moving smoke. 'And there's not much time left!'

He stiffened as the black-haired Korean woman left the small group by the hatch and moved quietly to the bulwark. Ignoring Cowley, she unwrapped an old blanket and laid it carefully across Lightfoot's body which had been moved into the shade of the boat's side. Haley shot a glance at Colquhoun's stiff face, but apart from a quick blink of his pale eyes there was nothing to give away his inner feelings.

Colquhoun saw Haley's apprehensive stare and kept his own gaze fixed on the open sea beyond the gently corkscrewing bows. He had carried Lightfoot's body to the bulwark himself. He had been surprised how light it had been. Now, as he let his eyes move to the blanketed shape, the shock seemed to affect him more deeply, and he was again reminded of his sense of loss. Before, as he had made himself stand rigidly behind the wheel staring at the mocking horizon, he had been able to glance at Lightfoot's body, to deceive himself for just a few more seconds. In the shade of the bulwark the boy had appeared to be asleep, or sheltering from the sun. The blanket made a stark difference. It was final.

He realised that he was gripping the spokes so tightly his hands were throbbing with pain.

Lightfoot had made him act. Had forced him to accept a role he had so long avoided. It was as if he had been betrayed and deceived by so many others in his short life that he was unable to see Colquhoun become another fallen idol. Even if it cost him his blood. He was suddenly conscious of the heavy watch in his trouser pocket, and he remembered Lightfoot's determined and angry face as he had thrust it into his hands. '*I want you to have it, see?*'

He felt the pain rising again to prick at his eyes and he said sharply, 'Take the wheel, Haley. I'm going to walk around for a bit.' He stepped down from the wheelhouse and immediately felt the sun across his bare shoulders like the cut of a whip.

Wolfe was sitting in the shade of the wheelhouse, his bound hands hidden behind his back. He looked up at Colquhoun's taut features and said, 'You'll see that I was right! He'll not come back for us now!' When Colquhoun failed to reply he shouted loudly, 'You'll regret this, Mr. Colquhoun!'

Colquhoun stopped and stared down at him. He still felt strangely calm, like a man under drugs, and he said, 'The only thing I regret is that I did not shoot you! But I intend to meet the *Temeraire*.' He looked away. 'If only to see you court-martialled!'

He walked slowly towards the bows where it had all started. As he passed the Koreans they bowed their heads, as if they too sensed his new and dangerous strength.

The little boat steamed on steadily, each turn of the screw piling the distance between them and the distant shoreline. Only the jagged mountains were visible now, detached from the horizon by a low bank of haze. Soon they would be too far out. They would be seen and singled out for closer inspection. If he had allowed Wolfe to have his way they might still be sneaking down the coastline itself, lost and safe amongst count-less similar craft. And Lightfoot would still be alive.

He stamped his foot with sudden anger. No! It was not like that. Just this once he had to be right!

Haley called from the wheelhouse. 'Would you come up here, sir? I think there's a small boat coming up astern!'

Colquhoun ran up the ladder and groped for the telescope as Haley added, 'Can't make it out myself. The haze is too thick back there.'

Colquhoun moved the telescope slowly and watched the glittering reflections playing across the water. A small boat might come too close for comfort. It might be as well to keep the Koreans in sight and let them know that they must behave quite normally, no matter what.

Haley started as Colquhoun snapped the telescope shut and threw it on the locker. 'What is it, sir?'

Colquhoun stared past him. 'Submarine! Dead astern! That was the conning tower you saw!' He watched the com-pass. 'Alter course slightly to port.' He waited a few moments and then trained the telescope once again.

This time he found it immediately. The submarine was

moving fast, her hull trimmed down so low that it was lost in a welter of spray thrown back from the bows. Only the conning tower seemed real. It cruised above the water like some strange war-machine, the white hats of the men on watch like tiny flowers on a sea-washed rock. As he studied the submarine Colquhoun saw the conning tower changing shape and becoming wafer-thin as when he had first seen it.

He said, 'She's altered course. She's coming after us.' There was neither surprise nor panic in his voice. Just a plain statement of fact.

Haley swallowed. 'I could go and tell the Koreans to act dumb, sir. I could make 'em understand!'

Colquhoun turned and studied him calmly. There was almost a wistful look in his eyes as he said, 'You really don't understand, do you, Haley?'

Haley shook his head. 'We could bluff it out, sir!'

'No. This is the same submarine which attacked the *Malange*.'

Haley stared at him. 'How can you be sure, sir?'

'Do you think I'm ever likely to forget, Haley?' Colquhoun looked emptily at Lightfoot's blanketed body and then said crisply, 'She must have been at the shallow end of the Wantsai Valley waiting for the trawlers to drive the *Pyramus* or the *Temeraire* across her sights!' He gripped the seaman's arm fiercely. 'God, man, don't you understand? The *Temeraire* will come straight into her! She'll surface to take us aboard, and she'll be a sitting target!'

Haley's face was drained of colour. 'What'll we do, sir?' He looked around the wheelhouse like a trapped animal. 'We can't do *anything*!'

Colquhoun picked up his Stirling and cocked it deliberately. 'There is a dinghy lashed forrard, Haley. It belongs to the fishermen. Get it ready for launching.'

Haley seemed dazed. 'Launching, sir?'

'I shall want the Koreans to leave the boat at once. We'll put them over the side before the submarine gets up to us.' He looked straight into Haley's eyes. 'You know what I'm asking, don't you, Haley?'

The man licked his lips and tried to grin. 'It had to be us, didn't it, sir?' He straightened his cap and added, 'I'll tell the others.' He turned to go and then said, 'The *Temeraire* wouldn't stand a chance, sir. We can't let these bastards use us as the bait!'

Colquhoun lifted the telescope and watched the submarine growing larger in the lens. It would be so easy to 'bluff it out' as Haley had suggested. *Temeraire* might not be able to make the rendezvous, and their deaths would be for nothing. Even if they delayed the approaching submarine, there was still the possibility that Jermain might not detect her presence in time. Again, their deaths would be in vain.

He picked up the Stirling and stared at it savagely. Then he shouted, 'Slow ahead, Nettle!' As the engine's roar subsided he added, 'Now get that boat over the rail, and be quick about it!'

He got a vague impression of the protesting fishermen and the stolid-faced woman with the baby hugged to her side as they were helped down into the tethered dinghy alongside. Then as a knife slashed away the line it grated down the side of the hull and curtsied astern on the fishing boat's wake. Colquhoun watched them drop further and further astern. Small, lost people caught up in someone else's struggle.

'Full ahead, Nettle! I don't care if you burst the engine apart now!'

Then he yelled through the window, 'The submarine will come up on our port quarter, Haley! You and Cowley keep in the bows out of sight. When I give the signal I want you to open fire on her conning tower with everything you've got!' He looked down at Nettle who sat perched on the edge of the engine hatch swinging his legs. 'You, too. Just concentrate on her bridge and keep her crew away from the deck gun!'

He turned back to watch the submarine again. It had increased speed, the wash from the lean hull brushing aside the bobbing dinghy like a leaf. He clamped his jaws tightly together. Soon now. The submarine was moving so fast that she would be overhauling the fishing boat as if she had been stationary.

Haley yelled, 'Smoke on the horizon, sir! Bearing green four five! It'll be that A/S trawler again, I expect!'

Colquhoun lifted his hand in acknowledgement. It made

little difference now. If he could lure the submarine close enough to attack her, he could make her submerge. It was unlikely that her commander would want to risk unnecessary damage to his periscopes, quite apart from possible casualties.

Colquhoun felt the sweat running free down his spine. No, the submarine's skipper would dive and finish off this irritating attacker with a single torpedo.

He raised his Stirling very slowly and held it against the side of the window. He watched the low bows and then the front edge of the conning tower moving into his vision, but he made himself wait just a bit longer, counting the seconds like a runner under the starting gun.

No matter how far from the rendezvous she was, *Temeraire*'s sensitive ears would detect the torpedo's explosion. He had a sudden picture of the cramped sonar compartment alongside Oxley and with Lightfoot just below him at the controls.

He rested his forehead on his wrist and wiped the mist from his eyes. When he looked up the submarine was drawing abeam, barely fifty yards away. He heard the squawk of a loud-hailer, saw the glint of sunlight on raised binoculars. There was no mistaking her now. She was the same boat.

His despair gave way to sudden fury, and as his finger tightened on the trigger he yelled, 'Open fire! Sweep her bridge!'

He heard himself yelling as the gun vibrated against his armpit, and through the drifting smoke he saw the figures crumple away from the conning tower like discarded puppets as the four Stirlings poured a deadly fire amongst them.

Colquhoun swung the wheel and sent the boat careering towards the grey hull, which even now was pulling away, the surprise giving way to trained reaction. The conning tower was already tilting, and across the gap he could hear the water roaring into her tanks as she started to dive. Two or three bodies floated free from the empty bridge, and as the sea cascaded over the periscope standards they twirled and pirouetted in a macabre dance before being sucked down to oblivion.

Colquhoun reloaded his gun and stared at the disturbed water. The submerged submarine would either move clear to fire her *coup de grâce*, or she might wait for the smokecloud on the horizon to come to her aid. Either way, there was nothing more to be done. He rested his chin on his forearm and watched the place where the enemy had dived.

*　　　*　　　*

The atmosphere in the *Temeraire*'s control room was so charged with suppressed tension that it was almost unbearable. Beside the chart table the navigator's yeoman busied himself aimlessly sharpening a pencil, until Mayo's glare quelled him too into silence. Jermain stood with his fists deep in his jacket pockets, his eyes on the clock. It seemed as if the hands were welded to the face, and he had to stop himself from checking with his own watch.

Oxley reported, 'Stronger diesel H.E. on same bearing, sir. Closing.'

Mayo let out a slow breath. 'Damn!' He glanced at Jermain's impassive features. 'A patrol boat, do you think?'

Jermain said, 'Check the range again!'

'Ten thousand yards, sir. The second vessel is moving fast. Around twenty knots. Still closing.'

Jermain felt the admiral at his side. He said quietly, 'It seems as if we might have to act fast, sir.'

Sir John Colquhoun stared at the plot table. 'This second ship. Do you think it's after the fishing boat?' He sounded strained to breaking point.

'We don't know for sure that the other one is *our* fishing boat, sir.' Jermain added gently, 'I'm going up to take a look round.'

Oxley's voice came like a slap in the face. 'More H.E. bearing green one six zero, sir! Range fourteen thousand yards! Fast diesel engines. Closing!'

The plot table hummed into life, its lights winking malevolently.

Jermain said slowly, 'One ahead and one astern. This second one might be the A/S boat we sighted earlier. She seems to be coming back for something.'

As if to confirm this Oxley snapped, 'Second H.E. sounds like the other A/S craft, sir. Still closing!'

Jermain made up his mind. 'Take her up to sixty feet! Make

it as slow as possible.' He lifted his arms as the deck tilted very slightly. 'Up periscope!' He crouched down with his head against the pad, his eyes staring into the churning panorama of sunlit water as the lens glided towards the surface. Hardly daring to breathe he swung the handles on to the given bearing and waited for the spray to clear from the glass. The others around him saw his mouth tighten with satisfaction.

'It *is* our boat!' He watched the little vessel move slowly into the cross-wires, her bows throwing up a tremendous moustache of white foam. The periscope was at full power, but with the heavy surface heat haze to contend with it was still difficult to obtain a hard picture. But it was the same boat. There was no doubt about it.

He swung the periscope round in another half circle and stared fixedly at the new menace astern. Here there was no haze, nothing to hide or soften the outline of the fast-moving ship. But she still had a long way to come. There was still time.

He turned back to watch the fishing boat. From the corner of his mouth he said, 'Where's the other ship now, I can't see anything!'

Oxley said, 'On the same bearing, sir. Closing fast!' He sounded unusually edgy. 'She's there all right!'

Jermain blinked his eyes and pressed his head harder against the rubber pad. Even allowing for the haze he should be able to see something. The sun was behind him, and the water was as calm as a millpond.

He cursed inwardly as spray twisted the little picture into interminglings of blue and silver. He could imagine Wolfe and the others watching each horizon, hanging on to hope, and yet not daring to take it for granted.

Then he tensed as the fishing boat's deck was further distorted by a drifting cloud of smoke. There were sudden, vicious pin-pricks of light too, matching the sunlight with their brilliance. Even as his mind grappled with this unexpected turn of events he saw the submarine. She had been in a direct line with the fishing boat, but now as the latter swung on some crazy collision course he could see the conning tower, the shine of spray on the smooth steel.

He straightened his back. 'Down periscope! There is a sub-

312

marine on the surface. Bearing red one zero. Same range as the fishing boat!'

There was a momentary shocked silence, and then Mayo snapped, 'Start the attack!'

Jermain gave him a quiet nod. 'Stand by tubes One and Two!' To the control room at large he said harshly, 'It's the same sub. Right now she's attacking the fishing boat, and it's my guess she's called up assistance.'

He stood quietly as the ranges and bearings rattled through the intercom. Then he said, 'Up periscope!'

'One and Two ready, sir. Bow doors open!'

He swung the handles very slightly from the previous bearing. The fishing boat was still afloat and unharmed, but the submarine seemed to have turned end on.

Oxley shouted, 'Diesels have stopped, sir! She's diving!'

'Down periscope! He watched the flickering lights on the plot table. 'He's either running away from Wolfe's Stirlings, or he'll haul off to fire a torpedo.'

Mayo said, 'More likely he'll wait for the A/S ship to arrive. He'll not want to waste a torpedo!'

Jermain nodded. 'That's what I think.' He rubbed his chin. 'In that case we must rescue Wolfe's party first. By the time we caught the submarine the surface ship would be here. Stirlings would be useless against *her*!'

'Submarine has dived, sir.' Oxley was in control again. 'Bearing green two five. Her course is zero nine zero. Depth steady at about one hundred feet.'

Jermain rested his hand lightly on Mayo's shoulder. 'Take over as Number One in the control room, Pilot.' To Drew he added, 'You get forrard. I want the torpedo department to run like clockwork if I give the order!'

Drew slipped from his seat. 'It will be a pleasure, Skipper!'

Another glance at the clock. 'Stand by to surface!'

The admiral said urgently, 'What can I do, Jermain? I can't just stand here. I'll go mad!'

Jermain picked up his glasses and checked their lenses. Quietly he said, 'I would like you to stay right here in the control room, sir. When we get started in a few minutes I want my men to be able to see you.' He let his eyes drop to the admiral's bright rectangle of decorations. 'They are all trained men, sir. But yours is the experience which will hold them together in a real emergency!' He turned away from the admiral's silent stare. He was not sure if the expression was one of pride or whether he was just grateful for being needed.

Jermain let his eyes move slowly over the assembled men. Look-outs, handling party below the main hatch, and the attack team around the plot table.

Then he knocked the clips off the lower hatch and started up the ladder. Over his shoulder he yelled, 'Surface!' He noticed that his voice sounded hollow inside the steel tower, and he tried not to picture what would have happened if he had not seen the gunfire aboard the fishing boat. He would have surfaced right on top of the submarine's sights. It would have been over very quickly, if they were lucky.

He forgot everything else as he knocked off the second lot of clips and ducked his head as the spray splashed down over his cap. His hands and feet moved automatically, his voice too was crisp and expressionless as he climbed the last few rungs to the cockpit with the lookouts and messengers panting behind him.

He swung his glasses to his eyes, searching astern for the approaching enemy. She seemed much closer, her bows high above a tremendous crescent of foam, upperworks glinting in the harsh sunlight. By comparison the little fishing boat still seemed a long way off.

'Full ahead!' He kept his glasses trained on her bows, and then breathed out with satisfaction as they began to swing towards him. 'They've seen us at last!'

He peered quickly over the screen as the *Temeraire* rose to her full buoyancy, her black flanks streaming with spray as she gathered speed and pushed harder into the clear water. There was weed on her plates too, and he could see a few bright scars left by the depth-charges. In spite of his inner anxiety the sight seemed to reassure him, and some of the watching lookouts saw him smile and run his hand along the top of the screen like a man stroking a great beast.

Never before, even on trials, had the *Temeraire* mounted such a surface speed. The great bow waves creamed back from her rounded stem, high sided and steep like ocean rollers. The whole fin vibrated wildly, and long streamers of spray floated

314

above their heads in ragged arrows.

A messenger shouted, 'Sonar still in contact, sir! Submarine now bearing green four five! Range four thousand yards! Her present course is still zero nine zero!'

Jermain banged his fist on the wet metal. The enemy commander must have heard the *Temeraire* by now. With all stops pulled and the damaged screw whining like a bandsaw, she would be hard *not* to hear!

He found himself smiling again. No wonder the other commander was clearing out of the area. For all he knew, the *Temeraire* might be after him!

He shouted, 'Continue tracking! He may decide to have a go!'

There was a high-pitched whistle and he ducked his head as a tall waterspout rose lazily midway between the submarine and the fishing boat. 'Port twenty!' He craned his head to watch the orange flash from the pursuing ship astern. Again the sharp, abbreviated whistle close overhead. He could almost feel the rush of air, taste the foul bite of cordite as the shell exploded on the water beyond the swinging bows.

'Steady! Steer two seven zero!' He lifted his glasses to watch the other ship. If only they could fire one torpedo at her. But there were too many in the game for that now. There was no time. No time left.

He snapped, 'Signal the fishing boat to lower their dinghy! We'll pick them straight out of the water!' He heard the clatter of the Aldis, and marvelled that the nineteen years old signalman was keeping his head.

He ducked his head again as another shell shrieked past the fin and ricocheted across the flat water before exploding with a sullen bang.

Through his glasses he could see the fishing boat's deck very clearly now. He could make out Haley's tall figure struggling with the *Temeraire*'s dinghy abaft the wheelhouse, assisted by Nettle and Cowley. Colquhoun appeared to be at the helm, and he could see Wolfe sitting on the deck below the ladder. He was the only one not employed, and Jermain said aloud, 'I think Number One must be wounded!'

The gap narrowed rapidly. It was far enough. With half a mile still between them Jermain rapped, 'Open the forehatch!

315

Stand by deck party to take on dinghy!' He saw one of the lookouts trembling uncontrollably and added calmly, 'No point in leaving anything lying about, eh?'

The man nodded and dragged his eyes from the last fall of shot. 'That's right, sir. We might as well keep the bastards guessin'!'

Jermain leaned forward to watch the big hatch being jacked open. Now the submarine was really vulnerable. She could not dive. She was a sitting duck.

'Watch out for aircraft!' Then he cupped his hands. 'I shall not stop the engine, so get ready to grab the dinghy!' He saw the huddled deck party watching him anxiously, their bodies frail and vulnerable to the screaming shellfire. Jermain made himself speak slowly, 'Remember all the practice you had with the C.N.D. dinghy! You should be able to do it blindfolded!' Mercifully, someone grinned and waved up at him. He snapped, 'Signal the fishing boat to bale out!'

He watched Colquhoun lean from his wheelhouse and raise his arm in reply to the brief message. There was a splash, and he saw Haley leap down into the dinghy, his hands already groping for the outboard motor.

There was a sharp crack astern, and the air was filled with screaming splinters. Jermain ducked his head as they clanged against the steel or thudded into the fin's fibreglass covering. He heard a sharp cry and turned to see the young signalman slipping down the side of the cockpit, his eyes wide and frightened as he stared at the blood which poured from his shoulder.

A lookout seized the boy and yelled, 'First-aid party on the bridge!'

The signalman looked dazedly at Jermain and said, 'It's okay, sir! I'm all right really!' Then he fainted.

Lieutenant Kitson struggled past the stretcher party and joined Jermain in the cockpit. He was carrying some glasses and peered quickly at the fishing boat. Between explosions he yelled, 'All electrical circuits are working well, sir!'

Jermain smiled. 'You already told me! But you might as well stay if you want to!'

Then he forgot Kitson's excited face as one of the deck party called, 'They haven't left the boat yet, sir!'

Jermain swore savagely. The shellfire was getting more accurate. It only needed one true hit to prevent them from diving. He levelled his glasses as Kitson said thickly, 'It's the first lieutenant, sir! He's fighting with Colquhoun!'

Jermain watched the little drama and felt his elation changing to dread. He could see Wolfe's mouth opening in a wild grin as he pushed Colquhoun back on the bulwark while the other sailors swayed helplessly in the dinghy.

One of the seamen was holding a limp body on the side of the dinghy, and Jermain guessed it was Lightfoot. It was strange he had not seen him earlier. But perhaps he had died when the submarine had made her first attack.

He felt the spray slashing over the bridge as another shell exploded astern. 'Starboard fifteen! Steer two nine zero!' When he looked up from the gyro repeater Wolfe had vanished, and then Jermain saw him slamming the wheelhouse door to seal himself inside. Colquhoun seemed to falter, and then as another shell filled the air with jagged splinters he leapt over the rail and cut the dinghy's line.

A messenger said urgently, 'Sonar reports submarine contact is turning, sir! Now bearing green six zero! *Closing!*'

Jermain gripped the screen with all his strength and concentrated on the small, gleaming dinghy. 'Come on! For God's sake, come *on*!'

Kitson said, 'Number One's steering the fishing boat, sir! What the hell has got into him?' Then he saw Jermain's face and added quietly, 'Poor bastard. It must have been too much for him.'

Jermain lifted his glasses and watched the dinghy as it scudded towards the onrushing submarine. The faces of the men leapt into focus, so that he could see each line of suffering and fear. Colquhoun crouched by the bow, with one hand on the dead sailor beside him. Haley was sitting upright, with his fingers round the tiller, his eyes already gauging the approach.

The other two were staring back at the fishing boat, which was still steaming on the same course, her diesel sending a steady plume of blue smoke over her wake.

Jermain said heavily, 'Slow ahead! Stand by on the forecasing!'

He felt the tension sapping his remaining strength as the

first grapnel missed its target. But the next fell beside Colquhoun, and as the line jerked taut the waiting seamen dashed forward to haul the dinghy up and over the curved hull.

A messenger, who had been stooped intently over his microphone, rolled his eyes and yelled, 'Sonar reports torpedoes approaching from starboard, sir!'

Jermain dragged his eyes from the gaping hatch and the dinghy which was still being manhandled below. 'Full ahead! Hard astarboard!'

It would not be in time. He could feel the urgent thrust of the screw and the sluggish swing of the bows.

Kitson seemed unable to take the glasses away from his eyes. 'I can see them, sir! Two torpedoes running just below the surface! Jesus! They're coming right at us!'

There was a dull clang from the casing, and a messenger said in a broken voice, 'Fore hatch shut, sir!'

Jermain raised his own glasses and watched the twin parallel lines streaking through the glittering water towards him. So it had all been in vain. He had brought the *Temeraire* and every man aboard to this.

He blinked as the left lens of his glasses hardened into a white, thrusting bow wave. Like a man in a trance he heard Kitson screaming, 'It's Number One! Oh Christ Jesus, *look at him*!' He was sobbing uncontrollably as the little fishing boat steamed purposefully across the *Temeraire*'s swinging bows, her blunt outline blotting out the twin white lines as she passed.

Jermain shouted, 'Clear the bridge! Stand by One and Two!' With his eyes still on the little fishing boat he pressed the diving button and heard the klaxon screaming below him.

Once, as the sunlight glanced off the boat's wheelhouse, he imagined that he could see Wolfe looking at him. He was standing quite still and relaxed, even as the two torpedoes bit into the frail hull and exploded in one deafening roar.

As the *Temeraire* filled her tanks and plunged into a steep dive, Jermain threw himself through the hatch. Above, patterned against the bright sky, he could see the remains of the shattered boat falling like so much matchwood. They seemed to fall very slowly, as if unwilling to return to the sea.

His feet thudded into the control room as the lower hatch

was slammed shut. Colquhoun was standing beside his father, his eyes dull with fatigue.

Jermain snapped, 'Hold her at sixty feet! The submarine is at periscope depth!' He waited, counting the seconds as the lights kept up their merry dance.

The intercom barked, 'Ready to fire, sir!'

Jermain dropped his hand and the speaker intoned, 'Fire One!' He felt the slight thud as the torpedo left the tube. 'Fire Two!' Then the voice said, 'Both torpedoes running, sir!'

'Up periscope!' He hardly recognised his own voice.

The sea was calm again, but for a few scattered pieces of bobbing flotsam. He moved the handles briefly to watch for the other ship. It had altered course, baffled by the *Temeraire*'s sudden dive.

He remembered Colquhoun's stricken face as he had clambered aboard with Lightfoot's body. There was a story there, he thought. But it could keep. Colquhoun had done well. They had all done well.

He tensed as a double explosion rumbled through the sea and battered against the *Temeraire*'s hull. Then there were other, disjointed sounds, terrible noises of tearing metal, accompanied by the jubilant inrush of water.

Then he saw it. Just briefly. Like the ending of a nightmare. The stricken submarine's stern was rising straight up out of the sea, her twin screws still turning, burnished in the sunlight.

Around him, excluded from what he could see through the periscope, the others watched his face and waited.

Jermain saw the grey hull begin to slide under in a welter of giant air bubbles and a thick, spreading blanket of black oil. It was like blood, he thought.

Then with sudden force the submarine gave up the fight and went into a steep dive. For many minutes they all heard her falling, down and down, the toughened steel screaming through the water as if in torment.

Jermain stepped back from the periscope and said, 'Bring her round to one seven zero. Dive to six hundred feet.'

When he looked again through the periscope he could see the water already closing over the upper lens to blot out the nodding flotsam and the spreading stain of oil.

Mayo asked quietly, 'Shall we attack the A/S trawler, sir?'

Jermain shook his head. It was almost an effort to reply. 'No, Pilot. We'll leave them to talk about it.' He looked around at the tired, watching faces. 'I think someone should talk about it!'

The *Temeraire* lifted her rudder and dived deep into the embracing darkness, and set course for home.

RENDEZVOUS -
SOUTH ATLANTIC

To the armed merchant cruisers
Rawalpindi, Jervis Bay, Laurentic,
Dunvegan Castle *and to all those other*
proud ships which sailed in peace but
went to war when they were most needed

I am the tomb of one shipwrecked;
but sail thou: for even while we
perished, the other ships sailed
on across the sea.
From The Greek Anthology

Contents

1 Scapa

The camouflaged Humber staff car ground to a halt, its front bumper within feet of the jetty's edge, and stood vibrating noisily as if eager to be off again.

The small Wren driver, muffled to the ears against the intense cold, made to switch off the windscreen wipers, saying, 'Well, here you are, sir. There'll be a boat across at any minute.'

She turned slightly as the car's only passenger said, 'Don't switch them off. Not yet.'

Oblivious to her curious stare, Commander Andrew Lindsay leaned forward to peer through the rain-slashed glass, his face outwardly devoid of expression.

Grey. Everything was grey. The misty outline of the islands, the sky, and the varied shapes of the ships as they tugged at their cables in the wind and rain. The waters of the great natural anchorage of Scapa Flow were the deeper colour of lead, the only life being that of swirling tide-race and the turbulent undertow.

Scapa. That one word was enough. To thousands of sailors in two world wars it spoke volumes. Damp and cold. Raging gales and seas so fierce as to need every ounce of skill to fight clear of rocks and surrounding islets.

As his eyes moved slowly across the anchored ships he wondered what his new command would be like. You could never tell, in spite of your orders, your searching through manuals and intelligence reports. Even at the naval headquarters in Kirkwall they had been unhelpful.

H.M.S. *Benbecula*, an armed merchant cruiser, had been fitting out for six months, and now lay awaiting her new captain. On the stormy crossing by way of the Pentland Firth from the Scottish mainland he had seen about a dozen young seamen watching him, their inexperienced eyes filled with what—curiosity, hope or, like himself, resignation? One thing was certain, they had all been as green as grass. In more ways than one, for within minutes of casting off most of them had been violently seasick.

And this was only September. The second September of the war.

The Wren driver studied his profile and wondered. Her passenger was about thirty-three or four. When she had picked him up by the H.Q. building she had seen him staring moodily at the glistening street and had sensed a sudden throb of interest. And that was unusual in Scapa. The Wrens were vastly outnumbered by the male services, and it had become hard to raise much excitement over one more newcomer. Yet there was something different about this one, she decided. He had fair hair, longer than usual for a regular officer, and his blue eyes were level and extremely grave. As if he were grappling with some constant problem. Trying to come to a decision. As he was at the moment as he stared over this hateful view. He had that latent touch of recklessness about him which was appealing to her, but at the same time seemed withdrawn. Even lost.

He said quietly, 'You can switch them off now. Thank you.'

Lindsay settled down in the seat, pulling his greatcoat collar about his ears. Grey and cold. Greedy and impatient to test him again.

He knew the girl was watching him and wondered idly what she was like under all those shapeless clothes and scarves. In her twenties probably, like most of the Wrens he had seen in the warm rooms of the H.Q. building. He smiled grimly. In her twenties. He had entered the navy as a twelve-year-old cadet in 1920. Twenty-one years ago. All that time without a break. Working and studying. Travelling and learning his trade. His smile vanished. Just for this. Command of some clapped-out merchant ship, which because of a few guns and a naval crew was classed as a warship. An armed merchant cruiser. Even the title sounded crazy.

'I think I can see a motor boat coming, sir.'

He started. Caught off guard. All at once he felt the returning anxiety and uncertainty. If only he was going back to sea in a destroyer again. Any destroyer would do, even one like the old *Vengeur*. But he must stop thinking like that. *Vengeur* was gone. Lying on the sea-bed in mid-Atlantic.

He saw the distant shape of the motor boat, her blurred outline scurrying above the white moustache of her bow wave. Soon now.

Warily he let his mind return to his last command, like a man touching a newly healed wound. He had been given her just two days after the outbreak of war. She had been old, a veteran V & W class destroyer built in the First World War, and yet he had come to love and respect her quaint ways and whims.

As the first nervous thrusts by friend and foe alike gave way to swift savagery, Lindsay, like most of his contemporaries, had had to start learning all over again. Theories on tactics became myths overnight. The firm belief that nothing could break the Navy's control of the seas was stretched to and beyond the limit of even the most optimistic. Around them the world went mad. Dunkirk, the collapse of Norway and the Low Countries, the French surrender with the subsequent loss of their fleet's support, piled one burden upon another. In the Navy the nearness of disaster and loss was more personal. Right here, within sighting distance of this quivering car, the battleship *Royal Oak* had been sunk at anchor by a

U-boat. The defences were supposed to be impregnable. That was what they always said.

And just six months ago, while he had been in hospital, the battle-cruiser *Hood* had been destroyed by the mighty German *Bismarck*. The Navy had been stunned. It was not just because a powerful unit had been sunk. In war you had to accept losses. But the *Hood* had been different. She had been more than just a ship. She had been a symbol. Huge, beautiful and arrogant, she had cruised the world between the wars, showed the flag in dozens of foreign ports, lain at anchor at reviews ablaze in coloured lights and bedecked with bunting to the delight of old and young alike. To the public at large she *was* the Royal Navy. Unreachable, a sure shield. Everything.

In a blizzard, just one shell had been enough to blast her to oblivion. From the hundreds of men who served her, only three had been found alive.

Perhaps his own *Vengeur* had been closer to reality, he thought vaguely. Old but well-tried and strongly built. She had served her company well, even at the last.

He could remember the moment exactly. As if it were yesterday. Or now.

His had been the senior ship of the escort to a west-bound convoy for the United States. Twenty ships, desperately needed to bring back the stores and needs of a nation alone and at war.

Two merchantmen had been torpedoed and sunk in the first three days, but after that it seemed as if the Atlantic was going to favour them. A great gale had got up, and for day after day the battered convoy had driven steadily westward, with *Vengeur* always hurrying up and down the straggling lines of ships, urging and pleading, threatening and encouraging. The rest of the escort had consisted of two converted trawlers and a patrol vessel which had been laid down in 1915.

It was all that the greatest navy in the world had to spare, so they had made the best of it.

Perhaps the invisible U-boats ran deep to avoid the storm and so lost the convoy, or maybe they went searching for easier targets. They would have had little difficulty.

But one U-boat commander had been more persistent and had managed to keep up with the ragged lines of merchantmen. He must have been trying for the most valuable ship in the convoy, a big, modern tanker which with luck would bring back enough fuel to carry the bombers across Germany and show *them* what it was like.

The wind had eased, and the sky had been clearer than for many days. It had almost been time to rendezvous with the American patrol vessels, an arrangement which made a lie to their neutrality, but one which was more than welcome to merchantmen and escorts alike.

There were three torpedoes, all of which missed the tanker by a narrow margin. But one hit the elderly *Vengeur* on the port side of her forecastle, shearing off her bows like a giant axe.

The ship's company had mercifully been at action stations at the time of the explosion, otherwise the watch below would have died or been drowned later when the forepart tore adrift.

As it was, the ship went down in fifteen minutes, with dignity. Or as the coxswain had said later, 'Like the bleedin' lady she was.'

Only five men had been lost, and all the remainder had been picked up from the boats and rafts by a Swedish freighter which had been an unwilling spectator to the sinking.

Lindsay dug his hands into his greatcoat pockets and clenched them into fists. Just one more sinking. It happened all the time, and the powers that be would be glad the *Vengeur* and not the big tanker had caught the torpedo.

It was later. Later. He gritted his teeth together to stop himself from speaking aloud.

The girl asked, 'Are you all right, sir?'

He turned on her. 'What the hell do you mean by that?'

She looked away. 'I'm sorry.'

'No.' He removed his cap and ran his fingers through his hair. It felt damp with sweat. Fear. 'No, I'm the one to apologise.'

She looked at him again, her eyes searching. 'Was it bad, sir?'

He shrugged. 'Enough.' Abruptly he asked, 'Are you engaged to be married or anything?'

She eyed him steadily. 'No, sir. I was. He bought it over Hamburg last year.'

'I see.' Bought it. So coolly said. The resilience of youth at war. 'Well, I'd better get out now. Otherwise the boat will go away without me.'

'Here, sir. I'll give you a hand with your bags.' She ignored his protests and climbed out of the car on to the wet stones of the jetty.

The wind slammed the door back against the car, and Lindsay felt the wind lashing his face like wire. Below the steps he could see the tossing motor boat, the oilskinned figures of coxswain and bowman.

He said, 'Maybe I'll see you again.' He tried to smile but his face felt like a mask.

She squinted up at him, the rain making her forehead and jaunty cap shine in the grey light. 'Maybe.'

'What name is it?'

She tugged down the sodden scarf from her mouth and smiled. 'Collins, sir.' She wrinkled her nose. 'Eve Collins. Daft, isn't it?'

She had a nice mouth. Lindsay realised one of the seamen was picking up his bags, his eyes on the girl's legs.

He said, 'Take care then.'

He walked to the steps and hurried down into the waiting boat.

The girl returned to the car and slid behind the wheel, her wet duffel coat making a smear across the worn leather. As she backed the car away from the jetty's edge she saw the boat turning fussily towards the anchorage. Nice bloke, she thought. She frowned, letting in the gear with a violent jerk, nice, but scared of something. Why did I give him my name? He'll not be back. She looked at herself in the mirror. Poor bastard. Like all the rest of us in this bloody place.

———————

Lindsay remained standing as the boat dipped and curtsied across the wind-ruffled water, gripping the canopy with both hands as he watched the anchored ships. Battleships and heavy cruisers, fleet destroyers and supply vessels, the grey metal gleamed dully as the little boat surged past. The only colour was made by the ships' streaming ensigns or an occasional splash of dazzle paint on some sheltering Atlantic escort. His experienced eye told him about most of the ships. Their names and classes, where they had met before. Faces and voices, the Navy was like a family. A religion. And all these ships, perhaps the best in the fleet, were tied here at Scapa, swinging round their buoys and anchors, waiting. Just in case the German heavy units broke out again to try and destroy the convoys, scatter the defences and shorten the odds against England even more.

Bismarck had been caught and sunk after destroying the *Hood*. But it had been a close run thing and had taken damn near the whole Home Fleet to do it. *Graf Spee* had been destroyed by her own people in Montevideo rather than accept defeat by a victorious but inferior British force. But again, she had done well to get that far, had sunk many valuable ships before she was run to earth. And even now the mighty *Tirpitz* and several other powerful modern capital ships were said to be lurking in Norwegian fjords or in captured French ports along the Bay of Biscay. Just gauging the right moment. And until that moment, these ships had to lie here, fretting, cursing and wasting.

He glanced at the boat's coxswain. Probably wondering what sort of a skipper they were getting. Was he any good? Could he keep them all in one piece?

The seaman said gruffly, 'There she is, sir. Fine on the starboard bow.'

Lindsay held his breath. For a moment she was just one more shadow in the steady downpour, and then she was right there, looming above him like a dripping steel cliff. Lindsay knew her history, had studied her picture and layout more than once, but after a low-lying destroyer, or any other warship for that matter, a merchantman always appeared huge and vulnerable. It took more than drab grey paint, a naval ensign and a few guns to change that.

Five hundred feet long from her unfashionable straight stem to her overhanging stern, and twelve-and-a-half thousand tons, she had steamed many thousands of miles since she had first slid into the Clyde in 1919. Born at a time of dashed hopes and unemployment, of world depression and post-war apathy, she had represented jobs to the shipyard workers rather than some source of a new hope. But she had done well for herself and her owners. Described in the old shipping lists as an intermediate liner, she had been almost constantly on the London to Brisbane run. Port Said, Aden, Colombo, Fremantle, Adelaide, Melbourne and Sydney. Her ports of call were like a record of the merchant navy itself, which in spite of everything had been the envy of the world.

Cargo, mail and passengers, she had pounded her way over the years, earning money, giving pleasure, making jobs.

After Dunkirk, when Britain had at last realised the war was not going to be won by stalemate, if at all, she had waited for a new role. The stately ocean liners had become hospital ships and troopers, and every other freighter, tanker or aged tramp steamer was thrown into the battle for survival on the convoy routes. *Benbecula* had done some trooping, but she was of an awkward size. Not suitable for big cargoes, too small for large numbers of servicemen on passage, she had been moved like a clumsy pawn from one war theatre to the next.

With the Navy stretched beyond safety limits she had been earmarked at last as an armed merchant cruiser. She could endure the heaviest weather and stay away from base far longer than the average warship. To patrol the great wastes of the North Atlantic off Iceland, or the barren sea areas of the Denmark Strait. Watch for blockade runners, report anything suspicious, but stay out of real danger. Any heavy naval unit could make scrap of an unarmoured hull like hers. *Rawalpindi* had found that out. And only some nine months ago the *Jervis Bay* had been sunk defending a fully loaded convoy a thousand miles outward bound from the American coast. The convoy had scattered in safety while the *Jervis Bay*, outgunned and ablaze, had matched shot for shot with a German battleship. Her destruction, her sacrifice, had brought pride as well as shame to those who had left the country so weak and so blind to its danger.

The motor boat cut across the tall bows and Lindsay saw the overhanging bridge wing, the solitary funnel and the alien muzzle of a six-inch gun below her foremast.

He said, 'She seems to have a list to starboard.'

The coxswain grinned. "S'right, sir. I'm told she nearly always has had. One of the old hands said she got a biff in some typhoon afore the war an' never got over it like.'

Lindsay frowned. He had not realised he had spoken his thoughts aloud. A slight list to starboard. And he was not even aboard her yet.

Again he sensed the chill of anxiety. He forced himself to go over the facts in his mind. Six six-inch guns, two hundred and fifty officers and ratings, most of whom were straight from the training depots.

The first lieutenant's name was Goss. John Goss.

The hull towered right over him now, and he saw the accommodation ladder stretching away endlessly towards several peering faces at the guardrail. How many passengers had swarmed up and down this ladder? Souvenirs, dirty postcards from Aden, a brass bowl for an aunt in Eastbourne.

Stop. Must stop right now.

He stood upright in the pitching boat as the bowman hooked on with studied ease.

As Lindsay jumped on to the grating the boat's mechanic hissed, 'Wot's 'e like, Bob?'

The coxswain watched Lindsay's slim figure hurrying up the side and replied through his teeth, 'Straight-ringer. A regular. Not like the last skipper.'

The mechanic groaned. 'Either 'e's blotted 'is copybook an' is no bleedin' good for nuthin' else, or we're bein' given some special, bloody-awful job! Either way it's no bloody use, is it?'

The coxswain listened to the squeal of pipes from the top of the ladder and said unfeelingly, 'Looks that way, so grab them bags and jump about.'

The other man muttered, 'Roll on my bleedin' twelve, and bugger all cox'ns!'

The coxswain tried to recall if there was a film on in the fleet canteen tonight. Probably full before he got ashore anyway. He glared at the dull sky and the rain. Bloody Scapa, he thought.

———————

Lindsay looked at the assembled side party, anonymous in their glistening oilskins. After the jetty and the boat, it seemed strangely sheltered here. The entry port was situated beneath the promenade and boat decks, and with the wind blowing across the opposite bow it was suddenly quiet.

'Welcome aboard, sir.' A tall, heavily built officer stepped forward and saluted. 'I'm Goss.'

Lindsay knew that Goss was forty-five, but he looked fifteen years older. He had a heavy jowled, unsmiling face, and in his oilskin he seemed to tower head and shoulders over everyone else.

Lindsay held out his hand. 'Thank you, Number One.'

Goss had not blinked or dropped his eyes. 'I've got one watch and the second part of port watch ashore on store parties, sir. We ammunitioned at Leith before we came here.' He moved his eyes for the first time and said almost fiercely, 'You'll not need to worry about this ship, sir.'

Something in his tone, the hint of challenge or aggressiveness, made Lindsay reply coldly, 'We shall have to see, eh?'

Goss turned away, his mouth hardening slightly. 'This is Lieutenant Barker, sir. Paymaster and supply officer. He's got the books ready for your inspection.'

Lindsay got a brief impression of a toothy smile, pale eyes behind hornrimmed glasses, and nodded. 'Good.'

Goss seemed very ill at ease. Angry, resentful, even hostile.

It had been a bad beginning. What the hell was the matter? Lindsay blamed himself. They were all probably more worried about their new captain than he had properly realised.

He tried again. 'Sailing orders will be coming aboard in the first dog watch.' He paused. 'So there'll be no libertymen, I'm afraid, until I know what's happening.'

Surprisingly, Goss smiled. It was more like a grimace. He said harshly, 'Good. Most of the hands are more intent on *looking* like sailors than doing anything useful. Bloody shower of civvies and layabouts!'

Lindsay glanced at his watch. It had stopped, and he remembered angrily that he had been looking at the clock on St. Magnus cathedral in Kirkwall to set the correct time when the Wren had arrived with her car.

Goss saw the quick frown. 'I'm afraid lunch has been cleared away, sir.' He hesitated. 'Of course I *could* call the cook and ——.'

Lindsay looked away. 'No. A sandwich will do.'

He could not even recall when he had last eaten properly. He had to break this contact. Find some privacy to reassemble himself and his mind.

'Then if you'll follow me, sir.' Goss gestured towards a ladder. 'The captain's quarters are below the bridge deck. Nothing's changed there yet.'

Lindsay followed him in silence. Changed? What did he mean? He saw several seamen working about the decks but avoided their eyes. It was too soon for quick judgements. Unlike Goss, who apparently despised men because they were 'civvies'. The Navy would be in a damn poor way without them. What did he expect for a worn old ship like this?

Aloud he asked, 'What about this list to starboard?'

Goss was already climbing the ladder. He did not turn round. 'Always had it'—— pause—— 'Sir,' was all he said.

The captain's quarters were certainly spacious and ran the whole breadth of the bridge. There was a ladder which led directly above to the chart room and W/T office, the navigation bridge and compass platform, and from it the occupant could see most of the boat deck and forward to the bows as well.

Goss opened the door, his eyes watchful as Lindsay walked into the day cabin.

After the *Vengeur* it was another world. A green fitted carpet and wood panelling. Good furniture, and some chintz curtains at each brightly polished scuttle. Above an oak sideboard was a coloured photograph of the *Benbecula* as she had once been. Shining green hull and pale buff funnel. Her old line, the Aberdeen and Pacific Steam Navigation Company, was also present in the shape of the company's crest and a small glass box containing the launching mallet used at her birth.

Goss said quietly, 'There are, *were* five ships in the company, sir.' He took off his oilskin and folded it carefully on his arm. He had the interwoven gold lace of a lieutenant-commander in the Royal Naval Reserve on his reefer. 'Good ships, and I've served in all but one of them.'

Lindsay looked at him gravely. 'Always with the one company?'

'Aye. Since I was fourteen. Would have been Master by now, but for the war.'

'I see.'

Lindsay walked to the nearest scuttle and looked at the swirling water far below. Goss's comment was part of the reason for his attitude, he thought. *Would* have been Master. Of this ship perhaps?

He turned and saw the books lined along a polished desk awaiting his scrutiny and signature. Neat and tidy like the oilskin on Goss's beefy arm.

He asked, 'Was this your last ship, Number One?'

Goss nodded curtly. 'I was Chief Officer. But when we stopped trooping and the Admiralty took over I stayed on with her. Being a reservist, they couldn't very well object.'

'Why should they *object*?'

Goss flushed. 'Not happy unless they're moving everyone about.'

'You may be right.' He turned away. 'Now if you'll arrange a sandwich I'll settle in while I'm reading these books.'

Goss hesitated. 'I hear you were in hospital, sir.' His eyes flickered. 'Lost your ship, I believe.'

'Yes.'

Goss seemed satisfied. 'I'll leave you then. Anything you want you can ring on those handsets or press the steward's bell, sir.'

The door closed silently and Lindsay sat down behind the desk. Not good, but it might have been a worse beginning. A whole lot worse. He leafed through the neat pages. Apart from Goss and himself there were seventeen officers aboard, including a doctor, and for some obscure reason, a lieutenant of marines. Most of the officers were hostilities-only. He smiled in spite of his taut nerves. *Civvies,* as Goss would have described them. A few, like Goss, including the engineer officers, Lieutenant Barker whom he had briefly met, and a Mr. Tobey, the boatswain, were Royal Naval Reserve. Professional seamen and well used to ships like *Benbecula.* That was something. The only regulars appeared to be the gunnery officer, a Lieutenant Maxwell, and two pensioners called back from retirement, Baldock, the gunner, and Emerson, a warrant-engineer. He paused at the foot of the page. And one solitary midshipman named Kemp. What an appointment for a midshipman, he thought bitterly. He saw himself in the bulkhead mirror and shuddered. Or Commander Andrew Lindsay for that matter.

The wind sighed against the bridge, and he was conscious of the lack of movement. A destroyer would be pitching to her moorings even here in Scapa Flow. He would have to meet his officers, explore the hull from bridge to keel. Get the *feel* of her.

He lowered his face into his hands. Must do it soon. Waste no time in remembering or trying not to remember. But he had got over the *Vengeur,* as much as anyone could who had seen a ship, his ship, die. But the rest. He hesitated, remembering the doctor's calm voice at the hospital. That might take longer. Avoid it, the doctor had said.

Lindsay stood up violently. Avoid it. How the hell could you? The man was a bloody fool even to suggest it.

He stared at a tall, mournful looking man in a white jacket and carrying a silver tray covered in a crisp napkin.

The man said, 'I'm Jupp, sir. Chief steward.'

Lindsay swallowed hard. The steward must think him

mad. 'Put the tray down there, and thank you, er, Jupp.'

The steward laid the tray down and said dolefully, 'I made 'em meself, sir. Bit of tinned salmon I'd been savin'. Some spam, and a few olives which I obtained from a Greek freighter in Freetown.' He looked at Lindsay, adding, 'Nice to have you aboard, if I may make so bold.'

Lindsay studied him. 'I take it you were with the company, too?'

Jupp smiled gently. 'Twenty-three years, sir. We've 'ad some very nice people to deal with.' The smile became doleful again. 'You'll soon settle in, sir, so don't fret about it so.'

Lindsay felt the anger rising uncontrollably like a flood.

'I'm really glad you've come to us, sir.' Jupp made towards the door.

'Yes, thank you.'

Lindsay stared at the closed door, his anger gone and leaving him empty. Jupp seemed to think he was joining the company rather than assuming command. Yet in spite of his jarring nerves and earlier despair he took a sandwich from the plate. It was thin and beautifully cut.

There was a small card under the plate which read, *'On behalf of the Aberdeen and Pacific Steam Navigation Company may we welcome you aboard the S.S. Benbecula.'* Jupp had crossed out the ship's title and inserted H.M.S. with a pencil.

Lindsay sank back into a chair and stared around the silent cabin. Jupp was at least trying to help. He reached for another sandwich, suddenly conscious of a consuming hunger.

So then, would he, he decided grimly, if only to hold on to his sanity.

———————

Jupp walked around the captain's day cabin, flicking a curtain into place here, examining an ashtray there, and generally checking that things were as they should be. It was early evening, but the pipe to darken ship had sounded long since as it seemed to get dark quickly in Scapa Flow. Not that it had been very light throughout Lindsay's first day aboard.

He sat at his desk, his jacket open as he pushed the last file of papers to one side. He felt tired, even spent, and was surprised to see that he had been working steadily for a full hour since his methodical tour around the ship.

The dockyard people at Leith had been very ruthless with their surgery, he thought. For once below 'A' Deck there appeared little left of the original internal hull. There was a well deck both forward and aft, but where the main holds had once been were now shored up with massive steel frames to support the main armament on the upper decks. There were four six-inch guns on the foredeck, two on either beam, and the remaining two had been mounted aft, again one on either side. There was not much alternative in a ship constructed for peaceful purposes, but it was obvious that at no time could *Benbecula* use more than half her main armament to fire at one target. There was an elderly twelve-pounder situated right aft on the poop, a relic of the ship's short service as a trooper, and on the boat deck itself he had discovered four modern Oerlikons. Altogether they represented *Benbecula*'s sole defence or means of attack.

Most of the original lifeboats had gone, and had been replaced by naval whalers, two motor boats and a number of Carley floats and wooden rafts. The latter were the only things which really counted if a ship went down fast.

She had a modern refrigeration space where he had found Paymaster-Lieutenant Barker and his assistants busily checking the last of the incoming stores. Barker had been a ship's purser before the war, some of that time in the *Benbecula*, and had spoken with obvious nostalgia of 'better days', as he had described them.

Many of the passenger cabins had been transferred into quarters for the ship's company, a rare luxury for naval ratings, even though the dockyard had seen fit to cram them in four or five to each space.

Accompanied by Goss, Lindsay had tried to miss nothing, had kept his thoughts to himself until he had completed his inspection.

Magazines for the six-inch guns had been constructed on the orlop deck below the waterline, with lifts to carry the shells and charges the seemingly great distance to the mountings above. The guns were very old. First World War vintage, they were hand-operated and almost independent of any sort of central fire control.

He had met Lieutenant Maxwell, the gunnery officer, although he had the vague impression the man had been waiting for him. Gauging the right moment to appear as if by accident.

Maxwell was a regular officer, but about the same age as himself. Thin featured, bony, and very rigid in his carriage, he never seemed to relax throughout the meeting. His knuckles remained firmly bunched at his sides, the thumbs in line with his trouser seams, as if on parade at Whale Island.

While they were speaking, Goss was called away by the duty quartermaster, and Maxwell said quickly, 'Pretty rough lot, I'm afraid, sir. But still, with a proper captain we'll soon whip 'em into shape.'

Lindsay had discovered that, unlike Goss, the gunnery officer had been referring to the R.N.R. officers and ratings of the ship's company. He had also gathered that Goss and Maxwell rarely spoke to one another.

Later, on the way to the boiler room, Goss had remarked sourly, 'Did you know, sir, Maxwell was on the beach for five years until the war? Made some bloody cockup, I expect. Damned unfair to have him put aboard *us!*'

Lindsay leaned back in the chair and interlaced his fingers behind his head. Goss probably thought the same about his new captain.

Jupp paused by the desk, his eyes glinting in the lamplight. 'I expect you'd like a drink, sir?'

'Thank you. A whisky, if you have it.'

Jupp regarded him gravely. 'I always manage to keep some for my captains, sir.' He sounded surprised that Lindsay should have doubted his ability to obtain something which was such a rarity almost everywhere.

Lindsay watched Jupp as he busied himself at the sideboard. *There* is a man who is happy in his work, he thought wearily.

Then he remembered Fraser, the chief engineer. Lieutenant-Commander (E) Donald Fraser had taken him on a tour around the boiler and engine rooms. He was a small, almost delicate looking man with iron grey hair, a sardonic smile, and a very dry sense of humour. Lindsay had liked him immediately.

Goss must be a good seaman, and Maxwell had sounded competent on matters of gunnery. Even Barker seemed shrewd and active in the affairs of his vital department. But Lindsay, even after much heart-searching, could not find much to like about any of them. Most ships' engineer officers were men apart, from his experience, defending their private worlds of roaring machinery from all comers, including captains, to the death. Fraser, on the other hand, was almost insulting about his trade and about the ships he had served. He had been at sea since he was seventeen. He was now fifty.

He had only been chief in the *Benbecula* for eight months, but had served before that in her sister ship, the *Eriskay*.

'Alike as two peas in a pod,' he had said without enthusiasm. 'Sometimes when I'm doing my rounds I almost forget I've changed bloody ships!'

When Lindsay had asked him about his previous service Fraser had said, 'I was with Cunard for ten years, y'know. Now there was a company!'

'Why did you leave?'

Fraser had run his wintry eye around the mass of glittering dials and throbbing generators before replying slowly, 'Got fed up with the wife. Longer voyages in this crabby company was the only peace I could get!'

As Lindsay had made to leave the engine room's humid air Fraser had said simply, 'You and I'll not fight, sir. I can give you fifteen, maybe sixteen knots. But if you want more I'll do what I can.' He had grinned, showing his small, uneven teeth like a knowing fox. 'If I have to blow the guts out of this old bucket!'

The whisky glass was empty, and he licked his lips as Jupp refilled it soundlessly from a decanter. He had hardly noticed it going down, and that was a bad sign. The doctor had said . . . he shut his mind to the memory like a steel trap.

Instead he turned over the rain-dampened envelope which the guardboat had dropped aboard during the first dog watch. Orders. But nothing fresh or even informative. The ship would remain at her present moorings and notice for steam until further notice.

Muffled by the thick glass scuttles he heard the plaintive note of a bugle. Probably one of the battleships. He felt suddenly tired and strangely cut off. Lonely. In a small ship you were always in each others' pockets. You knew everyone, whereas here. . . . He sipped the second drink, listening to the muted wind, the muffled footsteps of a signalman on the bridge above.

Jupp asked discreetly, 'Will you be dining aboard, sir?'

He thought suddenly of the small Wren with the wind-reddened face. He could go ashore and give her a call. Take her somewhere for a drink. But where? Anyway, she would probably laugh at him.

He replied, 'Yes.' He thought Jupp seemed pleased by his answer.

'I will try and arrange something special for you, sir.' Jupp glanced at the bulkhead clock as if troubled and then hurried purposefully away.

Lindsay switched on the radio repeater above the sideboard, half listening to the smooth, tired voice of the announcer. Air raids, and another setback in the Western desert. Last night our light coastal forces engaged enemy E-boats in the Channel. Losses were inflicted. The Secretary of the Admiralty regrets to announce the loss of H.M. trawler *Milford Queen*. Next of kin have been informed. He switched it off angrily without knowing why. Words, words. What did they mean to those who were crouching in the cellars and shelters, listening to the drone of bombers, waiting for their world to cave in on them?

There was a tap on the door. It was Fraser.

'Yes, Chief?' He thrust his hands behind him, knowing they were shaking violently.

The engineer officer held out a bottle of gin. 'I thought you might care to take a dram with me, sir?' His eye fell on the decanter. 'But of course if you were to offer something else, well now——.'

Lindsay smiled and waved Fraser to a chair, thankful he had come. Glad not to be alone on this first evening aboard. Knowing too why Jupp had been so concerned. Goss was first lieutenant and senior officer in the wardroom. He should have invited the new captain down to meet the other officers. Break the ice. Jupp would have been expecting it.

He looked at Fraser and realised he was studying him with fixed attention.

'Your health, Chief.'

Fraser held the glass to the light and said quietly, 'Ah well, we're both Scots, so there's some hope for this bloody ship!'

Beyond the tall sides of the hull the wind eased slightly, but the rain mounted in intensity, beating the black water like bullets.

Ashore, sitting in her cramped billet and darning a stocking, Wren Collins cocked her head to listen to it.

Aloud she said vehemently, 'Bloody Scapa!'

2 The nightmare

Andrew Lindsay awoke from his nightmare, struggling and tearing at the sheet and blankets, gasping
for air, and knowing from the soreness in his throat he
had been shouting aloud. Shouting to break the torment.
Hold it at bay.

Stumbling and sobbing in the pitch darkness he
groped his way across the cabin, crashing into unfamiliar
furniture, almost falling, until he had found a scuttle. He
could hear himself cursing as he fought to raise the heavy
deadlight and then to unscrew the clips around the glass
scuttle.

As he heaved it open he had the breath knocked from
him as with savage eagerness the rain sluiced across his
face and chest, soaking his hair and pyjamas until he was
shivering both from chill and sheer panic. He thrust his
head through the open scuttle, letting the rain drench
over him, feeling the cold brass rim against his shoulders.
The scuttle was large. Big enough to wriggle through if
you tried hard enough.

Breathing unsteadily he peered through the rain. The
sky was lighter, and he thought he saw the outline of
another ship anchored nearby. It was impossible to tell
what time it was, or how long the dream had lasted, or
when it had begun. He had never been able to tell. Just
that it was always the same.

Wearily he slammed down the deadlight and groped
back to the bunk where he switched on the overhead
reading lamp.

The sheet was damp, but not only from his rain-soaked body. He had been sweating as he had relived it. Sweating and fighting to free its grip on him.

He felt his breath slowing down and pulled his dressing gown from a hook. He was ice cold and shivering badly.

Around him the ship was like a tomb, as if she were listening to him. Not a footfall or even a creak broke the stillness.

Be logical. Face up to it. He went painstakingly through the motions, even filling his pipe unseeingly to steady himself. Suppose it would never loosen its grip? That the doctors had been wrong. After all, naval hospitals were overworked, too glutted with an unending stream of burned, scalded, savaged wrecks to care much about one more casualty.

He lit the pipe carefully, tasting the raw whisky from the previous night's drinking, and knowing he had been close to vomiting.

Across the cabin he saw his face in a mirror, picked out in the match flame as if floating. He shuddered. Drowning. The face was too young for the way he felt. Tousled hair, wide, staring eyes. Like a stranger's.

The tobacco smoke swirled around him as he stood up and walked vaguely back and forth on the carpet.

Perhaps if it had not happened right after the *Vengeur*'s sinking he would have been able to cope. Or maybe unknowingly he had already seen and done too much. Used up his resistance.

Feet clattered on a ladder overhead. The morning watchmen getting their cocoa carried to them while they tried to stay awake on the bridge.

It was strange to realise that throughout his life in the Navy he had been content with almost everything. Perhaps because it *was* everything to him. His father he could hardly remember. He had been wounded in that other war at Jutland and had never really recovered. His mother, worn out with worry for her husband, nursing

him, and hating the Service which had turned him into a
remote, broken man, had remarried almost immediately
after his death. Staying only long enough to carry out
her dead husband's wish, that Andrew should be entered
into the R.N. College at Dartmouth. She had married
a Canadian, a much older man with a thriving
business in Alberta, and had never returned. In her own
way she was getting as far as possible from the sea which
had taken her husband and separated her from her only
son.

Denied a normal home life, Lindsay had given everything to the Navy. In his heart he wondered if that
driving force, his inbuilt trust, had been the main cause of
his breakdown. For war was not a matter of weapons and
strategy alone. Above all it was endurance. To survive
you had to endure, no matter what you saw or felt. The
Atlantic had proved that well enough. Endurance, and
the grim patience of one vast slaughterhouse.

Could any one thing break a man? How many times did
he ask himself this same unanswerable question?

He sat down and stared at the glowing bowl of his
pipe.

The Swedish ship had taken *Vengeur*'s survivors into
New York. Had it been a British port things might have
been different. But to men starved of bright lights, kindness and a genuine desire to make up for their suffering,
it was another, unreal world. The cloak to hide, or at least
delay the shock of war.

After one week Lindsay and his men, some other
survivors and a large number of civilian passengers had
been put aboard a Dutch ship for passage to England. It
had an almost holiday atmosphere. The British seamen
loaded with gifts and food parcels, the friendly Dutch
crew, everything.

Lindsay had felt the loss of his ship much more once
the Dutch vessel had sailed to join an eastbound convoy.
Perhaps because for the first time he had nothing to do. A

passenger. A number in a lifeboat, or for a sitting in the
dining room.

He had shied away from the others, even his own
officers, and had found himself mixing more and more
with some of the civilian passengers. He had known it was
to help him as well as them. He needed to do something,
to occupy his mind, just as they required someone to
explain and to ease the anxieties once the land had
vanished astern.

There had been one family in particular. Dutch Jews,
they had been in Italy when war had begun, and unable
to reach home had started, as best they could, to escape.
They needed no telling as to what would happen if the
Germans got to them first. A nondescript Dutch Jew.
Plump, balding and bespectacled, with a chubby wife who
laughed a good deal. A quick, nervous laugh. And two
children, who were completely unaware of their parents'
sacrifices and strange courage on their behalf.

The family had got aboard a Greek freighter to Alex-
andria. Then in another ship via Suez to Durban, with the
little man using his meagre resources and his wife's
jewellery to oil the wheels, to bribe if necessary those who
were too busy or indifferent to care about them.

Finally they reached America, and after more delays,
examination of papers, and with money almost gone,
they got aboard the Dutch ship.

Lindsay had asked why they had not remained in
America. They would have been safe there. Well looked
after. It made more sense. The little man had shaken his
head. He was a Jew, but foremost he was Dutch. In
England he would soon find work, he was after all a
professional radio mechanic and highly skilled. He
would seek work to help those who had not given in. Who
were fighting and would win against the Nazis.

Almost shyly he had said, 'And I will know Holland is
not so far away. My wife and children will know it, too.'

The pipe had gone out, and Lindsay found he was

staring fixedly at the closed scuttle. Holding his breath.

It had been a fine bright morning and warmer than usual. He had been sitting in his cabin watching the horizon line mounting the glass scuttle, hanging motionless for a few seconds before retreating again as the ship rolled gently in the Atlantic swell. The previous evening he had been on the bridge with the Dutch master, who had told him that six U-boats thought earlier to have been near-by had moved away towards another convoy further south. This convoy was fast, and with luck should reach Liverpool in two more days.

The Dutch family had been getting visibly anxious with each long day, and Lindsay had called into their cabin before turning into his bunk to tell them the news. He could see them now. The two children grinning at him from a bunk, their parents sitting amidst a litter of shabby suitcases. They had thanked him, and the children had thrown him salutes as they had seen his men do.

That following morning he had wondered how he would pass the day. He had known that the Dutch family would be awake in their cabin, which was directly below his own. They had often joked about it.

At first he had thought it to be far off thunder, or a ship being torpedoed many miles away.

Even as he had walked to the scuttle there had been a tremendous explosion which had flung him on his back, deafening him with its intensity. When he had scrambled to his feet he had seen with shock that the sea beyond the scuttle was hidden in smoke, and as his hearing had returned he had heard screams and running feet, shrill whistles and the clamour of alarm bells.

Another explosion and one more almost immediately shook the ship as if she had rammed full-tilt into a berg. When he had regained his feet again he had found he could hardly stand, that the deck was already tilting steeply towards the sea.

When he had wrenched open the scuttle and peered into the smoke he had realised that the ship was already settling down, and when he had looked towards the water he had seen one of the sights uppermost in his nightmare.

The sea had almost reached the next line of scuttles below him. And at most of them there were arms and hands waving and clutching, like souls in torment. It was then he had realised that his own scuttle was just too small to climb through.

More violent crashes, the sounds of machinery tearing adrift and thundering through the hull. Escaping steam, and the banshee wail of the siren. It had taken all his strength to stagger up the deck to the door. The passageway had been full of reeling figures, forgotten lifebelts and scattered trays of tea which the stewards had been preparing at each cabin door.

Lindsay was on his feet again, pacing up and down as he relived each terrible minute. Fighting his way down companion ladders, looming faces and wild eyes, screams and desperate pleas for help, and with the ship dipping steadily on to her side.

Their cabin door had been open just a few inches, and he had heard the woman sobbing, the children whimpering like sick animals. In a shaky voice the little Dutchman had explained that the whole cabin bulkhead had collapsed, had sealed the door. They were trapped, with the sea already just a few feet below the scuttle.

Lindsay could hear himself saying, 'You must put the children through the scuttle.' It had been like hearing someone else. So calm and detached, even though every fibre was screaming inside him to run before the ship took the last plunge.

The other voice had asked quietly, 'Will *you* look after them?'

Lindsay could not remember much more. The next scene had been on the ravaged boat deck. Shattered lifeboats and dangling falls. Two dead seamen by a ventilator, and an officer falling like a puppet from the upper bridge.

Down on the water, littered with rafts and charred wood, with bodies and yelling survivors, he had seen the children float clear of the hull. Very small in their bright orange lifebelts. He had jumped into the water after them, but when he had looked back he had seen that the whole line of scuttles had dipped beneath the surface. But here and there he had seen pale arms waving like human weed until with a jubilant roar the pressure had forced them back out of sight.

Lindsay had swam with the children to a half-empty lifeboat, deaf to their terrified cries, and still only half aware what had happened.

The small convoy had scattered, and when he had stood up he had seen the nearest ship, a freighter, being bracketed by tall waterspouts, until she too reeled to explosions and was ablaze from bow to stern. Then and only then had he seen the enemy. Lying across the horizon like a low, grey islet, lit every so often by rippling orange flashes from her massive armament. The enemy never got nearer than about seven miles, and methodically, mercilessly she had continued to drop her great shells on the sinking ships, on the boats and amongst the helpless victims in the water. To the men behind those powerful rangefinders and gunsights the targets would have seemed very near. Close enough to watch as they died in agony under that clear sky.

Eventually, satisfied her work was done, the German raider had disappeared below the hard horizon line. Later it was said she was a pocket-battleship or perhaps a heavy cruiser. Nobody knew for sure. All Lindsay knew was that he had to stay five days in the boat with seven others who had somehow survived the bombardment. Five men and the two Dutch children.

A corvette had found them eventually, and the

children were buried at sea the next morning along with some victims from a previous attack. Lindsay had held them against himself for warmth and comfort long after they must have died from exposure, terror and exhaustion.

War was not for little children, as some smug journalist had written later.

Lindsay sat on the edge of the bunk and stared at the carpet. He had actually allowed himself to think about it. Just this once. What did he feel now? Despair, fear of what might happen next time? He rubbed his eyes with his knuckles, hearing a bugle bleating out reveille across the Flow. *Wakey, wakey! Lash up and stow!*

If he felt anything, anything at all, it was hatred.

The door opened an inch and lamplight cut a path across the carpet to his bare feet.

Jupp asked, 'Are you ready for some tea, sir?'

Lindsay shook himself. 'Thanks.'

Jupp padded to the table. 'I heard you about, sir, so I thought to meself, ah, the captain'll like a nice hot strong cup of char, that's what I thought.'

'Heard me?' Caution again, like an animal at bay.

'Thought you was on the telephone, sir.' Jupp's face was in shadow. 'I was already in me pantry, an' the old *Becky*'s a quiet ship, sir.'

He peered at the disordered bunk and pursed his lips. 'Dear me, sir, you've 'ad some bad dreams, and we can't 'ave that.' He grinned. 'I'll fix you some coffee an' scrambled eggs.' Disdainfully, 'Powdered eggs, I'm afraid, but there's a war on they tell me.'

Lindsay stopped him by the door. 'So I believe.' He saw the man turn. 'And thanks.'

'Sir?' Jupp's features were inscrutable.

'Just thanks.'

Somewhere above a man laughed, and the deck gave a small tremble as some piece of machinery came alive.

Lindsay walked to the scuttle, the hot cup in his hand. A new day. For him and the ship. The old *Becky*. Perhaps it might be good to both of them.

Lieutenant-Commander John Goss stepped over the coaming of Lindsay's cabin and removed his cap. 'You wanted me, sir?' His heavy face was expressionless.

'Take a seat.'

Lindsay stood by a scuttle watching the rain sheeting across the forecastle where a party of oilskinned seamen were working half-heartedly between the anchor cables. It was the forenoon, but the sky was so dull it could have been dusk. In spite of his bad night he was feeling slightly better. A good bath and Jupp's breakfast had helped considerably.

'I have sent round my standing orders, Number One, and I'd be obliged if you made sure that all heads of departments have read them.' He paused, knowing what was coming.

Goss said abruptly, '*I've* read them, sir. It's not that.'

'Well?' In the salt-smeared glass he saw Goss shifting his heavy bulk from one foot to the other. 'What's bothering you?'

'The watch bill. Action stations and the rest. You've changed my original arrangements.' In a harder tone, 'May I ask why?'

Lindsay turned and studied him calmly. 'Whether any of us likes it or not, Number One, this is a naval ship. As such she will have to work and, if necessary, fight as a single unit.'

Goss said stubbornly, 'I still don't see why——'

Lindsay interrupted, 'I studied your arrangements. You had put all the reserve people into one watch. The other watch was comprised almost entirely of hostilities only, new intakes, many of whom have never been to sea before. Likewise the allocation of officers.' He added slowly, 'Just what do you think might happen if the ship is caught napping and with two R.N.V.R. officers on the bridge, neither of whom has had the slightest experience?'

Goss dropped his eyes. 'They'll have to learn, sir. As I did.'

'Given time they might. But they'll have to be taught, like the rest of us. So I've allowed for it in my planning. A sprinkling in each part of both watches.'

'Yes, sir.' Goss looked up angrily. 'There's this other order. About the accommodation.'

Lindsay glanced at the ship's picture on the bulkhead. The *Benbecula* as she had once been. He could understand Goss's feelings, but like the ship's role they had to be overcome.

'Yes. Tell the chief bosun's mate to get his people to work right away. I want all the old titles removed or painted out, understood?' He saw Goss's eyes cloud over and added quietly, 'To the ship's company as a whole, as a *whole*, do you understand, *Benbecula* must represent part of the Navy. It is a wardroom, not a *restaurant* as the sign says. A chief and petty officers' mess, and no longer the cocktail lounge. Things like that can affect a man's attitude, especially a new, green recruit.'

'I don't need to be told about war, sir.'

Lindsay heard himself retort angrily, 'And neither do *I*, Number One, so do as I damn well say!'

When Goss remained stockstill, his cap crushed under his arm, he added, 'Whatever role we are given, wherever we are sent, things are going to be hard. If I am called to action I want a ship's company working as a team, one unit, do you understand? Not some collection of trained and untrained men, ex-merchant seamen and others brought back from retirement.' He was hoarse, and could feel his heart pumping against his ribs. The earlier sensation of control was slipping away, yet he had to make Goss understand. 'A ship of war is only as strong as her people, d'you see that? *People!*'

'If you say so, sir.'

'Good.'

He walked to a chair and slumped into it. 'You have been at sea long enough to know what can happen. The Atlantic is a killing-ground and no place for unwary idealists. I know how you feel about this ship, at least I think I do. You may believe that by keeping up the old appearances you'll make them survive. Believe me, you won't, quite the opposite. Many of the new hands come from training depots. Depots which up to a year or so back were holiday camps for factory workers and mill girls in the north of England. But after a while the trainees *believed* they were in naval establishments and progressed accordingly. Likewise this ship, so see that my orders are executed as of today.'

'Aye, aye, sir.' Goss sounded hoarse.

'I want to meet my officers today, too.' He glanced up quickly, seeing the shot go home. Goss looked suddenly uneasy. 'I've read all I can about them, but that is as far as it goes.'

'I'll arrange it, sir.' Goss sounded in control again. 'Eight bells?'

'Good.'

More calmly he continued, 'If the war gets no worse things are going to be bad. If it does,' he shrugged, 'then we'll be hard put to keep the sea lanes open. It's as simple as that.' Almost to himself he said, 'Once I thought otherwise. Now I know better. War isn't a game, and it's time we started breaking a few rules, right?'

Goss eyed him unblinkingly. 'Right.'

A telephone buzzed on the bulkhead and Lindsay seized it from its hook without leaving the chair.

'Captain.'

The voice said, 'Signal from shore, sir. Guardboat arriving with sealed orders forthwith.'

Lindsay looked at Goss's heavy face and thought about the voice on the telephone. What did he look like? What was his name? There was so much to discover. So little time.

'Thank you. Inform the O.O.D. please.' The phone went dead.

To Goss he said, 'Perhaps we shall know now.'

Goss looked around the cabin, his face suddenly desperate. 'They'll not be sending us to fight surface ships. Not after all that's happened, surely?' When Lindsay remained silent he said, 'One of our sister ships, the *Barra*, has got a nice billet at Singapore. She's an A.M.C. too, like us, but out there she'll be safe enough from these bloody U-boats.'

Almost gently Lindsay replied, 'Maybe you're right. But it's best to face the worst thing which can happen and plan from there.'

He turned away to hide his eyes, as the mental picture rose in his mind like some hideous spectre. The pale arms waving under the water. The soft, limp bodies pressed against his chest.

Goss opened the door. 'I——I'll carry on, sir.' Then he was gone.

Jupp entered the cabin by the other door and said, 'Guardboat's shoved off from the jetty, sir. I'd better start packin' up some of the glasses. They're hard to replace nowadays, and we don't want none of that issue stuff from naval stores.'

Lindsay relaxed slightly and smiled at Jupp's doleful face.

'What are you expecting?'

Jupp pouted. 'Sailin' orders they'll be, sir. We're off very soon now.'

Lindsay stood up. He was well used to lower deck telegraph and false *buzzes,* but the steward's tone made him ask, 'Have you heard something?' He smiled. 'You've a relative at H.Q. maybe?'

Jupp moved to another scuttle, his face grave. 'Look 'ere, sir.'

Through the steady downpour Lindsay saw a small boat chugging across the anchorage, several oilskinned figures crammed together for comfort like wet seals on a half-submerged rock.

Jupp said, 'That's the 'arbour-master's mob, sir. Earlier on I seen 'em checkin' our buoy and measurin' the distance to the next astern.' He glanced at Lindsay, his voice matter-of-fact. 'They'll be needin' it for another, bigger ship, I reckon. Stands to reason, don't it, sir?'

Lindsay nodded. 'Yes.'

Jupp asked, 'Will you be wantin' any letters taken ashore? If I'm right, that is.'

He shook his head. 'No. No letters.'

He walked towards his sleeping cabin and did not see the sadness in Jupp's deepset eyes.

———————

The *Benbecula's* wardroom, which was situated forward of the promenade deck, had once been the main restaurant for the passengers, and had been her pride and joy. It ran the whole breadth of the hull, and was panelled in dark oak. Most of the furnishings were drawn from the original fittings, and the chairs around the long polished table all bore the company's crest, as did the deep leather ones grouped by the stately coal stove at the after bulkhead. A few additional concessions had, however, been made. Officers' letter rack, a picture of the King, and a stand containing pistols which did little to alter the general appearance of wellbeing and comfort.

Sharp at noon Goss had arrived to accompany Lindsay to the wardroom and had said nothing as they passed two seamen who were busily removing the glass sign which proclaimed it to be a *Restaurant — First Class Only*. Lindsay doubted if the sign had ever been needed, for he had learned that *Benbecula* had never carried anyone but first class passengers. Except, that is, for emigrants to Australia, and it was hardly likely they would have misunderstood the rules.

As they entered all the officers rose to their feet, their expressions a mixture of curiosity, apprehension and expectancy. It was plain that Goss had already arranged them in some sort of order, while in the background two white-coated stewards hovered in readiness to serve drinks once the formalities were over.

Lindsay knew better than to expect a complete analysis at so brief a meeting. Some faces stood out more than others, however. There was a Lieutenant Stannard, the navigation officer, a lean, beanpole of a man with a skin like leather. A reservist, he was also an Australian who had served with the company before the war.

As Lindsay shook his hand he drawled, 'I sure hope we're going back on the Far East run, sir. The old ship can find her own way there by now.' He shrugged. 'Otherwise I'm not too optimistic!'

Maxwell was present of course, rigid as ever, and slightly apart from the professional seamen and the amateurs, like a disapproving referee at some obscure contest.

The ship's doctor, Surgeon-Lieutenant David Boase, returned Lindsay's handshake, and in answer to a question said, 'First ship, sir. I was at Guy's.'

Despite the red marking between his wavy gold stripes, Lindsay guessed that like so many of his contemporaries Boase was little more than a glorified medical student. But better than no doctor at all.

There were four sub-lieutenants, very new, and all but one of whom had never been to sea before except as ordinary seamen doing their obligatory service prior to going to *King Alfred,* the officers training establishment. The exception was named Dancy, a serious faced young man who said quickly, 'Actually, sir, I *have* done three months watchkeeping before joining this ship.'

Lindsay eyed him curiously. 'What ship?'

'The *Valiant*, sir.'

Lindsay was surprised. 'I'd have thought this is a bit of a change from a big battleship, Dancy.'

Dancy flushed. 'Oh no, sir. Not *that Valiant*. Actually she was an armed yacht at Bristol.'

The laughter helped to break the ice, and Goss said ponderously, 'Shall I call the stewards over now, sir?'

Lindsay nodded and let his eyes move round the faces which would become so familiar, given luck and time.

As Goss bustled away he saw Tobey, the big boatswain, talking with the two elderly warrant officers, Emerson and Baldock, and wondered what they thought about this appointment after their peaceful retirement.

Lieutenant Mark de Chair of the Royal Marines, a slim, elegant figure with a neat clipped moustache said suddenly, 'I expect you're wondering why I'm aboard, sir?'

Lindsay smiled. 'Tell me.'

'I was put here with my sergeant and thirty marines to man the ship's armament when we were trooping, sir.' He shrugged. 'The troops have gone, but their lordships in all their wisdom thought fit to forget us.'

'I've arranged for you to continue manning the after guns.'

Lindsay took a glass from a steward and waited until they were all silent again. A mixed wardroom, he thought. Like most ships these days, and yet. . . .

He said quietly, 'Well, gentlemen, I am sorry this has to be brief. I will have to get to know you better,' he paused, 'when we are at sea.' He felt the sudden expectancy move around him like a small wind. 'Our sailing orders have arrived.' He thought of Jupp by the scuttle. How right he was. 'We will slip from our buoy at 0800 tomorrow and proceed on independent patrol.'

He could see his words hitting home, affecting each and every one present in the way it would touch him. Fraser's relaxed indifference, his second engineer, Lieutenant (E) Dyke, frowning slightly as if going over his own watch-bill of stokers and mechanics. Barker biting his lip, squinting behind his glasses, seeing each sea mile steamed as so many sausages and tins of corned beef, rum and gallons of tea. Stannard, the navigation officer, balanced on his toes, thinking of his charts perhaps, or returning to his far off homeland. Maxwell, stiff and sphinxlike. And some of the rest, so young, so unsure that it made you feel sorry for them.

Lindsay continued, 'We will patrol the south-western approaches to Iceland, to extend when required into the Denmark Strait.' He had to steel himself to say the words. In his mind's eye he could see the raging desert of tossing whitecaps and dark-sided rollers, of shrieking gales, and ice. The Denmark Strait.

Stannard was the first to break the stunned silence. 'Jesus, sir, they sure believe in pitching us into the deep end!'

Goss muttered, 'We've had no time. No time to get things ready——' His voice trailed away.

Lindsay looked round their faces again, knowing it would be like this. He lifted his glass. 'To the ship, gentlemen.' As they drained their glasses without a word he added, 'And remember this. Our people will be looking to you after today. As I will. So let's not have too much despondency about, eh?'

He let his eye fall on Fraser. 'I'd suggest a party tonight——'

He turned as a figure stepped into the wardroom. It was Kemp, the midshipman, the only officer he had not met. Kemp had been acting O.O.D. during the meeting, and his face was pink with cold from the upper deck.

Kemp said, 'Signal from H.Q., sir.' He proffered a soggy sheet of pad. 'Would you report there at 1600, sir.'

Lindsay glanced at the signal, aware of all the eyes watching his face.

'Affirmative.' As the boy turned to go he added, 'You'll be allocated to dealing with ship's correspondence on top of your other duties.'

Kemp stared around the other officers and nodded. 'Yes, sir.'

Lindsay said, 'We're sailing at 0800 tomorrow. Iceland patrol, if you're interested.'

As the boy hurried away Lindsay noticed that one of the stewards had also gone. The news would be all over the ship by now, and perhaps it was better so. It would help prepare them for the formalities of getting under way.

He put down his glass. It was time to leave them to sort themselves out.

He said, 'There will be no shore leave, so inform your departments accordingly. Arrange for mail to be dropped tonight. After that,' he forced a smile, 'we are in business.' He nodded to Goss. 'Thank you. Carry on, please.'

Despite the rain and chill wind he made himself walk around the boat deck, his hands in his pockets, his head bowed against the weather. Part of the deck still bore the faded marks where handball had once been played in the Pacific sunlight. He walked past the hooded Oerlikons and climbed slowly up to the bridge. It would be strange to con a ship with the helmsman right there with you, he thought vaguely. It was a spacious bridge, the brass telegraphs and binnacle, the polished wheel deserted, as if waiting for the place to come alive again. Once the time came it would never be quiet, nor empty.

On either side of the wheelhouse the open bridge wings stretched out over the side, and he walked to the port gratings, his shoes squelching in rain puddles as he peered across at the murky shoreline.

A petty officer was leaning over the wing, the rain

bouncing off his oilskin and cap like hail as he stared at the water far below.

He swung round and saluted as Lindsay crossed to his side and said, 'Ritchie, sir. Yeoman of signals.'

He had a round, homely face, and Lindsay knew from experience that a yeoman of signals was just about one of the most important members of any bridge, no matter what ship.

'You've heard the news, Yeo?'

He nodded. 'Aye, sir.' Ritchie seemed oblivious of the rain. 'I'm not bothered.'

There was something strange about him. Remote.

Lindsay asked quietly, 'Had any leave lately?'

Ritchie looked away. 'Last month, sir.' When he faced Lindsay again there were tears running unheeded with the rain. 'Bloody street was gone, sir!' The words were torn from him. 'Nothing left.'

Lindsay stared at him. Helpless. 'Did you have——'

'Wife an' two kids, sir.' He brushed his face with his sleeve. 'All gone.' He recovered himself and said, 'Sorry about that, sir.'

'Yes.'

He remembered one of the children stirring in the lifeboat on the last night before the corvette found them. Dreaming perhaps. Like Ritchie's kids when the bomb had come down.

Ritchie said suddenly, 'You'd better get under cover, sir.' A smile creased his face. 'You'll be wanted on the bridge, not in the sickbay.'

Lindsay touched his arm. 'Yes.' As he turned to go he added, 'If you want leave I'll see if I can arrange it.'

Ritchie was looking skyward towards a slow-moving Walrus flying boat, his face like a mask.

'Thank you, sir, but no. You'll need a good signals department, I'm thinkin'.' He hesitated. ' 'Sides, I'd like the chance to get back at those bastards!'

Later when Lindsay went ashore to see the Chief of

Staff and to receive his patrol intelligence he remembered Ritchie's words and wondered if he too might be influenced by what had happened.

The Chief of Staff, a serious faced, urbane captain, was brief and to the point.

'Things are bad, Lindsay, very bad. There is talk of more German raiders breaking out, probably from French ports. However,' he glanced up at the great wall chart with all its coloured ribbons and flags, 'it is not unlikely they might try the longer way round.'

'The Denmark Strait.'

'Correct.' The captain eyed him distantly. 'I want no heroics. Any sighting report can be used right here in Scapa.'

Again he looked at the chart, and Lindsay saw the great clusters of crosses, each mark representing a ship sunk by enemy action. There must be hundreds, he thought.

The captain said, 'I know something of your experiences, and I'm sorry you've not been offered a command more fitting to your rank and knowledge. However,' there was that word again, 'in war we accept orders without question.'

A quick handshake, a fat envelope from a tired looking lieutenant, and it was over.

The staff car was waiting to take him back to the jetty, but there was a different Wren behind the wheel. She was pale and thin, and spent most of the journey sneezing into a handkerchief. When he asked her, she had never even heard of Wren Collins.

Between sniffs she complained, 'I've only just arrived at the base, sir. It's not fair really. Most of my friends have got draft chits to Ceylon.'

Lindsay thought of Ritchie and all those others like him. 'Yes,' he replied coldly. 'It really is too bad.'

On the way to the ship in the motor boat he thought of the next day and the days after that. How they would manage.

A motor fishing boat packed with libertymen on her way to Lyness wallowed past in the gloom and he heard the sailors singing above the din of rain and wind.

'Roll on the *Nelson,* the *Rodney, Renown,* this one-funnelled bastard is getting me down.'

He watched them in the rain and recalled the Chief of Staff's warning. *No heroics.*

But if these men could sing like that, there was still some spark of hope. For all of them.

3 Raider

Lindsay sat in his cabin, his legs thrust out in front of him, and peered at his watch. Half an hour to go. He made himself reach out for another cup of black coffee, sipping it slowly to clear his thoughts.

The ship around and below him was not so quiet as before. From the moment the hands had been called until the muffled pipe over the tannoy system, 'Special sea-dutymen to your stations!', there had been a feeling of nervous expectancy. As there always seemed to be when about to leave harbour. You never got used to it.

The cabin was dark, for the deadlights were still tightly shut, as they probably would be for most of the time. He glanced at his leather sea-boots and at the duffel coat and binoculars waiting on another chair. How often had he waited like this? he wondered. It would be strange to take *Benbecula* out of the Flow for the first time. Not that Lindsay was unused to handling big ships. He had served as navigation officer in a cumbersome submarine depot ship in Malta for two years, even though at heart he was still a destroyer-man. No, it was not that. It was going back. To the Atlantic and all it had come to mean to him.

The deck gave a nervous tremble, and he pictured Fraser far below in his inhuman world of noise and greased movement. Mouthing to his men in that strange engine room lip language, his eyes on the great dials above his footplate. It was lucky *Benbecula* was twin-screwed. Many ships built between the wars had only one propeller. Sufficient in peacetime perhaps, with tugs always on hand when entering and leaving harbour. He smiled grimly in

spite of his tense nerves. It would put a swift end to everything if he lost control in the Flow's perverse tide-races
before he had even got her clear.

More sounds now. Wires scraping along the forecastle,
the distant bark of orders. That would be Maxwell preparing to slip the final wire from the ring of their buoy. The
last boat had been hoisted inboard, the shivering seamen
picked up from the buoy where they had fumbled to
unshackle the massive cable while the spray had tried to
pluck them into the Flow.

Bells clanged overhead, and he guessed Goss was testing
the telegraphs, watching every move to make sure the
captain would find no fault with his precious ship.

He replaced the cup and stood up, patting his pockets
automatically to make sure he had all he required. Pipe
and pouch. And a small silver compass. He turned it over
in his hands under the deckhead light. Inscribed on the
back was, *'Commander Michael Lindsay. H.M.S.
Minden—1914.'* It was just about all he had to remind him
of his father now. He thrust it into his pocket, feeling the
newness of the jacket. Like everything else, his old clothes
were on the sea-bed in *Vengeur*.

There was a tap at the door and Goss looked in at him.

'Ready to proceed, sir.'

'I'll come up.'

He slipped into the duffel coat and slung his glasses
around his neck. As he picked up his cap he took a last
glance round the quiet cabin. It was time.

Goss followed him up the bridge ladder, between the
W/T office with its constant stammer of morse and crack-
ling static and the austere chart room, the deckhead lights
trained unwinkingly on the table and instruments.

He strode out to the bridge and crossed to the clearview
screens on the windows. Figures moved busily on the
forecastle, and a solitary signalman stood shivering right
in the bows, ready to lower the Jack when the slipwire came
free.

He turned and looked at the bridge party. Chief Petty Officer Jolliffe, the coxswain, whom he had already met briefly on his inspection, was standing loosely at the wheel, his eyes gleaming in the compass light as he idly watched the gyro repeater. He was a barrel of a man, but on the short side, so that his legs appeared too frail for his massive body and paunch. No trouble there. Jolliffe had been coxswain of a battle-cruiser and was used to the whims of big ships. At each brass telegraph the quartermasters lounged with their hands ready on the levers. On either bridge wing the signalmen stood by their shuttered lights and flags, the yeoman, Ritchie, with his long telescope trained towards the shore.

Lieutenant Stannard saluted formally and said, 'Wind's nor'westerly, sir. A bit fresh for my liking.' In the dull grey light he looked even more leathery, his eyes very bright below his cap.

Hovering in the background, two of the sub-lieutenants, Escott and Smythe, were trying not to be seen, their single gold stripes shining with newness.

Goss paced from side to side, his head thrust forward as if to discover some last fault. He glared at the two sub-lieutenants and barked, 'Get out on either wing, for God's sake! You might *learn* something!'

Seizing oilskins they fled away, and Lindsay saw one of the quartermasters wink at his mate.

Goss did no good at all by bellowing at them in front of the ratings, he thought. But there was not time for another confrontation now.

Ritchie yelled, 'Signal, sir!' A light winked impatiently through the rain. Like a bright blue eye.

'Proceed when ready!'

Lindsay tried not to lick his lips. 'Ring down standby.'

The bells were very loud, and he walked to the port door of the wheelhouse and peered over the screen towards the forecastle party. Maxwell was squinting at the bridge, his sodden cap tugged over his eyes as he awaited the order.

Lindsay relaxed slightly, tasting the blown salt on his lips, feeling his cheeks tingling in the crisp air.

'Very well, Yeoman. Make the affirmative.'

Seconds later a red flare burst against the leaden clouds and drifted seaward on the wind.

Stannard called, 'That was the signal from the boom vessel, sir. Hoxa gate is open for us.'

He sounded cheerful enough. Lindsay had heard him bawling some Australian song at the wardroom party when he had turned into his bunk. Every other word had been obscene. But he appeared to have avoided any sort of hangover. Which was more than could be said for Dancy, the sub-lieutenant *with* experience. His face was the colour of pea soup as he staggered aft along the boat deck where the marines and some of the hands had fallen in for leaving harbour.

Feet thumped above the wheelhouse where Chief Petty Officer Archer and his boatswain's mates were assembled to pipe as and when they passed any other ship. The Navy never changed. No matter what.

Lindsay lifted his hand and watched Maxwell point with his arm to indicate that the buoy was close up under the starboard side of the stem.

Once free, the wind would carry the ship abeam like a drifting pier, Lindsay thought. But there was plenty of room. Had wind and tide been against them, he would have had to contend with the nearby battleship and three anchored cruisers. He could see several tiny figures watching him from the battleship's quarterdeck and her name gleaming dully in the morning light. *Prince of Wales.* The ship which had been in company with *Hood* when she had been blown to oblivion. She had been too new, too untried to be much help, and Lindsay wondered briefly how he would have felt, had he been in her at the time.

'Slow ahead together.'

He saw the telegraphsmen swinging their brass handles and turned away to make a chopping motion with his hand towards Maxwell in the eyes of the ship. He saw a petty officer swing his hammer, heard the clang of steel as the slip was knocked away, and the instant rush of activity as the oilskinned seamen tumbled aft, dragging the mooring wire with them. The buoy appeared immediately, as if it and not the ship had taken wings.

Jolliffe intoned, 'Both engines slow ahead, sir. Wheel's amidships.'

'Port ten.'

He raised his glasses and watched the low humps of land beginning to drift across the bows. It was strange to have the great foremast right in front of the bridge with all its tangle of rigging and derricks. Standing at one side of the bridge it made the ship feel lopsided, Lindsay thought. The list to starboard did not help either.

He heard Goss say in a fierce whisper, 'She's making too slow a turn.'

He glanced at him. Goss seemed to be thinking aloud. All the same, he was right.

'Increase to fifteen. Starboard engine half ahead.'

That was better. A noticeable crust of white spray was frothing back from the stem now, and he could feel the bridge vibrating steadily to the additional thrust of screws and rudder.

Two incoming trawlers pounded past the port side, their spindly funnels belching smoke, their ensigns little more than scraps of white rag, after another anti-submarine patrol.

'Midships. Slow ahead starboard.'

Lindsay watched the nearest trawler as it rolled dizzily in the cross-current, showing its bilge. God knows what they're like in open water, he wondered.

Faintly across the water he heard the shrill of a pipe. Somebody, somehow was trying to pay respects to the *Benbecula* as she towered past on her way to the gate.

Overhead he heard Archer bellow *'Pipe!'* And the answering squeal from his line of boatswain's mates.

From aft another shout, that would be Mr Baldock, the elderly gunner. 'Attention on the upper deck there! Face to port an' salute!'

On the forecastle the seamen were still fighting with the seemingly endless mass of uncoiled wire, like people caught by some deadly serpent.

Lindsay steadied his glasses and watched the land closing in on either bow where the humps of Flotta and South Ronaldsay crouched on guard of the Sound. He could just make out the hazy shape of the boom-defence vessel, and beyond her another A/S trawler, sweeping to make sure no U-boat would slip inside while the gate was open.

'Take her out, Cox'n.'

There was no point in confusing the helmsman with unnecessary orders now. Jolliffe could see as well as anyone what was required. He was easing the spokes back and forth in his great red fingers, his eyes fixed on the channel.

A signalman said, 'I think someone's calling us up, Yeo!'

Ritchie was through the door and across to the opposite bridge wing in seconds.

'Where, lad?' His telescope was swinging round like a small cannon. Then, 'Gawd, you need yer eyes testin', it's a bloody car flashin' its lights!'

Lindsay walked to the open door as the yeoman exclaimed, 'You're right, lad, it *is* callin' us.' He looked at Lindsay. 'He'll cop it if the officer of th' guard spots 'im!'

Lindsay raised his glasses as the signalman, mollified, reported, 'He says *Good Luck*, sir.'

A hump of land was cutting Lindsay's vision away even as he steadied his glasses on the distant lights. The battered staff car was parked dangerously close to the sea's edge, and he could picture her as she sat muffled to her ears. Watching the old ship edge towards the boom gate.

He said, 'Acknowledge.' He knew they were staring at him. 'And say *Thank You*.' The lamp started to clatter, and then the car was lost from sight.

He saw one of the sub-lieutenants put out his hand to the screen as the deck lifted to the first low roller. On the bow the boom vessel was puffing out dense smoke as she started to set her machinery in motion again. A man waved from her bridge and then scuttled back from the rain.

Lindsay stooped behind a gyro repeater and said, 'Starboard ten.' The dial ticked gently in front of his eyes. 'Midships. Steady.'

'Steady, sir. Course two-two-zero.'

Stannard said quietly, 'New course in fifteen minutes, sir. Two-five-zero.'

'Very good.'

Lindsay walked out to the wing and rested his gloved hands on the screen. Already the land had fallen away to port, and he could see the whitecaps cruising diagonally towards the ship in an endless array. He felt for his reactions, then banged his gloved hands together, making a signalman start violently. He felt all right. It was amazing.

He thought suddenly of the girl in the car. She must have got up specially and wangled her work-sheet to get to that point in time to see them sail. He was being stupid, but could not help himself.

A telephone buzzed and Stannard called, 'From masthead, sir. Ship closing port bow.'

Lindsay glanced up at the fat pod on the foremast. It was hard to get used to after the congested layout of a warship's bridge and superstructure.

Goss asked, 'Fall out harbour stations, sir?'

But Lindsay was watching the approaching ship through his glasses. She would pass down the port side with a good half cable to spare. It was not that. He felt the tightness in his throat as she loomed slowly and painfully out of the rain and spray.

A cruiser, she was so low in the water aft that her quarterdeck was awash. Her mainmast had gone, and her after turret was buckled into so much scrap. She had received a torpedo which had all but broken her back, but she was fighting to get back. To get her people home.

A destroyer was cruising watchfully to seaward, and two tugs followed close astern of the listing ship. Like undertakers men, Lindsay thought with sudden anger.

He snapped, 'No, Number One! Have the hands fall in fore and aft! And tell the buffer I want the best salute he's ever done!' He saw Goss's face working with confusion and doubt. Probably thinks I'm mad.

As seamen and marines ran to fall in on the *Benbecula's* decks, Lindsay walked to the end of the wing and raised his hand to his cap as the cruiser moved slowly past.

The pipes shrilled and died in salute, and then Lindsay saw a solitary marine, his head white with bandages, walk to the cruiser's signal platform and raise a bugle to his lips. The *Still* floated across the strip of tossing grey water, and above the neat lines of sewn up bodies on the cruiser's deck. Along the *Benbecula's* side the lines of new, untried faces stared at the other ship in silence, until the bugle sounded again and Archer yelled, 'Carry on!'

Stannard said quietly, 'That was quite a scene, sir.'

Lindsay looked past him at the young signalman who had seen the car's lights. He was biting the fingers of his gloves and staring astern at the listing cruiser.

'It will do them good!'

He had not meant to speak so harshly, nor were they the words he had intended. So nothing had changed after all. Not the bitterness or the shock of seeing what the Atlantic could do.

Stannard said, 'Time to alter course again, sir.'

Lindsay looked at him, seeing the hurt in his eyes. 'Very well, take the con.' To Goss, 'Fall out harbour stations, if you please. We will exercise action stations in ten minutes, right?'

Goss nodded. 'Yes, sir.'

The *Benbecula's* straight stem lifted and then ploughed sedately into a low bank of broken rollers. Spray dappled the bridge windows and made the anchor cables look like black glass.

Later, as she came around the south-western approaches to the Orkneys, past the frozen shape of the Old Man of Hoy, she rolled more steeply, her forward well deck catching the incoming sea and letting it sweep lazily to the opposite side before gurgling away through the scuppers.

Then at last she turned her stern towards the land and headed west-northwest, and by noon, as the watch below prepared to eat their meal and the other half of the ship's company closed up at defence stations, she had the sea to herself.

Lindsay remained on the open wing, his unlit pipe in his teeth, his eyes fixed on the tossing wilderness of waves and blown spume.

He was in the North Atlantic. He had come back.

———————

'Char, sir?'

Lindsay turned in his tall chair and took a cup from the bosun's mate of the watch. As he held the hot metal against his lips he stared through the streaming windows and watched the solid arrowhead of the bows etched against the oncoming seas.

For eight days since leaving the buoy the scene had hardly changed. The weather had got colder, but that was to be expected as hour after hour the ship had ploughed her way to the north-west. And apart from some armed trawlers and a solitary corvette, they had sighted nothing. Just the sea, with its endless panorama of wavecrests and steep rollers.

He felt the deck vibrate as the stem smashed through one more bank of cascading water, and saw the feathers of spray spurting up through the hawsepipes as if from powerful hoses.

Stannard walked across the bridge, his lean body angled to the uneven motion.

'First dog watchmen closed up at defence stations, sir. Able Seaman McNiven on the wheel.' He looked through a clearview screen. 'I guess we've arrived.'

Lindsay nodded. 'Yes.'

An invisible dot on the ocean. The starting leg of the patrol area. Area Uncle Item Victor. A sprawling parallelogram which measured five hundred by three hundred miles. As far north as the Arctic Circle between Iceland and Greenland. It had been impossible to get an accurate fix, and their position was obtained by the usual method, described by navigators as 'by Guess and God'. Dead reckoning. Except that in this case you could not afford to be too casual, or you might end up dead in another sense.

'Very well, Pilot. Bring her round to three-five-zero. Revs for ten knots.'

He heard Stannard passing his orders, the instant reply from the engine room bells to show that Fraser's people were wide awake.

When the ship turned slightly to port the motion became more unsteady and violent, the waves piling up against the starboard bow before exploding high over the rails and hissing viciously across each open deck. Below there would be more wretched sufferers retching and groaning at this added onslaught, he thought.

He watched a tall greybeard of a wave surging down the starboard side, taking its time, as if to find the best place to attack. Just level with the bridge its jagged crest crumbled and broke inboard, the shock transmitting itself through the whole superstructure like something solid. It was almost pitch dark beyond the bows, with only the wavecrests to determine sea from sky.

Lindsay ran his fingers over the arms of the chair and recalled Goss's face when he had told him what he required. Goss did not seem to understand that it was no good trying to act as if everything was normal and routine.

The watches changed, the relieved men scampering thankfully below to cabins and messdecks for some brief respite, but Lindsay had been on the bridge almost continuously since leaving the Flow. 'I want a good strong chair, Number One.' That had been the first day out, and the shipwrights had built it during one watch from solid oak which had lain hitherto unnoticed, in a storeroom. Bolted to the deck it gave Lindsay good vision above the screen and was within reach of the bridge telephones. But Goss had stared at it with something like horror.

'But, sir, that timber was being saved! You just can't get it any more.' Like Jupp and his damn glassware.

But if he was to keep going, to hold on to the vital reserve which might be demanded in the next hour or minute, he *needed* a good chair.

It was strange how Goss avoided facing the truth about the ship and her new purpose. Or maybe he wanted the captain to crack under the strain so that he, after all, could take command.

Lindsay thought too of the practice drills he had carried out on passage to the patrol area. In spite of the severe weather he had put almost every part of the ship through its paces. Gun and fire drill. Damage control and anti-aircraft exercises, until he had seen the despair, even hatred on the faces around him.

Maybe Goss had some justification for expecting him to crack, he thought bitterly. Once or twice he had heard himself shouting into a telephone or across the open wing to some unfortunate man on the deck below.

The gun drill had been the worst part. Pathetic, he had called it, and had seen Maxwell's rigid face working for once with something akin to shame. While mythical targets had been passed down from the so-called control position above the bridge, the crews of the six guns had endeavoured to locate and cover them with minimum delay. But each gun was hand-operated, and valuable time was lost again and again while Maxwell and the assistant gunnery officer, Lieutenant Hunter, had shouted themselves almost hoarse with frustration and despair. In most warships, and certainly all modern ones, it was possible to train all major guns, even fire them, direct from the control and rangefinder above the bridge. One eye and brain, like that of a submarine commander at a periscope. But *Benbecula*'s firing arrangements had not even begun to reach a stage where some hope was justified. The six-inch gun crews had no protection from the weather, and had to crouch behind the shields, shivering and cursing as ranges and deflections were passed by telephone and then yelled to them above the din of sea and wind. And having no power at each mounting it also meant that the big shells and their charges had to be manhandled and rammed home with sheer bodily strength. If the deck chose to tilt the wrong way at the moment of loading it could mean disaster for an unwary seaman. The massive breech block of such a gun could swing shut, despite the normal precautions, and bite off a man's arm like a horse snapping at a carrot. It was hardly likely to encourage the gun crews to take risks, but on the other hand it reduced the speed of loading and firing to a dismal crawl.

A telephone buzzed at the rear of the bridge and the bosun's mate called, 'Number Three Carley float is comin' adrift, sir.'

Stannard opened his mouth and shut it. He crossed to the chair and said quietly, 'Can't very well send the lads out in this, sir. Shall I tell the buffer to scrub round it until daylight?'

Lindsay tried to answer calmly. 'Do it now. The boat deck is miles above the waterline. Pass the word for lifelines to be rigged. That should do it.'

Stannard remained beside the chair, his dark features stubborn. 'In my opinion, sir——'

Lindsay swung round, seeing in those brief seconds the pale faces in the background, watching and listening.

Sub-Lieutenant Dancy, Stannard's assistant for the watch, the signalman, the men at the telegraphs, all parts of the ship. Extensions of his own thoughts and interpretations.

'Just *do* it, Pilot!' He could not control it any longer. 'With the sort of results I've been getting since I took command, I think liferafts are about the most useful things we've got! By God, do you imagine *this* is bad?'

Stannard stood his ground, his face angry. 'I merely meant——' He shrugged. 'I'm sorry, sir.' He did not sound it.

'Well, listen to me, will you?' He kept his voice very low. 'The weather is going to get worse, much worse. Before long we will have both watches on deck with steam hoses to cut away the ice. We are up here to do a job as best we can. It does not mean being battened down below and weeping for mother every time it bloody well rains!'

Stannard turned and beckoned to Dancy. 'Go yourself, Sub. Tell the buffer to take all reasonable precautions.' He kept his back to Lindsay. 'No sense in killing anyone.'

Lindsay leaned back in the hard chair, feeling its arms pressing into his ribs on one side then on the other as the old ship rolled heavily in the troughs. He wanted to go out on the wing in spite of the weather and watch the men detailed to replace the lashings on the Carley float. At the same time he knew he must stay where he was. Let them get on with it. Allow them to hate his guts and so work better for it, if that was what they needed.

He peered at his watch. In fifteen hours they would officially relieve another armed merchant cruiser from this patrol. They would not see her, however, which was probably just as well. It would do no good for some of the ship's company to see what the other A.M.C. looked like at close range. How they would be looking themselves after a few weeks of this misery.

The telephone buzzed again. 'Float's secure, sir.'

'Very good.'

Lindsay rubbed his chin, feeling the bristles rasp against his glove. He felt strangely relieved, in spite of his forced calm.

Dancy entered the bridge, his figure streaming, his face glowing with cold. He sounded pleased with himself.

'Not too bad, sir.' He clung to the voicepipes as the deck tilted and shuddered sickeningly beneath him. 'But by God it's parky out there!'

Stannard said shortly, 'I'm going to the chart room, Sub. Take over.'

Dancy stood beside the chair and rested his hands below the screen. Lindsay glanced at him curiously. Like the others, he knew little about him. Young, serious looking, but little else to give a clue. Without his cap and duffel coat he might even be described as nondescript.

He asked, 'What were you before you joined, Sub?'

Dancy said vaguely, 'I—I wrote things.' He nodded. 'Yes, I was a writer, sir.'

Lindsay watched his profile. His own information described Dancy's previous calling as bank clerk. But if he wanted to see himself as something else, what did it matter? Nothing which had happened before the Germans marched into Poland made any sense now. All the same. . . .

'Tell me about it.'

Dancy frowned. 'Well, I've always had this terrific feeling about the sea, sir. My parents didn't really want me to go into the Navy, and after school I tried my hand at writing.'

'Books?'

Dancy sounded uncomfortable. 'Not books, sir.'

'What then?'

'Things, sir'. Dancy looked at him desperately. 'About the sea.'

Stannard came back suddenly. 'Sir? Sickbay has just called. The doc wants,' he hesitated, 'he *asked* if you could change course for about twenty minutes. A seaman's fallen down a ladder and broken his hip. Doc says he can't fix it with all this motion.'

Lindsay looked at him. He could see the man's resentment building up. Waiting for him to refuse the doctor's request. *He must think me a right bastard.*

'Very well, Pilot. But work out the additional revs we will need to make up time, and inform the chief.'

Stannard blinked. 'Yes, sir. Right away.'

As he vanished, Dancy said seriously, 'Of course, I had to do other jobs as well. For a time, that is.'

Lindsay slid from the chair, wincing as the stiffness brought pain to his legs.

'Well, there's a job for you now.' He waved around the bridge. 'Take over. I'm going to my cabin for a shave.' He saw Dancy's face paling. 'Just call pilot if you can't cope.' He tapped the brass telephone by his chair. 'Call *me* if you like.' He grinned at Dancy's alarm. 'Good experience later on for your writing, eh?'

With a glance at the gyro he walked stiffly to the ladder abaft the wheelhouse and did not look back.

Dancy remained staring fixedly at his own dim reflection in the spray-dappled glass. He felt riveted to the deck, unable to move. Even his breathing had become difficult.

Very cautiously he looked over his shoulder. The quartermaster's eyes glittered like stones in the dim compass light, the rest of the bridge party swayed with the ship, like silent drunks.

Nothing had changed, and the realisation almost unnerved him. *He* was in sole command of this ship and some two hundred and fifty human beings.

The quartermaster, for instance. How did he see him? he wondered. Authority, an officer in whose hands he was quite willing to entrust his life?

He asked suddenly, 'How is she handling, Quartermaster?'

The seaman, McNiven, stiffened. He had been watching the ticking gyro, holding the staggering ship dead on

course, so what the hell was wrong with Dancy? His eyes
flickered momentarily from the compass, sensing a trap of
some sort.

'All right.' He waited. 'Sir.'

He had been thinking about his last leave in Chatham.
The girl had seemed fair enough. But after a few pints
under your belt you could get careless. He stirred uneasily,
just as he had when the bloody Aussie navigator had
spoken to the skipper about the sickbay. Suppose that
bloody girl had given him a dose? What the hell should he
do?

Dancy said, 'Oh, in that case,' he smiled through the
gloom, 'carry on.'

McNiven glared at Dancy's back. Stupid sod, he
thought. *Carry on.* That's all they can say.

Unaware of the quartermaster's unhappy dilemma,
Dancy continued to stare straight ahead. It was true
what he had told the captain. Partly. He had always loved
the sea and ships, but his parents' means and open opposition had prevented his chances of trying for Dartmouth.
At the bank he had often met a real naval officer. He
used to come there when he was on leave to draw money,
and Dancy had always tried to be the one to serve
him. He had listened mesmerised to the man's casual
comments about his ship, and the exotic places like Singapore and Bombay, Gibraltar and Mombasa. And later he
had let his craving, his desperate imagination run
riot.

He sometimes told himself that but for the war he would
have gone raving mad at the bank. Mad, or turned to
crime, robbing the vault, and making old Durnsford, the
manager, beg on his knees for his life. He knew too that if
the war had not come to save him he would have stayed on
at the bank. No madness or crime, just the miserable day to
day existence, made endurable only by his imagination.

At *King Alfred* when he had been training for his temporary commission he had met another cadet of about his

own age. An Etonian, someone seemingly from another planet, he had transformed so much in Dancy's caution and suburban reserve. And it had been catching. When Dancy had gained the coveted gold stripe and had been sent to the little armed yacht at Bristol, the first lieutenant had asked him about his earlier profession. *Profession.* He could still remember that moment. Not job or work. Or business, as his mother would have described it. It had seemed quite natural to lie. 'I'm a writer,' he'd said. It had been easy. The officer had been impressed, just as Commander Lindsay had been. Writers were beyond the reach of Service minds. They were different and could not be challenged.

Stannard slammed back through the door and stared at him.

'Where's the cap'n, for Chrissake?'

'He left me in charge.' Dancy's eyes wavered under the Australian's incredulous gaze.

Stannard muttered, 'Must be off his bloody head!' He looked at McNiven. 'I'm going to alter course to zero-two-zero in half a sec. I'll just inform the sickbay.' He glanced at Dancy. 'In *charge.* Jesus!'

Lindsay completed the shave and studied his face critically in the mirror. There were shadows beneath his eyes and his neck looked sore from wearing the towel under his duffel coat. But the shave, the hot water refreshed him, and he wondered how the surgery was going on the seaman's hip.

He glanced towards his other cabin and pictured the bunk beyond the door. The warm, enclosed world below the reading lamp. Perhaps later he might snatch some proper sleep.

Jupp padded into the cabin and laid a silver coffee pot carefully between the fiddles on a small table.

He said, 'The old girl's takin' it quite well, sir. Not too bad at all.'

Lindsay sat in a chair and stretched out his legs gratefully.

'At least the decks aren't awash all the time. That's something.'

The telephone rattled tinnily, and when he clapped it to his ear he heard Stannard say, 'The doc's reported that he's finished, sir. I'm about to alter course, if that's all right by you?'

'Good. Carry on, Pilot.'

He felt the deck tremble, a sudden tilt as the helm went over, and saw the curtains on the sealed scuttles standing out from the side as if on invisible wires. The sea boomed along the hull, angry and threatening, and then subsided with a slow hissing roar to prepare another attack.

The telephone buzzed again.

'Captain.' He raised the cup to his lips, watching Jupp as he stooped to pick a crumb from the carpet.

Stannard sounded terse. 'W/T office has picked up an S.O.S., sir. Plain language. It reads, *Am under attack by German raider.*' He paused, clearing his throat. 'Seems to be a Swedish ship, sir, probably a mistake on the Jerry's part——'

Lindsay snapped, 'Keep on to it!' He dropped the cup unheeded on the tray. 'I'm coming.'

He bounded up the ladder and found Stannard waiting outside the W/T office door. Two operators were crouched below their sets, and Petty Officer Telegraphist Hussey had also appeared to supervise them, his pyjamas clearly visible under his jacket.

He saw Lindsay and said awkwardly, 'Was just having a nap, sir. Had a feeling something like this might happen.' He was not bragging. Old hands often found themselves called to duty by instinct, and Lindsay had no intention of questioning it.

Lindsay asked, 'What do you make of it?'

From the door Stannard said, 'She gave a position, sir. I've got it plotted on the chart. She's about ninety miles due north of us.'

Hussey looked up from his steel chair. 'Someone's acknowledged, sir.'

Lindsay bit his lip. 'That'll be *Loch Glendhu*, the other A.M.C.'

Hussey added after a pause, 'Dead, sir. Not getting a peep now.'

Stannard said uneasily, 'That might mean anything.'

'Let me see your calculations.' Lindsay brushed past him into the chart room. In spite of the steam pipes it was damp and humid, the panelled sides bloomed with condensation.

'*Loch Glendhu* should be pretty near there, sir, according to our intelligence log.' Stannard seemed calm again, his voice detached and professional.

Lindsay stared at the neatly pencilled lines and bearings on the chart. *Loch Glendhu* was bigger than *Benbecula* and better armed. But no match for a warship. Perhaps she would haul off and report to base for instructions.

'Keep a permanent listening watch for her. Tell Hussey to monitor everything.'

What the hell was a Swedish ship doing up here anyway? Probably using the Denmark Strait as a matter of safety. Bad weather was better than being sunk by mistake in the calmer waters to the south.

'Lay off a course to intercept, Pilot.'

He recalled Fraser's words. *I can give you sixteen knots.* It would take over five hours to reach the neutral ship's position. Longer if he waited for instructions from some duty officer in the Admiralty operations' room. Five hours for men to die beyond reach or hope.

He realised that he was sweating badly in spite of the unmoving air, could feel it running down his spine like iced water. Without effort he could see the low grey shape on the horizon, feel the breath-stopping explosions as the raider's shells had torn steel and flesh to fragments all around him. He tried not to look at the nearest scuttle with its sealed deadlight. Tried to shut it from memory.

Lindsay asked, 'Have you got it yet?'

Stannard put down his brass dividers and looked up from the chart. 'Course would be zero-one-zero, sir.'

Lindsay nodded. 'Not would be, Pilot, *is*. Bring her round and get the chief on the telephone.'

He realised that Goss was on the bridge, his heavy face questioning and worried.

He said, 'The A.M.C. we're relieving is probably going to assist another ship, Number One.'

Goss nodded jerkily. 'I know. I just heard. Neutral, isn't she?' It sounded like an accusation.

'Nobody's neutral up here.'

Stannard called, 'The chief's on the phone, sir.'

Lindsay took it quickly. '*Loch Glendhu*'s in trouble, Chief.'

Fraser sounded miles away. 'I'll give you all I've got. When you're ready.'

Lindsay looked at the others. 'We'll see what we can do.' To Stannard he added, 'Right. Full ahead together.'

The telegraphs clanged over, and far below, enshrouded in rising steam on his footplate, Fraser watched the big needles swing round the twin dials and settle on FULL.

Slightly below him he saw his assistant, Lieutenant Dyke, grimacing at him and shaking his head. His lips said, 'She'll knock herself to bits.'

Fraser's lips replied, 'Bloody good job.'

Then the noise began to mount with each thrashing revolution, the machinery and fittings quivering to join in with their own particular din, and Fraser forgot Dyke and everything else but the job in hand.

4 A ship burns

'Still nothing from W/T office, sir.' Stannard sounded wary.

Lindsay nodded but kept his eyes fixed on the ship's labouring bows. *Benbecula* was no longer riding each wavecrest but smashing through the angry water like a massive steel battering ram. The spray rose in an almost unbroken curtain around the forecastle, crumbling in the wind to rain against the bridge screens like pebbles, and the motion was savage. Every strut and frame in the superstructure seemed to be rattling and protesting, and as the sea sluiced up and over the well deck Lindsay saw the foot of the foremast standing like an isolated pinnacle in the great frothing white flood. He wondered briefly what the lookout would feel in his snug pod, and if the mast was quivering to the onrushing water.

A quick glance at his watch told him that they should sight something soon, if something there was. The hours since that short, feeble burst of morse had felt like days, and all the while the ship had crashed and rolled, pitched and battered her way forward into the teeth of sea and wind alike.

There was a metallic scrape above the bridge and he imagined Maxwell in his control position testing the big rangefinder, cursing his spray-smeared lenses. It was a good rangefinder, but in a war where weapons had long since outstripped the minds of those who planned day-to-day survival, it was already out of date. Even the old

Vengeur had been allowed some of the better sophisticated detection equipment, and newer ships were fitted with the latest, and even more secret, gear. But *Benbecula* was right down at the bottom of the list as far as that was concerned. Convoy protection, anti-submarine tactics and strikes on enemy coastal resources took all the precedence, which on paper was only right. But as he stared intently through the whirring clearview screen Lindsay wondered what the planners would think if they were here on the bridge instead of their comfortable nine-to-five offices. It was almost unnerving to imagine the radio operators at this very moment, at Scapa or down in the cellars of the Admiralty. Information and calls for help or advice. A convoy massacred, a U-boat sighted, or some maddening signal about clothing issue and the need to entertain a visiting politician. The telegraphists would be hardened to all of it. Probably sitting there right now, sipping tea and chatting about their girls, the next run ashore.

He glanced quickly around the bridge. Tense and expectant, a small, sheltered world surrounded by sea noise and the creaking symphony of metal under strain.

It was all over the ship by now, and he made a mental note to arrange for the tannoy system to be extended to all decks and flats so that if necessary he could speak to every available man himself.

He tried to remember the exact layout of his command, see it like some blueprint or open plan. They were all down there listening and waiting. Hearing the sea and feeling the hull staggering as if to fall apart under them. Warm clothing and inflatable lifebelts. Those little red lights which were supposed to show where a man was drifting in the water.

Stannard said, 'Time, sir.' He sounded less weary now. Alert, or maybe frightened like most of them.

Lindsay felt the sudden dryness in his throat. *As I am.*

'Very well, Pilot.'

He reached forward and held his thumb on the small red button. Just a while longer he hesitated. It was their first time together. As a ship's company. He cursed himself for his nagging anxiety and thrust hard on the button.

The alarm bells were muffled, but nevertheless he could hear them screaming away throughout the ship, and the instant clatter of feet on bridge ladders, the dull thuds of watertight doors slamming shut.

As messengers and bosun's mates hurried to voice-pipes and telephones the reports started to come in from every position.

'Number Six gun closed up!'

'Number Four gun closed up!'

'Damage control party closed up!'

The mingled voices and terse acknowledgements sounded unreal, tinny. Through the drifting spray he saw crouching figures hurrying towards the forward guns, and could almost feel the icy metal of shell hoists and breeches.

Stannard said, 'Ship closed up at action stations, sir.'

Lindsay eyed him searchingly. 'Good. Three minutes. Not at all bad.'

He swivelled in the chair and looked at the figures which had filled the bridge. His team for whatever would happen next.

Jolliffe on the wheel, wiping condensation off the gyro repeater with his sleeve. Quartermasters and messengers, signalmen, with Ritchie gripping a flag locker while he adjusted his night glasses. Stannard and young Dancy, and Lieutenant Aikman, listed as boarding officer, ready to fight, die, go mad, anything.

He turned back to the whirring screen. Goss was in damage control. All spare stokers and extra hands with him ready to shore up bulkheads, put out fires, hold the ship together with bare hands if necessary. And Goss was far enough from the bridge to survive and assume command should Lindsay fall dead or wounded. It was practical not to put all your eggs in one basket. Practical, but hardly comforting.

He thought of the marine lieutenant, de Chair, down aft with his two six-inch guns and the feeble twelve pounder. If he was inwardly resentful at being quarters officer of an ancient battery in an A.M.C. he gave no hint of it. Elegant, deceptively casual, he would be more use leading his marines in open combat, he thought.

Stannard replaced a handset. 'Nothing from masthead, sir.'

'Thank you.' Another glance at his watch. 'Reduce to half speed.'

No sense now in shaking the machinery to pieces. He felt the chair quiver with something like relief as the telegraphs clanged their reply.

The Swedish ship might be sunk, or in the confusion had given the wrong position. The enemy could have realised his mistake and ceased fire and already be many miles away, steaming for home like a guilty assassin.

And there had been no signal from *Loch Glendhu* either. But up here in the Denmark Strait you could never rely on anything. Only eyes, ears and bloody instinct, as someone had once told him.

The screen was squeaking more loudly, and he realised the glass was being scattered with larger, paler blobs than mere spray.

Stannard muttered, 'Bloody snow. That's just about all we need!'

It was more sleet than snow, but it could get worse, and if it froze the gun crews would be hard put to do anything.

The wavecrests were less violent, the troughs wider spaced, and he guessed the snow would be coming very soon now. He shuddered inwardly and wondered if the German invasion of Russia was facing this kind of weather. In spite of everything he was suddenly thankful to be here, enclosed by the ship, and not slogging through frozen mud, waist-deep in slush. A ship was a home as much as a weapon. A soldier fought often without knowing where he was, or if he was alone and already considered expendable by the master-minds of war.

The telephone made him flinch in his seat.

Stannard snapped, 'Very well. Good. Keep reporting.' Then to Lindsay, 'Masthead reports a red glow, sir. Fine on the port bow.'

Before he could reply the speaker at the rear of the bridge intoned, 'Control . . . Bridge.' It was Maxwell's voice, unhurried and toneless. 'Red two-oh. Range one-double-oh. A ship on fire.'

Lindsay swung his glasses to the screen. Nothing. Maxwell's spotters had done well to see it in such bad visibility. He slid from the chair and lowered his eye to the glowing gyro repeater.

'Port ten.'

'Port ten, sir. Ten of port wheel on, sir.' Jolliffe's voice was heavy. Like the man.

'Midships. Steady. Steer three-four-zero.' To Stannard he added, 'I hope your people know their stuff. I'm going to need a good plotting team when we clear this lot.'

He picked up another telephone and heard Maxwell's voice right in his ear.

'Guns, this is the captain. I'll not take chances. A diagonal approach so that you can get all the starboard battery to bear, right?'

Maxwell understood. 'Starshell on One, sir?'

'Yes.'

He heard the distant voices of the control team already rapping out ranges and bearings to the crews below.

'And you did well to find her. *Loch Glendhu* must have misread the signal, or buzzed off in pursuit.'

He replaced the telephone.

Dancy reported, 'Number One has loaded with star-shell, sir.'

The gunnery speaker again. 'All guns load, load, load, semi-armour-piercing!'

Lindsay had taken out his pipe without realising it and gripped it in his teeth so hard that the pain helped to steady him.

'Now, Pilot. Bring her round to three-two-five.'

Even as the wheel went over the speaker said, 'Range now oh-eight-oh.'

Four miles. But in this driving sleet it could have been a hundred. Lindsay concentrated his mind on the voices which muttered and squeaked on every line and speaking tube. He recalled the brand-new sub-lieutenants, down there acting as quarters officers on the forward arma-ment. The seasoned gunlayers and trainers knew what to do if anyone did, and the young officers were there to learn rather than do much more.

But Lindsay knew from bitter experience that time was not always kind. In the *Vengeur* he had seen one of the four-inch guns manned by a midshipman, two stokers and a cook when its real crew had been ripped to bloody remnants under an air attack. You could never rely on time.

'There it is!' Stannard craned forward. 'Starboard bow, sir!'

Lindsay held up his glasses and saw the flickering glow for the first time. It was reflected more in the low clouds than on the water, and the thickening sleet made even that difficult.

Stannard added grimly, 'The starshell'll scare the hell out of the poor bastards.'

'Better that than make a bad approach. If the snow comes down we might lose her altogether.'

Maxwell's voice sounded muffled as he spoke into his array of handsets. 'Number *One* gun. Range oh-seven-five.' One of the sub-lieutenants must have interrupted him for he rasped savagely, '*Listen*, for God's sake. Bearing is still Green oh-five, now get on with it!'

The crash came almost before the speaker had gone dead again, the sound of the shot coming inboard on the wind like a double explosion. When the shell burst it was momentarily like some strange electric storm. Lindsay realised that the gunlayer had applied too much elevation so the flare had burst in or above the clouds. Their bellies shone through the sleet like silver, and then as the flare drifted into view the sea was bathed with the hard, searing glare of a glacier.

The ship was already well down in the water, her tilting hull shining in the harsh glare, the smoke from her blazing interior pouring downwind in one solid plume, black and impenetrable. The fires were very low now, although here and there along the hull fresh outbursts shot skyward, hurling sparks and glowing embers across the water like tracers.

The flare was almost gone. 'Another!' Lindsay could not take his eyes from the dying ship. Knowing he was right. Willing otherwise. Sweating.

A door banged open and Mr. Tobey, the boatswain, entered the wheelhouse, the icy air following him as he sought out Lindsay's figure.

'Beg pardon, sir. I was just wonderin'. If those poor devils which is still alive can't understand our lingo, 'ow will we make 'em understand what we're doin'?' He did not see Lindsay's frozen expression. 'I got my people ready at the rafts and lines——'

Stannard said quietly, 'The midshipman on my plotting team can speak Swedish, I believe, sir.'

Lindsay let the glasses fall on to his chest. He had to draw several deep breaths before he could find his voice again.

'They will understand, Mr. Tobey.' He walked to the open door. 'She's *Loch Glendhu*.' He seized the frame to steady himself. 'I've met her before. I know her.'

Stannard said softly, 'Oh, my God.'

Tobey was staring past Lindsay at the flickering pattern of flames. 'Sea's quietened a bit, sir. The whalers could be lowered.'

Lindsay did not turn. 'Starboard ten.' He waited, his nerves screaming soundlessly. 'Midships. Steady. Slow ahead together.' Then he looked at Tobey's shocked face. 'Yes. Whalers and rafts. Call for volunteers.'

He swung round as a sharp explosion threw an arrowhead of fire high into the sky. A magazine perhaps. Not long now.

Ritchie stepped aside as Tobey ran past. 'Shall I call 'er up, sir?'

Lindsay said flatly, 'Just tell her to hold on.' He heard Ritchie jerking the lamp shutter, but as he had expected, there was no reply. He said, 'Keep trying. There'll be some left alive. They'll need all the hope they can get in the next minutes.'

Another face emerged in the gloom. It was Boase, the doctor. He said to Stannard, 'How many left, d'you think?'

It was too much for Lindsay's reeling mind. 'Where the hell do you imagine you are?' He was shouting but could not hold it back. Boase was like those other doctors. Ignore it. Forget it. Don't worry. The stupid, heartless bastards!

Boase fell back. 'I'm sorry, sir, I didn't mean——'

Lindsay shouted, 'You never bloody well do mean anything! This isn't some teaching hospital put here for your benefit! Not a Saturday night punch-up with a few revellers at your out-patients department while you play God!' He swung round and gestured towards the sea. Framed in the door, with the sleet glittering redly in the flames, it looked as if the sky was raining blood. 'Take a good look! There are men dying out there. Cursing the blind, ignorant fools who let them go to war in ships like that one. Like our own!'

A bosun's mate said hoarsely, 'Boats ready for lowering, sir.'

Stannard spoke first. 'Very well. Tell them to watch out for burning oil——'

Lindsay said, 'Stop engines.'

He wiped his forehead with his hand. The skin was hot, burning, despite the cold air from the door. It was not the doctor's fault. It was unfair to take it out of him in front of the others. Unfair, and cruelly revealing about his failing strength and self-control.

The deck swayed very slowly as the ship idled forward, her screws stopped for the first time since leaving the Flow.

More sounds rumbled in the darkness, like a ship breaking up. Crying out in her own way against the fools who had let it be so. All the fires had gone but for one darting tongue which appeared to be burning right through the other ship's bilge plates as she started to roll on her side, the sea around her misty with steam and whipped spray.

Small lights glittered in a deep trough, and he saw one of the whalers pulling strongly towards the sinking ship. He gritted his teeth as another crash from the forward gun hurled a starshell high over the scene of misery and pain.

Along the *Benbecula*'s side the boatswain had lowered some of the rafts, to act as staging posts for the survivors before they were hauled bodily up her tall hull. He saw white jackets in the cold and wet, and hoped Boase was there too with his stretcher parties.

When he looked up at the funnel with its low plume of dark smoke he realised that one side of it was shining like ice in the glare. The snow had started. There was not much time left. In the whalers the volunteers would even now be watching the snow, fearing more perhaps for their own survival than those they had gone to save.

He thought too of the corvette's small quarterdeck on
that morning. The line of corpses awaiting burial, like
those aboard the listing cruiser at Scapa. And the two
small ones at the end of the line. Like little parcels under
the flag as they had gone over the rail. *Look after them.*
Well, they had gone where there was no more hurt. No
persecution.

Stannard said loudly, 'She's going!'

More frothing water, and the last flame extinguished
with the suddenness of death. Then nothing.

It seemed like an age before Stannard reported, 'Boats
returning, sir.'

He walked to the extent of the starboard wing and
peered down through the snow flurries. The boats were
crammed with bodies. Shining with oil. A familiar
enough sight in the Atlantic. Others clung around the
sides of the boats, treading water, their gasps audible
even on the wing. Here and there a red lifelight shone on
the water, others floated away unheeded, tiny scarlet
pinpricks, each marking a corpse.

He tried to tear his eyes from the struggling figures
below him. There was so much to do. A signal to be coded
and despatched, to inform those who were concerned
with what had happened. Start the wheels turning. The
Secretary of the Admiralty regrets to announce the loss
of H.M.S. *Loch Glendhu. Stop it.*

Lindsay thrust himself bodily from the wet steel and
turned to see Lieutenant Aikman staring at him.

'Go and make sure that everything's all right! If they
need more hands, take them from aft. I want those boats
hoisted and secured without delay.' He watched the
officer scurrying for the ladder. One more victim of his
own despair and blind anger.

Dancy said hoarsely, 'If I have to die, I hope it's like
that, sir.'

Lindsay looked at him for several seconds, feeling his
anger giving way to a kind of madness, with wild,

uncontrollable laughter almost ready to burst out. Then he reached out to pat Dancy's arm.

'Then we shall have to see what we can do. But before you decide anything definite, go and visit the survivors in the sickbay. Then tell me again.'

Stannard called, 'Ready to get under way, sir.'

Lindsay saw his own reflection in the glass screen, as if he was indeed outside himself, assessing his resources.

'Very well. Slow ahead together. Bring her round on course again.'

He saw Ritchie thumbing through a manual then holding his torch steady above one page.

He asked, 'How many, Yeo?'

Ritchie replied quietly, 'She 'ad a company of three 'undred, sir.'

Goss appeared through the rear door and said thickly, 'We've picked up thirty, sir.'

Lindsay seated himself carefully in the tall chair. Strange how light his limbs felt. As in the dream.

Goss seemed to think he had not heard. 'Only *thirty*, sir!'

'Thank you, Number One. We will remain at action stations for another hour at least. Pass the word for a good lookout while visibility holds.'

Not that they'll need telling now, he thought dully.

He heard Goss slamming out of the wheelhouse. Probably cursing me. The iron, cold captain that no pain, no sentiment can reach. God, if he only knew.

One hour later the snow came down, and within no time at all the ship was thrusting her way through a swirling, white world, enclosed and excluded from all else.

As the men left their action stations and ran or staggered below to warmth and an illusion of safety, Lindsay heard a sailor laughing, the sound strangely sad in the steady blizzard.

Horror from what they had witnessed was giving way

to relief at being spared. Later it would be different, but now it was good to hear that someone could laugh, he thought.

———

Goss clumped into the wheelhouse, shaking snow from his oilskin and stamping it from his heavy sea boots. The bristles on his chin were grey, almost white, so that in the hard reflected glare he looked even older.

'Ready, sir.' He watched as Lindsay slid from his chair and walked towards the starboard door.

The motion was steadier, and overnight the sea had lost much of its anger, as if smoothed and eased by the growing power of the snow. Yet there was some wind, and every so often the snow would twist into strange patterns, swirling around the bridge superstructure, or driving like a desert storm, parallel with the deck.

Lindsay rested one hand on the clip. Apart from a few short snatches in his chair, he had not slept, and as he stood by the door he could feel the chill in his bones, the inability to think clearly.

Goss's eyes, red-rimmed with salt and fatigue, followed him as he tugged open the door and stepped on to the open wing. Watching him. Searching for something perhaps.

The snow squeaked under his leather sea boots, but there was no ice as yet. He felt it touching his face, pattering across his oilskin as he moved slowly to the extremity of the wing. There was hardly any visibility, and when he peered down he saw the sluggish bow wave sliding past as the only sign that the ship was still thrusting ahead.

He raised his head and stared fixedly abeam, the snow melting on his lashes, running down his cheeks like the tears on Ritchie's face that day at Scapa. The yeoman was here now, his features like stone.

In spite of the snow and dirty slush there were many

others from the watch below. Dark clusters of men against the glittering, descending backcloth.

He heard himself say, 'I'll be about ten minutes, Number One.'

Is that all it took? He did not wait for Goss's reply but turned and clattered down the ladder, his boots slipping on the slush, his hands cold on the rungs, for he had forgotten his gloves. Down more ladders to the promenade deck. As he strode aft, his legs straddled against the steady motion, he saw flecks of rust showing already through the new grey paint. He paused and looked abeam. Out there, some one hundred and fifty miles away, was the western extreme of Iceland. The nearest land. Up here, the only land.

He quickened his pace, and when he reached the after well deck he had to steel himself again before he could climb down the last ladder where Maxwell and Stannard were waiting to assist with the burials.

There were only eight of them. Five of those who had been picked up alive. The others had been hauled aboard the whalers by accident. Only eight, yet the line seemed endless, so that in his mind's eye Lindsay could picture all the others which *Benbecula* had left in her wake. There had been three hundred in *Loch Glendhu*'s company, Ritchie had said.

He strode to the side and returned Maxwell's salute. Beyond the gunnery officer he saw more watching figures and Lieutenant de Chair with some of his marines.

God, how could he do it? Just ten minutes, he had told Goss, but he was already cracking. He could feel his reserve stripping itself away like a protective skin. Leaving him naked to their serious faces.

He cleared his throat. 'Let's get on with it.'

As he pulled the little book from his pocket he looked up, caught off guard as de Chair said quietly, 'Very well, Sarn't. Off coats.'

He stared, almost dazed, as the marines obediently stripped off their shining oilskins and formed into a tight, swaying line behind the canvas-covered bodies. He realised they were all in their best blue uniforms, that somehow they were shaved. In spite of everything. *Oh God, what are they doing to me?*

Blindly he thumbed open the book, the print dancing before him, the snow falling softly on his hands.

'Now.'

He removed his cap and squinted up directly into the snow. It was so thick that he could not see if the ensign was at half-mast or not. What the hell did it matter to these dead men?

Maxwell shouted towards the bridge, and Lindsay heard the distant clang of telegraphs as the engines fell silent once more.

He stared hard at the open page and then, with sudden resolution, thrust the book back into his pocket. He did not need it any more. He had spoken the words too often. Heard them more than enough to forget even if he wanted to.

'We commend unto Thy hands of mercy, most merciful Father, the souls of these our brothers departed, and we commit their bodies to the deep. . . .'

He licked his lips as the marines edged forward, their faces like Ritchie's had been as they raised the neat bundles beneath the two large ensigns.

It was always a bad moment. When you did not know any of these quiet bundles. Strangers . . . not even that. Only the uniforms had been the same.

One of them was *Loch Glendhu*'s captain, who had died within thirty minutes of being carried aboard. By rights he should have died back there on his bridge. He had been hit by several shell splinters and had been savagely burned before an explosion had blasted him into the sea. Even then he had refused to die. Maybe he had seen Ritchie's signal lamp, or the whalers coming for his men.

Or perhaps he needed to stay alive just long enough to tell what he knew. To pass on his dying anger and hatred.

Lindsay had left the bridge for a moment to visit him in the sickbay, had watched the other captain's mouth through the bandages as he had gasped out his short, bitter story.

There had been no Swedish ship. No neutral under attack. Just the big German raider, lying there waiting for them like a tiger shark. True, she had looked Swedish, with her painted flag and neutral colouring, but as *Loch Glendhu* had turned to offer help, the enemy's guns had opened fire from a dozen concealed positions, smashing through the hull, blasting men to pulp who seconds before had been preparing to lower boats, to give aid.

As *Loch Glendhu* had become a raging inferno and had begun to settle down, the raider had gathered way, pausing only to fire a few more shells and rake the shattered vessel with automatic fire.

The dying captain had said, 'It was my fault. Should have been ready. Expecting it. But it was something different. New.' Then he had died.

Lindsay had been speaking the familiar words even though his mind had been reliving those last moments. When he looked again the flags were being folded, the bodies gone.

He nodded to Maxwell, and within seconds the big screws had started to churn the sea into a busy froth. He replaced his cap, the rim cold around his forehead, like ice-rime.

The marines were struggling into their wet coats, Stannard was staring over the rail, his eyebrows white with snow.

It was done. Finished.

Again he returned Maxwell's salute and said, 'Thank you, Guns.' He looked at the others. 'All of you.'

Stannard fell into step beside him as they walked forward along the promenade deck.

Lindsay heard himself say, 'I will make that signal now, Pilot. Can't tell them much——' He shrugged, knowing Stannard was looking at him. *Thinks I don't care, or that I am past caring. Or searching for some explanation when there's none to offer.*

As they started up the last ladder Lindsay heard voices. Low voices made harsh with anger. He climbed on to the open wing and saw Goss hunched in one corner, his massive figure towering above Fraser, who was glaring up at him, his white overalls coarse against the swirling snow.

Lindsay snapped, 'What the hell is going on?' Beyond the others he saw that the wheelhouse door was closed so that the anger would remain unheard.

Goss whirled round. 'Nothing, sir!'

Fraser exploded, 'Nothing, my bloody arse!' He hurried towards Lindsay. 'I came on deck. Just to watch quietly when——' He glanced briefly aft. 'But there were too many of the lads there, and I wanted to be on my own.' He held up a greasy hand as Goss made to interrupt. 'I was forrard, by Number Two gun when the engines stopped.'

For an instant longer Lindsay imagined that Fraser's keen ear had detected some flaw in the engines' familiar beat.

The little engineer added slowly, 'I heard something sir.'

Goss said harshly, 'You can't be sure, for God's sake!'

Fraser looked at Lindsay, his tone suddenly pleading. 'I've been too long in my trade not to recognise a winch, sir.' He swung round and pointed into the driving snow. It was thicker and the forecastle only just visible. Beyond the bows it was like a white wall. 'There was a ship out there, sir. I *know* it!'

Lindsay stood stockstill, his mind filling with words, faces, sounds. The burial service. The marines in their blue uniforms. The snow. Two dead children.

Goss said thickly, 'Suppose you were mistaken, Chief?' When nobody answered he added in a louder voice, 'Might have been anything!'

Stannard was still on top of the ladder, unable to get past Lindsay. He called, 'But surely no bloody raider would still *be* here?'

Lindsay moved slowly towards the forepart of the screen. 'Why not?' His voice was so quiet that the others drew closer. 'He's done pretty well for himself so far. Sunk an A.M.C. without any fuss at all.' How could he sound so calm? 'He's probably sitting out the snow and preparing for *Loch Glendhu*'s relief. Us, for instance.'

Goss stared at him incredulously. 'But we don't *know*, sir!'

Stannard said, 'Could be. He'd listen for any signals. Just make sure there were no other ships around to spread the alarm——' He fell back as Lindsay thrust him aside and wrenched open the wheelhouse door.

As he tore off the dripping oilskin and dropped it unheeded to the deck he snapped, 'Back to your engine room, Chief. I want *dead slow*, right?' He looked at Stannard. 'Pass the word quickly. I want the hands at action stations on the double. But no bells or pipes, not a bloody sound out of anyone.' He sounded wild. 'Send them in their bare feet if necessary!'

Midshipman Kemp had emerged from the chart room and Lindsay seized his arm saying, 'Get the gunnery officer yourself, lad, and be sharp about it!'

The boy hesitated, his face very pale. 'Where is he, sir?'

'Down aft. He's just helped to bury some of our friends.' He looked coldly at Goss by the door. 'Well, I intend to bury some of those bastards if I can!'

He ignored the startled glances and walked to the front of the bridge.

The deck was trembling very gently now. Fraser must have run like a madman to reach the engine room so quickly.

Five minutes later Stannard said, 'Ship at action stations, sir.'

Lindsay turned and ran his eye over the others. Jolliffe had certainly been fast enough. He was still wearing old felt slippers and there were crumbs on his portly stomach.

'I need three good hands up forrard.' It was like speaking his thoughts aloud. Describing a scene not yet enacted. 'Right in the eyes of the ship. Yeo, send some of your bunting-tossers. They'll have keen ears and eyes. If,' he checked himself, 'when we run this bastard to ground I want to see him first. So he'll know what it's like.'

Ritchie buttoned his oilskin collar. 'I'll go meself, sir.' He beckoned to two of his signalmen. 'It'll be a pleasure.'

Like a towering ghost the *Benbecula* glided forward into the snow, her decks and superstructure already inches deep from the blizzard.

Apart from the gentle beat of engines, the occasional creak of steel or the nervous movement of feet above the bridge, there was nothing to betray her.

Lindsay took out his pipe and put it between his teeth, his eyes on Ritchie's black figure as it hurried between the anchor cables. Perhaps Fraser had been wrong. There might be nothing out there in the snow.

He thought suddenly of the dying captain. *Something different*, he said, ashamed perhaps for not understanding the new rules.

He gripped the side of his chair and waited. At least we will have tried, he thought.

5 Learning

Petty Officer Ritchie tore off one glove with his teeth and fumbled with the clip on the small telephone locker. He was as far forward in the bows as he could reach, and was conscious of the muffled stillness, as if the ship were abandoned in the steady snowfall. He wrenched the door open and clapped the handset to his ear. As he glanced aft he noticed the bridge was almost hidden by snow, with only the wheelhouse windows showing distinctly, like square black eyes.

'Bridge.' It was the captain's voice, and Ritchie could imagine him standing beside his chair as he had last seen him, peering down towards the forecastle.

'Yeoman, sir.' He turned his back on the bridge and stared over the steel bulwark. 'In position now.'

'Good.' A pause. 'I will keep this line open.'

Ritchie touched the snow which lined the bulwark like cotton wool. It felt stiffer. Maybe a hint of ice, he thought, as he moved his eyes slowly from side to side. Occasionally the wind became more evident as it twisted the snow into nervous, darting patterns, and he saw the sea moving slowly towards him, dark, like lead. Despite all his layers of clothing he shivered. He had heard the officers talking, and his own experience told him the rest. You could not serve on a dozen bridges over the same number of years without learning.

He held his breath as a shadow lifted through the snow, and then relaxed slightly. The wind had cut a path just long enough to reveal an open patch of water. A small, dismal patch which for a few seconds had become a ship. If there was a ship out there, he knew she could just as easily be listening and waiting for them.

The hunter once again. Right now those bloody Germans might be adjusting their sights, hands tightening on triggers and shells while *Benbecula*'s outline nudged blindly into their crosswires. Even if the captain was right, and they got off the first salvos, both ships might pound one another to scrap, sink out here, one hundred and fifty miles from land.

To his left he heard Cummings, one of the young signalmen, sniffing in the cold air, and wondered briefly what he made of it all. Six months ago he had been a baker's roundsman in Birmingham, and now . . . he shook himself angrily. What the hell difference did it make? It was odd the way the snow made you drowsy, no matter how tensed up you were.

God, the deck was steady. Hardly an engine vibration reached him in the eyes of the ship, and in the handset earpiece he imagined he could hear Lindsay breathing. A good bloke, he thought. Not condescending like some of the arrogant bastards he had met. Genuine, maybe a bit too much so. Like someone nursing an old hurt. Something which was tearing him apart, so that when he heard of others' troubles he felt it all the more. Like, the burial service, for instance. He started. Was that only moments ago?

He had seen it then as the captain had spoken the prayer over the corpses. The same expression he had witnessed in London at the mass burial. Almost the whole street. The whole bloody street. They had said the bombers had been making for the London docks, but they had hit his street just the same. The East End was never the most attractive of places. Terraced houses, every one the same as its neighbour, and each with its own backyard the size of a carpet. Madge had always insisted on calling it a garden. He felt his lips move in a small smile. A garden.

The burial had been worse because of the weather. Bright and sunny, as if the world wanted to ignore their little drama. Red buses passing the end of the street in regular procession, making for Bethnal Green Underground station. A barrage balloon, fat and shining in the sunlight like a contented whale. A workman whistling in the ruins of a church which had been blitzed the week before.

But the faces had been the same. Frozen. Like Lindsay's. He wondered if anyone else had noticed. Not Maxwell, he was sure of that. Stupid parade-ground basher. Should have been a bloody Nazi himself.

He stiffened. There it was again. His head swivelled round as he heard the faint but distinct clang of metal.

'Green four-five, sir. As far as I can tell. I 'eard metal.'

A small shudder ran through his boots and he guessed that the helm had gone over.

Then Lindsay said, 'Keep it up, Yeo.' Cool, unhurried, as if he was reporting on a cricket match.

Cummings whispered, 'What d'you think, Yeo?'

Ritchie shrugged. 'I dunno.'

He felt the sweater warm against his neck. Madge had made it for him from an old jumper she had unravelled to get the wool. He tried to control the sudden surge of emotion. He had to get used to it. Accept it. But how long would it take? Only yesterday he had heard Hussey, the PO telegraphist, describing his service in a China river gunboat before the war. He had said to himself, *I'll tell the kids about that, next leave*. It was small, unguarded moments like that which left him aching and lost.

The snow whipped against his cheek in a wet mould, as with sudden force the wind swept hard across the bulwark. He dashed it from his eyes, and when he looked again he saw the other ship.

It was incredible she could be so close, that she had been there all the while. She lay diagonally across *Benbecula*'s line of advance, the stern towards him, her tall upperworks and poop gleaming like icing on a giant cake.

He said hoarsely, 'Ship, sir! Fine on th' starboard bow! Range about two cables!'

As the endless seconds dragged past he kept his eyes fixed on the other vessel. She was big right enough, probably a liner, with two funnels and a large Swedish flag painted on her side. As he watched he saw part of her upper bridge move slightly, and realised it was being lifted bodily by one of her forward derricks. The chief had heard a winch. The Germans were changing their appearance already. Preparing for their next victim. There was a sudden flurry of foam beneath her high counter where seconds earlier the enemy's hull had rolled, drifting on the sluggish rollers.

He rasped, 'Down, lads! She's seen us!' He grabbed Cummings' sleeve and dragged him gasping to the deck. ''Old yer 'eads down, and keep 'em there till I tells you different!'

Cummings lay beside him, his body only inches away, eyes filling his face as he gasped, 'I—I'm going to be sick!'

Ritchie opened his mouth to say something but heard the sudden tinkle of bells at the nearest gun and changed his mind.

———————

Like the yeoman, Lindsay had seen the other ship's blurred outline with something like disbelief. Perhaps the snow was passing over, but it gave the deceptive impression of leaving one opening, an arena just large enough to contain the two ships, while beyond and all around the downpour was as thick as before.

'Port fifteen! Full ahead both engines!'

The sharpness of his voice seemed to break the shocked stillness in the wheelhouse, and the figures on either side of him started to move and react, as if propelled by invisible levers.

'Midships! *Steady!*'

Jolliffe muttered, 'Steady, sir. Course three-five-five.'

Voicepipes and handsets crackled on every side, and he heard Maxwell shouting, 'Commence, commence, commence!' And the instant reply from the fire gongs.

By turning slightly to port Lindsay had laid the enemy on an almost parallel course some four hundred yards away. He watched the sudden flurry from her twin screws, saw her poop tilt slightly to their urgent thrust, and knew that in spite of everything his small advantage could soon be lost.

Then, with bare seconds between, the three starboard side guns opened fire. Number Three which was furthest aft fired first, and he guessed the marines had been quicker to translate the shouted instructions into action. The six-inch shell screamed past the bridge, the shock-wave searing against the superstructure like an express train charging through a station. The other two guns followed almost together, the smoke pluming across the deck, the savage detonations shaking the gratings beneath Lindsay's feet and bringing several gasps of alarm.

'She's turning away!' Lieutenant Aikman almost fell as Number Three gun hurled itself inboard on its recoil springs and sent another shell screaming across the grey water.

Tonelessly the voice of a control rating said, 'Over. Down two hundred.'

The deck was quivering violently now as the revolutions mounted, and the bow wave ploughed away on either beam like a solid glass arrowhead.

'Starboard ten.' Lindsay dropped his eye to the gyro. 'Midships.' He saw droplets of his sweat falling on the protective cover. 'Steady.'

When he raised his head again the enemy was nearer, the bearing more acute.

A bosun's mate shouted, 'Number Three gun 'as ceased firin', sir. Unable to bear!'

Lindsay looked at Stannard. It could not be helped. If

he hauled off again to give the marines a clear view of the enemy the other ship would escape in the snow. She was big. About seventeen thousand tons. Big, modern and with all the power required to move her at speed.

The two forward guns, their view unimpeded by the superstructure, fired again. The long orange tongues leaping from their muzzles as the shells streaked away towards the enemy.

Through the snow flurries Lindsay saw a brief flash, like a round red eye, and heard Maxwell yell, 'A *hit!* We hit the bastard!'

She was pulling away with each second, her funnels already hidden by the snow.

Lindsay dashed his hand across his forehead and waited, counting seconds, until the guns fired once more. Longer intervals now. He pictured the shell hoists jerking up their shafts, cooks, stewards, writers and supply ratings cursing and struggling to feed the guns with those great, ungainly missiles while the hull shook around them. And in the engine and boiler rooms Fraser's men would be hearing the explosions above the din of their machinery, watching the tall sides and praying that no shell came their way. The inrush of water, the scalding steam. Oblivion.

The snow lifted and writhed above the enemy ship, and Lindsay saw the telltale orange flash. The other captain had at last got one of his after guns to bear.

The shell hit the *Benbecula*'s side like a thunderclap, the shock hurling men and equipment about the bridge, while above the starboard bulwark the smoke came billowing inboard in a solid brown fog.

Lindsay gripped the voicepipes and heard splinters ripping and ricocheting through the hull, and tasted the lyddite on the cold air.

But the guns were still firing, and above the din he heard layers and trainers yelling like madmen, the rasp of steel, the clang of breech blocks before the cry, *'Ready!'*

Aikman called, 'Damage control reports a fire on A deck, sir. Two casualties.'

'Very well.'

Lindsay raised his glasses and studied the enemy. Nearly gone now, her shortened outline was just a murky shadow in the snow.

He had to chance it. 'Port ten.' To Aikman he snapped, 'Tell the gunnery officer to bring Number Three to bear.'

He watched the ticking gyro. 'Midships.' He did not wait for Jolliffe's reply but strode to the starboard side, feeling the icy wind clawing his face through the open window.

de Chair's gun reopened fire even as the enemy settled on the *Benbecula*'s starboard bow, and the shell hit her directly abaft the bridge. This time the explosion was more dramatic, and Lindsay guessed the exploding shell had also ignited either a small-arms magazine or some signal flares.

The snow seemed to glow red and gold as the flames licked greedily around one of the tall funnels, starting more scattered explosions to litter the churned water alongside with falling fragments.

The enemy fired again, and as before her gunnery was perfect. The shell hit *Benbecula*'s side further aft, exploding deep inside the hull and sending white-hot splinters scything in every direction. Some burst upwards through the boat deck and cut a whaler in halves, leaving bow and stern dangling from the davits like dead fruit.

Stannard said hoarsely, 'Snow's getting heavier again.' He ducked involuntarily as a shell exploded alongside, the flash masked instantly by a towering white water-spout. Bridge and wing were buried under cascading water, and Lindsay heard Jolliffe cursing one of the quartermasters who had fallen against the wheel.

Lindsay rubbed his glasses and peered after the enemy in time to see her fading completely into another squall. Only the glare of her fires was still visible, and he heard several small explosions on the wind as de Chair's last shell continued to spread its havoc between decks.

Aikman reported, 'Damage control have A deck fire under control, sir. Second hit was also A deck. No fire, but four men wounded.'

Another telephone jarred the sudden stillness and Stannard said, 'It's the chief, sir. He asks if he can reduce revs. Starboard shaft is overheating. Nothing serious, he thinks, but——'

Lindsay realised the Australian was staring at him and then his reeling mind recalled what he had been asked.

'Thank you, Pilot. Reduce to slow ahead.'

No sense in tearing the engines to pieces for nothing. The enemy would not come back for another try. Not this time. It was too risky.

He added slowly, 'Get a signal coded up right away. To Admiralty. Advise on our position, course and approximate speed of enemy.' He rubbed his eyes, forcing his mind to respond. 'Tell them we have engaged enemy raider and obtained two hits. Extent of her damage not known.'

Stannard lowered his pad. 'Is that all, sir?'

Lindsay walked to the door and wrenched it open as thankfully the bridge messengers started to close the glass windows again.

'Mention that *Loch Glendhu* has been sunk, and check with the sickbay for a list of survivors.'

He heard Stannard leave the wheelhouse and leaned over the wing to watch some of the damage control team scurrying along the forward well deck, bowed against the wind. Or fearful perhaps the enemy could still see them.

He was shaking uncontrollably, yet when he looked at his hands they seemed quite steady. Perhaps it was in his mind.

There were clangs and shouts, more orders as seamen and stokers ran to deal with damage and plug up the gaping splinter holes.

Goss appeared suddenly in the wheelhouse door. 'Nobody dead, sir.' He sounded accusing. 'One man's lost a foot, but the doc says he'll live——' He swung round as Ritchie pushed his way to the door.

Ritchie said harshly, 'There was *one* killed, sir.' He paused, recalling the astonishment on the boy's face. The eyes glazing with drifting snow. He said, 'Ordinary Signalman Cummings, sir. Shell splinter got 'im in the spine.' *But for his body, I would have got it.* 'I didn't realise he'd bought it till I told 'im it was all over.'

Lindsay nodded. Bought it. What the Wren had said at Scapa.

'You did bloody well, Yeo.'

Ritchie shrugged. 'It's a start.'

Goss cleared his throat noisily. 'About the *damage*.'

'Yes?'

'It's a dockyard job, sir.'

Lindsay could feel his nerves dragging like hot wires. He wanted to shake Goss, hit him if necessary to make him understand.

Instead he said flatly, 'No, it isn't, Number One. It's *yours*, until we hear to the contrary.'

Goss spoke between his teeth. 'If the snow hadn't eased at that moment we might have run straight into that German!'

Lindsay swung on him. 'Well, at least we'd have sunk the bloody thing! Now, for God's sake get on with those repairs!'

He turned to watch some seamen carrying a limp body aft from the forecastle. Cummings. Was that the man's name?

Dancy poked his head through the door. 'The chief has said everything's all right, sir.'

Lindsay looked at him. He had forgotten all about Dancy. But he seemed steady enough for his first action.

'Thank him for me, Sub. And fall out action stations.'

He realised Dancy was still there, staring at him as if for the first time in his life. 'Well?'

Dancy flushed. 'I—I'm sorry, sir. It's just that I wouldn't have believed it possible.' He seemed quite oblivious of Lindsay's grave face or Ritchie's despairing glance. 'To handle a ship like this, to outmanoeuvre that German——'

Lindsay held up his hand. 'Write about it one day, Sub. Tell your mother if you like, but spare *me*, will you?'

Dancy withdrew, and seconds later the upper deck tannoy grated, 'Fall out action stations. Starboard watch to defence stations.' The merest pause, then 'Up spirits!'

Lindsay looked at Ritchie, feeling the grin spreading across his face, pushing the despair aside like the wind had laid bare the enemy.

'Good advice, Yeo.' He walked towards the wheelhouse again. 'I think we deserve it!'

Ritchie watched him and then shook his head. You'll do, he thought. For me, and this poor old ship. You'll do.

Sub-Lieutenant Michael Dancy pushed aside the heavy curtain and stepped into the wardroom. With only half the deckhead lights in use the wardroom looked cosy and pleased with itself, the oak panelling gleaming softly in welcome. Just over an hour to midnight, and as Dancy had the middle watch he saw no point in trying to sleep.

By the fat coal stove he saw Barker in conversation with Boase, the doctor, although the latter's face was so expressionless it seemed hardly likely he was doing more than listening.

Barker was saying, 'We had some very rich passengers, of course. None of those save-up-for-the-cruise-of-a-lifetime types. Real class.'

Boase eyed him wearily. 'Good.'

The ex-purser lowered his voice. 'Like this ship today. I'm not saying that some of these temporary chaps don't mean well.' He winked. 'But you know what they say about the sow's ear, eh?'

Boase yawned. 'Nobody's more temporary than I am.'

Barker shot him an ingratiating smile. 'Ah, but you're *professional*, it's quite different!'

Dancy turned away. Quite apart from disliking Barker, he could not bear to watch him and the doctor sipping their drinks by the fire. Normally Dancy did not drink much. Before the war he had been unable to afford it, except at Christmas time, and in any case his mother disapproved, hinting darkly at a nameless uncle who had *gone off the rails*. After being commissioned and sent to the armed yacht he had been involved in several minor drinking bouts, most of which had ended in dismal failure and agonising sickness.

But tonight he did feel like it. A celebration all of his own.

He sat in a deep chair with his back to the others and stared unseeingly at the swaying curtains which partitioned off the dining space, half listening to the wind sighing against the hull. It was difficult to accept that only this morning they had been in action. Had fired and been fired upon. Had buried a young signalman, their first real casualty, and *he* had lived through all of it.

Dancy felt as if his lungs were too large for his body, that he wanted to shout or laugh out loud. What did that old woman Barker know about it anyway? He was more concerned with corned beef and the issue of clothing than the business of fighting. While Barker had been hidden below, he, Michael Dancy, had been up there beside the captain, seeing it, feeling it, and not breaking as he had once thought he would.

He heard the bell go and knew the others were ringing for more drinks. But he must go on watch soon, and had been left in no doubt by the first lieutenant what would happen to a watchkeeping officer who drank.

He tried to assemble his memories into order, to capture each moment. He smiled. As a writer should. But it was still difficult. It had been so swift, with the din and smells all mixed together in his mind. And all the while this great ship, and she was enormous after the armed yacht, had wheeled and pounded through the snow, guns blazing and—— He turned his head angrily as Fraser entered the wardroom and threw himself into a chair, prodding the bell push in the same movement.

Barker said, 'Of course, Doc, that was *why* the company was such a success. We only had the five ships, but there was true devotion, a sense of service and loyalty so lacking today.'

Fraser had his eyes closed. 'Crap,' he said.

Barker glared at him. 'How can you say such a thing?'

The engineer opened his eyes as a steward glided into the lamplight. He said, 'I want a treble gin.' Then to Barker he added slowly, 'The reason this company was a success, and I'm not denying it, was the fact that the owners were the meanest set of skinflints ever dropped the wrong side of a blanket!'

Boase stirred uneasily and glanced from one to the other.

Fraser continued calmly, 'See all this panelling, Doc?' He waved one hand and displayed the black grease on his fingers. 'All the pretty cabins? Well, it only went down as far as B deck. The rest, the crew's quarters and the poor emigrants section, was like the bloody Black Hole of Calcutta!' He looked at Barker's outraged face. 'Man, you're daft if you think loyalty played any part. Men needed work, and had to lick boots to get it. But you wouldn't know anything about that!'

The steward was just placing the brimming glass beside him when the bulkhead telephone buzzed impatiently. The steward said, 'For you, sir.'

Fraser seized the phone and jerked his head to the other voice. 'Yes. Yes. Oh, Jesus, not that freshwater pump again. This bloody ship'll be the death o' me!' He dropped the phone and downed the gin in one long swallow.

As he walked to the door he added, 'One thing. If I run short of hot air for the boilers, I'll know where to come!' The door slammed behind him.

Barker stood up, visibly shaken. 'I'll turn in now.' He looked round the wardroom. 'I might have to check some ledgers first, of course.'

As he hurried away Boase said softly, 'Of course.'

Then he smiled at Dancy. 'You look ready to do great deeds.'

Dancy replied coldly, 'I have the middle.'

'Ah.' Boase squinted at the clock. 'Think I'll go to bed, too.'

Dancy opened and then shut his mouth. *Go to bed.* Boase had not even learned the right terms. Funny chap. Very cool and distant, yet they said he had sawn off a man's foot and saved his life.

'Anything more, sir?' The steward yawned ominously.

'No. You can turn in.'

The steward's eye dropped very slightly to the single stripe on Dancy's sleeve. 'You doing Rounds then, sir?'

Dancy looked away. 'Well, no, not exactly.'

The steward slammed into his pantry muttering, 'Then I'll wait for someone who *is*.'

The door opened again and Dancy saw it was Kemp, the midshipman. Apart from the other sub-lieutenants, Kemp was the newest officer in the ship. In addition, he was the only one upon whom Dancy could exercise his scanty authority.

The boy said quietly, 'I—— I was just looking to see if——' his voice trailed away.

Dancy frowned. 'Sit here if you like.' He glanced at his watch for several seconds. 'I've got the middle.'

Kemp nodded. He was a slightly built youth, even slender, and his even features were extremely pale. But unknown to the young midshipman he possessed one tremendous gift, one glittering asset which Dancy could never hold or share. He was a regular and had been to

Dartmouth. Dancy had already discovered that he was the son of a senior officer, one of a family of naval men. He seemed to epitomise all Dancy's peacetime dreams, but at the same time did not really fit the role.

He asked casually, 'Your old man, pretty senior, I believe?' Old man sounded just right, he thought. Assured. A man of the world.

Dancy had learned his etiquette the hard way. Once in the armed yacht there had been a party and several women had been invited as guests. He had asked one very poised young lady about her father and she had replied, 'Oh, Daddy's a sailor.'

He had been horrified. 'Not an *officer*?'

She had stared at him as if he had spoken some terrible obscenity. 'But of course, silly! What else?'

Yes, Dancy was learning.

Kemp replied, 'He's a captain. Shore job at Rosyth.' He sighed. 'He was beached between the wars for several years.'

Dancy nodded gravely. 'I'll bet he's glad to be back.'

Kemp looked at him, his eyes strangely sad. 'Glad? That's an understatement.'

'Yes.' Dancy was getting irritated without knowing why. It was like talking to a stone wall. 'You sound as if you're unhappy about the ship or something.'

'I am.' He shrugged. 'Not the ship exactly. It's the Service. I hate it.' Now that he had begun he seemed unable to stop himself. 'I never wanted to enter the Navy. Never. But he kept on at me. Kept on reminding me of my obligations, my duty.'

Dancy said, 'I expect it was all for the best.' God, he sounded like his own father. He tried again. 'But surely he knew the Navy well enough to understand, eh?'

Kemp stood up violently, a lock of hair falling across his eyes. 'My father understands nothing about me, and cares less! He's a stupid, pompous bigot, so stop asking about him will you, *please*?'

Dancy was aghast. 'There's no call to speak like that! By God, if I'd had half your chances in life——' He checked himself hastily. 'What I mean is, if I'd not taken another profession I'd have wanted to enter the Service.'

Kemp's hands were shaking at his sides. 'Well, you got there in the end, didn't you, *sir*!'

As he ran for the door he almost collided with Stannard who was carrying his cap and duffel coat and wearing his scarred sea boots. He watched the midshipman run past and said dryly, 'Hell, that young fella's keen to go somewhere.'

Dancy said angrily, 'Doesn't know when he's well off.' It was like a betrayal, a broken image. 'I'll be watching him in future.'

The Australian grinned lazily. 'You do that, Admiral, but in the meantime shift yourself to the bridge, chop, chop!' He gestured to the clock. '*Our* watch, I believe?'

Dancy's frown faded. Stannard was a bit coarse at times, but he was all right. He had been on the bridge with him. Never got in a flap.

Stannard paused by a screen door and looked at him searchingly. 'Ever had a woman, Sub?'

Dancy stared at him. 'Well, I——that is——'

Stannard pursed his lips. 'Have to do something about that then!'

Outside the night was black. No stars or snow. Just the wind and the drifting feathers of spray above the guardrail.

Dancy buttoned his bridge coat and followed the lieutenant to the ladder. That was more like it. He was accepted.

———————

Jupp stopped beside Lindsay's littered desk and placed a large china mug carefully on a mat before removing its lid.

He watched Lindsay and said, "Ot soup, sir. Just th' job before you turn in.'

Lindsay leaned back in his chair and smiled wearily. 'Smells fine.'

Feet scraped on the ladder overhead and he heard muffled voices and more footsteps clattering hurriedly from the bridge. The watch was changing. Midnight.

The soup was very hot, and Lindsay realised he was ravenous, that he had hardly eaten since the brief action with the enemy. It had been a long day. Inspecting damage between decks, checking the progress of repairs, burying Cummings in another quick service at the rail. Poor Cummings, he had not even got used to living.

It was quite impossible to learn anything about the damaged raider. The Admiralty had merely acknowledged his signal. He felt vaguely bitter about it, yet knew it was because he was tired. Worn out. It was unlikely anything could be done about the other ship. It had been too stormy for flying off aircraft, and the sea was a big place. The German was probably steaming like hell for base, to some secluded Norwegian fjord where she could lie up and lick her scars.

He gripped the mug more tightly. At least she had not got completely away with it. Her captain might remember this day as he dropped his own men over the side with a prayer or some jolly Nazi song. He realised Jupp was still watching him, his hooded eyes worried.

The chief steward said, 'The lads took it right well, I thought, sir.'

Lindsay nodded. 'Yes.'

He recalled the great blackened areas on A deck where the shells had exploded. Buckled frames, and plates like wet cardboard. A ventilator so riddled with splinters it had looked like one huge pepper pot. The damage was bad, but had *Benbecula* been a destroyer those two big five-point-nine shells would have broken her back like a carrot. He had visited the sickbay, giving the usual words, seeing the grateful smiles from the wounded men who were not too drugged to understand him. Their immediate shock had given way to a kind of pride. They were probably dreaming of that first leave, the glances of admiration and pity for their wounds. Except the one without a foot. He had been a promising tennis player before the war.

The telephone buzzed. It was Stannard.

'Middle watch at defence stations, sir. Time to alter course in seven minutes.'

The next leg of the patrol. It would be a beam sea, uncomfortable, as they were cruising at a mere seven knots.

'I'll come up, Pilot.' He hesitated. 'No, you take her. Call me if you want anything.' He dropped the handset. Stannard was competent, and it did no good to have a captain breathing down their necks all the time. Let them learn while there was still time.

There was a tap at the door and Maxwell peered in at him. 'You wanted me, sir?'

The gunnery officer's face was red from the wind, but his uniform was impeccable. As usual he wore a bright whistle chain around his neck, the end of which vanished into the breast pocket of his reefer, and Lindsay was reminded of the leather-lunged instructors at the gunnery school.

'Yes, Guns. Sorry to keep you from your bunk after you've been on watch. Just a couple of points.'

Maxwell removed his cap. He had a very sharp, sleek head. Like a polished bullet.

He said, 'Would have been earlier, sir. Hate unpunctuality. But my relief was late.'

'Late?' That was not like Stannard.

Maxwell did not blink. 'One and a half minutes, sir.'

Jupp hid a grin and slid from the cabin.

Lindsay looked at the lieutenant thoughtfully. An odd bird even for his particular trade. Maxwell had made some error or other before the war and been allowed to leave the Navy without fuss. It would not have been difficult when the country was more concerned with cutting down the services than facing the reality of a new Germany.

He said, 'Whenever we return to base I want you to do something about the armour plate on the bridge. Lowering the windows in action prevents injuries from glass splinters, but it's not enough. The watchkeepers and gunnery team must have proper protection.'

A small notebook had appeared in Maxwell's hand as if by magic. He snapped, 'Right, sir.'

'The W/T office needs it also, but I'll get on to Number One about that.' It was amazing how little attention had been given to such matters, he thought. 'Then there are the bridge machine guns. Old Lewis guns from World War One by the look of them.' He watched the pencil scribbling briskly. 'See if you can wangle some Brownings from the B.G.O.'

Maxwell eyed him wearily. 'Wangle, sir?'

'Then I'll give you a chit, Guns, if it makes you happier.'

Maxwell showed his teeth. 'Go by the book, that's me, sir. Follow the book and they can't trample you down.'

'It's happened before then?'

Maxwell swallowed hard. 'It was nothing, sir. Bit of a mix-up back in thirty-seven. But it taught me a lesson. Get it on paper. Go by the book'

Lindsay smiled. 'And they can't trample you down, eh?'

'Sir.' Maxwell did not smile.

A man entirely devoid of humour, Lindsay decided. He said, 'The gunnery this morning was erratic. The marines got off two shots to every one from forrard. Not good enough.'

Maxwell said swiftly, 'My assistant, Lieutenant Hunter, is R.N.R., sir. Keen but without proper experience.' He let the words sink in. 'But I'll get on to him first thing tomorrow.'

The deck quivered, and Lindsay saw the curtains begin to sway inwards from the sealed scuttles. She was turning.

He said, 'You deal with it, Guns. It's your job.'

Maxwell's mouth tightened into a thin line. 'I did not mean to imply——' he stopped.

'Carry on then.'

As the door closed Lindsay stood up and walked slowly into the other cabin. The small reading light gleamed temptingly above his bunk, and Jupp had put a Thermos beside it, wedged carefully between two shoes, in case the motion got too bad. In spite of his dragging weariness Lindsay smiled at the little gesture. Jupp would make a damn good valet, he thought.

He lay down on the bunk fully clothed, and after a few seconds hesitation kicked off his sea boots.

It never stopped. Demands and questions, jobs needing attention, reports to be checked and signed. His eyelids drooped as he thought back over the day, the enemy ship's outline looming through the snow. The anguish of sudden fear, the cruel ecstasy at seeing the shell burst on her upperworks.

He listened to the sea booming against the side, the darting spray across the scuttles, and then fell into a deep sleep.

How long he slept he did not know. All he understood was that he was fighting with the blanket, kicking and gasping as the nightmare flooded around him more vividly than ever.

He rolled on to his side, half blinded by the reading light which was shining directly into his eyes, and as the madness retreated he heard a voice, remote but insistent, which seemed to be rising from the bunk itself.

'Officer of the watch.' It was Stannard, and Lindsay stared at the telephone as it swung back and forth on its flex, the voice repeating 'Officer of the watch' like some cracked record.

He must have knocked it off in his nightmare, in his terror to escape from the torture.

He seized it and said, 'Captain.'

Stannard said, 'I'm sorry, sir. I thought you were calling me.'

Lindsay fought to keep his tone even. 'It's all right, Pilot. What time is it?'

'0350, sir. I'm just calling the morning watch.' A pause. 'Visibility as before. Wind's still north by east.'

'Thank you.'

He lowered the phone and lay back again. God, how long had the line been open? What had he been saying? He rubbed his eyes, trying to clear his mind, remember.

Then he swung his legs from the bunk and groped for Jupp's Thermos. What would he do? *Bomb-happy*, some people called it. He might even have said it once about others. He shuddered violently, pulling at the Thermos cap. Not any more.

Up on the bridge Dancy was standing beside the voice pipes and turned as Stannard replaced the telephone.

Stannard did not look at him. 'Sure. Just the skipper asking about the time.'

When Dancy had turned away he bit his lip with sudden anxiety. He should not have listened. Should not have heard. It was like falling on a secret, laying bare something private or shameful.

Heavy boots thumped on the ladder as Goss mounted to take his watch. Stannard thought of that desperate, pleading voice on the telephone and thanked God he and not Goss had heard it. Things were bad enough without that. They needed Lindsay, whatever he was suffering. He was all they had.

He faced Goss's heavy outline and said, 'Morning, Number One.'

Goss grunted and waited until Stannard had made his

formal report. Then he moved to Lindsay's chair, and after a small hesitation climbed into it.

Stannard walked to the ladder. Goss's action was almost symbolic, he thought.

Throughout the ship the watch had changed, and in bunks and hammocks men slept or lay staring at the deckhead reliving the fight. Drowsy cooks tumbled cursing from their snug blankets and made their way to the waiting galley with its congealed grease and dirty cups left by the watchkeepers. Barker sprawled on his back snoring, a copy of *Lilliput,* and not a ledger, open on his chest to display a voluptuous nude. In the sickbay an attendant sat sleeping beside the man who had lost his foot, and in another white cot a wounded stoker was crying quietly on his pillow, even though he was asleep. In his cabin, Midshipman Kemp was wide awake, looking up into the darkness and thinking about his father. Further aft, in the chief and petty officers' mess, only a blue police light glowed across the tiered bunks. Ritchie slept soundlessly, while on a shelf beside his bunk the pictures of his dead family watched over him. Jolliffe, the coxswain, was having a bad dream, his mouth like a black hole in his heavy face. His teeth, like his slippers, were within easy reach should the alarm bells start again. In the stokers' messdeck, Stripey, the ship's cat, lay curled into a tight ball inside someone's metal cap box, his body trembling gently to the steady beat of the screws.

Indifferent to all of them, the *Benbecula* pushed slowly across a steep beam sea, her shape as black as the waters which were hers alone.

6 Officers and men

If the Icelandic patrol known as Uncle Item Victor had been created solely to test man's endurance it was hard to imagine a better choice. By the middle of October, a month after their clash with the German raider, *Benbecula*'s ship's company had reached what most of them imagined was the limit. To the men at the lookout and gun positions it appeared as if the ship was steaming on one endless voyage to eternity, doomed to end her time heading into worse and worse conditions. Only the bridge watchkeepers really saw the constant changes of course and speed as the old ship ploughed around her desolate piece of ocean.

During the whole of that time they had sighted just one ship, a battered little corvette which had been ordered to rendezvous with them to remove the wounded and the handful of survivors from *Loch Glendhu*. For two whole days the ships had stayed in company, hoping and praying for some easing of the weather so that the transfer could be made. Even some of *Benbecula*'s most dedicated grumblers had fallen silent as hour by hour they had watched the little corvette lifting her bows towards the low clouds, lurching and then reeling into troughs with all but her bridge and squat funnel submerged.

Then, during a brief respite, and with *Benbecula* providing some shelter from the wind, the transfer had taken place.

Even then, and in spite of Fraser's men pumping out gallons of oil to settle the waves, it had nearly ended the lives of some of them. Lindsay had ordered the remaining whaler to be lowered, as a breeches buoy or any sort of tackle was out of the question. The boat had made three trips, rising and vanishing into the troughs like a child's toy, reappearing again with oars flashing like silver in the hard light as they battled towards the corvette.

Then with a defiant toot on her siren the corvette had turned away, her signal lamp fading as she pushed into yet another squall which must have been waiting in the wings for the right moment.

Alone once more they settled down to their patrol, or tried to. But it was a bitter world, an existence and nothing more. The weather was getting much colder as winter tightened its grip, and each dawn found the superstructure and gun barrels gleaming with ice, the signal halliards thick and glittering like a frozen waterfall. If watchkeeping was bad, below decks was little better. Nothing ever seemed to get dry, and in spite of the steam pipes the men endured damp clothes and bedding while they waited their turn to go on deck again and face the sea.

Once they rode out a Force Eleven storm, their greatest threat so far. Winds of almost a hundred knots screamed down from Greenland, building the waves into towering, jagged crests, some of which swept as high as the promenade deck, buckling the guardrails before thundering back over the side. Patches of distorted foam flew above the bridge and froze instantly on guns and rigging, so that the watch below were called slipping and cursing to clear it before the weight of ice could become an additional hazard.

The ship seemed to have shrunk in size, and it was hard to find escape. Tempers became frayed, fights erupted without warning or real cause, and Lindsay saw several resentful faces across the defaulters' table to show the measure of their misery.

Much of the hatred was, of course, directed at him. He had tried to keep them busy, if only to prevent the despair from spreading over the whole ship.

Fraser had been a tower of strength. Like scavengers, he and some of his artificers had explored the bowels of the ship, even the lower orlop, and with blow torches had cut away plates from unused store rooms. They had skilfully reshaped them before welding them in the flats and spaces damaged by the enemy shells. He had even created his own 'blacksmith's shop' as he liked to call it, where his men were able to cut and repair much of the damaged plating and frames which otherwise would have waited for the dockyard's attention. For to Fraser the enforced isolation seemed to act as a test of his personal resources and ability, but when Lindsay thanked him he had said offhandedly, 'Hell, sir, I'm only trying to hold the old cow in one piece until I get a transfer!'

The outbreaks of anger and conflict were not confined to the lower deck. In the wardroom Maxwell had a standing shouting-match with Goss, while Fraser never lost a chance to goad Barker whenever he began to recount stories of his cruising days.

There had been one incident which lingered on long after it had happened. Like the rest of the ship, the wardroom was feeling particularly glum about the latest news of their relief. Another A.M.C. should have relieved them on the sixteenth of the month. Due to unforeseen circumstances, later discovered to be the ship had run into a pier, the relief was to be delayed a further week. Another seven days after what they had already endured was not much to those who arranged such details. To most of the ship's company, however, it felt like the final blow. Some had been counting the days, ticking off the hours, willing the time to pass. As a stoker had said, 'After this, even bleedin' Scapa'll suit me!'

In the wardroom it had been much the same. At dinner, as the table tilted sickeningly from side to side, the crockery rattling in the fiddles, the little spark had touched off a major and disturbing incident.

One of the sub-lieutenants, a pleasant faced youngster called Cordeaux, had been talking quietly to Dancy about gunnery. He was quarters officer of Number Two gun, which had still to be fired in anger, and because of the icy conditions had had little opportunity to watch its crew at drill. Dancy had turned to de Chair who was sitting beside him moodily staring at some greasy tinned sausages on his rattling plate.

'You're better at gunnery, Mark.' Dancy had nudged Cordeaux. 'The marines always are!'

de Chair had emerged from his brooding thoughts, and in his lazy drawl had begun to outline the very points which had baffled Cordeaux.

Maxwell had been sitting at the head of the table and had said sharply, 'By God, I'm just about sick of hearing how bloody marvellous the marines are at gunnery!' He had jabbed his fork towards the startled Cordeaux. 'And you, Mister, can shut up talking shop at the table! I know you're green, but I'd have thought good manners not too hard to imitate!'

Cordeaux had dropped his eyes, his face scarlet.

Then de Chair had turned slowly and said, 'He was speaking to me, Guns. As it happens, I do not believe that something concerning our job is a blight on the dinner table.' He had eyed him calmly. 'More useful than some of your topics, I'd have imagined. Your mind hardly ever seems to move beyond certain sexual activities, all of which put *me* off my dinner!'

Nobody spoke.

Then Maxwell had smiled. 'We are edgy tonight! Are you a bit peeved because the captain hasn't put you in for a medal because of your *superb* gunnery? Bloody luck is more like it!'

de Chair had stood up very slowly, his neat figure swaying easily with the deck. 'Perhaps. But at least I have so far confined *my* gunnery to killing Germans.'

Maxwell's face had been suddenly drained of colour. 'What the hell d'you mean?'

The marine had moved towards the door. 'Just stay off my back, Guns, or by God you'll regret it!' The words had hung in the air long after de Chair had left.

Maxwell had said haltingly, 'Can't imagine what the bloody man is talking about.'

But nobody had looked at him.

Barker had not been present on that occasion, but had received news of the flare-up within the hour. One of the stewards had served in the ship in peacetime and had been well trained by Barker in such matters. In fact, when he had been the ship's purser Barker had evolved an almost foolproof intelligence service. The ship's hairdresser had hoarded vital information about the rich female passengers, the senior stewards had hovered at tables and around the gaming room just long enough to catch a word here, a tip there. There were others too, and all the information went straight to Barker.

With the hopeless mixture of hostilities only ratings, regulars and ex-merchant seamen he had found it harder to rebuild his network, but he was starting. He disliked the regular naval officers, mainly because they made him feel inferior, or so he believed. For that reason he was glad to obtain the news of a clash between de Chair and Maxwell. Of Lindsay he knew nothing as yet. Very controlled, and from what he had heard, extremely competent. Nobody's fool, and with a sharp edge to his voice when he needed it. Midshipman Kemp, at the bottom of the scale, was the son of a senior officer. Kemp, in Barker's view, was worth watching. Any connection with a senior officer was always useful. The midshipman himself was not. Rather shy, not exactly effeminate, but you could never be sure. He had discarded Emerson, the warrant engineer. A pensioner, he was old, fat and dull. He dropped his aitches, referred to his far off wife as 'me old woman', and was generally distasteful.

But Maxwell now, here was something. Goss had hinted that the lieutenant had been under a cloud before the war, but Barker had always imagined it to be connected with some minor breach. Slight discrepancy in mess funds, or found in bed with his C.O.'s wife. Nothing too damning. But from what the steward had heard and seen it now appeared very likely that Maxwell had been involved in a serious accident.

He would, however, treat de Chair with an even greater respect from now on, even if he was a regular. de Chair was exactly like some of the passengers whom Barker had served in the better days of cruising. Outwardly easy-going, deceptively relaxed, but with all the toughness of arrogance and breeding just below the surface. Not a man to trifle with.

It was a pity about Jupp, he had thought on more than one occasion. As chief steward and a personal watchdog over the captain, Jupp should have been the mainspring of the whole network. Barker had served with him twice before, and knew better than to try and force the man to betray his trust. It could be dangerous to push him. You could never be entirely sure how much a senior steward knew about his purser. Barker owned a boarding house in Southampton and another in Liverpool. People might suggest it impossible to acquire such property on his pay alone. They would have been right, too.

The only officer in the ship with whom Barker shared some of his confidences was Goss. Not because he particularly liked him, in fact, he usually made him feel vaguely uneasy. Goss had somehow never bothered to rise with his rank, not, that is, in Barker's view. Beneath warm, star-filled skies in the Pacific, with all the magic of a ship's orchestra, the gay dresses and white dinner jackets,

Barker had always felt in his element. But once or twice at the chief officer's table in the dining room he had squirmed with embarrassment at Goss's obvious lack of refinement. Big, self-made, meticulous in matters of duty, Goss seemed unable to put on a show for the passengers at his table. Barker had seen the quick smiles exchanged between them as Goss had told some ponderous story about raising an anchor in a gale, or the time he had fought four drunken stokers in a Sydney bar and knocked them senseless. He was a difficult man to know, harder still to befriend.

But he *was* the first lieutenant, and in Barker's eyes still the senior chief officer in the company. Once the war was over, breeding or not, Goss would get a command. With his seniority plus war experience the company could hardly avoid it. When that happened, Barker would be ready for his own step up the ladder, if he had anything to say about it.

So without too much hesitation he had made a point of visiting Goss that same night. Goss, he knew, had the middle watch, and as was his normal practice stayed in his roomy cabin out of sight until a few minutes before the exact time due on the bridge.

It was not that Goss openly discouraged visitors to his private domain, it was just that his attitude was generally unwelcoming, like some trusted curator of a museum who resented visitors on principle.

If the rest of the ship had been altered and scarred by the Navy's ownership, Goss had somehow retained his old surroundings more or less as they had always been, so that his cabin was, in its own way, a museum, a record of his life and career.

There were many framed photographs of the ship and other company vessels in which he had served over the years. Pictures of groups, large and small, officers and owners, self-conscious passengers and various happenings in several ports of call. A blue and white house-flag of the company adorned one complete bulkhead, and the shelves and well-polished furniture were littered with models and mementos and more framed pictures. One of them showed Goss shaking hands with old Mr Cairns, the head of the company, who had died just a few weeks before the war.

Whenever Barker visited the cabin he always looked at that particular picture. It was the only place where he had seen Goss smile.

Goss had listened to Barker's casual excuse for the visit without emotion. Stores had to be raised from an after hold the following day and would the first lieutenant arrange some extra working parties for the task? It had all sounded innocent enough.

As he had gone through the motions Barker had studied Goss's heavy features with methodical interest. He had been sitting in one of his fat leather chairs, his jacket hanging neatly on a hook behind the door, his cap and binoculars within easy reach. But without a collar or tie, in his crumpled shirt and a pair of old plimsolls, he had looked like one of his own relics. Had Barker possessed an ounce of sensitivity he might have felt either concern or even pity, but instead he was merely curious. Goss, the great unbreakable seaman, looked old, tired and utterly alone.

Goss had said eventually, 'That all?'

'Of course.' Barker had walked round the chair, steadying himself against the table as the ship rolled wearily into one more trough. 'Oh, by the way, I *did* hear something about Maxwell. Seems he was in an accident of some sort.' A carefully measured pause. 'de Chair was saying a few words on the matter at dinner. Pity you weren't there yourself.'

'Accident?'

Barker had shrugged carelessly. 'Gunnery, I believe. Probably shot some poor sod by mistake.'

'Probably.'

Barker had been astounded at Goss's indifference. He had merely sat there staring into space, one foot tapping slowly on the company carpet, a sure sign he wished to be left alone. It had been altogether quite unnerving.

'Just thought you'd like to hear about it.'

Goss had said slowly, 'You know, Henry, I was thinking just now.' He nodded heavily towards the photograph. The one with the smile. 'Old Mr Cairns was a good owner. Hard, some said, and I daresay he remembered the value of every rivet down to the last halfpenny. But he had an eye for business, and knew every officer on his payroll. Every one, even the bloody apprentices. Now he's dead and gone. And it looks as if the company'll never survive either.'

Barker had gone cold. 'But after the war there'll be full compensation, surely? I——I mean, the government can't just take the ships, work the life out of them, and then give nothing back afterwards!'

Goss had heaved himself upright, so that his massive head had almost touched the steam pipes. 'Even if we win the war, and with some of the people I've seen aboard this ship I am more than doubtful on that score, things will never be the same. Mr Cairns' young nephew is in the chair now. Snooty little upstart with an office in London instead of down where the *ships* are. Had him aboard for our last peacetime trip.' His features had hardened. 'All gin and bloody shrimp cocktails, you know the type.'

Barker had swallowed hard. He knew. He liked to think of himself like that.

Goss had rambled on, as if to an empty cabin. 'I was promised the next command, but I 'spect you knew that. Promised. I'd have had the old *Becky* by now, but for the bloody war.'

There had been something like anguish in his voice which had made Barker stammer, 'Well, I'll be off then. Just thought I'd fix up about tomorrow——' He had left the cabin with Goss still staring fixedly at the framed photograph.

As the door had closed Goss had taken a small key from his pocket, and after a further hesitation had opened a cupboard above his desk. Inside, gleaming from within a protective oilskin bag, was the cap. The company's badge and the captain's oak leaves around the peak were of the best pre-war gold wire, hand woven by a little Jewish tailor in Liverpool.

After locking the cupboard again he had slumped into the chair and lowered his face into his hands.

'I'd have had this ship by now. It was a *promise*.'

The words had hung in the sealed cabin like an epitaph.

———

A week later, as the *Benbecula* headed south-east away from the patrol area, those who were on deck in the bitter air saw the other armed merchant cruiser steaming past less than a mile distant. Even without binoculars it was possible to see the fresh paint around her stem, evidence of her collision with the pier, her guilt which had allowed an extra week in harbour while *Benbecula* endured the gales and the angry seas.

Lindsay sat in his tall chair and watched the other ship until she had passed out of his line of vision. The obvious excitement he had felt all around him as he had given orders to leave the patrol had momentarily given way to a kind of resentment as the relief ship had forged past. Not so much perhaps because she was late, but because she was heading into what appeared to many was calmer weather. The wind was fresh but no longer violent, so that the watch below was called less often to hack and blast away the clawing ice from decks and guns. To the men who imagined they had now seen and endured everything the Atlantic could offer, it seemed unfair their relief should get it so easy.

Lindsay sat back and looked at the hard, dark horizon line. With the ship so steady it made the list all the more apparent. The horizon seemed to be tilting across the bridge windows like an endless grey hill.

Behind him he could hear a signalman talking quietly with Ritchie, the occasional creak of the wheel and Maxwell's clipped voice from the chart room door. The afternoon watch was almost finished, and the sky above the horizon was already duller with a hint of more snow. It was natural for the new hands to complain about the other A.M.C.'s luck, he thought. The more seasoned men would know the real reason for the change. Ice. Before winter closed in completely there would be plenty about to the west and north, some perhaps as far down as this. He had already discussed it with Goss, but as usual it was hard to fathom the extent of his words.

Lindsay had been a first lieutenant himself to several commanding officers, and he could not get used to Goss's total lack of feeling for his new role. A first lieutenant in any naval vessel was the link between officers and captain, the one man who could and should weld the ship into one tight community. Goss was not a link. He was like a massive watertight door which kept his captain even more aloof and remote than usual.

There was no doubting his efficiency in seamanship and internal organisation. But there it ended, and unless he could bring himself to change his days were numbered afloat, Lindsay decided.

Maxwell crossed to his side and stood fidgeting with the chain around his neck. 'D'you think there's any chance of leave, sir?'

Lindsay watched the lieutenant's reflection in the salt-smeared windows.

'Unlikely, Guns. A lick of paint, a few bits of quick welding and we'll be off again, in my opinion.'

Strange about Maxwell, he thought. He had been very quiet lately. Too quiet.

Maxwell said, 'Oh, in that case——' He did not go on.

'You worried about something?'

'Me, sir?' Maxwell's fingers tugged more insistently at the chain. 'No, I was just thinking. I might put in for an advanced gunnery course. Not much scope in this ship.'

He spoke jerkily, but Lindsay thought the words sounded rehearsed. As if he had been planning the right moment.

'And you want me to recommend you?'

Maxwell shifted his feet. 'Well, in a manner of speaking, yes, sir.'

Lindsay took out his pipe. It couldn't be much fun for Maxwell. A gunnery officer of the old school, who because of time lost on the beach was watching men far more junior being appointed to brand-new warships just as fast as they were built. But there was more to it than that. Maybe it was his assistant, Lieutenant Hunter. Only a temporary officer perhaps, and in peacetime the owner of a small garage many miles from the sea, but Hunter had got to grips with the ancient armament as if born to it. Probably because he had not had many dealings with any other kind, or maybe, like Fraser, his natural mechanical bent made him accept the old guns like some sort of personal challenge rather than an obstacle.

'I'll think about it, Guns. But I need either you or a damn good replacement before I recommend anything, right?'

Maxwell nodded. 'Yes, sir.'

The duty bosun's mate said, 'Beg pardon, sir, but Number Six gun 'as just called up. They say one of the liferafts is workin' adrift again on th' poop.' He sounded disinterested. Ten more minutes and he would be in his mess. Hot sweet tea and then his head down until suppertime.

Maxwell glared. 'Right, tell Lieutenant Aikman to deal with it.'

The man continued to stare at him, the telephone in his first. 'But you sent 'im to the chart room, sir.'

Maxwell nodded jerkily. 'Oh, yes.' To Lindsay he added, 'He's fixing the plot.'

Lindsay turned slightly to study him. Maxwell was not usually rattled.

He asked, 'What about young Kemp?' He had appointed the midshipman to Maxwell's watch for the experience, as well as to keep him from being bored to death by the ship's correspondence duties.

Maxwell nodded. 'Yessir.' To the seaman he barked, 'Mr Kemp is up in control. Pass the word for him to lay aft, chop, chop. The buffer will let him have a couple of hands.' He added angrily, 'Bloody well get a move on!'

Lindsay faced forward again, troubled by Maxwell's sudden irritation. Perhaps it was his own example which had done it. Maybe his outward mask of self-control was not so strong as he believed.

He heard the bosun's mate passing the order on the handset, his voice sullen.

Maxwell returned to his side and said vehemently, 'Number Six gun, was it. Those marines are just trying to rile me.' He seemed to realise he had spoken aloud and swung away, adding sharply, 'Pipe the port watch to defence stations. And I'll see that rating who was smoking on duty in five minutes, got it?'

The bosun's mate faced him coldly. 'Got it, *sir*.'

Lindsay thought about Goss and came to a decision. Maxwell's attitude was dangerous and could not be tolerated. But it was the first lieutenant's job to deal with internal grievances, and deal with them he would.

By the time Midshipman Kemp had made his way aft to the poop the daylight was almost gone. As he groped along the guardrail he could feel the ice-rime under his

glove and wished he had put something warmer than an
oilskin over his other clothing. The sea looked very dark,
with deep swells and troughs, through which the ship's
wake made a frothing white track, fading eventually into
the gathering gloom.

Beside the covered twelve-pounder he found Leading
Seaman Swan waiting for him, one foot on the lower
guardrail while he stared astern with weary resignation.

Kemp asked, 'Where are the others?'

Swan straightened his back and looked at him. He was
a big man, his body made even larger by several layers of
woollens beneath his duffel coat. He had already done
several repair jobs about the upper deck in the freezing
weather and was just about ready to go below. His neck
and chin felt sore, mainly because he had started to grow
a beard, and the cold, damp air was playing havoc with his
patience. Kemp's arrival did nothing to help ease his
irritation. Swan was a regular with seven years service to
his credit and was normally quite tolerant of midshipmen
in general. They were the *in-betweens*. Neither fish nor
fowl, and were usually taken at face value by the lower
deck. Hounded by their superiors, carried by petty
officers and leading hands, midshipmen were more to be
pitied than abused. But just this once Swan did not feel
like carrying anyone, and Kemp's obvious uncertainty
filled him with unreasoning resentment.

He replied offhandedly, 'They'll be here any second.'
He waited for Kemp to pull him up for omitting the
sir.

Kemp shivered and said, 'What's the trouble anyway?'

The leading seaman gestured with a massive, leather-
gauntleted fist towards the nearest raft. It was poised
almost vertically on two wooden skids, so that in a real
emergency it could be released to drop straight down
over the port quarter.

'Trouble with some of these bloody O.D.'s is that they
paint everything. Some idiot has slopped paint all over

the lines, and in this sort of climate it only makes 'em fray more easily.' He saw Kemp's eyes peering doubtfully at the heavy raft and added harshly, 'Not that it matters much. What with paint and the bloody ice, I doubt if the thing would move even if Chatham barracks fell on it!'

Two seamen loomed up the poop ladder and he barked, 'Where the hell have you been? I'm just about two-blocks waiting in the sodding cold!'

The first seaman said, 'The officer of the watch 'ad me on the rattle for smokin'.' He looked at Kemp. 'That's wot.'

Swan waited for Kemp to say something. Then he said angrily, 'Well, just you wait here. I'm going to get some new lines. You can start by checking how many of the old ones are frayed, right?'

As he stamped away one of the seamen muttered, 'What's up with Hookey then? Miserable bastard.'

Kemp gripped the guardrail with both hands, willing himself to concentrate on the raft. He knew the two seamen, like Swan, were testing him, that almost any other midshipman from his class would have snapped back at them. Won their obedience, if not actual respect. It was always the same. He seemed unable to face the fact he was here, that no amount of self-deception would change it. He could almost hear his father's resonant voice. 'I can't think where you get it. No moral fibre, that's you. No *guts!*'

He heard one of the seamen duck behind the twelve-pounder gunshield and the rasp of a match. If Kemp was unwilling or unable to act, they were quite happy to wait for Swan's return.

One of them was saying, 'Did you 'ear about that stoker in Scapa?' Ad a cushy shore job stokin' some admiral's boiler, an' they found 'im in 'is bunk with a bloody sheep!'

The other voice said, 'Never! You're 'avin me on!'

'S'truth.' He was enjoying the much-used yarn, especially as he knew the midshipman was listening. 'When

the jaunty slapped 'im on a charge he told 'im that he
didn't know it was a sheep. But that 'e'd been so long in
Scapa 'e thought it was a Wren in a duffel coat!'

Kemp thrust himself away from the rail. 'That's
enough, you two!'

They both stared at him in mild surprise.

'Start working on those lines!'

One of them said, 'Which lines, sir?'

The other added, 'Can't see much in this light, sir.'

Kemp felt the despair rising like nausea. It had been
the same when Dancy had been questioning him about
his father. It was always like that.

He seized the nearest seaman's sleeve and thrust him
towards the raft. 'Get up there and *feel* them one at a
time!' He swung on the second man. 'And you start
freeing the ice from the metal slips. Swan will probably
want to splice them on to the new lines.'

Behind his back the seaman on the raft made an
obscene gesture and then looked away as Kemp returned
to the rail.

Kemp was shivering uncontrollably beneath the oilskin. He knew it was partly because of the cold, but also
due to his inability to play out his part as he knew he must
if he was to keep his sanity. Kemp was an only son and in
the beginning had been prepared to try and see his
father's point of view. From as far back as he could
remember it had been like that. The tradition, the house
full of naval portraits and memories, even now he could
understand his father's desire to see him following the
family's heritage. Perhaps if he had known what he had
wanted to be, had found someone to help and advise him,
then his father might have relented. But at eighteen
Kemp was still unsure. All he did know for certain was he
did not want or need the Service, and that his father had
become more than an adversary. He was the very symbol
of all he had come to hate.

When he had been appointed to this ship he had

known his father's hand was in it. *To knock some sense into him. Smooth the rough edges.* In some ways Kemp had almost believed it himself. The officers were so unusually mixed and totally different from those he had met before.

He was not so inexperienced that he could not recognise the antagonism and occasional enmity between the officers, but when it came down to it they all seemed to be the same. In the action, as he had crouched inside the chart room he had heard their voices. Flat, expressionless, moulded to discipline, no matter what the men really thought behind the words.

He looked up startled as Swan bounded up the ladder carrying a huge coil of line.

Swan shouted, 'What the *hell* are you doing up there, Biggs? Come down immediately and fix a lifeline, you stupid bugger!'

Even as he spoke the other seaman inadvertently cut through a lashing with his knife. Perhaps because his fingers were cold, or maybe the icy planking beneath his boots took him off balance, but the result was the same, and immediate. The end of the severed lashing, complete with a metal shackle, slashed upwards like a frozen whip, cutting the seaman Biggs full in the face as he made to scramble back to the deck. Kemp stared horrified as the man swayed drunkenly, his duffel coat pale against the black sea at his back. Then as Swan flung himself on to the raft Biggs fell outboard and down. One second he was there, the next nothing. He had not even had time to cry out.

Swan pushed Kemp aside and groped for the handset by the twelve-pounder. But the canvas cover was frozen iron-hard, and with a sob he ran for the ladder, yelling to the nearest marine gun crew as he went.

Kemp gripped the rail and peered down into the churning white wash. But he did not know where to look. Where would Biggs be? Below, staring up at his ship as she faded into the darkness? Or already far astern, choking and crying out in terror? He began to fumble with a lifebuoy and was still struggling with its lashing as Swan came aft again.

Swan said hoarsely, 'Forget it. He'll have been sucked into the port screw.'

The other seaman, who was still standing transfixed with the knife in one hand, said brokenly, 'We're turnin'! The wheel's gone over!'

Kemp stared at the ship's pale wake as it began to change into a wide sweeping curve. In a moment he would wake up. It was a mad dream. It had to be.

Right in his ear Swan said, 'They'll have to go through the motions. Even if he missed the screws he'll be a block of bloody ice in minutes!'

A marine corporal from Number Six gun clattered on to the poop and snapped, 'Captain's compliments, Mr Kemp, and he wants you on the bridge right away.' He looked at Swan. 'You, too.'

The man with the knife said in a small voice, 'Worn't my fault, Hookey!'

Swan looked at Kemp with savage contempt. 'I know. You were obeying orders!'

Kemp tried to speak, his mind reeling with shock. 'I——I'm sorry——I was only trying to. . . .'

Swan gestured astern. 'Tell *him,* sir! He'll be bloody glad to know you're sorry, I don't think!'

All the way along the upper deck Kemp was vaguely aware of silent, muffled figures watching him as he passed. No matter what had really happened, he was already condemned in their eyes. Their silence was like a shouted verdict.

As they reached the door at the rear of the bridge Kemp heard Lindsay's voice, very level, as if from far away.

'Another five minutes, Pilot. Then bring her back on course.'

Then Stannard's voice. 'If he'd had a lifejacket on, sir, with a safety lamp——'

Lindsay had turned away again. 'But he hadn't.'

Stannard saw Kemp's outline in the door and shrugged. There seemed to be nothing left to say.

7 A Wren called Eve

The Chief of Staff looked up from his desk as Lindsay entered the office, and then waved to a chair.

'Take the weight off your feet. I'll not keep you a minute.'

Lindsay sat. After the bitter air across the Flow as he had come ashore in the motor boat the office seemed almost tropical. It was evening, and with windows sealed and a great iron stove glowing pink with heat, he felt suddenly drowsy.

The grave-faced captain was saying into a telephone, 'Very well, Flags, if you say so. Another draft coming in tonight. Get on to stores and find out about kitting them up. Right.'

He put down the telephone and shot Lindsay a brief smile. 'Never lets up.' He groped in a drawer and took out two glasses and a bottle of Scotch. 'The sun, had it been out today, would be well over the yardarm by now, eh?'

Lindsay relaxed slightly, hearing the wind hissing against a window, the clatter of a typewriter in the next room.

Benbecula had picked up her buoy that morning, and while he had stood on the bridge wing to watch a fussy tug assisting the forecastle party with the business of mooring, he had allowed a grudging admiration for the Flow. The snow had held off, and it was not raining either. In the hard morning light there had even been a kind of primitive beauty. The cold, pewter water and hunched brown islands were as uncompromising as ever, but seemed to say, we were here first, so make the best of us.

The whisky was neat and very good.

The captain said, 'I didn't call you over until now because I thought you'd have enough to do. Anyway, it gave me time to study your report.' He smiled and some of his sternness faded. 'You did damn well to have a crack at that raider. Against all sane instructions, of course, but I'd have done the same.'

Lindsay replied, 'I wish I could have finished him.'

'I dare say. We had a couple of clear days recently and the R.A.F. got a reconnaissance flight going. Your raider is holed up in Norway, if you're interested. She's the *Nassau*, seventeen thousand tons, and fairly new. Used to run to the East African ports.' He refilled the glasses. 'Intelligence have reported she's completely converted as a raider.' He added wryly, 'Of course, they didn't tell us anything about her until a few days ago.'

Lindsay nodded. He had been expecting the captain — his name was Lovelace — to go for him, to attack him for taking independent action. But now he could understand. As *Benbecula* had entered the boom gate he had been watching and waiting for orders to moor on some vacant buoy, wherever was convenient to the harbour-master rather than the returning A.M.C. He need not have bothered, as the Flow had been almost deserted.

The officer who had come aboard from the guardboat to collect Lindsay's despatches and mail had said, 'Several of the battlewaggons have sailed for the Far East and others to the Med. The shop window's a bit bare at the moment.'

So even if *Benbecula* had complied to the letter of her orders, to stand off and await assistance, there would have been little available. No heroics, Lovelace had said at their other meeting. Now it looked as if heroics were just about all they had.

As if reading his mind the captain said, 'We're tightly

stretched. Things are getting bad in the Med. and we've
had some heavy losses in Western Approaches. My operations staff will let you have all the backlog when you're
ready for it.' He looked grave. 'We have not released the
news of *Loch Glendhu*'s loss to the public as yet. The less
the enemy knows about our meagre resources the better.
Of course, the German radio has been playing it up. They
claim they sank a heavy cruiser. Maybe they really believe
it, but my guess is it's all part of the probing game.
Testing our strength.'

Lindsay felt suddenly depressed. The endless strain,
the continuous effort needed to pull his new command
into a fighting unit were taking their toll.

He said, 'It all sounds pretty hopeless.'

Lovelace paused with the bottle in mid air above Lindsay's glass. 'Come on, man, I thought you Scots could
drink!' With his eyes on the bottle he added slowly, 'Hard
luck about losing that chap overboard. Still, you were
damn lucky with your previous casualties. And with a
partly trained company like yours I'd have expected ten
times the number.'

'Yes.' He let the neat whisky burn across his tongue,
recalling Kemp's pale face, his wretchedness as he had
stammered out his story of Biggs' death. The leading
hand, Swan, had been stiff, even angry. *'Mr Kemp's got no
idea of things, sir.'*

Things, as Lindsay well knew, needed time to be mas-
tered. Kemp had had very little. But he also lacked
something else. Perhaps he did not care.

Lovelace asked, 'What have you done about the midshipman?'

'Nothing, sir. It was an accident due more to ignorance
than carelessness. I doubt Kemp will ever forget it.'

He thought of Fraser's reaction. 'Just one of those
things,' was all he had said.

Lovelace nodded, apparently satisfied. 'Fine. I should
keep Kemp busy, Make him jump about. If I transferred

him elsewhere it would do him more harm than good.'
He shot Lindsay a searching glance. 'Unless, of course,
you want him shifted?'

'No. I'll see how it works out.'

'Good. Especially as I'll have to take some of your
people anyway. Tobey, your boatswain, and a few other
key ratings. I need them as replacements. You'll have to
fill the gaps from the next incoming draft.' He smiled
grimly. 'Straight from the training depot, naturally.'

The telephone buzzed and Lovelace snapped, 'I will
see the commanding officer of *Merlin* in three minutes.
Tell him to warm his backside on your fire until I'm
ready.'

Lindsay stood up. 'Any orders for me, sir?'

'Soon.' Lovelace looked distant again, already grappling with the endless complications of his office. 'I've
told the maintenance commander to do all he can. The
repair ship is standing by to help, but anything she or
your people can't manage will have to wait. I'm afraid a
week is about all you can expect, so work along those
lines. I hear you've completed refuelling, so you can allow
local leave whenever it suits you.'

Lindsay picked up his cap. The whisky was burning his
stomach like fire. All a question of priorities, and his old
ship was very far down that list. A week, and back to
patrol duty. Ice. Men being worn out by cold and endless
discomfort. They were the dangerous times, when small
personal needs blunted a man's vigilance. Maybe *Loch
Glendhu*'s people had been like that. Too tired, too beaten
down by the seemingly futile patrol to see their peril until
it was beyond their scope.

He said, 'Thank you for the drink, sir.'

Lovelace grinned. 'My pleasure. I hear so much gloom
that it's a real prize to meet somebody who's achieved
something at last!'

Lindsay left the office, and as he walked through the
adjoining room he saw the officer who was waiting for the

next interview. A full rank junior to Lindsay, yet he commanded the *Merlin*, a new and powerful fleet-destroyer which was lying quite near to *Benbecula*'s buoy. He watched Lindsay pass, his face curious. When he had left the room Lindsay could imagine the little scene. The young lieutenant-commander would ask politely who he was. The Chief of Staff's secretary would tell him. In the mind of the *Merlin*'s captain a whole new picture would form. Nobody to bother with. Just the captain of that old A.M.C. Looked all right, and seemed bright enough, but with a command like her he must have something wrong with him.

He stood stockstill in the deserted passageway, spent and despairing. *Damn them. Damn them all to hell.*

'Are you all right, sir?'

Lindsay swung round and saw the girl standing just inside the blackout curtain by the main entrance. As before she was muffled to the ears, and her feet and legs were encased in a pair of muddy rubber boots.

He stared at her for several seconds. 'Yes, thank you.' He tried to smile, seeing the doubt and concern in her eyes. 'A bit bushed, that's all.'

She took off her jaunty cap and shook out her hair vigorously. 'I saw you come in this morning.' She was still studying him, her eyes troubled. 'We all heard about what happened.'

A door opened and closed with a bang and another Wren, also heavily covered in duffel coat and scarf, passed Lindsay without a glance. As she reached the door the Wren called Eve Collins tossed her an ignition key and said, 'Thanks for relieving me early, Sue. Watch out for ice on the roads.'

The other girl paused and looked at Lindsay. 'Do it for me sometime.' Then she was gone, the blackout curtain swirling momentarily in a jet of cold air.

She said quietly, 'I'm glad you made it back all right, sir.'

Lindsay recalled the flashing headlights on the shore, the signalman who had seen them.

He said, 'One of the bunting tossers read your message when we left Scapa. It was nice of you to see us off.'

She grinned. 'Thank him for me, will you? My morse isn't too hot.'

Then she saw his expression and added huskily, 'Was *he* killed?'

'Yes.' He tried to shut it all from his aching mind. Ritchie's face. The wet oilskins by the rail. *We commit his body to the deep.*

He said abruptly, 'I wonder if you'd care to have a drink with me?' He saw the sudden surprise and added, 'Maybe we could get a meal or something?'

She replaced her cap very slowly. 'I'm sorry. I really am.'

'You've *got* a date?' It was all suddenly clear. The other Wren relieving her early. *Do it for me sometime.*

She did not smile. 'Something like that.' She looked away. 'I can break it though——'

'No. It's all right.' He thrust his hands into his greatcoat pockets, trying to sound casual. That it did not matter. He did not even know why it had all become so urgent and important. 'Forget it.'

The curtain swirled inwards again and a R.A.F. flight-lieutenant blundered into the lamplight, banging his gloved hands together.

'I guessed you'd take half the night to get changed! I've got a car outside. I'll run you to your billet.' He saw Lindsay and said awkwardly, 'Oh, sorry!'

She said, 'Jack, this is Commander Lindsay.' Then she turned to him again, her voice very quiet. 'The fighter boys are giving a dance at the field. Why don't you come, too? It might be a change from——' She looked at the flight-lieutenant. 'What do you say, Jack? It would be all right, wouldn't it?'

'Of course.' He did not sound very enthusiastic.

Lindsay smiled. 'I must get back to my ship. They'll be waiting to hear the news.' He looked at the R.A.F. officer and back to the girl. 'But thanks again. Enjoy yourselves.'

Then he was outside in the darkness, the icy wind driving down his throat, making his eyes water like tears.

In the passageway the flight-lieutenant spread his hands. '*So?*'

She tightened her scarf and frowned. 'So nothing. He's a good bloke, that's all.'

He grinned. 'A full commander, too. By God, Eve, I admire your sense of priorities!'

Out on the roadway Lindsay heard her laugh and the sound of the car driving away. He had made an idiot of himself, and it mattered. It mattered so much he could feel it like pain.

Aloud he said, 'You bloody fool. You stupid bloody fool!'

Then he quickened his pace and turned once more towards the sea.

———————

Lindsay was working at his desk when Goss, followed by Fraser, entered his day cabin.

'Sit, gentlemen.' He pressed the bell beside his desk and added, 'Nearly noon. We'll have a drink.'

He watched Goss's heavy features as he selected a chair, noting the deep lines around his mouth and eyes. It had been a busy time for the whole ship, but the effect on Goss was even more noticeable. Captain Lovelace had been right about the timing, he thought bitterly. *A week is about all you can expect.*

He looked at the two men and said slowly, 'I have just received our orders. We are at forty-eight hours notice for steam.'

Fraser muttered, 'A week and a day. That's all they've given us.' Then he grinned. 'Generous bastards!'

Lindsay turned to Goss. 'What about you, Number One? Are you all buttoned up?'

Poor Goss, he had taken the time in harbour badly. Lindsay had watched him arguing with engineers and workers from the repair ship, seen him following the mechanics and welders between the *Benbecula*'s decks like an old hen trying to protect its chickens from a pack of rampaging foxes. But for Fraser's excellent work on repairs while the ship had been returning to the Flow it was hard to see how they could have managed. The shell holes in the hull had been covered by new plates, and with the aid of fresh paint the outer damage would pass unnoticed to all but an experienced eye. Inboard, the repairs had been equally brief, a case of patch up and hope for the best, as one dockyard official had described it.

Jupp padded into the cabin and opened the drinks cabinet as Goss replied, 'I've done my best, but it's nowhere near ready. Those butchers have made more mess than they've repaired. We should have gone down to Greenock or Rosyth.' He glanced at the nearest scuttle and added harshly, 'The weather's worse, too.'

Fraser grimaced. 'Proper ray of sunlight, you are!'

Lindsay said, 'I believe we may be at sea for Christmas.'

He watched his words affecting each of them in different ways. He had been at sea for nearly every Christmas he could remember, but this was different. Most of the ship's company had not, and after the misery of the last patrol, Christmas in the Arctic wastes might seem like a final disaster. He followed Goss's stare to the scuttle. The sky was very pale and without colour. Inside the cabin it was humid with steam heat, but beyond the toughened glass the air would be like a razor.

Fraser asked mildly, 'Is it definite, sir?'

Lindsay glanced at Jupp's stooped shoulders and smiled. 'The chief steward informs me that it is so.'

Jupp bowed over the desk with his tray of glasses and

eyed him calmly. 'I saw the turkeys meself, sir. Bein'
stacked up ready for Mr Barker's people to collect 'em.'
He shook his head. 'A sure sign.'

Fraser grinned. 'Very.'

Goss did not seem to be listening. 'Same patrol?'

'No.' Lindsay held up his glass to the light. 'Further
south-west than Uncle Item Victor. But that is just
between us.'

Goss shuddered. 'Nearer Greenland. There'll be ice
about.'

The three of them lapsed into silence, so that the
muffled shipboard noises intruded like whispers.

Lindsay watched as Jupp refilled his glass and wondered if the chief steward had noticed he was drinking
more lately. He should have gone ashore, if only to
stretch his legs or to find a change of scene. But apart
from two official visits to the headquarters at Kirkwall he
had remained on board immersing himself in the business of preparing his ship for sea again. He knew he had
stayed too much alone, that it had solved nothing.

He realised too that something had to be done to break
the gloom which hung over his command like a threat,
especially with the added prospect of Christmas at sea.
He had granted shore leave as often as possible, but the
libertymen had soon discovered the scope of enjoyment
in Scapa was almost nil. There had been several fights,
drunkenness and two cases of assault on naval patrol-
men. Few of the defaulters brought before him for
punishment had offered a reason for their behaviour,
and he knew that all these things were just symptoms of
frustration and boredom. The stark thrill of being spared
Loch Glendhu's fate, of hitting at the enemy, had soon
vanished when back in harbour. Anywhere else and it
might not have mattered. But here, in this dismal place it
was taking its toll.

He said suddenly, 'I thought we'd have a party before
we sail. It will help make up for Christmas.'

Fraser eyed him curiously. 'It'll pass the time.'

But Lindsay was watching Goss. 'It's rather up to you, Number One. If you think you've too much on your plate we'll scrub round it, of course.'

Goss stirred in his chair. 'I *am* very busy, sir.' He was pondering on Lindsay's words, his eyes far away as he continued, 'Who would be coming anyway?'

Lindsay tried to keep his tone matter of fact, knowing Fraser was watching him. He hoped Goss would not see through his little game as easily as Fraser was obviously doing.

He said, 'Oh, all the usual. Base staff, some of the people who have been helping us. That sort of thing.'

Fraser said over the rim of his glass, 'I think it might be too difficult. Number One's people have still got a good bit of clearing up to do. In any case, who'd want to come to a ship like this? There's a damn great carrier here now and——'.

Goss swung towards him angrily. 'That's all you bloody well know! How many ships like this one have *you* seen then, eh?' Some of his drink slopped on to his thighs but he did not notice. 'A carrier, you say? Well, that's just another warship, and most people are sick to death of them up here!'

Lindsay asked quietly, 'You're in favour?' He saw Fraser drop one eyelid in a brief wink.

Goss recovered some of his old dignity. 'Well, if you think——' He darted a glance at Fraser. 'Yes, I am, sir.'

'That's settled then. I'll leave it to you. Two days is not long to arrange it, but I expect you'll manage.'

Goss pushed his empty glass towards Jupp. 'Manage?' He frowned. 'I've seen the main saloon filled to overflowing in my day. A prince, his whole retinue, and some of the richest passengers we've carried, all eating and drinking fit to bust.' He nodded firmly. 'We'll show 'em.' He stood up violently. 'So if you'll excuse me, I think I'll find Barker. Go over a few things with him.' He did not mention the patrol at all. 'Carrier indeed! Who the hell wants to see that!' He left the cabin with unusual speed.

Fraser signalled for another drink and then said quietly, 'I've not seen him like that for years. My God, sir, you don't know what you've sparked off.'

Lindsay smiled. 'I hope you're right, Chief. This ship needs something, so we'll make a start with the party, right?'

Fraser grinned. 'Right.'

Lindsay did not have much time to think about the proposed party. Almost to the hour of its starting he was kept busy dealing with the ship's affairs as with growing speed sailing preparations were completed. Fresh supplies and ammunition. A new whaler to replace the one destroyed by shellfire, as well as the promised turkeys, which were whisked away by Barker's men to the cold storage room before any could go astray. And of course there were the new ratings who arrived in dribs and drabs in the ferries to take the places of more seasoned men needed elsewhere.

The *Benbecula*'s company watched the new arrivals with all the usual interest. The men who had made just one patrol, who had been drafted straight from shore training establishments, now stood like old salts and eyed the newcomers with a mixture of contempt and assured superiority. Lindsay had watched some of them from the bridge. Their brand-new greatcoats and gasmask haversacks, their regulation haircuts and general air of lost confusion marking them out from all the rest.

He had heard Archer, the chief boatswain's mate, bellowing at them, 'Come on then, jump about! Drop yer bags 'n'ammicks and get fell in while I gives you yer parts of ship!'

Archer seemed to have grown in size since the

commissioned boatswain, Tobey, had left for another ship, but quite obviously relished his new powers.

When one pale-faced recruit had said timidly, 'I thought we were coming to a warship, P.O., not a ——' he had got no further.

Archer had roared at him, 'This 'ere is an' armed merchant cruiser, see? Any bloody fool can 'andle a battleship, but this takes *seamen*, got it?' As he had been about to turn away he had added loudly, 'And I'm not a P.O., I'm the *chief bosun's mate*, so don't you bloody well forget it!'

The little seaman had tried to escape after the rest of the draft but Archer's voice had pursued him like an enraged walrus. 'An' get yer bloody 'air cut!'

It was dark in the Flow when Goss came to Lindsay's quarters. 'Ready for you in the wardroom, sir.'

Lindsay noticed Goss was wearing a new uniform and his cheeks were glowing from a fresh shave and bath. There was something else, too. A kind of defiance.

When they reached the wardroom Lindsay was astounded. It was difficult to believe he was in the same ship. Everything shone with polish and small coloured lights, and two long tables were groaning under such a weight of sandwiches, canapés and so many tempting morsels that he could pity the officers and their mess bills when the reckoning was made. Most of the stewards who had been with the company before the war were wearing their old mess jackets and maroon trousers, and as Lindsay followed Goss's massive figure towards the assembled officers he saw three other stewards waiting self-consciously with violins and a piano which had certainly not been present before.

Goss turned and faced him grimly. 'Well, sir?'

Lindsay kept his face impassive. 'It's not Navy, Number One.' Then he reached out and touched Goss's forearm. 'But it's bloody marvellous! I knew you'd do your best, but this is more than that!'

Goss stared at him uncertainly. 'You like it then?'

Barker appeared at his side, beaming. 'Just like the old days!'

Goss ignored him. 'You *really* like it, sir?'

'I do.' Lindsay saw Jupp making towards him with a tray. 'It's what I needed. What we all need in this bloody war!' And he knew he meant it.

Goss snapped his fingers at a steward and said, 'I heard a boat alongside. The first guests are arriving.' Then he strode away, his eyes darting across the laden tables to ensure nothing had been eaten.

Fraser watched him go and then said, 'You've made his day.' He looked at Lindsay searchingly. 'I'm drinking to you.' He lifted a glass. 'That was a damn nice thing you just did.'

In no time at all the wardroom seemed to get crowded with visitors. As the din of conversation and laughter mounted and the trio of musicians did their best to rise above it, Lindsay was conscious of the impression Goss's party was having. What had started almost as a joke was gathering way, so that he too could sense a kind of pride for the way this old ship, his ship, was hanging on to her past and so giving pleasure to the present.

Faces swam around him, handshakes and slaps on the shoulder marked each new arrival. Officers from the base and other ships. Some nursing sisters and the wives of senior officers and officials added the required feminine interest, and the plentiful supply of drink did the rest. There were several Wrens, too, but not the one he had been waiting to see. He knew it was pointless to try again, just as he realised he wanted very much to meet her once more before the ship sailed.

His own officers appeared to be enjoying themselves. de Chair, impeccable as ever in his best blue uniform, was entertaining two of the women. Stannard and Sub-Lieutenant Cordeaux seemed to be having a drinking contest, while Dancy was speaking gravely to a blonde nurse on the trials of being surrounded by so much literary material.

She was saying huskily, 'It must be marvellous to be a real writer.'

He looked at her and nodded, his eyes already glazed. 'It can also be a *great* responsibility.'

Even Emerson, the elderly warrant engineer, was coming out of his shell. He was talking with the wife of a dockyard manager, his voice loud with enthusiasm.

'Yeh. So I says to me old woman, what about a run to Margate? An' *she* says—' he paused to dab the tears from his eyes, '—*she* says, wot d'you think I am? A bloody rabbit?'

Behind him Lindsay heard Dancy's nurse ask, 'Is he really an officer?'

Dancy said thickly, 'One of my best, actually.'

And through and above it Goss moved like a giant, his voice carrying over all else as he received his compliments and replied to many of the questions.

'Yes, I recall the time when we were at Aden, that was quite a trip.' Or, 'She was the best paying ship in the line. Always popular on the Far East run, was the old *Becky.*'

Lindsay took another drink, trying to remember how many he had swallowed so far. Goss was really enjoying himself. It was just as if the opportunity to show what his old ship could do had released some of the pressure.

Jupp said quietly, 'There has just been a telephone call, sir. Captain Lovelace will be coming aboard shortly.'

But Lindsay was looking past him towards the door. Boase, the doctor, was greeting several latecomers and leading them to the tables. One of them was the Wren called Eve.

At first he could not be certain. Without her scarves and baggy coat she looked quite different. For one thing, she was much smaller than he had imagined, and her hair was cut very short, giving her a sort of elfin simplicity.

He pushed through the press of figures and saw Boase stiffen and say, 'Oh, this is the captain.'

She held out her hand. It was small and very warm. 'I know.'

Lindsay said, 'I'm glad you could come.'

She had hazel eyes, very wide. And she was studying him with that same mock gravity he had remembered so vividly from their first meeting in that wet, quivering staff car.

She said, 'It's like nothing I've ever seen. She's a *beautiful* ship.'

He realised with a start he was still holding her hand and said awkwardly, 'Here's a steward. Take a drink from the tray and tell me what you've been doing.'

She smiled up at him. 'Not much.' She lifted the glass. 'Cheers.'

Boase had sunk back into the crowd but Lindsay had not even noticed. He said, 'I'm sorry I was a bit stupid the other night. You must have thought——'

She interrupted quietly, 'I thought you looked worn out. I was sorry, too. About that dance.'

Lindsay glanced round. 'Have you brought him with you?' He forced a smile. 'He seemed a nice chap.'

'You hated him, and it showed!' She laughed at his confusion. 'But he's not with me.' The laugh wavered. 'He was a friend of Bill's. The one who was killed.'

Then she waved her glass to another Wren who was in deep conversation with Lieutenant Hunter. 'Watch it, Judy! You know what they say!' The mood had changed again.

Lindsay guided her to the bulkhead. 'We're leaving tomorrow, but I imagine you know. I was wondering. About that meal I promised you?'

She looked at him with new concern. 'Oh, I forgot to tell you. I've been drafted.'

'*Drafted?*' The word hung between them like a shutter.

'Well, I've been trying for ages to go on a signals course.

I should have gone when I joined, but I had a driving licence, you see.'

Lindsay did not see. All he knew was he was losing her almost before he had found her. 'Licence?'

She wrinkled her nose. 'Yes. So they made me a driver. You know how it is.' She staggered against his arm. 'Oops. I'm getting tipsy already!' Then she saw his face and added, 'Well, my draft-chit has at last arrived. I'm being sent on some new course.' She faltered. 'In Canada.'

Lindsay looked away. 'I'm very glad for you.'

'No you're not.' She rested a hand on his sleeve. 'Neither am I. Now.'

Canada. Not even where he could visit her. He cursed himself for allowing his disappointment to show. It wasn't her fault. It wasn't anyone's fault.

He said, 'You didn't come aboard to be miserable. Come and meet the others.'

She shook her head. 'I can only stay a little while. They're shipping me out tonight. I expect I'll be joining a convoy at Liverpool.' She was not smiling. 'Rotten, isn't it?'

'Yes.' He wanted to take her away. Free himself and her from the noise and enjoyment which hemmed them in like a wall. 'I shall miss you.'

She studied his face for several seconds. 'You mean it, don't you?'

Maxwell's polished head moved from the crowd. 'Sorry to interrupt, sir, but Captain Lovelace is here.' He kept his eyes on the girl. 'He has an important visitor with him.'

'Tell him I'll be right over.' As Maxwell hurried away he said urgently, 'You won't leave the ship without saying goodbye?'

She shook her head very slowly. 'No. Of course not.' She tried to bring back her cheeky grin. 'I'll go and yarn with your delicious doctor.' But somehow the grin would not come.

Lindsay moved through the crowd and found Lovelace speaking with Maxwell, his serious features breaking into a smile as he said, 'Ah, Lindsay, I'd like you to meet Commodore Kemp.'

The other guest was a sturdy, thickset man, who nodded abruptly and said, 'Quite a party. Never think you'd been in action, what?'

Lovelace eyed him coolly. 'No. You've done a marvellous job, Lindsay.'

Lindsay was still watching the commodore. There was something aggressive about him. Intolerant. Like his words. 'Are you joining the base, sir?'

The commodore took a glass from a steward and regarded it critically. 'I'm here to co-ordinate new strategy.' He glanced at Lindsay again. 'Still, this is hardly the time to discuss Service matters, what?' He did not smile.

Lindsay felt suddenly angry. Who the hell did he think he was anyway? He thought too of the girl, of the fading, precious minutes.

The commodore said abruptly, 'Where is that son of mine then?'

Kemp. Of course. He should have guessed.

'I'm afraid I don't know, sir.'

'*I* would want to know where every one of my officers was, at any time of the day or night.'

'Come along, sir, why not meet some of the other guests?' Lovelace sounded tense. 'I'm sure the captain doesn't bother about one more midshipman, eh?'

Kemp stared at him bleakly. 'I *want* to see him.'

Lindsay sighed. 'I'll send for him.' It was his own fault. After all, Kemp had come a long way to see his only son. It was not much to ask.

He heard the commodore say, 'Young fool. When I heard about his latest failure I thought I'd explode!' He stared round at the shining panels and glittering lights.

'Under these circumstances, however——'

Lindsay turned sharply, 'Are you here on official business, sir, or as a guest?'

Kemp looked at him with surprise. 'As a guest of course!'

Lindsay said quietly, 'Then, sir, may I suggest you start acting like one!' Then he turned on his heel and walked away.

The commodore opened and closed his mouth several times. 'The impertinent young——' He turned to Lovelace again. 'By God, there will be a few changes when I'm in control, I can tell you!'

Lindsay almost collided with Jupp as he pushed between the noisy figures by the door.

Jupp said, 'Beg pardon, sir, but the young lady 'as gone. There was a call from the shore. Somethin' about 'er draft bein' brought forward an hour.' He held out a paper napkin. 'She said to give this to you, sir.'

Lindsay opened it. She had written in pencil. *Had to go. Take care of yourself. See you in Eden. Eve.*

Then he hurried out and on to the promenade deck, the breath almost knocked from him by the bitter air. He found the gangway staff huddled together in their thick watchcoats, banging their hands and stamping their feet to keep warm.

The quartermaster saw Lindsay and said, 'Can I 'elp, sir?'

'The last boat, Q.M. Can you still see it?' Beyond the guardrail the night was pitch black.

The quartermaster shook his head. 'No, sir. Shoved off ten minutes back.' His breath smelt strongly of rum.

Lindsay felt the napkin in his hand and folded it carefully before putting it in his pocket.

'Thank you. Goodnight.'

The quartermaster watched him go and said to his companion, 'Funny lot.'

The bosun's mate looked at him. 'Who?'

The quartermaster reached for his hidden rum bottle. 'Officers, of course! Who the bloody else!'

Lindsay walked back into the noisy wardroom and noticed that Commodore Kemp was speaking to his son in a corner. Several of the guests were showing signs of wear, and when they reached the cold air outside they would know all about it.

He reached Goss's side and said, 'I'm going to my cabin, Number One. You take over, will you.'

Goss nodded, watching him strangely. 'Good party, sir.'

'Yes.' Lindsay looked at the door, as if expecting to see her there again. 'Very good party.'

Then he saw Jupp and said, 'I'll have some whisky in my cabin.'

'Now, sir?'

'*Now.*'

He walked out of the wardroom and climbed the companion ladder which now seemed very quiet and deserted.

8 A small error

The telephone above Lindsay's bunk rattled tinnily, and without switching on his overhead lamp he reached up and clapped it to his ear.

'Captain?'

Stannard sounded off guard. He had probably imagined Lindsay to be fast asleep.

'Time to alter course, sir.'

Lindsay held up his watch and saw the luminous face glowing in the darkness. Four in the morning. Another day.

'Very well, Pilot. What's it like up top?'

Not that it would have altered in the three hours since he had left the bridge. Nor had it changed much in the days and the weeks since they had slipped their buoy in Scapa. Ten days to reach the patrol area and another twenty pounding along the invisible lines of its extremities while the sea did everything possible to make their lives a misery. Even now, as he listened to Stannard's breathing and to the dull boom of waves against the hull, he could picture the water sluicing across the forward well deck, freezing into hard bulk, while the blown spray changed the superstructure and rigging into moulds of crude glass. Men frozen to the bone, slipping and cursing into the darkness with hammers and steam hoses, knowing as they toiled that they would be required again within the hour.

Stannard replied, 'Wind still nor'west, sir. Pretty fresh. It might feel easier when we turn into it.'

'Good. Keep me posted, Pilot.' He dropped the handset on its hook and lay back again on the pillow.

What a way to fight a war. Mile upon wretched mile. Empty, violent and cold. He heard feet overhead, the muffled clatter of steering gear as Stannard brought the old ship round on the southernmost leg of her patrol. Right at this moment of time Stannard's little pencilled cross on the chart would show the *Benbecula* almost five hundred miles south-west of Iceland, while some seven hundred and fifty miles beyond her labouring bows was the dreaded Cape Farewell of Greenland. It was not a patrol area, he thought. It was a wilderness, a freezing desert.

One more day and they would be in December, with still another month to go before they could run for home, for Scapa and its weed-encrusted buoys.

He turned on the bunk and heard the small pill jar rattle beneath the pillow. The sound was like a cruel taunt, and he tried not to think of Boase's reserved voice as he had handed them to him. Enough to make you sleep for four hours at least. Deep, empty sleep which he needed so desperately. Pitifully. Yet he knew he was afraid to take even one of them. In case he was needed. In case. . . . He rolled over to his opposite side and thought instead about opening a new bottle of whisky. It was no use. He could not go on like this. He was slowly destroying himself, and knew he was a growing menace to all those who depended on him at any hour of day or night.

Whenever he fell into the bunk for even a few moments the nightmare returned with the regularity of time itself. Again and again and again he would awake, sweating and frightened. Shaking and knowing he was beaten.

Perhaps if they were on convoy duty it might have been different. The daily check of ships under escort, the careful manoeuvres with massive merchantmen charging blindly through fog or pitch darkness for fear of losing the next ahead. The search for stragglers, and the triumph at watching the lines of weatherbeaten charges plodding past into harbour and safety.

But here there was nothing, and he knew it was affecting almost every man aboard. Tension flared into anger. Someone just a minute late on watch would be cursed by the waiting man with all the hatred and venom of an enemy. Lindsay tried to break the deadly monotony and discomfort by speaking daily to the ship's company over the new tannoy system. He occasionally left the bridge to do his rounds, to visit as many parts of the ship as he could between other duties, but he could feel the hopelessness of it just the same. Even the pathetically early Christmas decorations in some of the messes seemed to make a mockery of their efforts to stay sane.

The telephone jarred into his thoughts like a gunshot. It was Stannard again.

'Sorry to bother you, sir.' His Australian accent was more pronounced than usual. 'There's a westbound convoy altering course to the south-east of us. W/T office is monitoring all traffic as you instructed.'

'How far away?'

Stannard sounded vague. 'Approximately five hundred miles, sir.'

'Anything else?'

'Admiralty reports a deployment of seven plus U-boats converging ahead of convoy's original course, sir.'

'Very well. Keep a good listening watch.' He heard the line go dead.

As he lay back he thought of the countless times he had heard such warnings himself when he had commanded the *Vengeur*. Except that now there were more U-boats, bigger and better organised than before. He could imagine the heart-searching which would be going on at this moment as the commodore and escort commander of that unknown convoy examined and discussed the latest information. Alter course. Run further north to avoid the eager U-boats. Lose time certainly, but with luck the ships would be saved from destruction. U-boats rarely wasted their efforts and fuel by sweeping too far from the main convoy routes. And why should they? Their growing toll of sinkings was evidence of their harvest.

But in the Atlantic you could never be really certain. Time and distance, speed and visibility were so different here from the calm efficiency of the plotting rooms in the far off Admiralty bunkers.

But it was not *Benbecula*'s concern. The convoy, like all the others at sea at any given time, must depend on its own resources.

He closed his eyes and tried to dismiss it from his mind. But try as he might he could not put aside a sudden feeling of uneasiness. Doubt or instinct? It was impossible to describe.

He switched on the light and swung his legs off the bunk, feeling automatically for his sea boots. It was no surprise to hear the discreet knock at the outer door and to see Jupp's mournful face peering in at him. Perhaps he could not sleep either.

'Will you be wanting an early breakfast, sir?' His eyes flickered swiftly across the disordered bunk. 'I 'ave some coffee on the go.'

Lindsay shook his head, steadying his legs against the tilting deck. 'I think I'll make do with coffee for now.'

Jupp vanished just as quietly and returned in minutes with a pot of fresh coffee.

He said, 'Blowing a bit up top, sir.' He glanced with obvious disapproval at Lindsay's soiled and crumpled sweater. 'I could get you some more gear from my store.'

Lindsay smiled. 'Later.'

He swung round as the handset rang again. 'Captain?'

Stannard said, 'W/T office has just received a signal for us, sir. Top Secret. I've got Aikman on to it right away.'

Lieutenant Aikman, who was listed as boarding officer, had the additional chore of decoding the more secret and difficult signals, and would not thank Stannard for hauling him from his warm bunk.

Lindsay swallowed some coffee and then asked, 'Any news of the convoy?'

'Six more U-boats reported to the south of it, sir. I've marked 'em on my chart, so it also gives us a fair idea of the convoy's position.'

Lindsay nodded. 'Good. That was sensible.' There was more to Stannard than he had imagined.

He replaced the handset as Jupp said, 'Marvellous 'ow the Admiralty know all them things, sir.'

Lindsay shrugged. 'They've the Germans to thank for that. Admiralty intercepts signals from seagoing U-boats to German naval headquarters and passes the information on to the convoys. Got it?'

Jupp looked doubtful. 'Not quite, sir.'

Lindsay groped for the nearest dry towel and wound it round his neck. 'If a U-boat sights a convoy her skipper flashes the news to Germany. The German operations staff then signal all U-boats in the vicinity to home on to it like a pack of wolves.'

As he buttoned his jacket he was thinking of those submarines. Seven plus ahead of the convoy's previous course. Now six more to the south. It was a formidable force, but fortunately there was still time to take avoiding action. Thanks to the radio operators at the Admiralty.

Jupp handed him his cap and glasses. 'It's all too much for me, sir. Makes me feel old.'

Lindsay brushed past him. 'You'll never get old. You're like the ship. Rheumaticky but reliable!'

As he hurried up the companion ladder he realised with a start that it was the first time he had attempted to make a joke about anything since . . . he shut the other picture from his mind.

By the chart room he paused and glanced inside. Stannard was stretching across the big table, his fingers working deftly with dividers and parallel rulers. He made some small notations on the chart and then straightened his back. Seeing Lindsay in the doorway he said, 'Oh, good morning, sir.' He grinned. 'Although it's as black as a boot outside.'

Lindsay leaned on the table and studied the neat lines and bearings.

Stannard said, 'As far as I can make out the convoy has made a really drastic alteration of course.' He tapped the chart with his dividers. 'They are steaming almost nor-'west and really cracking it on.'

'What do we know about it, Pilot?'

Lindsay knew what the convoy's commodore was doing. He had already passed out of effective range of air cover from England and was heading further north in the hopes of getting help from the longe-range bomber patrols from Iceland. There were so many dead patches where aircraft could not reach to carry out sorties and anti-submarine attacks. Like the vast area now covered by *Benbecula*'s endless vigil.

Stannard said, 'I looked at the intelligence log, sir. Seems it's a fast westbound convoy. Only ten ships, according to the last information.'

The door banged open and Aikman, his pyjamas covered by a duffel coat, stepped over the coaming.

'Bloody hell, Pilot! Can't you let a bloke get some shut-eye!' He saw Lindsay and flushed. 'Sorry, sir!'

Lindsay smiled. 'I know how you feel.' He was still thinking about the convoy. 'What does the signal say?'

Aikman ran his fingers through his tousled hair. 'Three German heavy units have left Tromso, sir. Last reported heading south along the Norwegian coast. Further information not yet available.' He looked up as Lindsay turned to face him. 'There's a list of deployments too, sir.'

Lindsay took the long, neatly written signal and read it very slowly. It might be nothing. The enemy could be moving three important warships south to Kiel or to the

Baltic for use against the Russians. They had been *seen*
steaming south, but that could have easily been a ruse to
confuse the Norwegian agents who must have flashed the
news to the Admiralty in London. Perhaps they were
going to make another attempt to break into the Atlantic
in strength. He ran his eye over the deployment information. A cruiser squadron was already on its way from
Iceland, and more heavy units had left Scapa Flow. He
found he was reading faster as the mental picture began
to form in his mind. Almost every available ship was
being sent to forestall anything which the three German
units might attempt. He thought of the deserted buoys at
Scapa. The place would really be stripped bare now.

He looked at Stannard. 'I want you to make notes on
this signal. You'll need help with it, so I'll stay on the
bridge awhile until we hear something more.'

Stannard nodded and picked up a telephone. He said,
'Bosun's mate? Get the navigator's yeoman double quick.
And tell Midshipman Kemp I want him here, too.' As he
dropped the handset he was already searching through
his chart folios until with a grunt he dragged one out and
laid it on the smaller chart table by the bulkhead. 'Just so
as I can plot what's happening off Norway, sir.' He
grinned and added, 'Not that we'll be involved, but it
helps to pass the time.'

Lindsay eyed him gravely. 'Good thinking. But don't
bank on the last part too much.'

As he walked towards the wheelhouse Lindsay was
thinking of the carefully detailed information in the
signal. What Stannard did not yet realise was that apart
from *Benbecula* and two patrol vessels in the Denmark
Strait there was hardly a single ship within five hundred
miles of the convoy and its escorts.

He found Dancy standing in the centre of the bridge
staring straight ahead through a clearview screen.
Beyond the toughened glass there was little visible but the
dark outline of the forecastle framed against the

oncoming ranks of white-topped waves. Past the pale crests there was complete darkness, with not even a star to show itself through the thick cloud.

Dancy stiffened as Lindsay lifted himself on to the chair.

Lindsay remarked, 'How is the ice on deck, Sub?'

Dancy replied, 'The middle watch had it cleared before we came up, sir. But there is some forming below Number Two gun mounting, I think. I'll get the hands on it in half an hour.' He hesitated. 'If that is all right, sir?'

Lindsay looked at him. How much more confident Dancy had become. Probably through working with Stannard.

'Fine,' he said.

Stannard entered the wheelhouse a few minutes later but he was no longer so untroubled. 'I've marked all of it on the charts, sir.' His palm rasped over his chin. 'If those three jokers make a go for the Atlantic, which way will they come, d'you reckon?'

Lindsay shrugged. 'They'll know they've been seen on the move and will not waste time trying for the Denmark Strait this time. Quite apart from the problems of drifting ice, they'll imagine we've a mass of patrols there already waiting for them.'

Stannard said quietly, 'If they only knew!'

Lindsay nodded. 'My guess is they'll head for the Rose Garden.'

'Sir?' Dancy sounded puzzled.

Stannard understood. 'That's the area between Iceland and the Faroes, you ignorant oaf!'

Dancy replied carefully, 'All the same, it'll be hard to slip past our ships, surely?'

'Over four hundred miles, Sub?' Lindsay looked away. 'It's a pretty wide gap.'

He settled back in the chair and waited until the others had moved away. He did not want to talk. He wanted to think, to try and explain why he felt so uneasy. Involved.

On the face of it, Dancy's youthful optimism should be justified. The Navy had been planning for such an eventuality since the *Bismarck*'s breakout. But this was a very bad time of the year. Visibility was hopeless and air cover restricted accordingly. It was just possible the Germans might make it. If so, where would they go, south to prey on the convoys from the Cape, or further west in search of more rapid results?

Aikman entered the wheelhouse, his eyes glowing faintly in the shaded compass light. 'Another signal, sir. Two more U-boats reported to south of convoy.'

Stannard snapped, 'Give it to me. I'll put it on the chart.'

Lindsay's voice stopped him by the door. 'While you're there, Pilot, get me a course and speed to intercept the convoy.' He hesitated, feeling Stannard's unspoken warning. 'I mean to intercept the convoy *if* it comes as far north as our patrol limit.'

Stannard said, 'Right away, sir.'

Aikman asked, 'They'll never come right up here, surely, sir?'

Lindsay looked at him. 'Wouldn't you if you had fifteen odd U-boats coming after you?'

Aikman nodded glumly. 'I suppose so.'

Somewhere below the bridge the tannoy speaker squeaked into life. 'Cooks to the galley! Forenoon watchkeepers to breakfast and clean!'

Lindsay looked at his watch. Nearly three hours since Stannard had called him on the telephone about the change of course. It seemed like minutes.

Stannard came back and said, 'Course to intercept would be one hundred degrees, sir. Revs for fifteen knots.' He paused, his voice empty of everything but professional interest. 'If the convoy maintains its present course and speed we should make contact at 2000 tonight.' He stood back, his face hidden in shadow as he waited for Lindsay's reaction. Then he added slowly, 'Of course, sir, we'd be out of our allotted area by noon if you decided to act on it.'

'Yes.' He thought of the two lines which Stannard must have drawn on his chart. Two converging lines. One the *Benbecula,* the other a handful of desperate, valuable ships. The convoy's original track was straddled by U-boats. To the south the gate was also closed. But if the convoy came further north and the German heavy units burst through the patrol lines, they would need all the help they could get.

He said, 'Very well. Bring her round to one-zero-zero. Call up the chief before you ask for maximum revs, but warn the engine room what to expect.'

He could feel the sudden expectancy amongst the shadowy figures around him. Moments before they had been lolling and swaying with the regular motion, half asleep and dull with boredom. His words had changed all that in an instant.

'Port fifteen.' Stannard rested one hand on the gyro, his eyes watching the quartermaster as he began to turn the wheel.

Below decks, as the forenoon watchkeepers queued for their greasy sausages and powdered egg, their sweet tea and marmalade, they would feel the difference and cling to their mess tables until the turn was completed. Only the seasoned men would guess what was happening. The others would merely curse the officers on the bridge for deliberately trying to ruin their breakfast.

'Midships.' Stannard had his eye down to the gyro. 'Steady.'

'Steady, sir. Course zero-nine-five.' The quartermaster sounded breathless as the ship rolled heavily across a steep trough.

'Steer one-zero-zero.' Stannard looked up as small tinkling sounds echoed above like tiny bells. More ice forming on the control position and rigging made by the spray flung high over the bows.

A telephone buzzed and Stannard said, 'Yes, Chief.' He looked at Lindsay. 'For you, sir.'

Fraser sounded irritable. 'What's all this I hear about full revs, sir?'

Lindsay turned his back to the others and spoke very quietly into the mouthpiece. 'There may be a convoy coming into our pitch, Chief. There are three bandits at large from Norway and a whole pack of U-boats to the south. I thought our presence might cheer 'em up a bit. Pilot will give you the details. I just wanted you to know the rest of it first.'

There was a long pause. 'Aye, sir. Ring down when you're ready. I'll give you everything I've got.'

Lindsay handed the telephone to Stannard and said, 'I'm going below. I have a feeling this is going to be a long day.'

Two hours later Jupp stood beside Lindsay's table and eyed him with grave approval. Lindsay had shaved, taken a quick shower, and had allowed Jupp to supply him with a freshly laundered sweater. But 'it was the fact that he was eating his first complete breakfast since taking command which was obviously giving the steward so much pleasure. He even felt better, but could discover no cause for it.

Beyond the bulkhead he could hear hammers banging away the ice and the squeak of metal as the gun crews tested their weapons and made sure the mechanism had not frozen solid overnight. It was still dark on deck, and would be for most of the day. He could feel the ship's stern lifting slowly to the following sea, while the bows crashed and vibrated like dull thunder, throwing up the spray in long tattered banners as high as the foremast derricks.

There was a tap at the door and Petty Officer Ritchie stepped over the coaming, his cap beneath his arm. He too looked brighter and more relaxed than Lindsay could remember. Perhaps, like himself, he craved to be doing something, if only to keep his inner hurt at bay a while longer.

'Good morning, Yeoman. Anything new?'

Ritchie took a pad from his pocket. 'Not much, sir. No more U-boat reports. And there's nothin' about the three Jerry ships neither.' He leafed through the pad. 'Bad weather over the Denmark Strait, so all air patrols is grounded.'

'That follows.' Lindsay gestured to Jupp for some more coffee.

Ritchie added, 'Some more information about the convoy, sir. Ten ships and three escorts.'

'Only three?'

Ritchie grimaced. 'Well, sir, it's a fast convoy apparently. Mostly tankers in ballast and two personnel ships. One of 'em's got a party of Wrens aboard it seems. A complete signals course.'

Lindsay stared at him, suddenly ice cold. It was more than a coincidence, surely. The feeling. The nagging instinct that something was wrong. Like the dream. Only this time it was real.

'Give it to me.' He took the pad, his eyes darting across Ritchie's round handwriting as if to see something more than the bare details.

Ritchie watched him curiously. 'I did 'ear they was sendin' some Wrens to Canada, sir. Wouldn' 'ave minded an instructing job out there.'

Lindsay stood up. 'Get back to the bridge, Yeo, and tell the W/T office I want every channel open. Anything,' he paused, holding Ritchie's eyes with his own, '*anything* they hear I want to know about. Then pass the word for Lieutenant Stannard to report to me.'

Ritchie looked as if he were about to ask a question, but as he glanced past Lindsay he saw Jupp give an urgent shake of the head and decided against it.

Jupp watched the door close and asked, 'More coffee, sir?' When Lindsay remained staring at the bulkhead he added gently, 'She'll be safe, sir. They'll not take chances with a ship full of women.'

Lindsay turned slowly and looked at him. Poor Jupp, what did he know of the Atlantic?

He said quietly, 'I expect you're right. And thank you.'

Jupp had been expecting Lindsay to fly at him for his foolish comments and had been prepared for it. But he had been determined Lindsay should not be dragged down by the sudden despair which was stamped on his face. The fact that Lindsay had spoken so quietly was in some ways much worse. Jupp was deeply moved by the discovery, as he was troubled by the realisation he could do nothing to help.

In his private office below the bridge Lieutenant Philip Aikman carefully locked the secret code books inside his safe and took a quick glance at himself in the bulkhead mirror. He was past thirty, and occasionally worried about a certain flabbiness around his chin and waist. He liked to take care of himself whenever possible, but with the *Benbecula* rolling drunkenly through trough after trough it was not easy to exercise in comfort and work up a sweat without being watched by prying eyes.

Unlike most of the other officers aboard, Aikman really enjoyed his appointment to the ship. *Benbecula* was not involved with complicated manoeuvres of fleet actions. She was remote from all but the rarest chances of air or U-boat attack, which suited him just fine.

He slipped into his duffel coat and arranged his cap carefully on his fair hair at what was a jaunty angle, but not enough to draw sarcasm or a harsh reprimand from Goss.

In civilian life Aikman had been manager of a small but busy travel agency in the London suburbs. Holidays for middle class families in Brighton and Torquay. Weekends for the less fortunate in Southend and Selsey

Bill. It never varied very much except when someone came to see him for advice on something more daring. France or Italy. A cruise to the Greek Islands or the ski slopes of Switzerland. Aikman knew every place, almost as if he had visited each one himself.

His education was scanty, but he made up for it by his sharp attention to detail and manner. He watched and listened to those who came to his shop to book their holidays, and never pushed himself further than was necessary to gain more information from them when they returned to tell him of his satisfactory, or otherwise, arrangements.

Deep inside he yearned to be part of the world he sold and traded in his shop. That unreal world of laughing girls on posters holding beach balls and calling you to sunshine and endless enjoyment. Of the white-hulled liners anchored in glittering bays and harbours, surrounded by boats of eager wogs and, of course, more smiling girls.

When war came he volunteered for the Navy without really knowing why. He never lost a chance in seeking someone who could help him reach his new goal, a commission, and when luck came his way he seized it with both hands. In the early months, the phoney war as it was called by all those not made to fight in it, there was much confusion, as a peacetime Navy became swollen in size and purpose. By chance he saw and confronted one of his old customers, a retired captain of some age who was now back in the Service, and like it had become larger than life. Aikman had always flattered him, and when the old captain asked casually if he was interested in a job on Contraband Control, Aikman jumped at it.

One advantage Aikman had over the younger officer candidates was that he had experience of life outside the Navy or some public school. Without a blush he completed his forms, adding a list of languages which he spoke fluently and more of which he had a fair knowledge. In fact he spoke only one, his own, and even that was limited. But as he had told his customers often enough. *'Everyone* speaks English!' His supreme confidence and smooth acceptance of his new work somehow carried him through. In the early part of the war, when maritime neutrals still outnumbered the combatants, he was required to board and search their ships to make sure no war materials were being smuggled to the enemy. To his surprise, he found everyone *did* speak English, well almost, and when a rare ignorance spoiled his approach Aikman would soon discover another officer or a steward who could give him his necessary information. In fact, he did so well he gained a second stripe almost before the first one had become tarnished.

But when he was transferred to a troopship and later to *Benbecula* he felt a pang of relief. Luck could not last forever, and here he was really safe. The officers were nicely mixed, and only a few like Maxwell, the gunnery officer, and Goss, the first lieutenant, ever bothered him. He had not a specified job, other than as boarding officer, until of course the captain had made him his senior decoding officer, an untouchable and unreachable position. It suited him very well indeed.

He stepped over the cabin coaming and winced as the wind smashed him back on the wet steel. Over the weather rail the sea was sinking and then surging high against the hull, and he had to run like mad to reach the bridge ladder without getting soaked.

He entered the chart room and shook his cap carefully on the deck. Stannard was not there, and only Midshipman Kemp and Squire, the navigator's yeoman, were working on the two charts.

Kemp was well bred, you could see it in the fine clear skin and sensitive mouth. He had an important father too, Aikman had learned from someone, and he guessed there might be a next step for him there if he played it carefully.

He said casually, 'I've just decoded that last top secret one.' He laid the pad on the chart. 'It states, two repeat two of the German heavy units have entered the Skager-rak, so you'd better note it in the pilot's log.'

Kemp looked up, his eyes rimmed with fatigue. 'Just two of them?'

Aikman gave a grave smile. 'It stands to reason that if two of them have gone to earth the other will be close behind.' He shrugged. 'If not, I imagine the Home Fleet can take care of that bugger!'

Kemp thrust the pad to Squire. 'You do it, will you?'

'I said as much to Pilot.' Aikman yawned hugely. 'When he got me out of my pit at the crack of dawn. Still, there you are.'

He walked to a salt-stained scuttle and peered down at the leaping, jarring wave crests. It was just past noon, yet the sky was dull grey, like a London fog in winter. He watched the rivulets of spray running down the glass and freezing into small distorted worms.

'Nasty. But I've seen worse.'

Behind his back Squire looked up and grinned. Pomp-ous twit. Sounded like a proper old sea-dog. He lowered his head again and reached for his pencil. Squire had been a merchant seaman, but now that he was officially in the Royal Navy for the duration of the war was as determined as Aikman to better himself. There the simi-larity ended. He was a dark haired seaman of twenty-eight years, with the quiet good looks of a scholar rather than a sailor. He had worked hard and had gained the coveted appointment as Stannard's personal yeoman, a step, as the Australian had explained more than once, which would land him a bit of gold lace if he kept his nose clean. So there it was.

He paused, the pencil in mid air. He was too tired. Too worn out by the cold and damp of his endless visits to the bridge. He tried again.

As Aikman walked across the passage to visit the W/T

office Squire said quietly, 'These two Jerry ships, sir. How can they be in the Skagerrak?'

Kemp, who had been brooding about his father and their last angry confrontation, turned and looked at him warily. 'Why not?'

Squire studied him thoughtfully. He liked Kemp, but as an officer he was bloody useless.

Patiently he said, 'If three of them left Tromso last night, how can two have reached as far south as Denmark in that time?' He put down the pencil. 'It's not possible, sir, unless they grew wings!'

Aikman's voice was loud in the passageway and Squire said, 'You'd better tell him, sir. It could be important.'

'Tell him what?' Aikman was back, smiling at them with assured ease.

Kemp looked at the signal pad. 'The yeoman says that these ships could not have reached the Skagerrak so quickly, sir.'

'What?' Aikman was still smiling. 'That's bloody rubbish, lad.' He crossed to the table. 'If their lordships tell us they've got there, then who are we to question them, eh?' He laughed. 'Would you like me to make a special signal to the First Sea Lord? Tell him that Mr Midshipman Kemp and Acting Able Seaman Squire are of the opinion his information is all to hell?'

Kemp dropped his eyes. 'I was only saying what——'

Squire interrupted, 'I think you should check the original signal, sir.'

'Do you?' Aikman felt a sudden twinge of alarm. They were all reacting wrongly. He was losing control. 'As it happens, Squire, I do not require any advice on my department!'

'Sir.' Squire looked away, hurt and suddenly angry. What the hell was the matter with Aikman? He glanced at Kemp's strained face. And he was little better. He should have spoken out, done the job Stannard had entrusted him with.

He said stubbornly, 'When the navigating officer returns, sir, I shall have to tell him.'

'You *do* that small thing, Squire!' Aikman shot him a withering stare. 'I may have some things to tell him, too!' He stamped out of the chart room and slammed the door.

Kemp shrugged. 'Phew, you've really upset him now.'

Squire did not look at him. The first thing he had done wrong. Spoken out against an officer. He must be mad. Even Stannard would be unable to wipe that from his record.

At that very moment Stannard was standing beside Lindsay's tall chair, his eyes fixed beyond the bows and the steady panorama of cruising wave crests.

He said, 'Well, sir, I have to tell you that we should make a turn. Even allowing for dead reckoning and little else, I'm sure we're miles over our patrol line.'

Lindsay nodded slowly. Stannard was right, of course. All the forenoon as he had sat or paced the creaking, staggering bridge he had listened to the intermittent stream of incoming signals, The convoy had made another turn to westward, its commodore apparently satisfied the U-boats had given up the chase. There had been several reports of ice to the south and south-east of Cape Farewell from the American ice patrols, but every captain had to be prepared to take avoiding action in these waters.

He replied, 'Well, if anything had happened we'd have been better placed to go and assist.' It sounded as lame as he knew it was.

Aikman strode on to the bridge and reported, 'Two enemy units have been sighted in their own waters, sir. The third is still unaccounted for.'

Stannard grinned. 'That settles it then. I'll go and lay off a new course.'

Lindsay glanced at Dancy. 'Ring for half speed.'

He settled down again in the chair and thought of the

convoy and the party of Wrens who were probably quite unaware of their momentary danger.

He realised that Aikman was still beside him, and when he turned saw his face was deathly pale, as if he was going to be sick. 'What's wrong?'

Aikman spoke between his teeth. 'There's been a mistake, sir. Not important now as the enemy ships are back in safe waters, but——'

Lindsay asked, 'What sort of mistake?'

'I was called here this morning and told to decode that first signal.' He was speaking mechanically, as if he had lost control over his voice. 'I was tired, I'd been overworking, you see, sir, and I must have confused the times of origin.'

Lindsay gripped the arms of the chair. 'You did what?'

'Well, sir, it was just a small slip.' A bead of sweat ran from under Aikman's cap. 'But the three German ships left Tromso twenty-eight hours *earlier* than I calculated.'

Lindsay saw Dancy watching him over the gyro, his face like a mask.

'But two of them are back in their own waters.' Lindsay forced himself to speak gently, knowing Aikman was near breaking. 'Is *that* part right?'

Aikman nodded. 'Yes, sir.'

The sliding door at the rear of the wheelhouse crashed open and Stannard said harshly, 'Own waters be damned! They're in the Skagerrak, and that was how Squire knew *he,*' Stannard pointed angrily at Aikman's rigid shoulders, 'had made a cock of the decoding!'

'Easy, Pilot!' Lindsay slid from the chair, his mind working wildly. 'This won't help anything.'

Stannard crossed the bridge and said to Aikman, 'You stupid bastard! Why the hell did you take so long to find out?'

Aikman faced him, his lips ashen. 'Well, they're back now, so what are you trying to make trouble for?'

Lindsay's voice silenced all of them. 'In twenty-eight

hours quite a lot might have happened.' He looked at Stannard. 'See what you can find out about the convoy.' Then he looked at Aikman. 'I just hope to God I'm wrong. If not, you'd better start praying!'

Aikman walked from the wheelhouse, his eyes unseeing as Stannard came back from the W/T office.

He said quietly, 'Convoy is now steering two-seven-five, sir. Fifteen knots. Should pass within fifty miles of our southernmost leg at 2000.'

Lindsay waited, knowing there was more.

'A Swedish freighter reported sighting an unidentified ship in the Denmark Strait the night before last, sir. That is all the information available.'

Lindsay walked past him and gripped the rail beneath a clearview screen. Almost to himself he said, 'So while every available ship is out searching for the three from Tromso, one other slips quietly through the Denmark Strait. He's been there, sitting patiently and waiting while the U-boats did the hard part for him.' He swung round on Stannard and slammed one fist into his palm. 'Like beasts to the slaughter!'

Stannard stared at him. 'Oh, my Christ!'

Lindsay turned away. 'Bring her round on to your new course. Maximum revs again, and I'll want the hands to exercise action stations in thirty minutes before the light goes!'

He gestured to a bosun's mate. 'Get the first lieutenant and gunnery officer.' As the man ran to his telephone he looked at Dancy. 'And you, Sub, pray for a snowstorm, anything, if you've nothing else to do.'

Below in his small office Aikman sat on the edge of his chair, the knuckle of one finger gripped tightly between his teeth to keep himself from sobbing aloud. The mistake which he had anticipated and then ignored had at last found him out. He still did not understand exactly what had happened up there on the bridge, but knew it was far more terrible than even he imagined.

Overhead a tannoy speaker blared, 'Hands will exercise action in thirty minutes. Damage control parties will muster on A deck.'

Aikman stared at the speaker, his eyes smarting from the strain. What the hell was happening? There was no real danger now, surely? Two ships had been found, and probably the other one too by now.

Tears ran unheeded down his cheeks. That fool Stannard and his stupid, crawling yeoman were responsible. The signal could have been filed and forgotten like so many others. And now, whatever happened, his small world was broken and lost to him forever.

9 The trap

Lindsay made himself sit very still in his chair as the deck lifted, hesitated and then swayed through another steep roll. Apart from the shaded compass lights the bridge was in total darkness, and because the sea had moderated during the afternoon and evening the shipboard noises seemed all the louder. Steel creaked and groaned as if in pain, and above the bridge the long necklaces of iced spray on stays and rails rattled and tinkled in tuneless chorus.

The *Benbecula* had turned in a great arc, so that she was now heading once again towards the southern extremity of Greenland. All afternoon they had listened to the crackle of morse from the W/T office and watched the mounting clips of signals. The third German ship, a cruiser, had at last been sighted entering the Skagerrak like her consorts, so whatever doubt had remained in Lindsay's mind had almost gone. This was no slapdash operation for morale or propaganda purposes. The German navy was showing what it could do when it came to co-operation between all arms of the service.

But for the twenty-eight hours delay things might have been very different. He could have taken *Benbecula* at full speed to the northern span of her patrol area, where there was the best chance of contacting any ship which might come through the Denmark Strait. If only the neutral freighter had reported seeing the fourth ship earlier, but the unknown vessel had made good use of time and the carefully planned ruse to draw off the Home Fleet's reserves, and by now could be almost anywhere.

The Admiralty was suspicious, too. *Benbecula* had

received more signals giving details of the convoy's course and approximate position. The best Lindsay could do was to keep on a slowly converging track, putting his ship between the convoy and whatever was likely to come down from the north-east.

The ten ships and their escort were now in a position on *Benbecula*'s port bow. It was impossible to fix the exact distance. It could be thirty or one hundred miles away.

He watched the spray lift over the stem and drift lazily towards the revolving screens, saw the quick pinpoint of light from one of the guns as a quarters officer made some frantic inspection in the freezing air. The sea was very much calmer, moving towards them in a great humped swell with only an occasional whitecap to betray its anger. There were several reports of ice, and Lindsay knew the smoother surface was evidence enough that there was some quite near. He half listened to the engines' muted beat and imagined Fraser on his footplate, watching the dials set to the present reduced speed and waiting to throw open the throttles at a second's warning.

He thought too of the girl out there in the blackness. It seemed incredible that it could be so. She was probably fully dressed and in her lifejacket, talking quietly and listening to the unfamiliar orders and sounds around her. One good thing was that the convoy consisted of fast ships. It was not much but. . .

He turned on his chair and rapped, 'Time?'

A signalman said, 'Twenty-one 'undred, sir.'

Feet thumped overhead where Maxwell and his fire control team had been sitting and shivering for several hours.

He darted a quick glance around the bridge. Dancy and Petty Officer Ritchie. Stannard just by the rear door, and the signalmen and messengers arranged at telephones and voicepipes like so many statues. The coxswain was leaning slightly over the wheel, his heavy face set in a frown of concentration as he watched the ticking gyro repeater. The tension was almost a physical thing.

Watertight doors were closed, and apart from the bridge shutters every hatch and scuttle was tightly sealed.

Lindsay felt his stomach contract painfully and realised he had not eaten since breakfast.

The buzz of a telephone was so loud that a seaman gave a yelp of alarm.

Stannard snatched it and then said quickly, 'Signal from convoy escort to Admiralty, sir.' He paused, listening to the voice from behind the W/T office's protective steel plate. *'Am under attack by German raider. One escort in sinking condition. Am engaging.'* He swallowed hard. *'Require immediate repeat immediate assistance.'*

Lindsay did not turn. 'Full ahead both engines.'

Stannard shouted above the jangle of telegraphs. *'Admiralty to* Benbecula, *sir. Act as situation demands. No assistance is available for minimum of twelve hours.'*

Dancy whispered, 'God!'

Another telephone buzzed and Lindsay heard Dancy say, 'Masthead. Yes. Right.' Then he said, 'Gunflashes at Red two-oh.'

The bridge was beginning to vibrate savagely as the revolutions mounted.

Then Stannard again. 'Admiralty have ordered convoy to divide, sir.'

Dancy called, 'Masthead reports that he can see more flashes, sir.'

'Very well.'

Lindsay forced his spine back into the chair, willing his mind to stay clear. The flashes were a guide, but with the low cloud and possibility of ice about it was impossible to gauge the range.

The control speaker intoned, 'We can see the flashes too, sir. No range as yet.'

With the freezing spray splattering over the bridge it

was hardly surprising. Maxwell's spotters probably had their work cut out to keep even the largest lens free of ice.

'Any more news from the escort?'

'No, sir.' Stannard had the handset against his ear.

Lindsay pounded the screen slowly with his gloved fingers. Come on, old girl. *Come on.* He recalled the words from the Admiralty. *Act as situation demands.* Would they have said it if they had known *Benbecula* was so close?

Dancy asked quietly, 'D'you think it's the same one that sank *Loch Glendhu,* sir?' He sounded hoarse.

'Yes. That last effort was just a rehearsal. Maybe this is, too.'

Someone gasped as a bright orange light glowed suddenly in the blackness ahead. It seemed to hang like a tall, brilliant feather of flame, until with equal swiftness it vanished completely.

Stannard said, 'That's one poor bastard done for.'

Maxwell's voice made him look round at the speaker. 'Approximate range is three-double-oh, sir. Bearing Red one-five.'

Lindsay clenched his fingers to steady himself. Fifteen miles. It might as well be double that amount.

Stannard was by his side again. 'We're a lot closer than I calculated, sir.' He seemed to sense Lindsay's despair and added, 'We might still be able to help.'

Another bright flash against the unmoving backcloth. This time it seemed to last for several minutes so that they could see the underbellies of the clouds shining and flickering as if touched by the fires below.

Out there ships were burning and men were dying. Lindsay stared at the shimmering light with sudden anguish. It had been so well planned, with the methodical accuracy of an assassination.

The fire vanished, as if quenched by a single hand.

Lindsay looked away. If she was in that ship, please God let it have been quick. No terror below decks with the ship falling apart around her. No agony of scalding steam, of shell splinters. Only the freezing sea, just for this once being merciful.

Stannard took the handset from a messenger before it had stopped buzzing. 'To us from Admiralty, sir. Convoy has divided. The two personnel ships with the commodore aboard have turned north. The tankers and remaining escort have headed south.' He sounded surprised. 'Enemy has ceased fire.'

Lindsay stood up and walked slowly across the violently shaking gratings. Of course the German had ceased fire. He had destroyed two or more in the convoy. The U-boats would be waiting for the tankers now. The raider could take his time. Follow the two helpless ships as far as the ice, and then. . . .

He swung round, his tone harsh. 'Come to the chart room, Pilot. We'll alter course immediately.'

'Are you going after them, sir?'

Lindsay looked at him. 'All the way.'

Ritchie watched them leave the wheelhouse and then crossed to the gyro, straddling his legs as the ship crashed violently in the heavy swell.

'What d'you think, Swain? Will we make it?'

Jolliffe's face remained frozen in the compass light like a chunk of weatherworn carving. 'I'll tell you one thing, Yeo. If we gets stuck up there in the bleeding ice it'll be like shooting fish in a barrel.'

Dancy heard his words and walked quickly to the forepart of the bridge. He watched the spray rattling against the glass and thought of men like Jolliffe and Ritchie. Professionals, yet they were worried. He gripped the rail and shivered uncontrollably. Knowing he was at last afraid.

———————

Down in the ship's damage control section Goss sat in a steel swivel chair, his hands on his thighs, his head jutting forward as he stared grimly at the illuminated ship's plan on the opposite bulkhead. This compartment had altered very little since her cruising days, and apart from additional titles and new functions, the plan, the various sections throughout the hull had not changed. Coloured lights flickered along the plan showing watertight compartments and bulkheads, stores and holds, the complex maze of passageways and shafts which went into the body of a ship.

The damage control parties had been at their stations for hours, and behind him Goss could hear some of the stokers and seamen chattering together, their voices almost lost in the pounding rumble of engines and the whirr of fans.

In another seat at the far end of the plan sat Chief Petty Officer Archer, his head lolling to the unsteady rolls, his cap tilted to the back of his head as he waited with the others for something to happen.

Goss did not like Archer, and already there had been several flare-ups between them. With Tobey, the ship's boatswain, who had been drafted to *more important duties*, as the dockyard had explained, Goss had got on very well. Not on a sociable level, of course, but professionally, which was all Goss required in any man. Tobey was a company officer, one who had served in the line for many years, most of them in the *Benbecula*. He *knew* the ship, every rivet of her, like his own skin, and had nursed her over the thousands of miles they had steamed together. Being sparing with paint and cleaning gear, avoiding waste in materials by keeping an eagle eye on the seamen to make sure a proper wire splice was used instead of merely signing a chit for a whole new length of it. But at all times he had kept the ship perfect, a credit to the company.

He darted a glance at Archer. He on the other hand was a regular Navy man. He knew nothing of making do with meagre resources, with a clerk in the company office checking every item and expense. He had lived off the taxpayer for too long, and cared nothing for economy. When Goss had got on to him about the constant increase of rust streaks on the superstructure, Archer had merely ordered his men to slop on more paint. Hide it, cover it up, until somebody else made it his business to deal with properly. Someone else, in Archer's view, was the dockyard, any dockyard. He was not concerned.

He sat bolt upright in his chair as the deck and fittings gave a sudden convulsion, and above the engines' confident beat he heard a drawn-out, menacing roar.

A seaman called, 'What was that, Chief?'

Archer looked at Goss, his eyes anxious. 'I'm not sure.'

Goss listened to the sound as it faded and then stopped altogether. 'We must be pushing through some drift ice.'

He licked his lips. The captain must be stark, staring mad to drive the ship like this with ice about.

Archer said quietly, 'Well, I expect they know what they're doin'.' He did not sound very convinced.

A door opened and a seaman staggered into the compartment carrying a huge fanny of cocoa. Feet scraped and mugs clattered as the men hurried to meet him, their concern temporarily forgotten.

Goss glared at the clock. It was six in the morning. Nine hours since the bridge had reported sighting gunflashes and had rung down for full speed. The old *Becky* must have covered nearly a hundred and forty miles in that time, and it was a wonder the boilers hadn't burst under the strain. A further scraping roar echoed around the hull, and he gripped the arms of his seat as he pictured the surging slabs of ice dashing down the ship's flanks, fading into the wash astern.

He could feel his palms sweating, and knew from the stricken silence behind him that the others were watching him.

He said gruffly, 'She can take more than this, so get on with your bloody cocoa!'

Goss tried to shut them all from his mind, close them out, as he often did when he was worried. He thought back to that last cruise, before the war had changed everything. Even by looking at the damage control plan he could bring back some of it. The passengers had often come down here on one of the little conducted tours which had always been so popular. The ladies in the silk dresses, with tanned shoulders, the men in white dinner jackets wafting the scent of rich cigars as they listened to some earnest junior officer explaining the ship's safety arrangements. It had all been a bit of a joke to them, of course. Like the boat drill, with the stewards taking as many liberties as they dared when they *assisted* some of the younger women with their lifejackets. But Goss had never looked on it as anything but deadly serious. He had been in one ship when fire had broken out and the lifeboats had been lowered with minutes to spare. An ugly episode. He looked along the plan, his eyes dark. In those days, of course, one of the main points to be watched was the watertight door system. It did not actually *say* anything about it on the plan, but Goss had known that if *Benbecula* had begun to sink it would have been his job to ensure the emigrants and other poorer passengers were not released by his system of doors until all the first class had been cleared into the boats. He had always disliked the tours down here, just in case some clever bastard had noticed the obvious.

He felt the chairback pushing against his spine and saw a pencil begin to roll rapidly from the table. The helm had gone over, and fast. He thrust himself forward and gripped the table, as with a grinding vibration more ice came roaring against the ship's side. But this time it did not pass so quickly. Even as he staggered to his feet the whole compartment gave a tremendous lurch, so that men fell yelling and cursing amidst the widening stain of spilled cocoa. An overhead light flickered and went out, and flecks of paint chippings floated down like a toy snowstorm. The deck shook once more and then the noise subsided as before.

But Goss was already reaching for his array of buttons, his eyes fixed on the neatly worded compartment on the port side where a red emergency bulb had begun to flash.

'Pumps! Come on, jump to it!' He snatched up a telephone and shouted, 'Give me the bridge.' He saw Archer and a mechanic fumbling with the pump controls and added violently, 'Yes, the *bridge,* you bloody idiot!'

Benbecula had hit hard and was flooding. It was all he knew. All he cared about.

'Bridge? Give me the captain!'

Lindsay watched the foreshortened figures of some seamen slipping and sliding across the forward well deck. Because of the thin coating of ice their black oilskins made them stand out like so many scurrying beetles as they began work with their hammers to clear the wash ports and scuppers before the task became impossible.

Dancy was saying, 'Masthead? Yes, you can be relieved now.'

Lindsay thought briefly of the masthead lookout. Even with his electric heater he had to be relieved every hour if he was to keep his circulation going. He peered at his luminous watch. Six o'clock. It did not seem possible they had been charging through the darkness for so many hours. He walked to the port side to watch as more fragments of broken ice materialised out of the black water and swirled playfully along the side. Nothing dangerous, in fact it was unavoidable. It looked more menacing than it was, and in the darkness gave an impression of great speed and size.

Stannard said, 'We should sight something soon.' But nobody answered.

Hardly anyone had said much as hour by hour the ship

had pounded into the night. The noise and violent shaking had thrown most of them inwards on their own defences, and even the men with cocoa and huge chunky sandwiches who had come and gone throughout the agony of waiting had passed without more than a quick, anxious word.

Stannard said, 'I'd like to go and check the chart again, sir.'

'Yes.' Lindsay thrust his hands into his pockets, feeling the gratings under his sea boots jerking as if being pounded by unseen hammers. 'Do that.'

Maybe the German had indeed turned away and run for base. He might think the Home Fleet was better deployed than it was, and feared a quick and overwhelming reprisal. And where were the two ships?

A telephone buzzed and a messenger said urgently, 'It's the doctor, sir.'

Lindsay tore his mind from the mental picture of the chart, the course which he and Stannard had evolved to contact the two ships.

'What does *he* want?'

The seaman, hidden in the darkness, answered, 'He asked to speak with you, sir.'

Lindsay swore silently and groped his way across the deck. It was slippery from the constant comings and goings of slushy boots, and added to the streaming condensation from deckhead and sides it filled the bridge with an unhealthy, clinging humidity.

He snatched the handset. 'Captain. Can't it wait?'

Boase sounded edgy. 'Sorry, sir. It's Lieutenant Aikman. He's locked himself in his cabin. One of my S.B.A.'s tried to make him open the door. I think he's upset.'

'*Upset?*' The word hung in the air like one additional mockery. 'What do you want me to do, for God's sake?' Lindsay made an effort to steady his voice. 'Do you really think he's in trouble?'

Boase replied, 'Yes, sir.'

As Lindsay stood with the telephone to his ear, his eyes staring at Ritchie's shadowy outline by the nearest window, the hands of the bulkhead clock showed eight minutes past six.

At that precise moment in time several small incidents were happening simultaneously. Small, but together they amounted to quite a lot.

Able Seaman Laker, known to his messmates as Dracula because of his large protruding teeth, was just being relieved from the crow's-nest by a seaman called Phelps. As they clung together on the swaying iron gratings outside the pod Laker was shouting in the other man's ear about the stupid, bloody maniacs who had fitted such a piddling little heater for the lookout's survival. Neither of them was paying much attention to the sea beyond the bows.

On the forward well deck another seaman fell from a bollard and slithered like a great black crab across the ice and came up with a thud against a hatch coaming, dropping his hammer and yelling the most obscene word he could think of at such short notice.

The lookouts on Numbers One and Two guns turned to watch him, drawing comfort from the man's clumsy efforts to regain his feet, while the rest of the deck party paused to enjoy the spectacle as well.

On the bridge Dancy was remembering Aikman's stricken voice, his pathetic self-defence under Stannard's anger and the captain's questioning. He had not heard what Boase was saying, but he could guess. He did not know Aikman very well, but realised probably better than the others that he was, like himself, acting a part which had suddenly got beyond him. He turned to peer at Lindsay's vague outline at the rear of the bridge, wondering what it was Aikman had done to excite Boase and make him risk disturbing the captain.

All small incidents, but as Dancy turned once more to his clearview screen he saw in that instant what a momentary lack of vigilance had created. Looming out of the darkness was a solid wedge of ice. In his imagination he had often pictured icebergs as towering and majestic, like white cathedrals, and for several more seconds he was totally incapable of speech or movement.

Then he yelled, 'Hard astarboard!' He heard the wheel going over, the sudden gasps of alarm, and then added wildly, 'Ice! Dead ahead!'

Lindsay dropped the telephone and hurled himself towards the screen, his voice sharp but level as he shouted, 'Belay that! Wheel amidships! Both engines *full astern!*'

Ignoring the clang of telegraphs, the violent response of reversed screws and the clamour of voices from all sides he gripped the rail and stared fixedly at the oncoming wedge of ice. It was difficult to estimate the size of it. It was not very high, probably about ten feet, and some eighty feet from end to end. Against the dark backcloth of sea and clouds it appeared enveloped in vapour, like ice emerging from a giant refrigerator. He felt the engines shaking and pounding in growing strength to stop the ship's onward dash, and found himself counting seconds as the distance continued to shorten. Dancy should not have put the helm over. If the ship had hit an ice ledge with her bilge it would slit her open like one huge can. But if he had not even seen it the ship would have smashed into it at full speed, with terrible results.

Stannard came running across the bridge, then stood stockstill beside him, his voice strangled as he said, 'We're going to strike, by Jesus!'

It seemed to take an eternity for the ice to reach them. The engines were slowing them down, dragging like great anchors so that the bow wave was falling away even as the ice became suddenly stark and very close, the jagged crest of it looming past the port bow as if drawn by a hawser.

The crash, when it came, was muted, but the sensation

transmitted itself from the keel to the flesh and bones of every man aboard.

The ice turned slowly as the ship surged against it, making a kind of clumsy pirouette with pieces breaking adrift and sliding haphazardly into the dwindling bow wave.

'Stop engines!'

Lindsay ran to the port door and tugged it open. As he hurried to the unprotected wing he felt the wind across his face like a whip, and under his gloved hands the rail was like polished glass. He watched the ice moving away while the ship idled forward sluggishly, the deck under his feet very still, as if the ship herself was holding her breath, feeling her hurt.

There was more ice nearby but just small fragments as before. It was a piece of bad luck which had brought that one heavy slab across their path without anybody sighting it.

Stannard called, 'First lieutenant's on the phone, sir.'

Lindsay strode into the bridge again, feeling the heated air enclosing him like a damp towel.

Goss was very brief. 'Flooding in Number Two hold, sir. I've got the pumps working on it, and I'm waiting for a report from the boiler room. Their main bulkhead is right against that hold.' He paused and then said thickly, 'I knew something like this would happen.'

'Any casualties?'

'I don't know yet,' The question seemed to catch Goss off guard.

'Well, get on with it and let me know.' He replaced the handset very slowly.

He knew what Goss was thinking. What most of the others were probably thinking, too. That their captain was still unfit for command. Even this one. Especially this one. He felt the pain and despair crowding his brain like blood and he had to turn away from the others, even though they could not see his face.

Jolliffe said, 'We're drifting, sir. Ship's head is now three-three-zero.'

Stannard said quickly, 'Very well, Cox'n.'

A messenger called, 'Engine room reports no damage, sir.' He gulped. 'To the bulkhead, I mean, sir.'

Stannard remarked softly, 'Once saw a great berg down off South Georgia. Big as Sydney bridge it was, and all covered with little penguins.'

Lindsay said flatly, 'Penguins?' He did not even know he had spoken.

'Yes. There were these small killer whales about, you see, and the penguins would push one of their cobbers off the berg every so often as a safety measure. If the little chap survived they all dived in. If he was eaten they'd just wait there like a lot of unemployed waiters and stand around a while longer before they pushed another one over the edge.'

Nobody laughed.

Lindsay thought suddenly of Aikman, and was about to tell Stannard to call up the doctor when Ritchie snapped, 'Listen! I 'eard a ship's siren!'

Once more Lindsay was out in the freezing air, as with Ritchie and Stannard he blundered through the opposite door and on to the starboard wing.

'And there's another!' Ritchie was peering over the wing like a terrier at a rabbit hole.

Stannard said quickly, 'Same ship.' He too was bending his head and listening intently. 'When I saw those penguins I was doing a spell as third officer in a whale factory ship. Some masters used their sirens to estimate the closeness of heavy ice. Bounce back the echoes, so to speak.'

Lindsay heard it again. Mournful and incredibly loud in the crisp air. The echo threw back its reply some ten seconds later.

Dancy joined them by the screen. 'I——I'm sorry about that helm order, sir. I lost my head.'

Lindsay did not take his eyes from the bearing of the siren. 'You were quite alone at that moment, Sub.' He heard Dancy's breathing, knew how he was suffering. 'And if we had not stopped the engines we would have drowned out that siren.'

'Damage control says the pumps are holding the intake, sir. No apparent danger to boiler room bulkhead.' The seaman waited, gasping in the cold air. 'And only one casualty. Man on A deck broke his wrist.'

· Lindsay nodded. 'Good.' He tried to rub the ice from the gyro repeater below the screen but it was thick like a Christmas cake. 'We'll try and close on that siren, Pilot. Warn control in case of tricks. And we'll have some extra lookouts on the boat deck.'

Stannard was listening to his voice when his face suddenly lit up in a violent red flash. The savage crash of gunfire echoed across the water, lighting up the scattered patches of ice, painting them with scarlet and yellow as again and again the guns tore into the darkness, blasting it aside in short, violent cameos.

Lindsay dashed through the open door, his glasses banging against his chest as he shouted, 'Half ahead together!' Around him men were slamming the new steel shutters, and he added, 'Leave the centre one!' As he cranked it open he felt the air clawing his face and lips, heard the sudden surge of power from the engines as once more the ship began to push forward.

'Steer for the flashes, Cox'n!'

He tensed as a ball of fire exploded and then fanned out to reveal the outline and angle of a ship. She was less than two miles away, her upper deck and superstructure burning fiercely in a dozen places. There was ice all around her, small fragments and heavier, more jagged prongs which seemed to be enclosing her like a trap. Another ripple of flashes came from her opposite beam, and Lindsay saw the telltale waterspouts shooting skywards and one more bright explosion below her bridge.

The siren was bellowing continuously now, with probably a dead man's hand dragging on the lanyard, but as the *Benbecula* gathered way Lindsay thought it sounded like a beast dying in agony.

Crisp and detached above the din he heard a metallic voice intone, 'Control to all guns. Semi-armour-piercing, load, load, load.'

More thuds and clicks below the bridge, and somewhere a voice yelling orders, shrill and momentarily out of control.

'Target bears Green two-oh. Range oh-five-oh.'

Lindsay raised his glasses as Maxwell's voice continued to pass his information over the speaker. Five thousand yards. Maxwell's spotters had done well to estimate the range on the flashes alone.

'Port ten.' He watched the ticking gyro. 'Midships. Steady.'

Jolliffe replied heavily, 'Steady, sir. Three-one-zero.'

Almost to himself Lindsay murmured, 'That'll give the marines a chance to get on target, too.'

More flashes blasted the darkness aside and joined with those already blazing on the helpless ship. He could see her twin funnels, the great pieces of wreckage falling into the fires and throwing fountains of sparks towards the clouds. Not long now.

To Dancy he snapped, 'Pass the word to prepare that signal for transmission.'

Stannard said thickly, 'Aikman's got the code books, sir.'

Lindsay kept his glasses trained on the other ship. Was it a trick from the reflected fires, or was she starting to settle down?

He said harshly, 'Tell the W/T office to send it plain language. What the hell does it matter now?'

Stannard nodded and handed his pad to a messenger. 'Give this position to the P.O. Tel. He knows what to do.'

Maxwell's voice again. 'Starboard battery stand by.'

Lindsay lowered his glasses. 'Open fire.'

Maxwell waited until the hidden raider fired again and then pressed his button. The bells at each mounting had not rung for more than a split second before all three starboard guns roared out together, their long tongues flashing above the wash alongside.

Lindsay held his breath and counted. He shut out the bellowed commands, the click of breech blocks and the chorus of voices on the intercom. Someone at the Admiralty would be listening to all this, he thought vaguely. They would be plotting Stannard's position and rousing out some senior officers from their camp beds in the cellars. *From* Benbecula *to Admiralty. Have sighted enemy raider. Am engaging.*

Not much of an epitaph. But it might be remembered.

'Up five hundred. Shoot!'

Again the guns belched fire and smoke, the bridge jerking violently as the shock made the steel quake as if from hitting another berg.

'The other ship's going down, sir!' Dancy was shouting, his voice very loud after the crash of gunfire.

'Yes.'

Lindsay watched rigidly as the stricken ship began to tilt over towards him. She must have been hit badly, deep inside the hull, and the fires which he had imagined to have begun on her superstructure had in fact surged right up through several decks. He could see the gaping holes, angry red, the criss-cross of broken frames and fallen masts, and found himself praying there was nobody left to die in such horror.

More distant flashes, and this time he heard the shells pass overhead almost gently, the high trajectory making them whisper like birds on the wing.

Maxwell's bells tinkled again, and seconds later Lindsay heard him shout, 'One hit!'

A fire glowed beyond the sinking ship, just long enough for Maxwell's guns to get off another round each.

Then it died, and Lindsay guessed the enemy had turned end on, either to close with this impudent attacker or to run, as before.

He would have picked up the short signal and would probably be wondering what sort of ship he was tackling. Benbecula's name was not on the general list, as far as he knew, and it might take the German time to realise what was happening.

'Enemy has ceased fire, sir.' Maxwell seemed out of breath.

'Very well.' Lindsay watched the dark line of the other ship's hull getting closer and closer to the sea. 'Tell Number One to prepare rafts for lowering.'

Dancy asked, 'Will we stop, sir?'

Lindsay rubbed his eyes and then raised the glasses again. 'Not yet.'

A sullen explosion threw more wreckage over the other ship's side, and he imagined he could see a flashlight moving aft by her poop. One lonely survivor, he thought dully.

'Slow ahead together.' He heard men pounding along the boat deck. 'Starboard fifteen.' He watched the steam rising like a curtain, and knew the sea was exploring the damage, quenching the fires too late.

As if from a great distance he heard Stannard say, 'We *can't* stop yet, Sub. We'd be sitting ducks if that bastard is still about.'

'Yes, I understand.' But from his tone it was obvious Dancy did not. Like the others, he was probably thinking of the people who were trying to escape the flames only to face being frozen to death in minutes.

Lindsay climbed on to his chair and stared through the slit in the steel shutter. The slit was glowing red from the other ship's fires, like a peephole in a furnace door. Like a fragment of hell.

He looked at the gyro repeater again. 'Midships.'

They had almost crossed the ship's stern when with a

great roar of inrushing water she turned over and dived, the fire vanishing and plunging the sea once more into darkness.

Lindsay looked at his watch. Seven fifteen.

'Prepare both motor boats for lowering, Pilot. Each will tow a raft. Number One will know what to do.'

'I can see some red lights on the starboard beam, sir.' Ritchie lowered his telescope. 'Might be in time for 'em.'

'Yes.'

Lindsay heard the rumble of power-operated davits, the protesting squeaks from the falls as the two motor boats jerked down the ship's side. If their motors would start under these conditions it would be a miracle.

'Ready, sir.'

'Stop engines.'

Another set of sounds as the boats were slipped and took the released rafts in tow. Both motors were working, and Lindsay thanked God for an engineer like Fraser who kept an eye on such details.

'Sky's a bit brighter, sir.' Stannard looked at Lindsay's unmoving outline against the shutter.

The enemy had gone. Lindsay did not know how he could be sure, but he was. Slipped away again. Just like that last time. Leaving death in his wake. Blood on the water.

He stood up suddenly. 'Yeoman, use the big searchlight. Tell the gunnery officer to expect an attack, but we'll risk it.'

He walked to the door and then out on to the open wing. The searchlight's glacier blue beam licked out from the upper bridge like something solid, and as it fanned down across the heaving water where the two boats and their tows stood out like bright toys, he saw the endless litter of flotsam and charred wreckage. Chairs and broken crates, empty liferafts and pieces of canvas. Here and there a body floated, either spreadeagled face down in the water or bobbing in a lifejacket, its eyes like small stones as the beam swept low overhead.

There was a stench of oil and burned paint, and as the boats moved apart to begin a closer search Lindsay stood and waited, his body almost frozen with cold, but unable to move.

Stannard strode on to the gratings and said, 'The first lieutenant has reported that Aikman has tried to kill himself. Cut his wrists with some scissors. But he's still alive, sir.' He stared past Lindsay as a boat stopped to pull someone aboard.

Lindsay nodded. 'He couldn't even do that properly, could he?'

He too was watching the motor boat as it gathered way again towards another dark clump in the water. The other personnel ship was probably further to the northwest, waiting for some light before attempting to brave the ice and the possibility of a new attack. She would have seen the gunfire, and may have thought it was a second enemy ship making the assault.

A torch stabbed across the water and Ritchie said, 'One boat 'as got eleven survivors, sir.' He turned as the second boat's light winked over the lazy swell. 'She's got eighteen, though Gawd knows 'ow she's managed to cram 'em in.'

Lindsay wanted to ask him to call up the boats, to ask what was uppermost in his mind. But he was afraid. Afraid that by showing his fear he might make it happen. She could be in the other ship. Frightened but safe. Safe.

The search continued for a full hour. Round and round, in and out of the great oil stain and its attendant corpses and fragments.

'Recall the boats.' Lindsay wiped the ice rime from his eyebrows, felt the pain of cramp in his legs and hands. 'Tell the sickbay to be ready.'

Entry ports in the hull clanged open and ready hands were waiting to sway the first survivors inboard.

Goss came to the bridge and said, 'Boats secured, sir.

I've had to abandon the two rafts. They're thick with ice. I'd never get them hoisted.' He watched Lindsay and then added, 'There are five women amongst 'em. I don't know if they'll survive after this.'

Lindsay gripped the screen. So the Atlantic had cheated him after all. He said, 'Take over the con and get under way. I'm going below.'

By the time he reached the sickbay he was almost running, and as he stumbled past huddled figures cloaked in blankets, the busy sickberth attendants, he saw a young girl sitting on a chair, hair black with oil, her uniform scorched as if by a hot iron, her face a mass of burns.

Boase looked across her head and said tersely, 'We'll do our best, sir.'

Lindsay ignored him, his face frozen like a mask as he stared around at the scene of pain and survival. One body lay by the door covered in a blanket. One bare foot was thrust into the harsh light, and with something like madness Lindsay pulled the covering from the girl's face. She was very young, her features pinched tight with cold, captured at the moment of death. The sea water had frozen around her mouth and eyes so that she seemed to be crying even now. He covered her face, and after a small hesitation pulled the blanket over the protruding foot. As his fingers touched it he felt the contact like ice itself.

Without another word he turned and began the long climb to the bridge. The engines were pounding again, leaving the fragments floating and bobbing astern in their wake. She was with them. Back there in the Atlantic. Alone.

Take care, she had said. Will see you in Eden.

He reached the bridge and said, 'Fall out action stations and secure.' He looked at Stannard. 'We will steer north-east for an hour and see what happens.'

Stannard asked quietly, 'What about Aikman, sir?'

Lindsay did not hear him. 'Take over, Number One. I'm going below for half an hour.' He left without another word.

Goss grunted and walked to the empty chair. Stannard sighed and turned towards his chart room.

Only Ritchie knew what was wrong with the captain. Jupp had explained. Not that it helped to know about it, Ritchie thought.

10 Christmas leave

Lindsay removed his cap and tucked it beneath his arm as he stepped into Boase's sickbay. A week had passed since the survivors had been pulled aboard, and in that time the doctor and his staff had done wonders. Three of the survivors had died of their injuries and two more were still dangerously ill, but under the circumstances it was a miracle any had endured the fires and the freezing cold.

Boase was washing his hands, and hurried across when he saw Lindsay. He looked very tired but managed to smile and say, 'Nice of you to look in, sir.' He eyed Lindsay's strained features and added, 'Wouldn't do you any harm to rest for a bit.'

Lindsay looked around the long sickbay. The neat white cots, an air of sterile efficiency which he had always hated. The five girls had survived, and that was the biggest surprise of all. Maybe they were tougher than men after all, he thought wearily. Four of them were sitting in chairs, watching him now, dressed in a colourful collection of clothing which the ship's company had gathered. The fifth Wren was in a cot, her burned face hidden in bandages, her hands outstretched to the sides of the blankets as if to steady herself. She had nice hands, small and well shaped. Boase had told him she cried a lot when the others were asleep, fearful of what her face would be like when the bandages came off.

All told there were only thirty survivors. From what he had gleaned Lindsay had discovered the ship had carried a company of one hundred and fifty as well as some forty Wrens en route for Canada.

He cleared his throat. 'As you know, we have been ordered to proceed direct to Liverpool, where you will be landed and my ship can receive repairs.'

Lindsay looked slowly around the watching faces. The Wrens, their eyes just a bit too bright. Holding back the shock which would grow and sharpen as thankfulness for survival gave way to bitter memories for those who had died. The men, young and old alike, some of whom had probably been bombed or torpedoed already in the war, watching him, recalling their own moments, like the ones when a motor boat had come out of the searchlight's great beam to snatch them to safety.

He continued, 'I have just received another signal from the Admiralty. The Japanese have invaded Malaya, and yesterday morning carried out an air attack on Pearl Harbour in the Pacific.' He tried to smile as they stared at each other. 'So the Americans are in the war with us. We're not alone any more.'

He nodded to Boase. 'I'll leave you in peace now.'

Lindsay did not even know why he had come down to tell them the news. Boase could have done it. It was just as if he was still torturing himself by wanting to be near someone who had been with Eve when she had died. What did Malaya and Pearl Harbour mean to them at this moment anyway? The sea was all they understood now. During the night, before sleep relieved them, they would be thinking of it just beyond the sides of the hull. Waiting.

He recalled the atmosphere in the sickbay when *Benbecula* had sighted the second personnel ship two days after the attack. She had been edging through some drift ice, and her relief at seeing *Benbecula*'s recognition signals had been obvious to everyone aboard. Except here, in the sickbay. Was it that they felt cheated? Did they think it so cruelly unfair that their friends had been slaughtered while the other ship had escaped with little more than a bad scare? It was hard to tell.

The other ship had been ordered to Iceland and would

be in Reykjavik by now with another escort. *Benbecula* had not been short of company either. As she turned and steamed south once more she had been watched by two long-range aircraft, as well as a destroyer on the far horizon. But it was all too late. And the evidence of it lay and sat around him listening to him as he said, 'And remember, you'll all be having Christmas at home.' He turned to leave, the words coming back to mock him like a taunt. Christmas at home.

Something plucked at his jacket and when he looked down he saw it was the Wren's hand, the girl with the burned face.

As he bent over the cot he heard her say, 'Thank you for coming for us.' He took her hand in his. It felt hot. She said, 'I saw you when I was brought here. Just a few seconds——'

Boase shook his head. 'That's enough talking.'

But her voice had broken Lindsay's careful guard like a dam bursting. Still holding her hand he asked gently, 'Did you know Wren Collins? Eve Collins?'

'I think so. I think I saw her by the lifeboats when——' She could not go on.

Lindsay released her hand and said, 'Try and sleep.' Then he swung round and hurried from the sickbay with its clean, pure smells and shocked minds.

He found Goss and Fraser waiting for him outside his day cabin. 'Sorry you were kept so long.' He could not look at them. 'I just wanted to go over the docking arrangements at Liverpool.' He remembered the other thing and added quietly, 'By the way, Number One, you told me when I took command that one of *Benbecula*'s sister ships was an A.M.C. in the Far East.'

Goss watched him closely. 'The old *Barra*, sir. That's right.'

'Well, I'm afraid she's been sunk by Jap bombers off Kuantan.'

He saw Goss's face crumple and then return swiftly to

the usual grim mask. 'That's bad news, sir.' It was all he said.

Lindsay could feel the agony inside his skull crushing his mind so that he wanted to leave the others and hide in his sleeping cabin.

In a toneless voice he said, 'Right then, we'll start by discussing the fuel and ammunition. We must arrange to lighten ship as soon as we pick up the tugs.'

Fraser took out his notebook but kept his eyes on Lindsay's face. You poor bastard, he thought. You keep fighting it and it's tearing you apart. How much more can you take?

Goss was thinking about the *Barra*. He had been third officer in her so many years back. Her picture hung in his cabin beside all the others. Now she was gone. He looked desperately around the cabin. *Benbecula* could go like that. In the twinkling of an eye. Nothing.

Lindsay was saying, 'And there's the matter of leave. We should get both watches away for Christmas with any luck.'

Goss said, 'I'd like to stay aboard, sir.'

Fraser looked at him. Oh God. Not you, too.

Lindsay made a note on his pad. 'Right then. Now about Number Two hold——'

In his pantry Jupp listened to the muted conversation and walked to a scuttle. Below on the promenade deck he saw a figure in a duffel coat walking slowly aft. He knew from the bandaged wrists it was Lieutenant Aikman. He saw two seamen turn to watch Aikman as he shambled unseeingly past them, and wondered how he would be able to survive after this.

He returned to his coffee pot and hoped Fraser at least would remain and talk with the captain. He had seen what the girl's death was doing to Lindsay and knew he must not be left alone. He had heard him whenever he had turned into his bunk, which was not often. Fighting his nightmares and calling her name like a lost soul in hell.

Whenever he was alone Lindsay seemed to be searching through his confidential books and intelligence logs, totally absorbed, his eyes filled with determination, the like of which Jupp had never seen.

Maybe when the ship was in dock the captain would find some comfort at home. He frowned as he recalled hearing that Lindsay had no proper home to go to.

The bell rang, and with a flourish he picked up his coffee pot and thrust open the pantry door. Something might turn up. And until it did, Jupp would make sure Lindsay would have his help, just as long as he needed it.

———————

The wardroom stove glowed cheerfully across the legs of the *Benbecula*'s officers as they waited for the stewards to open the bar. The ship felt rigidly still, for she was moored to a wharf awaiting the next move to dry dock, and some of the officers glanced repeatedly through the rain-dashed scuttles as if unable to accept the fact. Murky grey buildings, motionless in the rain, instead of a tossing wilderness of angry wave crests. Tall cranes and gantrys and the masts of other ships, instead of loneliness and complete isolation.

Dancy listened to the clink of glasses and squeak of bolts as the stewards opened their pantry hatch, and tried to think of some special, extravagant drink to mark his return to the safety of harbour. While the ship had crept through the morning drizzle and mist and tugs had snorted and puffed importantly abeam, he had watched the great sprawling mass of Liverpool opening up before him with something like wonder. There had been little for him to do at the time so he had been able to let his ready imagination encompass everything he saw and felt. Relief, sadness, excitement, it had all been there, as it was now. Around him on the bridge he had watched his companions, faces and voices who had become real and very close to him. Stannard at the gyro taking careful, unhurried fixes while the ship glided up channel. Ritchie and his signalmen peering through their glasses at the diamond-bright lamps which winked from the shore. Down on the forecastle he had seen Goss waving his arms as he strode amongst the busy seamen at the wires and fenders, while from the upper bridge the pipes shrilled and twittered in salute to passing or anchored warships. Cruisers and sturdy escort vessels. Destroyers and stumpy corvettes, all showing marks of the Atlantic weather, the seasoned look of experienced and hard-used warriors.

Lindsay had been sitting in his chair for most of the time. He had seemed very remote, even aloof whenever someone had attempted to make personal contact with him. But Dancy had watched him, nevertheless, and had tried to draw from him some of the strength he seemed to give. He had seen the twin towers of the Royal Liver building loom above the mist and had felt the infectious excitement and purpose of this great port. Headquarters of Western Approaches Command, it was also one of the main doors through which came the very life blood of a country at war.

Stannard crossed to his side and held his hands above the glowing stove. 'Well, Sub, we've made it. All snug and safe. Until the next bloody move!'

He sounded relaxed, and Dancy envied him for it. Stannard was really important, a man who could work out a position when there was neither star nor sun to help him. When the deck was trying to stand on end while he plotted and brooded over his charts and instruments.

A steward said, 'Orders please, gentlemen.'

Dancy and Stannard stood back to wait for the first rush to subside.

'What do you think about the Japs, Pilot?'

Stannard looked at him thoughtfully. 'God knows. We were always told that if Malaya or Singapore were attacked the enemy would come from the south.' He shrugged. 'Still, I. guess they've got it in hand by now. When I think of the places I've been out East, it makes me puke to picture those little yellow bastards clumping all over them.'

Then he brightened and added, 'Now, about that drink. Have it on me.'

Dancy frowned. 'A brandy and gin.'

Stannard stared at him. *'Mixed?'*

'Mixed.'

'You greedy bastard!' Stannard waved to a harassed steward. 'I hope it chokes you!'

The door banged open and Goss marched towards the fire.

Stannard asked, 'How about joining us, Number One?'

Goss did not seem to hear. Turning his back to the fire he barked, 'Just pipe down a minute, will you!'

They all paused to look at him, suddenly aware of the harshness in his tone.

Goss said, 'We've just had news from the Far East. The Japs are still advancing south into Malaya.' He swallowed hard. 'And they've sunk the *Prince of Wales* and *Repulse*.' He did not seem able to believe his own voice. 'Both of 'em. In less than an hour!'

'Jesus.' Stannard stared at Dancy. 'Those two great ships. How the hell *could* they wipe them out so easily?'

Goss was staring into space. 'They had no air cover and were overwhelmed by enemy bombers.'

'It's getting worse.' Stannard downed his drink in one swallow. 'I thought it would have been a fleet action at least.' He sounded angry. 'What's the matter with our blokes out there? No air cover, they must be raving bloody mad!'

Goss continued, 'There'll be leave for three weeks. If you'll all see Lieutenant Barker about your ration cards and travel warrants after lunch we can get it sorted out without wasting any more time.'

Dancy looked at his glass. Goss's news had left him confused and feeling vaguely cheated. They had done so much, or so it had seemed. The quick, savage gunfire in the darkness, the handful of gasping, oil-sodden survivors, it had all been part of something special. The brief announcement about the two great capital ships sunk in some far off, unknown sea had changed it in an instant. That was the real war, the swift changing balance of sea power which could and might bring down a country, a way of life for millions of people. It made his own part in things appear small and unimportant.

Stannard said quietly, 'Drink that muck, Sub. I think I feel like getting stoned.'

Dancy touched the drink with his tongue. It tasted like paraffin.

Stannard was saying, 'My brother's out there in an Aussie battalion.' He looked away. 'To think his life depends on those stupid Pommie brasshats!' He faced Dancy and smiled. 'Sorry about that. You're quite a nice Pommie, as it happens.'

Dancy watched him worriedly. 'Thanks.'

Then he said quickly, 'What about coming home with me, Pilot? My people would love to fuss over you. Christmas is pretty quiet but——' He hesitated, realising what he had done. All his carefully built up disguise as the intrepid writer would be blown to ashes when Stannard met his parents.

Stannard eyed him gravely. 'No can do, Sub.' He was thinking of the girl he had met on his last leave in London. She had a small flat in Paddington. He would spend his leave with her. Have one wild party and make it last until the leave was over. He added, 'But thanks all the same. Maybe next time, huh?'

Dancy nodded, relieved and saddened at the same time. He could imagine what Stannard had in mind. And he thought of his own house. The Christmas decorations, his mother complaining about rations, his father telling him how the war should be waged, where the government were going wrong.

He said, 'Maybe we could meet up somewhere? Just for a drink or something.'

'Yeh, why not.' Stannard grinned lazily. 'I'll give you a shout on the blower when I get fixed up.' She would probably have forgotten him by now anyway. But she was a real beaut. Long auburn hair, and a body which seemed to enfold a man like silk.

A steward called, 'Ambulances 'ave arrived to take your people away, sir.' He waited until Boase had extracted himself from the group by the bar. 'The P.M.O. is comin' aboard.'

Dancy said, 'Let's go and see them leave, Pilot.'

Stannard nodded. 'I was feeling very sorry for myself just now.' He nodded again. 'We'll go and cheer them up a bit, eh?'

They grabbed their caps and hurried to the promenade deck. There were plenty of the ship's company with the same idea, Dancy noticed. A ragged cheer greeted the first of the survivors, as on stretchers or walking with white-coated attendants from the base hospital they started to move towards the gangway.

Stannard muttered quietly, 'Oh Jesus, there's Aikman.'

Dancy turned and saw the lieutenant walking slowly along the deck, a suitcase in his hand, a sickberth petty officer following him at a discreet distance.

Stannard bit his lip. Aikman was going ashore for observation. That was typical of Lindsay, he thought. Most other skippers would have slapped him under arrest to await court-martial for negligence and God knows what else. But Lindsay seemed to realise Aikman could not be punished more than he was already. He would probably be kept in hospital and then quietly dropped. Kicked out. Forgotten.

He said impulsively, 'Poor bastard.'

Dancy looked at him, recalling Stannard's bitter anger

on the bridge. His contempt for Aikman's pathetic efforts to cover his mistake.

Stannard strode forward and asked, 'You off then?'

Aikman stopped as if he had been struck. When he turned his face was very pale, his eyes shadowed by dark rings, like a man under drugs.

He said thickly, 'Yes. I——I'm not sure quite what——' He could not go on.

Dancy watched Stannard, wondering what he would say next. Aikman looked terrible, far worse than immediately after he had tried to kill himself. He had remained in his cabin, one of Boase's S.B.A.'s with him the whole time. Now he was slipping away, with not even a word from the other officers.

Stannard thrust out his hand and said quietly, 'Good luck, mate. I'm sorry about what happened.' He turned away as if to watch the ambulances on the jetty. 'Could have been any one of us.'

Aikman seized his hand and said brokenly, 'But it wasn't. It was me.'

There were tears running down his cheeks, and the petty officer said cheerfully, 'Come along, sir, we don't want to keep 'em all waiting, now do we?'

Dancy looked at Stannard. It was like hearing a teacher speaking to a backward child. He said quickly, 'So long, sir.' Then he saluted and watched Aikman being led down the gangway and into one of the ambulances.

Stannard said, 'When you're in a war you think sometimes you might get bloody killed or have a bit shot out of yourself.' He shook his head as they turned back towards the wardroom. 'You never think about this side of it.'

———

Lindsay's cabin was filled with swirling tobacco smoke and the smell of whisky. The dockyard officials in their blue serge suits, some officers from the base engineering department, a lieutenant of the intelligence section, there seemed to be an endless array of alien faces.

He held a match to his pipe and watched the flame quivering above the bowl. It was shaking badly, and he had to force himself to hold it still. He saw Fraser talking with another engineer and knew from the slur in his voice he was halfway to being drunk. Lindsay had already had more drinks than he could remember yet felt ice-cold sober. He did not even feel tired any more, just numb. Empty of anything which he could recognise.

Lindsay had been down to see the survivors over the side and had spoken to most of them. A handshake here, a quick thumbs-up there. They had all responded by playing their allotted roles. It was the unspoken word and unmade gesture which had moved him. The glances from some of the Wrens as they had looked down at the solid, unmoving jetty. The wounded sailor on a stretcher who had looked up at the grey sky and had stared at it with something like awe. And the girl with the bandaged face who had been carried by two S.B.A.'s on a kind of chair over the gangway with all the others.

It was almost as if she had sensed Lindsay was there, and had reached out to hold his hand. Nothing more. Just a quick contact, not even a squeeze, but it had told him so much.

Now they were all gone and the old ship was waiting patiently for the next phase to begin. Repairs and all the indignities of dry dock. Then back again. To the Atlantic.

If Goss had not been so determined to stay with the ship he knew he would have done so. He did not want to go anywhere else. Not to spend his leave in some hotel with all its Christmas noise and urgent gaiety. He would have to go somewhere. He thought of Aikman's face as he had explained what was arranged for him. But you never knew with men like Aikman. He might go under completely. He could just as easily grow a new outer covering and start all over again. Given time, he might even believe he had been blameless, that everyone else had caused the mistake. Lindsay hoped it would be the latter. Aikman was too weak and insecure to carry the brand entirely for what had happened.

He realised with a start that the earnest young lieutenant from Intelligence was speaking to him.

'I shall make a *careful* study of all your considerations, sir.' He nodded gravely. 'I feel sure that something very useful may come of them.'

Lindsay regarded him evenly. The lieutenant was a temporary officer with a beautifully cut uniform and perfect manners. Perhaps a journalist in peacetime who had found his niche on the staff. He certainly appeared to be enjoying his role. He even spoke with a conspiratorial confidence, like some master-spy in a pre-war film.

Lindsay found himself wondering why he had bothered to compile such a lengthy report. Probably to retain his own sanity. He knew he needed some new purpose if he was to keep from cracking apart. And if hatred was a purpose then he might be halfway there.

He said, 'I believe that if we can discover more about the German raider, the man who commands her, then we might learn something.' He stopped. It was obvious from the lieutenant's polite smile he was already thinking of something else. He added, 'With the Japs in the war we won't be able to rely too much on American protection on the other side of the Atlantic. They'll need all their spare ships in the Pacific until they can get on their feet again.'

The lieutenant looked at his watch. 'I am sure we can rely on that very point being watched by the powers-that-be, sir.'

'I'm sure.' Lindsay signalled to Jupp with his empty glass. 'Like they watched the Denmark Strait and the fjord where this bastard raider was anchored. Oh yes, I'm sure we can rely on *them.*'

Fraser said unsteadily, 'What about some food? My guts feel like a rusty oil drum.'

The sudden silence which had followed Lindsay's angry outburst broke up in laughter, and Lindsay saw Fraser watching him grimly.

The lieutenant stood up and said, 'Well, I'll be on my way, sir.' He forced a smile. 'I'm sure you're sincere, sir, but——'

Fraser took his elbow and pulled him away from the table. 'Look, sonny, if you want to play games, that's all right with me.' He tried to focus the lieutenant with his eyes. 'But don't come aboard *this* ship and try it, see?' He gestured with his glass, whisky splashing across the carpet. 'That man you were being so bloody patronising to has done more, seen more and cares more than you'll ever know! While you sit on your bum, sticking pins in some out of date map, it'll be men like him who get on with the job!'

The lieutenant looked down at him, aware that some of the civilian dockyard men were grinning at his confusion. 'Well, *really!* I don't see there's any occasion to speak like that.'

Fraser lurched away. 'Piss off!' He collapsed into a chair and added as an afterthought, 'And stick *that* on your bloody map!'

The others were leaving now. Most of them were used to dealing with men like Fraser. Western Approaches was unkind to those who served there. Death and constant danger had long since pared away the outward niceties and veneer of normal behaviour.

When they had all gone Lindsay said, 'Chief, I think you are one of the most uncouth people I have ever met.'

Fraser grinned. 'Could be.' He was unrepentant.

Lindsay held out his glass against the grey light from a scuttle. 'You'll be going home as soon as we've docked, I suppose.'

Fraser nodded. 'Aye. I'll have a good row and get this damn ship out of my system.' He grimaced. 'Still, I'll be there for Hogmanay. The wife'll have forgiven me by then.'

'Do you always have an argument when you go on leave?'

Jupp said, 'I think the chief engineer 'as dropped off, sir.' He removed the glass from Fraser's limp hand and added, 'I'll bring 'im some black coffee.'

Lindsay stood up. 'No. Let him sleep. He's done enough for ten men. His second can take over when we shift berth.'

'And when will that be, sir?'

'Tomorrow. Forenoon.'

Lindsay listened to the mournful bleat from some outgoing tug. It reminded him of the sinking ship. The siren going on and on as the shells blasted her apart.

He could hear muffled laughter from the wardroom and imagined them making plans for their unexpected leave. Wives and parents, girl friends and mistresses. Dancy's iceberg, as it had come to be known, had done them all a bit of good. Well, most of them. There were some, like Ritchie, who had nowhere to go. Wanted nothing which might remind them of what they had lost. And there was Goss. He had nothing but the ship, or so it appeared.

He said, 'I'm going ashore.' He had spoken almost before the idea had come to him. He had to get away, just for a few hours. Go where he knew no one and could find a moment of peace. If there was such a thing.

Jupp regarded him sadly. 'Aye, aye, sir. I'll run a bath for you.'

He hurried away to lay out Lindsay's best uniform and to make him some sandwiches, knowing the captain would not wait for a proper meal.

Lindsay walked to a scuttle on the outboard side and watched a rusty freighter being edged by tugs into the mainstream. But he was thinking of the signal and of the two ships lost on the other side of the world. Especially the *Prince of Wales*. He could see her clearly in his mind as she had been at Scapa Flow.

The memory of that windswept anchorage brought it all back again in an instant. The staff car. The girl with her duffel coat and jaunty cap.

He was still thinking about her as he left the ship and walked slowly along the littered jetty, his greatcoat collar turned up against the drizzle.

By a crouching gantry he paused and looked back. *Benbecula* seemed very tall and gaunt, rising like a wet grey wall above the winches and coiled mooring wires, the nameless piles of crates and the clutter of a seaport at war. From this angle her list to starboard was all the more apparent, so that she appeared to be leaning against the wet stonework, resting from the ordeal which men had thrust so brutally upon her.

How was it that Lieutenant de Chair had described her? *Long-funnelled and rather elderly.* It suited the old ship very well, he thought wearily.

Right aft an oilskinned seaman readjusted the halliards on the staff so that the new ensign flapped out with sudden vigour against the grey ships and sky beyond. But it took more than a flag to change a ship into a fighting machine. Just as it needed something extra to transform men into one company. Like Aikman, he thought. You could not expect a man to catch the same train to work day after regular day and then change into a dedicated, professional fighter. He strode on towards the gates. And when it was all over, would Aikman and Dancy, Hunter and Boase, and those like them, ever be able to break free from all this and return to that other, almost forgotten existence?

Then he stopped and took another look at his ship. It was up to him and the *Benbecula* to try and make sure they got the chance, he thought.

He showed his identity card to the dockyard policemen and then stepped outside the gates, suddenly confused and uncertain. Perhaps he was wrong. Maybe he was the one to be pitied and who needed help.

Some sailors disentangled themselves from their girl friends and saluted him as he passed, and he tried to read their faces in that small moment of contact.

Respect, envy, disinterest. He saw all and none of it. They were home from the Atlantic and were making the best of it. In a way, that answered his question, and he quickened his pace to look for a taxi.

11 Memories

During the forenoon of the second day in January 1942, His Majesty's Armed Merchant Cruiser *Benbecula* was warped from dry dock and made fast to her original jetty. In Western Approaches Command her appearance excited little comment, and if there was any reaction at all it was one of impatience. Impatience to be rid of her so that the dock, jetty and harbour services could be used again for the procession of damaged ships which came with every incoming convoy.

All leave for the ship's company was due to expire at noon, and as officers and ratings returned to Liverpool, with varying degrees of reluctance and according to the success or otherwise of their unexpected freedom, they could only stare at their floating home with a mixture of surprise and apprehension. For in their absence the old ship had shed her drab grey, and now rested at her moorings with an air of almost self-conscious embarrassment. From stem to stern, from the top of her single funnel to the waterline she was newly covered with dazzle paint. Green and ice-blue, strange angular patches of black and brown made it difficult to recognise her as the same ship. Only her list remained to prove her true identity, and as one amazed stoker remarked, 'She looks like some old Devonport tart in her daughter's summer dress!' There were other comments even less complimentary.

Lindsay had returned from leave several days earlier, and as he sat in his cabin studying the piles of stores folios, signals and the latest Admiralty Fleet Orders he heard some of the raised voices and remarks, and could appreciate their concern.

As usual, nobody knew what role was being cast *Benbecula*'s way. It was someone else's department. The dockyard people had made good the damage below the waterline and had added some of the extra refinements he had been asking for since taking command. There was an additional pair of Oerlikons on the boat deck, which he had *not* requested, so it rather looked as if the ship would be working within reach of enemy aircraft, at least for some of the time. Fresh armour had appeared abaft the bridge and wheelhouse, previously regarded as a very tender spot should an attacker be fortunate enough to approach from astern. Several new liferafts, an additional generator in the engine room and a generous repainting job in the lower messdecks showed the dockyard manager had not been idle, even allowing for Christmas.

For Lindsay the leave had been a strange and frustrating experience. Far from seeking seclusion in some hotel as he had first considered, he had instead gone south to London. After several attempts he had managed to obtain an interview at the Admiralty with a fairly senior intelligence officer. As he had expected, the department had heard nothing from the suave young lieutenant in Liverpool, nor did they know anything of Lindsay's report and suggestions about the German raider. Looking back, the intelligence officer had been extremely courteous but vaguely unhelpful. He had known very little about the raider, other than she was the *Nassau* which had sunk *Loch Glendhu* as well as the recent losses. She had not returned to Norway, and even now, as Lindsay sat staring at the littered desk, nobody had heard or seen anything of her at all.

But when Lindsay had persisted with his theme, that the Germans were planning another series of widespread attacks on Allied commerce to thin the resources of escort vessels and air patrols as well as to aid their new Japanese ally, the officer had been more definite. He was being hard-pressed to the limits of his department. There was no evidence to suggest that Lindsay was right. And anyway, the war was quite difficult enough without adding to it with *ifs* and *maybes*.

Lindsay groped for his pipe, remembering London. The ruined buildings, the gaps in small terraced houses where the bombs had carved a path like some giant axe. Sandbags around stately Whitehall offices, policemen in steel helmets, the blackout, and the wail of air-raid sirens, night after night, with hardly a break.

The people had looked tired and strained, as with each new day they picked their way over rubble and firemen's hoses to queue with resigned patience for buses which still somehow seemed to run on time.

And everywhere there were uniforms. Not just the three services, but all those of the occupied countries as well. Poles and Norwegians, Dutch and Czechs, whose alien uniforms seemed to show the extent of the enemy's successes.

When not waiting in an Admiralty lobby or going through the latest intelligence reports in the operations room, Lindsay had found himself walking. He still did not know how far he had walked nor the full extent. The East End and dockland. Green Park and the scruffy gaiety of Piccadilly. Quiet, faceless streets south of the river, and the proud skyline of the city darkly etched against the night sky with its criss-cross of searchlights and sullen glow of burning buildings. He had been bustled into an air-raid shelter by an indignant warden who had shouted, 'Who do you think you are, mate? God or something? You'll get your bloody head blown off if you walk about while there's a raid on!'

He had sat on a bench seat, his back against the cold concrete, while the shelter had quaked and trembled to the exploding bombs. Beyond the steel door, where the same warden had stared at him fixedly as if to discover the reason for his behaviour, he had heard the clang of fire bells, the shrill of a police whistle. But inside the crowded shelter he had found the same patience, the sense of oneness which had made such a mark on his memory.

From the day he had entered the Navy as a cadet Lindsay had been trained in all matters of the sea and, above all, sea warfare. Ship-handling and seamanship, gunnery and navigation, the complex management of groups of vessels working together in every conceivable condition which past experience and history could offer.

Nobody had said anything about the other side of it. At Dunkirk and Crete, Norway and North Africa, the lessons had been hard and sharp. Terrified refugees on the roads, scattering as the Stukas had sliced through them with bombs and bullets. Soldiers queueing chest-deep in the sea to be taken off devastated beaches by the Navy, which like London buses always managed to reach them in time. But at what a price.

The loss of his own ship, the agonising memory of the sinking transport which refused to leave him in peace, had all left their scar on Lindsay. But this last visit to London had shown him more than anything else that he knew nothing of the other war at all. It was not a battle to be contained in a gun or bombsight, with an enemy beyond reach or personality. It was right here. It was everywhere. No one was spared, and he knew that if these people with whom he had shared an air-raid shelter and all the others like them were to lose faith and hope the end was even closer than some imagined. It was amazing they had not given up already, he thought. Yet in the battered pubs with their shortages and watery beer he had heard plenty of laughter and optimism. Although on the face of it he could find no reason for either. The war was going badly, and the first breath of relief when it was learned that, willingly or otherwise, the Americans were now firm allies, was now giving way to an awareness that the real struggle had not even begun.

Even the newspapers found it hard to explain the daily events in Malaya. In a month the Japanese had driven almost the full length of the peninsula, smashing resistance and leaving a wake of horror and butchery which was impossible to measure.

During his leave Lindsay had toyed with the idea of finding out where Eve Collins had lived. He would visit her parents. Would make and hold on to some small comfort by the contact. He had dismissed the idea almost immediately, despising himself for his own self-pity. What would he have said? That he saw the ship burn with their daughter condemned to a hideous death? That he was there, a witness who should have been able to help but could not?

No, it was better to leave them to their own resources. After the harsh cruelty of an official telegram they would have to draw upon each other for strength. With time, even this unreality might ease and they would be able to think of her memory without pain, as countless others were having to do.

There was a tap at the door and Goss walked heavily into the cabin.

He said, 'Eight bells, sir. Still seven absentees, but there's been a train delay. They might be on that.' He opened his notebook. 'One call from the R.N. hospital. Able Seaman McNiven is detained in the V.D. wing for treatment.' He closed it with a snap. 'I've detailed another A.B. to replace him as quartermaster, sir.' He did not sound as if he cared much about McNiven's unhappy predicament.

'Thank you.' Lindsay eyed him steadily. Goss looked very strained, and he could imagine his feelings about the ship's new appearance. 'I expect we shall be getting our orders shortly.'

Goss nodded. 'Yes.'

It was as hard as ever to make contact with Goss.

Lindsay said, 'We will be taking on fuel and ammunition

this afternoon. We'll work into the dog watches if necessary. If there's an air-raid on the port we don't want to be
sitting ducks.'

In the distance he heard a man laugh, and pictured the
returning hands far below his chair as they struggled out
of their best uniforms, folding them carefully into kitbags
and lockers until the next time. They would all be telling
each other of their leaves. Their conquests and their fail-
ures. Their families and their expectations for the next
leave. It was always the same.

Goss said suddenly, 'I've been ashore a few times. Made
it my business to find out where we're going next.'

Lindsay asked, 'Discover anything?'

He sighed. It seemed to come from his very soul. 'Snotty
lot of bastards, sir.' His eyes gleamed. 'But I did hear we
might be going south.'

Lindsay nodded. 'Could be.' He had already noted the
extra fans and ventilation shafts, and the bright dazzle
paint pointed to something more than another Icelandic
patrol. He realised too that he did not care where it was,
except for one thing. The faint, impossible chance of
meeting that raider again.

Goss said, 'If we do.' He moved slightly so that Lindsay
could no longer see his face. 'I don't think we'll ever get
back.'

Lindsay turned in his chair. Goss was deadly serious. As
he always was. He was also more troubled than he had ever
seen him.

Goss continued in the same empty tone, 'While you were
away, sir, they got the old *Eriskay*. Torpedoed her. Didn't
say where.'

Without asking, Lindsay knew the ship must be another
of Goss's old company.

Goss said, 'Only three left now.' He moved restlessly to a
scuttle, his face very lined in the grey light. 'They'd no
right to put them where they can't survive. It's always the
same.' He turned, his eyes in shadow. 'The big warships

swing round their buoys in harbour. The best destroyers stay with 'em just in case they might be in danger. While the poor bloody escorts which should have been on the scrap-heap years ago,' he took a deep breath, 'and ships like the *Becky* are made to take the brunt of it!' He clenched his big hands as if in pain. 'It's not bloody right, sir! It's not bloody fair!'

Lindsay watched him gravely. Goss's sudden outburst was both vehement and moving. He knew he was hitting not only at the nameless warships but at the Service which controlled them. Perhaps indirectly at him, too.

'I've seen people in London, Number One, who are in much the same position. They've no choice.' He hardened his voice. 'Any more than we have.'

Goss recovered himself. 'I know that.'

The deck gave a delicate tremor, and Lindsay wondered if Fraser was already in his engine room, testing some machinery or the new generator.

He said, 'Well, carry on, Number One. We'll make an early start after lunch.' He saw Ritchie peering in the door and added, 'Come in, Yeo.' He watched Goss stride past Ritchie and wondered why he could not face the inevitable.

Ritchie said, 'New batch of signals, sir.'

'Thanks.' He flicked over the top one. 'Good leave?' He looked up, seeing the distress on the man's round face, cursing himself for his stupidity. 'I'm sorry. That was bloody unforgivable.'

Ritchie smiled. 'S'all right, sir.' He added, 'I'm not sorry to be back.' He glanced around the cabin. 'I stayed at the Union Jack Club. Better'n nothing, I suppose.'

Lindsay thought of his own leave. The endless walking, the visits to the Admiralty. The nights when he had at last made good use of Boase's pills. Now, with the ship needing him once more, he wondered what the first night would bring. Perhaps he would be safe.

Ritchie said, 'Signal 'ere from H.Q., sir. Ops officer

comin' aboard at 1400.' He added quietly, "E's bringin' the commodore with 'im.'

Lindsay looked up. 'Kemp? I thought he was staying at Scapa?'

Ritchie shrugged. 'You know 'ow it is in the Andrew, sir. They give you tropical rig and sends you to the Arctic. Train you for torpedoes and make you a cook!' He grinned. 'They call it plannin'!'

Lindsay smiled up at him. It was good to see him again. Something familiar. To hold on to.

'We shall just have to see what it is in our case.'

'There's another signal about A.B. McNiven, too.' Ritchie leaned over to open the pad. 'A shore patrol caught 'im breakin' into a chemist's shop. Poor chap probably thought 'e could cure a dose with stickin' plaster.' He became formal again. 'An' Mr. Aikman's replacement is due this afternoon.'

Jupp entered the cabin and hesitated. 'Pardon, sir.'

Lindsay stood up. 'I think we'll have a drink.' He looked at Ritchie. 'What about it, Yeoman? Just to start things off again.'

Ritchie grinned. 'Well, if you say so, sir. Never bin known to refuse.'

Jupp darted a quick glance at Lindsay and saw the smoother lines around his mouth and eyes. The tablets had done some good then. He looked at the petty officer as he stood beside the desk, pleased yet awkward with the captain's invitation. He thought too of Ritchie's family photographs in the P.O.'s mess and wondered how he had endured the past three weeks.

He straightened his stooped shoulders. 'Comin' right up, sir. An' as we're safe in 'arbour, the *best* glasses!'

Immediately after lunch, while the cranes dipped and swayed back and forth overhead, the ship's company turned to for work. There was a keen wind across the port and they needed little encouragement to make the business of loading stores and ammunition as brisk as possible.

On the outboard side an oiler nestled against the fenders while the pulsating fuel hoses pumped *Benbecula*'s life-blood into her bunkers, her skipper already watching other ships nearby with signal flags hoisted to show they too were demanding his services.

Throughout the ship, above and below decks, officers and ratings busied themselves with their allotted duties, their faces absorbed as they relived some incident or memory of their leave.

Fraser stood by the guardrail above the oiler, his gloved hands on his hips as he watched the chief stoker checking the steady intake. He had done it so often, in so many ports, he could gauge the fuel supply almost by the jerk of the hoses. He was thinking of his family in Dundee. It had all turned out to be quite different from what he had expected. For years he had been almost a stranger in his own home. A man who came and went, season by season. Back and forth to the other side of the world, a life which he could share with no one outside whatever ship he happened to be serving.

But this time he had been shocked to find his wife was suddenly growing old. And his two children had seemed like strangers, even embarrassed by his forced familiarity. There had been no tours around the pubs as in the past. No quiet anger on his wife's face as he staggered home in the early hours. For three whole weeks he had tried to make up for it. Had tried to rediscover what he had never known he had possessed. She had understood. No arguments. No quarrels about other ships' officers who lived in the district, whose wives had always told her how well their men were doing. Better ships than Fraser's. Promotion, more opportunities, fancy jobs on shore or in some harbour authority.

It had been a close, warm Christmas, and unlike any other leave when New Year had been involved, neither

Fraser nor his wife had budged from their fire. As they had listened to the welcome to the New Year on their radio they had held hands, both realising perhaps that it was not merely the end of a year but also of this leave.

He had heard himself say, 'If anything happens to me, will you let young Jamie follow the sea if he's so inclined?'

Their son was eleven but had seemed so much older this time.

She had replied, 'Don't talk like that, Donald. It's not like you to fret so. What have they done to make you like this?'

'I didn't mean to worry you, lass.'

She had poured him a full glass of whisky. 'Drink this, Donald. Jamie's like his father. I'll not stop him.'

And when he had made to leave he had stared around their small house as if trying to remember everything at once. Then he had kissed her and had gone down the path without looking back.

The chief stoker squinted up at him, his eyes red in the wind. 'That feels better, eh, sir? The old girl'll take us anywhere!'

Fraser regarded him dourly. 'She'd bloody well do just that, Usher! I'll not forgive her if she conks out now!'

Above on the boat deck Lieutenant Maxwell was staring up at the twin mounting which had appeared abaft the bridge superstructure.

His assistant, Lieutenant Hunter, was saying, 'I've checked the communications, sir, and the siting of the mounting is quite good, too.' He was careful to say little, knowing how scathing Maxwell could be.

Maxwell bobbed his bullet head. 'Good. Fine. As it should be.' He had hardly heard a word Hunter had said.

He still could not accept it. It was like a bad dream which refused to be broken even when the sufferer was endeavouring to burst awake and free himself from it.

If he had telephoned first he would never have known. He felt the sweat gathering under his cap, hot in spite of the bitter wind. He rarely bothered to telephone or send a letter about leave. Decia, his wife, always seemed to be home anyway. She had money of her own, plenty of it, thanks to her rich father, and was quite content to entertain her friends rather than go visiting.

It might have been going on for months. Years. He felt the anxiety and disbelief churning his insides as if he were going to vomit.

On the last link of his journey down to Hampshire the train had been held up for several hours because of a derailment further along the line. Without lights or heating, the occupants of his compartment had sat in resentful, shivering silence. Then when at last he had reached his station there had been no taxi or hire-car available. The aged porter had said sourly, 'Don't you know there's a war on?' Stupid old bastard.

Maxwell had been almost out of breath by the time he had walked the five miles to his house. His case had been heavy, filled mostly with duty-free cigarettes and a length of silk which he had obtained in Liverpool from an old contact. For Decia.

Inside the front door the house had been as quiet as a grave, and for a few moments more he imagined she might have been away. The housekeeper lived out, for now that factories and the services offered either better money or a more exciting life, servants were almost impossible to find. Decia often complained about this fact, as she did about other things, too.

Then he had heard her laugh. A long, excited, sensuous sound.

He did not remember running upstairs or how long he had waited outside the bedroom door. In his mind he could only picture the scene captured in the bedside lights like some hideous tableau.

Decia sitting up and staring at him, her naked body like gold in the lamplight, her hair across her shoulders in a way he had never seen before. And the man, open-mouthed and transfixed, one hand still thrust against her thigh. He had tumbled from the bed, blurting out senseless, meaningless words, groping for his trousers, falling, and then sobbing with terror as Maxwell crossed to his side.

The worst part of it was that Maxwell had been unable to hit him. Maybe in his heart he had known that if he had once started he would have killed him there and then. The man was paunchy and ridiculous. Not even young, and had been in tears as he had babbled for forgiveness.

Maxwell had slammed the door behind him, hearing the man stumbling downstairs, the sounds of his feet across the gravel drive, and then silence.

In the bedroom there had been no sound either. Just her breathing and his own heart pounding into his ribs like a hammer.

'Why?' The one word had been torn from him even before he had recovered his reason. 'In Christ's name, *why?*'

Instead of trying to cover her body she had leaned back, her eyes suddenly calm again.

'Why not? Did you imagine I'd be able to go on living like this without a *man*?'

Maxwell had turned towards the door. 'Man? You call that a man?'

She had said, 'He made a change.'

Even as he stood stockstill below the twin Oerlikons Maxwell could not believe. She had not been afraid or repentant. Had not even bothered to conceal what she had done, perhaps many times with others.

'You bitch!' He had almost choked. 'You bloody, spoiled whore!'

Still she had not flinched, and when she had spoken her voice had been scathing, taunting.

'What did you expect? That I could just sit here while you go playing the little hero again? But for this war you'd still be living on my money, pretending to be the retired gentleman, when we both know you were thrown out of the Navy! I'm only surprised they took you in the first place!' She had mocked at his anguish. 'God Almighty, *look* at you! No wonder we're losing the war!'

'I was not thrown out.' He had heard his excuses pouring from his lips, just as he had told them to himself over and over again. 'It was an accident. Someone else——'

'Someone else? Oh, it would be. It always is when you make a mistake.'

She had let her shoulders fall back over the pillows, her perfect breasts firm in the bedside lights.

'You're a failure. Just as you're a failure in bed!'

He had almost fallen on top of her, his eyes blinded with tears and desperation, his hands groping for her as he had pleaded, 'You're wrong. You know you are. I've had bad luck. I've tried to make you happy.'

And all the time she had just laid there, her eyes almost disinterested as she watched his hands running over her shoulders and breasts.

'You make me sick.'

Everything else had been lost in a blur. Like a film out of focus. He could still hear himself screaming down at her, saw her amused contempt change to sudden fright as he had swung back his arm and then struck her across the mouth. She had rolled on to her side, gasping with pain, only to rock back again as he had hit her once more. How many times he had struck her he could not recall. But he could see her doubled over the side of the bed, her cheeks puffed and swollen, her beautiful lips running with blood.

That last sight had frozen him, chilled his fury as if he had been drugged. Hesitantly, almost timidly he had put one hand on her quivering shoulder.

Before he could speak she had turned and looked up at him, her hair disordered across her bruised face, partly hiding one eye which was already closing from his blows.

'Better now, little man?' The tears had been running down her face to mingle unheeded with the blood on her lips. Perhaps she had expected him to kill her and no longer cared.

Maxwell remembered only vaguely leaving the house. Even as he made to close the front door he had heard her call after him. Just one word which hung in his brain even now. *'Bastard!'*

The leave had been spent in a small hotel. He had tried phoning her. Had even written several letters and then torn them up. After having her telephone hung up on him he had tried to get drunk. He had almost gone mad in his hotel room, drinking and going over it all again and again. The nightmare had been made worse by the other hotel guests singing Christmas carols, their curious or amused stares as he had sat at his table for an occasional meal. Once he had taken out her picture from his wallet and torn it in half, cursing her and her beautiful body until someone had banged on the wall and yelled, 'Pipe down, chum! Who've you got in there? A bloody tiger?'

The sudden interruption had sobered him, and with pathetic despair he had dropped to his knees, gathering up the fragments of her picture, and had tried to fix them together as he had mumbled her name.

Hunter watched him carefully. He disliked Maxwell but his present mood was almost unnerving. Perhaps he had gone round the bend. It could happen, they said. Or maybe he had heard some bad news.

He asked, 'Everything all right at home?'

Maxwell turned on his heels like a bullfighter, his face screwed up with sudden anger.

'You mind your own damn business, right? Do your job and keep the guns in order, that's all I want from you!' He swung away and marched violently towards the bridge, his shoes clicking across the worn planking as if he were on parade.

Hunter shook his head and smiled to himself. That was

more like it. Better the bastard you knew than some nut case.

Lieutenant de Chair was passing and drawled, 'Back to normal, I see?'

Hunter grinned. 'One big happy family.'

The marine lieutenant rested his hands on the guardrail and watched a staff car driving towards the main gangway.

'Let's hope it stays that way, old son.'

A marine driver opened the car door and a stocky figure climbed out to stare up at the ship's side, the dull light glinting on his oak-leaved cap and the single broad stripe on his sleeve.

de Chair added quietly, 'I should tell young Kemp to watch out.' He walked casually aft saying over his shoulder, 'Some sort of god has just arrived!'

———————

Commodore Martin Kemp selected an armchair and sat down very exactly. Without his cap he became just as Lindsay had remembered him from the wardroom party at Scapa. Stocky, even heavily built, he looked like a man who took some pains over his appearance. His features were very tanned, so that his keen blue eyes and the few remaining wisps of grey hair stood out as if independent from the rest of the mould.

He said briskly, 'I expect you're wondering why I've come bursting in like this. I *could* have arrived quite unannounced, of course.'

Lindsay watched him impassively. The *of course* was somehow typical of the man, he thought.

He said, 'I would be ready to receive you at any time, sir.'

Kemp grunted. 'Yes. I expect so. Wasn't trying to catch you out.'

'Would you care for some refreshment, sir?'

He shook his head. 'No time.' He studied Lindsay calmly. 'But if you feel *you* would like a drink, don't let me stop you.'

Lindsay sat down and tried to relax. He must not let Kemp get under his skin so easily.

'What is it you want to see me about, sir?'

Kemp interlaced his fingers carefully across his stomach. Lindsay noticed how erectly he sat in the chair. There was not a crease in his uniform, and he guessed that he made a point of appearing alert whenever he was with his subordinates.

'As you know, Lindsay, I have been doing a good deal of work on co-ordination.' A small sigh. 'A hard, thankless task.'

'I did hear something about it, sir. But I've been away for several weeks, and of course there has been leave for the whole ship since we came to Liverpool.'

Kemp's eyebrows lifted. 'Away? Oh yes. The patrol.'

Lindsay took out his pipe and gripped it until Kemp's casual dismissal of the patrol faded into perspective. Perhaps being recalled to the Service after retirement, the fast-moving rate of the war, the sudden jump into his new work were hard to bear for him, too. There were plenty like Kemp. So grateful to be needed again, yet unwilling to bend in the face of the changes which war had hurled against the country and the world.

Kemp continued, 'That was a bad show about the convoy. Its commodore did not throw much light on the matter.' He shrugged. 'Past history now.'

Lindsay thought of the girl with the bandaged face. The blazing ship, and that last pathetic signal from the convoy escort. *Am engaging.*

He said quietly, 'It was murder. In my opinion, our people will have to start thinking like the enemy and not of acting out the war as if it is a game.' He could feel his hands trembling. 'To see men die and be helpless to aid them was bad enough. To know it was because of carelessness makes it all the worse.'

Kemp smiled. 'You are still on your hobby horse? I've been hearing about your assault on the Admiralty. I'd have thought you'd find a better way of spending your leave.' He shrugged. 'No matter. I came to tell you your new assignment. Not partake in amateur strategy.'

Lindsay replied, 'You don't believe that ships and men's lives are important then, sir?'

Kemp smiled again. He looked more at ease than when Lindsay and the side party had met him at the gangway.

'Look, Lindsay, you've had a bad time. I make a point of knowing everything there is to know about my officers. Especially *commanding* officers.'

Lindsay looked away. *My* officers. So Kemp was taking the reins.

He said, 'I am involved, sir. I cannot just ignore it.'

'Of course not. Admirable sentiment. However, you must allow me to understand the overall position and what must be done to contain whatever the Hun intends to do.'

Lindsay watched him with sudden realisation. There was something old-world about Kemp. He may have been able to obtain this new appointment through his past knowledge or record, but his manner, his form of speech were as revealing as a Cockney barrow-boy trying to masquerade as a bishop. The *Hun,* for instance. It had a First World War, Boys' Own Paper ring to it. God, if Kemp thought he could introduce cricket into the Atlantic he was in for a shock. He felt the anger rising like a fever. But Kemp would not be the one to suffer.

'Drastic situations call for drastic measures, Lindsay. I will be speaking with everyone concerned tomorrow, but I felt you should be put in the picture first.' He hesitated. 'Well, I mean, this ship is hardly a front-line warrior, eh?'

Lindsay said quietly, 'They are using old pleasure boats,

paddle-steamers for minesweeping, sir. China river gun-boats for covering the army's flanks in the Med. *Benbecula* is not alone when it comes to unpreparedness.'

'Well, we can't all have the plum commands.' Kemp's smile was still there but it was without warmth. 'We need every ship we can get. Every man-jack who can serve his country to step in and fill the breech.'

Lindsay wanted to laugh. Or cry. 'And the breech is a big one, sir.'

Kemp let his hands move up and outwards to the arms of his chair. 'I think I am a tolerant man, Lindsay. Do not overtax me. There is vital work to be done and without wasting any more time.' He stood up and walked to a scuttle. 'The situation in Malaya is grave, more so than I would have thought possible. Of course I realise the Japanese have only been facing our native troops for much of the campaign, but I still feel that in my early days we would have given any attacker out there very short shrift indeed.'

Lindsay watched his profile. Native troops. Why not just let him talk. Get it over with and send him away happy.

Instead he said abruptly, 'The troops are from many parts of the Commonwealth. Indians and Australians, as well as our people. I understand the Indian infantry have not been trained in tank warfare. Have never even seen one. They were told no attacker could use them in the jungle. I suppose the Japs didn't know that though.'

Kemp swung round. 'That's probably a damned rumour!' He calmed himself with a quick effort. 'One thing is certain, however. Singapore will be held. It is a sad business to lose so much of Malaya, but with Singapore made even stronger than before we can soon retake the initiative on the mainland.'

Lindsay massaged his eyes. What was Kemp saying? That *Benbecula* was to go to the Far East? If so he was deluding himself more than ever.

Kemp became very grave, so that his eyes seemed to sink into the wrinkles like bright buttons.

'Reinforcements will be sent forthwith. A fast convoy is being mustered and will sail in four days. It is a vital convoy. Armoured vehicles and anti-aircraft weapons. Troops and supplies, and everything else they'll need for a siege.'

Lindsay tensed. 'Around the Cape, sir?'

'Of course. Did you imagine I would direct it through the Med. to Suez? We'd have every bomber and submarine attacking it all the way.'

Lindsay replied, 'I know, sir.'

'Non-stop to Ceylon.' Kemp seemed satisfied Lindsay was now in full agreement. 'From there the troops and supplies will go on in smaller ships with fresh escorts. The FOIC in Ceylon is ready to act and will get them moving within two days of our arrival.' He rubbed his hands. 'That will keep the moaning minnies quiet when they see what can be done with a bit of initiative and drive.'

Lindsay said, 'It's thirteen thousand miles to Ceylon, sir. Even allowing for minimum changes of course to avoid U-boat attacks, breakdowns and delays it will take nearly seven weeks to get there.'

'*Really?*' Kemp's eyebrows seemed to rise a full inch. 'I am glad you have such a quick grasp of routes and distances. But I hope you are not suggesting that Singapore will have sunk without trace before that time?' He laughed quietly. 'And there will be no delays. This is an important job. We will have a heavy escort, and will go through regardless of what the Hun can throw our way.'

Lindsay stood up. 'Look, sir, my idea about this German raider was not just born on the spur of a moment. I believe it is the start of something fresh. Something which could put our convoys into real danger. We're fighting on two oceans now. Even the Americans can't be expected to help us until they've replaced some of their losses at Pearl Harbour.'

Kemp picked up his cap and eyed it critically. 'I am not concerned with the American Navy, Lindsay. How they fight their war is their affair. Personally I have greater respect for the Japanese. I worked with them in the last war. Courageous, plucky little chaps. Plenty of guts.' He sighed. 'But fate can be unkind, as we have seen.'

Lindsay could feel his mind reeling. It was like part of a badly acted play. Dinner jackets in the jungle. The captain on his bridge saluting as the ship went down.

He said, 'I'm afraid I can't agree, sir.'

'That is hardly my worry, Lindsay.' He smiled grimly. 'I know you're fretting about having this old ship to command. With any sort of luck I may be able to help towards something better.' His smile vanished. 'But I intend to see that my arrangements *work*. I do not expect to hear any more of this defeatist talk from you or anyone else.'

Lindsay followed him from the cabin. 'Would you like to see your son, sir?'

Kemp did not turn. 'When he has achieved something worthwhile, yes. Then I'll see him with pleasure.'

Lindsay saluted as Kemp hurried down the gangway and then turned abruptly towards the bridge. The commodore had a new appointment and expected everyone to work, or die if necessary to make it a success.

He stopped and looked up suddenly at the masthead pennant flicking out to the wind. He had just remembered Goss's words. *I don't think we'll ever get back.* ·

Then he thought of the commodore and quickened his pace again. I'll get them all back, if it's only to spite that pompous fool, he thought.

And if Commodore Martin Kemp was coming along for the ride he might at last realise what he was up against. Or kill all of us.

Jupp was waiting for him and said, 'South Atlantic then, sir?'

Lindsay sat down wearily. 'Who says?'

Jupp showed his teeth. 'Some fur-lined watchcoats 'ave just arrived, sir. The pusser 'as 'ad 'em on order for weeks.' He spread his hands. 'If they sends us that, then we just 'ave to be goin' to the sunshine, it stands to reason.'

Lindsay nodded. 'Except for the word *reason*, Jupp, I'm inclined to agree.'

12 Convoy

'Forenoon watch closed up at defence stations, sir.' Stannard saluted formally and waited for Lindsay to comment.

Lindsay glanced at the gyro repeater and then climbed on to his chair and stared at the grey horizon for several seconds.

'Very good, Pilot.'

He waited for Stannard to move away again and then lifted his glasses to study the regularly spaced lines of ships. The convoy had been at sea for four whole days and as yet without a sign of trouble. The first two days had been very rough with gale force winds and visibility down to four miles. Maybe the U-boats had run deep to stay out of the savage buffeting which such seas could give their slender hulls, or perhaps they had just been lucky. The convoy was small but weighty nonetheless. The ships were steaming in three columns, the centre one being led by a modern heavy cruiser mounting twelve six-inch guns, a formidable looking vessel which represented the main escort. She was followed by two oil tankers and then the most hated member in the group, a large ammunition ship which steamed directly ahead of the *Benbecula*. The two outer columns were led by troopships, followed at prescribed intervals by freighters, the decks of which were covered by crated aircraft and armoured vehicles of every kind. They were well down in the water, and Lindsay guessed their holds were also crammed to capacity.

The destroyer escort was impressive. Six of them, none more than a year old, an unusual state of affairs with so many shortages elsewhere, and evidence of the importance placed in the convoy's safety and protection.

It was strange how the weather had eased. That too was rare for January. The horizon was sharply defined and very dark, and as Lindsay steadied himself in his chair he thought it made *Benbecula*'s list all the more obvious. The horizon line appeared to be on the tilt with the ships balanced on it and in danger of sliding uncontrollably abeam.

He readjusted the glasses to watch one of the escorts zig-zagging some five miles ahead of the convoy. He could see the great white surge of her bow-wave creaming away from her raked stem, the lithe hull almost hidden as she sped protectively across the convoy's ponderous line of advance. Just the sight of her plucked at his mind and made him remember his own destroyer and the others which he had served before her. Fast, aggressive and graceful. They above all had managed to retain the dying art of ship design. The cruiser on the other hand was like some grey floating fortress. Bridge upon bridge, her triple gun mountings and secondary armament giving her an air of massive indestructibility.

Some signal flags broke from the yard of the troopship leading the starboard column. The commodore was urging some unfortunate captain to keep station or make better speed. He could picture Kemp up there, revelling in his new power. It was to be hoped he was equally aware of his great responsibility.

All around them the horizon was bare, with the enemy-occupied coastline of France some thousand miles away on the port beam. Apart from the distant shapes of the prowling destroyers the sea was theirs alone. Not even a gull, let alone a spotting aircraft to break the dull overcast sky as a warning of impending danger.

Seventeen ships in all. He saw some anti-aircraft guns

aboard the cruiser swivel skyward, their crews going through the daily drills. Unconsciously he touched the gold lace on his sleeve. She was the *Madagascar*, nine thousand tons, and capable of tackling almost anything but a battleship. Had things been different he might have been on her bridge right now, or one like it. Doing what he had been trained for. What he had lived for.

He looked round the bridge, seeing the worn panelling, the usual scene of watchkeeping monotony. Quartermaster on the wheel, telegraphsmen swaying with the easy roll, their eyes lost in inner thought. A signalman was sitting on a locker splicing a worn halyard, and Ritchie was leafing through the morning watch reports with little on his face to show what he was thinking. A bosun's mate, a messenger gathering up the chipped enamel mugs, everything as usual.

Dancy was out on the open wing, his glasses trained on one of the ships. Stannard leaned against the screen, his face set in a tight frown.

Lindsay eased forward to watch some seamen who were working on the well deck, taking the rare opportunity to dab on some fresh paint under C.P.O. Archer's baleful eye. It was very cold, but after the ice and the constant hazards of working on a slippery deck with seas breaking over their numbed bodies they would find it almost normal.

He lifted his glasses and trained them on the commodore's ship. She was the *Cambrian*, a handsome twin-funnelled liner which had once plied between England and South America. Commanding the *Benbecula* had made a marked difference where merchant ships were concerned. Before, Lindsay had seen them as charges to be protected. Names on a convoy list to be chased or reprimanded as the occasion demanded. The slow ones, and those which made too much smoke. The ones who strayed out of their column or crept too close on the next ahead. With so many ex-merchant service people around him every day and night he was seeing them differently. They spoke of their past records, their cargoes and passengers. The carefree cruises or months in harbour without charter, and the dockside thronged with unemployed, hungry seamen. Rogue ships and bad skippers. Fast passages or valuable time and freight lost while searching for some other ship in distress. Shifting cargo in a Force Nine gale, miserly captains who kept their crews almost on starvation diet for their own ends. It was so remote from the regulated world of the Royal Navy. It was like re-learning everything just by listening to others.

Stannard had worked in a whaling fleet and on the frozen meat trade before joining the company. The second engineer, Lieutenant Dyke, had originally gone to sea in a Greek ship running guns to the Republicans in the Spanish Civil War. To them the ships they met in convoy were like old faces, old friends, with characters to match.

Stannard was studying the next ship ahead. 'Down two turns.' He looked at Lindsay and gave a wry smile. 'Don't want to be too near that joker if she gets clobbered.'

Lindsay nodded. He had seen an ammunition ship go up. She had been two miles away, yet the noise, the savage pressure on his ears had been almost unbearable. One great ball of fire, rising and expanding like another sun. When the smoke and steam had faded there had not even been a stick or spar to mark where the ship had been. What sort of men were they, he wondered, who would go to sea again and again knowing they were the targets?

He saw a small hatch open on the forward hold and Lieutenant Barker clambering on deck to stand shivering in the wind. He had been checking his stores again, no doubt. He did not seem to trust anybody where they were concerned. Barker had returned from leave in a very shaken state of mind. Lindsay had heard that he had some private property in England. Boarding houses or something of the sort. But when he had gone to make his usual inspection of his other source of income he had been horrified to find them commandeered by the military. Every room filled with soldiers. Paint scratched, floorboards used for firewood. The havoc had been endless. Jupp had casually mentioned it to Lindsay. It seemed to amuse him.

A destroyer on wing escort turned in a wide arc to begin another zig-zag and he watched her with silent fascination. Then he remembered that she was the *Merlin* and recalled her young commander waiting in the office at Scapa. That day when he had seen Lovelace. When he had met the girl in the passageway. He thrust his hands into his pockets and stared fixedly at the sloping horizon. It seemed so long ago. And it felt like yesterday.

'Signal from commodore, sir.' Ritchie was wide awake. 'Alter course in succession to two-two-zero.'

'Acknowledge.' He heard Stannard moving swiftly to the gyro.

Ritchie steadied his telescope. 'Execute.'

Like ponderous beasts the ships moved slowly on to their new course. A destroyer swept down between the lines, a signal lamp flashing angrily at a rust-streaked freighter which had edged badly out of station. As she dashed abeam of *Benbecula* her loud-hailer echoed across the churned water, 'You have a bad list, old chap!'

Stannard snatched a megaphone and ran to the open wing. 'You have a loud voice, *old chap!*' He sounded angry.

Lindsay watched him thoughtfully. Like Fraser, Stannard was often quick to malign the *Benbecula*. But if anyone else tried it he became protective, even belligerent.

He came back breathing hard. 'Stupid sod!'

Lindsay asked, 'Have you heard how your brother is getting on?'

'Not much.' Stannard stared gloomily towards the

nearest ship. 'He is always a cheerful cuss. I think he *enjoys* being in the army.'

Lindsay could tell Stannard wanted to talk. He seemed on edge, different from before his leave.

'Your people are in Perth, I believe?'

'Yeh. My dad runs a sale and repair business of agricultural gear. He'll be missing young Jason, I guess. He's twenty-five almost. It was bad enough for my folks when I scarpered off to sea.' He turned his head sharply. 'Watch your helm, quartermaster! You're snaking about like a whore at a christening!'

'Aye, aye, sir.' The man sounded unmoved. Nobody seemed to mind Stannard's occasional bursts of colourful language.

He continued, 'Most of Jason's mob come from Perth or nearby.' He gave a brief smile. '*Nearby* means a coupla hundred miles either way in Aussie.'

Lindsay thought of the news reports, the confused despatches he had read in the London papers. It sounded as if the Japs were right across the Malay Peninsula, cutting it into halves with a line of steel.

Ritchie called, 'Signal from *Merlin*, sir! Aircraft bearing zero-eight-zero!'

Before anyone could move the control tannoy reported, 'Aircraft at Red one-four-oh. Angle of sight one-oh.'

Stannard said harshly, 'That *Merlin* must have good RDF. She's two miles on our starboard quarter.' He shook his fist at the deckhead. 'Why the hell don't they give us something better? We might just as well have a pair of bloody opera glasses!'

Lindsay strode to the port wing and levelled his glasses over the screen. It was not hard to see it now. A black splinter etched against the sky, seeming to skim just clear of the horizon line itself.

He heard Dancy at his side fumbling with his glasses.

'Don't bother, Sub. It'll be a Focke Wulf reconnaissance

plane. Long-range job. It'll not come within gunshot unless by accident.'

Very faint above the sea noises and muffled engines Lindsay heard the far off notes of a bugle. The cruiser was doing things in style. Within seconds the A.A. guns would be cleared away and tracking the distant aircraft. It was always good experience for the crews. He rubbed his eyes and lifted the glasses once more to watch the enemy aircraft. How small it looked and near to the sea. Both were illusions, as he knew from bitter experience. The Focke Wulfs were like great eagles, huge whenever they came near enough to be seen properly. They could cover many hundreds of miles of ocean, where there were no fighter planes to pluck them down and no guns to reach them as they circled so lazily around a convoy, their radio operators sending back the vital information. Position, course and speed. It never varied. Even now, somewhere out there in the grey Atlantic a U-boat commander would be awakening from a quick nap by one of his officers shaking his shoulder. *Convoy, Kapitan.* And the signals from his H.Q. would waste no time either. Attack, attack, attack.

'Signal from commodore, sir.' Ritchie stood in the doorway. 'Maintain course and speed. Do not engage.'

Do not engage. Lindsay felt despair like pain. What did the bloody fool imagine they could do?

Dancy said, 'Is it bad, sir?'

'Bad but not critical, Sub.' He looked at him calmly. 'We will be altering course at dusk. That may throw them off the scent. If we can keep up this speed we should soon be out of range even of that high-flying bastard!' He had spoken with unconscious venom and realised Dancy was watching him with obvious surprise. Surprise that the cool-headed commander should possess any feelings. That he could hate. He added slowly, 'He'll keep up there as long as he can. Flying round and round and watching us. He may be relieved by one of his chums. It happens.'

Dancy turned towards the distant cruiser. 'She's got an aircraft, sir. I saw it on the catapult.'

Lindsay laughed. 'A poor old Walrus. Better than nothing, but that bastard would have it down in flames before you could blink.'

'Makes you feel a bit naked, sir.'

Lindsay walked towards the wheelhouse. 'Keep an eye on him, Sub. I'm going to check the chart.'

Dancy stood at the end of the wing watching the aircraft. How slow it seemed. But it was very real. The enemy. Something you could see. Not like the haphazard flash of guns in the night. The terrible leaping reflections on the ice as a ship had burned and died before his eyes. There were real Germans over there. Sitting on little stools. Drinking coffee perhaps as they peered towards the convoy. How would the ships look, he wondered? Little dark shapes, betrayed by their long white wakes and a haze of funnel smoke. Impersonal. Remote. Did they hate the men in the convoy? Did they feel anything at all as they listened to the plane's operator hammering away at his morse key?

He thought suddenly of his leave. His mother had prompted, 'Go on, Mike, tell us what it was like.' She had laid the table, spread out the best cups and plates. The sandwiches and home-made cakes. His sister and her boy-friend had been there too. His father and one of his friends from the bowling club at the Nag's Head at the end of the road. Tell us what it was like. . . .

He had tried to describe the ship, the first sight of floating ice, the party at Scapa. He had started to tell them about the captain. About Lindsay who had just left his side.

His mother had remarked, 'I expect he's a proper toff, eh, Mike? Not one of our sort.'

His father had eyed her reprovingly. 'Now, Mother, Mike's as good as anyone now that he's an officer.'

It had ended there, or almost. His mother had started

on about the reduced rations, how hard it had been to get enough even for this welcome-home tea party. They should have more consideration for those who had to stay at home and *take it*.

His father had got out his *Daily Mail War Atlas*. 'In my opinion, we should never have trusted the Froggies. It was just the same in the last lot. No guts, the lot of 'em.'

Dancy had recalled Lindsay's face at the burial parties. His quiet voice. And all at once he had not wanted to tell them anything. To share what they could never understand because they did not really want to.

Stannard came out on the wing and screwed up his eyes to search for the aircraft. It was almost abeam, parallel with the port column of ships.

'He's flaming confident.' He looked sideways at Dancy's grim face. 'I hope he runs out of gas without noticing!'

They lapsed into silence, watching the Focke Wulf until it was hidden by a freighter and the overlapping superstructure of the leading troopship.

Dancy said uneasily, 'With an escort like ours we *should* be all right.'

'Too right. The destroyers can cope with the subs. And the big cruiser can beat the hell out of the captain's raider.'

'Is that how you see it?'

'The raider?' Stannard shrugged, remembering with sudden clarity Lindsay's agonised voice on the telephone as he relived the nightmare or whatever was trying to destroy him. 'Every man has to have something in a war. Something to hate or hope for. A goal, personal ambition, who knows?' He glanced round quickly to make sure the nearest lookout was out of earshot. 'Sorry I couldn't give you a ring, Sub. Got a bit involved. You know how it is. Still, I expect you had some little sheila to keep the cold out, eh?'

Dancy tried to grin. 'I did all right.' He did not want to

think of his leave. Or how hurt he had been when
Stannard had failed to call him on the phone. Just for a
drink. Anything. He watched Stannard's clean-cut
profile. Lucky devil. There was something about him. A
sort of carefree recklessness which would appeal to
women very much, Dancy decided.

The closest he had got to female company had been a
friend of his sister. They had made a foursome, which
had of course included his sister's boy-friend. He was not
in the armed forces but employed on some reserved job
in an aircraft factory. Plenty of money, a loud laugh, and
his sister appeared to adore him.

The other girl had been called Gloria. They had gone
to a local dance, and Dancy had been so desperate for
enjoyment that once again in his young life he had mixed
his drinks. Recklessly he had invited the girl back to his
home. His sister and her friend had vanished halfway
through the dance so he had the sitting room marked
down in his mind as a suitable place for improving his
relationship with Gloria. She was young and quite pretty
and had giggled nervously when he had said casually,
'We'll have a tot together. Some of the real stuff I brought
back with me.'

The warmth of the fire, the scent of her hair and body,
the gin, all seemed to combine against him. When he had
kissed her it had still appeared to be going well enough.
When he had put his hand on her breast she had pushed
him frantically away, jumping up with such force that the
gin and glasses had scattered over the floor with a crash
loud enough to wake the dead.

It had in fact awakened Dancy's mother. He could see it
all clearly in his mind as if it was happening this very
instant. Feel the humiliation and embarrassment as his
mother had switched on all the lights and had stood in the
doorway in a dressing gown, her hair in curlers, as she
had snapped, 'I don't expect this sort of thing in *my*
house! I don't know what sort of people you've been

mixing with in the Navy, but I'll not stand for filth under this roof!' To make it worse, Gloria had been violently sick. Altogether it had not been a successful leave by any standards.

Stannard raised his glasses and studied the ammunition ship for several seconds. 'Check her bearing again, Sub. I think she's off station.'

He heard Dancy return to the wheelhouse and sighed. I must be losing my touch, he thought. He had never believed in coincidence, love at first sight, we were meant for each other, and all the other sentiments he had heard voiced in so many ports of call.

But it had happened to him. Just like that. There was no future for either of them. It was hopeless. Best forgotten. Equally he knew he was involved completely. No matter which way it ended.

He had had a couple of drinks at the railway hotel before getting a taxi to the flat. It was all exactly as he had remembered. As he had nursed it in his aching mind throughout the patrols and the freezing watches, the sights of death and pitiful survival.

But another girl had opened the door. When he had identified himself she had said calmly, 'Oh, *she* left some weeks back.'

Stannard had been dumbfounded. No message. Nothing. Not even a goodbye.

The girl had said, 'But if you like to come back in an hour I'll be free.' She had smiled, and in that instant Stannard had realised his dream had been something more than he had bargained for. 'We're kept pretty busy you know.' She had reached out to touch his shoulder strap. 'But for a nice lieutenant like you I'll break all the other appointments, okay?'

He had left without a word, his mind a complete blank.

As he had reached the stairway she had called after him, 'What d'you expect? Betty Grable or something, you stuck-up bleeder!'

And then, a few days later, as he had been walking aimlessly down a London street searching for a bar he had visited some years before, an air-raid had started. Within minutes, or so it had seemed, bombs had begun to rain down, the far end of the street had been filled with dust, smoke and crashing debris. With vague, scurrying figures he had run into a shelter, amazed that he had seemed to be the only one who did not know where to go or what to do.

The All Clear had sounded thirty minutes later. It had been a hit-and-run raid, a warden had said in an authoritative tone. 'Lost 'is bleedin' way more, likely!' a disgruntled postman had suggested.

But when Stannard had emerged from the shelter it was almost dark, and as the other strangers had melted away in the gloom it had begun to pelt with rain.

It was then that he had noticed her. She had been standing under the doorway of a bombed shop clutching a paper bag against her body and staring at the rain in dismay. Without hesitation he had taken off his greatcoat and slung it across her shoulders before she could protest.

'Going far? Well, I'll walk you there, if you like. We'll be company for each other if there's another raid.'

And that was how it had all begun. She lived at a small house in Fulham, close to Putney Bridge. At the door she had looked at his dripping uniform and had said quietly, 'Would you like to come in for a minute? I owe you that at least.'

Her name was Jane Hillier, and she was married to a captain in the Royal Armoured Corps.

As Stannard had given her his jacket to hang by the fire he had seen her husband's picture on the sideboard. A nice looking chap standing with some other soldiers in front of a tank.

'I'd offer you a meal but I'm afraid I've only got some Spam until the shops open tomorrow.'

She was dark and slim, and very attractive. She had

opened the rain-splashed parcel and taken out a small, brightly coloured hat.

'I was being extravagant. I wanted everything to be just right.'

Stannard had glanced at the photograph but she had said quickly, 'No, he's all right. It's not that. But he'll not be coming home. Not yet anyway. He's in the Western Desert. I've not seen him for two years.'

Stannard had walked to his suitcase. 'I've got something better than Spam. I was bringing it for——'

Then she had smiled. For the first time. 'So we were both let down?'

Try as he might, Stannard could not remember the exact moment, the word or the sign which had brought them together.

As he leaned against the screen watching the distant aircraft while it reappeared around the port quarter all he could recall was her body, naked in his arms, her fierce passion as she had given herself, pulling him to her as if there were only minutes left before the world ended. Outside the room the sirens had sounded and somewhere more houses had been bombed to fragments. Once, as Stannard had lain awake staring up into the darkness he had felt her crying against his shoulder, very softly, like a child. But she had been asleep, and he had wondered if, like himself, she was thinking of that other man, the face in the photograph, somewhere in the desert with his tank.

The next day he had collected his things from his hotel and had stayed at the little house near Putney Bridge until the end of his leave.

She had said, 'I'm not sorry for what we did. You know that, don't you?'

As he had stood by that same front door a lorry packed with soldiers had rattled past the house, and Stannard had heard the wolf-whistles and cheerful yells of admiration with something like hatred.

'It wasn't just because you, *we* were lonely. You must know that, too.' The seconds had ticked away. Where were the words when you needed them? 'I don't know how, Jane. But we'll sort this out. I must see you again. *Must.*'

On the crowded train he had tried to rationalise his feelings. Collect his arguments. It was over. An episode, inevitable in this bloody war. He had wanted her. She had been starved of love for two years. That was all there was to it.

When Lindsay had told him of the convoy and the long haul around the Cape to Ceylon he had tried again. Time and distance would end it. But in his heart he knew he would have to see her again, if only to be sure.

Feet moved on the gratings and Lindsay said, 'We've had a signal from Admiralty, Pilot. Four plus U-boats in our vicinity. You'd better put your plotting team to work.' He watched Stannard's strained face. 'You bothered about something?'

Stannard looked at him. 'I'm okay, sir.' He forced a grin. 'Just thinking that I *could* have stayed with my dad selling tractors instead of all this!'

Lindsay watched him leave. He's like the rest of them. Like me. Sick and tired of being on the defensive. Worn out by retreat and vague plans for hitting back at an invisible enemy.

'Signal from commodore, sir.' Ritchie grimaced. 'To *Benbecula.* Make less smoke.'

'Acknowledge, Yeoman.'

Lindsay glanced up at the tall funnel, garish in its new paint. No more smoke than usual. No more than anyone could expect from a ship which should by rights be ending her days quietly somewhere in the sun. Where war meant only a fight for better freight or cheaper running costs.

Maybe the commodore had seen in the curt Admiralty signal some small hint of what he was up against. Not pins

and paper flags on a map. Not a glib daily communique
for the press and the civilians who were *taking it* as best
they could. Out here it was very real. A killing ground
where there were no rules and no standards. A place
where the horizon never seemed to get any nearer, where
the only quick escape was straight down, to the bottom.

He saw two destroyers wheeling in a flurry of spray and
foam to take station on the port quarter, to begin yet
another sweep, listening for the unseen attacker, preparing to strike and kill if the opportunity offered itself.

He glanced at his watch. There was still plenty of time.
The hunters and the hunted knew their various skills,
just as they understood how easily their roles could be
changed.

'I'm going below, Pilot. Call me if you hear anything.'

Stannard watched him climb down the bridge ladder.
Then he turned and stared at the hard horizon. The little
house so close to Putney Bridge suddenly seemed very
far away. A memory, which somehow he must hold on to.
No matter what.

─────────

It was at dusk when the first torpedoes streaked into
the convoy. During the afternoon there had been numer-
ous reports of U-boats in the vicinity, and later still a
destroyer, the *Merlin,* had made a contact.

Aboard the *Benbecula* at the rear of the convoy the
hands had been sent to action stations, but with nothing
to do but wait had stared into the gathering gloom,
listening to the thundering roar of depth-charges. They
had seen tall columns of water bursting skyward even as
the destroyer had swung round for another run-in across
the hidden submarine. She had soon been joined by the
other wing escort, and again the charges had thundered
down, the explosions booming against the *Benbecula*'s
lower hull as if she too was under attack.

In the engine room Fraser had seen several of his men

pausing at their work to look up at the oil-streaked sides, imagining perhaps that a torpedo was already speeding towards them.

On the bridge it was all remote and vaguely disconnected with attack or defence. The three lines of ships plodded on towards a darkening horizon while the other destroyers tore back and forth like nervous dogs around a valuable flock of sheep.

Merlin had reported she had lost contact. There had been some oil sighted but no one paid much attention to that. The U-boat might have been damaged. It could have been a ruse to allow her commander to take evasive action. Either way, *Merlin*'s swift attack had given the convoy more time.

Lindsay sat on his tall chair and watched the ships on either bow. They were already losing their identity as darkness closed in. They were moving faster now, making a good fourteen knots in response to the commodore's signals.

Dancy said, 'It looks as if we may have given them the slip this time, sir.' He sounded very tired.

Lindsay shrugged. 'If the escorts can keep them down, yes. But if they surface they can make a fair speed, too.' He looked at Dancy. What with having the forenoon watch and being called to his action station on the bridge soon afterwards he was showing the strain.

Stannard snatched up a handset as its shrill cry shattered the stillness in the enclosed bridge.

He swung towards Lindsay, his voice urgent. 'Masthead reports torpedoes approaching on the port quarter, sir!'

Lindsay jumped from his chair. 'Full astern!'

When he reached the bridge wing he saw the pale white lines cutting across the dull water, his brain recording their bearing and speed even as he noted the urgent flash of signal lamps, the muffled squawk of the R/T speaker as the alarm ran like wildfire along the lines of ships.

'Stop engines!'

He craned over the screen, straining his eyes to watch the nearest track as it sped straight for *Benbecula*'s port bow. Nothing happened. The nearest torpedo must have missed the ship by less than twenty feet.

'Resume course and revs, Pilot!'

He waited a few more seconds, half expecting to see another torpedo coming out of the gloom. Slamming the engines astern for just those few minutes must have thrown the enemy's sights off balance.

There was a single, muffled explosion which seemed to come from miles away, like thunder on a range of hills. As he ran through the bridge to the starboard wing he saw a searing column of fire, bright red against the clouds, a billowing wall of smoke completely hiding the victim from view.

Lindsay crouched over the gyro repeater on the bridge wing and took a quick bearing. The torpedo must have run diagonally right through the convoy, hitting a freighter just astern of the commodore's ship. There were no more explosions, and he guessed the U-boat commander had fired at extreme range, fanning his torpedoes in the hopes of getting a lucky hit.

Depth-charges boomed and echoed across the water, and over the R/T Lindsay heard an unemotional voice say, 'Have contact. Am attacking.'

The freighter astern of the torpedoed ship was already swinging wildly out of line, the side of her tall hull glowing scarlet in the flames of her burning consort, the fires reflecting in her scuttles and ports so that her cabins appeared to be lit from within.

A destroyer was charging down the lines of ships, and faintly above the grumble of depth-charges and engine room fans Lindsay heard her loud-hailer bellowing, 'Keep closed up, *Pole Star*! *Do not heave to!*'

Stannard said thickly, 'God, look at her!'

The stricken freighter was beginning to heel over, and

in the leaping flames and sparks it was possible to see the
deck cargo starting to tear adrift and go crashing through
the tilting steel bulwarks as if they were matchwood.
Army lorries lurched drunkenly overboard, and from aft
another column of fire burst out of a sealed hold, the
flames licking along the upper deck and setting several
lifeboats ablaze.

The destroyer swept down *Benbecula*'s side, her wash
surging against the hull plates like a great wave breaking
on a jetty. Just briefly before she vanished astern Lindsay
saw her gun mountings swinging round and the crouching seamen on her quarterdeck beside the depth-charge
racks.

Dancy called, '*Pole Star*'s stopping, sir.'

Someone else said hoarsely, 'He's going to try and pick
up survivors!'

Lindsay gripped the screen and watched the sinking
freighter swinging helplessly abeam in the heaving water.
The other ship, *Pole Star*, obviously intended to ignore
the escort's order, and already he could see a boat jerking
down its falls, so clear in the reflected fires it could have
been midday.

'Starboard ten.' For a few seconds nobody moved or
spoke.

Then Jolliffe said, 'Starboard ten, sir. Ten o' starboard
wheel on.'

Lindsay watched the bows swinging very slowly
towards the burning ship. 'Midships.' The bows were still
edging round until the motionless *Pole Star* suddenly
appeared in direct line with the stem.

'Steady.' Lindsay hurried out on to the wing again.
Over his shoulder he snapped, 'Yeoman, make to *Pole
Star*. Resume course and speed. Do not stop.'

He heard Ritchie's shuttered lamp clicking busily but
kept his eyes fixed on the ship ahead.

Stannard exclaimed, 'We'll ram her if we keep on this
course, sir!'

'Exactly.' Lindsay did not move.

Several miles astern a starshell burst almost level with the clouds, and he heard the immediate crack of gunfire. That destroyer must have caught one on the surface.

Ritchie said, '*Pole Star* requests permission to pick up survivors, sir.'

'Denied!'

Stannard looked at Dancy's stricken face and shrugged. If Lindsay did not check *Benbecula*'s onward charge they would hit the other ship fine on her port quarter. At nearly fifteen knots, *Benbecula* would carve through her poop like an axe into a tree.

'*Pole Star* is under way again, sir.' Ritchie had to clear his throat before adding, 'She's turnin'!'

'Port fifteen.'

Lindsay stayed by the screen, his heart pounding in time with the engines. The *Pole Star*'s master had ignored a necessary signal to try to save a few lives. It had taken the sight of *Benbecula*'s massive bows to make him change his mind. As the freighter turned heavily on to her proper course the sinking ship drifted into view down her starboard side. Lindsay watched the blazing hull fixedly as if under a spell. When *Pole Star* moved clear it was like the opening door of a furnace. Most of the freighter was ablaze now and she was going down by the stern, her poop and after well deck blanketed in steam as the beam sea eddied and swirled over the heated metal.

A signalman called, 'Sir! There's men in the water! I can see 'em by a raft!'

Ritchie said harshly, 'Just you watch the commodore's ship, Bunts!'

But the signalman turned towards him, his voice breaking. 'But, Yeo, there's blokes down there! I saw one wavin' at us!' He sounded close to tears.

Ritchie strode across the vibrating gratings and gripped his arm. 'Wot d'you want us to do, lad? Bloody well stop and get *our* arse blown off!' He swung him almost savagely. 'Up at the 'ead of the convoy there's two troopers with Gawd knows 'ow many squaddies on board, see? If we're goin' to get through we've got to stick together!'

The signalman was little more than a boy. 'I know that, Yeo.' He dashed one hand across his eyes and picked up his Aldis lamp. 'It's just that——'

Ritchie interrupted gently, 'You don't 'ave to spell it out, lad.' He sighed as the signalman moved slowly to the opposite side of the bridge. Away from the drifting inferno which was now almost abeam. He could feel the furnace heat on his face through the wheelhouse door, caught the foul stench of charred paint and woodwork. A ship dying. One more for the scoreboard.

The bosun's mate by the voicepipes said bitterly, 'Look at the skipper. Just standin' there watchin' 'em fry! The cold-blooded bastard!'

Ritchie pivoted on his heels and thrust his face within inches of the seaman's. 'If I 'ear you talk that sort of squit again I'll 'ave you on a charge!' He turned slightly to watch Lindsay's head and shoulders silhouetted against the angry glare. ''E's worth twenty of your sort, an' you'll eat your bloody words if you lives long enough!'

Lindsay heard none of it. He watched the other ship's bows begin to rise slowly above the litter of drifting flotsam, heard the dull roar of inrushing water, the screech of machinery tearing free to crash through the burning hull to speed its end. Some sort of fighter plane had broken from its crate and was suspended across one of the blazing holds. In the red glow it looked like a charred crucifix, he thought dully.

With a final roar the ship slid steeply under the surface, leaving a maelstrom of exploding air bubbles and frothing foam. Then nothing.

A messenger said, 'Captain, sir. From W/T office. Six plus U-boats in convoy's vicinity.'

Stannard snapped, 'Very well. Tell my yeoman in the chart room.'

He walked out to the wing, sucking in the cold air like a man brought back from drowning.

He said, 'Poor bastards. D'you think the escorts will be able to find any of them, sir?'

Lindsay's shoulders seemed to sag. 'Listen.' Astern the depth-charge explosions were rising to a drumming crescendo.

Stannard opened his mouth and then closed it, his mind suddenly sickened. The depth-charges would do what the torpedo had failed to accomplish. He had seen many hundreds of dead and gutted fish left in the wake of a depth-charge attack. Men in the water would fare no better, except they would know what was coming.

Lindsay continued to stare astern, his mind still cringing from the suddenness of death. He should be used to it. Hardened, as his half-trained company imagined him to be. But you never did get used to it. Close the ranks. More speed. Don't look back. His mouth twisted in a tight smile. That was the most important bit. Don't ever look back.

Stannard saw the smile and said quietly, 'I'm sorry, sir. I didn't understand.'

Lindsay turned his back on the sea and looked at Stannard's dark outline against the dazzle paint.

'Stop thinking about those men, Pilot.' He saw Stannard stiffen and added coldly, 'Another few feet and it would have been us. Think about that and about how you would have reacted then.'

An hour passed with nothing to break the regular beat of engines, the sea noises beyond the bridge. In the new darkness it looked as if the lines of ships had drawn closer together for mutual support. Another illusion.

Ritchie found Lindsay in his chair. 'From escort, sir. No survivors.'

Half to himself Lindsay said, 'And no U-boat sunk.'

'No, sir.'

Lindsay turned in the chair. 'Pass the word to

Lieutenant Barker to get some hot soup around the ship for all hands. Sandwiches as well.'

As Ritchie beckoned to a messenger Lindsay heard Stannard mutter, '*He* should have thought of that already himself!'

Lindsay turned and stared at the screen, the black blob of the ammunition ship's stern which seemed to be pivoting on *Benbecula*'s jackstaff.

'Pilot, come here.'

'Sir?' Stannard crossed to the chair.

Lindsay kept his voice very low. 'You have the makings of a good officer, a *naval* officer I'm talking about now.' God, how difficult it had become to keep his voice level. 'You are a good navigating officer too, and God knows that's something in a ship like this.' He turned and studied Stannard's face, pale in the darkness. 'But try not to be too clever for your own good. Don't get too hard or you'll grow brittle. Brittle enough to break when you're most needed.'

'I only meant——'

'I don't give a damn what you meant! For all you know, Barker may be dealing with the men's food right now. He may just as easily have fallen down a hatch and broken his neck.'

Stannard said abruptly, 'I *have* apologised.'

'That's fine then.' Lindsay turned back to the screen. 'Just one thing more, and then carry on. If a piece of Krupp steel comes through that screen or a shell bursts above your head on Maxwell and his spotters, things could change for you and *fast*.' He waited a few more seconds, feeling Stannard's resentment and uncertainty. 'You will be in command at that moment. Alone on this bridge maybe. Perhaps for just a few seconds until the next shell. Or maybe you'll have to nurse this old tub a thousand miles without help from anyone.'

Stannard nodded slowly. 'I think I *do* understand, sir. I'm sorry.' He smiled sadly. 'When you've always had a captain or someone to give orders and get you out of a jam it's hard to see yourself in that position.'

Lindsay nodded and took out his pipe. 'We'll say no more about it.'

But Stannard said, 'I was wrong about Aikman, too. I'll never forget how he looked when he left the ship.'

'I was the one who made the mistake, Pilot.' He heard Stannard's quick intake of breath. 'Surprised? That I can be wrong?' He gave a short laugh. 'I used to think much the same about my first captain. He died at Narvik. He turned out to be just a man after all. Like the rest of us.'

Dancy called, 'The first lieutenant's on the phone, sir. Wants to know if he can fall out action stations.'

'No.' As Dancy turned back to his telephone he added quietly, 'Cold and uncomfortable it may be. Cursing my name and birth they most certainly are. But if we catch a torpedo I want our people, or as many of them as possible, *on deck*, where they've got a chance.'

Jupp appeared at the door behind the helmsman carrying a tray. "Ot cocoa, sir?'

Lindsay looked at Stannard, feeling the nervous tension dragging at his mind like one huge claw. 'You see, Pilot? Someone remembered us!'

Stannard walked to the starboard side where Dancy was peering through his night-glasses at the ship ahead.

'I wish you'd heard some of that, Sub.' He kept his voice very quiet. 'Sometime in the future you could have tried to write it all down.'

Dancy lowered his glasses. 'He cares, doesn't he?'

Stannard nodded slowly. 'By Christ, and how he cares. I saw his face when we steamed through those wretched devils in the drink back there. I've sailed with some skippers in my time, but never anyone like this.'

Dancy said simply, 'I was scared to death.'

Stannard took a cup of cocoa from Jupp and held it in his gloved hands. And so was he, he thought wearily. Lindsay was making himself watch those men die with something like physical force. Testing his own reserves and hating what he was doing.

He thought suddenly of a captain he had once served in a ship on the meat-run from Australia. They had gone to assist a Portuguese vessel which had lost her rudder in a storm off Cape Finisterre. And what a storm. Stannard had been a green third officer at the time, and the thought of standing by a crippled ship in such mountainous seas had made him swear it would be his last voyage, if he ever managed to reach port. The old captain had stayed on the bridge for three days without a wink of sleep, never resting until they had lifted off every man from the stricken ship. And that was after several attempts to take her in tow.

There had been a doctor travelling as a passenger on board at the time and Stannard had heard him say to the skipper, 'You *must* get some rest! Or *your* life will be in danger next!'

The skipper, a man of few words on most occasions, had regarded him indifferently. '*My* life, doctor?' He had walked up the pitching deck to the screen again. 'My life is obligations. Nothing else counts.'

Stannard had had his own troubles at the time and had not fully grasped the significance of those words.

He watched Lindsay as he craned over the gyro repeater, the unlit pipe still jutting from his mouth. But he understood now well enough. Perhaps better than any other man aboard.

13 Abandoned

Thirteen days out of Liverpool found the convoy steaming due south, with the Cape Verde Islands some three hundred miles on the port beam. All the colours had changed, yet few aboard the *Benbecula* had noticed the exact moment the transformation had come about. Instead of leaden grey the sea had altered its face to a deep blue, and above the spiralling mastheads the sky was of paler hue with just a few frayed banners of cloud to break its washed-out emptiness.

Lindsay sat in his chair feeling every movement as the ship heaved up and over in an uncomfortable corkscrewing motion. There was a stiff breeze to ruffle the blue water with a million busy cat's-paws, and with a quarter sea to add to the ship's plunging lifts and rolls he could feel the chair pressing into his body as if the bones were pushing through his skin.

Thirteen days. Long days and longer nights, with hardly a break for the men who came and went about their duties like dull-eyed robots.

Not only the weather had changed. The convoy was steaming in just two lines, and it was smaller. The day after the first ship had been torpedoed the *Pole Star* had received a similar fate. Except that the attack had been better planned and controlled, possibly by three U-boats simultaneously. She had taken two torpedoes in her side and had started to sink in minutes. Even before the bow-wave around her rust-streaked stem had died away a third torpedo had struck her dead amidships, blasting her into halves, the forepart sinking immediately, the stern section remaining afloat just long enough for a destroyer to scrape alongside and lift off the remaining survivors. That same day one of the escorts had been hit, the explosion shearing off her forecastle as cleanly as a giant welding torch, laying bare her inner hull for a few more minutes until she rolled over and disappeared with her straight white wake still marking where she had dived.

Encouraged by their success the U-boats had made a surface attack under cover of darkness, only to be caught and pinned down by starshells from one of the other destroyers. She had dropped far astern of the convoy to pick up some survivors sighted by the cruiser's Walrus flying-boat. In fact, they were from some other convoy, and they had *not* survived. Eight men in a scarred lifeboat who had not waved or cheered as the destroyer had come to find them. They must have been dead for several weeks. Just drifting with the currents and winds, already forgotten by the living world they had left behind.

The destroyer had chased after the convoy and even as she had been about to make the recognition signal had detected the surfaced U-boats directly across her bows.

In the eerie glare of drifting flares she had opened fire with every gun which would bear. One U-boat had managed to dive without being hit, but another had been seen to receive several shells so close alongside it was more than likely she would never reach home. But the third had been even less fortunate. In the eye-searing flares her commander may have misjudged the destroyer's bearing and distance. Or perhaps his stern tube had been unloaded and he was trying to engage with his bow torpedoes. Whatever the reason for his sudden turn, the result of it had been swift and definite.

At twenty-five knots the destroyer had rammed her just abaft the conning tower, riding up and over the low whaleback of her casing with a scream of rending steel which had been heard even aboard the *Benbecula*. Like a gutted shark the U-boat had rolled over, breaking apart as the destroyer continued to grind and smash across her.

When daylight came the men on the rearmost ships of the convoy had lined the guardrails to cheer the victorious destroyer, the sound wild and almost desperate as she had turned away for the dangerous passage to Gibraltar. With her bows buckled almost to her forward bulkhead and her forecastle gaping open to the sea she would be out of the war for some time to come. She had made a sad but defiant sight as her low silhouette had finally faded astern, and there were few men in the convoy who had not prayed for her survival.

Nothing else had occurred for two whole days. Then one of the tankers had been hit by a long-range torpedo, her cargo spilling out around her broken hull like blood, until with a great roar the oil had caught fire, encircling the ship in a wall of flames which had almost trapped one of the escorts which was attempting to pick up some of her crew.

Lindsay put a match to his pipe and tried to concentrate his mind on the ships ahead. Without such constant effort his eyes seemed to droop, so that he had to drag himself to his feet, move about like some caged animal until his circulation and brain returned to life.

Thirteen days. Two escorts gone and three merchant ships. The two remaining lines were led by the commodore's troopship, *Cambrian,* and the cruiser *Madagascar.* Just four ships in each line, with *Benbecula* now steaming directly abeam of the ammunition freighter. The early fear of having her in the convoy, and so close to the *Benbecula* for most of the time, had given way to a kind of nervous admiration. Day in, day out, through the U-boat attacks and the desperate alterations of course and speed, she was always there. Big and ugly like her name,

Demodocus, she had, according to Goss, been sailing
under almost every flag in the book since she had been
laid down some four years before the Great War. A
coal-fired ship, she was usually on the receiving end of
some caustic signal about making too much smoke, but
either her master didn't give a damn or as Fraser had
suggested, her chief engineer had his work cut out just to
keep the boiler from bursting.

He saw some off-watch seamen sprawled on the forward hold cover. In the bright sunlight their faces and
bared arms looked very pale, almost white. He was thankful that for the past twenty-four hours there had been
neither an attack nor any more reports of U-boats from
the Admiralty. The hands had been able to get some rest,
enjoy a properly cooked meal, and above all to be spared
the jarring clamour of alarm bells.

He could hear Stannard moving about the chart room.
It was not his watch, so he was probably getting his
personal log up to date.

Lieutenant Maxwell had the forenoon watch, and he
was out on the port wing staring at the ammunition ship,
his cap tilted over his eyes against the glare. His assistant,
Lieutenant Anthony Paget, did not seem to know where
to stand. Afraid perhaps of disturbing his captain he
stayed on the starboard side of the bridge, but at the same
time he seemed unwilling to stray out of Maxwell's vision,
just in case he was needed.

Paget was Aikman's replacement. He appeared a pleasant enough chap, Lindsay thought. He had obtained his
watchkeeping certificate in a corvette but had been in the
Navy for only eighteen months. Before the war he had
been a very junior partner in a firm of solicitors in Leeds.
It was his father's business, otherwise he might have
found it more difficult to get that far, Lindsay decided.
He seemed rather shy and hesitant, and his previous
captain had written in his personal report, 'Honest and
reliable. But lacks qualities of leadership.'

But he was one of *Benbecula*'s lieutenants now, and more to the point, his watchkeeping qualifications would help to spread the load more evenly in a wardroom where most of the junior officers had no experience at all.

Petty Officer Hussey, the senior telegraphist, walked to Lindsay's side and saluted.

'Just the usual bulletins, sir. No U-boat reports.' He flicked over the neatly kept log. 'It seems that the Japs are still advancing though.' He held the log in the sunlight and squinted at it. 'Says that they've reached a place called Batu Pahat.' He grinned. 'Could be in Siberia as far as my geography is concerned, sir.'

The rear door slammed back. 'What was that?' Stannard stood in the reflected sunlight, his brass dividers grasped in one hand.

Lindsay said quietly, 'Batu Pahat.'

Stannard seemed to stagger against the voicepipes. 'But that's only sixty miles from Singapore, for God's sake! It can't be true. No army could move that fast!'

Paget said timidly, 'It's in the south-west corner of Malaya, sir.'

Stannard looked at him unseeingly. 'I know.'

Paget nodded eagerly. 'I read somewhere that there's a prosperous coastal trade for rubber and——.'

Lindsay said, 'Would you ask the chief bosun's mate to come to the bridge, please?'

As the lieutenant scurried for the rack of telephones Stannard said, 'Thanks, sir. You didn't have to do that. He didn't mean anything by it.'

'I know.' Lindsay watched him gravely. 'But sometimes one extra word is enough to drive a man mad.' He smiled. 'I expect your brother has been pulled out by now anyway. If Singapore Island is to be the real holding-point it would be the obvious thing to do.'

Stannard nodded. 'I guess so. But all these reports.' He shook his head. 'Surely to God the people in charge out there can see what's happening?'

Lindsay looked away. 'Some people never read the words, Pilot. They just check the commas!' He rubbed his eyes. 'Forget that. They're probably doing their best.'

Paget returned. 'C.P.O. Archer is coming right up, sir.'

'Good.' Lindsay settled down again on the chair. 'Now I'll have to think of something to tell him.'

'Yes, sir.' Paget looked completely lost.

A signalman shouted, 'Signal from escort, sir! *Merlin* has strong contact at zero-nine-zero. Closing!'

Paget stared at him, his mouth hanging open.

Lindsay snapped, 'Sound action stations!' He felt the sweat gathering under his cap. 'Well, jump to it, man!'

As bells shrilled through the ship he stood up and walked to the port wing where Maxwell was still looking at the ammunition ship.

'What's the matter, Guns? Didn't you hear that?'

Maxwell stared at him. 'Yessir. Sorry, sir.' He turned and ran for the control position as Hunter and the spotting team came pounding up the other ladder from the boat deck.

Ritchie was already here, brushing crumbs from his jacket and still chewing as he snatched his telescope and shouted, 'From commodore, sir. Alter course to two-five-zero!'

'Acknowledge.'

Lindsay gripped the screen, feeling the ship vibrating under his fingers as the voicepipes and telephones burst into life once again.

Ritchie's telescope squeaked as he readjusted it on the leading ships. 'Execute in succession, sir!'

Stannard was already at the gyro compass, his face expressionless while he studied the column wheeling slowly to starboard. The ship directly ahead was the convoy's remaining oil-tanker, a smart, newly built vessel which had already narrowly avoided a torpedo in the earlier attacks.

Ritchie said, '*Merlin*'s got 'er black pennant 'oisted, sir! She's goin' in for a kill!'

A messenger muttered, 'We *hope!*'

'Starboard ten.' Stannard's mouth twitched as a pattern of depth-charges exploded somewhere on the port quarter. The *Merlin* was moving at full speed and swinging in a wide arc while the sea erupted in her curving wake like some impossible waterspout.

'Midships.' Stannard twisted his head quickly to watch the straight black stem of the *Demodocus* following round in obedience to the signal. More explosions, and a second escort came tearing back down the column, racing for the great spreading area of churned water where the last charges had exploded.

As she ploughed through the white froth Lindsay saw the charges fly lazily from either beam, while two more rolled from her quarterdeck rack into her own wash. He could picture them falling through the untroubled depths, ten feet a second, and then. . . . Even though he was expecting it he flinched as the charges detonated and hurled their fury skyward. How long the columns of water seemed to hang there before subsiding into the growing area of foam and dead fish.

'*Madagascar*'s signallin', sir!' The man's voice was almost shrill. 'Torpedoes approachin' from starboard!'

Already the cruiser was turning her grey bulk towards the invisible torpedoes, while far away across the commodore's bows a destroyer was turning to race in to give additional cover.

'Must be two of the bastards, sir!' Stannard raised his glasses and added sharply, 'Watch the ship ahead, Cox'n. Follow her like a bloody sheepdog, no matter what happens!'

'Aye, aye, sir.' Jolliffe eased the spokes and kept his eyes fixed on the oil-tanker.

'Missed her anyway!' Dancy swung round as a double explosion rattled the bridge screen and brought down some flecks of paint on to his cap.

The freighter astern of the cruiser had been hit. The torpedoes must have passed between the two troopships in the starboard column, missed the cruiser, and struck the other vessel as she attempted to follow her leader in the turn.

She was already staggering to port, thick smoke billowing from her side, her bridge wing hanging towards the sea in a tangle of twisted metal and broken rigging.

A great flurry of froth rose around her counter and Stannard said, 'She's going astern. Her skipper must be trying to get the way off her to save the bulkhead.'

Lindsay held the glasses jammed against his eyes while the gratings jerked and vibrated to the thunder of depth-charges. He saw tiny figures running along the freighter's boat deck, while further aft there were others struggling to slip one of the heavy rafts over the side. There was a sudden internal explosion, so that the bridge superstructure appeared to lift and twist out of alignment, the funnel buckling and pitching into the smoke as if made of cardboard.

Whatever had caused the explosion must have killed everyone on the bridge, Lindsay thought. Or else the controls had been shattered by the blast. Whatever it was, the ship was still churning astern, her engine room probably too dazed or desperate to know what had happened on deck.

The freighter which had been following the torpedoed ship had at last understood the danger and her captain was reducing speed, his bow-wave dropping while the distance between him and the runaway freighter continued to diminish.

One of the lifeboats had reached the water, only to be upended by the reversed thrust, hurling its occupants overboard to vanish instantly in the churned wash from the propellers.

The other seamen had at last succeeded in releasing

the liferaft, but could only stand huddled by the guard-rails as their ship continued to forge astern. She was heeling very slightly and certainly sinking, but as the convoy fought to maintain formation she was still a very real menace.

'Commodore's signalled *Rios* to take evasive action, sir!'

The *Rios* was the one astern of the torpedoed freighter, and with something like a prayer Lindsay watched her turn unsteadily and head diagonally from the broken column.

'Torpedo to port, sir!' Dancy had the masthead telephone gripped in his fist so tightly his knuckles were white. 'Two cables!'

Lindsay lifted his glasses and saw the flurry of excitement on the ammunition ship's bridge. It must be running straight for her.

A man screamed, 'If she goes up we'll go with her!'

'Silence on the bridge!' Jolliffe's voice was like a saw, but his eyes stayed on the ship ahead.

It was more of a sensation than a sound. Lindsay saw the other ship stagger, her foremast and derricks falling in tangled confusion even as the tell-tale column of water shot violently above her fore deck.

In those few seconds nobody spoke or moved. Even breathing seemed to have stopped. As the *Demodocus* started to slow down and fall past *Benbecula*'s port beam, to those who were able to watch her it felt as if there were just seconds left to live. The sea and sky, the depth-charges and fast-moving destroyers, none of them counted for anything now.

The torpedoed freighter, her screws still dragging astern, ploughed very slowly beneath the surface, her hull breaking up as she dived for the bottom. But it was doubtful if any man on *Benbecula*'s decks even saw her last moments or the few struggling figures caught in the last savage whirlpool above her grave.

Lindsay lowered his glasses and rubbed his eyes, the movement making Dancy jerk with alarm.

The old *Demodocus* was still there. There was plenty of smoke rising above the hidden wound, and as he held his breath he heard the discordant grinding of her port anchor cable running out. The explosion must have blasted away a capstan or sheered right through the forepart of the lower hull.

'They're callin' us up, sir.' Ritchie cradled the Aldis on his arm and watched a small winking light from the other ship's bridge.

'Have fire in forrard hold.' He took another breath. 'Am holed port side but pumps are coping.' He gasped and then shuttered an acknowledgement before saying thickly, 'An' 'e says that there *is* a God after all!'

A telephone had been buzzing for some seconds. Or minutes. Nobody seemed to understand anything any more.

Then a messenger said, 'W/T office reports that the escorts have sunk another U-boat, sir. Definite kill.'

Lindsay wiped his face with his hand. It was clammy.

'That will keep them quiet for a bit.' He felt unsteady on his feet. As if he was recovering from some terrible bout of fever.

'From commodore, sir.' Ritchie was very calm. "E's callin' up the ammo ship.' He smiled grimly. 'Can't never pronounce *'er* name, sir. 'E's enquirin' about damage, sir.'

Lindsay walked out on to the port wing and looked at the other column. The cruiser, the *Rios*, which had narrowly avoided being rammed by the sinking freighter, and now, dropping still further astern, the ugly bulk of the ship whose name Ritchie could not pronounce.

Eleven left of the seventeen which had headed so bravely from Liverpool.

Ritchie said suddenly, 'She's tellin' the commodore she can only manage five knots till they've carried out repairs,

sir. But the fire's almost under control. There was no
ammo in *that* 'old, sir.' He watched the slow winking light.
'But the next 'old is filled to the brim with T.N.T.'

Lindsay looked at Stannard. 'Near thing. She may still
have to abandon. Tell Number One to warn the boat
crews and lowerers.'

A destroyer was edging past the *Demodocus*'s hidden
side, her raked masts and funnel making a striking
contrast to the bulbous hull and outdated upperworks of
the ammunition ship. As she moved into full view Lindsay saw she was the *Merlin*.

Her loud-hailer squeaked and then boomed into life. 'I
have a message for you, Captain!'

Lindsay trained his glasses on the slow moving
destroyer. The open bridge with the officers and lookouts
standing down from their last battle, their last kill.

Her captain's face swam into the lenses, reddened by
sea and wind, but the same man he had seen in the office
at Scapa. He, at least, had something to be proud of. He
had sunk a U-boat and damaged at least one other.

Lindsay picked up the megaphone and shouted, 'Well
done, *Merlin!*'

As he said the words he felt a new upsurge of resentment and despair. To this young destroyer officer *Benbecula* would not be seen as anything more than just
another charge to be escorted and protected. A big,
vulnerable liability.

The loud-hailer continued, 'From the commodore.
You will stand by *Demodocus* and act as her escort. He
feels the risk to the troopships is too great to slow down.'
He added almost apologetically, 'The cruiser too is some-
what naked under these conditions.'

Behind him Lindsay heard Dancy whisper fiercely,
'What's he saying? No escort? We're being left behind?'

The destroyer was starting to gather speed again. The
voice called, 'By dawn tomorrow you should be joined by
other escorts. But I'm pretty sure there are no more

U-boats in the vicinity now. If there are, they'll keep after the convoy.'

Lindsay lifted one hand to him. 'Good luck!'

He watched the destroyer surging ahead. Good luck. That young man certainly had that, and more. But it was hard to hide the hurt, the knowledge that he could have been on that bridge. Being useful.

He turned his back on the other ships. 'Signal *Demodocus* to take station astern. Find out her exact speed and reduce revs accordingly.'

Stannard was still watching the oil-tanker. She was drawing away so fast it made it appear as if *Benbecula* was going astern. Lights were flashing and more signal flags were breaking from the commodore's yards. The escorts re-formed and the cruiser altered course to lead the single line of merchantmen like an armoured knight watching over his private possessions. In fifteen minutes the convoy was so far away that the ships which had been old friends had lost their meaning and personality. In an hour there was little to see at all. Just a smudge of smoke on the horizon, a single bright flash of sunlight on the bridge screen of an escort as she turned in another sweep for echoes from below.

Ritchie said quietly, 'Now *'ere's* a fine thing, Swain.'

Jolliffe darted a glance at the officers and nodded. 'I know. A D.S.O. for the commodore, D.S.C. for the escort commander, and medals all round, I shouldn't wonder.' He grinned. 'An' us? We'll be lucky if we *sees* the bloody dawn tomorrow, let alone a soddin' escort!'

Stannard said, 'Look at the damage, sir.'

Lindsay followed him on to the port wing and studied the ship astern. It was a great gash, as if another vessel had rammed her at full speed. Smoke was still billowing from the hole and the deck immediately above. But there was less of it, and he could see plenty of activity on the forecastle where men were working to clear away some of the debris from the fallen derricks. It must be like standing on one gigantic floating bomb, he thought. And if the fire got out of hand again or the next bulkhead became overheated, that would be that.

He said, 'Fall out action stations.'

Stannard looked surprised.

'Well, Pilot, if there *is* a U-boat about we can't see it, and we can't damn well hear it, so where's the point of wearing everyone down for nothing.' He touched Stannard's arm. 'Anyway, if there *was* one of the commodore's *Huns* about, I think he would have announced his presence by now.'

Stannard nodded. 'I guess so.'

'But double the lookouts and keep all short-range weapons crews closed up.'

Stannard hurried away as Goss mounted the bridge ladder and stood breathing heavily for several seconds. Then he swivelled his head slowly from side to side as if still unable to grasp that the convoy had vanished.

Ritchie called, 'Ammo ship 'as R/T contact now, sir.'

Lindsay strode quickly to the W/T office where Hussey and his telegraphists slumped wearily in their steel chairs.

Hussey said, 'Here you are, sir.' He handed a microphone to Lindsay and added shortly, 'Permission to smoke, sir? My lads are just about dead beat.'

Lindsay nodded and snapped down the button. '*Benbecula* to *Demodocus*. This is the captain speaking. How is it going?'

The telegraphists looked up at the bulkhead speaker as a tired voice replied, 'Thanks for staying with us. We're not doing too bad. But the collision bulkhead is weeping a bit and I've got the hands shoring it up as best they can. There's still a fire in the forrard hold, and we've no breathing apparatus. Nobody can work down there for more'n minutes at a time.' They heard his sigh very loud on the speaker. 'Can't make much more'n four knots. If that bloody bulkhead collapses the hold will flood. With the weight of cargo forrard it'll damn near lift my arse out of the drink! Then he laughed. 'Still, better that way than how the Jerry intended, eh?'

Lindsay said, 'Keep a good lookout astern, Captain. I'm going to drop a boat and send some breathing gear and extra hands.'

'I'm obliged.' A pause. 'A doctor too if you can spare him. Mine was killed by the blast and I've twelve lads in a bad way.'

'Will do.' Lindsay saw Ritchie in the doorway. 'Tell the first lieutenant. Quick as you can.'

He hesitated and then spoke again into the microphone. 'At the first sign of trouble, Captain, bale out. I'll do what I can.'

The speaker went dead and he returned to the bridge wing.

Goss said, 'I've got things going, sir. Boat will be ready for lowering in five minutes. I'm sending Lieutenant Hunter to take charge. Doc's already on the boat deck.' He added, 'I'll go myself if you like.'

'No.' Lindsay watched the port motor boat swinging clear of its davits. 'I need you here.'

Goss shrugged. 'Won't make much difference anyway if another U-boat arrives.'

It took another half-hour to ferry the required men and equipment to the other ship and recover the motor boat. Groups of unemployed seamen and marines crowded the *Benbecula*'s poop to watch the activity as hoses were brought to bear on the burning hold and a winch came to life and started to haul some of the debris clear of the fore deck.

All afternoon the work continued while the two ships ploughed across the blue water at little more than a snail's pace.

Aboard *Benbecula* the atmosphere was unreal and strangely carefree. In close convoy, with U-boats reported in every direction, death had seemed very near. But like most men in war, it had to happen to others, never to you. Now, without escort or aid of any kind, the mood was entirely different. Men went about their duties with a kind of casual indifference. Like people Lindsay had seen in the London air-raids. They could *do* nothing, so what the hell, the mood seemed to suggest.

C.P.O. Archer and his men had checked the liferafts for instant lowering, and as the sun began to dip towards a hazy horizon most of the ship's company appeared to accept the inevitable.

The last dog watch had almost run its course when a signalman said sharply, 'There's someone callin' us up, sir!'

Ritchie had been squatting on a flag locker, legs outstretched as if asleep, but he was across to the open wing before Lindsay could move from his chair.

'I don't see nothin'!'

The signalman pointed. 'There. On the upper bridge, Yeo.'

Lindsay trained his glasses and saw one of the ammunition ship's officers dimly outlined against the outdated compass platform, his arms moving very slowly like a child's puppet.

Ritchie raised his telescope and muttered, 'Bleedin' semaphore! 'Ow the 'ell does 'e expect me to read that in this light?'

Lindsay steadied his feet on the gratings. There was a lazy swell and the breeze had dropped considerably. At such slow speed it was difficult to hold the glasses on the tiny dark figure.

Ritchie gasped and said, "E says there's somethin' astern, sir. Five miles or thereabouts.' He looked quickly at Lindsay's set features. 'Could be a submarine.'

Lindsay lowered his glasses. The ammunition ship had become part of the scene. Familiar. Almost part of themselves. It seemed impossible that anything could happen now. Just like this.

He said, 'That captain is a very clever man, Yeoman.' He watched Ritchie's telescope wavering in the motion like a small cannon. 'Most men as tired and worried as he must be would have used a lamp, or even worse, the R/T.'

Goss came hurrying from the chart room. 'What's it doing?'

Lindsay said, 'Go aft, Yeoman, and keep contact with the bridge by the poop telephone.'

To Goss he added, 'Reduce to dead slow and close the gap. We *must* keep visual contact. Their lookouts may be able to see the U-boat, but if we try and turn they'll know we've spotted them.'

Stannard asked, 'Why doesn't the bastard fire, sir?'

Goss nodded. 'Christ knows we're moving slow enough. He could catch us up in no time.'

A messenger called, 'W/T office reports no signals, sir.'

Lindsay nodded slowly. It could just be possible the U-boat had been damaged in that last attack. Maybe she could not dive, or perhaps her torpedo tubes had been put out of action by depth-charges. But she was back there all the same. Limping along like a wounded wolf, and every bit as dangerous.

He glanced quickly at the masthead pendant. It was flicking out very gently towards the stern. The wind was still coming from the south-east.

He turned and stared unblinkingly at the dipping sun. It was too high. The slow-moving ships would stand out against the horizon as perfect targets for another half-hour, maybe longer.

'I think the U-boat is going to close and use his deck gun.'

Even as he spoke his thoughts aloud he knew he was committing himself. All of them.

Goss stared at him. 'But if they get one shell into that bloody ship——.' He could not go on.

Stannard said tersely, 'Shall I signal them to abandon, sir? We could drop all our boats and rafts and maybe come back for them later.'

Lindsay was still watching the ship astern. Big, solid and black. That U-boat commander would recognise her all right. Would probably know her lethal cargo down to the last bullet. It would make up for the way his own command had been mauled. The terror of his men as the charges had rained down from the hunters on the surface.

'Leave her, you mean?' He spoke very quietly. 'Run away?'

Goss said, 'It's not that. We've the ship to consider. Our own people.'

A signalman called, 'The yeoman says that the ammo ship can still see the U-boat, sir. On the surface. Full buoyancy.'

Lindsay thought briefly of the *Demodocus*'s master. A man he would dearly like to meet. Someone who, despite the hideous death which was so close to him and his men, could note the small but vital details. No U-boat would chase after its prey fully trimmed to the surface. It would be ballasted well down with just part of the casing and conning tower visible. It *must* be damaged. It was their only hope.

'Tell the yeoman to use his Aldis. It should be masked from the U-boat by the other ship. I want the *Demodocus* to start another fire. It'll be damn dangerous. But her captain will know the risks without my telling him. Oily rags, anything, but I want plenty of smoke.'

He pushed past the others and snatched up the engine room handset. 'Chief? This is the captain.'

Fraser chuckled. 'I thought you'd forgotten us.'

'Listen. I want you to make smoke, everything you can do to produce the biggest fog in creation! Just as soon as I give the word!'

'Aye, sir.' Lindsay heard him yelling to his assistant,

Dyke, above the roar of fans. Then he asked calmly, 'Might I be told the reason, sir?'

'Yes. We're going to engage a surfaced U-boat.'

He dropped the handset as Stannard said, 'They've got a fire going already. God, I'd have thought the worst if I'd not heard your order.'

Lindsay saw the pall rising rapidly astern. 'Sound action stations.' He grasped Goss's arm. 'I'm going to go hard astarboard in about ten minutes.' He saw Goss's anxious features and wondered if he was fearing for his life or that of the ship. 'The fact that the U-boat's made no W/T signals doesn't mean she won't very soon. Her radio may be damaged, but if they once get it going again we're done for.' He had to yell above the alarm bells. 'So go to damage control, and *pray!*'

Dancy called, 'Ship at action stations, sir.'

'Very good. Tell control to stand by. Maxwell will have to engage with the starboard battery.'

He looked at Stannard. 'Inform the chief. Make smoke now.'

He turned to watch the thick greasy cloud which started to gush over the funnel's lip almost before Stannard had replaced the telephone. He made himself wait a few more minutes, feeling the ship heaving uneasily beneath him, trying to estimate her turning circle under such desperate circumstances.

'Ready, Cox'n?'

Jolliffe nodded. 'Ready, sir.'

'Pilot?'

Stannard forced a grin. 'As I'll ever be, sir.'

Lindsay took out his pipe and thrust it between his teeth.

'Stop starboard. Full ahead port.' He counted more seconds, feeling the deck shuddering violently to the added thrust on one shaft. 'Hard astarboard!'

He glanced through a stern scuttle at the dense smoke. Already the angle was changing. 'Starboard engine full astern!'

He turned again to face the empty sea beyond the bows. Perhaps it could not be done. There was nothing in the book to say it should even be attempted. But there was little in any of those books about the war either, he thought.

'Midships! *Full ahead together!'*

14 Hitting back

Heeling steeply to the violent thrust of screws and rudder the *Benbecula* thrashed round until she was steering almost the reverse of her original course. Lindsay stood in the centre of the bridge, his glasses level with his chin as he waited for a first sight of the enemy. The fore deck was almost hidden in a thick, choking fog from the funnel, as caught by a sudden down-draught and aided by the change of direction the wind fanned Fraser's screen over the ship in a solid wall. Lindsay knew they must be passing the *Demodocus* somewhere to starboard, although her improvised smokescreen was so thick she could have been a mile away or fifty yards. Even with the doors closed Lindsay could taste the acrid stench, just as he could hear the lookouts on the upper bridge retching and gasping above the din of racing engines. He lowered his eyes a few inches to the gyro.

'Steer zero-one-zero!'

He heard Jolliffe's quick reply but kept his eyes fixed on the thinning pall of smoke across *Benbecula*'s line of advance. Soon now and he would know if he had been right. Justified.

The U-boat commander may have seen the two ships as stragglers from the convoy, which indeed they were, and was so confident that he considered it wasteful to use his remaining torpedoes.

Lindsay dashed a trickle of sweat from his eyes. If that was the case, and the U-boat was undamaged, one salvo from her bow tubes would be enough. With *Benbecula* working up to her maximum revolutions the effect would be too terrible to contemplate.

Maxwell's voice came over the bridge speaker, detached and toneless. 'Starboard battery stand by.'

Lindsay dropped his gaze to the fore deck and saw the two starboard guns moving their muzzles slightly, like blind things in the swirling smoke. Further aft de Chair's marines would have to remain inactive for the present. Their starboard gun could not bear on the target if Lindsay's calculations were correct. *If, if, if.* The word seemed to hammer in his brain as if someone had shouted it aloud.

Slivers of spray spurted over the bows, and he knew that Fraser's gauges were well into the danger mark now. The old ship was shaking and groaning to the whirling screws and the whole bridge seemed to be quaking under the strain.

Maxwell's voice cut above the other sounds, as if he had the handset right against his lips. 'Submarine on the surface at Green two-five! Range oh-eight-oh!'

Lindsay gritted his teeth, willing the smoke to clear so that he could see what Maxwell and his spotters had sighted from their precarious position above the bridge.

There was a brief flash beyond the smoke and seconds later the sound of a shellburst. For an instant longer he imagined the enemy had already anticipated his move, was even now slamming a shell towards *Benbecula* to make her sheer away and present a perfect target for torpedoes.

Through the smoke there was another flash, the sullen bang of an explosion.

Lindsay glanced at Stannard and said, 'He's shooting at the ammunition ship!'

When he turned his head again he saw. the U-boat. Even at ·four miles range her austere silhouette was exactly as he had pictured it in his mind. The dying sunlight seemed very bright on the slim conning tower, so that it looked as if it was made of pure copper.

Then the bells rang below the bridge and both six-inch guns fired in unison.

It seemed an age before the shells reached the narrow target. Then as Lindsay jammed his glasses against his eyes he saw twin columns of bursting water astern of the U-boat, very white against the darkening horizon.

'Over. Down two hundred.' Maxwell could have been at a practice shoot. Lindsay had never heard him so cool.

He watched the sudden reaction on the U-boat's fore deck, holding his breath. She was turning, steering almost on a converging course now. But she was still high on the water, the bow-wave creaming along her rounded saddle tanks as she completed the slight turn.

The bells sounded once more and both guns lurched back on their springs, the shockwaves rattling the bridge screens like gale-force winds.

Lindsay bit his lip as both shells ploughed into the sea to the right of the target.

There was an answering flash from the U-boat's deck gun, and he felt the hull shudder as the shell ploughed alongside and exploded, hurling up a great column of water and smoke as splinters clanged over the bulwark.

Lindsay felt very calm. Whatever happened in the next few moments would decide the fate of his own ship and that of the damaged *Demodocus*. But one thing was certain. The German captain could not dive, nor could he use torpedoes. He would have done both by now if it was humanly possible. Lindsay could imagine the consternation on that conning tower as Maxwell's six-inch shells ripped down on them, getting closer with each agonising second. And it must have all looked so easy. Just two more stragglers from a convoy and not an escort within miles.

Smoke funnelled back from the bows, and Lindsay heard the screeching crash of a shell exploding between decks.

'Range oh-six-two.'

He banged the teak rail by the screen with his clenched

fist. The U-boat showed no sign of turning and her gun was firing with even greater rapidity than before. Just one good shot and *Benbecula* could be slowed or stopped while the German manoeuvred to a more favourable position. Right ahead of the bows where not a single gun would bear.

A shell ripped past the bridge and exploded somewhere astern. It made a terrible sound, like tearing canvas, and so close that a gyro repeater on the starboard wing exploded like a small bomb, the fragments thudding into the door and steel plates overhead.

Lindsay heard a man cry out and Maxwell snap, 'First aid party on the double!'

Stannard yelled wildly, 'We've straddled the bastard!' He was almost sobbing with excitement as two waterspouts bracketed the U-boat, burying her after casing beneath tons of falling spray.

Two tiny figures pitched from the bandstand abaft her conning tower, where a four-barrelled Vierling pointed impotently at the sky, and vanished into the falling deluge of water. One of the shells must have exploded close enough to rake the stern with splinters.

Stannard said tightly, 'She's turning, sir!'

The bridge speaker intoned, 'Target has altered course. Moving right. Number Three gun stand by to engage!'

Lindsay said, 'I think his steering is damaged.'

The U-boat's forward gun flashed once more, and he felt the deck jump beneath him as a shell exploded inside the hull.

From the boat deck an Oerlikon opened fire, the tracer drifting like lazy red balls towards the U-boat before pitching down into the darkly shadowed troughs.

Maxwell sounded furious. 'Number Three Oerlikon *cease firing!*'

Lindsay could imagine the lone Oerlikon gunner losing his self-control. Even the knowledge that his gun was almost useless above a thousand yards, his training and Maxwell's discipline were not enough under such circumstances. Just to see the enemy. To watch him in the sights and be doing nothing about it was too much for any man.

He flinched as the two forward guns belched fire yet again. He had lost all idea of time and distance covered. His brain and hearing seemed lost in the crash of guns, the blasting returns from the U-boat.

A tall waterspout shot skyward beyond the German's hull and the other shell exploded directly against her side. It must have hit a saddle tank just beneath the surface, and for several seconds Lindsay imagined she had been blasted apart. As spray continued to fall he saw the black hull sliding clear, heard Stannard gasp, 'Oh, the bastards! They're still afloat!'

Lindsay steadied his glasses, waiting for some sort of reaction to take hold of him. He heard himself say, 'She's going over. Look, Pilot, the gun's crew are baling out.' Why was his voice so flat? So empty of excitement?

He moved his glasses very slightly to watch more dark shapes tumbling from the conning tower which was already tilting towards him. The way was off the hull and gigantic air bubbles were exploding on the surface alongside, like obscene glassy creatures from the depths.

'Reduce to half speed. Starboard ten.'

He swung around as the second gun on the well deck lurched inboard, the shell exploding alongside the U-boat's listing hull like a fireball.

Lindsay shouted, 'Cease firing!' He lowered his eye to the gyro. 'Midships. Steady. Steer zero-four-five.'

That last one had been more than enough. The U-boat's bows were lifting very slowly above the dotted heads in the water. Greedily the sea was already clawing along her buckled after casing, dragging a corpse with it as it advanced.

Lindsay watched without emotion. The Atlantic was

having another victory. It was as impartial as it was ruthless.

Dancy called, 'Damage control reports flooding in Number Three hold, sir. There's a fire on B deck, too.'

Lindsay kept his eyes fixed on the submarine. In the powerful lenses he could see the weed and slime on her exposed hull. She had probably been at sea for weeks, months. Maybe she would have been on her way home by now but for her commander's determination. The sight of two helpless, ungainly targets.

Almost distantly he asked, 'Is Number One coping?'

'Yessir.' Dancy's voice was shaking with emotion or barely suppressed excitement. 'But one man has been killed, sir. Twenty more wounded by splinters or burns.'

'Very well. Make a signal to *Demodocus* and request they send the doc to us as soon as possible.'

He turned and looked through a quarter scuttle. The black ammunition ship looked even darker now against the shadows. But she had stayed to watch the fight, even though she would have been blown to hell if *Benbecula*'s tactics had failed.

There was a yell, 'There she goes!' And from the upper deck Lindsay heard more shouts and then wild cheering as the submarine began to slide under the surface. For just a few more seconds she hung with her raked stem pointing straight at the sky, holding the last tip of sunlight from the horizon, as if burning from within. Then she vanished.

The cheering faltered and died, and Lindsay saw some of the seamen lining the guardrails to watch in silence as a patch of oil continued to spread across the water, making an even greater darkness, like the shadow of some solitary cloud. 'Slow ahead both engines.'

He let the glasses drop against his chest. He could almost feel what those men were thinking, their confusion and uncertainty. This was their first victory, probably one of the few occasions in which a ship built for peace had destroyed one created for war. Now it had happened, their emotions were lost in shock and disbelief.

Stannard said, 'Light's almost gone, sir.' He watched Lindsay's impassive face, waiting for a reaction.

Ritchie called, 'Motor boat from the ammo ship approachin', sir!'

'Very well. Pass the word to Number One's people to assist the doctor aboard.'

Lindsay walked slowly to the open door and stared at the shattered gyro repeater. There was a scorched black scar on the plating. The shell had been that near. Twenty feet and it would have exploded inside the wheelhouse. He thought of Stannard and Dancy, Ritchie and all the others who would have died with him.

Stannard joined him by the screen. 'Stop engines, sir?'

Lindsay watched the dark shape of a power boat chugging towards the side. 'Yes.' He knew Stannard was still there. Waiting. He added shortly, 'Put a party of our people in the boat and send it to pick up survivors. If there are any.'

He gripped the rail until the pain steadied him. He heard the telegraphs clang again, the sigh of water against the hull as the ship began to slow down. They had been made to steam past sinking ships. Men like themselves crying out and dying while they and other ships in convoy had obeyed the signal. Keep closed up. Don't look back.

Now there *was* time, and for a while anyway they were safe from further attack. So they would obey the code. Play out the game. Except that this time the survivors would be German and not their own.

Goss came up to the bridge and said, 'Fire's out, sir.' He sounded incredibly tired. Beaten. 'The pumps are holding the intake in the hold but the marines' messdeck has been destroyed. God, it looks like a pepperpot on the starboard side!'

Ritchie called from the wheelhouse, 'Ammo ship 'as just called us on R/T, sir. That one shell the Jerry slung at 'er seems to 'ave put 'er shaft out of line. 'Er chief says 'e don't reckon on bein' able to get even steerage way now.'

Lindsay removed his cap and turned to face the cool evening breeze. After all that, they would have to leave the other ship. Abandon her.

Aloud he said, 'If I'd known that before, I'd——'

Goss said, 'You'd have let those Jerries drown, sir?'

Lindsay looked at him, trying to control his aching mind. 'I think I would.'

Goss watched the motor boat as it started back for the *Benbecula's* tall side. 'Not many of 'em left anyway.' He turned towards Lindsay. 'The *bastards!*'

Ritchie asked quietly, 'Any reply for the ammo ship, sir?'

Goss said, 'Could we stand by her till morning, sir?'

'Yes.' Lindsay replaced his cap. 'It would be safer than trying to transfer her crew in the dark.'

'I wasn't thinking of that.' Goss sounded strangely calm. 'We could take her in tow.'

Lindsay stared at him. 'Do you mean that?'

'I know we're not rigged for it. The old *Becky* was built for better things.' He spoke very quickly, as if he had made up his mind despite doubts and inner arguments. 'But with some good hands I could work all night an' lay out a towing cable. There's not much aft to help secure it, but I thought——'

'The twelve-pounder gun?'

'Yessir. It'll probably never fire again, but it'd make a damn fine towing bollard.'

Lindsay turned his face away. 'As far as I know it never *has* fired.'

There was so much to do. Plans to make and the damage to be inspected and contained. The wounded, too. And the men who had died.

But all he could think of now was Goss's voice and his

obvious conviction. It was even more than that. It was the first time since he had taken command that Goss had openly shared their mutual responsibility.

He nodded. 'Then we'll do it. At least we'll have a damn good try.' He beckoned to Stannard. 'Tell *Demodocus* we will stand by until first light. Explain what we are going to attempt.' He checked him. 'No, tell them what we are going to *do!*'

Goss shrugged his shoulders inside his heavy watch-coat. 'There may be fresh escorts coming for us tomorrow. But I expect they'll be sent from Freetown. Probably never find us anyway.' He tugged down the peak of his cap and stared at the promenade deck. 'Now I'll go and see what C.P.O. bloody Archer really knows about seamanship!'

Lindsay stood on the gratings to watch the motor boat riding on the swell against the ship's rough plates.

'Number One.'

'Sir?' Goss paused, his foot in mid-air.

'Tell doc to make some arrangements for the German survivors. His sickbay must be getting rather crowded.'

'I'll lay it on.' He waited, knowing Lindsay had something more to say.

'And thanks, Number One.'

Goss swivelled around on the top of the ladder, squinting at Lindsay's silhouette dark against the sky. Then without another word he clattered down the ladder and vanished into the gathering darkness.

Lindsay took out his pipe and tapped it against the damp steel. Goss had his pride. It was unshakable, like his faith in this old ship. Just for a few seconds he had almost overcome it. But not quite.

He sighed and walked into the wheelhouse. 'Slow ahead both engines. Take the con, Pilot, until we can work out the drift. We don't want to ram the poor old *Demodocus* after getting this far.'

Stannard smiled gravely and walked to the compass.

He had heard most that had been said on the scorched starboard wing. He knew what it had cost Goss to make his suggestion about towing. He could have remained silent, and Lindsay would have abandoned the other ship. God knows, he's done enough for all of us, he thought, without that.

But Goss loved this ship more than life itself, and if he had to tow that bloody hulk with his bare hands to prove what his *Becky* could do, then Stannard had no doubt he would attempt that, too.

A telephone buzzed and the bosun's mate said, 'Sick-bay, sir. The doctor says there's one Jerry lieutenant amongst the survivors. 'E sends 'is thanks for us pickin' 'im up.' He waited. 'Any reply, sir?'

Stannard looked at Lindsay. 'Sir?'

'Just tell doc to do what he can for them.' He walked towards the chart room. 'But keep that bastard lieutenant off my bridge, *understood?*'

As the seaman spoke rapidly into the telephone Lindsay added from the doorway, 'What do they expect? A handshake? All pals again now that it's over for them?' His voice was quiet but in the sudden stillness it was like a whip. 'Well, not for me, Pilot. But if you happen to bump into this polite little German lieutenant on your rounds, you may tell him from me that I only picked them up for one reason. And that was to see what they *looked* like.'

'And now, sir?'

'Now?' He laughed bitterly. 'Now, I don't care. I don't give a damn.'

He seemed to realise they were all staring at him and added curtly, 'We will remain at action stations, but make sure the watchkeepers and lookouts are relieved as often as possible. Gun crews can sleep at their stations. And see what you can do about some hot food and have it sent around. There could be another U-boat about, although I doubt it.'

Stannard replied quietly, 'I'll do that, sir.' He watched Lindsay stagger against the open door, feeling for him, imagining what the strain was doing to him. He hesitated, 'And congratulations, sir. That was a bloody fine piece of work!'

Lindsay remained in the doorway, his face in shadow. 'You did well, Pilot.' He looked slowly around the darkened bridge. 'You all did.' Then he was gone.

Dancy moved to Stannard's side and said softly, 'I thought we'd had it.'

Stannard watched the pale arrowhead of foam riding back from the bows. 'Me, too. Now that we're still alive I don't really know if I'm on my arse or my elbow!'

Dancy nodded and ran his fingers along the smooth teak rail beside Lindsay's chair. It was impossible to understand. To grasp. In convoy he had been hard put to keep his fear from showing itself. Every minute had been an eternity. When on one occasion the ship's company had stood down from action stations he had been unable to go to his cabin, when moments earlier it had seemed the most important, the most vital goal in his existence. Sheer terror had prevented his going. He had found himself thinking of the brief Admiralty signals. Instead of six U-boats in the convoy's vicinity he had begun to think of the men inside them. Six submarines. That meant a total of some four hundred men. Four hundred Germans somewhere out there in the pitiless ocean, waiting, preparing to kill. To kill him. Even as he had crouched, sweating and wideawake below the bridge, he had imagined a torpedo already on its way. Silent and invisible, like those four hundred Germans.

The sudden action with the surfaced U-boat had changed all that, although he could not explain why or how. It was as if he had been pushed beyond some old protective barrier into another world. A no-man's-land. What was it the captain had called it? A killing ground. Sense, hope and reason were unimportant out here. Just the men near you. The ship around all of them. Nothing else counted.

Stannard said, 'Go and check around the messdecks, Sub. Make sure we're not showing any lights.'

Dancy replied, 'I could send someone.'

Stannard shook his head. 'You go. Walk about for a bit. It'll do more good than standing up here thinking. You can think too much.'

Jupp came into the wheelhouse. 'I've brought some sandwiches for the cap'n, sir.'

Stannard strode to the chart room and pulled open the door. Lindsay was sprawled across one of the lockers, one hand still reaching for a folio, his cap lying where it had fallen on the deck. He closed the door gently.

'Leave them, Jupp. I'll see he gets them later.'

Jupp nodded. 'Yessir.' Like Dancy, he did not seem to want to go.

Stannard said, 'Let him rest while he can. Christ knows, he's earned it.'

Steel scraped on steel and he heard Goss's resonant voice roaring along the promenade deck. He was at it already. Wires and strops, cable and jacks, it was something Goss had been doing all his life.

Stannard walked unsteadily across the gratings, massaging the ache in his limbs. He must have been standing as stiffly and rigid as one of de Chair's marines, he thought vaguely. *You did well, Pilot.* The words seemed to linger in his mind. Yet he could hardly remember moving throughout the action, giving an order, anything. Once he had thought of the girl in London, had tried to see her face.

He sighed. There was still a long, long way to go before they reached Trincomalee in Ceylon. And after that, where?

A signalman said, 'Ammo ship on the starboard bow, sir.'

Stannard shook his weariness away and hurried to the

screen. Time enough to worry about a future when this lot was finished.

'Port ten.' He rubbed his eyes. 'Midships.'

The watch continued, and in the dimly lit chart room Lindsay slept undisturbed either by dreams or memory, his outflung arm moving regularly to the motion of his ship.

———————

At first light the next day the business of passing a towline was started. It took all morning and most of the forenoon, with motor boats plying back and forth between the ships to keep an eye on the proceedings. It took hours of backbreaking work and endless patience, and while Lindsay conned his ship as close as he dared to the drifting *Demodocus*, Goss strode about the poop yelling instructions until his voice was almost a whisper. Twice the tow parted even as *Benbecula*'s engines began to take the strain, and each time the whole affair had to be started from scratch.

The after well deck and poop were scarred and littered by wires and heavy cable, and the twelve-pounder gun mounting soon took on the appearance of something which had been squeezed in a giant vice.

But the third time it worked.

Ritchie said, 'Signal, sir. Tow secured.' He sounded doubtful.

'Slow ahead together.'

Once more the increasing vibration while very slowly the great length of towing cable accepted the strain.

Lindsay watched the other ship's massive bulk through his glasses, his eyes on an officer in her bows who was holding the bright flag above his head. Seconds, then minutes passed, with the *Demodocus* still apparently immobile in the shallow troughs, as if gauging the exact moment to break free again.

Quite suddenly her angle began to alter, and Lindsay saw the bright flag start to move above the officer's head in a small circle. Reluctantly the other vessel swung ponderously into the *Benbecula*'s small wake, her siren giving a loud toot as a mark of approval.

The tow did not part again, and when two destroyers found them on the following day both ships were still on course, the cable intact.

The senior destroyer made a complete circle around the two ships and then cruised closer to use a loud-hailer.

'Jolly glad we found you! It looks as if you've had a bad time!'

Lindsay raised his megaphone. 'Have you a tug on way?'

'Yes!' The other captain brought his ship even closer, and Lindsay saw the seamen lining her guardrails to look at the jagged splinter holes along *Benbecula*'s side. He added, 'You're damn lucky to be afloat! There was a report of a surfaced U-boat shadowing the convoy. But we'll take care of the bugger if she comes this way!'

Lindsay said quietly, 'Bring them on deck, Sub.'

He did not speak again until the German seamen and their lieutenant had been hurried on to the forecastle and lined up in the bright sunlight. He waited just a few more seconds and then called, 'We met up with her.' He saw their heads turn to stare at the small group on the forecastle. 'But thanks for the offer.'

Another day passed before a salvage tug appeared to take the crippled *Demodocus* in tow. They had made use of the time by ferrying ten badly wounded men to one of the destroyers. In Freetown they could get better attention, although it seemed to Lindsay as he watched them being lowered into the boats alongside that those who were conscious did not want to leave.

And when the tow was released he had that same feeling. He had still not met the ammunition ship's master and probably never would. But as she wallowed slowly abeam while the tug's massive hawser brought her under control Lindsay saw him standing on his bridge, his hand raised in salute. Along the upper deck his men waved and cheered or just watched the strange ship with a list to starboard and her dazzle paint pitted with splinter holes until she was lost in a sea haze.

Goss came on to the bridge, his hands filthy, his uniform covered in oil and rust. He shaded his eyes to watch the little procession as it turned eastward and then said gruffly, 'Well, *that* showed 'em.'

Stannard and Dancy were beside Lindsay, while the new lieutenant, Paget, was hovering nervously some feet away. But they all saw it. Even Jolliffe, who had been on the wheel with hardly a break, feeling the strain, nursing his helm against the tremendous weight of the tow.

Goss turned to face Lindsay and said, 'I don't reckon you could have done better, even if you'd been in the company.' Then he held out his hand. 'If you wouldn't mind, sir.'

Lindsay took it. He could see the faces around him, blurred and out of focus, just as he could feel the power of Goss's big fist. But he could not speak. Try as he might, nothing would come.

Goss added slowly, 'We've had differences, I'll not deny it. She should have been my ship by rights.' He stared up at the masthead pendant. 'But that was in peace. Now I reckon the old girl needs both of us.'

Lindsay looked away. 'Thank you for that.' He cleared his throat. 'Thank you very much.' Then he strode into the wheelhouse and they heard his feet on the ladder to his cabin below.

Goss was looking at his grimy fist, and then saw Paget staring at him with something like awe.

'What the bloody hell are you gaping at, *Mr* Paget?' He bustled towards the ladder muttering, 'Amateurs. No damn use the whole lot of 'em!'

Stannard looked at Dancy and then said quietly, 'They

always said there was *something* about this ship, in the company.' He glanced around him as if seeing her for the first time. 'Well, now I believe it. By God, I believe it!'

Then he looked forward and added, 'Now get those bloody Jerries below decks. I'd forgotten all about them!'

As Dancy hurried away he heard Stannard murmur, 'A will of her own, they used to say. And by God, I've just seen her use it!'

15 The dinner party

Lindsay stood on the gratings of the starboard bridge wing and watched the seething activity along the jetty below him. There seemed to be hundreds of coloured dockyard workers running in every direction at once, although from his high position Lindsay could see the purpose as well as the apparent chaos.

Heaving lines snaked ashore, seized by a dozen brown hands, all apparently indifferent to the hoarse cries from *Benbecula*'s petty officers, as very slowly the hull touched against the massive piles which protected it from the uneven stonework.

The lines were followed by heavy mooring wires, the eyes of which were cheerfully dropped on to huge bollards along the jetty, with no small relief from the officers on the forecastle and poop, as with tired dignity *Benbecula* nudged a few more feet before tautening springs halted her progress altogether.

A messenger called, 'Back spring secured, sir.' He was staring at the shimmering white building beyond the jetty and harbour sheds, handset pressed against his ear. 'Head spring secure, sir.'

Lindsay saw Goss waving from the forecastle, his bulk even more ungainly in white shirt and shorts.

'All secure fore an' aft, sir.'

'Very well.'

Lindsay leaned still further over the screen, feeling the sun across his neck as he watched the mooring wires slackening and tautening in the gentle swell.

'Out breast ropes. Then tell the buffer to rig the brow.'

He could see other white uniforms on the jetty amidst the busy workers, faces raised to watch as *Benbecula* handed over her safety to the land once again.

'Ring off main engines.'

He heard the telegraphs clang, the dials below swinging to *Finished with Engines*, where no doubt Fraser and his men would give a combined sigh of relief,

It had been a slow passage to the jetty. The whole of Trincomalee seemed to be packed with shipping of every description, so that even the two tugs which had been sent to assist had not found the last few cables very easy. Warships and supply vessels. Troopers, their rigging adorned with soldiers' washing like uneven khaki bunting, harbour craft and lighters, as well as an overwhelming mass of local vessels of every kind. Dhows and sampans, schooners and ancient coasters which looked as if they had been born in the first days of steam.

The gratings gave one last quiver and then lay still beneath him.

Ritchie said, 'One of the troopers is the *Cambrian*, sir.'

'Yes.'

Lindsay did not turn. Perhaps, like himself, the yeoman was thinking back to those first days out from Liverpool, with the commodore's ship leading the starboard line. Remembering the explosions and fires flickering across the dark water. The wasted effort, and the cost.

He heard Stannard speaking into a voicepipe and tried to imagine what he was thinking.

And at one time it had at last seemed that everything was going to be all right. A change of luck, if you could call it that.

After leaving the ammunition ship they had continued into a kinder climate, with something like a holiday atmosphere pervading the ship for the first time. Eighteen days out of Liverpool they had crossed the Equator and all work had stopped for the usual boisterous ceremony of Crossing the Line. He could see it now. Jolliffe as Neptune in a cardboard crown and carrying a deadly-looking trident, his heavy jowls hidden in a realistic beard made of spunyarn. His queen had been one of Boase's S.B.A.'s, a girlish-looking youth whose sex, it had often been said, was very much in doubt anyway.

Sunshine and blue skies, bodies already showing a growing tan, and an extra tot of rum to complete the ceremony. It had seemed a sure sign for the better.

They had paused in Simonstown to replenish the fuel bunkers, and the ship's company had swarmed ashore to see the sights and gather all the usual clutter of souvenirs which would eventually find their way to mantelpieces and shelves the length and breadth of Britain.

Barker had arranged for buses to take libertymen on to Cape Town in a manner born. For just that one day he had not been the supply officer to an armed merchant cruiser. He was a ship's purser, and took as many pains to make the short trips and tours successful as if every man had been a first class passenger.

Then they were at sea again, and Lindsay could recall exactly the moment Stannard had come to his cabin. *Benbecula* had rounded the Cape and was steaming north-east into the Indian Ocean for the last long haul of her voyage.

All at once their own small world had been changed. The outside events, the war, all that went with it had come crowding in once more.

The Japanese had not been halted. That strip of water between Singapore Island and the mainland was not an English Channel as everyone had claimed it to be. The enemy had crossed it and were already advancing into the island itself. It was impossible but it was happening.

Stannard had stood in the sunlit cabin watching Lindsay as he had read the signal.

'What d'you think, sir? Will they pull our lads out?'

Looking back to that moment it was hard to remember what he had really believed. Not another retreat, surely? For this time there could be no Dunkirk with friendly white cliffs within reach of those brave or foolhardy enough to try for them. No sane man would write off the whole garrison. Not an army. It was inconceivable, just as now, standing on the sunlit bridge he could see it had been inevitable.

There had been a security clampdown on signals and little more was heard of that other war. *Benbecula* had continued across the Indian Ocean, enjoying perhaps the waters which had once been so familiar to her well-worn keel. They had passed several convoys heading in the opposite direction. Meat and grain from Australia and New Zealand, oil from the Gulf. The very stuff of survival for the people who waited in England for those ships to arrive.

The *Benbecula*'s people had watched them pass. Had waved and laughed at the usual exchange of crude or witty signals. Inwardly they had thought of that other ocean which still lay awaiting those convoys. Which they had endured and somehow survived to get this far.

Lindsay had watched Stannard going about his duties with growing concern. And he was not the only one with Singapore on his mind. Several men had brothers and friends there. Some even had fathers and uncles on the island, so great were the demands of war.

Then, just a week ago, while *Benbecula* had been passing within visual distance of the Seychelles, the news had broken. Singapore had fallen. The Gibraltar of the Far East, as it had been so often described by the press, had surrendered. And with it, every man who had been unable to escape on the few vessels left afloat by Japanese bombers.

Commodore Kemp's fast convoy, or the remains of it, still lay in Trincomalee with many other ships which had been expecting to go to Singapore's aid. Many a soldier would be thanking God right now that they had not arrived in time to be sacrificed for nothing.

Stannard came out to the wing and saluted. He was wearing sun-glasses and it was impossible to read his expression.

'All secure, sir. Permission to clear the bridge?'

'Carry on.' He hesitated and then said quietly, 'Look, Pilot, it may not mean your brother is still out there. He might have been one of the lucky ones.'

Stannard looked down at the milling figures which were struggling to assist Archer's seamen with securing the brow.

'I don't know whether I wish him dead or a prisoner. You've heard what the Japs have been doing to prisoners.' He added with sudden bitterness, 'And it seems to me the chance of our ever retaking Singapore, or any other bloody place for that matter, is pretty remote.'

'I know how you must feel.'

Stannard turned. 'Yes. I know how I feel, too. It's Jason I'm thinking about. Never been out of Aussie in his life. He's not like us. He's just a kid.' He saluted. 'I'll carry on then, sir.' Then he swung round and hurried into the wheelhouse.

Goss had appeared on the wing, his red face running with sweat. 'What's up with him then?'

'His brother.'

Goss nodded. 'Yes. I forgot.' He sighed. 'I reckon the dockyard people will be aboard to see about the damage, sir.' He glared at the crowded jetty below. 'We'll have to screw everything down to stop those bloody wogs from stealing it!'

'You deal with it.'

Lindsay watched him wearily. Goss had withdrawn into his old shell. Or partly. But there was a difference now. An unspoken understanding. One which had been sealed with a handshake. Lindsay knew he did not have to ask. It was unbreakable. Like the man.

'Aye.' Goss jerked his thumb vaguely. 'What'll they do with all these troopships and the squaddies?'

Lindsay watched some uniformed figures starting towards the brow. The first visitors. Questions and reports. Assessments and promises.

'Who knows? India maybe. South to Australia if the Japs look like getting that far.'

Goss scowled. 'It's all getting too big for me.' He too was watching the white figures at the brow.

'I'll go an' see 'em aboard, sir.' He showed his teeth. It was almost a grin. Then he pointed to the tall funnel where a grey submarine had been painted with a swastika below it. 'Reckon that'll take some of the starch out of their breeches!'

Maxwell climbed to the bridge and saluted. In his shorts and gleaming white shirt he looked as thin as a stick. A ramrod.

'I'm O.O.D., sir. The ambulances are arriving for our wounded. And an escort for the Jerries.'

'Good.'

Lindsay watched him march away. He had changed, too. He still made a lot of noise but was withdrawn and seemed to avoid the other officers whenever possible.

He had expected to hear of Maxwell's boasting about the accuracy of his guns and the sinking of a U-boat. Also that for once, the marines had been left out of it.

When he had congratulated Maxwell he had replied curtly, 'What I was trained for, sir. Given time, you can even teach a block of wood to shoot straight.' And that was all he had said.

Lindsay looked up at the painted U-boat and wondered why he had kept the prisoners aboard. He could have dropped them at Simonstown or passed them to the destroyers which had come to search for him and the *Demodocus*. He had seen them once or twice as they were exercised on the after well deck. A dozen in all, including the lieutenant who took his walks alone but for an escort.

He had even used his binoculars to study them without knowing why. What had he expected to see? Some sign of a master race? Superior beings which in captivity could still display their arrogance? For the most part they had looked very ordinary.

So perhaps he was getting like Goss and his submarine painted on the funnel. He wanted to show the Germans off like trophies. Heads taken in battle. Scalps.

He ran his hand over his neck and shuddered. The sun must be hotter than he had realised.

He glanced briefly at the wheelhouse, deserted now and strangely peaceful. Then he ran lightly down the bridge ladder and then another to A deck where an entry port had been opened to receive the heavy wooden brow from the jetty. He passed groups of ratings who had been dismissed from duty, already on their way below to prepare for shore leave. They seemed cheerful, even jubilant, and he could guess that they were still reliving their small victory. But once ashore they might find it even smaller, he thought. Other events had already outweighed and outreached one sunken U-boat, no matter what the circumstances had been.

Further aft some marines were busy polishing boots, apparently determined to retain their usual smartness in spite of having their messdeck blasted to blackened fragments.

He paused and looked at the smoke-grimed paintwork, the bright scars of deflected splinters, and was suddenly moved. After a destroyer, he had seen this ship as the end of the line. A limbo from which there was no return, and in which he could find no future.

Now he knew differently. And when the U-boat's last shell had shaken the bridge beneath his feet he had felt something more than anxiety. Affection, love, there was no proper word for it. But it was there all the same.

Maybe most of his officers had been appointed to her because they were not much use for anything better. The majority of the ratings had been untrained to the ways of war, so they too had been sent to make up the required numbers. His own appointment he understood well enough and had accepted it.

But somehow, back there over the hundreds of miles from the Arctic Circle to Ceylon, they had come together, and that was more than could be said for many ships.

Like Goss, *Benbecula* was all he had. Now, he needed her to go on living.

Goss was waiting by the entry port, an elegant lieutenant in white drill at his side.

The latter saluted smartly and announced, 'Commodore Kemp sends his compliments, sir, and would you join him at his residence for dinner?'

Lindsay nodded. 'Very well.'

'The admiral would like to see you too, of course, sir. But he sends his regrets and is unable to do so until tomorrow. You will be informed of the time, of course, sir.'

Of course. 'Thank you.'

The lieutenant gazed around at the nearby splinter holes. 'The wires were fairly humming about your U-boat, sir.' He sighed. 'But we are rather involved with this other unhappy affair at present.'

Boots clumped on the planking as the German prisoners marched towards the entry port, some military policemen bringing up the rear. Lastly, their lieutenant, who had miraculously retained his cap after jumping from the sinking submarine and being hauled into the motor boat, walked alone towards the sunlight.

Seeing Lindsay and the others he threw up a stiff salute which was returned with equal formality by Kemp's lieutenant.

The German made as if to speak but Lindsay turned away until he heard the footsteps recede down the brow.

He heard the lieutenant say testily, 'That man over

there! Don't you know you should stand to attention
when an officer passes, enemy or not?'

That man there was unfortunately Fraser. Hatless, his
boiler suit almost black from a recent inspection in the
bilges, he was leaning against a ventilator shaft, his slight
body bowed with fatigue. He stood up very slowly and
stared at the angry lieutenant.

'*One*, I don't salute any bastard who's been trying to
blow my backside off! And *two*, I don't take orders from
some snotty-nosed little twit like you!'

Goss said gravely, 'This is Lieutenant-Commander
Fraser. The chief engineer.'

The lieutenant blushed. 'I—I'm sorry, sir. I didn't
understand.'

Fraser stared at him calmly. 'You wouldn't.'

The lieutenant turned desperately to Lindsay. 'I'll tell
the commodore, sir.' He darted a frightened glance at
Fraser. 'I have to go now.'

Goss looked down at Fraser and said, 'Amazing. I'm
surprised he didn't recognise a real gentleman when he
saw you like that.'

Fraser eyed him with equal gravity. 'In my book a
gentleman is someone who gets out of his bath to have a
pee.'

Goss turned to Lindsay. 'Now you see why we used to
try and keep the engineers away from the passengers in
the company, sir? Their *refinement* might have made some
of them feel inferior.' Then he turned and walked slowly
towards the bridge.

Fraser gaped after him. 'Well, I'll be damned! He made
a joke! Not much of one maybe, but he *made* it!'

Lindsay smiled. 'And you asked for it, Chief. If you
insult another up-and-coming admiral I may not be able
to save you.'

Fraser shrugged. 'When the likes of that upstart are
admirals I'll either be tending my garden at home or six
feet under it.' He chuckled. 'But fancy old John Goss

cracking a joke.' He was still chuckling as he walked towards his quarters.

Maxwell crossed the deck and saluted.

'I've assembled the dockyard people for you in the wardroom, sir.'

'Good idea. It never hurts to soften them up with a few drinks before asking their help.'

He paused by a screen door. 'Is there anything wrong, Guns? Any way I can help?'

Maxwell stiffened. 'Wrong, sir? Why should there be?' He stared at a point above Lindsay's shoulder. 'All the starboard watch and second part of port watch for liberty this afternoon, sir?'

Lindsay studied him thoughtfully. 'Yes. Have it piped.'

He would have to keep an eye on Maxwell. He was so tensed up he might well become another Aikman. He smiled bitterly. Or Lindsay.

He straightened his shoulders and pushed open the wardroom door.

'Now, gentlemen, about these repairs.'

———

Commodore Kemp's temporary residence was situated several miles from the naval base, and after the crowded, jostling streets, the seemingly endless numbers of servicemen, it gave an immediate impression of peaceful seclusion. A staff car, driven by a bearded Sikh corporal, had collected Lindsay at the jetty at the exact minute prescribed, and as it left him standing just inside the open gates Lindsay wondered how he had arrived without a fatal accident. The Sikh had driven with expressionless abandon, as if every street had been empty, using the car's horn as the sole form of survival.

It was a very attractive house, white-walled and fringed with palms. There was a colourful, well-tended garden, and he could imagine the number of servants required to keep it so.

A house-boy in white tunic and scarlet sash took his cap and ushered him into a cool, spacious room where the commodore was standing with his back to a large portrait. It depicted a bearded Victorian who was staring steadfastly into the distance, arms folded, and with one foot on a dead tiger.

Kemp waited for Lindsay to reach him and then offered his hand. 'Good to see you safe and well.' He snapped his fingers to the servant. 'You'll have a drink before dinner, I imagine.'

'Thank you, sir. Scotch.'

Kemp was smoking a cigar and gestured for Lindsay to sit in one of the tall gilt chairs.

'Nice place, eh? Belongs to a tea-planter. He stays up-country for most of the time. Just comes here to get away from it all.'

Lindsay tried to relax. The whisky was good. Very good. Kemp certainly appeared to be enjoying his new role. Relishing it, as if the house and all it entailed were his by right.

'I was damn glad to hear about your U-boat.' Kemp's eyes followed the cigar smoke until it was plucked into a nearby fan. *Merlin*'s captain was pretty sure he'd done for that one, otherwise I'd never have left you without another escort, naturally.'

Lindsay thought of the convoy receding over the horizon. The sense of isolation and danger.

'But your ships got through all right, sir.'

Kemp shrugged. 'Lost the other freighter, I'm afraid. She had a bit of engine trouble. Her master signalled that some of our depth-charges had exploded too close for comfort.' He poured himself another drink without calling for the servant. His hand was shaking. 'But I *knew* there was no real risk of more U-boats attacking us, so I pressed on. The convoy was vital, as you know. Anyway, there were more escorts on way from Freetown, plus two destroyers from the inshore squadron.'

Lindsay watched him over his glass. 'You left him behind.'

Kemp looked uneasy. 'It should have been safe enough. But the destroyers could find no trace of the poor chap. Must have had an explosion aboard. Anyway, can't be helped. All water under the bridge, as they say.'

Lindsay swallowed his drink and held the glass out to the impassive servant. Kemp had abandoned the freighter. Just like *Benbecula* and the ammunition ship.

'Didn't she send any distress signals, sir?'

'No.' Kemp sounded too casual. 'Nothing.'

'That's strange.'

Kemp stood up and walked to one of the wide windows. 'Well, there's damn all we can do about it now.' He turned, his face set in a smile again. 'Now, about you. I gather you've had the repair yard hopping like mad all day. They'll do what they can, of course, but I can't promise too much. It'll have to be a patch up job. I've been informed that your damage is largely superficial where the hull is concerned.'

'We'll manage, sir.' He tried to hide his bitterness.

Kemp nodded. 'That's the spirit. Front-line ships are right at the top of the list, I'm afraid. But I don't have to tell you that.'

'I was wondering about the next assignment, sir.' He saw the decanter hovering above Kemp's glass.

'Well, we can't talk shop tonight, eh? This is a sort of celebration for you. A welcome back.' He became serious. 'Of course, with Singapore in the enemy's bag there's nothing for all these reinforcements we brought out from U.K. I've seen the admiral and his Chief of Staff, and I gather we'll be expected to help in another convoy.' He sounded vague. 'I daresay the troops will be a godsend elsewhere, anyway. Things have been getting a bit grim in North Africa to all accounts.'

Lindsay watched him as he took another drink. *You don't care. Don't give a damn about anyone but yourself.*

Ships left without help, men dying, none of it counted. It was outside, beyond Kemp's vision, and interest too for that matter.

Kemp seemed to realise Lindsay was studying him and said with forced cheerfulness, 'But you shouldn't complain.' He wagged his glass. 'I'll not be surprised if you get a decoration for saving the ammunition ship and sinking the U-boat. Promotion too, I wouldn't wonder. Now that you've overcome your, er, past problems, I see no reason why you should not be given something better.'

'There are several of my people I'd like to recommend for——'

Kemp frowned. 'Well, we must wait and see. Nothing definite, you understand. Everything's in turmoil here, and ·it sounds as if the whole naval structure is being changed. *Merlin*'s captain is being promoted and is to be given one of these new escort groups. Killer-groups, they're being called. Nice young chap. Should do well.' He stared vaguely at Lindsay's glass. 'But for your early setback I daresay you'd have been on the list for something of the sort, too.'

Lindsay replied calmly, 'I lost my ship, sir. I was blown up in another. Many have suffered the same fate.' His voice hardened. 'Many were less fortunate.'

Kemp seemed to have missed the point. He nodded gravely. 'I know, Lindsay. We who face death and live to fight again rarely realise how narrow the margin can be.'

Lindsay fixed his eyes on the portrait opposite his chair. His immediate anger at Kemp's words was already giving way to a new realisation. Not merely that Kemp was drunk but that he needed to be so. *We who face death.* Kemp had not been to sea in wartime before this last convoy. Had it really been the vital need of ships and men for Singapore which had made him drive them without letup? Or was it his own fear, his new understanding that he had been left behind by war, of a role he only vaguely recognised?

Another house-boy appeared in the doorway. 'Dinner served, sir.' He grinned from ear to ear.

Kemp lurched to his feet. 'Impudent lot. Still, they have their uses. Mean well, I suppose.'

He paused beside the table and added abruptly, 'When we meet the FOIC tomorrow, I'd be obliged if you'd not mention your ideas about commerce raiders and so forth. He's quite enough on his plate at the moment. He'll not thank you for wasting his time.'

'Even if it means saving ships and men, sir?'

Kemp seemed to have difficulty in holding him in focus. 'That last freighter sank by accident, Lindsay!' He was shouting. 'And that's all there is to it!'

Lindsay stood stockstill. He had not even been thinking about that unfortunate ship, except for the fact Kemp had left her unaided. But now it was out in the open and there was no avoiding the truth. Kemp actually *believed* what he had been telling him, yet was equally prepared to ignore it for his own survival. He needed things to stay as they were, like stopping the clock, just long enough for him to achieve some better appointment elsewhere.

As he followed Kemp's thickset figure across a marble floor to the dining room his mind was already working on this frightening possibility.

The terrible news about Singapore could be all it needed to make the Germans take full advantage of their ally's victory. For the next few months naval resources would be stretched far beyond safety limits as troops and supplies were re-deployed to meet the new dangers. The Japs might invade India and march on into the rich oil-fields of the Middle East. They could have it planned for months, even years with the Germans, so that an eventual link-up between their forces was made a brutal fact. One vast pair of steel pincers biting through Russia and the Middle East, to carve the world in halves.

Inside the tea-planter's cool house it all seemed so clear and starkly obvious he was almost unnerved. It must be just as plain to those in real authority. Unless. . . . He looked at Kemp's plump shoulders. In past wars it had always taken several years to rid authority of men like him. It was said that in the old battlefields of Flanders the ploughs were still churning up countless remains of the men thrown away by generals who had believed cavalry superior to machine-guns and barbed wire. And admirals who had scoffed at the trivial consequences of submarine warfare.

He was surprised to find he was not the only guest for dinner. A bearded surgeon-commander from the admiral's staff, the commodore's aide who had wilted before Fraser's verbal barrage and an elderly major of artillery were already standing around a well-laid table. Midshipman Kemp was also present, standing apart from the others, and there was a dried-up little woman acting as hostess, introduced as the surgeon-commander's wife.

In spite of the fans it was very hot, and the ample helpings of varied curries did little to help matters. Beyond the shuttered windows Lindsay could see the last rays of bronze sunlight, the palms very black against the sky.

There was a lot to drink. Too much. Lindsay was astonished at the way the commodore could put it away. Wine came and went with the soft-footed servants, while his voice grew louder and more slurred.

Beside Lindsay the midshipman ate his meal in silence, his eyes rarely leaving the table until his father suddenly said, 'By God, Julian, don't pick at your food! Try and *eat* like a man, if nothing else!'

Lindsay recalled the boy's face after the action. Tight-lipped but strangely determined. Stannard had told him how the midshipman had worked with his plotting team. How he had been sick several times but had somehow managed to keep going. And all that time he had probably been picturing his father speeding to safety with the heavy escort. Leaving him alone, as he had always done.

Lindsay leaned back in his chair. He felt light-headed but no longer cared.

'Actually, sir, he did very well on this last trip.' He knew the boy was staring at him, that the surgeon's wife had paused in her apparently insatiable appetite with a fork poised in the air.

The aide said swiftly, 'Good show. I remember when I was at Dartmouth I———'

The commodore said flatly, 'Hold your noise!' To Lindsay he added, 'You don't know my son or you might think otherwise.'

He signalled for more wine, unaware of the sudden tension around the table.

'My *son* does not like the Service. He would rather sit on his backside listening to highbrow music than do anything useful. When I think of my father and what he taught me, I want to weep.'

The army major dabbed his chin with a napkin.

'Spare the rod, eh?' He laughed, the sound strangely hollow in the quiet room.

'I think he's old enough to know his own mind.' Lindsay could feel the anger returning. 'When the war's over he'll be able to make his choice.'

'Is that what you think?' The commodore leaned forward, his eyes red-rimmed in the overhead lights. 'Well, I'm telling you, Commander Lindsay, that I will decide what he will or will not do! No son of mine is going to bring disgrace on my family, do you hear?'

'Perfectly, sir.' He gripped his glass tightly to prevent his hand from shaking. 'But at present he is under my command, and I will assess his qualities accordingly.'

The commodore shifted in his chair and then snapped, 'We will take our port in the next room.'

Lindsay stood up. 'If you will excuse me, sir. I would like to be excused.'

The surgeon's wife said hastily, 'You must be worn out, Commander. If half of what they're saying about you is true, then I think you should get some rest.'

The commodore only succeeded in rising to his feet with the aid of a servant's arm.

'You *are* excused.' He faced Lindsay and added thickly, 'And as far as I'm concerned you can——' He turned and walked unsteadily to the door without finishing it.

Lindsay left the room and waited for a house-boy to fetch his cap. He heard footsteps and saw the young midshipman staring at him.

'I'm sorry, sir. I'd not have had this happen for anything.'

Lindsay forced a smile. 'Forget it. My fault entirely.'

'You don't understand, sir.' Kemp's face was tight with concern. 'I *know* him. He'll try and get his own back on you.' He dropped his eyes. 'He's not like you, sir. If he were, I'd never have needed to be told to enter the Navy.'

The boy's sincerity, his shame and humiliation, made him appear even more defenceless than usual.

Lindsay said quietly, 'That was a nice compliment. One which I happen to value very much.'

He took his cap and walked quickly into the garden.

Behind him the boy stood staring at the open door long after Lindsay had disappeared in the shadows.

A slow, lurching taxi carried Lindsay back to the base, his head lolling to the jerky motion, his throat parched in spite of the wine.

By the time he had found the jetty a moon had appeared, and in the pale light he could see the *Benbecula* resting against the piles, the dazzle paint strangely vivid and garish. A sentry paced back and forth on the gangway, and in the glow of a blue police light he saw the quartermaster drooping over his desk, probably engrossed in a book or some old letter from home.

It was very still, and after lighting his pipe Lindsay walked the full length of his ship, from her towering straight stem to her outmoded poop where the ill-used twelve-pounder pointed at the moon like a rigid finger. Then with a sigh he walked up the steep brow, nodding to the startled quartermaster and then walking forward towards his quarters.

As he passed a door he heard the crash of breaking glass. It was Stannard's cabin, but as he made to reach for the clip he heard Dancy say, 'I'd leave him, sir.'

Dancy had been leaning against the rail, his body merging with the deep shadows.

He added quietly, 'There was a message sent aboard just after you left, sir. Pilot's brother is aboard one of the hospital ships.'

Lindsay watched him. 'He got away then?'

Dancy did not seem to hear. 'He went across right away. He's been in there drinking ever since.' Dancy rested his elbows on the rail and added, 'He saw him all right. But he'd got no arms!' His shoulders shook uncontrollably. 'And he can't see either, sir!'

Lindsay stared past him towards the distant buildings, so white in the moon's glare.

'You've been here all the time?'

Dancy nodded. 'Just in case, sir.'

Lindsay touched his arm. 'I'll not be turning in yet. Come and have a drink in my cabin when he's asleep.' He waited. 'If you feel like it.'

Dancy straightened his back. 'Thank you, sir.'

Lindsay walked on towards the bridge ladder. In just one evening he had learned a lot about his officers. And himself.

16 A miracle

For three more days no fresh instructions were sent to *Benbecula* or any intimation of what her next duty might be. Lindsay had still not had the expected interview with the admiral or even his chief of staff, but at first this omission had not troubled him. Indeed, when he thought about it at all, he was almost relieved. The local naval staff had enough work on hand as it was, and he was being kept more than busy with his ship's repairs.

But it was concerning *Benbecula*'s repairs and general replenishment which at last gave him a hint that something was happening outside his own knowledge. Small items for the most part, which added together grew into a definite pattern.

Lieutenant Hunter had called on him to complain of his inability to secure any six-inch shells to replace those fired, although he had been told that plenty were available.

When Lindsay had asked, 'Have you spoken to Guns about this?' Hunter had sounded guarded.

'Well, sir, he has been a bit preoccupied lately. Anyway, I can deal with it once I've got the authority.'

Maxwell had been acting even more strangely, that was certain. He had stayed ashore every night, although nobody had seen him or knew where he went.

Goss too had been perturbed by the apparent lack of attention which was being paid to his list of repairs by the dockyard staff. That was normal enough on its own. Goss saw every dockyard worker as a potential thief, layabout and someone bent on spoiling his ship's appearance and efficiency. But it was true that some of the work had been skimped rather than properly rectified.

Lieutenant Barker had much the same tale. Stores were difficult to obtain, and apart from the basic rations of food and clothing, very little seemed available for the *Benbecula*.

Added together, Lindsay felt it was more than mere coincidence.

The ship's company on the other hand accepted the situation with obvious delight. Trips ashore, strange sights of native women and rickshaws, elephants and snake charmers, all helped to make each day an event.

Stannard had been ashore very little. In fact, apart from occasional duties he hardly seemed to leave his cabin.

Lindsay had seen him alone after the night of the commodore's dinner party and had asked if he could do anything.

Stannard had replied, 'They've sent Jason to a hospital, sir. He's being sent up to another one at Karachi tomorrow. After that, they say it'll take time.' He had looked at Lindsay with sudden anguish. 'Just tell me how I'm to write to the old man, sir. Can you imagine what it will do to him?'

After that brief interview Lindsay had seen little of him. Even Dancy seemed unable to reach him or help ease his despair.

Perhaps when they got back to sea things might change. Lying alongside a jetty in the blazing heat was no help to anyone tortured with such thoughts as Stannard.

On the morning of the fourth day the summons to naval H.Q. was received, and with Jupp hovering around him like an anxious hen Lindsay changed into a white uniform which he had not worn since the outbreak of war.

Jupp remarked, 'A bit loose around the middle, if I may make so bold, sir. You should've let me get it fixed sooner.'

He handed Lindsay his dress sword, adding, 'Not been feedin' yourself enough, sir. Too much worry is bad for you.'

Lindsay looked at himself in the bulkhead mirror. Even in war the formalities had to be observed. To show there was no crack in the foundations.

He grinned. 'I shall eat better when I know what's going to happen.'

He waited, half expecting Jupp to supply a rumour or at least some reason for the sudden call to H.Q. But Jupp seemed concerned only with his appearance, the impression *Benbecula*'s captain would make when he got there.

At the gangway Goss had to shout above the rasping rattle of a rivet-gun.

'You won't forget about my paint, sir? We're getting very low, and I'm not happy about the port anchor cable.'

Lindsay smiled briefly. The side party stood in a neat line, the bosun's mates wetting their calls on their lips ready to pipe him over the side.

Lieutenant Paget, who was O.O.D., stood very erect, his eyes fixed on Lindsay with something like terror, as if he expected the brow to collapse or one of the side party to run amok in his presence.

He said, 'I'll do what I can. I've a few questions of my own, too.'

Then with one hand to the oak-leaved peak of his cap and the unfamiliar feel of his sword in the other, he hurried down the brow where a car was shimmering in heat-haze to carry him to the presence of the mighty.

But he was met by a harassed flag-lieutenant who hurried to explain that the admiral would not, after all, be able to see him. The F.O.I.C. had been whisked away to some important conference. It was one of those things. Unavoidable.

Lindsay spent a further twenty minutes in a small room before the lieutenant reappeared to usher him into an adjoining office. The Chief of Staff came round a big desk and shook his hand.

'Sorry about this mix-up, Lindsay. Bad times. But I have no doubt you've seen enough of admirals anyway.' He smiled. 'As I have.'

Lindsay took a proffered chair and watched him as he stared out of a window towards the harbour.

The other man said slowly, 'Also, we've been waiting for instructions from Admiralty. Certain recommendations have been made, and it's my duty to inform you of them.' He turned and studied Lindsay thoughtfully.

'The war's speeding up. Increased submarine activity and long-range aircraft have made previous ideas obsolete. Almost overnight, in a manner of speaking.'

Lindsay tensed. He had been expecting a hint of orders, even acceptance of his own recommendations for some of *Benbecula*'s company. But something in the Chief of Staff's tone, his attitude, seemed to act like a warning. He was troubled. No, he was embarrassed.

'My staff are arranging your orders, Lindsay. But I think it best all round if you know without any more delay.' He sat down behind the desk and looked at his hands.

'*Benbecula* will return to U.K. as soon as the dockyard say she is seaworthy.'

Seaworthy. Not ready for action or patrol duty. She merely had to be able to make the passage home.

Lindsay asked tightly, 'And then, sir?'

'Rosyth. I gather they want her as a sort of depot cum accommodation ship for incoming drafts, replacement personnel and so forth.' He flicked over some papers. 'Your first lieutenant will be promoted to commander upon arrival there. He will also assume command from that time.' He tried to smile. 'Bit of a rough diamond, I gather, but he should be all right for the job.' He dropped his eyes again. 'It seems very likely that your promotion is already on its way here. I'm glad for you. You've more than earned it.'

Lindsay felt as if the walls were moving inwards. Crushing the air from his lungs.

'And *my* appointment, sir?'

The Chief of Staff did not look up. 'The Navy's growing every day. Recruits are flooding the depots like ants. We're having to cut courses rather than lengthen them, and they need the very best help they can get.' He plucked at the litter of papers. 'I detest this job. I entered the Service to feel a ship around me. I know this work is important and I'm doing more good here than I would be on the bridge of some cruiser in Scapa Flow.' He shrugged. 'But I still find it hard to take.' His eyes lifted to Lindsay's face and he added quietly, 'As you will, at first.'

'Shore job?'

'They're putting the finishing touches to a new training depot on the east coast. Hasn't got a name yet, but I've no doubt their lordships will have dreamed up something grand by the time you take command.'

Lindsay was on his feet without noticing he had moved from the chair. East coast. Shore job. Probably a peacetime holiday camp or hotel converted for training purposes. A white ensign on a flag mast. A ship's bell by the main gate. A temporary illusion for temporary sailors.

He said, 'I thought I was going to get——'

The Chief of Staff watched him sadly. 'I know. You can appeal against the decision of course, but you know as well as I do what weight it will have.'

Lindsay crossed to the window and stared blindly at the courtyard below. He could see the new depot as if he had actually visited it already. Could almost hear voices saying, 'The new captain? Oh yes, came to us because he's a bit bomb happy.'

Most of the officers who commanded such establish-

ments were old, retired and brought back to the Navy to
help spread the load. Men like Commodore Kemp.

He heard himself ask, 'I take it this was Kemp's idea,
sir?'

'You know I cannot discuss confidential reports.' The
Chief of Staff added, 'But you may draw your own conclusions.'

'I *will* appeal.' He turned away from the window and saw
the other man give a brief shake of the head.

'It is your privilege. However, as there is a war on, and on
the face of things you are being given a just promotion, I
think you should be warned against such a course of
action.'

A telephone rang impatiently and the Chief of Staff
snapped. 'No. *Wait.*' He slammed it back before adding
quietly, 'I do not know Kemp very well. I would go further.
I do not *wish* to know him very well. But from what I hear of
him I would say he is not the sort who would act without
apparent justification.'

Lindsay strode to the desk and leaned on it, his voice
almost pleading. 'But there must have been signals, sir?
Some hint of all this?'

'Again, they are confidential. But there was a full report
made to Admiralty.' He looked away. 'Including one from
the staff medical officer.'

Lindsay straightened his back, sickened. He recalled the
bearded surgeon with the wife who could not stop eating.
Kemp must have planned the whole thing. Must have
worked on his first dislike which their meeting at Scapa
had begun.

He remembered the midshipman's voice when he had
said, *He'll try and get his own back on you.*

Or maybe he had started it all himself when he had
defended the boy at the dinner table. Had walked into the
trap which he had sprung by his own carelessness.

In those dragging seconds he could even see the looming bulk of the *Benbecula* leaning against the piles in the

bright sunlight. Now even she was being taken. That realisation most of all was more than he could bear.

'Look, Lindsay, try not to take this too badly. The war is
not going to end next week. And who knows, you'll probably find new orders in England which will make all this
seem like a bad dream.'

A bad dream. It seemed to linger in his mind. Perhaps
someone aboard his own ship had made the first move.
Had listened to his ravings as he relived the nightmare.
Had recorded every small action or mood in order to
destroy him.

He thrust out his hand. 'I will leave now, sir.' He met
the other man's troubled gaze. 'I would not have been
in your shoes for this. Thank you for trying to spare my
feelings.'

The Chief of Staff smiled. 'I have tried. But I feel like an
executioner nonetheless. I only hope the men who pass
through your hands appreciate what you will no doubt
offer them.'

'And what is that, sir?'

'I am not going to indulge you with all the trite words of
leadership and example. You'll get plenty of those later.'
He sat down again, his eyes suddenly distant. 'Give them
the same sense of value, of *belonging* as you have to the old
Benbecula. That'll be more use than a room full of
admirals.'

Lindsay picked up his cap and walked slowly to the door.
It was over. For him and the ship.

He said, 'I will try to remember that. There will be plenty
of time from now on.'

Outside, the flag-lieutenant handed him an envelope
and said, 'Here's a brief rundown on appointments, sir. It
will be all right to mention them to your people if you so
wish.'

Lindsay walked through the building without another
word. He got vague impressions of men at desks, the
chatter of telephones and typewriters. A different sort of

war. One he would soon be joining or watching from the sidelines.

He returned the salutes of two marine sentries and headed for the parked staff car.

He must hold on. Just long enough to reach his cabin. Hide, like Stannard and Maxwell. But he knew it was only a deception. For there was nowhere he could hide from himself.

———————

Goss stood a few paces away from Lindsay's desk, his face hidden while he listened to the neatly typed instructions.

'So you will have the ship after all, Number One.' Even as he said it Lindsay thought this bare fact was the only shred of comfort which really affected him. 'And with promotion, you should be well placed after the war with another shipping company when you may be competing with younger men.'

He did not know what he had expected. Goss's silence was like something physical. He turned in his chair and asked, 'Aren't you pleased? I thought it was what you wanted?'

Goss opened his big hands and closed them again. 'I always wanted the *Becky*. Ever since I can remember.' His fingers clenched into tight fists. 'But not like this!'

'She'll be safe as a depot ship. No more convoys. No being left alone with nothing but a few First World War guns to hit back.'

Goss said quietly, 'A ship dies when she's inactive. I've seen a few good ones go like that during the depression.' He seemed to be struggling with his words. 'A ship should be at sea. She needs it. It's her life. Her purpose for being.' He turned slightly so that Lindsay saw the emotion on his heavy features. 'Like an old man who takes to his chair. He starts to die from then on. He can't help it.'

Lindsay tore his eyes away from Goss's despair. 'I'll leave it to you to tell the others. You can use this list. Stannard's to go on an advanced navigation course. He'll probably be appointed to a new destroyer. de Chair and his marines are to be sent to Eastney Barracks for re-allocation, and Maxwell's to get his half stripe. He'll be going to Whale Island for an instructor's course.'

He wondered how he could keep his voice so level when his whole being was screaming like a tortured instrument. Calm, even matter-of-fact. It had to be that way. The only way.

He recalled the time his mother had made her decision to leave for Canada. For good. He had wandered round the old house, watching the familiar things which he had always taken for granted, going under the auctioneer's impartial hammer. Things he had known all his young life. Things he had loved.

It was like that right now. Familiar faces being parted and sent to the winds.

'Young Dancy is going on a navigation course, too. His work with Stannard will stand him in good stead. The other young subs are being transferred to escort vessels when they return from home leave. Hunter is to be gunnery officer in one of the Western Approaches ships.'

Goss asked abruptly, 'What about Fraser?'

'The chief is transferring to a fleet repair ship.'

'I see.' Goss walked a few paces and stopped, as if uncertain where to go. 'Isn't *anyone* staying from the old company?'

'Dyke will take over the engine room, although being a depot ship his duties will be pretty limited.' He added, 'I thought you disliked Fraser?'

Goss said vaguely, 'Dyke can't do the job. It takes a proper chief engineer. She's old. She must have proper care.' He added with sudden fierceness, 'No, I've never liked him much. But he's a good chief. The best in the company, and no matter what he's told you, he bloody well cares about this ship right enough!'

'I know that, too.' Lindsay stared at the papers on his desk. They were blurred, like those on the Chief of Staff's desk. 'You're keeping Barker. He's getting a half stripe like Maxwell.'

Goss walked to the desk and stood looking down at Lindsay for several seconds.

'And *you're* on the beach, sir. I know a lot of people'll only see your extra stripe and envy you, most likely. But I know different. I'm not a clever man an' never was. I sweated blood to get where I am, and saw many a useless bastard get promoted over my head because I'm slow by nature. I'm slow, and I take my time. I've never been able to afford mistakes. There's not been a captain in the company I've not envied, nor one whose job I've told myself I couldn't do better given the chance.' He rested his hands on the desk. 'But I've not envied you, because I couldn't have done what you've had to do. No matter what I've kidded myself on that score, I know that, and nobody can tell me otherwise.'

Lindsay did not look up. 'Thank you.' He heard Goss moving restlessly to an open scuttle.

Goss added slowly, 'Christ, she can feel it already. Poor old girl, she can *feel* it.'

Lindsay lurched to his feet. 'For God's sake, Number One, we have to carry out orders. Nothing else *can* matter. Ships don't feel. They're steel and wood, pipes and machinery, and only as good as the men who control them.' Even as he said it he saw the other man shaking his head.

'It's no use talking to me like that, sir. You don't believe it either. She feels it all right.' He swung towards the scuttle, his eyes staring into the harsh sunlight as he shouted, 'Those toffy-nosed bastards who sit in their offices will never understand, not if they live a million bloody years! I don't know much but by the living Jesus I know ships! And above all I know this one.' When he spoke again he was very calm. 'Sorry about that. I should be used to kicks at my time of life.'

Somewhere a tannoy bellowed, 'Hands to dinner. Leave to port watch from 1400 to 2300. Chief and petty officers 0830 in the morning. Ordinary Seaman Jones muster at the quartermaster's lobby for mail.'

Goss moved to the door. 'Can you see her tied up to some stinking pier, full of gash ratings and layabouts, sir? With nothing to do, no use any more?' He waited, staring at Lindsay's lowered head. 'No, and no more can't I.'

As the door closed behind him Jupp entered the cabin and asked, 'Will you be wantin' your lunch now, sir?'

Lindsay shook his head. Goss had known. Must have known. One more minute and he would have broken down.

'Fetch some whisky, please.'

Jupp picked up the dress sword from a chair where Lindsay had thrown it and replied, 'If you'll pardon the liberty, sir, it's not fair.'

'Just the whisky.'

Jupp hurried away. For once in his long life he could think of nothing to say or do which would help him understand what was happening.

In his pantry a young steward said, 'What's up, Chiefy? The end of the world comin'?'

Jupp looked at him and saw the steward pale under his fierce stare. 'For once in your miserable life, I reckon you're right.' He picked up a clean glass and held it automatically to the light before putting it on his silver tray.

The steward stammered, 'I was only jokin', Chiefy!'

Jupp placed the decanter carefully on the tray and thought of Lindsay in the next cabin staring down at his desk.

Aloud he said, 'You don't joke, son, when someone's dyin'.'

But the steward had already gone.

Lindsay could not remember how he had reached this particular restaurant. He seemed to have been walking for hours, his feet taking him down narrow streets and away from the main crush of people and tooting vehicles. It appeared to be quite a small building. The upper part was an hotel under the same ownership and bore a sign depicting a bejewelled elephant and the words 'English and French dishes. Only the best.'

It was evening and the sun already hidden beyond a towering white temple on the opposite side of a dusty square. He guessed the hotel would probably look very shabby in harsh sunlight.

But it was quiet and seemed almost deserted. No uniforms or familiar faces like those he had seen at the Naval Club where he had paused for a drink. He had recognised several people there. From the past. From other ships and forgotten places. They had meant well but always he seemed to see the questions in their eyes. Curiosity, sympathy? It was hard to tell. He had finished his drink and started walking again. He realised now that he was very tired, his shirt clinging to his back like a damp towel.

A board creaked beneath his feet as he thrust through some bead curtains and dropped into a chair at one of the small cane tables. There were fortunately only two other occupants and neither gave him more than a cursory glance. Their conversation seemed to consist entirely of the latest rubber prices. The cost of local labour. The general inefficiency of transport. He guessed they were both planters, so familiar to each other that neither appeared to listen to what the other was saying.

A smiling waiter bowed beside the table. 'Sair?'

Lindsay stared at the proffered menu, realising for the first time that he had been drinking heavily since noon. Since he had seen Goss. But the drink did not seem to have had any real effect, other than to make the thought of food impossible.

'Perhaps the commander would wish to order later?'

He looked up at the second figure who had appeared. Either the newcomer was cat-footed or Lindsay was more drunk than he imagined. It seemed impossible he could have missed seeing such a man. He was gross, his huge body impeccably covered in a cream linen suit, his girth encircled by a crimson sash to match a small fez which appeared minute on his round head. A chair groaned loudly as the man sank into it.

'A drink first, maybe?' He snapped his fingers. 'I have some gin.'

Lindsay eyed him dully. He wanted to leave right now. He did not wish to talk. There was nothing to say.

The man announced calmly, 'I am the owner.' He waved a plump hand, several rings glinting in the coloured lanterns overhead. 'And bid you welcome.'

The waiter was pouring out two glasses of neat gin. On the bottle he saw the words. *Duty Free. H.M. Ships only.*

'Thanks.' He took a glass, wondering what it would do to his stomach.

The owner sipped at the gin and smiled. 'My religion regards gin as an evil. However.' He took another sip. 'One must adapt to the country's ways, eh?' He watched Lindsay unblinkingly. He had very dark, liquid eyes, like those of a younger man encased in a grotesque mask.

He continued in the same gentle tone, 'I am Turkish. Once, although some may find it difficult to accept, I was in the Grand Cavalry. A Captain of Horse.' He chuckled, the sound rising from a great depth. 'Now it would take more than one beast to carry me, you are thinking?'

Lindsay smiled. 'I am sorry. I am bad company.'

'Only loneliness is bad, Commander.' He signalled to the waiter. 'I fought your people on the Dardanelles in that other war. I learned to respect their courage, even though their leadership was less inspiring. So when I had to flee my own country I decided to come here. Halfway between two ways of life. East and West. I will be happy to end my life here.'

Lindsay felt the gin scraping his throat like fire. 'I really must go.' He tried to smile. 'As I said, I am bad company.'

The man shook his head. 'Not yet. It is not time.'

'Time?'

The man smiled gently. 'Do not play with fate, Commander. You will have one more glass, and then, perhaps, it will be time.'

Lindsay stared at him. He must have misheard or had finally taken leave of his senses. He looked quickly around the room but it was quite empty. The two planters had vanished.

The man said quietly, 'It is all right, Commander. They were there. They have gone up to their rooms for an arrangement with some women.' He wrinkled his nose disdainfully. 'They drink a lot first and then their women begin to appear beautiful again!' It seemed to amuse him greatly.

Lindsay sighed and raised the glass to his lips. What would they be doing aboard the ship? Some might be celebrating their forthcoming promotions and appointments. Others would be ashore, making the most of the last few days in Ceylon. Back in England it would be cold and grey. Air-raids and ration queues. Tired faces and pathetic bravery. The memories of Ceylon would become precious to many of *Benbecula*'s company in the months or years ahead.

The massive Turk snapped his fingers and as if by magic the gin bottle disappeared.

'I must go to the temple and make amends, Commander.' He stood up and took a deep breath. 'I have enjoyed our little talk.' He held out one fat hand. 'Maybe you will come again. But I think not.'

Lindsay groped for his cap, thinking he should offer to pay for the drinks but knowing also that the man would resent it.

He heard him add quietly, 'Now, you may leave. Somehow, I feel that your hurt will be easier to carry.'

Lindsay thanked him and walked out into the purple gloom, his mind still dazed by the unexpected encounter. Perhaps the man was crazy. Why the hotel was so deserted.

He lurched against a shuttered shop front and gasped. But the gin was real enough.

At the end of the street he saw bright lights and the hurrying criss-cross of crowds. Perhaps he might find a taxi. He could not face fighting his way back to the base through those same cheerful throngs of people.

But there was no taxi available, so with tired determination he increased his pace, shutting his ears to the din of voices and music, car horns and rickshaw wheels, while he tried to concentrate on the gross Turk who had once been a Captain of Horse at the Dardanelles.

'Hey, mate, got a light?'

He stopped to face two Australian soldiers who were clinging to each other for support. He took out his matches and waited while one of them made several attempts to light their cigarettes. Their voices reminded him of Stannard.

The first soldier squinted at Lindsay's shoulder straps. 'Pommy sailor, eh?' He grinned. 'But never mind, mate. You got me an' my cobber out of Singapore.' He laughed as if it were one huge joke. 'Leastways, somebody did!' They staggered away, their bush hats strangely alien against the coloured lanterns and bazaars.

He took out his pipe and then realised the soldiers had left without returning the matches. He was still patting his pockets when a taxi scraped against one of the nearby stalls and sent a mountain of fruit cascading under the wheels. A crowd gathered in seconds, prepared to be freely amused by the fierce exchange between driver and merchant. He tried to free himself from the growing crush but it was impossible. Above those around him he saw two impassive faced policemen forcing their way through the crowd towards the taxi which was now completely hemmed in by spectators.

He saw a dark doorway and decided to make for it. The police would take several minutes to clear the crowd. He might even find some matches. Two white figures were already in the doorway, probably with the same idea as himself. An eddy of figures pressed against him and he felt himself being pushed slowly towards another shopfront. He gave up. It was hopeless, and he was feeling worse. Sick.

Yet even through the excited babble of shouts and jeers he seemed to hear a voice. It was like part of a dream. A nerve laid bare in his memory.

'Commander! Commander Lindsay!'

All at once he was fighting his way back through the crowd, pushing with all his strength even though he knew it was just one more crack in his reserve.

A policeman grabbed at his arm, yelling at him, but he knocked him aside, his ears deaf to the roar of voices, his eyes blind to everything but the doorway and the two figures in white.

Against the darkness they seemed to hover like ghosts, and in those last desperate moments he imagined he had at last gone mad.

Gasping with exertion and almost sobbing he burst from the crowd and threw himself into the opening. Then he stood quite still. Afraid to blink or breathe, even though it was just one more dream.

She said, 'I *knew* it was you!'

Very slowly he reached out and put his hands on her shoulders. *'Eve.'* He felt her shiver under his grip. 'Eve. I thought——' She was still staring up at him, her face

almost hidden in shadow. The other Wren had moved
away and stood uncertainly by the shopfront. Then he
pulled her to him. Holding her tightly as he murmured,
'Oh Eve. All this time.'

She said quietly, 'You're not well.' To the other girl, 'Tell
that policeman to get us a taxi.' Then she pressed her face
into his chest and whispered, 'It's a miracle. We were
trying to get back to the base. Then this crowd, and I saw
you. I had no idea you were here.' She trembled. 'I still
can't believe it.' Then she looked up at him again, her eyes
very large in her face. 'You didn't get my letter then?'

He stared at her, still fearful it would suddenly end.
'We've had no mail except local letters.'

'And you thought I was in Canada!' She laughed, her
eyes shining with sudden tears. 'There was a last minute
mix-up. My medical report got confused with another
Wren's, and by the time it was sorted out the convoy had
sailed without me. So they sent me here instead. I'll bet
they're laughing like hell about it in Canada.'

She reached up to touch his face. 'You're like ice! Tell
me, what happened?'

'The convoy.' He could feel his body trembling violently. 'It was attacked. The ship with the Wrens aboard was
destroyed. I was there. I saw it.' He felt her hair with his
fingers. 'Burning. I tried to find you.' He broke down and
whispered, 'To bring you back.'

A policeman shouted, 'What's going on here?'

The other Wren replied just as loudly, 'Get a taxi and
don't be a bloody fool!'

Lindsay heard all of it but was conscious only of the girl
pressed against his body. He had to hold on to her. Otherwise. . .

She asked, 'Is the taxi coming, Marion? We must get him
to his ship quickly. He's ill.' She touched his face again, her
hand very gentle. 'It'll be all right now. My poor darling,
I'm so sorry!'

'Here's the taxi!'

Lindsay remembered very little of the journey. There was some sort of argument at the dockyard gates, a pause while the other Wren hurried away to make a telephone call.

Then she said, 'We can't come any further. Regulations. We've been on four days leave. Should have been back hours ago.' She pulled his head down on to her shoulder, speaking very softly. 'Or else I would have known you were here. Would have seen your ship come in.'

The other girl came back and peered into the taxi. She said vehemently, 'I spoke to the Third Officer and explained. Silly cow!'

Eve whispered, 'You'd never believe her father was a lord, would you?' She was half laughing, half crying.

The other Wren added, 'Then I got the sentry to put me through to the ship. Just as you said. I wouldn't speak to anyone else but him.'

Feet scraped in the darkness and Jupp loomed above the girl's shoulder.

'Ah, there you are, sir!' He saw the girl and nodded gravely. 'I'm so glad for you, Miss. For you both.'

She said, 'Take good care of him.' As Lindsay tried to keep hold of her arm she added, 'It will be all right, darling. I shall see you tomorrow. I promise.'

'Come along, sir.'

Jupp helped him from the taxi, the driver of which was watching with fixed fascination until the Wren whose father was a lord snapped, 'Our quarters, and double quick!'

Lindsay realised they had reached the brow. At the far end of it he could see the same quartermaster. The same blue light.

Jupp said evenly, 'Just a few more paces.' He moved back. 'On your own, sir.' He followed Lindsay, his eyes fixed on his shoulders, willing him up the endless length of brow.

The quartermaster had been joined by the O.O.D. It

was Stannard. He saw Lindsay and Jupp's set face behind him and snapped, 'The captain's coming aboard!' Then he stepped between the quartermaster and the entry port and said quietly, 'Welcome back, sir.'

Jupp smiled but kept his eyes on Lindsay.

'I think some 'ot soup might do the trick, sir.'

Stannard watched them fade into the shadows. Paget had been O.O.D., but when Jupp had come to him to ask for his help he had sent the lieutenant away, although he could not recall what for. He had been in his cabin drinking with Dancy at the time. Not talking, just drinking in companionable silence.

He was touched in some strange way that Jupp had chosen him. Had trusted him to share his secret.

Paget came back breathing fast. 'I couldn't find it, Pilot.'

'What?'

'What you sent me for.' Paget stared at the gangway log. 'The captain's aboard then?'

'Yeh.'

'And I missed him.' Paget sounded cheated.

'Shame, isn't it?' Stannard walked towards his own quarters whistling quietly to himself.

Jupp had succeeded in getting Lindsay to his cabin without meeting anyone else.

He waited until he had dropped on to his bunk and then said, 'I'll fetch the soup, sir.'

Lindsay's eyes were closed. 'Don't bother. I'm all right.'

'I 'ad it ready. It's no bother.' He saw the reading-lamp shining directly across Lindsay's face. 'I'll switch it off.'

'No. Leave it.' He opened his eyes. '*You* saw her, didn't you?'

'Course I did, sir!' He grinned broadly. 'Don't you worry, light or no light, she'll see you tomorrow, if I 'ave to fetch 'er meself, an' that's a fact!'

Lindsay's eyes closed again. 'There was this Turk. He made me stay there. Said it wasn't time. Something about fate. I wanted to go and yet I couldn't move. Kept on about the time and the Dardanelles.'

Jupp waited as Lindsay's words grew quieter and his features became more relaxed.

'Was trying to find some matches. And then I heard her call my name.' His voice trailed away.

'That's right, sir.' Jupp watched him sadly. 'I don't understand a word of it but I'm sure you're right.' He snapped off the light and padded from the cabin.

In his pantry he sat down on a stool and stared at the soup which was simmering on a small heater. He'll not be wanting it now. He cocked his head to listen but heard nothing. Just the creak of steel, the muffled sounds of a sentry's regular footsteps.

Then he groped into a locker and took out a bottle of Drambuie. It was his one weakness for special occasions. He wiped a clean glass and held it to the light before pouring himself a generous measure.

For to Jupp it was a very special occasion indeed.

CR

17 The house by the sea

Petty Officer Ritchie waited until he heard Lindsay's voice and then stepped into the cabin.

'Good mornin', sir.' He placed his signal pad on the desk and then handed him a sealed envelope. 'Just arrived from H.Q., sir.'

As Lindsay slit open the envelope Ritchie darted a quick glance at Jupp. He had already heard about Lindsay's return on board. Jupp had awakened him just before dawn to tell him. He saw the untouched breakfast on the cabin table and Jupp's obvious anxiety.

Lindsay said, 'Orders. You'd better ask Number One to come and see me as soon as he's finished with Morning Colours.' He stared at the carefully worded instructions. Four days time. It was not long.

The bulkhead telephone buzzed and he made himself sit very still until Jupp announced, 'Just the O.O.D. About requestmen an' defaulters.'

'I see.'

He tried to hide the disappointment and to concentrate on his written orders. Work was to be completed before sailing time but leave for the ship's company could continue at the captain's discretion. Further information would be forthcoming etc. etc. etc.

Beyond the cabin a bugle blared the 'Alert' and on the tannoy system a voice bellowed, 'Attention on the upper deck. Face aft and salute!'

Lindsay stood up and walked slowly to an open scuttle,

feeling the morning sunlight on his face. As he listened to one of de Chair's marine buglers he could picture the ensign rising at the taffrail, while the Jack was hoisted in the bows. Once at sea the ensign would be replaced by one of the well-worn ones, tattered and stained, which Ritchie retained for harder use.

He had awakened in his bunk with Jupp touching his shoulder, a cup of black coffee poised and ready. For just a few seconds he had been gripped with something like terror until Jupp had grinned at him.

''S'all right, sir. It *'appened* just like you remembers!'

As he shaved and dressed and the ship had come alive around him for another day he had tried to piece it all together in his mind. Each small moment, so that he could hold it intact forever.

To think that mere seconds had saved them. Another moment and they might never have met. The letter which she had written had probably been lost or bogged down in some forgotten mail office. If he had not stayed in that strange restaurant. If, if, if. . . . It seemed unending.

Goss appeared in the doorway, 'You wanted me, sir?'

'Orders, Number One. Four days notice.'

'Not much. Still a lot of work undone. I suppose they don't care any more.'

'Well, do what you can. They might still cancel the orders.'

Goss shook his head doubtfully. 'I went ashore last night and met an old mate of mine. He says there's a big convoy being assembled. Any time now, it seems.'

It made sense. Every available escort would be required if the convoy was to be a large one.

He replied, 'Leave will be granted as before.'

Goss nodded. 'Good. Gives me room to get things sorted out with most of the jolly jacks ashore.'

The telephone buzzed again. Jupp's face was expressionless. 'It's the Signals Distribution Office, sir.'

He handed the phone to him and said breezily, 'Now, Mr Goss, what about a cuppa while you're 'ere?'

Her voice seemed right against his ear. 'Sorry about the deception, although this *is* the S.D.O.' Then she asked quickly, 'Are you all right?'

'Yes. Never better.' Goss, Jupp and the cabin had faded away. 'When can I see you?'

He heard a typewriter clattering in the background as she replied, 'Now, if you like. At the gates. I must see you as soon as possible.' She added very clearly, 'There isn't much time, is there?'

'No.' He glanced quickly at his watch. 'I'll be there right away.'

When he had replaced the handset he saw Goss watching him, a cup like a thimble in his large hand.

'I'm going ashore, Number One. Not for long.'

Goss nodded. 'I can cope, sir.' He studied Lindsay over the rim of the cup. So that was it. Well, bloody good luck to him.

Jupp asked, 'Nice coffee, Mr Goss?'

Goss stayed poker-faced. 'Very nice.' Surprisingly, he winked. 'Better for some though, eh?' Then he followed Lindsay from the cabin.

At the brow he stood beside Lindsay and looked at the busy jetty below.

'By the way, sir, if, and I say *if* you were thinking of taking a bit of leave yourself.' He waited until Lindsay was facing him. 'Then we can manage quite well.' He shrugged. 'After all, the sooner I get used to carrying the weight on my own the better, so to speak.'

'Yes. Thank you.' He turned to watch a column of soldiers marching along the next jetty, their bodies deformed by packs and weapons. 'I may hold you to that.' Then he saluted and ran quickly down the brow.

She was waiting just outside the gates, looking very young in her white uniform. But exactly as he remembered her.

She said, 'There's a little Chinese restaurant just up the road. It's quiet.' She shot him a quick glance. 'Not too bright either.'

As they hurried past the dock-bound vehicles and groups of saluting sailors she added breathlessly, 'I had to pinch myself this morning. Even now I'm afraid I'll wake up.'

The restaurant was just as she had described it. And at such an early hour quite empty.

They were ushered to a table and he said quietly, 'My God, you're even more beautiful than I remembered.'

'It must be darker in here than I thought!' Her voice was husky, and for a few moments neither of them spoke.

Then she removed her cap and shook out her hair. That too was like a touch against his heart.

'I'm working in the S.D.O.' She did not look at him. 'So I know about your orders. Four days.' She fell silent until a waiter had brought some tea. 'I will be going, too. Back to old England.' She faced him and reached out to grasp his hand. 'Maybe we'll be in the same convoy.' She squeezed it gently. 'Don't worry. It won't be like that other one. It can't be.'

'No. But why are you going back so soon?'

She wrinkled her nose. 'I was sent here with some others for the Singapore operation. We were to work here on communications. Now that's all over we're going home again. Maybe I'll even get my proper signals course now.' She dropped her eyes. 'I'm sorry. I was forgetting about those other Wrens. It must have been terrible.'

He started to speak but she tightened her grip on his hand.

'Just a minute. There's something I must tell you. I don't know what you'll say or think but I must say it.'

He waited, suddenly tense.

'You remember my friend Marion?'

'The one whose father is a lord?'

'Yes, that Marion. Her father's terribly rich. But she's very nice.' She seemed suddenly nervous. 'He has business out here. Her father. There's a place down the coast. We stayed there during the last leave.' Her hand trembled slightly. 'I can get leave again now that I'm on draft.' Then she turned and looked directly into his eyes. 'If you'd like that.'

'You know I would, Eve. If you're sure——'

She stared down at their hands on the table. 'I'm sure. It's just that I'm afraid of losing you again. This way we'll know.' She tried to laugh. 'I was also scared you'd think I was in the habit of taking all my commanders to a coastal villa!'

'When can you leave?'

She looked up again, her eyes very bright. 'Today. And you?'

He remembered Goss's words. Perhaps he knew about it, too. Maybe the whole ship did.

'This afternoon. How do we go?'

'I can get a car. Or rather Marion will. She can get anything.'

'I'm beginning to like her, too.'

She replied quietly, 'We'd better go now. There are things I must do.' She replaced her cap and added, 'At least you'll know you've got a good driver.' She faced him and he saw the colour on her cheeks. 'The best in Scapa, they used to say!'

'They were right.'

Outside the restaurant the sunlight was almost blinding.

He said, 'I'll phone your quarters.'

'Yes. Then I'll pick you up.' She grinned. 'That sounds bad.'

'Not to me.' He touched her bare arm. 'I love you.'

A working party of seamen marched along the road, and as they passed the petty officer bawled, 'Eyes left!'

When he turned again she saluted him too and said, 'And I you, *sir!*'

He watched her until she had disappeared into a nearby building and then hurried through the gates after the working party. Even when he reached the top of the brow he was still expecting something to go wrong. A change of orders. A staff conference. Some crisis which would hold him aboard like one last cruel trap.

Goss listened to his instructions and said, 'Where will you be staying, sir? In case I need to contact you.'

'I'll telephone the ship when I know the number where I can be reached.'

He saw Stripey, the ship's cat, sauntering up the brow after a brief visit to the dockyard.

Goss nodded. 'Then I suggest you get going, sir.'

In his cabin as he threw a few things into a case he kept one ear for the telephone.

Jupp helped him pack, and as he was about to leave said, 'Perhaps you'd take this too, sir.' He held out a tiny silver replica of the *Benbecula*. It was less than two inches long but perfect in scale and detail. He added awkwardly, 'It was made by the *Becky*'s boatswain many years back. Shouldn't be tellin' you this o'course, but 'e 'ad to melt down four silver teapots from the first class dinin' saloon to complete it.'

Lindsay stared at him. 'But you'll want to keep this!'

'I was savin' it, sir.' He shook his head. 'Maybe this is what for. Anyway, I reckon she'd appreciate it.'

Lindsay placed it inside the case. 'She will. As much as I do.'

Jupp shifted from foot to foot. 'Well, this won't get the work done. Chatterin' like this.' He hesitated. 'An' good luck, Cap'n.'

'I shall miss this sort of treatment when I go back to the real Navy.'

Jupp grinned. 'I'll probably take a pub after this lot's over, sir. You can come an' see me sometimes.'

'It's a promise.'

Jupp followed him to the ladder and watched as he hurried down to the promenade deck. It was strange to be parted from the little silver ship after all these years, he thought vaguely. But the girl for whom it had been intended had not waited for him. His lip curled with disgust. She had married a bloody bricklayer, and it served her right.

He heard the trill of pipes and gave a deep sigh of relief. Lindsay had got away all right. He loped into the cabin and picked up the telephone.

''S'all right, Bob. You can reconnect the phone now. All's well.'

Then humming cheerfully he went to his pantry to find the bottle of Drambuie.

———————

The car was a very old open M.G. but the engine sounded healthy, and when they had cleared the town limits the miles began to pass more quickly.

Once, as they swung around a wide curve above the sea she asked, 'Why are you staring at me? It's not fair. I have to watch the road.'

Lindsay rested his arm along the back of her seat, his fingers touching her hair as it ruffled in the wind. He had never seen her out of uniform before. At the dockyard gates he had almost walked past her. The dress was pale green and very simple. It was, she had explained, straight off a stall, and had proved it by removing a price tag which had been dangling from the hem.

'I'm enjoying it. So you drive and I'll stare, okay?'

Another time, while they waited for some cattle to wander aimlessly across the road, they held hands, oblivious to the heat and dust or the native driver who paused to study them.

Green hills with trees almost touching above the road

changed in seconds to long open stretches and only an occasional building or bungalow to show any sign of life. The dust poured back from the wheels in an unbroken yellow bank, the car jerking violently across deep ruts and loose stones with careless abandon. Climbing in low gear then roaring down again, with quick flashes of dark blue between the tall palms to show that the sea was never far away.

Then another road, narrower than the main one, and the girl had to reduce speed to take an increasing number of bends.

She said, 'What you were saying about the ship. Is it definite?'

He nodded. 'Yes.'

She reached out and grasped his hand, keeping her eyes on the road. 'You feel bad about it, don't you?' She hesitated. 'Maybe I can get transferred near this place you'll be going.'

She must have been thinking about Canada again for she added, 'I'm not jolly well going away from you again, if I can help it!'

'You'd better have a word with Marion! She's bound to know about these matters.'

She laughed, showing her even teeth, and shouted above the engine, 'She did that already for another girl. Told her to get herself pregnant to avoid going overseas.'

'And did she?'

'Shouldn't think so. You should have seen her bloke. Like a rhinoceros!'

The car stopped eventually on the crest of a small hill. Below, Lindsay saw a crescent of beach, the sea making a necklace of surf to the next headland. There was some sort of building set amongst the palms. It looked as if it had been there since time began.

'Is *that* it?'

She turned and studied him gravely. 'You are nutty.

'That's an old temple.' She let the car move forward again and called, 'There, *see!*'

The house was inside a low wall, painted white and partly screened by a line of trees. It looked very cool and inviting.

Lindsay could see no sign of life, and even when the car halted outside the gates nothing moved.

She said, 'An old chap and his son look after things most of the time. When proper visitors come here they have more servants, of course.'

'It's marvellous.'

She jumped from the car and dragged at his arm. 'Brother, you ain't seen nothing yet!' She was laughing. Like a tanned child. Watching his face as she pulled him towards the house.

There was only one storey, and the whole house seemed to have been built of stone and marble. Even in the days of cheap labour it would have cost a small fortune.

She said, 'Ah, here he is.'

The head servant was grey-bearded and extremely wrinkled. He must be about eighty, Lindsay thought.

He said, 'Welcome back, Missy. I have sent my son for your luggage.'

The girl looked at Lindsay. 'You'll be wanting a telephone?' She gestured to a door. 'In there.' For an instant her face clouded over. 'Don't go back. No matter what. Even if the base is on fire!'

'What will you be doing?'

She ran her fingers through her hair. 'Ugh, the dust! I'm going to have a swim. Then we'll have something to eat.' She made a mock curtsy. 'Anything *sir* desires.'

Lindsay walked into a low-ceilinged room. There was little furniture but what there was looked old and hand-carved. An unlikely brass telephone stood beside the window, and he imagined someone in the past sitting there. Listening to a voice from the outside world. Who would ever want to leave such a place, he wondered?

The line was surprisingly clear, and after a short delay he was connected to the ship's telephone.

'This is the captain. O.O.D., please.' He waited, picturing the sudden bustle on the upper deck, and tried to control a pang of apprehension.

But it was not the O.O.D.

Goss sounded calm and matter-of-fact. 'Everything's all right this end, sir. Two marines just brought aboard drunk. And I'm about to kick the arse off a thieving coolie I found in the bosun's store.' He paused. 'A normal day, in other words.'

Lindsay looked at the number on the telephone and gave it to Goss. Then he said, 'Thanks for holding the fort.'

'No bother, sir.' There was a pause and the sound of someone else murmuring in the background. Then Goss said abruptly, 'Just heard where I can lay my hooks on some paint. Can't stop, sir. Might lose it!' The line went dead.

'I take it from your cat's smile that the base is *not* on fire?'

He swung round and saw her framed in the open doorway. She was wearing a black swimsuit which made her limbs appear even more tanned.

'You're staring again!'

He walked towards her. 'As I told you. You're very lovely. Especially today.'

She put her hands on her hips and tried to frown. 'My mouth is too wide, I'm covered in freckles and I've got a figure like a boy.' She watched him as he put his hands on her shoulders. 'And I love you, even if you are a liar.'

'I'm surprised they allowed you in the Wrens.' Her skin was very smooth. 'You must need glasses.'

She dropped her head against his chest. 'A nice liar.' Then she pushed him away. 'Get your pants, or whatever commanders wear for informal occasions, and join me on the beach.' She paused and looked back at him, her cheeks flushed. 'Old Mohammed will tell you where your gear is stowed.'

'Is that *really* his name?'

But she was already running out into the sunlight, her bare legs like gold against the nodding palm fronds.

The old man was waiting at the door of an end room, the swimming trunks in his hands.

He said impassively, 'The young missy is very much alive. It pleases me to see her so.'

Lindsay threw off his soiled shirt. 'Was she unhappy?'

'I think lonely. But that is gone now.' He picked up the shirt and added, 'I will have the women attend to this for you.'

Lindsay watched him walk slowly down the hallway. Old but very dignified. Another Jupp perhaps.

Then he turned and looked around the room. The green dress lay on a chair beside the bed. He touched it. It was still warm. Then he opened his case and took out the silver model. On a teak table was the girl's wristwatch. After a second's hesitation he put the little ship beside it. Four silver teapots, Jupp had said. It must have taken some explaining at the time.

With a smile he turned and ran down the hallway, the floor very cool under his bare feet.

He found her standing waist deep in the sea, her slim body being pushed from side to side in the deep swell.

'Come *on*!' She was squinting into the sunlight and he wished he had brought a camera. 'There you go! You're *doing* it again!' Then she laughed, the same sound he had heard that night at Scapa Flow, and plunged into the water.

When finally they emerged dripping and gasping from the sea the light was already fading. The tall line of trees was topped in the last of the sun's rays, their shadows like black bars across the house.

She threw him a towel and began to rub another one vigorously over her hair.

She said suddenly, 'I haven't asked yet.'

He turned but she had her back to him. 'What?'

'How long?'

'Two days.' He saw her shoulders stiffen, the skin still shining with droplets of spray.

Then she replied quietly, 'We'll make it last, won't we?'

Her shoulders were shaking now as if from a chill breeze, but when he put his arm around them she said, 'I'm not going to cry.' Then she twisted on his arm and looked up at him. 'I'm so happy. I can't tell you.'

He picked up his towel. 'By the way. The old man was quite upset when I called him Mohammed.'

She stared at him, appalled. 'You *didn't*!' Then she saw his face and exclaimed, 'You beast! I'm not speaking to you again, ever!' She chuckled. 'Although I suppose he *is* pretty old!'

Together they ran up the shelving beach and into the house. Several lights were already burning, and in the low-ceilinged room a table was laid and a bottle of wine stood chilling in a silver bucket beside it. They stood side by side in the doorway just staring at the table and the quiet room. Then he slipped his arm around her shoulders again, the damp skin almost cold under his touch.

He heard her say, 'It's quite marvellous. I didn't know things like this could happen.'

'Nor me. I have a feeling that your friend Marion has had a hand in it.'

'Yes. I was thinking the same thing.' She moved away, light on her feet, before he could reach her. 'I'm going to change. I shall try and look like a lady, just for you.' She paused. 'Then you can get into something. But not uniform. This once.'

'I wasn't going to.' He smiled. 'This once.'

'Help yourself to a drink over there. Not too much. I want to share everything.' She ran down in the hallway towards the bedroom. 'God, I feel wicked! I really do!'

The old servant appeared silently with a bath robe. 'I will call you when missy is ready, sir.'

'You've done a fine job here. Thanks very much.'

The man shrugged. 'It is nothing.' But there was a hint of a smile as he walked away as dignified as ever.

Lindsay was stooping at a drinks cabinet when she burst in on him again. She was still wearing the swimsuit and was holding the silver ship in her hands.

'This is a wonderful present, darling!' She ran to him and kissed him impulsively on the cheek. Her face was wet, but it was not spray this time.

'It was Jupp's. He wanted you to have it.'

'Bless him.' She stood back and studied him for several seconds. 'And you.' Then she walked away again, very slowly, holding the ship against her body like a talisman.

The dinner, like everything else, was perfect. While Lindsay had been changing into shirt and slacks, candles had appeared on the table, and while the old man and his son waited on them, he and the girl sat facing each other, aware of nothing but each other. In the distance an animal was howling in the darkness and insects maintained a steady buzzing attack on the screened windows. But beyond the circle of candlelight nothing was real or important.

She was wearing a dress of soft yellow which left her shoulders bare. In the candlelight her face was very clear, her expression changing to match their mood with each passing moment.

Only once did she touch on that other world.

'When is it all going to end? It might be years yet.'

'Don't think about it.' Their hands clasped across the table. 'Think about us.'

After that they said very little, and when the table was cleared, the coffee cups empty, Lindsay could sense yet another change in her mood.

She walked to the door and said, 'Don't look at me. I——I don't want to make a fool of myself.' She turned towards him, her voice very low. 'But it's so little time.' Her lip quivered. 'And I want you so badly.' When he made to speak she added quickly, 'Just give me a few minutes.' Again she tried to laugh. 'I'm a bit fluttery inside!'

Lindsay sat in the quiet room listening to the insects against the screens. The animal had stopped howling, so that the silence seemed all the more intense.

Then he blew out the candles and walked from the room. One light still burned in the hallway and beneath the bedroom door was another.

She was lying quite motionless in the bed but her eyes followed him as he moved into the lamplight and stood looking down at her.

A black nightgown lay across a chair and she said, 'It belongs to Marion.'

He sat down on the edge of the bed and touched her hair.

She added quietly, 'But I don't want anything belonging to anyone else. You don't think I'm silly?'

'No. Of course I don't.' He leaned over and kissed her forehead. 'I think you're very special.'

'I just want you to be happy with me.' She dropped her eyes to his hand as he pulled the sheet gently from beneath her chin. 'I don't want to spoil *anything.*'

Then she closed her eyes and lay still as he dragged the sheet away and sat looking at her, his hand moving gently across her body. She did not move until he had slipped out of his clothes and lay down beside her, an arm beneath her head, his other hand around one of her breasts. Then she opened her eyes and watched him, her breath warm against his face.

'Two days and three nights.'

He felt her body go rigid as he moved his hand across the gentle curve of her stomach, and when he lowered his head to her breast he could feel the heart beating like a small trapped animal. Beating to match his own.

Her arms came up and around his head, her fingers gripping his shoulders with sudden urgency as she whispered, 'Oh, God! I do love you!'

The fingers seemed to be biting into his flesh as he moved his hand still more, feeling her come alive to his touch, the need and the desire breaking down their reserves like an unspoken word.

As he rose above her she threw open her arms and stared up into his face, her mouth moist in the lamplight.

Then he was falling, feeling her arch to receive him, holding him, dragging him down and down, until the fierceness of their love left them entwined in the soft glare like statuary.

The next thing Lindsay realised was that he was awake, his head cradled against the girl's hip while she ran her fingers gently through his hair. The lamp was out and through the shutters he could see the faint gleam of dawn.

She whispered, 'You cried out, my darling. Just once, and then you were still again.'

He kissed her hip and felt a tremor run through her. Was the nightmare gone at last? Had it found the one, unmatchable strength and left him in peace?

He kissed her again and said, 'I want you.'

She pulled his head across her stomach, moaning softly as he postponed the moment a while longer.

Later, as they lay and watched the first yellow sunlight through the shutters, she said simply, 'I don't feel like me at all. Strange, isn't it?'

'Whoever you are, I think you're wonderful.'

He thought he heard footsteps in the hallway. The clatter of cups. He almost expected to see Jupp peering around the door.

He dragged the sheet over their bodies and said,

'Cover yourself, you shameless creature.' He kissed her hard on the mouth. 'Or we may be asked to leave.'

She took the mood, swinging her legs over the bed and seizing her robe from a chair.

'Lay another finger on me and I'll——' She ran back to him and held him against her. 'I'll probably let you do anything you like with me.'

And that was how it continued for the next two days and nights. Moments of peace and intimate silence. Swift, exploring passion which left them both breathless and limp like young animals. The sun and blue sea, the isolation and the sheer perfection of it all was like a backcloth to their own happiness.

When they climbed into the old car again Lindsay said quietly, 'I will never forget this place.' He squeezed her hand. 'One day I'll remind you of it. When you start getting fed up with me.'

She looked at the house. The old man and his son had made their farewells as if to allow the moment of departure a certain privacy.

'They'll put a plaque up there one day.' She shook the hair from her eyes. 'To Wren Eve Collins, who fell here.'

They smiled at each other and he said, 'Time to move.'

The car jolted up the hill past the ruins which they had not found time to visit.

They hardly spoke during the return journey, and once when he had seen a tear on her cheek she had reached out for his hand, saying, 'I'm all right. Don't worry, my darling.' She had placed his hand on her thigh and continued to drive along the dusty road above the sea. 'It's just me. I'm selfish, pig-headed and silly.'

He gripped her leg, knowing she felt as he did. 'And perfect.'

The first buildings of the town swung into view as she said, 'I'll drop you at the gates.'

He nodded. 'Right. I'll ring you as soon as I know what's happening.' The car stopped, the bodywork glittering in the harsh sunlight. She kept both hands on the wheel.

'You're not sorry?'

'Grateful.' He watched her turn to look at him. 'And happy.'

She revved the engine. 'Me too, as it happens.'

The car moved away into the traffic and Lindsay walked towards the gates.

He returned the sentry's salute. 'Good morning.'

The marine watched him from the corner of his eye. 'Good for some,' he said.

18 Passage home

Goss's private information proved to be very true. Within twelve hours of the libertymen returning aboard, the last few missing ones being found and delivered by shore patrols, *Benbecula* was steaming out of harbour.

The day prior to sailing Lindsay had attended a conference at the H.Q. building, and from it had gleaned some importance of the ships being allotted to the convoy. Troops, munitions, oil and food, it was to be organised like some vast relay race. The first leg across the Indian Ocean was more or less straightforward, as Japanese submarines had so far made little or no impression there. Once around the Cape more escorts would be joining and leaving the convoy, like guards changing on a valuable treasure, and a powerful cruiser squadron would be at sea the whole time, never too far away to give support against heavy enemy units.

Off Gibraltar the convoy would be reorganised. Some ships would slip under the Rock's own defences with supplies for the fleet and the desert army. Others would be joining with another convoy to head westward to America. The bulk of the ships would press on for the last and most hazardous part, to run a gauntlet between U-boats and German long-range bombers.

The fact that so much care was being shown for the final part of the voyage was proof of the importance given to it. It was hinted that an aircraft carrier and her escorts would be available to provide vital round-the-clock air cover, something almost unheard of.

Once at sea, *Benbecula* joined with other naval vessels in sorting out and organising the ships into three columns. There were twenty-four to be escorted in all. Lindsay had been in far larger convoys but somehow this one seemed so much bigger. Perhaps the size and majesty of individual ships made up for actual numbers. The four troopers, for instance, were ocean liners of repute before the war. Large, well-powered and new. The other ships were as varied as their flags, but unlike most other convoys Lindsay had seen, were fairly modern vessels, well able to keep up a good pace under almost every circumstance.

As they had gathered, from Colombo and Bombay, from Kuwait and as far away as New Zealand and Australia, he had been conscious of the variation. Almost every flag seemed to represent a country occupied by an enemy. French and Dutch, Danish and Norwegian, there seemed unending colours on hulls and flags. There were several British ones and two Americans, and Lindsay wondered what it must feel like to be at sea, depending on your own resources but free, while your homeland was under the enemy's heel.

Goss's special information had omitted one fact, however. Because of the convoy's changing shape and size it would be necessary to retain one naval officer in sole charge, in a ship which would be employed for the whole of the journey. *Benbecula* was that ship. Commodore Kemp was to be senior officer.

Maybe Kemp was still unsure of Lindsay's reaction, or perhaps he was at last aware of his own unpopularity with higher authority. Either way, he appeared content to stay at a distance, keeping his contact with Lindsay to a bare, cool minimum.

When he had first come aboard he had said, 'You command the ship. I will control the overall pattern of events.'

Now, four days out, and steaming south-west across

the blinding blue glare of the Indian Ocean, Lindsay
wondered what the commodore had been offered as his
next appointment. A lot would no doubt depend on the
success of the convoy, although with such a well planned
series of escorts it was hard to see how things could go
wrong.

He walked to the extent of the port wing and stared
astern at the great panorama of ships. *Benbecula* was
leading the starboard line, while one of the big troopers
led the centre. The port column was headed by a dazzle-
painted cruiser. He let his eyes move along each ship, and
wondered how many would survive the whole war. Oil-
tankers and freighters, grain ships and ore carriers, while
in the centre the four stately liners carried the most
precious cargo of all. Even without binoculars it was
possible to see the packed masses of men on their decks,
like pale khaki lines over every foot of open space. The
second troopship was partly hidden by the leader, and he
wondered where Eve was at this moment. Peering at the
Benbecula? Resting in her cabin or chatting to the irre-
pressible Marion? He could not see the ship without
seeing her face in his mind.

Because of the convoy conferences, the planning and
last minute organisation he had only been able to meet
her twice, and then briefly.

As he strained his eyes towards the ship he thought of
all the coincidences which had brought and held them
together. Even the mistake at Liverpool which had sent a
girl to her death and kept Eve safe seemed like part of
some uncanny plan.

Through the open wheelhouse door he heard Stannard's voice as he handed over his watch.

'Course still two-two-zero. One-one-zero revs.'

He heard Hunter's muffled reply.

Stannard walked on to the wing and stared at the ships.
'Quite a sight, sir.'

Lindsay glanced at him. He looked strained and

sounded as much. He had not spoken of his brother again and made an obvious effort to be his old self. But the signs were only too clear. Perhaps when he got involved with the new navigation course and his next ship he might be too busy to brood.

'How does it feel, sir?'

Lindsay saw the Australian's eyes move to his shoulder straps. The fourth gold stripe was very bright and new against the others.

The unexpected promotion had been one of the first things which Goss had mentioned when he had returned from the two days leave. You never really knew a man like Goss. If he was deadly serious or trying to hold on to a secret joke.

He had said, 'Two bits of news, sir. One good. One not so good.'

The good news had been Lindsay's advancement to captain. The bad had been Commodore Kemp's arrival on board.

He smiled. 'I don't feel any different.'

It was true. Once, years back, he would have imagined that reaching the coveted rank was all a young officer could wish for. He had changed. Everything seemed and felt different now.

Stannard seemed surprised. 'It's just that I've never seen you looking so well, sir. I guess I'll never know the strain of command. Not sure I want to.'

Lindsay looked at the ships. 'I am getting married when we reach the U.K.'

Stannard gasped. 'Well, Jeez, that is, I'm very glad, sir.' He held out his hand. 'Hell, that's good news.'

'You're the first to know.' He wondered why he had told Stannard. Just like that. Seeing his obvious pleasure made him glad he had.

'Certainly sudden, sir.'

A signalman called, 'From the *John P. Ashton*, sir. Permission to reduce speed. Engine failure.'

Lindsay nodded. 'Affirmative. Better now than when we run into trouble.'

The ship in question was an American destroyer, and apart from *Benbecula* the oldest in the convoy. They had been launched the same year, and Lindsay could sympathise with her captain's problems. She was one of the old four-pipers, now on way to be handed over on loan to the Royal Navy for anti-submarine duty. She was not the first to change flags by this arrangement, but unlike the others she had been on picket duty at Singapore when the Japanese had struck. Now, rolling unsteadily above her own image, she was falling away on the convoy's flank, her captain no doubt praying that the fault was nothing fatal.

Ahead of the convoy two other destroyers were barely visible in sea haze, but Lindsay knew one to be the *Merlin*. Her captain would be thinking, too. Of his next command. Not one ship but a group. A positive job. Something which really mattered.

For the first time since rejoining the ship he felt the return of resentment and bitterness. Ashore, he had tried to hide his feelings from Eve, guessing she was probably grateful for his new appointment. You could not get drowned or burned alive in a training depot. Unless you were born unlucky.

But now, as he watched the escorting cruiser, the wink of signal lamps, he knew the same feeling.

He saw de Chair standing on the forward deck watching some of his marines exercising with Bren guns. In their shorts and boots, their bodies tanned from Ceylon's swimming and sunlight, they looked like strangers.

'From *John P. Ashton*, sir. Am under way again.' The man paused. 'This chicken is ready for the pot.'

Stannard said, 'What a helluva name for a ship. I wonder who he was.'

Lindsay grinned. 'Old or not, she'll be very welcome. Just about anything afloat is wanted now.'

Stannard looked up at the masthead and said quietly, 'Except the *Becky*. They don't want her any more.'

Lindsay looked away. 'I know how you feel.' What he had said once before to Stannard. 'But there's nothing we can do about it.'

Stannard sighed. 'Well, I think I'll get my head down, sir. Plenty to do later, I guess.'

Lindsay waited until he had left the bridge and then raised his glasses to study the second ship of the centre column. It was just possible he might catch a glimpse of her.

———

Eighteen days out of Ceylon the convoy was off the Cape of Good Hope and heading north-west into the Atlantic. Each day was much like the preceding one. Drills and general routine, with the weather still warm and friendly. The leading destroyers had been relieved by another pair from Cape Town, and the Royal Indian Navy sloop which followed them this far had returned to her own country. The cruiser was still with them, and surprisingly, so was the *John P. Ashton*. She had had two minor breakdowns but always she seemed to manage to be there when a new dawn broke.

As the forenoon watch took stations around the ship, Lindsay climbed up to the bridge and found Commodore Kemp sitting in his chair staring at the open sea across the bows. Goss had the watch but was on the starboard wing, apparently staying as far as possible from his superior. The latter had hardly shown himself throughout the voyage so far. He had a large cabin aft, formerly an extended stateroom for very important passengers, which was still retained for much the same reason, although Lindsay suspected Goss's sentiment had a good deal to do with it.

Kemp turned as Lindsay saluted formally. 'I was going to send for you.' He turned to stare forward again. 'I've just had a top secret signal from Admiralty.' He sounded hoarse, and Lindsay wondered if he was drinking heavily in his private quarters. 'Been a spot of bother off the Cape Verde Islands. A freighter has been sunk. Believed to have been shelled by a surface ship.' He shifted his shoulders beneath the spotless drill jacket. 'Not our problem, naturally, but it's as well to know these things.'

Lindsay watched him narrowly. 'Was that all, sir?'

'Admiralty appears to think there may be some connection with another report. A cruiser was badly damaged by a mine. Too far out in the Atlantic for a drifting one from a field. Dropped with some others apparently, on the off chance of hitting any stray ship in the area.'

Lindsay clenched his fists to steady himself. 'It must be that raider again. Has to be.'

Kemp replied evasively, 'We don't know that for certain. Nobody does. Anyway, if the two attacks *are* connected, the Hun is in for a shock. This convoy is on the top secret list and so is our additional cruiser screen. If the enemy tries to tangle with us, I can whistle up enough heavy guns to cut him into little shreds!' He swivelled in the chair and glared at him. 'Satisfied?'

Lindsay caught the smell of brandy. 'Not entirely.'

He walked to the teak rail and ran his hands along it. 'Was there any other information from the freighter before she was silenced?'

Kemp swallowed. 'She was a Greek. Said she was going to the assistance of a Spanish merchantman which was in difficulties.'

Lindsay bit his lip. How long would it take for people to realise and see through this simple trick? Without effort he could visualise the savage gunflashes against the drifting ice, the burning hull and the Wren who was blind.

Kemp was right about one thing. If the raider came upon this convoy, even the one cruiser in company should be more than a match. But with the distant screen as well she would not stand an earthly, even of getting in range.

Kemp appeared to think his silence was an acceptance and added curtly, 'In another week we'll be meeting with a heavy additional escort from Freetown.' The thought seemed to give him new confidence. 'Like a clock, that's how I like things.'

The rear door slid back and Midshipman Kemp walked into the wheelhouse.

The commodore watched him make a few notations in the bridge log and said, 'Ah, Jeremy. There you are. Wondered what you were doing.' He gave a careful smile. 'Been hiding from me, eh?'

The boy looked at him. 'Sir?'

The commodore spread his hands. 'I shouldn't be at all surprised if you have a pleasant surprise waiting for you in England. I'm not promising anything, of course, but if I put a word in the right direction, I believe you may get something to your advantage.' He beamed around the quiet wheelhouse. The impassive quartermaster, the signalman, a bosun's mate who was looking anywhere but at him.

The midshipman asked flatly, 'Is that all you wanted, sir?'

The commodore swung away. 'Yes. Carry on.' As the door slid shut he snapped, 'Bloody ungrateful little tyke!'

Jupp came from the port wing carrying a tray covered with a napkin. He saw Lindsay and showed his teeth.

'Coffee and a sandwich, sir.'

Kemp said coldly, 'What about me?'

'Sir?' Jupp placed the tray carefully on a vibrating flag locker. 'I will inform your steward that you wish 'im to fetch somethin' for you.' He looked at the man's angry face. 'Sir.'

The commodore thrust his thickset body from the chair and stalked to the door. As he disappeared down the ladder Lindsay seemed to feel the men around him come to life, saw the quartermaster give a quick wink at the signalman.

He said, 'It won't do, Jupp.' He smiled gravely. 'And it won't help either.'

Jupp folded the napkin into four quarters. 'I'm not with you, sir? Did I do anythin'?'

Lindsay grinned. 'Get back to your pantry while you're still alive!'

Goss re-entered the wheelhouse and yawned hugely. 'God, it smells better in here!'

Lindsay turned away. They were all at it. Even Goss. For the ship and for him. It was the only way they knew of showing their true feelings.

Jupp was still hovering by the flag locker. 'Beggin' yer pardon, sir, but I 'ave to report some missin' gear from the wardroom.'

Goss interrupted calmly, 'Not to worry. I expect some bloody coolie lifted it. Or maybe it went down a gash chute by accident.'

Lindsay did not know how to face them. 'Silver teapots?'

Jupp sounded surprised. 'Well, as a matter of fact, yes, sir.'

Goss sighed. 'One of those things.' He walked to the wing again, his face devoid of expression.

Lindsay began to see more and more of the commodore in the days which followed. He said little and contented himself with examining incoming signals or just sitting in silence on the bridge chair.

That he was growing increasingly worried became obvious as news was received from the Admiralty signals of a new and changing pattern in enemy activity. It seemed there was no longer any doubt that all the incidents were linked. A German raider was at large, and more to the point, was the same one which Lindsay had last seen off Greenland.

Her captain was a man who appeared to care little for his own safety. Several times he had barely missed the searching cruisers and the net was closing in on him rapidly. The last sinking had been three hundred miles north-east of Trinidad, and because of it some small convoys had been held up for fear of another attack. There were too few escorts available on the opposite side of the Atlantic, and the U-boat menace further north made the hope of any quick transfer of forces unlikely. Badly needed convoys were made to stay at anchor or in port while the cruisers increased their efforts to hunt the German down once and for all.

Two days before the anticipated meeting with the Freetown escorts Kemp sent for Lindsay in his quarters. He was sitting in a deep sofa, the deck around his feet covered with signals and written instructions. He seemed to have aged in the past week, and there were deep furrows around his eyes and mouth. He did not ask Lindsay to sit down.

'Another sinking report.'

Lindsay nodded. He had seen it for himself. A Danish tanker sailing in ballast without escort had been shelled and sunk barely a hundred miles from the previous sinking. This time the Danish captain had managed to get off more than a cry for help. There was now no doubt the raider was the same ship.

He replied, 'The German's working south, sir. Trying to catch the Americas trade as much as possible.' He added, 'He'll sink a few more poor devils before he's run to earth.' He did not try to hide the bitterness.

Kemp picked up a signal and then dropped it again. 'I know he can't get at us.' He looked up, his eyes blazing. They've ordered our cruiser screen westward. Taken it away from my support!'

Lindsay watched him coldly. 'Yes, sir. I heard.'

'Didn't even consider what I might think about it.'

'They've no choice. If the raider continues to move south or south-east the cruisers will have him in the bag. He can't run forever.'

'This is a valuable convoy. Perhaps vital.' He seemed to be speaking his thoughts aloud. 'It's wrong to expect me to take all the responsibility.'

Lindsay said, 'Was that all you wanted, sir?'

The commodore watched him with sudden anger. 'I know what you're hoping! That I'll make some mistake so that you can crow about it!'

'Then you don't know me at all.' Lindsay kept his voice level. 'When you are in charge of any convoy there is always the risk of change and sudden alteration in planning. It doesn't necessarily go like a *clock*.'

There was a tap at the door and Stannard stepped into the cabin.

Kemp glared at him. 'Well?'

'Another signal from Admiralty, sir. Request you detach the cruiser *Canopus* and destroyer escort immediately.' He looked at Lindsay. 'They are to leave with all speed and join in the search.' He shrugged. 'It seems that the net is tightening.'

Kemp nodded. 'Execute.' As the door closed he muttered, 'Now there's just this ship until the Freetown escorts arrive.' He looked up. 'When will that be?'

'Forty-eight hours, sir. We crossed the twentieth parallel at noon today.'

Lindsay left him with his thoughts and returned to the bridge. The cruiser was already moving swiftly clear of her column, and far ahead of the convoy he could see the two destroyers gathering speed to take station on her.

'Signal the freighter *Brittany* to take lead ship in the port column.' He raised his glasses and watched the lamp winking from the other vessel's bridge.

He said, 'It seems we're in charge of things, Yeo.'

Ritchie, who was keeping an eye on his signalman,

nodded. ''Cept for the Yank, sir.' He jerked his thumb over his shoulder. '*She's* still with us, more or less.'

Lindsay smiled. There was no real danger but it was strange that in a matter of hours their hidden strength had melted away to leave the two oldest ships as a sole protection.

'Signal the *John P. Ashton* to assume station ahead of the convoy.'

Ritchie said, 'She'll blow 'er boilers, sir.'

'Her captain will know he's the only one now with submarine detection gear. He won't have to be told what to do.'

Later, as the elderly destroyer thrashed past the other ships he saw her light blinking rapidly and heard Ritchie say, 'Signal, sir. This must be Veterans Day.' He shook his head. 'He ain't kiddin' either.'

When darkness fell over the three columns the American four-piper had retained her position well ahead of the convoy. Lindsay hoped she did not break down overnight. She stood a good chance of being rammed by several of the big ships if she did. With that in mind, her engineers would no doubt be doubly careful.

He was lolling in his chair, half sleeping, half listening to the engines' steady beat, when Stannard roused him again. He was actually asleep when the watch had changed and had heard nothing at all. He had been dreaming of a sunlit beach. The girl, wet with spray and warm in his arms. Laughing.

He straightened himself in the chair. 'Yes?'

Stannard had his back to the shaded compass light and Lindsay could not see his face.

'Just decoded an urgent signal, sir. Admiralty. If you come into the chart room you can read it.'

'Just tell me.' He waited, almost knowing what he would say.

'R.A.F. reconnaissance have reported a large German unit at sea. Out of Brest, sir.'

Lindsay stared at him. 'When was this?'

'That's just it. They don't know. Weather has been very bad for aerial photography and the flak has been extra thick around Brest lately. The Jerries have been using all sorts of camouflage, nets and so forth. All they do know for sure is that one large unit is not there any more.'

'When was the last check made?'

'Two weeks back, sir.' Stannard sounded apprehensive. 'Won't affect us, will it? I mean, this is a top secret convoy.'

Lindsay slid from the chair. 'Nothing's that secret. How can you hide twenty-four ships and God knows how many people?' He added sharply, 'Send someone to rouse the commodore. He'll want to know.'

As Stannard hurried to a telephone Lindsay walked out on to the port wing. He could see the nearest troopship quite clearly in the moonlight, her boat deck and twin funnels standing out against the stars like parts of a fortress.

A mistake? It was possible. The Germans were always trying to move their heavy units to avoid bombing raids. They had to keep them afloat and to all appearances ready for sea. Just by being there they were a constant threat. Enough to tie down the Home Fleet's big ships at Scapa and others further south. Having the whole French seaboard as well as their own, the enemy were more than able to extend the menace.

He gripped the screen and tried to clear his mind of the nagging doubt. Just suppose it was part of a plan? That the raider's attacks on *Loch Glendhu* and the other convoy had been a working-up for all this? At best, it would mean the Germans had been right in assuming that a single raider could tie down a far greater mass of ships than her worth really suggested. At worst . . . he gripped the screen even tighter. Then it would mean that every available cruiser had been withdrawn from this convoy to search for a red-herring. The raider would be caught and sunk. He stared fixedly at the troopship. But in exchange for their sacrifice, the Germans might hope for the greatest prize of all. A whole convoy. Men, supplies, vital materials and. . . .

He swung round as a man called, 'Commodore's comin' up, sir.'

Stannard joined him by the screen. 'What shall we do, sir?'

'Wait, Pilot.' He did not look at him. 'And hope.'

———————

The following morning was another fine clear one. Even during the last part of the morning watch the sun gave a hint of the power to come and the horizon was hidden in low haze, like steam.

Maxwell was officer of the watch, and as Lieutenant Hunter started the daily check on the columns and bearing of the various ships nearby, Maxwell stayed by the screen, staring at the tiny shape of the American destroyer directly ahead. The haze was playing tricks with her upperworks and spindly funnels. As if she had been cut in halves, with the upper pieces replaced at the wrong angle.

He glanced at Lindsay but he was still asleep in his chair, one arm hanging down beside it like that of a corpse. He returned to his thoughts, unconsciously clasping his hands behind him as if on parade.

Soon now he would be getting his half stripe. Without effort he could see himself at the gunnery school on Whale Island. The toiling ranks of marching officers and men. The bark of commands and snap of weapons. It would be like picking up the threads all over again. With luck, further advancement would follow automatically, and people would forget the one mistake which had cost him so much time.

Maxwell had been young and newly-married to Decia

when it had happened. Her family had been against the marriage from the start but had put a brave face on things when it had come about.

As gunnery officer in a destroyer he had been in charge of a practice shoot, a normal, routine exercise. His assistant had been a sub-lieutenant, a spoiled, stupid man whom he should never have trusted. Perhaps he had been thinking about his new bride. The excitement and sudden prosperity the marriage had brought him. He was a proud man and had at first disliked the idea of having a rich wife while he lived on a lieutenant's meagre pay.

Whatever he had been thinking about, it had not been the shoot. The sub-lieutenant had made a serious mistake with deflection, and instead of hitting the towed target, the shell had ploughed into the tug and killed seven men.

The sub-lieutenant had been dismissed the Service with dishonour. But he had been inexperienced, a nervous breakdown following the accident had more than proved the point to the court's satisfaction. So if Maxwell had not directly pressed the trigger, he was certainly recognised as the true culprit. Only his excellent record had saved him from the same fate. To be required to resign was a lesser punishment in the court's eyes, but to Maxwell it spelled disaster.

Returning to the Navy because of the war, he had half expected that his past would be buried. Another chance. One more fair opportunity. He had been wrong. One empty job after another, until finally he had been appointed to *Benbecula.* The bottom rung of the ladder.

He swayed back on his heels. But when he reached Whale Island again no one would sneer or cut him dead. *He* would be the man who had sunk a U-boat and made history. Ancient six-inch weapons with half-witted conscripts behind them against the cream of the German Navy. And it had been his eye and brain which had done it.

Then he thought of Decia. The nightmare vision of the bedroom and the man on his knees pleading with him. It would all be too late. He would not have her. Not see the admiration and envy on the faces of brother officers when he entered a room with her on his arm.

The telephone by his elbow made him start. 'Officer of the watch?' His eye moved to the pod on the foremast as he formed a mental picture of the lookout.

'Aircraft, sir. Green four-five.'

Lindsay was awake. 'What was that?'

Maxwell kept his eyes on the foremast. 'Say again.'

'I'm sure it was an aircraft, sir.'

Maxwell covered the mouthpiece and looked at Lindsay. 'Bloody fool says there's an aircraft on the starboard bow, sir.' He frowned. 'Fifteen hundred miles from the nearest land and he sees an aircraft! Must be the bloody heat!'

Lindsay moved from the chair and took the handset. 'Captain here. What exactly can you see?'

The seaman sounded flustered. 'Can't see nothin' now, sir.' Then more stubbornly, 'But it was there, sir. Like a bit of glass flashin' in the sun. Very low down. Above the 'aze.'

'Keep looking.' To Maxwell he added, 'It's disappeared.'

Maxwell sniffed. 'Naturally.'

Hunter came out of the sunlight, folding his shipping lists. 'Could be a *small* plane, sir.' He smiled awkwardly as they looked at him. 'But I was forgetting. There are no carriers hereabouts.'

The phone rang again.

Lindsay took it quickly. 'Captain.'

'Just saw it on about the same bearin', sir. Just one flash. Very small, but no doubt about it.'

Lindsay handed the telephone to Hunter. 'Inform the commodore that I would be grateful of his presence here.' He waited for Maxwell to pass his message. 'Very well, Guns.' He glanced towards the nearest troopship. 'Now you can sound off action stations.'

For a moment longer nobody moved. Then Maxwell asked, 'But, sir, *why?*'

'It may give us,' he paused, recalling the deserted restaurant, the gross Turk at his table, 'it may give us *time.*'

Maxwell shrugged. Without another word he pressed his thumb hard on the red button.

————————

Dancy rubbed his forehead with a handkerchief. In spite of the bridge air ducts it was stifling.

He asked quietly, 'Do you reckon anything will happen?'

Stannard glanced at the commodore's bulky shape in the chair, at Lindsay who was standing just outside the starboard door.

'I dunno. This waiting makes me sweat a bit.'

The ship had been at action for two hours, although it seemed much longer.

Without warning the commodore heaved himself from the chair and snapped, 'Chart room.' He waited until Lindsay had followed him and added, 'You, too, Pilot.'

In the chart room it was even hotter with every scuttle and deadlight clamped shut.

The commodore said, 'Nothing.'

Stannard looked at Lindsay. He seemed very composed, even calm.

'The lookout was certain about the plane, sir.' Lindsay watched him across the table. 'He is an experienced rating.'

'I see.' The commodore's hands fluttered vaguely and then came to rest on the chart. 'What do you suggest?'

Lindsay relaxed slightly. 'If I'm right, sir, it would be inviting disaster to make a radio signal for assistance. One, we know the Freetown ships will not make contact before tomorrow at the earliest. Two, if there is an enemy ship out there, it might be in total ignorance of our position.'

'Well?'

'I suggest you should alter course to the east'rd, sir. Or turn one hundred and eighty degrees and *then* call for assistance. Increase to maximum speed. It would give us time and room to manoeuvre.'

'Do you know what you are asking?' Kemp's voice trembled. 'For me to run away from a shadow! You must be out of your mind!'

Lindsay said patiently, 'That aircraft was probably catapulted from its parent ship. If so, you can expect the worst.' He added with sudden sharpness, 'What is the alternative? Head on into destruction?' He spoke faster as if to prevent interruption. Stannard saw his hands clenched into fists against his sides, could almost feel the effort he was making to break Kemp's resistance. 'Think, sir, of the effect it will have if we allow this convoy to be decimated. Quite apart from damage to morale on top of the Singapore disaster, the actual losses would be terrible. These troops are vital for the next few months, and for all we know, so too are the supplies and equipment.'

Kemp took a few paces to the bulkhead and turned his back on them. 'Can't do it. It's too big.' He added hesitantly, 'We have to take the risk.'

'There have already been too many of those, sir.' Lindsay spoke very quietly. 'Admiral Phillips took a risk with *Repulse* and *Prince of Wales* but they were both sunk, and Singapore fell just the same. We took risks by sending an army to help the Greeks when anyone but a fool should have seen it was impossible to stop the rot there. Result, we lost more men and plenty of good ships trying to get them away at Crete.'

'You're accusing me of risking this convoy. Is that it?' Kemp still did not turn.

'I do not see you have any choice but to take evading

action *now*, sir.' When the commodore said nothing he persisted, 'If you wait, it will be useless trying to scatter the convoy. We have a whole day of clear visibility——'

Kemp faced him abruptly. 'Leave me to think.'

Stannard asked, 'What about my plotting team, sir?'

Kemp shouted, 'Let them wait until I am ready! Now for God's sake *leave me alone*!'

Stannard followed Lindsay into the passageway and thrust past the waiting midshipman and his yeoman. Under his breath he muttered, 'Stupid bastard!' Then he slammed the door behind him, making one of the messengers jump with alarm.

Above the bridge in his armoured control position Maxwell heard the door slam. His shirt was wringing with sweat, and the backs of his spotting team and Lieutenant Hunter immediately below his steel chair looked as if they had just emerged from the sea. In the Denmark Strait they had somehow kept going with thick clothing and the small electric heaters. In this glare there was no defence at all against the sun.

Hunter twisted round and looked at him. 'No more aircraft. No bloody anything. So why can't we fall out action stations?'

Because that stupid commodore can't make up his mind, that's why. But aloud Maxwell replied sharply, 'For God's sake, don't you start!'

Hunter shrugged and reached out to open a small observation slit on the port side. It made a very small breeze, but the sight of the nearest troopship was somehow reassuring. The same view, day after day, after bloody day. He felt Maxwell stirring behind him and smiled. Whale Island. Maxwell would love that. All mouth and trousers, like the rest of his breed.

For a split second he imagined an aircraft had dived from the sky, although it was impossible. The screaming roar seemed to press down on him, until his mind was a complete blank. Then came the explosions, and as he stared incredulously at the troopship he saw the towering waterspouts rising beyond her, higher and higher, until they shone like white silk in the sunlight.

As the tall columns began to subside he saw the tell-tale pall of black smoke, growing and rising against the clear sky like a filthy stain. A ship on the port column had been hit. But with what? It had all been just a matter of seconds. Seconds in which everything and each man around him seemed suspended in time and space.

Then Maxwell yelled, 'Don't gape at me! Start tracking!' He punched the shoulder of the nearest seaman. 'Come on, *jump* to it!'

He pressed his eyes to his powerful sights as the control position turned slightly on its mounting. He blinked in the harsh light and rubbed his forehead with his wrist. Nothing. The horizon was still hazy but not that much. You should be able to see something. He felt a chill run down his spine as he picked up the handset and reported, 'Captain, sir. Those shells came from below the horizon.' He heard Hunter gasp. 'No target, sir.'

Lindsay heard his flat voice and then ran to the wheelhouse door. The ship which had been straddled by three or more heavy shells was falling out of line, her upper deck burning fiercely beneath the towering smoke pall.

He snapped, 'Make the signal.' He scribbled a brief addition before Ritchie dashed to the W/T office. 'At least someone will know what's happening.'

He heard the commodore pushing through the bridge watchkeepers, his voice shaking as he called, 'What was it? Where is the enemy?'

Again that screaming roar, and Lindsay tensed, imagining the projectiles hurtling down from their high arc of fire. He had been right. Three columns of water shot above the far line of ships.

He shouted, 'I've reported we are under attack!' He did not take his eyes from the burning freighter.

'Yes, yes.' Kemp seemed unable to think clearly. He was also peering at the ship, at the smoke and flames which had now engulfed the whole of her poop.

Lindsay said, 'Spotting plane. It was just a freak hit.' He glanced at the other man's stricken face. 'But I'm afraid we can't rely on luck any more.'

Then he left the commodore on the gratings and entered the wheelhouse. It was too late to turn the convoy now. At any second the other ship would show herself. But to shoot this far and with such accuracy she must be big. Too big.

He saw the faces of the men around him, watching, waiting for his decision.

He said quietly, 'As soon as we know the enemy's bearing we will make a signal to the convoy. To scatter.'

Kemp's shadow filled the doorway. 'I did not order that!' He was tugging at his collar. 'I demand to be informed!'

'Then I am informing you now, sir. Do you have any objections?'

Kemp dropped his eyes. 'I suppose some will get away. There's nothing we can do.'

Lindsay eyed him calmly. Christ, how could he feel so remote?

He said, 'As you told me when you came aboard, sir. This is my ship. When the convoy scatters, *your* control will be at an end.'

Kemp stared at him, his eyes watering with fixed concentration. 'There's still the American destroyer!'

For once Lindsay did not bother to hide his contempt. 'You'd send *her*, would you?' He turned his back. 'She'll be needed anyway, to shadow the enemy when it's all over.'

As if to mark the finality of his words, the tannoy speaker intoned, 'Control to bridge. Enemy in sight!'

19 'They made it safe . . .'

The burning freighter had dropped a mile astern of the convoy when the port column of ships wheeled away in response to Lindsay's signal, their rising wash giving evidence of increasing speed.

'From *John P. Ashton*, sir.' Ritchie steadied his telescope. *'Request permission to engage the enemy.'*

The bridge shivered as another salvo came screaming out of the sky. The shells exploded in an overlapping line of spray and dirty smoke, a mere cable from the leading troopship.

'Negative.' A near miss from one of those shells would sink the elderly destroyer. 'Make to the second column to scatter *now*.'

Stannard muttered fiercely, 'They can't get far. Christ, those bastards are shooting well.'

Another sullen roar enveloped the bridge and he saw the shells explode where the big liner might have been but for the change of course.

Lindsay slid open a shutter on the starboard side and raised his glasses. At first he saw only haze and the clear blue sea below the horizon. Behind him he heard Hunter's voice on the speaker.

'Green three-oh. Range one-eight-oh.'

Then quite suddenly he saw the enemy ship. She was a darker blur in the horizon haze, but as he watched he saw the ripple of orange flashes which momentarily laid bare her superstructure in the powerful lenses. He tried not to swallow, although his throat was like a kiln. He knew those nearby were watching him. Trying to gauge his reactions.

A cruiser at least. He heard the screaming whine of shells as they tore down over the scattering ships, the tell-tale shiver as they exploded harmlessly in open water.

'Make the signal to our column. Tell them to be as quick as possible.'

The enemy fired again, and the rearmost ship in the column was straddled by three shells. As she steamed stubbornly through the falling torrents of spray he saw she had been badly mauled. Her boat deck looked as if it had been crushed by an avalanche of rock.

'All acknowledged, sir.' Ritchie scribbled automatically on his pad. Not much point. Nobody would ever read it.

There was a sudden silence in the wheelhouse as Lindsay said, 'Give me the mike.' He took it from Dancy, seeing in his mind the men throughout his command.

'This is the captain speaking. We are under attack by a heavy enemy warship which is now about nine miles off our starboard bow. She is big and therefore fast. With bad visibility or darkness the convoy might have been saved by scattering.'

He paused as the sea erupted far away on the port quarter, smothering another ship with those deadly waterspouts. Across the distance he heard the jolting metallic cracks, like a woodsman using an axe on a clear day. The sounds of jagged splinters biting into her hull.

He continued, 'To have even a hope of escaping, these ships must be given *time*.'

Lindsay snapped down the button and looked at Ritchie. 'Very well, Yeoman. Hoist battle ensigns.'

The commodore, who had been staring at the freighter with the smashed boat deck, swung round and shouted, '*Stop!* I order you to——.'

Lindsay interrupted harshly, 'I intend to give the convoy as much of a chance as possible. With or without your help, sir.'

Ritchie pushed between them and grasped the wrist of

a young signalman. 'Come on, boy! Somethin' to tell yer kids!'

Lindsay stooped over the gyro. 'Starboard ten. Midships. Steady.'

'Steady, sir. Course three-four-zero.'

'Full ahead both engines.'

Stannard listened to the urgent telegraphs. 'Shall I call up the chief, sir?'

'No. He knows what's happening up here.' Lindsay felt the gratings shaking and rattling under his feet. 'He *knows* all right.'

As the ship heeled slightly on to her new course Lindsay saw a dark shadow fall briefly across the screen. He looked up at the great ensign climbing the foremast and at some of the gun crews turning to watch it.

He heard Ritchie remark, 'Funny, really. Bin in the Andrew all these years an' never seen 'em 'oisted before.'

When he turned again Lindsay saw that the sea astern seemed full of ships moving away on differing bearings and angles. Once more the air cringed to the ripping passage of shells, and again they exploded close to a careering tanker.

'Aircraft, sir. Dead ahead.'

He watched the sliver of silver above the horizon as it moved calmly in the sunlight. The enemy's eye, unreachable and deadly. Reporting each fall of shot. Standing by to pursue and guide the cruiser like a pilot fish with a shark.

Too fast for Maxwell's ponderous guns. Out of range for the automatic weapons.

But as yet nobody aboard the enemy ship appeared to have noticed the *Benbecula*'s challenge. Maybe they imagined she was out of control or trying to escape in the wrong direction.

Stannard said tightly, 'Maxwell's guns will never even mark the bastard at this range.'

Lindsay did not look at him. He picked up a handset,

feeling it shaking violently as the bridge structure hummed and vibrated to Fraser's engines.

'Guns? Captain. Commence firing with the starboard battery.' He waited, shutting out Maxwell's protest. 'I know the marines can't get their guns to bear. But we *must* draw the enemy's fire from those ships. I will try to close the range as quickly as possible.'

He replaced the handset and heard the fire gong's tinny call, the immediate crash of guns as One and Three lurched inboard together.

'Short.'

He lifted his glasses in time to see the thin feathers of spray falling in direct line with the enemy's hazy outline. But she was much clearer now. Bridge upon bridge, her turrets already swinging as if to seek out this sudden impudence.

Dancy watched transfixed as the sea writhed like surf across a reef before bursting skyward on the starboard beam. He imagined he could feel the heat, taste the foul stench of those great shells.

He realised that Stannard's fingers were around his wrist, his voice intense as he whispered, 'Take this letter. Keep it for me.' He looked him in the eyes. 'Just in case, eh, chum?'

Dancy made to reply and then felt himself falling as the whole bridge shook to one terrible explosion. He felt Stannard and a signalman entangled around his legs, and even when the deafening explosion had stopped it seemed to linger in his ears like pressure under water.

He saw shocked faces, mouths calling silent orders, and the starboard door pitted with bright stars of sunlight. He pulled himself upright as his hearing returned and saw that the stars were splinter holes, and then almost vomited as he stared aghast at the bloody shape beneath them.

Lieutenant Paget had been sent to assist on the bridge and had been almost cut in half by the explosion. Yet as his hands worked like claws across his torn body his screams grew louder and louder, like those of some tortured woman.

'Starboard twenty!' Lindsay locked his arm around the voicepipes as the helm went over. 'Stand by, the port battery!' He wiped paint dust from the gyro with his elbow.

'Midships. *Steady.*'

'Steady, sir. Course zero-three-zero.'

Jolliffe had to grit his teeth as a signalman wrapped a bandage around his arm. A small splinter had laid it open after passing cleanly through the screaming lieutenant a few feet away.

The port guns hurled themselves back on their springs, their muzzles angled towards the sky in their efforts to hit the enemy.

Lindsay made himself ignore the cries and screams until they became fainter and suddenly stopped. He knew that a stretcher party had entered the bridge but did not turn his head as he concentrated every fibre of his mind on the other ship.

'Range now one-six-oh.'

He moved his glasses carefully. Eight miles separated the armoured cruiser and the garishly painted ship with the list to starboard. The enemy had got the message now all right. She had turned towards *Benbecula* using her two forward turrets alternately. The six guns fired with regular precision so that her bridge seemed to dance in the flashes as if ablaze.

When at last he glanced over his shoulder he saw that Paget's corpse had been removed. Just a brush-stroke of scarlet to show where he had been torn down.

As the gunfire mounted Lindsay changed course at irregular intervals, their progress marked by the curves in their seething wake. Starboard battery and then port. Two by two against the German's six.

Maxwell remarked over the speaker, 'She's the *Minden.*

Eight-inch guns, twelve torpedo tubes.' A brief sigh. 'Estimated speed thirty-three knots.'

Lindsay bit his lip to hide his despair. A miniature battle-cruiser as far as *Benbecula* was concerned.

A telephone buzzed, the sound muffled by explosions, the roar of fans.

'W/T have received a signal about that other raider, sir!'

Lindsay blinked as the sea beyond the bows vanished behind a towering wall of spray. He felt the hull buck to the shockwave as if she had been struck by a bomb.

'Read it!'

The man tore his eyes from an observation slit and crouched over his telephone.

'*Raider sunk. All available assistance on way to help you.*' And a few seconds later. 'Cruiser *Canopus* calling us, sir. *What is your position?*'

Lindsay saw the sea erupt again. Much closer this time. 'Tell her our position is *grim*!'

Stannard touched the man's arm. 'Here. I'll give it to W/T.'

Lindsay called, 'How are the ships, Sub?'

Dancy ran aft and peered through the *Benbecula*'s drooping plume of funnel smoke. In those seconds he saw it all. The scattered ships, so very small beneath the great ensign on the mainmast. The twisting white wake, the sea, everything.

'Troopships out of range, sir. The rest well scattered.'

'Good.'

'Range now one-five-oh.'

All four guns were firing and reloading as fast as they could move, with Maxwell's spotters yelling down bearings and deflexions with each veering change of course.

In the engine room Fraser clung to the jerking platform and watched his men swarming around the pounding machinery like filthy insects. In damage control Goss sat unmoving in his chair, facing the panel, hands folded across his stomach. Throughout the ship, above and below decks, behind watertight doors or on exposed gun platforms, every man waited for the inevitable. Meeting it in his own way.

Far astern, and spread fanlike towards the horizon, the once proud convoy had long since lost its shape and formation. The first ship to be hit had sunk, but the others which had received near misses still managed to maintain their escape, some leaving smoke-trails like scars across the sky.

Aboard the second troopship the decks and emergency stations were crammed with silent figures, mis-shapen in lifejackets as they stood in swaying lines, as they had been since the attack had begun.

A deck officer at his boat station said suddenly, 'God, look at the old girl! I'd never have believed it!' In spite of the watching soldiers he took off his cap and waved it above his head. But his voice was just a whisper as he called, 'Good luck, old lady!'

The small party of Wrens packed at the after end of the boat deck huddled even closer as the distant ship was again straddled by waterspouts.

The one named Marion slipped her arm around her friend's shoulders and said, 'Don't cry, Eve.'

She shook her head. 'I know I'm crying.' She strained her eyes to try and see the ship with the stubborn list and outdated stern. 'But I feel like cheering!'

Something like a sigh transmitted itself through the watching soldiers.

A voice called, 'She's hit!'

When the sound finally reached the scattered ships it was like a roll of thunder. Even the officers with binoculars could hardly distinguish one part of *Benbecula* from the next because of the dense smoke.

Marion tightened her grip. 'But they're still firing. How can they do it?'

The Wren called Eve did not answer. She was seeing

the little villa, the table in candlelight. And him sitting on the bed. Looking at her. Holding her.

Another set of explosions rumbled across the sea's face. More muffled now as the distance steadily mounted between them.

A man said, 'Direct hit that time. Must be.'

'Would you like to go below?' Marion stared sadly at the great spreading smokestain far astern. 'It's safe now. They made it safe.'

'No.' She shook her head. 'He'll know I'm here. I'm sure of it.'

'So am I.' Together they stayed by the rail in silence.

———————

'Shoot!'

Maxwell was hoarse from yelling into his mouthpiece. The compartment seemed full of smoke and the din was unbearable as time and time again the ship rocked to the enemy's salvos.

'Why can't we *hit* her?' Hunter shouted through the tendrils of smoke below Maxwell's chair. 'We're down to six miles range, for Christ's sake!'

The starboard guns crashed out again and Maxwell cursed as his shells exploded into the haze.

'Up two hundred!'

He was still speaking when the next salvo straddled the ship in a vice of steel. He saw Hunter lurch in his chair to stare up at him, his expression one of horror even as the blood gushed from his mouth and his eyes lost their understanding forever.

Two of the seamen were also down, and the third was crawling up the side of Maxwell's chair holding his hip and sobbing with agony.

'First aid party to Control!' Maxwell sighed. The line had gone dead. He stood up and hung his microphone on the chair, then giving the wounded seaman a vague pat on the head climbed out into the sunlight.

Figures blundered past him in the smoke and a man yelled, 'Up forrard! Starboard side!'

Number One gun was still firing when Maxwell arrived, and he found Baldock, his elderly warrant officer, giving local orders to its crew. The other gun was in fragments, hurled inboard above a deep crater around which human remains lay scattered in bloody gruel.

Baldock shouted, 'Both quarters officers are done for on this side!'

Maxwell nodded, feeling very detached. 'You carry on here then.'

He strode to the opposite side where he found the young sub-lieutenant in charge sitting on a shell locker, an arm across his face like a man in the sun.

'All right, Cordeaux?'

The officer stared at him. 'Yes, sir.' Then he saw a spreadeagled corpse at the opposite gun. Headless, it still wore a jacket. Like his own, with a single wavy stripe.

A shell whimpered close overhead but Maxwell did not flinch. 'Luck of the draw, my boy.' He adjusted his cap. 'I'm going aft to see the bootnecks. Keep at it, eh?'

The youth watched him leave and then groped for his helmet. In front of him the gunlayer and trainer, the gloved seamen who worked the breech were all waiting as before. They were going to die. All of them. Like his friend who now lay headless and without pain.

The gunlayer said thickly, 'We're turnin' again, sir!'

Cordeaux heard himself say, 'Stand by, Number Two.' Then with the others he watched the bows start to swing to starboard.

———————

'Midships!' Lindsay had to yell to make himself heard. The enemy gunners were shooting rapidly and he knew that *Benbecula* had been badly mauled. But the noise was too great, too vast to recognise or distinguish. Time no longer meant anything, and as he conned the vibrating ship, swinging her drunkenly from bow to bow, he was conscious only of the distance which still separated the ill-matched enemies.

'Wheel's amidships, sir!' Jolliffe was clinging to the wheel, his face ashen from loss of blood.

Ritchie climbed up beside him and said, 'We'll go together, eh, mate?'

The coxswain peered at him glassily. 'Cheerful bastard!'

Ritchie looked away. Christ Almighty. The poor old sod still thinks we're going to survive!

Lindsay swung round as sunlight lanced through the smoke and he saw the spotter plane flashing down the starboard side less than half a mile distant. The little seaplane looked near and remote from the crash and scream of gunfire. Like a child's toy, her approach made soundless by the din. As it tilted slightly he saw the black cross on one stubby wing, and imagined he could see a helmeted head in the cockpit. Watching with the patient indifference of a cruising gull.

Somewhere aft an Oerlikon came to life, the bright tracer licking out through the smoke, making the seaplane veer away, startled, disturbed. Too far away for good shooting, but Lindsay could understand the Oerlikon gunner's gesture. Strapped in his harness, vulnerable and helpless as the ship came apart around him.

Stannard shouted in his ear, 'The ships'll be safe now!' It was more like a question.

Lindsay looked at him. 'There's still too much daylight left.'

He watched the seaplane turning for another run. But for the plane the ships would have been beyond reach by now. But once *Benbecula* had been destroyed the German captain would be in pursuit again. What had Maxwell said? It was hard to think. To remember. *Thirty-two knots.*

The deck canted violently and a wall of flame shot skyward from the forecastle.

Telephones buzzed and he heard men yelling over the remaining voicepipes.

'Bad fire forrard, sir! Number One gun knocked out. Mr Baldock has been killed.'

Lindsay dragged himself across the littered gratings. 'Who's still down there?'

Stannard called, 'Young Cordeaux, sir.'

Lindsay wiped his face with his hand. Just a boy. And Baldock was gone. He should have been at home with his grandchildren.

A savage explosion tore down the ship's side, filling the air with splinters and heavier fragments. Cabins and compartments, machinery and bulkheads felt it as the scything onslaught expended itself through the hull. The funnel was streaming tendrils of smoke and steam from countless holes, and Lindsay saw that the mainmast had gone completely.

Not long now. Something splashed across the nearest telegraph which still pointed to *Full Ahead,* and glancing up he saw blood dripping through a split in the deckhead. Probably Hunter's, he thought wearily.

When he dropped his eyes he saw that the chair was empty. For an instant he imagined the commodore had been cut down by a splinter.

Stannard called harshly, 'He ran below, sir! Puking like a bloody kid!'

Lindsay shrugged. It did not seem important now.

He raised his glasses again. There was so much smoke that it was hard to see beyond the bows. Smoke from guns and bursting shells. From the ship herself as she defied the efforts of hoses and inrushing water to quench the creeping fires.

The range was less than six miles. It was impossible to know how many times they had managed to hit the enemy. If at all. The cruiser was still coming for them, moving diagonally across the bow, her turrets tracking *Benbecula*'s approach with the cool efficiency of a hunter awaiting a wounded beast to be flushed from cover.

A pencil rolled across the counter beneath the screen and for a brief second he stared at it. The list which had defied owners and shipyards for years had gone at last. Goss had probably flooded the magazines nearest the fires, the weight of water bringing the old ship upright with kind of stubborn dignity. How would she appear to the enemy and the German gunnery officer? This battered, half-crippled ship, limping towards destruction but refusing to die. What would they feel? Admiration, or anger at being delayed?

He clenched his jaw again as more explosions made the hull quake. Not *delay*. The German must be held off until help arrived.

'Where's *Canopus* now?'

Stannard glanced at him. 'W/T office is badly hit, sir. Can't be sure of what's happening.'

Lindsay opened his mouth to speak and then found himself face down on the gratings with someone kicking and struggling across his spine. There was smoke and dust everywhere. He could hardly breathe and felt as if the air was being sucked out of him.   Near his face small things stood out with stark clarity. Rivets, and pieces of his watch which had been torn from his wrist to shatter against the steel plates. A man's fist, and when he turned his head he saw it belonged to Jolliffe. The coxswain had been blasted from the wheel and lay with his skull crushed against the binnacle.

Lindsay lurched to his feet, spitting out dust and blown grit, searching for the remains of the bridge party. He saw Stannard on his back, blood running between his legs, and Dancy kneeling over him.

Ritchie was already dragging himself to the wheel and managed to croak, 'Got 'er, sir! Steady as she goes!' He grinned. 'To 'ell!'

Stannard opened his eyes and stared at Dancy. 'Easy,

mate. I'm all right. Christ, I can't feel much of anything!'

Two more figures entered the smoke-filled compartment, slipping on blood and broken panels, groping for handholds. Midshipman Kemp and Squire, the navigator's yeoman.

Lindsay said, 'Man those voicepipes!'

Kemp nodded wildly. 'I've sent for the first aid party, sir!'

Dancy crouched over the Australian, holding him as the deck jerked to another shellburst.

'You'll be fine. You see. We can be in England together and——'

Stannard looked past him at Lindsay and grimaced. 'The letter. See she gets it, will you? Don't want her to think I've forgotten——'

His head lolled to one side and Lindsay said, 'Leave him, Sub. He's gone.'

Dancy stood up, shaking badly. Then he said, 'I'm okay, sir.' He tried not to look at his friend on the gratings. 'Later on I'll——' He did not finish it.

The rear door rattled across the splintered gratings, and Boase with two stretcher bearers ran into the wheelhouse. Boase looked deathly pale, his steel helmet awry as he peered round at the chaos and death. A signalman had been pulped against the rear bulkhead, a messenger lay dead by his feet but totally unmarked.

In an unexplained lull of gunfire Kemp shouted wildly, 'Go on, Doc, show us what you can do!' He shook Squire's restraining hand from his arm and continued in the same broken voice, 'You're bloody good at offering advice to others!'

Boase stood with his arms at his side, his helmet jerking to the relentless vibration.

Lindsay snapped, 'Get a grip on yourselves!'

Kemp's face seemed to crumple. 'He was helping my father and that surgeon to ruin you, sir. Was giving a bad report so that you'd be finished.' Some of the fury came back to his face as he yelled at the stricken doctor, 'You rotten, cowardly bastard! You're like my father, so why don't you run down and hide with him?'

Squire took Boase's wrist and pushed him towards the grim-faced stretcher bearers. 'Get him away, chum.' He turned his face to the screen as Boase allowed himself to be pulled from the door. A long thread of spittle was hanging from his chin.

A bosun's mate said, 'First lieutenant on the phone, sir.'

Lindsay took it. 'Captain.'

Goss sounded far away. 'Forrard bulkhead is badly cracked. If it's not properly shored the whole thing will go.' He coughed harshly and added, 'There's a bad fire here, too. No room for any bloody thing.'

Lindsay forced his brain to react to Goss's brief summary. It must be bad to have got him out of damage control in person.

'You want me to reduce speed?'

Goss waited a few seconds. 'Yes. At full revs she'll go straight to the bottom if this lot caves in.' Another pause. 'We'll need fifteen minutes. No more just yet.'

Fifteen minutes. He could as easily have asked for a week.

Dancy was watching him, another telephone in his fist. 'It's the chief, sir. Two pumps out of action. Engine room is flooding.'

Lindsay jumped as a shell exploded somewhere aft. He heard heavy equipment falling between decks, the tearing scrape of splinters ricocheting from the ravaged hull.

'Yes, Chief.'

Fraser seemed very calm. 'I can still give you full speed, sir. But I'm warning you that things could get dicey down here.'

'Yes.' Even the one word seemed an effort. 'Get all your spare hands out right away and put them in damage control. It may not be long now.'

'Aye.' Fraser shouted something to his assistant and then added, 'She's not doing so badly though.' The line went dead.

Lindsay stared at the handset and then said, 'Ring down for half speed.'

Dancy swung the telegraphs and stood looking at Hunter's blood on his fingers.

'They'll have us cold now, sir.'

Another shell ploughed into the forecastle, the splinters bursting out across the well deck even as the mast and derricks began to stagger drunkenly over the side. Rigging, spars and one complete winch vanished through the broken plating, smearing the remains of Cordeaux and his gun crew as they passed.

Lindsay felt someone tying a dressing around his forearm and realised he had been hit by a small splinter. Maybe when Stannard had been killed. He could not remember. There was no real pain. Just a numbness which seemed to begin behind his brain and probed right through his aching limbs like a fever.

'Enemy's ceased fire, sir.' The remaining bosun's mate leaned against the screen as if about to collapse.

Lindsay moved automatically to the port door and knocked off the clips. When he wrenched it open he found he was looking straight down at the deck below through a tangle of blackened, twisted steel and wood. The port wing had received a direct hit. The shell which had killed Stannard, Jolliffe and the others in the bridge had carved the wing away like so much cardboard. How he and Dancy had survived was a miracle.

He felt the salt air driving the smoke from his lungs and tried to steady his glasses on the enemy. The ship was so slow now, and he could feel the deck under his feet moving ponderously and in time with each trough. She must be filling badly, he thought. Heavy in the water. Nearly finished.

He heard Goss clattering through the bridge but kept

his glasses trained on the enemy. The cruiser had all but stopped too, less·than four miles away. He could see the scarlet flag at her gaff, the haze of gunsmoke above her turrets.

Behind him he heard Goss mutter, 'The bastard's picking up his seaplane, sir.'

Lindsay saw the little aircraft bobbing on its floats as it manoeuvred delicately towards the ship's massive grey hull. A derrick had already been unlimbered by the mainmast and was swinging outboard in readiness for the pick-up.

Perhaps the sight of these calm, practised movements did more to break Lindsay's reserves than any act of expected violence. The cruiser was confident of the victory. She could afford to ignore the blazing, shell-pitted ship without masts or ensigns, and would soon be off again after the convoy. Because of *Benbecula*'s challenge many of those ships would survive. But some would not, and with sudden anger Lindsay shouted, 'Stop the starboard engine!'

Goss stood aside as he hurried into the wheelhouse.

'Stand·by to abandon ship. Get the wounded on deck and cut loose the rafts.' They were all staring at him. 'Jump to it!'

The telegraph clanged, and with a brief shudder the starboard screw spun to a halt.

Dancy called, 'The enemy are training their tubes on us, sir!'

Lindsay ran to the shutters. Even without the glasses he could see the gap in the cruiser's silhouette where one set of torpedo tubes had been swung out across the side.

The cruiser's captain was not even going to allow them time to clear the ship of wounded. Maybe he knew that help was already on its way, perhaps just below the horizon, and time was more important than a handful of madmen who had tried to prevent his conquest. Or then again he might want to do it. To wipe out the insult of this delay to a set plan.

Goss muttered, 'There's no time to get the lads off, sir.'

He watched the bows labouring very slowly to starboard as the port screw continued to forge ahead. He had guessed Lindsay's intention almost as soon as he had seen his face. Knew what he would do even in the face of death. He was surprised to find he could understand and meet the inevitable. Just as he had accepted the ruin of his cabin. He had been chasing after his damage control parties, plugging holes, dragging the sobbing wounded out of mangled steel, repairing obsolete pumps and trying to stay alive in a prison of screaming splinters and echoing explosions. The cabin had been torn apart by splinters, his pictures and relics just so much rubbish. Anger, despair, resentment; for those few moments he had known them all. It was like seeing his life lying there amidst the wreckage. Carefully he had unpinned the company flag from the bulkhead, and with it across one arm had crunched out of the cabin. His foot had trodden on the picture of himself and the old company chairman.

Aloud he had murmured, 'Chief was right. You *were* a mean old bastard!' Then without looking back he had got on with his work.

Goss had seen the commodore crouching on a broken locker pleading with a young S.B.A. to treat his wound. The S.B.A. had been more than occupied with other injured men and had retorted shrilly, 'You're not wounded! For God's sake leave me alone!'

No wonder the midshipman was the way he was. With a father like that it was a marvel he was still sane.

And now the noise and din were all but over. Already the sky was showing through the drifting pall of smoke, and the water between the ships was no longer churned by the racing screws. In fact, Goss decided, it looked very cool and inviting. With narrowed eyes he watched the little seaplane etched against the cruiser's side, imagining some officer giving the orders to hoist it inboard, maybe under the eyes of the captain. Like Lindsay.

Goss shook his head angrily. No, not like him.

Then he heard himself say, 'I'm ready to have a go if you are.'

Lindsay met his gaze and said quietly, 'It's only a faint chance.'

'Better'n sitting here waiting to be chopped.' Goss walked aft. 'I'll tell de Chair. Maxwell, too, if he's still in one piece.'

Lindsay touched the screen. It was warm. From sun or fires it was impossible to say.

'Stop port.'

Before the last clang of the telegraph he had the telephone against his ear.

'Chief? Listen.' Through the open shutter he saw the seaplane rising up against the grey steel. A toy.

Dancy stood by the voicepipes listening to Lindsay's even voice. Knowing he should understand as Goss had done. But the quiet, the painful heaviness of the ship beneath him, the stifling smell of death seemed to be muffling his mind like some great sodden blanket.

Lindsay joined him by the voicepipes and groped for his pipe. But it was broken, and he said, 'Disregard the telegraphs. Hold this phone, and when I give you the signal just tell the chief to let her rip.'

Before Dancy could speak he added to Ritchie, 'Just keep her head towards the enemy's quarter. I'm going to give the after guns a chance. Only one of them will bear. But if we miss I'm going to turn and try again.' He smiled grimly. *There'll be no second go. By that time we'll be heading straight down.*

Somewhere below a man cried out in agony and feet crashed through the wreckage to search for him.

Aft on the well deck Goss found Maxwell squatting on the side of a gun mounting, his cap over his eyes as he stared at the glittering water. Between the two guns the wounded lay in ragged lines, moaning or drugged in silence. A few exhausted stokers and seamen waited in little groups, and some marines were looking down at de Chair in the shadow of a shattered winch. His face was enveloped in dressings, through which the blood was already making its mark.

His hands moved slightly as Goss said, 'You are to engage with Number Six gun. Captain's orders.'

Two men carried a corpse and laid it by the rail. It was Jupp. Even with his face covered Goss would have known him anywhere. He sighed.

The marine sergeant said, 'Right, sir.'

But as he made to move Maxwell bounded over the coaming and threw himself against the big six-inch gun.

'No!' He thrust the gunlayer aside and crouched in his seat as he added petulantly, 'Check your sights!'

A young marine bugler at Goss's side said shakily, 'Anythin' I can do, sir?'

Goss tore his eyes from Maxwell's frenzied movements, his hands as they darted across his sighting wheels. *Gone off his head.* 'Yes. Why not.' Carefully he unfolded the company flag and added, 'Bend this on to that radio antenna. We've no ensigns and no bloody masts.' He forced a grin. 'I guess the old *Becky* would rather end her days under her right colours anyway!'

Another marine had found a telephone which was still connected with the bridge and stood outlined against the sky like an old military memorial. Only his eyes moved as he watched the little bugler clamber up to the boat deck and seconds later the big flag billow out from its improvised staff.

The sergeant rubbed his chin. 'The Jerries'll think we've gone nuts!'

Goss eyed him impassively. 'It's what I think that counts.' Then he strode forward towards the bridge.

He found Lindsay just as he had left him. 'Ready, sir.'

Lindsay nodded. 'Chief says the engine room is flooding faster. Without those two pumps——' He broke off and stiffened as the seaplane rose out of the cruiser's shadow and swung high above the rail.

He turned and looked at Squire. 'When I drop my hand.'

Squire swallowed hard and glanced quickly at Kemp. 'All right, sir?'

The boy stared at him, his stained face like a mask. But he jerked his head violently and replied, 'Fine. Thank you. Fine.'

Lindsay concentrated on the distant warship. He saw some of the *Benbecula*'s rafts drifting haphazardly in the current. They might help. The German captain would probably imagine that some of the survivors were trying to escape.

Gently. Gently. How slowly the seaplane was moving on its hoist.

He held his breath and then brought his hand down in a sharp chop.

Squire gasped, *'Now!'*

Along the remaining telephone wire and into the ear of the motionless marine. Across the littered deck and pitiful wounded, past Jupp's still body and the blinded marine lieutenant to where Maxwell was poised over his sight like an athlete awaiting the starter's pistol.

Just one more agonising split second while the cruiser's upper deck swam in the crosswires like something seen through a rain-washed window. Maxwell had to drag his mind from the others around the gun, the trainer on the opposite side, the men waiting with the next shell and the one to follow it. This was the moment. *His moment.*

'Shoot!'

He felt the sight-pad crash against his eye, the staggering lurch of the gun recoiling inboard, and was almost deafened by the explosion. He had forgotten his ear plugs, but ignored the stabbing pain as he watched the shell explode directly on target.

There was one blinding flash, and where the seaplane had been hanging above its mounting there was a swirling plume of brown smoke. It was followed instantly by another, darker glare, the flames spreading and dancing even as the breech was jerked open and the next shell rammed home.

On the bridge Lindsay had to hold down the sudden surge of excitement. The seaplane had been blasted to fragments and the whole section below it was ablaze with aero fuel.

He shouted, 'Now, Sub!'

The gun crashed out again and drowned Dancy's voice, but far below them Fraser had heard, and as he threw himself on his throttles the screws came alive, churning the sea into a great welter of spray, pushing the old ship forward again, shaking her until it seemed she would come apart.

The sudden fire on the cruiser's deck had done its work. The torpedo crews were being driven back while their comrades with hoses and extinguishers rushed into the attack.

Maxwell's next shell was short, the explosion hurling the spray high above the enemy's side, the flames dancing through the glittering curtain like bright gems.

Lindsay pounded the screen with his fist. The revolutions were speeding up, and already the cruiser had dropped away on the port bow. But not fast enough, and already he could see her forward turret turning in a violent angle to try and find the hulk which had returned to life.

On his steel seat beside the one remaining gun which would bear, Maxwell took a deep breath. He ignored the bright flashes as the enemy fired, did not even see where the shells went as he concentrated on the column of smoke just forward of the cruiser's mainmast. Just the one set of tubes would do. Six torpedoes in a neat row, all set and ready to deal *Benbecula* a death blow. Except that now they were unmanned, abandoned because of his first shot. In spite of the tension he could feel the grin spreading right across his face. If Decia could see him now. If only——

'*Shoot!*'

The two ships fired almost together, the shockwaves rolling and intermingling until the noise was beyond endurance.

Maxwell did not see what happened next. His gun, the crew and most of the marines at the opposite mounting were blasted to oblivion by the explosion. In seconds the well deck and poop were ablaze from end to end, the scorching heat starting other outbreaks below and as high as the lifeboats.

Lindsay felt the shock like a blow to his own body, knew that the ship had done her best and could fight no more. So great was the onslaught of metal that he was totally unprepared for the wall of fire which shot skywards above the billowing smoke. Then as a down-eddy parted the huge pall he saw the cruiser's raked stem moving steadily into the sunlight, the forward turret still trained towards him, her grey side reflecting the bright wash of her bow wave.

The first cries of despair gave way to a lingering sigh as the cruiser emerged fully from the smoke. Her bow wave was already dropping, and as the smoke swept clear of the upper deck Lindsay saw that her stern was awash. The torpedoes must have blasted her wide open with greater effect than if they had been fired into the hull. It was impossible.

Lindsay felt Dancy gripping his shoulders and Ritchie croaking in either joy or disbelief. Throughout the battered hull men were cheering and embracing each other, and even some of the wounded shouted up at the sky, crazed by the din but aware that despite all they had endured they were still alive.

The cruiser was slewing round, her bilge rising to blot

out the chaos and torment on her decks as she started to roll over. More explosions echoed across the water, and even at such a distance Lindsay heard heavy machinery and weapons tearing adrift to add to the horror below decks.

There was no hope of saving any lives. *Benbecula* was devoid of boats, and most of her rafts were either lost or destroyed in the savage battle.

Steam rose high above the cruiser's bows as very slowly they lifted from the water, a black arrowhead against the horizon and clear sky. Then she dived, the turbulence and spreading oil-slick marking her last moment of life.

Dancy asked thickly, 'Shall I get our people off, sir?' He seemed stunned. 'We could build rafts.'

Fraser, without orders, had already cut the speed to dead slow, and Lindsay guessed that many of his men would have thought their end had come when Maxwell's gun had been smashed, to say nothing of the German's violent ending.

'Yes.' He touched his arm. 'And thank you.'

But Dancy did not move. He looked as if he was doubting his own reason. 'Sir! Listen!'

Feebly at first. Little more than a murmur above the hiss of flames, the occasional crackle of bursting ammunition, Lindsay heard the sounds of Fraser's pumps.

He took the handset. 'Chief?'

Fraser was chuckling. 'The old cow! I told you, didn't I?' He sounded near to tears. 'Bloody old cow judged it right to the last bloody moment——' His voice broke completely.

Lindsay said quietly, 'If we can get these fires out and hold the intake we might keep her afloat.' He lowered the handset very gently.

Then he walked out on to the remaining wing and gripped the screen with both hands. Slowly he looked down and along his command. The death and the terrible damage, even the leaping fires on the well deck could not disguise the old ship's familiar outline. Hoses which had been lying smouldering came to life again, and more men emerged like rats from their holes to control them. He saw a stoker, his head bandaged, carrying the ship's cat and standing it down by a cup full of water. Then he stood back to watch the cat's reactions, as if witnessing the greatest miracle in the world.

Three hours later, as the ship struggled forward at a dead slow speed, her hull cloaked in smoke and escaping steam, a lookout reported another vessel on the horizon. It was the *Canopus*, hurrying back in the vain hope of saving some of the convoy.

The sight of the riddled, fire-blackened ship with some unfamiliar flag still flapping jauntily above the destruction made her captain believe the worst had happened.

Ritchie lowered his telescope and reported, "'E wants to know, sir. *What ship are you?*"

Goss, bare-headed and black with filth from top to toe, was sipping tea at the rear of the bridge. He looked at Lindsay's tired face and winked.

Then he said to Ritchie, 'Make to *Canopus. This is H.M.S.* Benbecula.' He turned away in case Lindsay should see his eyes. *'The finest ship in the company.'*